A
KINGDOM
OF
FLESH
AND
FIRE

Also From Jennifer L. Armentrout

Fall With Me
Dream of You (a 1001 Dark Nights Novel)
Forever With You
Fire In You

By J. Lynn
Wait for You
Be With Me
Stay With Me

A Blood and Ash Novel
From Blood and Ash
A Kingdom of Flesh and Fire

The Covenant Series
Half-Blood
Pure
Deity
Elixer
Apollyon
Sentinel

The Lux Series
Shadows
Obsidian
Onyx
Opal
Origin
Opposition
Oblivion

The Origin Series
The Darkest Star
The Burning Shadow

The Dark Elements

Bitter Sweet Love
White Hot Kiss
Stone Cold Touch
Every Last Breath

The Harbinger Series
Storm and Fury
Rage and Ruin

A Titan Novel
The Return
The Power
The Struggle
The Prophecy

A Wicked Novel
Wicked
Torn
Brave
The Prince (a 1001 Dark Nights Novella)
The King (a 1001 Dark Nights Novella)
The Queen (a 1001 Dark Nights Novella)

Gamble Brothers Series
Tempting The Best Man
Tempting The Player
Tempting The Bodyguard

A de Vincent Novel Series
Moonlight Sins
Moonlight Seduction
Moonlight Scandals

Standalone Novels
Obsession
Frigid
Scorched
Cursed

Don't Look Back
The Dead List
Till Death
The Problem With Forever
If There's No Tomorrow

Anthologies
Meet Cute
Life Inside My Mind
Fifty First Times

A KINGDOM

OF

FLESH

AND

FIRE

#1 *NEW YORK TIMES* BESTSELLING AUTHOR

JENNIFER L. ARMENTROUT

A Kingdom of Flesh and Fire
A Blood and Ash Novel
By Jennifer L. Armentrout

Copyright 2020 Jennifer L. Armentrout
ISBN: 978-1-952457-11-1

Published by Blue Box Press, an imprint of Evil Eye Concepts,
Incorporated

Acknowledgments from the Author

This book wouldn't be in your eager (hopefully) little hands if it weren't for the amazing team at Blue Box Press and everyone who played a role in getting this book ready. Thank you Liz Berry, Jillian Stein, MJ Rose, Kimberly Guidroz, Chelle Olson, Jenn Watson, Kevan Lyon, and Stephanie Brown. A huge thank you to JLA Reviewers and JLAnders for being the most awesome, supportive and kind readers. Last but not least, thank you to you, the reader. None of this would be possible if it weren't for you.

Dedication

To you, the reader

Vodina Isles

Undying Hills

MASADONIA

STROUD
SEA

Pensdurth

Blood Forest

New
Haven

Dead Bones Clan

Three Rivers

Whitebridge

Spessa's End

Niel Valley

CARSODONIA

KINGDOM OF
SOLIS

Willow Plains

Elysium Peaks

N

W   E

S

WORLD MAP

EVAEMON

KINGDOM OF
ATLANTIA

Mountains of Nyktos

stelands

Skotos Mountains

n Bay

Saion's Cove

SEAS OF
SAION

Isles of Bele

Chapter 1

"We go home to marry, my Princess."

As in get married?

To *him*?

Suddenly, I thought of all those girlish fantasies I'd had before I learned who I was and what was expected of me—daydreams given life because of the love my parents had for one another.

Never once did those little-girl dreams include a proposal that wasn't remotely an actual proposal. Nor did they incorporate it being announced at a table full of strangers, half of which wanted me dead. And those dreams surely hadn't involved what had to be the kingdom's worst—and possibly most insane—non-proposal of marriage to a man currently holding me captive.

Perhaps I had some sort of ailment of the brain. Maybe I was experiencing hallucinations brought on by stress. After all, there had been so much painful death to process. His betrayal to deal with. And I'd just learned I was descended from Atlantia, a kingdom I'd been raised to believe was the source of all the evil and tragedy in the land. Stress-induced hallucinations seemed a far more believable reason than what was actually happening.

All I could do was stare at the larger hand holding my much smaller one. His skin was slightly darker than mine as if kissed by the sun. Years of wielding a sword with deadly, graceful precision had left his palms callused.

He lifted my hand to an indecently well-formed and full mouth. To lips that were somehow soft yet unrelentingly firm. Lips that had spun beautiful words into the air and whispered heated, wicked promises against my bare skin. Lips that had paid homage to the many scars that riddled my body and face.

Lips that had also spoken blood-soaked lies.

Now, that mouth was pressed against the top of my hand in a gesture that I would've cherished for an eternity and thought exquisitely tender just days or weeks ago. Simple things like hand-holding or chaste kisses had been forbidden to me. As were being wanted or feeling desire. I had long since accepted that I would never experience those things.

Until *him*.

I lifted my gaze from our joined hands, from that mouth that was already curving up on one side, hinting at a dimple in the right cheek, and from the slowly parting lips that revealed just a hint of fatally sharp fangs.

His hair brushed the nape of his neck and toppled over his forehead, and the thick strands were such a deep shade of black, it often shone blue in the sunlight. With high and angular cheekbones, a straight nose, and a proud, carved jaw, he often reminded me of the large, graceful cave cat I had seen once in Queen Ileana's palace as a child. Beautiful, but in the way all wild, dangerous predators were. My heart stammered as my eyes locked onto his, orbs a shade of stunning, cool amber.

I knew I was staring at Hawke—

Coldness poured into my chest as I stopped myself. That wasn't his name. I didn't even know if *Hawke Flynn* was merely a fictitious persona, or if the name belonged to someone who had most likely been slaughtered for their identity. I feared it was the latter. Because *Hawke* had supposedly come from Carsodonia, the capital of the Kingdom of Solis, with glowing recommendations. But then again, the Commander of the guards in Masadonia had turned out to be a supporter of the Atlantians, a Descenter, so that too could've been a lie.

Either way, the guard who'd pledged to protect me with his sword and with his life wasn't real. Nor was the man who had seen me for who I was and not just *what* I was. The Maiden. The

Chosen. Hawke Flynn was nothing more than a figment of fantasy, just like those little-girl dreams had been.

Who held my hand now was the reality: Prince Casteel Da'Neer. His Highness. The Dark One.

Above our joined hands, the curve of his lips grew. The dimple in his right cheek was apparent. It was rare that the left dimple made an appearance. Only genuine smiles brought that out.

"Poppy," he said, and every muscle in my body knotted. I wasn't sure if it was the use of my nickname or the deep, musical lilt of his voice that made me tense. "I don't think I've ever seen you so speechless."

The teasing glimmer in *his* eyes was what snapped me out of my dumbfounded silence. I pulled my hand free, hating the knowledge that if he had wanted to stop me from pulling away, he could've easily done so.

"Marriage?" I found my voice, if only to say the one word.

A glint of challenge filled his gaze. "Yes. Marriage. You do know what that means?"

My hand curled into a fist against the wooden table as I held his stare. "Why would you think I wouldn't know what marriage is?"

"Well," he replied idly, picking up a chalice. "You repeated the word as if it confused you. And as the Maiden, I know you've been...sheltered."

Under my braid, the nape of my neck started to burn, likely turning as red as my hair in the sunlight. "Being the Maiden or sheltered does not equal stupidity," I snapped, aware of the hush that had settled over the table and the entire banquet hall—a room currently full of Descenters and Atlantians. All who would kill and die for the man I openly glared at.

"No." Casteel's gaze flickered over me as he took a sip. "It does not."

"But I am confused." Against my fist, I felt something sharp. With a quick glance down, I saw what I had been too shocked and disturbed to notice earlier. A knife. One with a wooden handle and a thick, serrated blade, designed to cut through meat. It wasn't my wolven bone dagger. I hadn't seen that since the stables, and it cut me deep to think I may never see it again. That dagger was more than a weapon. Vikter had gifted it to me on my sixteenth birthday, and it was my only connection to the man who was more than a guard. He had assumed the role my father should've occupied if he'd lived. Now, the dagger was missing, and Vikter was gone.

Killed by those who supported Casteel.

And based on the fact that I'd shoved the last dagger I'd gotten my hands on deep into Casteel's heart, I doubted the wolven-bone blade would be returned anytime soon. The meat knife was a weapon, though. It would have to do.

"What is there to be confused about?" He placed the chalice down, and I thought his eyes warmed like they did when he was amused or...or feeling a certain way I refused to acknowledge.

My gift swelled against my skin, demanding I use it to sense his emotions as I flattened my hand over the meat knife. I managed to shut off my abilities before they formed a connection to him. I didn't want to know if he was amused or...or *whatever* at the moment. I didn't care *what* he was feeling.

"As I said," the Prince continued, dragging one long finger over the rim of his cup. "A marriage can only occur between two Atlantians if both halves are standing on the soil of their home, Princess."

Princess.

That annoying and yet somewhat slightly endearing pet name of his had just taken on a whole different meaning. One that begged the question: How much had he known from the beginning? He'd admitted to recognizing who I was the night at the Red Pearl, but he claimed he didn't know that I was part Atlantian until he bit me. Tasted my blood. The mark on my neck tingled, and I resisted the urge to touch it.

How much of that nickname was a coincidence? I wasn't sure why, but if that was yet another lie, it mattered.

"Which part confuses you?" he asked, amber eyes unblinking.

"It's the part where you think I would actually marry you."

Across from me, I heard the choked sound of someone trying to conceal laughter. I flicked a look at the handsome face of a tawny-brown-skinned, pale-blue-eyed wolven—a creature able to take the form of a wolf as easily as they could assume the form of a mortal. Until a few days ago, I'd believed that the wolven were extinct, killed off during the War of Two Kings some four hundred years ago. But that was yet another lie. Kieran was just one of many, very alive wolven—several of which sat at this table.

"I don't *think* that you will," Casteel replied, thick lashes lowering halfway. "I know."

Disbelief thundered through me. "Maybe I wasn't clear, so I will try to be more explicit now. I don't know why you'd think, in a million years, that I'd marry you." I tipped toward him. "Is that clear enough?"

"Crystal," he responded, eyes heating to a warm honey hue, but there didn't seem to be any anger in his stare or tone. There was something else entirely. A look that made me think of warm skin and how those rough, callused palms had felt against my cheek, gliding over my belly and thighs, grazing much more intimate places. The dimple in his cheek deepened. "But we shall see, won't we?"

A hot, prickly feeling spread over my skin. "We shall see absolutely nothing."

"I can be very convincing."

"Not *that* convincing," I retorted, and he gave a noncommittal murmur that sent a bolt of pure rage streaking through me. "Have you lost your mind?"

A deep belly laugh came from farther down the table. I knew it wasn't the fair-haired Delano. That wolven appeared as if he'd just witnessed a massacre, and his neck was next on the line. Maybe I should be afraid, because wolven weren't easily scared, especially not Delano. He'd defended me when Jericho and the others came for me, although he and the Atlantian, Naill—who currently sat on one side of him—had been sorely outnumbered.

The Dark One wasn't someone most would dare to anger. He was an Atlantian, deadly, fast, and impossibly strong. Hard to wound, let alone kill. And as I learned just recently, capable of using compulsion to enforce his will upon others. He'd killed one of the most powerful Dukes in all of Solis, thrusting the very cane Teerman often used on me through the Ascended's heart.

But I felt no fear.

I was too furious to be scared.

Sitting on Delano's left was the source of the laugh I'd just heard. It had come from the mountain of a man, the one called Elijah. I didn't think he was a wolven. It was the eyes. All the wolven had the same wintry blue eyes. Elijah's were hazel, a color more gold than brown. I wasn't the only one staring at him now. Several gazes had landed on him. I took the opportunity to slide the meat knife off the table, hiding it under the slit in my tunic.

"What?" Elijah stroked his dark beard as he met the many stares. "She's asking what most of us are thinking."

Delano blinked and then slowly looked at Elijah. Casteel said nothing. His tight-lipped smile spoke volumes as the piercing weight of his gaze moved from me to farther down the table.

Fingers stilling on his beard, Elijah cleared his throat. "I thought the plan—"

"What you think is irrelevant." The Prince silenced the older man.

"You mean the one where you thought to use me as bait to free your brother?" I demanded. "Or has that magically changed in the last couple of hours?"

A muscle popped along Casteel's jaw as the full focus of his attention returned to me. "You should eat."

I almost lost it right then and threw my scavenged knife at him. "I'm not hungry."

His gaze dipped to my plate. "You've barely eaten."

"Well, you see, I don't have much of an appetite, *Your Highness.*"

His jaw tightened as his eyes met mine and held. The golden hue of his irises had chilled. Goosebumps prickled my skin as the air around us seemed to thicken and become charged, filling the room. There hadn't been an ounce of respect in my tone. Had I pushed Casteel too far? If so, I didn't care.

My fingers tightened around the handle of the blade. I was no longer the Maiden, bound to rules that prevented me from having a say in matters of my life. I would no longer be controlled. I could and would push harder than this.

"She asks a very valid question," someone said from the end of the table. It was a man with short, dark hair. He looked no older than Kieran, who, like Casteel, appeared to be in his early twenties. But Casteel was over two hundred years old. The man could be even older, for all I knew. "Has the plan to use her to free Prince Malik changed?" he asked.

Casteel said nothing as he continued watching me, but the utter stillness that crept into his features was a far better warning than any words could be.

"I am not trying to question your decisions," the man stated. "I'm attempting to understand them."

"What do you need help understanding, Landell?" Casteel leaned back in the chair, his hands resting lightly on the arms. The way he sat as if completely at ease, raised the tiny hairs all over my body.

A tense moment of silence descended, and then Landell said, "We have all followed you here from Atlantia. We stayed in this archaic, cesspool of a kingdom, pretending loyalty to a counterfeit King and Queen. Because, like you, we want nothing more than to free your brother. He is the rightful heir."

Casteel nodded for Landell to continue.

"We have lost people—good people trying to infiltrate the Temples in Carsodonia," he said. I tensed as images of the sprawling, midnight-hued structures formed in my mind.

If all that Casteel had alleged was true, the purpose the Temples served was another lie. Third sons and daughters weren't given over during the Rite to serve the gods. Instead, they were given to the Ascended—the vamprys—becoming nothing more than cattle. Much of the pile of lies I'd been fed my entire life was terrible, but that was possibly the worst of them all. And as revolting as what Casteel claimed was, I feared it was the truth. How could I deny it? The Ascended had told us that the Atlantians' kiss was poisonous, cursing innocent mortals and turning them into these decaying shells of their former selves— vicious, blood-hungry monsters known as the Craven. But I knew that to be untrue. The Atlantians' kiss wasn't toxic. Neither was their bite. I was proof of both of those things. Casteel and I had shared many kisses. He'd given me his blood when I was mortally wounded. And, he'd bitten me.

I did not turn.

Just like I hadn't turned when I was attacked by the Craven all those years ago.

And it wasn't like I hadn't begun to develop suspicions about the Ascended before Casteel entered my life. He had only confirmed them. But was it all true? I had no way of knowing. My fingers ached from how tightly I held the knife.

"We haven't found any leads on where our Prince is being held, and too many will never return home to their families," Landell continued, his voice steadying with each word, thickening with anger I didn't need my gift to sense. "But now we have something. Finally, something that could be used to gain knowledge of your brother's whereabouts—to possibly free him, keep him from being forced to make new vamprys, living through the kind of hell you're all too familiar with. Instead, we're going home?"

I knew of some of that hell.

I'd seen the numerous scars all over Casteel's body, the brand in the shape of the Royal Crest on his upper thigh, just below his hip.

But Casteel said nothing in return. No one spoke. There was no movement, not from those at the table or the ones near the hearth at the back of the banquet hall.

Landell wasn't finished. "The ones hanging on the walls of the hall outside this very room deserve to be there. Not just because they disobeyed your orders, but because if they had succeeded in killing the Maiden, we would've lost the one thing we could use. They put the heir in jeopardy for vengeance. That is why I believe they deserve their fate, even though some of them were friends of mine—friends of many at this table."

I will kill them.

That was Casteel's promise when he saw the wounds the others had left behind. And he had. Mostly. Casteel had staked those Landell spoke of to the wall. All were dead now, except for Jericho. The ringleader was barely alive, suffering a slow, agonizing death to serve as a reminder that I would not be harmed.

"You can use her," Landell fumed. "She is the Queen's favorite—the Chosen. If they were ever to release your brother, it would be for her. Instead, we're going home for you to marry?" He jerked his chin toward me. "*Her*?"

The distaste in that word stung, but I'd been on the receiving end of far more cutting remarks from Duke Teerman to show even a flicker of reaction.

Across from me, Kieran's head snapped in Landell's direction. "If you have any intelligence, you would stop speaking. Now."

"Let him continue," Casteel interjected. "He has a right to speak his mind. Just as Elijah did. But it seems as if Landell has more to say than Elijah, and I would like to hear it."

Elijah's lips pursed, and he emitted a low whistle, eyes widening as he leaned back in his chair, dropping an arm over the back of Delano's seat. "Hey, sometimes I speak and laugh when I shouldn't. But whatever you plan or want, I'm with you, Casteel."

"Are you serious?" Landell's head whipped toward Elijah as he shot to his feet. "You're okay with giving up on Prince Malik? You're fine with Casteel bringing her back home, to our lands, and marrying her, making her the Princess? An honor meant to bring all of our people together, not to divide them."

Casteel moved slightly, his hands sliding off the arms of his chair.

"As I just said, I'm with Casteel." Elijah lifted his gaze to Landell. "Always, and no matter what he chooses. And if he chooses her, then we all do."

This was…that was entirely ridiculous, the whole argument. It didn't matter. And I didn't care why there was a need to bring the people of Atlantia together because Casteel and I weren't getting married. I didn't get a chance to point that out, though.

"I do not choose her. I will *never* choose her," Landell swore, the skin of his face thinning and darkening as he scanned those who sat around him. Wolven. He was a wolven, I realized. I adjusted my grip on the knife and tensed. "All of you know this. The wolven will not accept her. It doesn't matter if she has Atlantian blood or not. Neither will the people of Atlantia welcome her. She's an outsider raised and cared for by those who forced us back into a land that is quickly growing too small and useless." He stared down the table, looking at Casteel. "She didn't even accept you, and we're supposed to believe that she will bond with you?"

Bond? I glanced at Kieran and then Casteel. I knew that some wolven were bonded to Atlantians of a particular class, and it took no leap of logic to assume that Casteel being a Prince was just that. The two of them seemed the closest out of everyone I'd seen Casteel interact with, but I knew of no other bond.

However, again, it was irrelevant since we were not marrying.

"Are we supposed to believe that she is worthy of being our Princess when she flat-out denies you in front of your people while reeking of the Ascended?" Landell demanded. My nose wrinkled. I didn't smell like...like the Ascended. Did I? "When she refuses to choose you?"

"What matters is that I choose her," Casteel spoke, and my stupid, *stupid* heart skipped a beat, even though I did not choose him. "And that is all that matters."

The wolven's lips peeled back, and my eyes widened at the sight of his canines elongating. "You do this, and it will be the downfall of our kingdom," he snarled. "I will not choose that scarred-face bitch."

I flinched.

I'd actually *flinched*, cheeks burning as if I'd been slapped across the face. I lifted my fingers, touching the uneven skin of my cheek before I realized what I was doing.

Landell's hand dropped to his hip. "I'll see her dead before I stand by and allow this."

Seconds, mere heartbeats passed from when those words left Landell's mouth, and the frenzied stir of air as it lifted wisps of hair at my temples.

Casteel's chair was empty.

A shout, and then something heavy clanged off a dish. A chair toppled, and Landell...he was no longer standing by the table. His plate was no longer empty. A narrow dagger lay there, one designed for throwing. My wide eyes followed the blur that was Casteel as he pinned Landell to the wall, his forearm pressed into the wolven's throat.

Good gods, to be able to move that fast, that silently...

"I just want you to know that I'm not even particularly upset about you questioning what I intend to do. How you've spoken to me doesn't bother me. I'm not insecure enough to care about the opinions of little men." Casteel's face was inches from the wide-eyed wolven. "If that had been all, I would've overlooked it. If you had stopped after the first time you referenced her, I would've let you walk out of here with just your overinflated sense of self-worth. But then you insulted her. You made her flinch, and then you threatened her. I will not forget that."

"I—" Whatever Landell was about to say ended in a gurgle as Casteel's right arm thrust forward.

"And I will not be able to forgive you." Casteel jerked his arm back, throwing something to the floor. It landed with a fleshy smack.

My lips slowly parted as I realized what the lumpy, red mass was. Oh, my gods. A heart. It was an actual heart.

Letting go of the wolven, Casteel stepped back, watching Landell slide down the wall, the wolven's head lolling to the side. He turned to face the table, his right hand stained with blood and gore. "Does anyone else have anything they'd like to share?"

Chapter 2

A chorus of denials echoed through the banquet hall, but none of the men had so much as twitched in their seats. Some of them were even chuckling, and I...I stared at the red coursing down the length of Casteel's fingers, dripping onto the floor.

Casteel leaned forward, plucking up Landell's napkin. Strolling back to his chair, he idly wiped his hand clean.

I watched him sit, my heart thumping as he turned to me, his gaze sheltered by a fringe of heavy lashes.

"You probably think that was excessive," he said, dropping the crumpled, blood-stained napkin onto his plate. "It wasn't. No one speaks of you or to you like that and lives."

I stared at him.

He sat back. "At least, I gave him a quick death. There is some dignity in that."

I had no idea what to say.

I had no clue what to feel. All I could think was, *oh my gods, he just ripped a wolven's heart from his chest with his* bare *hand.*

The men who stood by the doors were picking up Landell when one of the men at the table asked, "So, when is the wedding?"

Laughter greeted the question, and there was a hint of a smile on Casteel's lips as he leaned toward me. "There is no side of you that is not as beautiful as the other half. Not a single inch isn't stunning." His lashes lifted, and the intensity in his stare held me captive. "That was true the first time I said it to you, and it is still the truth today and tomorrow."

My lips parted on a sharp inhale. I almost reached for my face again but stopped myself. Somehow, in the process of getting used to being seen without the veil of the Maiden, I'd forgotten about my scars—something I'd never thought possible. I wasn't ashamed of them, hadn't been for years. They were proof of my strength, of the horrific attack I had survived. But when I was unveiled in front of Casteel for the first time, I'd feared he would agree with what Duke Teerman had always said. What I knew most thought if they saw me unveiled or looked upon me now.

That half of my face was a masterpiece, while the other was a nightmare.

But when Hawke—*Casteel*—had seen the pale pink, jagged streak of skin that started below my hairline and sliced across the temple, ending at my nose, and the other that was shorter and higher, cutting across my forehead through my eyebrow, he had said that both halves were as beautiful as the whole.

I'd believed him then. And I'd felt beautiful for the first time in my life, something that had also been forbidden to me.

And gods help me, but I still believed him.

"What he said was more than an insult. It was a threat that I will not tolerate," Casteel finished, sitting back as he picked up his chalice with the same hand that had torn a heart free from its cage moments before.

My gaze fell to where the dagger still lay on Landell's plate. What the wolven would've attempted to do with that dagger shouldn't have come as a shock. It wasn't like I didn't know that many of those at this table would rather see me sliced into pieces. I knew I wasn't safe here, but all of them had seen the hall outside this room. They had to know what would happen if they disobeyed Casteel.

Some unconscious part of me still underestimated their hatred of anything that reminded them of the Ascended. And that was me, even if I hadn't done anything to them other than defend myself.

Conversation picked back up around the table. Quiet discussions. Louder ones. Laughter. It was like nothing had happened, and that rattled me. But what left me wholly unsettled was what I couldn't admit, even to myself.

Kieran cleared his throat. "Would you like to return to your room, Penellaphe?"

Pulled from my thoughts, it took me a moment to respond. "You mean my cell?"

"It's far more comfortable and not nearly as drafty as the dungeon," he replied.

"A cell is a cell, no matter how comfortable it is," I told him.

"I'm fairly certain this is the same conversation we had earlier," Casteel commented.

My gaze swiveled back to Casteel. "*I'm* fairly certain I don't care."

"I'm also sure that we came to the conclusion that you have never been free, Princess," Casteel tacked on. The truth of those words was still as brutal as it was when they had first been spoken. "I don't believe you would even recognize freedom if it were ever offered to you."

"I know enough to recognize that's not what you're offering," I shot back, fury returning in a hot, welcoming wave, warming my too-cold skin.

A faint smile appeared on Casteel's mouth, though it wasn't his tight, calculating one. My anger gave way to confusion. Was he purposely baiting me?

More than a little agitated, I focused on the wolven. "I would like to return to my more comfortable, not-nearly-as-drafty cell. I assume I won't be allowed to walk there myself?"

Kieran's lips twitched, but his expression smoothed out pretty quickly, proving that he had the common sense not to smile or laugh. "You would assume correctly."

Without waiting for His Highness to give permission, I pushed back my chair. The legs screeched across the stone floor. Internally, I sighed. My motions weren't as dignified as I wished, but I kept my head high as I started to turn.

One of the men who'd been at the door and had retrieved

Landell's corpse stalked across the banquet hall, headed straight for the Prince. He bent low, whispering in Casteel's ear as Kieran rose. Without waiting for Kieran, nor looking at the smear of blood across the wall, I took a step.

Suddenly, Casteel was at my side, his hand on my arm. Not having heard him rise, I swallowed a gasp of surprise and moved to pull my arm free as the man who'd spoken to Casteel stepped away.

"Don't," Casteel whispered, holding onto my arm. Something about his tone in that one word stopped me. I looked up at him. "We're about to have company. Fight me all you want later. I'll probably enjoy it. But do not fight me in front of him."

My eyes met his as knots formed in my stomach. Again, his tone struck a chord of unease within me as I looked at the door. Who was coming? His father? The King?

Casteel shifted so that he stood partially in front of me as a group of men filled the doorway. The sandy-haired man who walked in the center, tall and broad of shoulder, snagged my attention. I inherently knew that this was who Casteel had spoken of.

The man, his wealth of blond hair brushing a square, hard jaw, appeared much older than Casteel. If he was mortal, which I doubted, I would've pegged him for someone on the verge of approaching mid-life. I didn't think this man was Casteel's father. He looked nothing like him, but I supposed that didn't mean much.

He strode toward us. The heavy cloak he wore, dusted with melting snow, parted, revealing a black tunic with two gold lines overlapping across his chest. As he drew closer, I somehow managed not to gasp. It wasn't the pale blue eyes I associated with the wolven. It was the deep groove in the center of his forehead as if someone had attempted to slice open his head. I, of all people, knew better than to be surprised by scars. Shame crept up my throat as I averted my gaze. It wasn't that the injury was ugly. The man was handsome in a rugged way that reminded me of a lion. It was just a shock to see someone, a possible wolven, scarred. Vaguely, I became aware of Kieran coming to stand at my back.

"What in the gods' teeth is happening here?" the man demanded.

The breath I had taken got stuck as my gaze flew back to the man. His voice...it sounded so familiar to me.

"Or do I even want to know?" he continued, his brows lifting as he saw the blood on the wall. The others who'd traveled with them moved among those at the table, all except one. He was shorter than Casteel and more compact. His hair was a reddish-brown mop of waves, and his eyes were a brilliant gold like Casteel's. This one remained close to the man, and his gaze seemed to track every breath I took.

"I've just been doing a little redecorating," Casteel replied, and the wolven chuckled as the two males clasped hands.

I felt a catch in my chest again, a tug at my heart. His laugh...it was raspy and rough as if his throat weren't sure what to do with the emotion. Like Vikter's. My heart squeezed. That was why his voice and laugh sounded familiar to me.

"I didn't expect you to be here so soon, Alastir," Casteel said.

"We rode hard to get ahead of the storm headed this way." Alastir's gaze slid past the Prince to me. Curiosity marked his features, though not the flush of anger or the coldness of distaste. "So, this is her."

"It is."

Every muscle in my body tensed as Alastir's gaze lowered. His head tilted, and it took me a moment to realize that he was staring at my neck—

The damn bite!

My braid had slipped over my shoulder, revealing my throat.

The skin around Alastir's mouth tightened as his gaze shifted back to Casteel. "I feel like things have occurred since we last spoke."

Had Alastir been with Casteel's father when he left New Haven to speak with him? If so, where was the King?

"Many things have changed," Casteel answered. "Including my relationship with Penellaphe."

"Penellaphe?" Alastir repeated in surprise, one eyebrow arching. "Named after the Goddess of Wisdom, Loyalty, and

Duty?"

Since I very well couldn't stand there and ignore him, I nodded.

A faint smile appeared. "A fitting name for the Maiden, I imagine."

"You wouldn't think that if you knew her," Casteel replied, and I clamped my lips shut against a retort.

"Then I cannot wait to do so." Alastir's smile tightened.

"You will have to wait a little longer." Casteel glanced back. His eyes briefly met mine, but it was long enough for me to know that he wished for me not to challenge what he said next. "Penellaphe was just about to retire."

Kieran stepped closer, placing his hand on my lower back to urge me forward. I squelched the urge to refuse, having enough sense to realize that Casteel didn't want me around this man, and there was probably a good reason for that.

I walked forward, well aware of several gazes following me. I'd made it halfway to the door when I heard Alastir ask, "Is it wise to allow the Maiden to roam freely?"

I stopped—

"Keep walking," Kieran said under his breath. The handle of the knife I'd stolen dug into my palm.

"It wouldn't be wise to refuse her to do so," Casteel said with a laugh, and it took everything in me not to throw the blade at him.

Kieran kept pace with me as we passed the men who'd returned to standing sentry at the large wooden doors. Striding forward, I told myself not to look up, but my eyes lifted anyway as I passed the impaled body of Mr. Tulis.

Pressure clamped down on my chest. He and his wife had come before Duke and Duchess Teerman, pleading to keep their third-born son, their only remaining child, who had been *destined* to go into service to the gods during the Rite. I'd felt their soul-deep pain and desperation, and even without my gift, I would've been affected. I'd planned to plead their case to the Queen. To do something, even if I weren't successful.

But they'd escaped. His entire family, his wife and infant son, given a chance at a new life. And he'd taken that opportunity to deliver what would've been the wound that killed me if it hadn't been for Casteel.

I wanted to scream. I wanted to yell, *"why?"* as I stared at the pale face and the dried blood that stained his chest. Why had he made that choice? He'd thrown everything away for a short-lived sense of retribution. Against me, who had done nothing to him or his family. None of that had mattered in the end. Now, his son would grow up without a father.

But at least he would live. If he'd been given over in the Rite, he'd likely face a future worse than death. I had no idea how long the third sons and daughters survived within those Temples. Were they...fed upon immediately, even as infants? Small children? Third sons and daughters were given over annually, while the second sons and daughters were given to the Court between the ages of thirteen and eighteen. They lived—well, most of them. Some died at Court due to a sickness of the blood that took them during the night. Casteel had said the vamprys struggled to control their bloodlust, and I now doubted that there'd been an ailment that took them. Instead, it was like what had happened to Malessa Axton, who'd been found with a bite on her throat and her neck broken. It was never confirmed, but I knew Lord Mazeen, an Ascended, had killed her and left her body there, half exposed for anyone to find.

At least Lord Mazeen will harm no one else, I told myself as a savage wave of satisfaction flowed through me. I easily recalled the look of shock etched onto his face when I chopped off his hand. I'd never thought I would be glad to kill anything but a Craven, but Lord Mazeen had proven that false.

The violent joy came to a swift end as thoughts of the children crept back in. How could anyone, mortal or not, hurt young ones like that? And they had been doing it for years—hundreds of years.

Realizing I'd come to a standstill, I started walking again. Chest heavy, I didn't even bother to look at Jericho. I could tell by the pitiful whimpers coming from him that he was still alive.

I believed everyone deserved dignity in death, even him, but I didn't feel even one iota of empathy for what he'd brought upon himself.

And Landell? Did I feel sorry for him? Not particularly. What did that say about me?

I didn't want to think of that so I asked, "Who was that man?"

"His name is Alastir Davenwell. He's the advisor to the King and Queen. A close family friend. More like an uncle to both Casteel and Malik," Kieran said, and I jerked a little at the mention of Casteel's brother.

"Is that why Casteel didn't want me around him? Because Alastir is an advisor to his parents? Or because he too will wish to chop me into pieces?"

"Alastir is not a man prone to violence, despite the scar he carries. And while he knows his place with the Prince, he is loyal to the Queen and King. There are things that Casteel would not want to get back to his father or mother."

"Like the ridiculous marriage thing?"

"Something like that." Kieran shifted the conversation as we rounded the corner and entered the common area where the air was free of the stench of death. "Do you feel pity for the mortal? The one Cas helped escape the Ascended with his family?"

Cas.

Gods, that sounded like such a harmless nickname for such a dangerous man.

I glanced at Kieran as we entered the narrow stairwell, noting that he was without his short sword and bow as he moved in front of me. But he was far from defenseless, considering what he was. I didn't even bother to make a run for it. I knew I wouldn't make it more than a foot. Wolven were incredibly fast.

Kieran stopped without warning, spinning around so suddenly that I backed up, hitting the wall. He took a step toward me and dipped his head to mine. Every muscle locked as he inhaled deeply.

Was he…?

His head lowered, the bridge of his nose brushing my temple. He inhaled again.

"What are you doing?" I jerked to the side, putting space between us. "Are you *smelling* me?"

He straightened, his eyes narrowed. "You...smell different."

My brows lifted. "Okay? I don't know what to tell you about that."

He didn't seem to hear me as his eyes brightened. "You smell like..."

"If you say I smell like Casteel again, I will punch you in the face," I promised. "Hard."

"You do smell like him, but that's not it." He shook his head. "You smell of death."

"Wow. Thanks. But if I do, that is not my fault."

"You don't understand." Kieran eyed me for a moment longer and then turned, starting up the stairwell once more.

No. I didn't understand, and I really didn't want to.

I sniffed the sleeve of my tunic. It smelled like...roasted meat.

"Earlier, you said you didn't feel sympathy for any of them," he said as I followed him.

"That hasn't changed," I said. "They wanted me dead." We stepped out of the stairwell and onto the covered walkway. Damp, cold air greeted us. "But I can't help but feel pity for Mr. Tulis."

"You shouldn't."

"Well, I do." Shivering, I ducked my chin against the sharp gust of wind. "He was given a second chance. He threw it away. I feel pity for that choice and for his wife and son. And I guess I feel sorry for the families of any of them that are now on that wall."

Kieran fell into step beside me, taking the brunt of the wind. "The pity for the families is rightfully placed."

I stopped in surprise but said nothing.

"What?"

"Nothing," I murmured.

He issued a soft chuckle. "You think I'm not capable of compassion?"

I glanced out over the yard below. A fine layer of snow shone brightly in the moonlight. Beyond, I saw nothing but the thick darkness of the encroaching woods. It was strange to look out and not see a Rise, the often-mountainous walls constructed from limestone and iron mined from the Elysium Peaks. The sleepy town of New Haven had one, but it was much smaller than what I was accustomed to in both Masadonia and Carsodonia.

"I don't know what you're capable of," I admitted, touching the banister's cool wood as the wind picked up, lifting the shorter strands of my hair that had escaped my braid. "I hardly know anything about the wolven."

"My animal side doesn't cancel out my mortal one," he replied. "I'm not incapable of emotions."

My gaze cut to his. "I didn't mean it like that. I just…" I trailed off. What had I meant? "I guess I *did* mean it like that. I'm sorry."

"You don't need to apologize. It's not like you've met many wolven," he reasoned.

"Yes, but that's no excuse." I gripped the railing with one hand. "There are a lot of different people from various places that I haven't met and know nothing about. That doesn't mean it's okay to make assumptions."

"True," he replied, and I almost cringed. How many times had I made assumptions about the Atlantian people? The Descenters? Biases were taught and learned. Maybe that wasn't my fault, but that didn't make it acceptable.

But nobody at that table had even twitched in their seats as Casteel killed Landell. What did that say about them? "Is what happened tonight common?"

"Which part? The marriage proposal or the open-heart surgery?"

I shot Kieran a dark look. "Landell."

He studied me for a moment, and then his stare turned to the yard and the trees. "Not particularly. Even if you don't see this yet or don't want to, Cas is not a murderous tyrant. Honestly, it's rare that any question him. Not because what he does or doesn't do is always reasonable, but because he has no problem getting blood on his hands to assert his authority to get what he wants or to keep those he cares for safe."

There was a measure of relief, knowing Casteel didn't rip hearts out of chests often. That was a good thing…I guessed.

Although, I didn't dare believe that I fell into the category of those he cared for. I was someone he needed.

"What Cas did wasn't about Landell questioning him." Kieran angled his body toward me. "It wasn't as simple as Landell not being able to understand how or why the Prince would choose you. It wasn't even about him challenging Cas. Atlantians and wolven do anything to protect their home, and it was clear that Landell saw you as a threat to it," Kieran told me, and I wondered what I had to do with Landell's concern over their land growing too small and useless. "Cas was right to do what he did. If he hadn't, Landell would've thrown that dagger he pulled. There will be others who will want to do the same thing."

Dread settled in my bones. "Was Landell another warning, then? How many warnings will there need to be?"

"As many as are needed."

"And that doesn't bother you? Some of them are your friends, right?"

"If someone is idiot enough to insult and threaten you in front of Cas, it's likely someone I wouldn't have been particularly close to in the first place."

I almost laughed at that, but none of this was funny. "Everyone seems so full of emotion one moment and then absolutely apathetic the next."

"You haven't tried to feel my emotions to know what I am feeling?" Kieran asked, delivering another dose of the unexpected. My gaze cut to him.

Then I remembered that Kieran had been there when I used my gift to ease the pain of a dying guard. Still, it was bizarre to discuss this with anyone after spending so long forced to hide my abilities and never speak of them.

"Cas told me that it started with you only being able to sense and ease pain. But he also said that changed."

I nodded. "It did change, only a little while ago. I don't know why. I asked the Duchess about it because I thought maybe the first Maiden had been able to do the same." Tension crept up my neck. Duchess Teerman had told me that the first Maiden's gift had grown from sensing pain to reading emotions, and that the growth was because she was near her Ascension—like I was. Honestly, little was known about the first Maiden. Not even her name or what era she lived in. But the Duchess had insinuated that the Dark One had killed the first Maiden.

Casteel.

I shivered, and I didn't think it had anything to do with the cold. "I haven't tried to read your emotions. I try not to do that since it feels like an invasion to do so."

"Maybe it is a breach of privacy," he agreed. "But it would also give you an upper hand when dealing with people."

It could.

"Do you think he's told others?" I asked.

"Cas? No. The less others know about you, the better," he answered, and my brows rose. "I don't know of any Atlantian alive today who can experience what others feel."

"What does that mean?"

"I'm not sure yet." He started walking. "You coming? Or are you planning to stay out here and turn into an ice cube?"

Sighing, I pulled myself away from the railing and went to where he stood in front of the door.

He slipped a key from his pocket. "Your ability would especially help you when it comes to dealing with Cas."

"I have no intention of dealing with him."

A small smile appeared as he held open the door. I walked into the room, warmed by the heat of the fireplace. "But he has every intention of dealing with you."

Keeping the meat knife hidden under my tunic, I faced Kieran. "You mean he has every intention of using me."

His head cocked to the side. "That's not what I said, Penellaphe."

"Why not? Do you think he really has given up on his brother? I don't. He even said that I'm the Queen's favorite," I spat, the last two words acidic on my tongue. "This marriage thing has to be a part of the plan to get his brother back. Though why he didn't just fess up to that at the table, I have no idea."

"I don't think either of you knows the truth."

My spine stiffened. "What is that supposed to mean?"

Kieran eyed me. He was quiet for so long, the unease within

me tripled. "He told you the truth about the Ascended, didn't he?"

I wasn't sure what any of this had to do with what he'd said, but I answered. "The Ascended are...vamprys, and everything I've been taught—that everyone in Solis believes—is a lie. The gods never Blessed King Jalara and Queen Ileana. The gods aren't even—"

"No, the gods are real. They are *our* gods, and they now rest," he corrected. "You know the Ascended aren't Blessed. They are as cursed as those bitten by a Craven are. Except they don't decay. You know this, but do you understand?"

His words were like a punch to the chest. "My brother—" I cut myself off. I didn't need to talk about Ian. "I understand."

"And do you believe what Cas told you about the Ascended?"

I looked at the fire, not answering. On one hand, I'd seen the evidence of what Casteel claimed—saw it branded on his skin. The Ascended had held Casteel captive before they took his brother. He'd been tortured, forced to do and take part in things I knew were utterly horrific based on the few small details he'd shared with me. What I felt when I thought about that was too heavy and noxious to be called disgust. And the ache in my heart was only the beginning, knowing that Casteel's brother had been captured while freeing him.

I could be furious with Casteel.

I could even hate him.

But that didn't mean I didn't want to scream for all the agony Casteel had experienced and for what his brother was surely suffering at this very moment.

Did that mean that all Ascended were evil? Every last one of them, including my brother? I believed in what I saw proof of. But Casteel... I couldn't trust more than half of what left his mouth, and it wasn't like all Atlantians were utterly innocent.

"If you do believe him, then what are you fighting to go back to?" Kieran asked, and my gaze flew to his. "Isn't that what you're doing by refusing Cas?"

"Refusing to marry him has nothing to do with the Ascended, and everything to do with him," I argued. "He lied to me about *everything*."

"He didn't lie about everything."

"How do you know?" I challenged. "You know what? Don't even answer that. It doesn't matter. What does is that he plans to ransom me to the very people who did these horrible things to him and countless others. He plans to hand me over to the people who will most likely use me as a blood bag until I die. And even *if*, by some small chance, those plans have changed, they only did so because he realized I was part Atlantian. How is that any better? Why would I marry him?"

"Why would he marry someone he plans to ransom off?" he queried.

"Exactly!" Exasperated, I mashed my lips together as my focus shifted to the dark night beyond Kieran. "I don't even know why we're having this conversation."

He fell quiet again. "You push him like you have no fear, even after all you've seen?"

"Should I fear him?" I asked. An incredibly stupid part of me almost didn't want to know the answer. I'd trusted Hawke with my secrets, my desires, my body, my heart, my…life. I'd trusted him with *everything*, and nothing about him had been real. Not even the name Hawke.

I'd stumbled and tripped for him, and I was afraid that I would keep falling despite his betrayal. *That* was what I was afraid of.

"He has done things some might find unforgivable. Things that would haunt your sleep and leave you with nightmares long after you wake. He may hate being called the Dark One, but he has earned that name." Kieran's pale eyes met mine as a shiver curled its way down my spine. "But he's the one thing in all the kingdoms that you, and only you, never have to fear."

Chapter 3

If Kieran's words were meant to reassure me, they'd done the exact opposite.

Pacing in front of the narrow window that was too small to escape from, I stared at the door. It had been locked from the outside.

Just like a cell.

My hands curled into fists as I made another pass in front of the window, anger mingling with the ever-present unease. It wasn't what Kieran had said about Casteel earning the title of the Dark One. After how coldly and efficiently Casteel had killed Phillips, the guard who'd traveled with us from Masadonia, I already knew how he ended up with the nickname. Seeing him take out Landell was only further proof that he could—and would—kill without hesitation, but...

I stopped suddenly. I could also kill without too much reluctance. Hadn't I proven that with Lord Mazeen? When Jericho and the others came after me, I'd been prepared to kill. My gaze dropped to my hands. They too, were covered in blood, and I couldn't say it was just from self-defense and the necessity to survive. Lord Mazeen deserved the ending he got. The Ascended had taken the same perverse joy the Duke had when it came time for my *lessons*, but he hadn't attacked me when I turned on him. He'd insulted Vikter within moments of my guard and friend taking his last breath, and I didn't feel even a smidgen of guilt for how I handled it. Even if he hadn't been a vampry, he was still a monster. Maybe that was why I wasn't shocked by what Casteel had done in the hall.

And that quite possibly meant there was something wrong with me. Either way, it was what Kieran had said before he closed the door that made me angry.

That Casteel was the only person I never had to fear.

Kieran couldn't be more wrong.

I looked to the bed then, and my stomach dipped as if I were standing on the edge of a Rise. I could almost see us, our limbs entwined, and our bodies joined. An aching pulse rolled through me as I touched the bite mark on my neck. I shivered, then searched for a hint of disgust or even fear. I found none.

He'd bitten me.

And his bite had hurt, but only at first, and only for a few seconds. Then, it had felt…it had felt like being drowned in liquid heat. I had never felt something so intense in my life— hadn't even known something like that was possible. But it wasn't the effects of the bite that had led to what we'd done in the woods while the snow fell around and upon us. Our bodies had come together because of my attraction to him. Because how I felt for him had been greater than the truth of what and who he was. That was what drove this need to understand how he'd gotten to this point in his life and why he was doing what he was now. It was what fueled this desire to forget everything except for the bliss I'd felt while I was in his arms—his lips against my skin, and the peace and companionship I experienced when we were simply speaking to one another.

But I wasn't safe with him.

Even if Casteel never raised a hand to me, I couldn't forget what he was. What he'd caused. Vikter's death may not have come at the tip of Casteel's sword, but it had been the jagged blades of the people who followed him. And what of Loren and Dafina, the Ladies in Wait who had died during the attack at the Rite? They had been excited to Ascend, but I doubted they had known the truth. They hadn't deserved to die like they had, murdered by Descenters who most likely didn't even know their names. Again, it hadn't been by Casteel's hand, but the act was carried out in his name. How could I ever forgive him for any of that?

And what kept hurting every time I thought about him was that he knew how badly I desired freedom. To have the ability to simply choose something—anything—for myself. Whether it be something as simple as walking where I wanted, unveiled, or speaking to whoever I wanted. To something as important as choosing who I shared my body with. He knew how much that meant to me, and he was trying to take it away. My heart twisted so painfully, it felt like someone had thrust a dagger deep into my chest.

What, if anything, could he feel for me?

My heart *hurt* deeply, as if I were grieving someone who had died. In a way, it *was* like that. I mourned the loss of Hawke, and it didn't matter that he still lived and breathed. The Hawke I'd grown to trust, the man I'd shared my secrets with was gone. In his place was Prince Casteel Da'Neer, but I was still drawn to him. I still had that desire, need, and the...

That was why he was the most dangerous person in any kingdom. Because no part of me doubted that he planned to use me to free his brother, returning me to the same Ascended who had held him captive for five decades and who now held his sibling.

Pressure clamped down on my chest as I started pacing again, my thoughts shifting to Queen Ileana. My mother and the Queen had been close. So much so that when my mother chose my father over the Ascension, the Queen had allowed it. That was unheard of. Even rarer was how the Queen had cared for me after the Craven attack as if I were her own child. She had changed my bandages, sat with me when the nightmares of the attack came, and held me when all I wanted was to be hugged by my mother and father. She was the first to teach me not to be ashamed of the scars when others gasped and whispered behind their gloved hands. During those years, and before I was sent to Masadonia, she'd become more than a caregiver.

And according to Casteel, she had been the one who branded him with the Royal Crest.

I could easily remember her holding my hand as we traveled the Royal Gardens under the star-swept skies. Her patience and kindness had seemed never-ending, and yet the same hand that had held mine had sliced into Casteel's skin. If what Casteel said was true, the same softly spoken voice that'd told me stories of my mother when she was a little girl, running through the same paths we'd walked, had also fed an entire kingdom nothing but blood-soaked lies. If Casteel were telling the truth, she'd used the people's fear of the creatures she and others like her had created to control every single mortal.

And if it all was true, then had the Queen known the whole time that I was half-Atlantian?

Gods, that was almost too hard to process. But what of Ian? How could he have Ascended? Casteel had said that Ian had only been seen at night, and he believed that Ian *had* Ascended. Was it then like someone had suggested at the dinner? Was Ian my half-brother? I found it hard to believe that either of my parents would've had a child by someone else. Their love for each other was…well, it was the kind people only hoped to find for themselves.

Or I could be entirely naïve. Because if Ian wasn't their child, where did they get him? On the side of the road or something?

Casteel would likely think that I was being foolish.

Not that I cared what he thought. What the Queen knew and whether or not Ian was my half-brother, didn't matter. My gaze tracked its way back to the door.

I had to escape.

Even with the warning Casteel had left hanging in the hall, it was evident that his people still saw me as the figurehead for the Ascended. I didn't think Landell had said any lies when he spoke how my ancestry wouldn't matter to the Atlantian people. I doubted the new arrivals would want anything different than the others. It had sounded like Alastir believed I should be in a cell instead of roaming around.

As if I were allowed to do that.

And once he brought me to Atlantia, if that was truly what Casteel planned, I would be surrounded by them, and in an even more precarious position.

A small seedling of excitement took root in my stomach when I thought of Atlantia. I couldn't help but want to see the kingdom. Probably because I'd hardly seen anything in my life. But to be able to look upon a place that wasn't supposed to exist? That was something very few people would ever be able to do.

Sighing, I shoved those feelings and thoughts aside. There would be no escape if Casteel managed to take me to Atlantia.

Kieran had been wrong to assume that I was fighting Casteel to return to the Ascended. I was fighting him to return to my brother.

I had to get to Ian, but it had to be on my terms. If I somehow managed to live long enough for Casteel to exchange me, I would be going straight from one cage to another. That could only be an option of last resort. So, I needed to get to Ian my way.

And then what?

I knew I wouldn't be safe among the Ascended, but there *were* distant villages and towns I could try to carve out some kind of life in.

Slowly, I lifted my hand to my face, my fingers finding the longest scar. It would be hard to hide, wouldn't it? I would have to try, though. Because I refused to hide my face ever again. I couldn't live like that.

But that was a bridge I couldn't even begin to cross until I figured out how to escape, make my way to the capital, and find Ian without getting caught or killed.

We'd escape the Ascended together. Because even if Ian wasn't my full-blooded brother and had gone through the Ascension, he couldn't be like the rest. I refused to believe that. There was no way he would feed off the innocent and from *children*. There was no way that all Ascended were evil. Some had seemed rather normal.

But if they didn't feed off the third sons and daughters given to the gods during the Rite, then how did they survive?

They needed blood. If not, they would eventually die from whatever mortal wounds had plagued them before the Ascension. Ian had been healthy as a horse, but he would've been drained of nearly all his blood before feeding from an Atlantian to Ascend. That would've killed him, and could *still* kill him if he didn't feed.

I wanted to see for myself what Ian had or had not turned into. I would do everything I could to help him. But if he had turned into a monster who preyed on others? On children? Then what? My heart squeezed, but I took a deep, slow breath. I knew what I would have to do.

I would have to end it for him, and I *would*. Because Ian was a kind, gentle soul—always had been. He was a dreamer, destined to spin tales for the rest of his life. Not to become a monster. There was no way he would have wanted to become something so evil. Ending that nightmare for him would be the honorable thing to do.

Even if it killed a part of me.

My muscles tensed for action, and the room seemed three sizes smaller than before. I couldn't spend one more moment in here with these thoughts, not being able to do a damn thing.

I wasn't sure if I could resist Casteel.

If Casteel were right, I didn't think I would survive my time in Atlantia.

But I could find my brother.

"And I will not spend one more fucking moment in this room," I said out loud, stalking to the door. I leaned against it, listening for any sounds from outside. Hearing nothing, I rapped my knuckles on the wood. "Kieran?"

Silence.

Kieran wasn't standing guard by the door. He likely thought I was safely tucked away in the room. It wasn't like I could kick it down or climb out the stupid, pointless window. He probably thought there was no way out. And there wasn't, if one didn't have an older brother who had taught them how to pick locks.

My lips curved into a smile as I spun around. I grabbed the meat knife off the table and took it back to the door. The blade was thick near the handle, but the edge was thin enough to fit into the lock.

Kneeling, I slipped the point into the keyhole. Ian had taught me how to wiggle the knife around, applying pressure to the right and then the left, repeating until I heard the soft click. Before I requested to be moved to the older part of Castle Teerman that contained the old servants' access, allowing me to move about unseen, I was often locked inside my bedchambers while Ian was allowed out for schooling, to play, and to do whatever. He'd never told me how he learned to pick a lock, but he spent many, many afternoons teaching me.

"You have to be patient, Poppy," he'd said, kneeling beside me as I jammed the knife into the keyhole. He'd laughed as he placed his hand over mine. *"And gentle. You can't come at it like a battering ram."*

So, I was patient, and I was gentle. I wiggled the knife until I heard the soft snick of the point finding the tumbler. Grabbing the handle with my other hand, I exhaled deeply as the mechanism gave a little. I willed my hand to steady as I turned counterclockwise.

The handle turned, and the door cracked open. Cold air seeped in as I peeked outside, peering at the empty walkway.

A rush of euphoria hit me as I closed the door, scanning the room. The leather satchel was already packed with the meager items I'd brought with me. I went to grab it, but my gaze strayed to the bed, to the flannel nightgown left out by someone for me to wear. Snatching that off the bed, I started to shove it into the bag when I saw the thigh sheath lying on top. Quickly, I strapped that on and slipped the knife inside it, breathing through the pang I felt when I thought of my wolven bone and bloodstone dagger. Could it still be lying in the stables, lost under piles of straw and hay?

I crammed the nightgown into the bag and then dropped the strap over my head and across my chest. Turning, I picked up the heavy, fur-lined cloak. It was a drab, dark brown, chosen when we left Masadonia since it wouldn't catch the eye. Tossing it over my shoulders, my fingers were steady as I secured the buttons along the neck of the cloak, even though my heart pounded. I tugged on my gloves, wishing there were supplies in the room other than what I thought was liquor that sat on the table below the window. But I had gone without food before, usually when Duke Teerman was disappointed in something I did or didn't do. I could go without again.

I didn't have much of a plan, and very limited knowledge of the surrounding areas, but I knew that traveling east would take me closer to the Skotos Mountains. Supposedly, Atlantia lay—and thrived—beyond the cloud-capped peaks and the fog-drenched valleys. If I headed through the town, I could follow the road back to Masadonia, but that would take me straight through the Blood Forest. If I went southwest, through the woods, I would eventually reach…what was the town? My nose wrinkled as I tried to recall one of the maps I'd seen in the city's Atheneum. It had been old, the ink faded, but there had been a bridge drawn—

Whitebridge.

The town of Whitebridge was to the south, but I had no idea how far it would be on foot. Cursing my inexperience with horses, I sprang forward, opening the door. Walkway still clear, I slipped outside, closing the door behind me. I could lock it from the outside, but the time it would take to do that wasn't worth the seconds it would take for someone to unlock the door.

I hurried to the stairwell, sticking close to the wall. Stopping at the door, I listened for signs of life. When I heard nothing, I entered and raced down the steps, a surreal sense of deja vu hitting me as I reached the landing. I turned to the door that led outside, just like I had after stabbing Casteel.

I really hoped this had a different outcome as I pulled up the hood of the cloak, then reached for the door, opening it slowly.

A fine layer of snow crunched under my boot as I stepped out into the yard, the sound minuscule but sounding like a crack of thunder to my ears. Drawing in a deep breath, I reminded myself of all the times I'd snuck out onto the Rise without being seen, or moved throughout the castle and the city, never once being caught—until Casteel.

I wasn't going to think about that right now. I would think about how much I excelled at sneaking off, right under the noses of many.

I could do this.

My breath puffed out in small, misty clouds as I looked to the right, toward the stables. Could the wolven dagger really be in there?

Could I really be stupid enough to check?

Yes?

The dagger meant…well, it meant everything to me. But Ian was more important—my *freedom* was more important. Going to the stables was too much of a risk. There'd be stable hands there, Descenters and possibly even Atlantians or wolven.

I wasn't *that* stupid.

"Dammit," I muttered and then pushed away from the wall. I ran for the shadows, the edges of my cloak streaming out behind me as I avoided the lit torches and their buttery glow.

I didn't even realize I'd made it to the forest until the silvery moonlight became fragmented, leaving just enough light for me to not be taken out by a tree. I didn't slow. I ran faster than I ever had, keeping the pace to put as much distance between me and the keep as possible. When my boot snagged on an exposed root, bringing me down hard, my knees cracking off the frozen ground, I climbed back to my feet and ran some more, pushing past the pain and the cold, the damp air stinging my cheeks. I ran until the dull ache in my side turned into a stitch that forced me to slow. By then, I had no idea how far I'd traveled, but the trees were less crowded, and the snow-covered ground was untouched.

Panting as I rubbed at my side, I forged forward. There couldn't be more than a day's ride between New Haven and Whitebridge. So, on foot? A day and a half, maybe two if I rested. Once I got there, I could find the next group who was traveling toward the capital. I could get lucky. Maybe there wouldn't be a long wait. But if not? I would have to make do, though the real concern was if Whitebridge was as controlled by Descenters as New Haven was. If so, would they know who I was? I didn't think so. Very few people knew I was scarred. But if Casteel got word out, just like the Ascended would once we didn't show at our next outpost, I would be recognized. As far as

I knew, we hadn't planned to stop at Whitebridge, but whatever plans had been shared with the Duchess hadn't been real. But could I use my identity? If I could prove to any of the mortals or possibly the Ascended that I was the Maiden, then I was sure I could secure travel to the capital, and then I could escape once we were inside. That would be a risk, but nothing about this was safe. Only the gods knew what lived in these woods. Knowing my luck, probably a cantankerous family of very large, very hungry bears. I'd never seen a bear before, though, so that would be kind of an amazing sight to behold right before it chewed off my face. But at least I doubted—

The snapping of a branch stopped me as I climbed over a fallen tree. Looking down, I saw nothing but smooth snow and scattered pine needles. I held my breath, skin prickling as I strained to hear any other sounds. A cracking noise came again, this time closer, sending a rippling wave of wariness through me.

Spinning around, I scanned the trees and their low-hanging branches, weighed down by the snow and ice. Was that the cause of that sound? Branches breaking? I turned in a full circle, slower this time, my eyes watering from the cold air. My head jerked to the right. I squinted at the thicker, deeper shadows where the moonlight didn't quite penetrate. Reaching into the folds of my cloak, I pulled the meat knife out. I really hoped it wasn't a bear. I didn't want to have to kill the ursine. I almost laughed because I doubted the knife would do much against a bear. My muscles tensed as the shadow peeled away, slinking out from the gloom. I jerked back a step at the size of it, nearly as tall as a man, its tawny fur dusted with snow.

My heart sank all the way to the tips of my freezing toes as the wolven prowled forward, its muscles bunching and rolling under the heavy fawn-colored fur.

Kieran.

"Dammit," I growled, tasting fury in the back of my throat.

His ears flattened as he climbed halfway onto the fallen tree, the claws of his front paws ripping into the wood. He dropped his chin, those pale blue eyes alert as we stared at each other. He was waiting, probably for me to run, but I knew that wouldn't end well for me. The sense of hopelessness, of how unfair this was almost brought me to my knees.

But I stood my ground.

I would not give up.

The handle of the knife dug into my gloved palm as my heart slammed against my ribs. "I'm not going back to the keep," I told Kieran. "You will have to force me, and I will not make it easy for you. I will fight you."

"If you're looking for a fight..." came a voice that sent a shiver down my spine and then over my skin. My head jerked in the direction of the sound. "You'll fight me, Princess."

Chapter 4

Casteel, garbed in black, cut a striking figure silhouetted against the snow as he stalked forward.

He came to stand beside Kieran, and I saw that he was armed with his two short swords, the handles a deep chrome, and the blades a ruby-hued bloodstone.

The knife I held had never felt more pathetic than it did in that moment.

"I suppose I will need to add lock picking to the ever-growing list of attributes," Casteel drawled. "But what a very un-Maiden-like talent to have. Then again, I shouldn't be that surprised. You have many un-Maiden-like talents, don't you?"

I said nothing as my heart threw itself around my chest.

"Did you really think you'd escape me?" Casteel asked softly.

Anger was sharper than any blade, far more welcomed than the hopelessness. "I almost did."

"Almost means nothing, Princess. You should know that."

I did. "I'm not walking back to that keep."

"Would you prefer that I carry you?" he offered.

"I would *prefer* never to see your face again."

"Now, all three of us know that's a lie." Beside him, Kieran made a chuffing sound, and I considered chucking the knife at the wolven's face. "I'll make you a deal."

I stayed alert as he stepped over the fallen tree I had as if it were nothing more than a branch. "I'm not interested in any deals. I'm interested in my freedom."

"But you haven't heard what I have to offer." Reaching across his chest, he unstrapped one of the swords. "Fight me. You win, you can have your *freedom*." He tossed the sword so it landed in front of me.

Giving the weapon a quick glance, I laughed, the sound gritty against my skin. "As if he'll let me cause you any harm." I jerked my head to Kieran.

Casteel tilted his head as the wolven's ears perked. "Go back to the keep, Kieran. I want to make sure Poppy feels this is fair."

"Fair?" I seethed as Kieran hesitated for a moment and then pushed off the fallen tree. Twisting with all the grace of an animal, he loped off. "You're an Atlantian. How will fighting you be fair?"

"So you're afraid to lose, then? Or afraid to fight me?"

"Never," I swore.

He smirked as his eyes flared a heated ocher. "Then fight me. Remember what I said earlier? I want you to battle me. I look forward to it. I enjoy it. None of that was a lie. Engage me."

Of course, I remembered what he'd said, but there was no way I could beat him. I knew that. *He* knew that. However, there was no way I would stroll back to my cage either. Not when I'd spent my whole life in one.

Keeping my eyes on him, I slid the knife back into its sheath and unhooked the cloak, letting it fall to the ground. I immediately missed the warmth, but the garment would be too much of a hazard. I removed the satchel, as well, dropping it by the outer garment.

One of Casteel's eyebrows rose. "Is that all you were planning to escape with? Just some clothes? No other supplies? No food or water?"

"I couldn't risk being caught shopping from the pantry, now could I?" Watching him, I bent and picked up the short sword, holding it with two hands. It was nowhere near as heavy as a broadsword, but even as lightweight as it was, I didn't have the upper body strength of those who trained for years with them. Vikter had quickly erased the notion that I'd be able to wield either with one hand for any extended period.

"More like this was a poorly thought-out plan, one borne of panic."

"It was not borne of panic." Not exactly. Maybe a little.

"I don't believe that. You're smarter than this, Poppy." He unsheathed the other sword, sliding it free. "Too damn clever to run in the middle of the night with no food, no water, and nothing more than a paltry meat knife for protection."

I clamped my lips together as the heat of anger warmed my skin.

"Do you know how long it will take to get to Whitebridge on foot? That's where you were heading, wasn't it? Did you think about how cold it gets in the middle of the night?" he demanded, a hint of anger hardening his tone. "At any point, did you stop and think about the things that could be in these woods?"

I hadn't. Not really. And he was right. My plan wasn't all that well-thought-out. "Are you done talking yet? Or are you too afraid that I might actually beat you, so you won't shut up?"

"I like hearing myself talk."

"I'm sure you do." The snow picked up, spiraling across the ground.

"Ready?" he asked.

"Are you?"

"Always."

My gaze dipped to his sword. He held it pointed down, not at the ready. There was an insult there, whether he meant it or not. Blistering, smoky rage burned through me, spurring me into action.

Charging him, I jabbed for his midsection, but Casteel was fast, deflecting my attack with a simple swipe of his sword. "You should be aiming for my neck, Princess. Or is the sword too heavy for you?"

Lips thinning at the taunt, I swiped the sword high. He blocked it and struck out, not nearly as fast as he could, considering I could easily dance out of his reach.

"You've forgotten a lot of what I said to you." He prowled forward, cutting off my next blow with a swipe of his blade.

"Maybe I chose to ignore whatever it was you had to say." Eyes narrowing, I moved to the side.

"Either way, I'll do you a favor and repeat myself."

"Not necessary." I tracked his movements as he circled me. He was far more skilled with the sword, just like Vikter had been when he trained with me. What had he taught me? Never forget one of the most important weapons: the element of surprise.

Casteel stalked me, sword raised. "It seems entirely too necessary for me to repeat myself, considering your foolish behavior."

I would show him foolish behavior.

"Fight me. Argue with me. I won't stop you. But I will not allow you to put your life in jeopardy. And this? Tonight? Is the epitome of reckless, life-endangering behavior."

"You didn't want me to argue with you earlier," I reminded him, watching him carefully.

"Because, as I said, you can fight me, but not when it jeopardizes your life."

"So, my life was in jeopardy with Alastir?"

"I was working on ensuring that's not the case. Yet here I am instead, making sure you haven't gotten yourself killed."

"Only because you need me alive. Right? What good will a dead Maiden be as a bartering tool when it comes to freeing your brother?"

His jaw flexed. "So, you'd rather get yourself killed?"

"I'd rather be free," I gritted out as the wind blew a strand of hair across my face.

His upper lip curled, revealing one fang. "If you think running back to the Ascended will give you freedom, then I've overestimated your critical-thinking skills."

"If you think that's what I'm planning, then I've overestimated yours," I returned.

Casteel made his move then, swinging hard. I suspected he planned to knock the sword free from my hand. If he landed the blow, he would've, but I darted into the sword's path. Surprise widened his eyes as he drew the blade back like I knew he would. I was no good to him dead.

I dipped under his arm and spun, kicking out. My boot connected with his stomach, pushing a sharp curse out of him. Straightening, I swung the blade around. Casteel shifted to the side, narrowly avoiding a slice to the chest.

"Nice job," he remarked, his voice free of mockery.

"I didn't ask for your thoughts."

His blade met mine in a clang of bloodstone. For several heated moments, that was the only sound in the woods as we thrust and parried. A fine sheen of sweat dampened my forehead despite the cold, and even though all the running caused my muscles to now weep in protest, I refused to give in.

This wasn't a fight to the death. In the back of my mind, I knew this wasn't even a fight for freedom because no matter what deal Casteel made, he wouldn't let me go. This was about who disarmed whom first. Who drew first blood. This was about driving out the pent-up rage and the festering sense of helplessness that had resided inside me for far longer than I was comfortable admitting. And maybe, just maybe, that was why Casteel was allowing this.

The edge of my sword came close to nicking his left cheek as he swept the blade aside, the deflection sending an aching tremor up my arms. I was breathing fast while he showed no signs of tiring.

He moved around me in a slow circle, his sword once again lowered. "Did I frighten you tonight? With Landell?" he asked. The arrogance marking his features slipped away, revealing someone else entirely. "Is that why you ran? Are you scared of me?"

Startled by the question—by the way he almost looked afraid to hear my answer—I lowered the sword an inch.

It was a mistake.

Casteel struck as fast as a falcon with its prey in sight. He gripped my arm, spinning me so my back was to him. I tried to twist, but his arm clamped down on my waist, pulling me back against his chest. He pressed his fingers into my wrist, forcing my hand to spasm open. The sword fell to the snow.

"I had to do it," he said, dipping his head so his cheek pressed against mine. "No one, and I mean *no one*, speaks of you like that. Threatens you and lives."

My stupid, ridiculous heart skipped a beat. "That's so sweet," I said, and I felt his arm loosen around my waist. "But you cheated."

Jerking to the side, I slammed my elbow into his stomach as hard as I could. Casteel grunted, letting go. I whirled, striking fast instead of going for the sword he still held. My fist caught him in the corner of the mouth. The shock of pain flared in his eyes, and I spun, dipping low as I swung my leg around. He jumped, but I caught one leg, sweeping it out from underneath him. He went down, and a shout of victory burst from me as I popped to my feet and turned to him, breathing heavily.

Casteel dropped his sword as he rose onto one elbow, dragging his hand over his mouth as he stared up at me. Red smeared the back of his hand, and a sense of violent delight surged through me. He'd disarmed me first, but I'd made him bleed.

"Just so you know, I'd do it again—kill a thousand versions of Landell," he said, dampening some of the satisfaction I felt as I glanced at the sword he'd dropped. "And I wouldn't lose a moment of sleep over it. But you never need to fear me. Never."

My gaze flew to his. There was no smugness in his words, no teasing in his stare. "I don't fear you."

His brows furrowed in confusion, and I seized that moment, shooting toward the sword. I wasn't even exactly sure what I would do with it once I held it.

I didn't get to find out.

Casteel snagged me around the waist, moving so silently that I hadn't even heard him stand or come at me. He took me to the ground, twisting so he took the brunt of the fall. I ended up on top of him.

"This reminds me of the stables," he spoke to the back of my head, and whatever vulnerability had been in his voice moments before was now gone. He rolled me under him. "You were just as violent then as you are now."

His weight and the heat of his body against my back and the

iciness of the snow at my front was a shock to my senses, stunning me.

"Most wouldn't find that such an attractive quality." His voice was a warm whisper against my ear, invoking thoughts of tangled sheets and lush spice.

There wasn't an inch of space separating us. I could feel him along the length of my back, over the curve of my rear, and where one of his legs was shoved between mine. The decadent scent of him and the crispness of the snow filled every too-short, too-shallow breath as every part of my body became aware of his.

"But…" he said, his mouth brushing my jaw, followed by the graze of his sharp teeth, sending an illicit thrill through me. Would he bite me? An aching heaviness filled my chest and glided lower, igniting a burst of disbelief. Did I…? Did I want him to do that? No. Of course, not. I couldn't. His lips curved against my skin, against the healing bite mark. "I'm not most people."

"Most people aren't as insane as you," I said in a throaty voice that wasn't mine.

"That's not a very nice thing to say." He scraped harder with his sharp teeth, just below where he'd bitten me before, and I gasped as my body jerked. "And the truth is, you like my brand of insanity."

My blood pounded through me in a dizzying push. "I don't like anything about you."

He laughed as his lips skimmed the side of my throat. "I love how you lie."

"I'm not lying," I denied, wondering if he nudged my head to the side or if I had done that. It couldn't have been me.

"Hmm?" His lips hovered over the spot where my pulse fluttered wildly. "Your penchant for violence isn't anything to be ashamed of. Not with me. Haven't I told you it turns me on?"

"One too many times," I said, pushing off the ground and against Casteel. I felt him against me for a brief moment, felt the proof of his words. The tight throbbing response to the knowledge made me question my sanity.

Casteel hadn't expected the move, and he slipped to the

side—or maybe he was just humoring me. Probably the latter. Either way, I scrambled to my knees and turned on him, throwing a wild punch.

Casteel caught my hand. "Then I guess it would be repetitive of me to tell you how much you're turning me on now?"

"That and how incredibly disturbing it is."

He smiled up at me, his eyes twin golden flames. "I do so prefer hand-to-hand combat with you," he said, catching my other wrist when I swung my fist down. "I like how close it brings us, Princess."

I shrieked my frustration—my irritation—at him. At myself. "There is something so wrong with you!"

"Probably, but you know what?" He lifted his head off the ground. "That's the part you like the most."

"There is nothing—" My response died on the tip of my tongue. Under his head, the snow seemed to be rising off the ground, but that...that wasn't right. I lifted my gaze, seeing white, misty clouds rolling softly along the snow. *Mist.* "Do you see that?

"What?" Casteel twisted his head. "Shit. Craven."

My heart stammered. "I didn't think there were any Craven here."

"Why would you think there's no Craven here?" Disbelief rang in his tone. "You're in Solis. The Craven are everywhere."

"But there's no Ascended here," I argued as the mist thickened and spread. "How can there be Craven?"

"There used to be Ascended here." He sat up, bringing me closer. "They fed, and they fed a lot. Elijah and the others keep the Craven back, but with Whitebridge on the other side of these woods, and young, pretty girls blindly running through them in the middle of the night, it's not like they don't have a food source."

"I didn't run into the woods blindly," I snapped.

"But you did, and you didn't even realize there were Craven in these woods." His voice hardened with hints of his earlier anger. "And all you had was a damn meat knife. Why did you run, Poppy?"

A high-pitched shriek sent a bolt of dread through me. "Do you think now is a good time to have this conversation?"

"Yes."

I shot him an incredulous stare.

"No?" he said and then added a sigh. He rose as swiftly as the air, pulling me to my feet. Letting go of one of my arms, he bent and swiped up the sword he'd dropped.

Another shrill cry sounded, followed by the sound of snapping tree limbs, freezing the blood in my veins. "I think—"

Casteel hauled me against his chest without warning. Before I knew what he was even about, his mouth was on mine, stealing my breath and scattering my thoughts. The kiss was hot and raw, a clash of lips and teeth. I was reminded again of how, as Hawke, he'd held himself back when he kissed me, and how much he hid. It wasn't just the fangs, it was also the power—*his* power.

He lifted his mouth from mine, his eyes nearly luminous as he stared down into my wide ones. "But we will have that conversation later," he promised, thrusting the sword into my hand. "Make me feel incompetent and kill more than me, Princess."

For a moment, I was rooted to the spot where I stood, the hilt of the sword cold against my palm. The Cravens' screams jolted me from my stupor. I turned just as Casteel picked up the other sword. There was no time to think about anything, especially not the kiss. The mist grew, reaching our knees—

They streamed out from a cluster of trees, a tide of sunken, gray bodies, bared fangs, and blazing, coal-red eyes. I'd never seen the Craven so…decayed. Their skulls were bare of hair, or only patchy, clumpy strings remained. Ribcages were all but exposed through the ragged clothing they wore. They were so emaciated, so withered away that I couldn't help but feel pity for the mortals they used to be and the rotting corpses they'd become.

I braced as they spilled over the fallen branches and boulders. Because even in their condition, they were fast, and they would be deadly in their bloodlust.

The first to reach me may have been a woman once, given the faded yellow frock and the jeweled ring still on her finger.

She screamed, reed-thin legs pumping as she reached for me with outstretched hands, her fingers ending in razor-sharp claws that could easily shred skin.

I was proof of that.

Her jaw hung open, exposing the two elongated canines along the top, and the two that jutted up from the bottom. Meeting her halfway, I thrust the sword into her chest. Rotten blood spurted, filling the air with putridness. If the blade weren't bloodstone or a stake fashioned from the trees within the Blood Forest, she would've kept coming, tearing herself in two to get to me. I'd seen a Craven do that before. But the blade *was* bloodstone, and she was dead the moment the sword pierced her heart.

Yanking the weapon free, I turned as she crumpled to the ground. Casteel had lopped off the head of a Craven, another surefire way of killing them. I wasn't worried for him. I imagined it would take dozens of Craven, if not more, to overwhelm an Atlantian.

Piercing the chest of another Craven, I couldn't help but acknowledge that if there had been any semblance of truth behind the Ascended's claims of the Dark One controlling the Craven, I doubted they'd be trying to rip his skin open right now. I already knew that though, having seen the Craven go after him in the Blood Forest before. This was just more evidence of the truth he spoke.

And the lies I'd been told.

Fury energized me as I sliced the bloodstone through the neck of a Craven, severing its head. I whirled from the gore, only to come face-to-face with ghastly, inhuman eyes, and snapping teeth. A moment of pure, unadulterated terror swamped me when my gaze locked with the Craven's. It threatened to toss me back through the years to when I couldn't keep my grip on my mother's slippery, blood-soaked hand as the pain of the first claw and then the first bite turned into a never-ending nightmare.

I wasn't a small child now, incapable of defending myself. I wasn't weak. I wasn't prey.

With a rage-filled shout I barely recognized as mine, I jabbed the blade through the Craven's caved-in chest. The ungodly light went out in its eyes, the last vestiges of life.

"Six," Casteel called out. "You?"

"Four," I answered, calming myself as I almost wished I didn't know what he'd meant. I darted under the arms of another Craven, driving the sword deep into its back. "Five."

"Shameful," he teased, and I rolled my eyes.

A wailing Craven jerked my head around. It raced toward me, and I stepped in, gripping the hilt with both hands as I shoved the blade through its chin. Tearing the sword free, I saw that the mist was all but gone now.

Heart thumping as Casteel drove his blade through the last Craven, I lowered the sword. Taking a step back, I dragged in deep breaths. As he pulled his weapon free, his head swiveled in my direction. I didn't know if he was looking to see if I was still standing or to make sure I wasn't running away—or at him with the sword.

He didn't have to worry about the last two things. I was far too tired to run anywhere.

"I was hoping to have the chance to rescue you." Casteel bent, wiping his sword clean on the leg of the fallen's pants. "But you didn't need my help."

"Sorry to disappoint you." My gaze shifted to the Craven before me. He wore no shirt, and that was how I could see the wound on his stomach, four deep indentations along his waist that were an ugly shade of purple, whereas the rest of his skin was the color of death. He hadn't been fed upon by an Ascended. I wondered how old he'd been before a Craven's bite had cursed him. What had he done for a living? Was he a guard or a Huntsman? A banker? A farmer? Did he have a family? Children who had been ripped apart in front of him? "Did I tell you that a Craven bit me?"

"No," he answered quietly. "Where?"

"On my leg. Scarred as it is now, it looks like claws did it, but it was fangs," I said, unsure why I was talking or thinking about this. "I never understood why I survived the bite while everyone else bitten was cursed. I'd planned to tell you about it after we were…together, but things happened. I didn't say anything before because it was another thing I was told to keep silent about. The Queen told me it was because I was the Maiden, the one Chosen by the gods. That was why I didn't turn. But I wasn't chosen by anything or anyone." I looked over at him. "It's because I'm part Atlantian, isn't it?"

Slipping his sword into the scabbard as he walked toward me, he stopped beside me. "A Craven's bite does not curse an Atlantian, but in enough numbers, and I suppose depending on if they managed to sever our heads, they could kill us."

"I think the reason I was never allowed to use my gift or tell anyone about the bites is because those things are Atlantian traits," I said. "Maybe the Ascended were afraid that if people knew, someone would realize what that meant."

"Did anyone know?" he asked.

"Vikter knew about the bites and my gift, but Tawny didn't. My brother did—I mean, he *does*. He knows." My brows knotted. "And the Teermans."

"There are Atlantians among the Descenters. If one of them had become aware of your gift or the bite, they would've known." He lifted his hand to my cheek. I tensed as he smoothed his thumb down the side of my face to below the scar. "Craven blood," he explained, wiping it away. His eyes met mine. "If I'd known those marks were bites, I would've realized what you were right away."

"Yeah, well…." I trailed off. "Would that have changed anything?"

He didn't answer for a long moment, and then he said, "No, Poppy. You being mortal or half-Atlantian wouldn't have changed what was already happening."

"At least you're honest." An ache pierced my chest as I dragged my gaze from his and looked over the Craven. They'd come from the direction I'd been heading. I let out a heavy breath, knowing I wouldn't have survived. There was no way I could have taken on a dozen Craven by myself. And only with a meat knife. I could admit that. I would've died tonight, and that wasn't the kind of freedom I'd been looking for.

For some reason, I thought about what he'd said to me before, during what felt like a different life. "Do you remember saying that you felt like you knew me when we met?"

"I do."

"Was that a lie?"

His features hardened and then smoothed out. "Was it a lie to you?"

I shook my head no. "Why, then?"

Thick lashes lowered. "I think it's the Atlantian blood in us recognizing each other, showing the connection in a feeling that would probably easily be overlooked," Casteel said as I felt his hand over mine, over the one holding the sword. He slipped it from my grasp, and I didn't try to fight him. I watched as he cleaned the blade and then sheathed it next to the other.

I met his gaze again. "I'm not handing over the meat knife."

"I wouldn't expect you to." A long, silent moment passed between us. "It's time."

I knew what he meant. It was time to go back. And it was. The fight for *this* battle had left me. "I'll try to escape again."

"I figured as much."

"I'm not going to stop fighting you."

"I wouldn't want you to."

I thought that was weird. "And I'm not going to marry you."

"We'll talk about that later."

"No, we won't," I said, starting toward my cloak with weary steps. I drew up short, cursing under my breath.

"What?" Casteel followed.

"There's a dead Craven on my cloak." I sighed heavily.

"That was an especially inconvenient place for it to fall." He nudged it off the cloak, but the damage was already done. I could see and smell the rotten blood staining the garment.

"If I put that on, I will vomit," I warned him.

Picking up my satchel, he draped it over his shoulder as he rose. "You ran far. Farther than I thought you would get," he said. Since he wasn't looking, I allowed myself a small smile. "But I don't think you'll freeze to death on the way back. Then you'll rest," he said, facing me. "You'll need all your strength for the battles ahead, Princess."

Chapter 5

The trip back to the keep was quiet and long. The wind had picked up, battering both of us. I'd begun to wonder if the gods had awakened, and this was their punishment. After all, if everything Casteel and the others had claimed was true, wasn't I as counterfeit as the Queen and King of Solis? I'd done everything possible to handle how much the cold had begun to affect me, but it seemed impossible to hide anything from Casteel. Halfway through our journey, he ended up wrapping his arm around my shoulders, tucking me close to him as we forged forward, his body absorbing the brunt of the wind.

Gods help me, but I didn't resist. I chalked it up to being far too tired and cold. It had nothing to do with his lush scent masking the stench of the Craven. It didn't have anything to do with how…good it felt to lean on someone, for them to take the worst of the wind, to carry their weight and mine. Nor did it have anything to do with the simple luxury of being allowed this close to someone without fear of reprimand or being found unworthy.

Casteel was just…warm.

When we finally made it back to the keep, there was no telling what time it was. But despite my failure, I welcomed the warmth of the room. I was a walking ice cube, unable to feel my nose, and unsure if it was even still attached.

What I did not welcome was finding Kieran waiting inside

the room, sitting in the corner chair by the fire.

He looked up, one eyebrow raised. "What took you two so long? I was actually beginning to wonder if she beat you."

"You seem real concerned sitting there," Casteel replied, ushering me toward the fireplace. I allowed it, as I was shivering so badly, I swore my bones were trembling.

Kieran grinned. "I was beside myself with worry."

Casteel snorted. "We worked things out."

"No, we didn't," I gritted out between chattering teeth.

Ignoring that, Casteel pried my clenched hands apart. "We ran into some Craven," he told Kieran, tugging my damp gloves off. He dropped them onto the hearth. "A little over a dozen."

Kieran tilted his head at me as Casteel moved to the side, slipping off my satchel. "Wonder how that would've worked out for you with your meat knife."

"S-shut up," I stammered, holding my fingers as close to the fire as I could without shoving them into the flames.

"She knows it wouldn't have worked out all that well for her." Casteel shoved a hand through his snow-kissed hair, dragging the thick strands back. "That's why she's cranky."

"I doubt that's the only reason," Kieran remarked.

I shot him a look that would've withered him on the spot if he cared.

Apparently, he didn't care, at least based on how his grin kicked up a notch. "I had a bath drawn. The water would be warmer if you had simply come back without too much trouble."

I almost raced straight to the bathing chamber, but the way he said, "too much trouble" dripped with amusement. "Do you expect a thank you?"

"It would be nice," he replied. "Doubt I will get one, though."

Warmth crept back into my fingers in a prickly rush as I spared a quick, longing look toward the bathing chamber. "Your expectations would be correct, then."

"They usually are." He studied me for a moment and then rose from the chair. "I'll wrangle up some men and go out and take care of the Craven."

"I'll come with you," Casteel said, and I glanced over at him in surprise. He caught my stare before I could look away. "We don't let them lay out there and rot. They were once mortal," he explained. "We burn them."

The same was done in Masadonia whenever the Craven reached the Rise, but it was the fact that *he* was volunteering to go back out there that shocked me. I would've expected that from Hawke, but this was the Prince. And it was freezing out. Then again, he didn't appear even remotely fazed by the cold.

I bit down on my lip to stop myself from asking, but that didn't work. Curiosity always got the best of me. "Does the cold not affect you?"

"I have thick skin," he answered, and I frowned, not sure if that was true. "To go along with my thick skull."

Now that was something I was sure of.

"I would ask that you hold off on any more attempts at escape tonight. Make use of the bath and rest," Casteel said, and I gritted my teeth. "But in case you feel like testing out how much cold your body can withstand, just know that Delano will be standing guard outside this room."

Poor Delano, I thought. The last time he played guard, things hadn't exactly been easy for him—or me.

Casteel joined Kieran at the door. He was halfway out when I heard him say, "Behave, Princess."

A thousand retorts rose to the tip of my tongue as my head whipped toward him, but he was already closing the door. I let out a rather filthy curse, and as the lock clicked into place, I heard him laugh.

Instead of running and kicking the door like I wanted to, which would serve no purpose but to bruise my frozen toes, I tore myself away from the fire. Unhooking the thigh sheath, I placed it near the flames so it would dry. I left the knife on the small wooden table by the bed and then quickly stripped off my nearly frozen clothing. Leaving them in a pile by the fire, I hurried to the bathing chamber. Several oil lamps had been lit, casting a soft glow over the tub and several pitchers still full of fresh water. Dipping my fingers into the water, I was relieved to find that it was still warm.

I probably should've thanked Kieran since it had been a

considerate thing to do.

But he was also party to my captivity, so I shouldn't be too grateful. I *wouldn't*.

Rolling my eyes at myself, I stepped into the tub. As I sank into the warm water, wincing as it met my chilled skin and scraped knees, the reality of tonight set in like lead balls in my stomach. Neither Casteel nor Kieran had been anywhere near the room when I made my escape, and yet they'd still discovered my absence. Maybe I'd waited too long to leave, and one of them had already been on their way to my room.

I draped my braid over my shoulder as I grabbed the bar of lilac-scented soap and started scrubbing vigorously at my skin. It wouldn't have mattered if I had left sooner. They still would've found me, either alive or…torn to pieces by the Craven.

My escape had been foolish and ill-planned, borne of my need to find my brother and…yes, panic. Not because of what Casteel had done in the banquet hall, but because of the soul-crushing sense of helplessness and…

Letting the soap slip through my fingers, I lifted my hand to the bite on my neck. An achy pulse coiled low in my stomach. That. *That* had a lot to do with why I ran.

I opened my eyes, fishing the bar of soap from the water. In the quiet stillness of the room, I recognized the truth of my situation. Escape would be nearly impossible, even with longer lead time, supplies including bloodstone, and more amicable weather.

Kieran would track me.

Casteel would come for me.

Sighing, I leaned back against the tub and stayed in the water until I almost forgot how cold I'd been. Finally, I climbed out. After drying off, I pulled the nightgown from my bag, relieved to find that it was dry. I slipped it on and then climbed into bed, slowly undoing my braid. The ends of my hair were wet, but they'd dry. I curled up on my side, facing the door.

The warmth of the blankets lulled me to sleep, despite my racing thoughts. It couldn't have been more than an hour before a deep laugh from outside jolted me from my slumber.

Casteel.

He was here, outside the bedchamber. Why? My mind immediately went in several directions. One of those flashed images of him and I all twisted together—

I jumped from the bed as if the mattress had caught fire, grabbing the knife.

He couldn't be here to make sure I was still inside, not with Delano standing guard outside. Why was he here instead of his quarters when he had to be exhausted from the night's events?

My heart stammered.

He must have his own bedchamber…right? I looked around, my heart thumping. *This* was his bedchamber.

At the sound of the grinding of the lock, I turned.

The door swung open, letting in a gust of cold, damp air that ruffled the flames of the fireplace. And he…

Casteel prowled in as if he had every right to do so. He halted the moment he saw me and what I held, sighing heavily. Closing the door behind him, he was wise enough to not take his gaze off me.

"Poppy," he started. "As you know, it's been a long day and night. And while I'm relieved to see that you didn't manage to evade Delano, and despite that I think you look rather adorable in that gown, holding that tiny, little knife—"

I threw the blade, aiming for his head just like he'd told me to do.

Stepping aside, Casteel snatched the weapon out of the air. I knew how fast he was, but it was still shocking to see how quick he could be. It stole my breath even as an infuriating voice whispered in the back of my mind that I had *known* he'd easily avoid the knife.

A curse hissed through his teeth as his fingers closed around the blade. Blood trickled between his fingers, and I didn't feel even a kernel of guilt as he stared at his hand. Well, perhaps there was a tiny bit of remorse—no larger than the size of a gnat, though. He hadn't done anything at the *exact* moment in time to truly earn a knife being thrown at his face, but I was sure he would be more than deserving in a few minutes.

Slowly, he opened his fingers, dropping the knife to the floor. The blood-soaked blade clanged off the wood. "That is the second time you've drawn blood tonight." He looked over at me. A tense moment passed, and he then raised one dark brow. "You're so incredibly violent."

"Only around you," I shot back.

His lips curled into a half-grin, revealing the dimple in his right cheek. "Now, you know that's not true at all." Walking toward the basin just inside the bathing chamber, he washed his hand. "But you know what *is* true?"

My jaw ached from how tightly I was clenching it as I told myself not to ask. Maybe if I ignored him, he'd go away. Highly unlikely, but one could always hope.

Casteel looked over his shoulder at me, waiting.

Frustration burned through me. "What?" I demanded. "What's true?"

He smiled then, a real one. Both dimples were on full display, and they weren't the only thing. No longer needing to hide what he was behind a tight-lipped smile, there was a hint of fangs. My breath hitched in my throat. I didn't know if it was the fangs or the dimples. Or the genuine warmth in his smile—and I'd seen all his smiles to know which ones were real: The half-curl of his lips that said he was amused. The predatory one that reminded me of a large cat whose prey had made a foolish mistake. The cold curve to his mouth that never reached his eyes. The twist of a grin full of barely banked violence that was a promise of bloodshed. Those smiles may not have been directed at me, not even tonight when we squared off in the woods. But I'd seen them all.

But this was the kind of expression that softened the striking lines of his face and turned his eyes from cool amber to warm honey. And to me, it was the most dangerous of all his smiles. He wasn't mad I'd thrown a knife at him and made him bleed, but warning bells went off nonetheless. These kinds of smiles begged for me to forget reality and all the lies and blood that had been shed.

They made me think of him as *Hawke.*

Instinct triggered self-preservation even as his smile tugged at my foolish heart, and the sensation slid lower, spiraling tight.

Casteel turned to me, his hand open. There was no blood.

No wound except for a faint pink line across the center of his palm. "It still turns me on, Princess."

I exhaled a shrill breath. "I feel like I've said this a hundred times, but it needs to be said again. There's something wrong with you."

He lifted his shoulder in a half-shrug. "Some believe there's something wrong with all of us, and I tend to believe that."

"I didn't realize you were so philosophical." I glanced at the knife on the floor while he emptied the basin into a bucket. There was no way he'd forgotten that I had it, or that it lay there now. Was he waiting to see what I would do?

"There's a lot you don't realize about me," he replied, returning to the bedchamber to retrieve the pitcher of water warmed by the fireplace. "I cannot wait to return home, to the land where all you need to do for hot water is turn a faucet handle."

"I—what?" I turned to him. "What do you mean?"

The half-grin was back. "In Atlantia, all homes have running hot water that goes straight to their tubs and sinks."

"You lie."

He sent me a look as he placed the pitcher on the stand beside the basin. "Why would I lie about something like that?"

"Because you're a liar?" I reasoned.

Loosening the collar of his tunic, he tsked softly. "Poppy, you wound me. In my heart," he said, placing his hand over his chest. "Again."

"Don't whine. You'll heal. Again," I snapped. "Unfortunately."

He chuckled. "I'm not the only one who is a liar, it appears." Reaching down, he gripped the hem of his tunic. "You'd be very sad if I didn't heal."

"I wouldn't care—" My eyes widened as he pulled the tunic over his head. "What are you doing?"

"What does it look like?" He gestured at the tub. "I just had my hands all over what are basically rotten corpses. I'm washing up."

For a moment, I couldn't find any words as he turned, pouring the warm water into the tub. Partly due to disbelief, though also because he was…damn, his body was a work of art, even with numerous nicks and thin slices I could barely see in the soft lamplight. "Why are you doing that in here?"

"Because this was my room. And for what is left of tonight, which isn't very much, it's our room." He bent over the tub, picking up the pitchers of water I hadn't used. The muscles along his shoulders and back moved under the taut skin in interesting ways.

My heart clamored. "I used the water in the tub——"

"The water is clean enough," he interrupted. "And I've shared far dirtier water with far less intriguing people."

"Couldn't you go to another room and have a bath all to yourself? With fresh water?" I suggested. "I'm sure many here would be eager to serve their Prince."

"There are many here who would be glad to serve me." He looked at me, brows raised. "But leave you alone? When you could take all kinds of reckless, albeit exciting action? I don't think so. I can't have someone standing outside your room all night. They need their rest. I need to rest."

"Why? Because we're leaving tomorrow?"

"Not with the storm blowing in. It will make travel far too difficult," he told me. "You know, the same storm you would've gotten caught in if you did manage to escape." His hands lowered to the flap of buttons on his breeches——

I quickly looked away. "I can't believe you're doing this."

Casteel chuckled. "Not like you haven't seen it all before."

"That doesn't mean I need to see it all again," I shot back as I heard the soft rustle of fabric hitting the stone floor.

"Interesting word choices."

Telling myself I shouldn't and somehow being unable to resist, I peeked at the bathing chamber——

I caught sight of bronzed skin dusted with dark hair, strong thighs, and the sleek, muscled curve of his backside. His body truly was a work of art, all the nicks oddly adding to the perfection.

"You could've said you didn't *want* to see everything," Casteel continued, startling me enough that I looked away, cheeks flaming. Water sloshed against the sides of the tub as he climbed in. "You can look now. I'm...somewhat proper."

I folded my arms across my chest.

"Although, not nearly proper enough for your barely ex-Maiden eyes," he continued. This time I spun toward the bathing chamber. All I could see was the back of his head and the breadth of his shoulders, which was more than enough. "But I imagine your issue has nothing to do with what is proper or expected of you, is it? You've never been one to follow the rules."

I shook my head even though he couldn't see as he reached for the soap, lathering the bar between his hands. He was right. I didn't care about what was proper or expected, and that was long before he swept into my life like a fierce storm. But there was no way he was staying in this room with me. Tearing my gaze from him, I turned—

"Go for the knife." Casteel's voice stopped me.

My head snapped back in his direction as water splashed. How had he known?

"That's what you want, right? If it makes you feel safer, I don't have a problem with it." He splashed his face. Water ran down his neck and over the delineated lines of his shoulders. "Take it, Poppy."

My mouth dried. "You're not afraid I'll use it against you while you take your time bathing?"

"I'm counting on you to use it again. If you didn't, I'd be shocked. That's why I didn't bring my swords into the room. Figured you'd probably grab one of them."

I would if they were near. My hands opened and closed at my sides. He was offering me some level of protection, a sense of safety, and to some, that would be seen as a positive. Not to me. It was kind of offensive and pointless. He and I both knew the knife would only make him bleed temporarily.

I still hurried over to where the knife lay and picked it up, my rising irritation halting when I saw the blood on the blade. His blood. My stomach twisted as I rose.

"Do you want to know about the land of hot water that awaits with just the turn of a knob?" he asked amidst the trickling of water.

Yes, I did, even though I wasn't sure I believed that such a thing existed. Yet I said nothing as I picked up the towel I'd used earlier. I wiped the knife clean.

"It's boilers and pipes," he went ahead and explained. "The piping runs from the boilers that are usually in a room off the kitchen. From there, they carry the hot water to wherever it's needed."

Reluctantly, my interest had been piqued and was now stroked. "What do you mean by broilers?"

"They're like…large ovens where combustible material heats a storage tank of water." He rose without warning, and all that water sluicing down the gleaming skin of his back, between—

Heart pounding, I whirled away from the bathing chamber. A handful of seconds passed, and I looked over my shoulder just as he walked out of the smaller room, a towel tucked around his waist. He was… I had no words to describe his level of indecency. Or maybe I had too many words in my head—

Casteel smiled at me as he strode across the room, opening a narrow cabinet in the wall that I hadn't investigated. He pulled out what appeared to be black pants. "Electricity aids the broilers, and yes, in Atlantia, all homes and businesses, no matter who resides inside them, have power."

Fixing my gaze on the fire, I thought about what he'd said. If only what he claimed was true. That would probably be the first of many things that set the kingdom apart from the one I'd grown up in. Only the extremely wealthy or the well-connected had access to electricity in Solis. "How is that possible?"

"It may be a finite source here, but it doesn't need to be that way. The Ascended make it that way," he said, and a quick glance told me that he'd ditched the towel in favor of the pants he'd retrieved. They were looser than breeches, hanging indecently low on his hips, held up by some sort of drawstring that seemed to defy gravity. He gathered up our clothing, placing it all in a laundry hamper that he then placed outside the door. Closing the door, he said, "A crucial part of their all-encompassing control is creating a rift between mortals who have and mortals who have not."

He sat in the chair in the corner and leaned back, propping one ankle on top of his knee. In just those strange, loose pants, I'd never seen a more arrogantly at-ease male. His fingers slowly tapped the arm of the chair. "So, those who barely have enough to survive, turn their anger towards those who have more than they could ever need. And never towards the Ascended."

I couldn't exactly argue that point. The rift in Masadonia was clear and as wide as it was in the capital. While Radiant Row, where some Ascended and the wealthy lived, was only a few blocks long, it was an entire city within Carsodonia. And everything else was like the homes near the Rise in Masadonia, squat and stacked upon one another.

"But Atlantia is ruled differently?" I challenged, holding the knife against my chest.

"It is."

I thought of what Landell had said. "Sounded to me like there are problems in Atlantia."

His fingers stilled. "There are problems everywhere, Poppy."

"And what kind of problems is Atlantia having with limited space and useless land?"

His head tilted to the side. "Atlantia was once this entire landmass from the Stroud Sea to far beyond the Skotos Mountains. My people built cities and cultivated the lands that the Ascended now rule over. When my people retreated at the end of the War of Two Kings, they lost all of that land. We are simply running out of space now."

"And what happens if you run out of space?"

"I won't allow that to happen," he replied, straightening his head. "I thought you'd be asleep when I came back. You've probably had a far more tiring day than most of us."

"I was sleeping, but..." My gaze dropped to his chest, to the tightly coiled muscles of his stomach. The glow from the fireplace left very little to the imagination.

"I woke you? I'm sorry about that," he said, and the apology sounded genuine enough. "There's a lot we need to talk about, Poppy."

"There is." Namely, the whole marriage nonsense. "But

talking doesn't require you to be shirtless."

"Talking doesn't require any clothes at all." That smoky grin of his returned. "I can promise you that some of the most interesting conversations take place with no clothes to speak of."

Heat blasted my cheeks. "I'm sure you've had a ton of experience with those types of conversations."

"Jealous?" Propping his elbow on the arm of the chair, he rested his chin in his palm.

"Hardly."

The grin increased, and even though I couldn't see the dimple beyond the fingers splayed across his jaw and cheek, I knew it had to be there. "Then…distracted?"

"No," I lied, and then lied some more. "Not even remotely."

"Ah, I understand. You're dazzled."

"Dazzled?" A surprised laugh almost broke free. And there it was again, the slight widening of his eyes, the parting of his lips, and the absence of arrogance. It was like watching him slip off a mask, but I had no idea if what was revealed was just another mask, especially when the look disappeared as his features became unreadable again.

I exhaled slowly. "We don't need to talk about your over-inflated ego. That has been long since established. We need to talk about this whole marriage stuff. There is no way I'm—"

"We do need to talk about that, about our future. But not right now. It's late. I'm tired. And if I'm tired, you have to be exhausted," he said, and my eyes narrowed. "That's the kind of conversation we both need to be fully energized for."

"That conversation will take just enough time for me to say I'm not marrying you. Therefore, there is no future to speak of. Now the conversation is over and done with. See how simple that was?"

"But it's not that simple," he replied softly. "Why did you run tonight?"

Frustration began to burn a hole through me. "Could it possibly be because you're trying to force me to marry you? Did that never cross your mind?"

"Possibly." There was a stretch of silence as he stared at me.

"Do you know why I chose the name Hawke?"

My heart kicked at my chest at the unexpected change of subject. "I figured it was a name that belonged to whatever poor soul you most likely killed."

He laughed, but there was no humor. Suddenly, I realized that his laughs, like his expressions and even his smiles, were also like masks—each representing a different Casteel, a different truth or falsehood. "There was no poor soul who owned that name. Or at least not that I'm aware of. If there is or was, that would be a pure coincidence. But I chose Hawke for a reason."

I wanted to tell him that I didn't care, but I did. Oh gods, I wanted to know.

He lowered his hand. "In Atlantia, it is tradition to be given a second name, a middle one, so to speak. It's given in honor of a cherished family member or friend, usually picked by the mother, and it is a well-guarded secret only shared outside of the family with the closest of friends and with those who hold a special place in one's life. My mother chose my middle name in honor of her brother. His name was Hawkethrone. My full name is Casteel Hawkethrone Da'Neer. When I was a small child, my mother took to calling me an abbreviated form of that name. And so did my brother. They, and only they had ever known me as Hawke," he said. "Until you."

Chapter 6

Hawke…

The name didn't belong to someone else. It was real. Hawke was real?

"To be honest, the only time my mother calls me Casteel, it generally includes my full middle and last names, and it usually means she's irritated by something I did or didn't do," he continued. "Although Kieran doesn't call me Hawke, he knows the origin of the name. He was the one who chose the last name, Flynn. He thought it sounded like it fit with Hawke."

"We…we don't have middle names," I heard myself say.

"I know."

"Are you telling the truth now?"

His features tightened as some sort of emotion flickered across them. "I'm telling the truth, Poppy."

My gift pushed against my skin, and what Kieran had said about my abilities resurfaced. I'd said that I had no intention of handling the Prince, but my gift could tell me what he was feeling and maybe help me determine if he was lying. Lies and truths were so often tied to emotions, and a person could try to hide what they were feeling. Sometimes, they were successful, even with the most extreme mental anguish. But while people could lie to someone about what they felt, they couldn't lie to themselves.

Opening myself up was always easy. It required no effort.

My senses stretched out, and it was like a cord formed between Casteel and me, connecting us. It wasn't always like that, so singular. Sometimes, crowds overwhelmed me and pulled me in. Some people were projectors, their anguish so deep and raw that they formed the connection with me without trying. With Casteel, it took a few seconds for me to process what I was picking up from him. Emotions had a certain taste and feel to me, and what I felt now was both tart and tangy in the back of my mouth. Discomfort and...sadness.

His sorrow was familiar. It was always there, shadowing his every step, every breath. I often thought about how he could laugh and tease. How he could be so ridiculously vexing while feeling such grief. I wondered if the teasing and his all-too-easy laughter were also masks because I knew his pain started and probably ended with his brother.

I didn't know what the discomfort was tied to, but I didn't feel anything that made me think he wasn't telling the truth now.

And maybe...maybe that meant the name Hawke was real. That it wasn't a lie.

The next breath I took felt thin. "Why are you telling me this about your name? Why does it matter?"

He was quiet now, his features smoothing out. "Because knowing that Hawke is a part of my name, a part of me, matters to you."

"Can you read minds?" I asked, thinking I'd probably asked that before but I felt like I needed to ask again. Mind reading couldn't be too farfetched considering he could force his will upon others, and especially since what he said was true. It did matter to me. Why? I had no idea, because what did it change? At the end of the day...nothing.

A faint grin appeared. "No, I cannot, which is a disappointment when it comes to you. I would love to know what you're thinking—what you're really feeling."

Thank the gods he didn't know, because what I was feeling was messier than when I attempted to knit.

"I am Hawke," he said after a moment. "And I am Casteel. I'm not two separate people, no matter how badly you want to believe that."

I tensed, my grip tightening around the handle of the knife. I hated how well he knew me. "I know that."

"Do you really?"

A rush of frustration scorched my skin because I did often think of him as two different people, but mainly that there were simply different masks he wore, and there'd been one for Hawke.

But it didn't matter. It couldn't.

"I know you are the same," I said. "You are the one who lied to me from the beginning, and you're the one who is holding me captive now. It doesn't matter what name you used while doing it."

He arched a dark eyebrow. "Yet you haven't called me Hawke since you learned who I was."

The frustration quickly flamed into anger. "And why does that matter, *Hawke*?"

A smile crept across his lips then, one that showed the barest hint of fangs. "Because I miss hearing you say it."

I stared at him for what felt like a small eternity. "You're ridiculous, *Casteel*."

He laughed, and the sound was warm and deep and real. I felt his amusement through the connection, a sprinkling of sugar on my tongue. That almost angered me enough to do something very reckless with the knife yet again. Somehow, I managed to resist the impulse that proved just how violent I could be.

His humor faded. "I haven't lied to you since you learned who I was."

"How am I to believe that?" I demanded. "And even if you haven't, that doesn't erase those lies."

"You're correct. I don't expect you to believe, nor do I expect you to ever forget those lies," he said. Again, through the connection I had left open, I felt sadness with the fading taste of humor. "But I have nothing to gain from lies now. I have what I want. You."

"You do not have me."

One side of his lips curled up. "We'll have to agree to disagree on that. Ask me something, Princess. Ask me anything, and I will tell you the truth."

A hundred different questions arose. There was so much I

could ask him. Two things dominated.

Did you ever care for me?

Was any of it real?

I wouldn't ask those questions again. "And I'm just supposed to believe you?"

"Whether or not you do is up to you."

It wasn't just a question of me choosing to believe him, but I didn't point that out. There was another question that rose to the forefront, something I'd been thinking about earlier.

"Did you kill the first Maiden?" I asked.

"What?" Surprise filled his tone, and I also felt it through the cord—cool like a splash of ice water.

I told him what the Duchess had claimed about the first Maiden's abilities. "She said that the Maiden had been unworthy, even though she was still to be given to the gods. But her decisions and choices led her to the Dark One. To you." *Just like me.* "The Duchess basically said that the Dark One killed her."

"I don't know why the Duchess would tell you that. The only Maiden I have met is you," he answered, and I could feel the hot, acidic burn of anger radiating from him. "I don't even know if there truly was another Maiden."

I… I had not considered the possibility that there had been no other Maiden. That could explain why there was nothing written about her, not even a name. But for her to not exist at all?

"I have a lot of blood on my hands, Poppy. Sometimes, so much that I don't think they'll ever be clean. So much that I don't know if I ever want them to be."

My gaze shot to his.

"And I'm sure you've heard a lot about me—about the Dark One. Some of it is true. I kill the Ascended every chance I get, in Carsodonia and in every city I've visited. And, yes, I do find unique ways to end their lives. I am drenched in their blood."

Skin chilled, I was unable to look away. "You were responsible for Goldcrest Manor—Lord Everton?"

"Lord Everton was not alive when I left the city of Three Rivers. Nor were any of the mortals who aided him when it came to his penchant for feeding on young boys—a predilection that went beyond that. And as I'm sure you've realized, some mortals know the truth, and they helped to cover what happened in the Temples and what they did when there was no Rite."

I'd figured that the Ascended had help. They had to. The Priests and Priestesses in the Temples had to know. The Mistresses of the keeps and those who served the Ascended closely.

"And I'm sure you heard the rumor that my affair with Lady Everton was what allowed me to enter the manor?" he said. I had heard that. "I will admit that I've used every weapon I have. After all, the Ascended taught me that."

I flinched.

"She was known for her affairs. Servants helped to sneak her lovers inside the manor. Many never left, but I made sure she saw me. Eventually, she invited me to her bed, and that was how I gained entry. But I did not lay a finger on her in that way. Never." There was a low rumble in his tone. "And if she hadn't run as the flames began, she wouldn't have escaped either."

I didn't doubt that for one second.

Tipping forward, he held my stare. "It's not just the Ascended that stain my hands. There are innocents. Mortals and descendants of Atlantians alike, caught between what I want and me. Your guard, Rylan, was one of those."

My throat tightened.

"As were the ones who traveled here with us, and countless others. Each by arrow, poison, or fall. Anything that stood between you and me." He didn't look away, not for one second. "And Vikter? Those Ladies at the Rite? I didn't kill them, but you were right. Those who support me acted on their own, but they did so enflamed by my words, urged by my lead. So, their blood is on my hands, too. I should've taken ownership of that from the first moment."

A shudder worked its way through me, one of pain and sorrow. "Does any of it stain your soul?" I whispered.

"Much of it does." He sat back. "But this Maiden is not a part of that. If she did live, and she was like you—part Atlantian, and shared your gifts or something similar—she wasn't given to the gods. She was most likely used in the same way they plan to use you."

The breath that left me was ragged. "If...if they've had your brother, why would they have needed her?"

He eyed me from his chair. "Atlantians need Atlantian blood to survive. One who is only half-Atlantian can provide the necessary sustenance. That was how I was kept alive."

I swallowed thickly, hurting for him despite everything. Hurting for her, a woman I didn't even know, wasn't even sure existed. "She could've been held captive to...to feed him? To keep him alive?"

"Without Atlantian blood, we don't die," he said.

I frowned. "How could you not survive but still live?"

"Because what we become is not something I would compare to being alive," he answered. Before I could question that, he spoke. "If there was a first Maiden, she was either keeping my brother alive, or she was used in the same manner as he is. Possibly both. But either way, I imagine that she has long since perished. What you should be asking is why they need you. Why would they make you the Maiden, keep you closeted away, under their protection and under their ever-watchful gaze? Why did they wait until now for your *Ascension?*" He spat out the last word. "Earlier, after the Craven, you were right about why they forced you to stay quiet about being bitten and told you never to use your abilities. Someone could've discovered what you were, and that would have brought their entire house of bones down on them. So, why did they wait so long and take that risk? Please tell me that you've asked yourself these questions."

My skin chilled. "I have. They...they want to use me to make more vamprys. But why? They have—"

"And why do you think they waited this long?" he repeated. "Why did this supposed first Maiden conveniently disappear around the same time her abilities began to grow? There is no Ascension for you. The gods require no service. They waited so you could be useful to them." He sat forward. "There's a reason the Ascended wait until a certain age to Ascend. Do you know what happens when an Atlantian reaches the age of nineteen?"

I did. I'd read about it in *The History of The War of Two Kings and the Kingdom of Solis.* The answer had been in that damn book I'd been forced to read a hundred times. Probably the only part that was true. "An Atlantian reaches a state of maturity. You call it…the Culling, when they go through physical changes."

"And when certain other abilities begin to manifest or strengthen for some," he added, his eyes bright in the dimly lit room. "For me, it was compulsion. As a child, I could be somewhat persuasive, but once I went through the Culling, I could force my will onto another if I wished."

A hollowness spread in my stomach. "Then why haven't you just made me go along with whatever it is you wish for me to do?"

His brows furrowed together. "Because I may be a monster, but I'm not *that* kind of monster, Poppy."

There was a catch in my chest as I looked away from him.

"Besides, compulsions are temporary, only useful for immediate gains," he said. When I looked at him again, his expression had smoothed out. "And interestingly, just like you can't pick up on emotions from the Ascended, compulsions do not work on them either."

I cleared my throat. "Do you know why?"

"Some believe it's because they have no soul."

I thought of Ian and then shut those thoughts down. "So you think my abilities are changing because I'm going through the Culling?"

"A version of it, yes. Your blood wouldn't have been useful to them until you at least hit nineteen, even if your abilities took the next two years to morph."

As I processed what he was telling me, my brain went in one direction. "Will I develop…fangs?"

He lifted his brows. "Doubtful. Half-Atlantians don't need blood, so they don't need fangs."

"What about…immortality?"

"Would you not want that?"

I thought of the Ascended, of how long they lived, and I wasn't sure their lack of humanity was due to what they did to survive or because they lived to see everyone around them die several generations over.

"I don't know," I answered honestly. "Will I?"

He shook his head. "Only full-blooded Atlantians have what mortals would think of as immortality."

I wasn't sure if I should feel relieved or not. "Can I even Ascend then? Be made into a vampry?" I asked, thinking of Ian. If he were part Atlantian like me...

"I honestly don't know, Poppy. It is forbidden for any Atlantian to Ascend anyone with a drop of mortal blood in them. Even the half-Atlantians that live in Atlantia are not Ascended. They live and die just like mortals," he explained, and that was something I didn't know about those who lived in Atlantia. That not all Atlantians were like him. "I would imagine a half-Atlantian going through an Ascension would be the same as a mortal. They would become a vampry."

Meaning, they would be ruled by bloodlust, just not as consumed by it as a Craven. Pressure settled in my chest. "When a person is turned—made vampry—what happens to them?"

He was quiet for several moments before he said, "They are fed upon by other vamprys, brought to the brink of death by blood loss, and then fed blood from an Atlantian. Sometimes, the change is immediate. Other times, they can appear dead for hours. But they wake up and...they are hungry. As uncontrollable as a Craven, it often takes several Ascended to subdue them." His jaw worked as his gaze shifted to the fire. "Even after being fed, they're consumed by hunger. I've heard that it can take weeks, sometimes months for a newly made vampry to control his or her thirst."

A sinking sensation threatened to pull me through the floor. There had been a space of time after Ian's Ascension that I hadn't heard from him. It was when he'd married, and it had been months.

"And I know that for those who could not abide by what was now needed of them, they ensured that they would not harm another," he added quietly.

"How?" I asked, instinct telling me that the answer wasn't going to be an easy one.

"They choose to walk when the sun is at its highest. It doesn't take long, but it is not quick by any means. Nor is it painless."

Oh, gods.

Now that...*that* sounded like something Ian would do. But he was alive. He'd been sending letters. He had to be alive.

I swallowed. "Those you saw turned? Did all of them seem aware of what was happening?"

His gaze shifted back to me. "I know where you're going with this, and I don't think the answer will change things in the way you wish."

"Will you just answer the question?"

His lips thinned. "The Ascended held a ceremony for it. Mortals were brought in dressed in robes and wearing masks. Meaningless words were chanted, and candles were lit. Some seemed to know what would occur. Most appeared intoxicated. I had no idea if they knew exactly what was happening." His chest rose with a deep breath. "Some seemed drugged. I doubt they even knew if they were awake."

I stared at him, stuck in this terrible place between relief and horror. Suddenly, I understood why he hadn't wanted to answer the question. If Ian had been drugged to the point where he hadn't been aware—if others hadn't been aware of what was happening—that was far worse.

Casteel watched me silently. "There is no reason for an Ascended to turn a half-Atlantian. Doing so would taint the blood—the part they need to either turn other Ascended or to keep an Atlantian alive. That is why they made sure you were healthy and safe, why your precious Queen cared so tenderly for you," he said. My entire body went as taut as a bowstring. "Your blood meant nothing to them before now, and it would mean even less to them if you went through the Ascension."

So, Ian and I likely had different parents, either one or both. Because he had to have been turned. He'd been writing me letters, and Casteel claimed that Ian had only been seen at night. Unless—

Unless Casteel's contacts had seen someone else, and it hadn't been Ian sending those letters at all.

The pressure inside me increased, shifting to my stomach as I swallowed thickly. I couldn't even consider any of that right now while I was so far from Ian. The questions and the doubts would crush me.

And I already felt crushed.

I knew what they'd planned for me before, but to fully understand why they'd waited, why they did everything they had done, it sickened me to the point where I feared I might actually become physically ill.

"They were only keeping me alive until they..." I choked on my words as the weight of them threatened to crush me.

Casteel said nothing as he sat there, though that was probably for the best at the moment. I felt like a powder keg that had been lit. Inside me, disbelief and anger sparked. I'd been kept sheltered and virtually caged, cared for like some prized cattle until my blood had aged. Until it was useful—either to make more vamprys or to keep another alive to continue making more.

"I'm not a bottle of wine," I whispered.

"No," he said quietly. "You are not a bottle of wine, Poppy."

My head jerked up. "And you didn't know this when you came for me? You swear? You swear right here and now that you didn't know I was part Atlantian. That this is why they made me the Maiden. That I was being kept alive and sheltered from everything until I was...useful?"

His gaze met mine. "I swear to you, Poppy. I had no idea that you were Atlantian until I tasted your blood. I didn't even expect that was what you were when I learned of your gift. Maybe I should have." A shadow crossed his features, gone so quickly I wasn't even sure I had seen it. "But no Atlantian has been capable of such a thing for, well, for hundreds of years. I didn't know."

My senses were still open, and it took several moments to filter through what I felt to even make sense of his emotions. There was still the acidic taste of anger, the tart flavor that I associated with uncertainty, and the sadness that always lingered within him.

My gift wasn't a lie detector by any means, but I didn't think he was lying. Pulling my gift back was the hardest part because that didn't feel natural. What did was going to him and taking away the sadness, giving some temporary peace. My skin tingled with the desire to do just that, and it wasn't necessarily because it was him. The gift demanded to be used, to heal. I wrestled it back, exhaling raggedly as I sat on the edge of the bed.

"Now that you fully understand why they've done what they have to you and what they plan," Casteel said, his voice hardening in a way I rarely heard when he spoke with me. "Why in the hell would you run back to them, Poppy? Marriage to me or not."

I stared at Casteel, the meat knife loose in my hands. "I told you earlier, I wasn't running back to them."

"Then where were you running to? With no supplies, might I add."

"You don't need to add that. I'm well aware of what I left here with."

"If you weren't going back to the Ascended, where did you think to go? You were heading toward Whitebridge—to the south." His eyes were like shards of amber. "You weren't going back to Masadonia. I figure you were going to the capital. Why? Even knowing what you did then, why would you do that?"

"Why?" Anger flashed through me, hot and bright like the flames. "Are you seriously asking that question again?"

"Do I look like I'm joking?" he asked.

I was stunned into silence, but only for a moment. "Why would I stay here and let you turn me over to them? To the people you told me wanted to use me—to the people who abused and tortured you? Who are doing that to your brother? How does that make you any better? Safer? You're doing the same thing they did to me!" The back of my throat burned as a knot of ugly, painful emotion lodged there. "You're keeping me safe, well-fed, and caged until you can use me!"

A muscle flexed in his jaw.

"And then you announce that you're going to marry me." I shook my head, trembling. "What in the world would make you even say such an offensive thing?"

"Offensive? Come now, Poppy, I know deep down that you must be excited. Not everyone gets to become an actual Princess."

"I am not remotely—" I snapped my mouth shut, realizing he was *actually* teasing me. Was this all some grand joke to him?

"It's considered a great honor in Atlantia to be welcomed into the bosom of the noble, ruling family," he went on. "I think my mother is going to like you."

I shot to my feet. "We are not getting married!" Slamming the knife down, it scored deep into the wood of the table by the bed, the handle vibrating from the impact.

"On second thought, my mother is definitely going to like you," Hawke murmured, and right then, he *was* Hawke.

That was the bemused tone I was all too familiar with, and it threw me enough that it took a few moments to recover, to remember that it was simply another mask. "Why? Because I didn't throw it at your face this time?"

"She'll most likely be amused to hear that you have done exactly that," he said, and my brows knitted. "And she will be happy to know that you are capable of showing restraint."

"Now, I wish I hadn't shown restraint."

Casteel chuckled, and that too sounded so familiar, but it was Casteel's laugh that faded. It was his golden eyes that held an intense look of fascination. He was both Hawke and Casteel, but it was the latter that I now dealt with. He leaned forward in his chair, lowering both bare feet to the floor. "You are so incredibly beautiful when you're angry."

I refused to be flattered by that somewhat weird compliment. "And you're so incredibly disturbed."

"Been called worse."

"I'm sure you have." I folded my arms across my chest.

He rose from the chair, and for a moment, I got a little lost in all the bronze skin on display. "We'll talk tomorrow about our future—"

"There is no future to talk about. We're not marrying," I cut in.

"I think you'll find my reasonings impossible to refuse."

"Nothing is impossible."

"We'll see."

"No, we—what are you doing?" I demanded as he walked to the other side of the bed. "What are you doing?"

"Getting into bed."

"Why?" My voice pitched high.

He arched a brow as he pulled the blanket aside. "To go to sleep."

"I figured that out, thanks. But why do you think you get to sleep in the same bedchamber, let alone the same *bed* with me?"

"Because, as I explained earlier, this is my bedchamber."

"Then I will find another room."

"There are no other rooms available, Princess."

My hands dug into the blanket as my mind raced. "This isn't appropriate. I'm the Maiden. Or was. Whatever. I'm the definition of appropriate."

He stared at me. "Besides the fact that you are not the definition of appropriate, everyone in this keep knows that we've already shared a bed, Poppy."

"Well, that's just…" My face burned. "That's just great."

"I'm not leaving you alone."

"I'm not going to try to escape! I promise."

"I hope you don't think I'm foolish enough to trust your vow." Casteel picked up a rather flat pillow and fluffed it. "So, either it's me in here, or it's Kieran. Would you rather it be him? If so, I will summon him for you." He tossed the pillow toward the head of the bed. "But just so you know, he often slips into his wolven form and has a habit of kicking in his sleep."

My lips slowly parted. "What? Wait. I don't need an explanation of that. I don't want Kieran."

The hint of a smile was pure wickedness. "You want me."

"That is not what I said. You can sleep on the floor."

"I am not sleeping on the floor. And before you say it, neither are you." He slipped into bed with enviable grace. "No matter what you think you know of me, I hope you realize that I would never force myself on you, nor would I compel you to do something like that. I won't ever do something you don't want from me, and that's not just because I know what that feels like," he said flatly, and my heart squeezed. "It's because I've never been that kind of person."

"I don't think you would do something like that," I said quickly. And I didn't want to know. I…needed to know. "What did they do to you?"

"That's not something I really want to get into, Poppy."

I opened my mouth and then closed it. I could understand that. Respect it.

And as I remained where I was, I thought about what Kieran had said earlier about me being safe with the Prince. Unfortunately, I also remembered the effects of his blood, and how I all but begged him to touch me.

Not one of my finer moments.

Casteel had refused, though. He could've easily taken advantage of the situation, but what had he said? That he wasn't a good man, but that he was trying to be one. I thought of the shame I had felt inside him. He was both the villain and the hero, the monster and the monster-slayer.

But I wasn't afraid of him trying something with me. I was more afraid of myself—scared of how much my heart was pounding. The night we had been together, falling asleep in his arms had been...it had been just as beautiful as what we'd shared before that.

Only it hadn't been real.

The problem was that my heart didn't seem to understand that, at least not all the time. That was why it was pumping so fast now. To some—probably to most in the kingdom—sleeping beside someone didn't mean much of anything. But to me? It was as life-altering as holding hands, being able to openly touch another, or sharing dinner with someone—things other people often took for granted.

That was why sharing a bed with Casteel was dangerous.

I watched him let the blanket fall to his waist and then fold his hands under his head. Once he appeared comfortable, he said, "But, just so you know, if you want my lips on any piece of you, I'm more than willing to appease you."

My mouth dropped open.

"And my willingness to comply extends to my hands, my fingers, and my cock—"

"Oh, my gods," I cut him off. "You don't have to worry about that. I will never request your...your services."

"Services?" He tipped his head toward me. "That sounds so

dirty."

I ignored that comment. "You and I are never going to do anything like what we did before."

"Never?"

"*Never.*"

"Would you say it would be…impossible?"

"Yes. It's definitely impossible."

Hawke smiled then, and it *was* Hawke's smile. Dimples appeared in both cheeks, and I hated the catch I felt in my chest upon seeing them. Loathed that it made me see him as Hawke. "But didn't you just say nothing was impossible?" he all but purred.

I stared down at him, at an absolute loss for words. "I want to stab you in the heart right now."

"I'm sure you do," he replied, closing his eyes.

"Whatever," I muttered, accepting that I would have to deal with him. At least for the night or until I figured out how to escape. I scooted back, shoving my legs under the blanket. I threw myself down with enough force that it shook the bed.

"You okay over there? Sounds like you could've hurt yourself."

"Shut up."

He laughed.

With my back to him, I stared at the knife. The blade was bent. I sighed. A moment later, there was a click, and the room darkened. He'd turned off the oil lamp by his side of the bed.

His side of the bed?

We didn't have sides.

I tugged the blanket to my chin as I shifted my focus to the fireplace. My mind wandered back to something that shouldn't matter but did.

"Why did you tell me?" I whispered, not even sure if he was still awake or why I was asking. He'd already answered. "Why did you have to tell me that Hawke was your middle name?"

The fire crackled, spitting sparks, and I closed my eyes.

Seconds, maybe minutes later, Casteel said, "Because you needed to know that not everything was a lie."

Chapter 7

With all the stress and trauma of the last several days, it shouldn't have come as a surprise that the past found me in my sleep. Still, it was a shock to the senses.

Blood was everywhere. Splattered against the walls, running down them in thin rivulets, and pooling along the dusty wooden floor—under the lumps on the floor, misshapen and not right. The air was thick with the scent of metal. A smear of blue in the lamplight caught my gaze. A shirt. Hadn't the funny man who'd served our food that evening been wearing a blue shirt? Mr. La…Lacost? He told us stories about the family of mice that lived in the barn out back, who'd made friends with the kitties. I'd wanted to see them, but Papa had taken us back to our rooms. He hadn't been smiling or laughing at dinner. He hadn't since we left. He'd sat at the table, his gaze darting to the window in between every quick bite of food.

But Mr. Lacost's chest and stomach looked strange to me as I stood there, trembling. No longer round, it was sunken, jagged—

"Don't look, Poppy. Don't look over there," came Momma's hushed voice as she pulled on my hand. "We must hide. Hurry."

She pulled me down the narrow hallway, her hand wet against mine. "I want Papa—"

"Shh. We must be quiet." Her voice shook, sounding too thin. The arms of her dress were torn, the pale pink streaked with crimson. Momma was hurt, and I didn't know what to do. "We must be quiet so Papa can come and find us."

I didn't understand how being quiet would help Papa come to us. It was dark in the room we entered, and the sounds, the ragged breaths and moans, the continuous shouts and cries were loud. Papa had gone outside when they came, went out there with the strange man who'd seemed to know him. I wanted my papa. I wanted Ian, but he had left with the woman who smelled like sugar and vanilla—

A shrill sound pierced the darkness. Momma tugged hard on my hand, yanking me down to where she crouched. She opened a large cupboard behind me as someone screamed. Pots clattered off the floor as Momma tore them from inside the closet.

"Get in, Poppy. I need you to get in and be very quiet, okay? I need you to be as silent as a mouse, no matter what. Do you understand?"

Looking behind me at the small hole of darkness, I shook my head. Momma wouldn't fit in there. "I wanna stay with you."

"I'll be right here." Her hands touched my cheek. Her skin was damp as she turned my head towards her. "I need you to be a big girl and listen to me. You have to hide—"

The high-pitched howl came again, and I clamored for her, clutching at her sides. My fingers dug into the sticky waist of her dress. "You have to let go, baby. You need to hide, Poppy."

I held tighter, feeling wet warmth coursing down the sides of my face.

Momma jerked at the sound of something—a voice. Someone spoke, but my heart pounded too loudly in my ears for me to hear. It sounded like a rushing fall of water, and the nightmare sounds were louder, closer. Then, there was a voice again. And Momma, her hands were wetter, stickier...

Someone knocked a lamp over somewhere. Glass shattered. Momma yelled as her arms folded around me, the words mushed together, making little sense except for one—

Screams. Someone was shrieking. Momma? She was torn from me, her hands sliding down my arms, her fingers catching mine and then slipping. A body crashed into us—me—and I tottered to the side, losing my hold of Momma. Fiery pain sliced across my face, stunning me. I fell back. Hands grabbed at me. Hands that were too heavy. Hands that *hurt.* I screamed—

There was a voice again, somewhere in the darkness, living under the screams.

What a pretty little flower.
What a pretty poppy.
Pick it and watch it bleed.
Not so pretty any longer...
Poppy.

I jerked awake, a scream ringing in my ears, burning my throat as I gasped for air, struggling to move but unable. My arms were trapped against my sides, my legs tangled in thick warmth. My eyes peeled open, and it took a moment for my surroundings to make sense. I focused on the steady thumping under my cheek as I slowly dug out the thorns of panic and fear.

Faint gray light seeped in through the narrow window across from the bed. I wasn't at the inn, being ripped and torn into. I was in the keep, in bed, with a warm, hard chest against my cheek, a hand that continuously smoothed over my hair, a voice that whispered my name over and over, telling me it was okay, promising me that it was safe. I was nestled in his lap, held tightly to his chest as if he tried to keep the tremors at bay with his hold alone.

Casteel.

Reality came back to me in pieces as the disorientation from the nightmare eased, and I began to realize that he was slowly rocking us.

I knew I needed to pull away, should put some distance between us, but something about his embrace was grounding. Something that felt inexplicably right in the aftermath of the blood and terror. Maybe it was because I often woke alone after the nightmares, shaken and terrified, especially after Ian left for the capital. And even with my screams often waking Tawny, I never allowed such...comfort. I'd always been too embarrassed to seek it from my lady's maid. But there wasn't another option now, and it was the first time I'd ever been relieved to have the choice taken from me. I closed my eyes, letting the warmth of Casteel's body soak into mine.

A hint of shame sifted through me even though he'd known about the nightmares. Vikter had warned him about them, and I knew that Vikter had done so not for Casteel's benefit but mine. Sorrow tightened my chest. I missed Vikter, missed him so badly, and waking from these blood-soaked nightmares, the loss was raw.

But embarrassment also warmed my skin. How incredibly silly Casteel must think me to be suffering nightmares so many years later. I started to pull away. "I'm sorry," I said, wincing at the hoarseness of my voice. Only the gods know what kind of sounds I must've made to scratch my throat so raw. "I didn't mean to wake you."

"When I was younger and I left Atlantia for the first time, I saw a Craven outside a small village. I'd never seen anything scarier in my entire life. I didn't think there could be anything worse out there." Casteel's arms tightened around me. "Having been in its state for quite some time, it looked like a walking corpse. It was far more terrifying than anything my imagination could've created when I was a child. And hearing the way it wailed? I swore it would haunt my sleep, and it did. For weeks, even far away from any Craven, I woke in the middle of the night, swearing I heard it screaming."

The tremors were subsiding as he curved his hand around the back of my head. "But then I was captured. And the worst part? It was my fault. I was still young and foolish. I thought I could solve everything by taking out King Jalara and Queen Ileana myself. I truly believed I could do it. I got close—near enough to make my move. Obviously, I failed. And then I learned what true terror was. You asked me earlier what they did to me. They refused me blood, kept me on the edge, giving me just enough to survive—sometimes barely, but the constant low supply affected my ability to heal."

Bile crept up my throat, but I said nothing as I stayed in his arms.

"It takes a long time for that effect to occur, and they knew it. They didn't brand me before they knew the mark would remain." His chest rose against me. "When the ones they brought in to feed me were close to dying, no longer able to serve their purpose, they killed them right in front of me. Sometimes slowly, putting the same nicks and cuts into their skin until they died. Other times, they snapped their necks. But there were times that I was so hungry that I…" He swallowed. "It was me that tore into their throats and killed them. And they'd leave their bodies in there with me to rot. For days. Weeks. Nothing for me to stare at but the person I'd killed. Nothing to think about but what kind of life they'd lived before that moment, and what kind of future I'd stolen from them. Sometimes, the bodies would pile up, left in there long after the stench had passed."

Oh, my gods.

My eyes were open but unseeing as I listened to him. Was this also a part of the grief he carried with him? If so, I could understand why. All the terrible things he'd done or caused didn't matter in that moment. I couldn't imagine the suffering he must've endured. No one deserved that. Even those whose actions warranted death didn't deserve to be tortured, used, and abused.

And to be haunted by nightmares decades later? Centuries later? I didn't think I could deal with a hundred years of reliving the night the Craven attacked.

There was an emptiness to his voice as he continued. "And they did things to me—things that caused reactions I couldn't control. Females. Males. They made me—" He stopped, and I could feel his head shake. "I learned what true fear was."

A shuddering breath left me. "I…I'm sorry. I wish--"

"You have nothing to apologize for. It wasn't you, and I don't want that from you." His fingers curled around my hair. "I don't want pity."

"I don't pity you," I told him. "And I know I'm not responsible for what happened to you—and neither are you, even if your actions led to your capture. I still feel horrible for what was done to you."

"I don't want you to feel that. I just want you to know that I had nightmares, Poppy. For years after being freed, I woke in the middle of the night, thinking I was still in that cage, shackled by my wrists and ankles. Sometimes, things I did after being freed follow me into sleep."

His hand slid to my cheek, guiding my head back so my eyes met his. "So, I know all about how the past doesn't remain where it should. How it likes to pay visits when you're at your weakest. There is never a need to apologize, nor should you ever feel shame."

My heart twisted even as some of the discomfort lessened. "How...how did you survive what you did?"

"I don't think you'll like the answer," he said after a moment, looking away. "I promised myself that when I escaped, I would eventually watch the life seep from the soulless eyes of Queen Ileana and King Jalara." He dropped his hand. "That's how I survived."

I swallowed at the utter coldness of his tone. "Revenge, then." When he nodded, I wasn't sure how I was supposed to feel about what he'd said. Was I supposed to think poorly of him? I still didn't know how to reconcile what he'd told me about the Queen and what I knew, what I'd seen.

"How did you survive, Poppy?" His gaze swept back to mine, lashes lowered halfway. "How have you not let the night of the Craven attack make you afraid of everything? Because you are fearless, whether it be facing a swarm of Craven, staring into the eyes of a wolven, or when you push back at me, even knowing what I am."

His question caught me off guard, as did the knowledge that he saw me as fearless. "I...it's not that I'm without fear. I do fear things."

Interest sparked in his golden eyes. "I don't believe that."

There was no way I'd admit to him that I feared myself more than I could ever fear a Craven, wolven, or even him. "I survived because I refused to ever be helpless again. That kept me from caving to the fear. That's what helped me push through the pain of training with Vikter—the aches and bruises." I thought of the brand on Casteel's thigh, the pain he must have endured for something like that to scar when he healed so easily. "I can understand how the need for revenge helped you survive."

His head tilted as his lashes lifted, revealing his bright, intense gaze. "Is that how you're surviving right now? Picturing all the ways you will kill me?"

No. I wasn't thinking that at all. Maybe I should be, but I wasn't.

Slipping out of his embrace, I scooted over to my side of the bed. "I guess you'll just have to wait and find out."

A half-grin appeared, revealing the dimple in his right cheek. Too soon, it faded. "Do you remember anything from the nightmare?"

"I'm really trying not to think about it," I admitted, tugging the heavy blanket up to my chest.

He reclined back on an elbow, and my gaze dipped from his eyes to the lean length of his stomach. "You were speaking in your sleep."

"What?" That jerked my traitorous eyes back to his.

Casteel nodded. "You were saying something that reminded me of a…disturbing nursery rhyme, to be honest. Something about a pretty flower."

The moment those words left his mouth, the nightmare came back in a rush of startling clarity. "*What a pretty poppy. Pick it and watch it bleed,*" I murmured. "*Not so pretty any longer.*"

"Yes. That." An eyebrow rose. "And it's as disturbing as it was the first time around."

"I can't believe I was saying that."

"Neither could I when I heard it," he commented. "Has someone said that to you before?"

"I…" My brows furrowed as I shook my head. "I don't know. Sometimes, the nightmares I have of that night aren't exactly how things happened, but I don't remember ever hearing that before." I curled my fingers around the collar of the nightgown. "And I…I try not to think about it when I wake up. I could've heard it before and forgotten. Sometimes, it's—"

"Disorientating," he finished for me.

I nodded, sifting through what I remembered. Nausea rose as I did. I could almost smell the blood, feel my mother's wet hand against— "Someone spoke to my mother. In my nightmare. There was a voice right before the Craven reached us." My eyes widened. "I think it was the one who said the thing about the flower, and my mother responded. But I…"

Frustration ate at me as I tried to make sense of the garbled word I'd thought she said. It could've been more than one word. I could almost see her lips moving, but it could also be a false memory. "I don't… I can't remember."

"Maybe it will come to you later."

"Maybe." I sighed. "But I don't even know if what I heard was real."

"It might not be. Sometimes, things in the past seem to overlap one another in dreams. My capture often gets mixed up with Malik's." He eased onto his back, his eyes on the exposed beams of the ceiling. "The night of the Craven attack isn't the only ordeal you've been through."

My fingers slipped from the neckline of my gown. I knew at once that he was referring to the Duke. Heat crept up my throat, and I hated the shame that caused it—the humiliation of what he did to me that I'd been unable to stop. And as I'd just learned, if anyone knew how that felt, it was Casteel. He'd had it far worse than me, though. "How did you find out about the Duke? I never told you."

"About his *lessons*?" Tension bracketed his mouth. "Duke Teerman was feared but not respected among his Royal Guards. It took only the smallest of compulsions for one of them to share what they knew."

My mouth dried at the knowledge that he'd used compulsion, but it wasn't that he'd done it that caused the reaction. It was the reminder of what he could do. That kind of ability was frightening—and awe-inspiring. And not using it whenever he could was also impressive. I doubted that I'd have that kind of strength of character.

I frowned.

Was I actually complimenting his character? The man who had lied, kidnapped me, and held me captive?

I obviously needed more rest.

"The thing you repeated in your sleep?" he said, jarring me from my thoughts. "It sounded like something the Duke might've said to you. It's perverse enough for that bastard."

Casteel was right. It *was* perverse enough for Duke Teerman. The voice had sounded familiar. Could he be right? Was it the two...ordeals overlapping? There were times I didn't quite remember everything from the time spent in his private offices, when the pain of the canings had left me in a semi-lucid state.

"How often did he do it?" Casteel asked quietly. "Engage in his lessons?"

I clamped my mouth shut.

Casteel turned his head toward me. "I know what he did. I know that he wasn't always alone. And I know that, sometimes, it only lasted a half an hour. Other times, the guard lost track of the time." His features were sharp and stark. "And I know that he preferred to use the cane against bare flesh."

Pressure clamped down on my chest at the image of Lord Mazeen holding my hands to the table, preventing me from covering my chest, stopping me from any shred of dignity. "Whenever he was disappointed in me," I replied roughly. "He was often disappointed."

His lips thinned. "If I had known that Lord Mazeen joined him, he would've been staked to that wall right alongside the Duke."

I lifted my gaze to his. "I'm glad you didn't. If you had, then I wouldn't have gotten to see the look on his face when I sliced off his hand and then his head."

Casteel stared at me, the corners of his lips curving up. His lips parted, and I saw a hint of his fangs. The dimple in his right cheek appeared, and then his left. I felt a curling motion in my stomach. "So incredibly violent, my Princess."

The curl moved even lower. "I'm not your Princess."

He chuckled as he turned his head away. "You think you can go back to sleep?" he asked. "We probably have a couple more hours before Kieran or someone will be banging on this door to make sure you haven't found a way to murder me in the middle of the night."

I rolled my eyes.

"As soon as the storm blows over, we'll leave for Spessa's End."

I knew very little about Spessa's End. Only that it was a small town similar to New Haven, sitting on the edge of Stygian Bay. It was the closest town to Pompay, the last Atlantian stronghold during the war. One of the Priestesses had told me that Stygian Bay was the gateway to the Temples of Eternity, overseen by Rhain, the god of Common Men and Endings. She'd described the Bay as black as the night sky.

Lying down, I turned onto my side, but I didn't sleep. Instead, I stared at the dying flames, thinking of the Duke, the nightmare, and the knowledge that there would be little chance of escape between here and Spessa's End.

"You're not sleeping, are you?" Casteel asked sometime later.

"How did you know?"

"You're rocking over there like you're a babe being wooed to sleep."

"I am not—" I swallowed a groan as I realized that I was doing exactly that. I stilled my lower half. "Sorry. It's an old habit from when I was a child. I usually can't sleep after the nightmares," I admitted after a few seconds.

"Is that when you sneak off to explore the city?"

Since he couldn't see me, I grinned. "Sometimes. It all depended on how late it was."

"Well, there's no city for you to explore," he said, and I felt the bed shift as he moved. "I'm confident you remember how adept I am as a sleep aid."

Sparks danced over my skin. Of course, I remembered the night in the Blood Forest, when he'd slipped his hand between my thighs, and for the first time in my life, I'd discovered what pure pleasure was. I tried to block those images. "That's not necessary."

"That's disappointing."

"That's your problem—" I sucked in a sharp breath as I suddenly felt him against my back. I twisted. "What are you doing?"

"Holding you," he answered, curving an arm over my waist.

My heart bounced like a child's ball. "I don't—"

"That's all I'm doing," he cut in. "I sometimes find that being close to another helps me fall asleep."

I wondered how he'd gained that knowledge. Instead, I asked, "Then why didn't you suggest that in the Blood Forest?"

"Because this is not nearly as fun or interesting as what I did then," he replied. "I do have that diary around here somewhere. You know, the one with the throbbing co—"

"I know exactly which journal you're speaking of. And that won't be necessary either."

"That's all so disappointing." He settled his head behind mine as he all but pulled me down. "I need my sleep, and that's not going to happen when it feels like I'm on a boat." He paused. "A rickety one."

"I wasn't rocking that much!" I denied, wiggling to put space between us.

"I wouldn't advise that," he said, voice gruff as his arm tightened.

"Why?"

"Squirm a few more inches lower, and I'm sure you'll find out why."

My eyes popped wide as I grew very, very still. Was he...? Was he aroused? Simply because he was lying in bed next to me? Was that all it took? After what we'd just talked about?

I bit down on my lower lip. Sometimes, all it took for me was to look at him, and I'd feel a certain way. Knowing that he could experience all the want and desire after what he went through was a relief. What he felt now had nothing to do with what had been done to him. What I felt when he touched me had nothing to do with how I felt when the Duke placed his hands on me. I knew that.

And I shouldn't be shocked to discover that Casteel was attracted to me. That had been abundantly clear unless...that too had been an act.

No, I didn't think it was an act.

There'd be no reason to force the attraction now, especially not when it was just us—

"I can practically hear the wheels of your brain turning, Princess," he said.

"Why do you believe I'm thinking about anything?" I demanded.

"Because you couldn't be stiffer. Sleep, Poppy. We have a lot to talk about tomorrow."

The marriage.

Our future.

Two things that were irrelevant because the first was never going to happen, so there could be no future for us.

Besides, how was I supposed to sleep with him curled around me like one of those small, fluffy animals that lived in trees near the capital? What were they called? I couldn't remember. I'd only seen drawings of them in a children's book I'd once found in the Atheneum. They were cute and looked soft, but Vikter had once told me that they were vicious little creatures.

"Do you know what the fluffy animals are called that live in the trees near the capital?" I asked.

"What?"

"The ones that hang onto the limbs," I explained. "They're fluffy and cute, but are supposedly vicious."

"Dear gods, do I even want to know why you're thinking of the tree bears?"

"Tree bear?" My brow puckered. "That's the name?"

"Poppy," he sighed.

I rolled my eyes. "You remind me of a tree bear."

"I would tell you that I'm offended, but that requires speaking, which means neither of us would be sleeping."

"Whatever," I muttered.

Lying there stiffly, I debated snatching the meat knife and stabbing him in the arm with it. That seemed like a bit of an overreaction, but it was one I'd enjoy, at least in the moment.

I didn't know exactly when or how long it took, but somewhere between staring at the knife and doing everything not to rock, my eyelids grew heavy, and I did eventually sleep.

And I did not dream.

Chapter 8

The next time I saw Casteel, I was going to shove the stupid knife so far into his chest, he would have to dig it out.

Glaring at the door, guarded from the outside, I swallowed a shout of frustration and anger. With the exception of Delano arriving with lunch, I'd been locked up in this room all day, alone and going absolutely stir-crazy.

Casteel was gone when I woke, and that had been a welcomed discovery since waking up in his arms was not something I needed to experience again. The memories of such were already hard enough to forget. But hours later, as the snow fell steadily and the wind howled outside the narrow window, whatever gratitude I'd felt had shriveled up and died.

Delano had stood guard outside nearly the entire day. I knew because the last time I had pounded on the door, he'd answered through the heavy wood. He'd replied in virtually the same way each time I demanded to be let out.

"No one wishes to chase you through a snowstorm."

"I'd rather not be gutted by the Prince, so no."

"The Prince will return soon."

My favorite was when I'd said that I just wanted some fresh air. *"Nothing personal, but there is literally no way I would trust you enough to crack this door open to allow even an inch of fresh air to enter your chamber."*

How was that not personal?

I started toward the door, planning to bang my fist off it until the whole keep came running—

The door suddenly swung open as Delano rushed inside, hand on the hilt of his sword. He drew up short, eyes bright as he checked me over and scanned the room.

"Are you okay?" he demanded. Delano had the kind of face that often tricked you. Except for the nearly constant crease between his fair brows, there was a boyishness to his features. As if he would be grinning the second he thought you weren't looking. But in that moment, with the hard set to his jaw and the steeliness in his eyes I'd never seen before, he looked as if he were a breath away from lopping off someone's head.

"Other than being angry about being trapped in here? Yes."

His eyes narrowed. "You weren't yelling?"

My brows lifted. "Not externally. Did you hear me yelling?"

Delano's head tilted. "What do you mean by...not externally?"

"I was probably screaming internally for being locked in here."

"So, you weren't screaming?"

"No. Not out loud." I crossed my arms.

His already light skin seemed paler. "I thought... I thought I heard you calling my name." The crease between his brows deepened. "Screaming for help." Letting go of his sword, he ran a hand through his nearly white-blond hair. "It must've been the wind."

"Or your guilty conscience."

"Probably the wind."

I started toward him.

There it was, a flash of a grin. "Sorry to interrupt."

"Interrupt what? I'm stuck in this room. What could—?" I shrieked as the door closed and locked. "Now I am yelling!"

"It's the wind," he yelled back through the door.

I stomped my foot once and then twice instead of giving in to the urge to really scream.

Throwing myself onto the bed, I pictured all the different places I could stab Delano, but then I felt a little bad about that.

It wasn't his fault. It was Casteel's. So, I pictured putting as many holes in him as I could until I started to doze. I didn't fight it. Being unconscious was far better than rage-pacing. I had no idea how long I slept, whether it was minutes or hours, but when I opened my bleary eyes, a patchwork quilt had been draped over my legs, and I saw that I wasn't alone. Across from the bed sat Kieran, in the same chair as the night before, practically in the same position—one booted foot resting on a bent knee.

"Good afternoon," he said as I blinked slowly, looking between him and the quilt. "The quilt wasn't me. That was Cas."

He'd been in here? While I slept? That son of a—

"Though I'm glad you finally woke up. I was going to give you another five minutes before I risked life and limb to wake you. Unlike Cas, watching you sleep is not something I find all that entertaining."

Casteel watched me sleep? Wait. How long had Kieran been sitting there? "What are you doing in here?" I rasped.

"Other than wondering exactly what choices I made in my life that led me to this exact moment?" Kieran asked.

My eyes narrowed. "Yes. Other than that."

"Since I figured Delano would like a break and wondered if you might be hungry. I'm hoping that you are because I would like to eat, too."

My stomach immediately decided that yes, it would like some food, and grumbled loudly.

"I'll take that as a yes."

Feeling my cheeks flush, I shoved the blanket off and stood. "Am I actually allowed to leave this room?"

"Of course."

My brows lifted. "You say that as if I'm asking a stupid question. I've been locked in here all day!"

"If you could be trusted not to run, then perhaps you wouldn't be locked in here."

"Maybe if you weren't holding me captive, I wouldn't have to try and escape!"

"Good point."

I blinked.

"But it is what it is." Kieran arched a brow. "Do you wish

to leave the room and eat, or would you rather sit here and stew? Your choice."

My choice? I almost laughed. "I need to use the bathing chamber first."

"Take your time. I'll just sit here and stare at…nothing now."

Rolling my eyes, I started to turn, and then my stupid mouth opened. "Where is His Highness?"

"Highness? Man, I bet Cas loves being referred to as that." Kieran chuckled. "You miss him already?"

"Oh, yes. That's exactly why I'm asking."

He grinned. "He's been speaking with Alastir and several of the others in town. If he wasn't the Prince of Atlantia, with all his princely duties, I'm sure he'd be here…" His pale eyes glimmered. "Watching you sleep."

"Thank the gods that he has something to pass his time with then," I muttered.

Ignoring that, I hurried into the bathing chamber. I took care of my needs and then grabbed the brush from the small vanity. My hair was a mess from sleeping on it, and there was a good chance that I tore half of it out while trying to get the knots out. Once I finished, I placed the brush back and then looked in the small mirror, tilting my head to the side.

I wasn't looking at the scars, though I thought they seemed less noticeable somehow—could be the lighting. Rather it was my eyes that I stared at. They were green, passed down from my father to Ian and me. My mother's were brown, and I thought of how the Atlantians had golden or hazel-colored eyes. Had my mother's been a plain shade of brown? Or had they been a golden brown? Was I just assuming that all Atlantians had some shade of gold in their eyes?

Turning my head to the side, I saw that the bite mark was now just a pale purple bruise. It looked like one of the love bites I'd read about in Miss Willa Colyns' diary. I flushed as I quickly braided my hair. Once completed, I tossed the plait over my shoulder, hoping the thick tail would stay in place, concealing the mark.

My gaze lowered to my hands. *I have a lot of blood on my hands.*

As angry as I was at Casteel, his words still haunted me, as did what he'd shared about the time he'd spent as a captive. He didn't deserve that.

Part of me still couldn't believe that he'd taken ownership for Vikter and the others, and I couldn't help but wonder if their deaths were part of what stained his soul.

I also wondered if what he hadn't been able to control when he was held also darkened his soul.

If so, that sat even heavier on my heart, and I wasn't sure what to do with any of that. Horrific things had been done to him. He'd done terrible things. Neither canceled out the other.

Kieran was at least standing when I exited the bathing chamber. He faced the banked fire, and I wondered if that was as far as he'd moved.

"Do you ever get bored?" I asked.

"With what?" he replied, sounding as disinterested as possible.

"With standing around and waiting for me? It seems like you are tasked with doing so quite often."

"It's actually an honor to guard what the Prince values so highly," he replied. "And since I'm never quite sure what you're going to do from one second to the next, it's not even remotely boring. That is, except when you're sleeping."

I made a closed mouth sound of annoyance as my heart immediately went to war with my brain over why I was considered something the Prince valued. My heart, which gave a happy little flop, was obviously stupid.

I went to the fireplace and picked up the thigh sheath. Relieved to find the supple leather dry, I asked, "Have you seen my dagger?"

"The one fashioned from wolven bone?"

I cringed. "Yes, that one."

"I have not."

Feeling a bit contrite and insensitive, I turned to him. "About the…the handle. I have no idea how that came into creation or when. It was given to me as a gift—"

"I know," he interrupted. "Unless you are the one who carved it from the bones of a wolven, you don't need to apologize. I imagine it was created shortly after the War of Two Kings. Many of my kind fell during the battles, and not all the bodies could be retrieved."

I wanted to apologize again, especially when I thought about how families hadn't had the chance to honor their loved ones with whatever burial practices they observed. I resisted the urge to comment as I slipped the bent meat knife into the sheath, half expecting Kieran to say something, but all he did was smile faintly when I glanced at him.

"Ready?" he asked. When I nodded, he peeled away from the wall. "Lead the way."

I did just that, and it gave me great satisfaction to do so. Opening the door, I stepped outside and headed down the walkway. Why did it never feel nearly as cold when it snowed?

A better question resurfaced as I opened the door to the stairwell. "Are all Atlantians' eyes a golden shade?"

"That's an incredibly random question," he said, catching the door before it swung shut in his face. "But, yes, most Atlantians have some shade of gold in their eyes. Only those of the elemental bloodline have pure golden eyes."

I almost missed a step. "Elemental bloodline?" I asked, looking over my shoulder.

"Not all Atlantians are the same," he remarked. "Did your history books leave that out?"

"Yes," I grumbled, facing forward. The texts mentioned the wolven as being a part of Atlantia, but nothing had ever suggested there were different...bloodlines. "What is the elemental bloodline?"

"Those whose blood is purely Atlantian and can be traced back to the earliest known Atlantians," he answered. "Not descendants by blood but by creation."

"They were created by other...Atlantians?"

"Yes, by the deities, the children of the gods."

"Really?" I said doubtfully. "Deities?"

"Really."

My brows knitted as we reached the landing. I wasn't sure if I believed that, but what did I know? I looked back at him. "Are any of them still in Atlantia?"

"If there were, Cas would not be our Prince." A muscle flexed in Kieran's jaw. "The last of their line was gone by the end of the war."

"What does that mean? That Casteel wouldn't be the Prince?"

"They were deities, Penellaphe. The ones who created the elemental Atlantians. A drop of their blood is a drop from the gods. They would usurp any bloodline that sat on the throne."

"All because they can link their blood back to these…deities?"

"They ruled Atlantia since the dawn of time, up until the last of them died. They weren't just a bloodline," he said. "They *were* Atlantia."

Okay, then. "And Casteel is of the elemental line?"

"He is."

Well, if anyone would somehow be connected to deities and gods, it would be him. It explained his arrogance and high-handed attitude. "So, there are others who live in Atlantia? Besides the wolven?"

"There are," he said, surprising me. I half expected him to deem the information confidential. "Those with mortal blood, usually first or second-generation with one Atlantian and one mortal parent."

Those had been the half-Atlantians Casteel had spoken of the night prior.

"Very rarely does a third-generation or more removed have any discernible Atlantian blood or traits. But even though they have mortal lifespans, they aren't often plagued by illnesses or disease."

"Since their blood can feed one of an elemental line and be used to make vamprys, they don't need blood after their Culling, do they?" I asked, realizing I hadn't talked with Casteel about that part.

Kieran raised an eyebrow. "No. They do not need blood."

That was a relief, although Casteel's blood tasted nothing like I'd ever imagined. "Do those of the elemental line need food?" I'd seen Casteel eat. I'd actually seen the Ascended eat. "Do vamprys?"

"Those of the elemental line can go long periods without food but doing so requires them to take blood more often. Vamprys can eat, but they don't need to. Food does nothing to slake their bloodlust."

I stopped in the stairwell. "The ones who are part mortal...those are the ones with eyes that are hazel but more gold?"

"You'd be correct in your assumption."

"Then why are mine green? Neither of my parents had hazel eyes," I told him. "My mother could've had golden brown, but I'm pretty sure her eyes were just brown."

He glanced at the door. "If your mother or father had Atlantian blood in them, that doesn't mean they were purely Atlantian. They could've been second-generation and your memory of their eye color faulty."

I frowned. "I remember the color of their eyes."

He glanced down at me. "It's also possible that neither of them were your birth parents."

I almost tripped again. "Did they just find me in a field or something and decide to keep me?"

"Mortals often do inexplicable and strange things, Penellaphe."

"Whatever." A lot of things seemed impossible that I was working to accept. Both of my parents not actually being my blooded parents wasn't one of them. "Are there more...bloodlines?"

"There are."

I waited while he stared at me. "Are you going to tell me what they are?"

Amusement crept into his wintry eyes. "There were many bloodlines at one time. However, most have either died off naturally or were lost in the war. The changelings are another bloodline, although their numbers have significantly dwindled."

"Changelings?" I repeated slowly, having never heard the word before.

"Most are of two worlds, able to shift their forms."

"Like a wolven?"

"Yes. Some." His gaze swiveled to the door again, and his

eyes narrowed. "Many believe they are distant cousins of the wolven, the offspring of a deity and a wolven."

"What kind of forms can they shift into?" I asked, thinking of one of the stories Ian had sent, the one about the water folk. I almost asked if they could shift into part fish, but that was too ridiculous for me to even utter.

"Many different forms. But that will have to wait." He pressed a finger to my lips when I opened my mouth. "One second."

I frowned, but he moved his hand, brushing past me to open the door. I followed on his heels. When he came to a sudden stop, I almost walked right into his back.

"Kieran." The familiar, raspy voice caused my heart to lurch, even though I knew it wasn't Vikter. It was Alastir. "I've been wondering where you were today. I expected to see you with Casteel."

"I've been busy," Kieran answered. "Is Cas back already?"

"He's still with Elijah, speaking about...about the upcoming move." There was a pause as I peeked around Kieran. Alastir's hair was pulled back in a knot at the nape of his neck. Without the cloak, I saw that he wasn't without weapons. A dagger was strapped to one thigh, and a golden-trimmed scabbard held a sword on his opposite hip. Alastir also wasn't alone.

A man with auburn waves and the same vivid gold eyes as Casteel was with him. An elemental Atlantian, I now knew. His gaze slid from the wolven to where I stood, mostly hidden behind Kieran. One side of his lips tipped up.

Kieran moved to the side, blocking my view of the elemental.

"As I'm sure you know, there are concerns," Alastir continued.

"Concerns from Elijah or you?" Kieran asked.

"Concerns from all," Alastir answered. "It's a sizable group to move and keep healthy and whole during the trip. And once there..."

My mind rapidly turned that over. Were the people who lived in New Haven making the move to Atlantia? Even the Descenters, who were of no Atlantian descent? I thought the concerns had a lot to do with their limited land. But why were they going there now?

Kieran crossed his arms. "It needs to be done."

"Does it?" came the quiet reply from Alastir.

"I would think you of all people would know that it does," Kieran said as I silently stepped farther to the side. "To do nothing is cruel."

Alastir's features were somber as he said, "I agree. Doing nothing is cruel. My hesitation doesn't come from a place of apathy. Hell, you know I've spent the better part of my life locating our people and their offspring trapped in Solis and bringing them home." Alastir placed his hand on Kieran's shoulder. "My hesitation comes from a place of empathy. I hope you and Casteel realize that."

"We do." Kieran clamped his hand over the older wolven's forearm. "It's just a complicated situation."

"That it is." Alastir turned his head to where I stood. "But not nearly as complicated as this."

Kieran started to block me once more, and I'd had it with the ridiculousness. "He can see me standing behind you," I said. "You're a giant oaf, but not that giant of an oaf."

A wide smile broke out across Alastir's face, and the elemental behind him laughed.

Kieran sighed.

"I was hoping we'd get a chance to cross paths again without the Prince rushing you off." The wolven's smile tightened. "He does seem quite taken with you."

I tensed, immediately wanting to put out that based on what Casteel planned to do, he couldn't be taken with me. But recalling that Casteel had said that he was working on making sure my life wasn't in jeopardy with this man, I managed to keep that to myself. "I think he's far more taken with himself."

A loud laugh burst from the elemental. "I think I can now be counted as one of those taken with you."

My cheeks flushed, burning even deeper when Kieran said, "I would advise against saying that in front of Casteel."

"I like my head attached to my body, and my heart in my chest," the elemental responded. "I have no plans to repeat that."

"He did say you were…quite outspoken."

I crossed my arms. "More like warned you?"

"Something like that, but surprising nonetheless." Alastir's pale eyes danced with amusement. "We didn't get a chance to be properly introduced yesterday. I'm Alastir Davenwell and the one behind me is Emil Da'Lahr."

Emil grinned as he nodded in my direction. "I will forever think of Kieran as a giant oaf now, thanks to you."

"That's great," muttered the wolven standing beside me.

Sparing a quick glance at Kieran's stoic expression, I said, "I'm Penellaphe...Penellaphe Balfour."

Alastir's gaze sharpened on me as his brows narrowed. "Balfour?"

I nodded.

"That's an old name, one that goes back several hundred years in Solis," Alastir said.

How old was this wolven? "My father's family was involved in shipping. They were merchants."

"Casteel has told me that you are of Atlantian descent," Alastir said after a moment. "Which would explain why the Ascended have deemed you the Maiden and kept you close to them." His head tilted. He must've seen something in my expression, because he continued. "You've learned what they had planned for you."

A statement, but I nodded anyway.

"I am sorry for that," he offered softly, bowing his head slightly. "I cannot imagine what it must feel like to learn that those who cared for you did so for such abhorrent reasons."

It felt like the world was nothing but a violent lie.

"Your mother was close to the vampry Queen, and your father's family a friend to the King? Correct?"

Surprise flickered through me. "Did Casteel tell you that?"

A faint smile appeared. "I knew some of your background before I met you, Penellaphe. Word of a Maiden, one Chosen by the gods, reached Atlantia long ago."

That didn't make me feel entirely comfortable. "I guess that came as a shock to your people since your gods are asleep, therefore unable to choose anyone."

Emil chuckled. "That it did. We wondered if they had woken and forgotten about us."

"I think what is more of a shock is learning that you're of Atlantian descent," Alastir said, brows knitted. "Especially since your mother and father were so connected to the Blood Crown."

"The Blood Crown?"

"The Queen and King of Solis. The Royals," explained Kieran. "They're referred to as the Blood Crown."

I was sure there was disturbing accuracy behind that title.

"It leaves me with the question of how you're even here," said Alastir.

Kieran unfolded his arms. "What is that supposed to mean?"

"You can't tell me that neither you nor the Prince has wondered how the parent of someone of Atlantian descent survived long so close to the Blood Crown." Alastir looked at me. "It's not that they can sense us, but being that close, I imagine it would've been discovered."

"And they would've used one of them as what? A blood bag?" I finished.

Emil's brows rose. "That's one way of putting it, but yes."

"I don't know which one was Atlantian," I admitted. "Kieran seems to think that I was found in a field."

Emil sent a questioning look at the wolven.

Kieran sighed. "I did not say that. I merely suggested that one or even possibly both weren't her blooded parents."

"That's possible." A thoughtful expression entered Alastir's features. "I never heard what became of your parents. Are they still in the capital of Solis? If so, then I imagine the answer lies with them."

"My parents are no longer alive." Unsure if he knew of Ian, I didn't mention him. "They were killed in a Craven attack outside the city."

Alastir paled as he stared at me. "Is that...?" He trailed off, lines bracketing his mouth.

I had a feeling I knew what he had been about to ask. "It was how I was scarred," I told him, holding his stare.

The lines at his mouth deepened. "You wear your scars

proudly, Penellaphe."

"As do you," I murmured.

"I am sorry to learn of your parents," Alastir said. "I wish there was more I could say."

"Thank you," I murmured.

"We need to get going." Kieran touched my back lightly. "Excuse us."

Alastir nodded as both he and Emil stepped aside. "It was nice to speak with you, Penellaphe."

"You, too," I said, sending both men a small smile.

Kieran ushered me through the otherwise empty common area. I looked over my shoulder to see both males still standing there, watching us. I turned back to the hall. My steps slowed as I said in a low voice, "They...seemed nice. Are they?"

"They are both good men, loyal to Atlantia and the Da'Neer dynasty."

Dynasty. Is that what Casteel's family was? A dynasty?

"Come." He touched my back again. "We must eat. *You* must eat."

I forced my steps to keep pace with Kieran's as I momentarily forgot about Alastir. I couldn't see beyond the bend, but tiny knots tangled up my stomach. I didn't want to see the walls with the hanging dead again. "Why is everyone so concerned about me eating?"

"We want to take you to Atlantia. Not starve you."

Atlantia. My already churning stomach dipped. I knew so little about what rose from the blood and ash of war. "Do they really have running hot water there, available in...faucets?"

Kieran blinked once and then twice. "Yes. They do. It is probably the thing I miss the most when I am here."

"That sounds lovely," I murmured. "The hot water part. Not the missing it part."

"I figured that was what you meant."

As I neared the bend, I steeled myself for the grotesque sight of the bodies spiked to the walls. Was Jericho still alive? Had the others begun to rot? It was cool enough in here that the others would probably look as they had before, only grayer and waxier. My empty stomach churned as I stepped into the hall and lifted my gaze.

The walls were bare.

No bodies. No evidence of blood, nothing streaming down the walls and finding the tiny cracks in the stone to form little rivers. None on the floor, either.

I pressed my hand to my stomach. "They're gone."

"Cas had them removed last night after dinner," Kieran advised.

Surprise shuttled through me. "And Jericho?"

"He is no more. Casteel took care of him while you were running off to start a new life, one which would've ended in certain dismemberment and death at the hands of the Craven."

Ignoring that jab, I didn't know if I should feel as relieved as I did. "Did...did Casteel believe his warning was heard?"

"I believe he was more concerned about what you said than if his warning was left up long enough to be heeded." Kieran crossed through the open doors. "I, on the other hand, would've left Jericho up there for at least another day or so."

My mouth dropped open. I wasn't sure what shocked me more. That Casteel had acted upon what I'd said, or that Kieran would've left the traitorous wolven lingering in a painful state of almost death. "There should always be dignity in death," I said once I found my voice. "No matter what."

Kieran didn't answer as he led me to an empty table. The chairs from the night before had been replaced by a long bench. I sat as I looked around, spotting only a few people toward the back of the banquet hall, near the hearth and several doors. Where was everyone? With Casteel and Elijah?

I turned as Kieran sat beside me. "I don't think Casteel acted upon my words, but if he did, I'm grateful to hear that."

He rested an elbow on the table. "I don't think you realize how much sway you have over him."

I started to deny such a statement, but an older woman with a white smock covering the front of her soft yellow gown hurried to the table, carrying two plates. The scent of food caused my stomach to make itself known once more. She placed one in front of us, both full of fluffy mashed potatoes, roasted meat, and glistening rolls on the side. As inconspicuously as possible, I noted the color of her eyes. They were brown with no hint of gold.

"Thank you," I said.

There was a grunt of acknowledgment, but when Kieran offered the same thanks, he was given a warm smile and a sweet, "thank you." My lips pursed, but I didn't let it bother me as I snatched up the fork and started shoveling the potatoes into my mouth. Though it was a unique experience for me to even be able to look anyone in the face, or for them to see me, and for us to exchange even simple pleasantries. The mouthful of potatoes turned to sawdust on my tongue, so I guessed her response *did* bother me. A little.

Looking over at Kieran, I saw that he had been given a fork *and* a knife. My eyes narrowed. It was slightly thinner, but far sharper than my sad blade.

Finishing off the potatoes, I got back to my line of questioning. "She was mortal, wasn't she? The woman who brought the food to us?"

Cutting up his roasted meat into neat pieces that all appeared to be the same size, he nodded. "She is."

Then she must be a Descenter, a mortal of Solis. I used to wonder what sort of hardships someone had to face in their life to lead them to support the Dark One and the fallen kingdom. But that was before I knew the truth. Now, I wondered what hardship had awoken her to the truth.

"Are the people here planning to leave for Atlantia?" I asked.

"You put two and two together, I see."

"I'm smart like that."

He raised a brow.

"So, I'm right? Why are they leaving here?"

"Why would anyone want to remain under the control of the Ascended?"

Well, that sounded like a good enough reason. "But why now?"

"Sooner rather than later, the Ascended will realize that their Maiden is missing, and they will come looking for you. They will come here," Kieran said. "And there are far too many supporters in New Haven."

My gaze lifted to the now-empty hearth as I thought of all the filled homes along the street we'd come in on. "How many people live here?"

"Several hundred."

"Is there room for them in Atlantia?"

His gaze slid to mine, and I could tell he was working out that I knew about their land problem. "We will make room."

I had a feeling it wasn't that simple. I wanted to know what would happen if they weren't able to move them in time. I stopped before I could. It wasn't my problem. Their problems weren't mine.

Kieran had finally, after about ten years, finished cutting up his food. "May I have that? If you're done, that is? I'm not sure, but the last piece is a little thicker than the rest of the pieces."

Slowly, he looked over at me. "Would you like me to cut your food for you?"

"Would you like me to knock you off this bench?"

He chuckled deeply. "Cas is right. You are incredibly violent."

"No, I'm not." I pointed my fork at him. "I'm just not a child. I don't need someone else cutting my meat."

"Uh-huh." He handed the knife over, and I took it before he could change his mind.

I didn't take nearly the same amount of time to slice the tender meat, but I didn't hand the knife back over either. I kept it in my left hand as I speared the food with my fork. "Where is everyone?"

"Living their best lives, I suppose," he replied rather wistfully.

I shot him a dark look, but I was undaunted. "Anyway," I drew out the word, getting back to what we had been talking about before we ran into Alastir. "What do you call the ones who have mortal blood in them? The half-Atlantians? Like what would you call me?"

"Atlantian."

"Really?" I replied, picking up one of the rolls. "That makes things confusing."

"Not to me."

Rolling my eyes, I bit into the bread and almost moaned. It was so buttery, and there was a hint of sweetness I couldn't place. Whatever it was, it was amazing.

"The amount of blood someone has does not define an Atlantian," Kieran elaborated. "Those who are elemental are no more important than those who aren't."

I wasn't sure I believed that if those who were elemental were more powerful, lived longer, and were created by the children of the gods. "Do the changelings have longer lifespans? I'm guessing the wolven do."

"We do." He sighed, picking up his cup. "And they do."

"How long do they normally live?" I picked up a cloth, wiping my fingers, and then I reached down, unsheathing my ruined knife.

"Longer than you can comprehend." He stared straight ahead, chewing slowly.

"I can comprehend a long time. The Ascended live forever. The Atlantians—well, the ones who are of the elemental line, practically do, too." I placed the ruined knife on the table and slipped the other one under and into its sheath.

"Nothing lives forever. Anything can be killed if you try hard enough."

Overly proud of myself, I stabbed another piece of meat. "I suppose."

"But no matter how hard you try with that knife you just swiped," he said, and my eyes widened, "you will not be able to kill Cas with it."

My head swung in his direction. "I'm not planning to kill him with it."

"I would hope not." He looked at me from the corner of his eye. "It would probably only further endear you to him."

I gave a small shake of my head. "I'm going to ignore that incredibly disturbing possibility."

"Ignoring something doesn't make it less true, Penellaphe."

"Why do you call me Penellaphe?"

"Why do you have so many questions?"

My eyes narrowed. "Why can't you answer the question?"

Kieran leaned over, dipping his chin. "Nicknames are often reserved for friends. I don't believe you consider us friends."

What he said made so much sense that I wasn't quite sure how to respond. When I did, I doubted he would be happy to learn that it was another question. "Like how Atlantians only share their middle names with friends?"

"With *close* friends, yes." He studied me a moment. "I'm guessing Casteel told you his."

"Yes."

"Did that change anything for you?"

I didn't answer because I still didn't understand why it mattered to me. Or maybe I did, and I just didn't want to acknowledge it. Kieran didn't push it, and we finished what was left of our lunch in silence. I kept glancing toward the open doorway. Not that I was looking for Casteel, but I…I was looking for anyone. The few people who had been at the back of the room had all but disappeared.

I imagined Kieran was grateful for the reprieve, but sadly for him, it was short-lived. "You know what I don't understand?"

"Yet another question," he said, heaving an absurdly loud sigh.

I pretended not to hear his comment. "Alastir brought up a good point about my parents. I must be a second-generation, right? Since neither of my parents were full-blooded, like born in Atlantia as far as I know," I told him. "But Queen Ileana knew what I was…" I trailed off, frowning.

I truly had no idea if the Ascended knew what I was before or after the Craven attack. Surviving the Craven's bite and not turning would've been a dead giveaway to Queen Ileana.

"What?" Kieran prodded.

"I…I honestly can't remember being referred to as the Maiden or the Chosen before my parents left. But I was so young, and there are so few memories." And what I remembered of the night of the Craven attack, I couldn't exactly trust as real. "I don't know how they learned what I was. If it were my abilities before the attack or if it was after that."

"And you don't remember what made your parents leave the capital?"

"I remember them saying that they wanted a quieter life, but what...what if they knew what would happen to me? To their children?"

"And they were escaping the Ascended?" Kieran took a drink. "That's a possibility."

I glanced back at the doors. "Alastir helped to relocate Atlantians who were stranded in Solis?"

"He did, but if your parents were first-generation, unaware of what they were, I doubt they would've known how to even contact someone like Alastir. "

"How would they have contacted him?" I turned back around.

"They would've had to know someone who knew someone who knew someone, and through the whole chain of people, they'd have had to trust each and every one completely."

Considering how Descenters were treated, I couldn't imagine anyone having that kind of trust. But still, what if they had been seeking someone like Alastir? What if they'd left without even knowing that there were others out there that could help them? Would that have changed the outcome at all? Probably.

"Alastir did bring up another good point," Kieran commented.

"How either of my parents didn't end up being used to create more vampry."

"Unless..."

I knew where he was heading with that. "Anyway, back to my original question."

"Yay," he muttered.

"If my parents were first-generation, then I would be second."

His gaze flickered over my face, passing over the scars without even so much as a slight widening of the eyes. "*Assuming* that they are both your parents, yes. I would almost think your abilities would make you first-generation, but it's possible that you're second."

"And all Atlantians have golden eyes, in some shape or form," I said. "As I'm sure you can tell, I don't have golden eyes."

"No, you don't. But I never said all Atlantians have golden eyes. I said *most* do," Kieran said, toying with the fork. "Changelings don't, and they have no unique eye color. Neither did a few of the other bloodlines we believed had died off," he added, the fork stilling between his fingers. "Maybe we were wrong to assume that some of the older lines have ceased to exist. Perhaps you're proof of that."

Chapter 9

"You think I might be a descendent of one of the other bloodlines? Or…or a changeling?" A thousand thoughts entered my head all at once. "I can't change my form. I mean, I haven't tried. Should I?" My nose wrinkled. "Probably not. Knowing my luck, my other form would be a barrat." I shuddered. Barrats were rats the size of a small bear.

Kieran stared at me, his lips twitching. "You have a selective memory. I said *most* can shift forms, but not all. And it would be extremely doubtful that even a first-generation descendent of the changeling bloodline could do that."

"Sorry, I got hung up on the whole shifting forms part. What can the others do? The ones who don't shift?"

"Some have heightened senses—mental abilities. As those of an elemental line often do."

"Like…being able to tell the future or knowing things about people?"

He nodded.

The woman who'd been in the Red Pearl came to mind immediately. She'd known way too much for someone I'd never met before, and I'd wondered then if she'd been a Seer, but it seemed more likely that she had been working with Casteel. But she'd said something. It had been strange then, but virtually meaningless. What had it been?

You are like a second daughter, but not in the way you intend.

Had she meant second daughter as in…second-generation?

Either way, with my abilities, it would make sense that I had descended from such a bloodline. Being able to tell what others were feeling was a heightened sense.

"What about the other bloodlines?" I asked. "The ones that died off?"

"There were—" Kieran's head suddenly twisted toward the doorway. I followed his gaze, finding the area empty at first. However, within seconds, *he* appeared.

The breath I took sort of got stuck somewhere in my chest when I saw Casteel. Annoyed by the reaction and also somewhat awed by the idea that the mere sight of someone could cause such a physical response, I had to admit that he cut a striking and imposing figure dressed in black breeches and a tunic with a heavy, fur-lined cloak draped over his shoulders. As he strode forward, the cloak parted, revealing both of his short swords, sheathed close to the sides of his stomach, their deadly, sharp points were tucked away from his arms, and the serrated sides lay flat against him. His hair was windblown back from his face, sharpening the lines of his cheekbones.

Casteel had taken only a few steps into the banquet hall when he turned in our direction. His gaze found mine with unerring accuracy. The space between us seemed to shrink as he held my stare. My heart rate picked up, and my skin flushed.

I didn't remember falling asleep this morning, but I did recall exactly what it had felt like with his arm draped over my waist, his chest mere inches from my back. It had been an *experience* and would've been perfect if things were…different. If things were different, I would be looking forward to the many nights and mornings that surely awaited us. A sharp aching pulse rolled through me.

Casteel's lips rose, just a corner. I knew that if I were closer, I would see the dimple in his right cheek. It was almost like he knew where my thoughts had gone. Tearing my gaze from his, something occurred to me. Casteel did know.

Facing Kieran, I asked in a low voice, "Can he somehow sense…like what I'm feeling? Not like I can, but in another way?"

Kieran tilted his head toward mine, dark brows furrowing and then smoothing as a hint of amusement played across his lips.

Oh, no.

I tensed, instinctively knowing I probably wasn't going to like the answer.

"Atlantians of the elemental line do have heightened physical senses," he explained. "Their sight is far beyond what a mortal could even imagine, allowing them to see clearly even during the darkest hours of the night."

I already knew that.

"Their sense of taste is also heightened, as well as their sense of smell," he continued, his grin growing. "They can scent a person's unique scent, and that can tell a lot of things about someone and their body—where a person has been, what they last ate, or who they've been close to."

Relief began to seep into me. All of that didn't sound too bad—

"One could tell, in certain situations, if a person is unwell or injured or the exact opposite. Like, for example, if someone is…." He paused. "Aroused."

And there it was, what I feared.

Casteel could sense *arousal?*

Heat swept over every inch of my body, and I knew I had to be as red as the leaves within the Blood Forest. Oh, gods. That explained how he seemed to know exactly when I was lying about being attracted to him. But could he sense *that* from a distance? I doubted that.

"How is that even possible?"

"Each person has a unique scent. At certain times, the scent is stronger. Especially when someone is aroused."

"I wish you'd stop saying that word," I muttered.

"Why? There's nothing to be ashamed of," he responded. "It's probably one of the most natural things there is."

Natural or not, I now knew what it felt like to know someone could be privy to such intimate dealings. Feeling as if the tables had been turned on me, I picked up my cup and swallowed the sweet juice.

"Only the wolven have keener senses that allow us to track over longer distances," Kieran added. "And for longer periods."

I nearly choked on the juice.

The night in the Blood Forest came back to me in vivid, startling detail. Kieran had been keeping guard while Casteel…while he *helped* me sleep. At that time, I'd believed Kieran had been too far away to hear or see or *scent* anything.

I almost shouted a curse that would've shocked Vikter and then made him laugh.

"I'm curious," Casteel said, causing me to jump. I hadn't even heard him approach. "What are you two discussing that has Poppy looking as if she's five seconds away from crawling under the table?"

"Nothing," I said.

"I was just telling her about how you have heightened physical senses," Kieran answered at the same time as I did. "Like your ability to see better than her, and scent her arousal—"

"Oh, my gods!" I spun on the bench, swinging at Kieran, but he easily avoided my fist.

"I'm sorry." Kieran didn't look remotely remorseful. "I meant desire. She doesn't like the word arousal."

"Careful, Kieran," Casteel murmured, catching my hand before I could swing at Kieran once more. "She'll be threatening to stab you next."

The wolven grinned. "I'm pretty sure that's already happened."

"I hate you," I announced. "I hate you both."

Casteel chuckled. "That's a lie."

My gaze shot to his as I tugged on my hand. "You can't sense that."

He didn't let go of my hand. "Not through any type of heightened senses, but I know you don't nonetheless."

"Whatever you think you know is completely wrong. I absolutely loathe your very existence." I glared up at him. "And you can let go of my hand, please and thank you."

"Why do you think you loathe my very existence?" His eyes glimmered as a hint of a smile played across his lips. "And even though you asked oh so nicely, I fear that if I let go of your hand, either Kieran or I will be in grave danger."

Kieran nodded.

"Cowards," I hissed.

"Also, I like holding your hand," Casteel said, sucking his lower lip between his teeth—between his *fangs*.

"I don't care what you like. And I also can't believe you're seriously asking why I would loathe you. Do you have memory problems?"

"I think I have a very impressive memory. Don't you think so, Kieran?"

"There is very little you forget," the wolven answered.

Steam had to be billowing out of my ears. "Besides the fact that you've lied to me, kidnapped me, and planned to ransom me, you kept me locked in a room all day. How is that any better than what the Ascended did to me my entire life?"

The warmth and amusement vanished under the ice drenching Casteel's gaze. "Because this time, it is for your safety."

I laughed harshly. "Isn't that what they also claimed?"

A muscle ticked in his jaw. "The difference is that they were lying to you, and I'm not."

"There are those who would risk death to seek revenge against the Ascended," Kieran added. "He's trying to protect you."

"For what?" I shot each of them a withering stare. "So I stay alive long enough for him to trade me?"

Casteel arched a brow but said nothing.

Anger and embarrassment was a dangerous mix. I was furious over being locked up all day and embarrassed by the knowledge that both of these men knew how I responded to Casteel—how easily my body sang for him. "You're no better than the Ascended."

Casteel didn't move.

Kieran didn't speak.

Silence stretched out so long between us that unease blossomed, sending my heart pounding. I shouldn't have said that. I knew that the moment it left my mouth, but I couldn't take it back.

"I need to show you something," Casteel bit out, all but lifting me off the bench. He started walking, tugging me along behind him, his grip on my hand firm but not painful.

I struggled to keep up with his long-legged pace as he crossed the banquet hall. "There is nothing you can show me that I want to see."

"You won't want to see this. No one does. But you *need* to see it."

Confused by that statement, I looked over my shoulder to see Kieran leaning back, arms resting on the table, his long legs stretched out in front of him. He waved at me.

I did something that Ian had once taught me, something that I'd seen the guards do to one another—sometimes in humor and other times in anger. It was considered a foul gesture, and I'd never done it in my life.

I gave Kieran the middle finger.

Throwing his head back, the wolven laughed loudly and deeply.

Casteel glanced back at me, brows raised as his eyes flicked to Kieran. "Do I even want to know what you just did?"

"It's none of your business," I grumbled, cheeks feeling hot.

"You're in a lovely mood today."

"I'm beginning to doubt your comprehension skills. You've kept me—"

"Locked away in a room all day. I know," he interrupted as we walked through the empty hall. "I would've preferred not to. Believe it or not, the idea of keeping you confined is something I find distasteful."

I wanted to believe him. I really did, but I wasn't that naïve. "Then you can simply not do it."

He coughed out a dry laugh. "And risk you running off again, unprepared and unprotected? I think not."

"I'm not going to try to run away—"

Casteel laughed again, this time as deeply as Kieran had. I figured there was a good chance I might explode as we entered the common area. People lingered in the space, and I had no idea what they thought when they saw Casteel and I walk past them. I imagined one or both of us looked as if we were charging off to do battle.

Up ahead, one of the men by the door opened it for us, and I had no idea where we were going as Casteel led me outside. Regardless, I was glad he wasn't taking me back to the room. I'd definitely lose it then.

The snow was coming down in a light, slow flurry, having eased off a bit from before. We trudged through several inches on the ground as we crossed the yard.

"Why are we going into the woods?" I asked, wondering if I should be concerned, even though I knew I was no good to him dead.

"We aren't going very far." Having slowed down so I could walk at his side, he glanced over at me. "Are you cold?"

I shook my head.

"We won't be out here for very long," he said.

I lifted a hand as we walked, momentarily distracted by the snow. I watched it fall and melt against my skin. After a moment, I became aware of Casteel's intense gaze on me. Closing my hand, I lowered it to my side.

"It snowed in Masadonia, didn't it?" he asked quietly as we reached the edge of the forest. "Were you ever able to enjoy it?"

"It would've been unseemly for a Maiden to be romping around in the snow." I frowned as we stepped under the trees. Snow dusted large areas of the forest floor and drifted in higher piles where there were breaks in the trees. "But a few times when I was able to sneak out at night I saw it, but it wasn't often. A couple of times with Ian. Once with Tawny."

Tawny.

My heart hurt as I thought of her, almost wishing I hadn't. Gods, I missed her. She was the second daughter of a successful merchant, given to the Royal Court at the age of thirteen during the Rite. She had been tasked to be a companion of sorts to me, but she had become far more than that. I often worried that our friendship was nothing more than a task, a duty to her. But I knew better now. She genuinely cared for me.

"Everyone seemed to go outside in the snow," I continued. "So, going out without being seen wasn't always feasible."

"That's a shame. There are few things more peaceful than being out in the snow." Casteel's steps slowed, and then he stopped, letting go of my hand.

Palm still tingly from the contact, I crossed my arms over my chest as he bent. "Does it snow in Atlantia?"

"In the mountains, yes." He lifted a heavy branch and then swept the fine layer of snow off what appeared to be a wooden door in the ground. "My brother and I would sneak off quite a bit to go into the mountains when we knew it was snowing. Kieran would often come with us, as would…others sometimes." He tugged on an iron hook, pulling a door up. "I can make a mean snowball."

I stared at a dimly lit hole. Stone and earthen steps took form out of the shadows. "Ian taught me how to make snowballs, but I haven't thrown one in years."

He looked up at me, a slight smile on his lips. "I bet you're the type who packs the snow so tight that it leaves welts behind when it hits someone."

My lips twitched as I looked away, thinking the mask of the Prince had cracked a little just there, showing a peek of either Casteel or yet another mask.

"Knew it," he murmured and then cleared his throat. "I ran into Alastir before I came into the banquet hall. He told me he spoke with you."

"We did. Briefly." I glanced at him. "Kieran was there."

"I know." He watched me. "What do you think of Alastir?"

I thought about that for a moment. "He seems nice, but it's not like I know him." I lifted my gaze to his. "Kieran said you are close with him."

"I've known him my entire life. He's like a second father to Malik and me. To even Kieran. When I wanted to do something and my mother said no, and my father would ask what my mother said,"—a faint grin appeared—"which was usually no, obviously, I then went to Alastir."

"And what did he say?"

"Usually, yes. And if it was something reckless or if he thought I might find myself in trouble, he followed," he said. "Alastir found you very…unexpected."

"I thought you warned him about how outspoken I could be."

"Apparently, not well enough."

I took a deep breath. "Am I still in jeopardy with him?"

"Hopefully, not for much longer." Casteel turned to the earthen steps. Another long moment passed. "I know you hate being kept in a room, secluded. I didn't mean to leave you in there for that long."

Saying none of what I wanted to, I stared at his shoulder.

"I had to speak with Mrs. Tulis about her husband," he continued, voice soft. "About why what happened had to."

Mouth suddenly dry, I lifted my gaze to his.

"She was upset. Unsurprisingly. She couldn't believe that he'd taken part in what he did. I don't think she even believed me." He tipped his head back, squinting at the snow as it drifted through the trees. "I can't even blame her for doubting what I said. How often had she been lied to by the Ascended? Speaking with her took longer than I anticipated."

A smidgeon of guilt blossomed. "How...? Is she okay now?" I asked, wincing. Of course, she wasn't okay. Her husband was dead.

"I gave her the option to stay with the people of New Haven, promising her that no harm would come to her or, if she wished, I told her I would provide her safe passage to another town." He lowered his chin. "She is to let me know."

"I hope she chooses to stay," I whispered.

"As do I." He exhaled roughly. "Can you see the steps?" When I nodded, he said, "I'll follow you down."

I hesitated and swallowed thickly. I wasn't afraid of the dark or tunnels, but... "I've never been underground before."

"It's a lot like being aboveground."

I sent him a dry look. "Really?"

He chuckled then, and the sound was soft and real. "Okay. It's nothing like being aboveground, but we'll only be in a narrow tunnel for a very short distance and then you'll forget you're underground."

"I don't know about that."

"You will," he said, his tone quiet and heavy.

My eyes met his for a moment, and then I exhaled, nodding. I had no idea what we were doing, but I was curious. I was always curious. Carefully, I made my way down the steps, placing my hands on the damp, cool walls. Once I reached the bottom, I tried not to think about how I was underground. I took a couple of cautious steps forward. Lit torches spaced several feet apart cast light upon the stone and dirt floor and the low ceiling, continuing for as far as I could see. It wasn't as cold as I thought it would be.

The door clicked shut, and then Casteel landed behind me. I turned, wondering if he'd jumped, but he turned to face me. Suddenly, we were chest to chest. Under the scent of rich soil, there was the hint of him. Of pine and spice. His eyes met mine, and I quickly looked away, unsettled by...everything.

"What is this?" I asked, hoping my voice sounded steadier than it felt.

"It is different things to different people." Casteel stepped around me, his shoulder and hip brushing mine. I knew the shiver had nothing to do with the surroundings.

His hand curved around mine once more, and the spark of his skin touching mine traveled up my arm. "To some people, this is a place of reflection," he said as he began walking, and I wondered if he felt that charge of energy. We continued down the tunnel. "For some, it is a place to bear witness to what many strive to forget."

The shadows ahead disappeared as the tunnel came to an end. Several feet of stairs led down into a space that opened into what appeared to be some sort of circular chamber with high ceilings and...dear gods, it had to be the length of the keep itself. Dozens and dozens of torches jutted out from the stone, casting light across the chamber's walls. Only the center was in shadows. Within that gloom, there appeared to be several benches.

"To others, this is simply a tomb. Hallowed ground." Casteel let go of my hand. "One of the few places in all of Solis where those who have lost family members to the Ascended can mourn."

I was moving before I knew it, walking down the stairs and then onto the chamber's floor. Pedestals were situated every couple of feet, and upon them rested slender chisels and hammers. I went to the right, my gaze crawling over the wall—over what was etched into the stone. There were words. Names. Ages. Some with epithets. Others with none. As I drew closer, I saw sketches carved into the stone. Portraits rendered by capable, artistic hands. A shuddering breath left me as I followed the curve of the wall. The names...there were so many of them. They flowed over the surface, from floor to ceiling, but the dates were what formed a knot in my chest, each marking the birth and then the death. The realization that many shared the same death dates moved the knot to my throat, and the recognition of those dates caused the carvings in the wall to blur.

Quite a few of the death dates were sporadic, some several hundred years ago. While others were only a decade or five years ago, or last year, or...or a couple of months ago. But many others had dates that lined up with the Rites of the past.

And the ages...

My hand clutched at my chest. Two years of age. Seven months of age. Four years and six months of age. Ten years of age. And on and on. There were so many. *Thousands*. Thousands and thousands of children. Babies.

"They...they are from the Rites," I broke the silence, my voice thick and hoarse.

"Many are, but others are Descenters who were killed," he answered from somewhere behind me. "Some died of what the Ascended call a wasting disease, but in truth, it was due to uncontrolled feedings."

My eyes squeezed shut as Mr. and Mrs. Tulis appeared in my mind's eye. They had lost two children that way. Two.

"And some of the names, the ones you'll notice have no end dates?" He was closer now. "They represent those who've disappeared, presumed to have become Craven or are dead."

Opening my eyes, I blinked back tears. I stepped closer, reaching out to trace the grooves that formed cheeks and eyes, but stopped short. Below, set against the wall, were old, dried flowers. Some fresh ones. Pieces of jewelry that glimmered faintly in the firelight. A necklace. A bracelet. A ring. Two wedding bands laid to overlap one another. My hand shook as I drew it back to my chest. I stopped in front of a stuffed animal. An old bear with a pale ribbon as a crown. My throat burned.

"These are only a small fraction of the lives taken by the Ascended. There are large chambers with not a single space left for even one more name. And these are only the names of the mortals who were taken." Each word bitterly clipped. "In Atlantia, walls that travel as far as the eye can see carry the names of our fallen."

Swallowing hard, I spread my fingers over my cheeks, brushing away dampness as I stared at the bear.

"I am not without sin. I'm sure that I've caused names to be carved into different walls, but I am not them." His voice was quiet in the chamber, and yet it somehow still echoed. "*We* are not them. And all that I ask is that the next time you think I am no better than an Ascended, you think of the names on these walls."

The words *I know you're not like them* rose to the tip of my tongue, but I couldn't speak. I was barely holding it together.

"I can promise you that the vast majority of those I've killed, who've ended in tombs or on walls, deserved it. I don't lose a single moment of rest thinking of them. But the ones who were innocent?" Casteel spoke again, his voice low and as sharp as the chisels that awaited fingers shaking with grief. "The ones caught in the middle or who died by those who support me? I lose sleep over them—over the Lorens and the Dafinas of the world. The Vikters—"

"Stop," I rasped, unable to move for what felt like a small eternity.

Casteel quieted, and I didn't know if it was because he'd said all that he needed to or if it was a small gift that he was bestowing upon me.

My lips trembled when I was finally able to move again. I walked on, discovering fresher flowers, newer dates, and more common names—and far too many too-short date ranges, and ones left open-ended.

I don't know how long we stayed in there, but I felt like I needed to walk every foot of the chamber, see every name that I could read, commit as many to memory as possible, and bear witness just as others had to the horrific and painful loss of life.

Casteel had been right when he said that this was something no one wanted to see. I didn't, but I needed to see this. No one could fake this. They just couldn't.

Slowly, I turned around.

He stood by the entrance. "You ready?"

Feeling as if I'd just battled a legion of Craven, I nodded.

"Good." He waited until I joined him before he climbed the stairs. Neither of us spoke until we emerged to discover that day had long since given way to night.

I watched him close the door and move the limb over it. "Why did you remove the bodies from the hall?" I asked.

He remained kneeling. "Does it matter?"

"Yes," I whispered.

Lifting his head, he stared out over the moonlight-drenched snow. "I didn't lie when I told you that I had helped those cursed by a Craven die with dignity. I did. Because I believe there should be dignity in death, even for those I loathe. I'd forgotten that in my anger and in my—" He cut himself off and then looked up at me. "You reminded me that as Hawke, I believed in that."

As Hawke.

"Thank you," I said hoarsely. I wasn't sure if I was thanking him for remembering or for showing me what I never wanted to see but needed to.

His head tilted as he stared up at me, and then he rose. "Come," he said quietly. "We have a lot to discuss before it gets too late."

His proposal that wasn't a proposal.

Our future that really wasn't one.

I said nothing though as we walked back toward the keep, nor did I resist when he took hold of my hand once more. I had no idea why he did it. I doubted he feared I'd run. Maybe he simply liked holding my hand.

I liked my hand being held.

The last to do it so often was Ian, and that had only been when no one was around. But that felt nothing like this.

Maybe I liked it so much because my mind was still in that chamber—no, that *crypt* with no bodies, among all those people who would never hold hands again. Perhaps it was because my mind was still in the moment where Casteel remembered a part of him that was Hawke.

We didn't speak the entire walk back to the keep or up to the room. Once inside, he led me over to the hearth. I stood by it, letting the fire warm my chilled skin.

"Will we leave tomorrow?" I asked, breaking the silence.

"The storm is weakening, but it will have to clear a little from the roads." Flakes of snow melted and disappeared in the dark strands of his hair as he looked to the rattling window. "The wind should help with that…and possibly blow down this keep if it keeps up like this for another night."

I laughed out loud, thinking of the tale Ian had once told me he'd heard. Casteel turned to stare. "Sorry," I said. "I was just thinking about this story Ian once heard. About a wolf blowing down the homes of pigs. For some reason, I thought of a wolven doing that."

"You don't need to apologize," he said. "You're beautiful when you're quiet and somber, but when you laugh? You rival the sunrise over the Skotos Mountains."

He sounded so genuine, as if he truly meant that, and I couldn't understand it. "Why do you say things like that?"

His gaze searched mine. "Because it's the truth."

"The truth?" I laughed, stepping back from the fire. The burn was back in my throat, threatening to overwhelm me. "Will you add my name to the walls once you hand me over? I'll be dead eventually. That's the truth. So, don't say things like that."

"But it's not the truth. Not at all," he said, his gaze catching and holding mine. "It's why we must marry."

"Why are you so adamant about the marriage?" I demanded. "It makes no sense."

"But it does. It's the only way I can get what I want, and ensure you stay alive. Hopefully so you can live a long, *free* life."

Chapter 10

"What?" I repeated, this time barely above a whisper. Live a long life? Free? How was that possible if he got what he wanted—his brother's freedom in exchange for my captivity?

"Will you let me try to make sense of it for you? I'm not asking you to trust me."

"Trusting you is not something you have to worry about."

He leaned back, the line of his jaw hardening. "Neither am I asking for your forgiveness, Penellaphe."

The use of my formal name was jarring, sending my heart racing as it silenced all the bitter words rushing to the tip of my tongue.

"I know what I've done to you is not something that can be forgotten," he continued. "All I'm asking is that you listen to what I have to say. And, hopefully, we will come to an agreement."

I forced myself to nod. My need to understand what he was suggesting far outweighed my desire to argue with him. "I...I will listen."

There was a slight widening of his eyes as if he expected me to refuse, and then his brow smoothed. "Remember when I left to speak with my father? Of course, you do," he added after a moment. "That was when Jericho went after you." The line of his jaw tightened. "My father hadn't been able to show, sending Alastir in his place. There had been issues at home that he had to attend to."

"Issues with the wolven and running out of land?" I surmised.

He nodded. "Not now, but soon, with the scarcity of the land, we will have a lack of food and other resources."

A small part of me was surprised that he had answered the question. "When Alastir spoke to Kieran, it sounded like the people of New Haven would be leaving for Atlantia soon."

"They will be."

"Because you took me, and the Ascended will come here, looking for me."

His gaze met mine. "There were plans to move them to Atlantia before I took you. My actions move up that timeframe, but the lack of land wouldn't have been resolved before then."

I thought that over. "So, the resources are about to be stretched even further."

"They will be, but we're not at the breaking point. Not yet," he said. "Some want a more aggressive stance on alleviating our shortages. Many of the wolven are among that group, as many Atlantians are. Some of the conversations surrounding what should be done have grown heated, and that is why my father had to remain behind."

Casteel rose then, walking to a small table under the window. He picked up a glass decanter full of some kind of amber-colored liquid that I suspected was liquor. "Would you like a drink? If I recall, you liked to sneak a whiskey or two with Tawny."

Tawny.

I wanted to see her so badly, to know for sure that she was okay. But if she had been here…

I briefly closed my eyes, hoping Tawny was safe. More than ever, I was grateful that she wasn't here. She could've become an issue dealt with in the same way Phillips and the other guards had been.

Drawing in a deep breath, I opened my eyes and asked, "Would you have killed her? Tawny? If she had traveled with me, would you have killed her?"

Casteel paused as he reached for a glass and then gripped it, pouring the whiskey until the glass was half full. "I don't make a habit of killing innocent women." He poured a second glass. "I would've done all that I could to ensure that it would not have been necessary, but her presence could've caused a complication that I wouldn't wish to solve."

Meaning that, if he had to, he would have. However, he *had* ensured that the situation hadn't arisen by forbidding Tawny to travel with me. I didn't know how to feel about that. What was right or wrong there? None of this meant that Tawny was entirely safe, though. She was destined to Ascend.

But would her or any of the Lords and Ladies in Wait Ascend now that I was missing? All the Ascensions in the kingdom were tied to mine. They still had Casteel's brother, and they had to have another Atlantian to keep the Prince alive. Without me, they could proceed with the Ascension, unless…

Unless something had happened to Prince Malik? I swallowed hard as I shoved that question aside. It would do no good to ask such a thing, and I doubted Casteel hadn't already considered that.

He walked the glass of whiskey over to me, and I took it even though I hadn't asked for it. He moved to stand in front of the fireplace.

Sliding my thumb along the cool glass, I lifted it to my lips and took a small sip. The liquor burned the back of my throat, but the second drink was far smoother. I still had to clear my throat, though. Tawny and I would sneak drinks, and I had helped myself to a sip or five every once in a while, but not nearly enough for me to be used to it. "What do the issues your people are facing have to do with the whole marriage thing?"

"That's what I'm getting to." He turned toward me, propping one elbow against the mantel. "But first, my people will obey me to their deaths, both Atlantian and wolven." He swirled the liquid around in his glass. "I hope between that and the actions I took to remind them that you are not to be harmed, it will go a long way in aiding them in making smart life choices. However, these are not normal circumstances. You are not a normal circumstance."

"But I have done nothing to your people. I even tried to

save one."

"Many Descenters have done nothing to you, but you once viewed them all as evil and murderous," he returned. "You once believed that all Atlantians were nothing more than monsters, and yet an Atlantian had never harmed you."

I opened my mouth.

"It is the same, is it not? The Descenters and I represent death and destruction, although many of them have done nothing more than speak the truth." His gaze drifted to the softly rolling flames. "You represent a dynasty that has subjugated and decimated their families, stolen from them the lives of the ones they love, their gods, and even their rightful heir. You did none of those things, yet that is what they see when they look upon you. They see the opportunity to take their pound of flesh."

His words sat like stones in my liquor-warmed belly, and I couldn't stop myself from saying, "I'm sorry."

"For what?" His brows furrowed.

Wheezing from the huge gulp of the whiskey I swallowed, I blinked rapidly. "For what was done to your people," I told him, my voice hoarse. "To your family. To you. I know I said that last night, and you didn't want my apologies, but I need to say it again."

Casteel stared at me. "I think you've drunk enough whiskey." He paused. "Or maybe you should have more."

I snorted. Like a little piglet. "What you've done doesn't mean I can't still feel compassion." I started to take another drink but thought twice. Whatever kind of whiskey this was, it seemed to have a far quicker effect than anything I'd had before. "What you've done doesn't mean I suddenly don't know or care about what is right and wrong. What was done to your people is horrible." My gaze dropped to the golden liquid in my glass, thinking of all those names on the walls. Who knew how many were never listed? "And...and what is being done to the people of Solis by the Ascended is horrible. It is all terrible."

"That it is," he said quietly.

"I guess I get why they hate me." I thought of Mr. Tulis and took a larger drink. "I wish they didn't."

"As do I. Which is one of the reasons why we must marry."

My gaze flew to his as I almost choked. "That's the part I don't understand. How you've come to that conclusion or why. How will that get your brother back? How will that help with limited resources? How will I be...free?"

There was a sharpness to his gaze then. "There's a chance that some may still disobey my commands. Retribution can be a strong motivator. I, myself, love and enjoy the taste of revenge, as I know you do."

I started to deny that, but he'd been there when I turned on Lord Mazeen. He would know that my denial would be a lie.

"I must return home to help ease the concerns of the others, where you will be surrounded by many who believe that anyone from the Kingdom of Solis is the *lamaea* in the flesh."

"*Lamaea?*"

"It's a creature with fins for legs and tails for arms that hides under the beds of children, waiting until the lights are turned off. In the dark, it makes its way out from under the bed to then suck the life from them."

"Oh." My lip curled.

"It's not real. Or at least I've never seen one, but as a small child, both my brother and I fought to keep the lights on at night," he said, and I could see him as a precocious child, hiding under a blanket with wide, golden eyes.

My gaze snagged on how the muscles of his arm curled as he lifted the glass of whiskey to his lips.

Well, I could *almost* see him as such.

"Wait," I said, confused. "How does it get out from under the bed if it has fins for legs and tails for arms?"

His lips twitched. "I believe my mother once said it wiggled and slid, like a snake."

"That's extremely disturbing." My nose wrinkled as I glanced at the decanter of whiskey, wondering if I should have another glass. "I also don't understand the tails for arms part."

"No one does." He looked away, dipping his chin as he dragged his fangs over his lower lip. My gaze—my entire being—seemed to be snagged on that act. A subtle shiver danced over my skin, and again.

"The point I'm trying to make is that even though I have

ordered that no one is to harm you, you may still be in danger," he explained. "For some, the idea of revenge is far greater than the fear of certain death."

It took me a bit to pull my thoughts away from this *lamaea* creature and the glimpse of his fangs before I could focus on the point of this conversation. "And you believe that marrying me will remove me from danger?"

"Making sure that people know you are part Atlantian and will become my wife *should* make you off-limits. Especially to those who still have some fear of death and actual common sense." He took a drink. "You will no longer be the Maiden in their eyes. You will be my fiancée. In their minds, you will become their Princess."

I mulled over what he was saying, and I didn't know if it was weariness tugging at me or the liquor dulling my emotions, but I was able to process what he was telling me without throwing my glass at him.

Which I was sure he appreciated.

And probably why he offered the drink in the first place.

"What are you thinking?" he asked.

"If I should have another glass of whiskey."

"You can have whatever you want."

Whatever I wanted? I looked at him, and the wealth of want rising inside of me told me that another glass of whiskey wouldn't be wise.

Leaning over, I placed the empty tumbler on the table. "You're marrying me to...protect me. Is that what you're saying?"

"Yes, and no."

While there was warmth in my stomach, my chest felt ice-cold. "What does that mean?"

"It means that marriage will provide you with safety, and it will also provide me with what I want and what my kingdom needs."

"How will marrying me secure your brother's release or give your kingdom what it needs?"

He took another drink. "What do you think those who rule over Solis value more? The ability to create more vamprys or to remain living?"

I jerked my head back at the question. "I would hope the latter."

"I would hope so, too," he agreed, and a moment passed. "My father believes that Malik is either dead or beyond saving."

I sucked in a sharp breath. "He does?" When Casteel nodded, I didn't know what to say. "That...that is terribly sad."

The line of his jaw tightened. "It's the reality of the situation, and I cannot blame him for it, but I don't believe that Malik is lost. I *refuse* to believe it," he stated adamantly, and I hoped for his sake that he was right. "Many Atlantians want retribution. Not just for what the Ascended have done to their Prince, but for the countless lives they have taken, and the land and future they stole from us. My father is quickly becoming one of those who wants retribution. And the thing is, Poppy, we can take our revenge. Atlantia rose from blood and ash. We are no longer a fallen kingdom. Not by any sense of the word. We haven't been for a very long time. We are a kingdom of fire."

The tiny hairs all over my body rose.

"We may have retreated after the war, but we did so for the sake of our people and the lives of the mortals caught between us, but that did not mean we suffered. That we have become less than the kingdom we once were. In the time since the war, we've rebuilt our numbers, and we've stretched far and wide from Atlantia, entrenching ourselves in every city within Solis, opening the eyes of those who are ready to see the truth."

My heart rate picked up as I watched him lift the glass to his lips once more. "Many have spent the last four hundred years preparing to take back the kingdoms," Casteel said, and I might've stopped breathing then. "They want to make war with Solis, and if they succeed in convincing my father, countless people will die. Atlantians. Wolven. Mortals. The land will once again be soaked with blood. But this time, there will be no retreat. If my father is convinced to make war, Atlantia will not fall. We will not stop until all the Ascended, and those who support them, are nothing but ash."

"And...you don't want this? To take back the kingdom and end the Ascended?" I could understand if he did, but I couldn't stop thinking about Ian and Tawny, and all the innocent people who would be trampled in the process.

He eyed me over the rim of his glass. "Sometimes, bloodshed is the only option. If it comes to that, I will not hesitate to pick up my sword, but my brother will be one of the casualties. There is no way he will be kept alive if we go to war against them. I need to free him before that happens."

"And you think your people will not want to go to war if he's returned to you?" I asked.

"It's not only about him, but if I am successful, I believe so. If not, at the very least, it may give mortals time to prepare. To either choose their side or escape as far as they can to wait it out. I'd rather not subject this land to another several-hundred-year war."

He cared about the mortals? Even the ones who didn't support Atlantia? That sounded like the Hawke I knew, but not the one who earned the name the Dark One. Unsettled, I smoothed my hands over the hem of my tunic. "How will marrying me accomplish any of this? I'm just the Maiden—and you and I both know that means nothing. The gods did not choose me—"

"But the people of Solis don't know that," he countered. "To them, you are the Maiden. You *were* Chosen by the gods. Just like you are the figurehead of the Ascended to Atlantia, you are a symbol of them to the people of Solis." A half-grin formed. "And you are the Queen's favorite."

I shook my head. "All of that may be true, but I don't see how that accomplishes anything."

"You don't give yourself enough credit, Princess. You're incredibly important to the kingdom, to the people, but even more so, to the Ascended. You are the glue that holds all their lies together."

I stiffened.

"Imagine what will happen when the people of Solis learn of you, the Chosen Maiden, marrying an Atlantian Prince and not turning into a Craven? Not even after a wicked kiss?" He grinned at me, one dimple appearing. My eyes narrowed. "That alone will open many eyes. And through our union, we would be able to _y introduce the mortals to a world where the Atlantian people are not defeated and scattered to the wind. But it would also show them that the gods must approve of such a union. After all, based on what the Ascended have told them for generations, if the gods don't approve, they will seek vengeance. The people of Solis don't know that the gods sleep. And the Ascended rely on them never discovering that truth."

Nodding slowly, I thought about the people. "The people would think the gods approved."

"And what do you think the people would do if the Ascended turned on the one Chosen by the gods? The very gods who, according to the Ascended, keep the people of Solis safe from the Craven? If the Ascended turn on you, the kingdom built on lies will begin to crack. It will take very little to shatter the whole damn thing. And if I remember anything about Queen Ileana, is that she's a very clever woman. She knows this."

Jarred by him saying her name when he did so very rarely, I saw the thinning of his lips. "But not clever enough to know that the Kingdom of Atlantia has grown to the point where it's a considerable threat to their rule?"

"They know Atlantia still exists, and they've fortified their armies—their knights."

An icy shiver wrapped its way down my spine at the mention of the Royal Knights. They were the army of Solis, heavily armored, exceptionally trained, and utterly imposing. I'd only ever seen them in the capital, and even then, it was rare to see a knight since they were camped in the foothills of the Elysium Peaks. Many had taken a vow of silence.

"But we have been very careful to keep how much we've grown and accomplished quiet, making sure that the Descenters are seen as a ragtag group of people supporting a lone Prince who is hell-bent on securing the throne. They've grown complacent over the many years." He arched a brow as he took a drink. "And I do believe many scholars have said that the ego is the downfall of many, many powerful people. Even with the knights and the entirety of their guards standing behind them, it would not be enough for them to defeat us. This is where you come in. Or, more accurately, where *we* come in. Together.

Married. Joined. You and me—"

"I get it," I interrupted with a low growl.

The hue of his eyes deepened. "Even with all my considerable talent, I won't get anywhere near them or the Temples. I tried, many times while I was in Carsodonia, but you...you are my way in."

I exhaled heavily. "You think with me—by marrying me—you'll be able to negotiate the release of your brother."

"And bargain for the return of some of our land. I want everything east of New Haven."

"Everything east of New Haven. That would be...the Wastelands and Pompay. And farther south, Spessa's End...."

"And many more small towns and fields. Many of those places not even ruled over by a local Ascended," he said. "Many of those places they don't even use. It would be a fair request."

It was a fair request. Solis would still maintain the major trade cities and the farmlands outside of Carsodonia and Masadonia, among others. But...

"It won't be as simple as us sending a letter to them, announcing our nuptials." Casteel snagged my attention. "Once the Ascended realize that you've gone missing, they may believe you have come to an unfortunate end."

"At the hands of the Dark One?"

He inclined his head in my direction. "Or any number of very bad people. Either way, neither Queen Ileana nor any of the Ascended will believe that we have come together without seeing that you're still alive, healthy, and whole. We will meet with them on our terms and present them with their options."

"Give in to your demands or face war?" I finished. "War may come either way, but if they agree, we may buy the people of Solis some time."

Casteel nodded as he placed his arm back on the mantel.

"What you're requesting is fair. They have your brother, and the loss of land wouldn't hurt Solis that much," I said. "I would hope that they would have the common sense to agree. They may not be able to make more vamprys—that is if they haven't captured others to use for that." An image of Ian formed, and my stomach rolled. "And if they don't agree...then there will be war." My gaze lifted to his. "And if you meet with the King and Queen, and they agree, will you let them live?"

His chin dipped as a slow, cold smile spread across his striking face. "Once I have what I want and what my kingdom needs, they will not remain on Solis's throne. They will not remain breathing. Not them. Not her."

I looked away, tensing against the desire to recoil. I could understand it, especially after what they'd done to him. But it was hard to forget those months, those years after the attack, when all I had was Ian and Queen Ileana.

But I had seen the walls of the chamber underground. I'd seen Casteel's scars. I'd had my suspicions before I even met him. I knew that what he claimed was true. I didn't need to see or know anything else to believe that.

"And you plan to allow the Ascended to live? Who would rule Solis then?" I cut myself off because I wanted to ask: what about Ian?

"To prevent war and repeat history, they would have to be allowed to live. Things would have to change, though. No more Rites. No more mysterious deaths. They would need to control themselves."

"And you believe that can happen? You said it takes months, if not longer—"

"But they can control themselves. They already do in some cases, and a lot of Ascended are old enough to do so. They can make their bite pleasurable. They can feed without killing. I'm sure many would volunteer. Or the Ascended could even pay for the service. Either way, if they want to live, they will need to control their bloodlust. The fact that they are not the Cravens they create is proof that they can. They just never had a reason to do so."

"Do you think it will work?" I asked.

"It's the only way the Ascended have a chance of survival," he said.

But if he was wrong—if he failed? If his brother was already gone? I looked up at him and could say with a hundred percent certainty that he would kill them all or die trying.

My throat constricted. "And afterward, with or without your

brother, I'm free?"

He met my gaze. "You will be free to do as you choose."

"So, this marriage will not be...real?"

There was a beat of silence before he said, "It's as real as you believe anything about me is."

He wasn't looking at me then. His attention was once again fixed on the flames. The line of his jaw was like marble. "I truly have no idea what that's supposed to mean," I admitted, folding my legs under the blanket. "How will I be free if we marry?"

"I will grant a divorce if that is what you decide."

I gasped before I could stop myself. Divorces were practically unheard of in Solis. They had to go before the Court to even petition to have one, and it was, more often than not, rejected. "Is divorce common in Atlantia?" I asked.

"No," he answered. "What is uncommon is for two Atlantians to marry who don't love one another. But when people do change along with their love, they may divorce."

I got snagged on the whole part about marrying when there was no love being uncommon. If it was so rare, then how could he so easily go into a union with someone he obviously didn't love? The answer was easy. He would do anything for his brother.

"So, this marriage isn't real." I drew in a shallow breath. "And what if I refuse? What if I say no?"

"I hope that won't be the case, especially after everything you've seen. But this way, you won't be used to send a message to the Ascended, and you won't be used by them. It's a way out." He dragged a hand through his hair. "It's not a perfect one, but it is one."

It...it was a way out. A windy, twisting one, but I knew that if he had never come for me, I would be in Masadonia, veiled and suspicious, but having no real idea of the horror that was happening—the future I was going to meet. Casteel wasn't a blessing in disguise. I didn't know what he was, but nothing would have been okay if he hadn't entered my life.

I lifted my chin. "And what if I still say no?"

"I won't force you to marry me, Poppy. What I already have to force from you is...distasteful enough, given everything that was taken from you before you even met me." His chest rose with a heavy breath. "If you refuse, I don't know. I'll have to find another way to free my brother and somehow hide you away so that no one, including my people, can get their hands on you."

Surprise flickered through me, and without thinking, I reached out to him, reading his emotions, searching for a hint of scheming or slyness. Anything to indicate that he wasn't being truthful. What I felt was sadness, heavier and thicker than before, and I tasted something sour in my mouth, something that left me with the sensation of wanting to shed my skin.

Shame.

I felt shame coming from him, and it wasn't buried deep. It was there, just below the surface. "You…you don't like this, do you? The situation I'm in—that we're in."

A muscle flexed in his jaw once more, but he said nothing.

"That's why you aren't just hauling me straight to the capital right now, demanding the exchange," I said. "That would be quicker. It would be easier—"

"There would be *nothing* easy about giving you to them." His eyes flashed an intense amber before he looked away. "And stop reading my emotions. It's a bit rude."

My brows lifted. "And forcing me to drink your blood wasn't?"

"I was saving your life," he groused.

"Maybe I'm saving yours by reading your emotions," I shot back, pulling my senses back in.

Casteel pinned me with a dry look. "Please explain how you came to that conclusion."

"Because it's a relief to know that you wouldn't force my hand in marriage." And it did loosen some of the tension knotting in my chest. "It doesn't change the lies and everything else, but it does at least dampen my near murderous rage." And the soul-shattering disappointment, but I wasn't sharing that. "So, I might not actually try to sever your head while you sleep."

His lips twitched. "But no promises?"

I didn't dignify that with a response. "So, you will tell everyone we're getting married, and I'm supposed to act as if that is the case when we're around others? Then once we're married, we will go to the capital?"

Casteel lifted his head, gaze focused on the wall across from him. "Yes, but we will have to be convincing. It's not as simple as telling the world we're to be married. We must marry as soon as we arrive in Atlantia. Before I take you to my parents."

My stomach hollowed. "Do you think it's wise to marry before you even tell the King and Queen you're engaged?"

"Not particularly." There was a flash of a boyish grin, one I imagined he wore quite a bit when he was younger and about to do something he knew he would get in trouble for. "My parents will be…displeased."

"Displeased?" I choked on a laugh. "I have a feeling there will be a stronger emotion."

"Quite possibly. But my parents will seek to delay the marriage until they are sure it's true. We cannot afford the time it will take to gain their permission—permission I do not need," he said. "As I said before, my people want retribution. If they think this is a ploy to get back a Prince they have already mourned, and if they value revenge over life, they will try something. Once you become my wife, you will be protected."

"Your people seem…" I trailed off. His people seemed barbaric, but mine weren't much better. Whether I claimed the Ascended as my people or not, I had been raised by them. And wouldn't I be just as violent if I lived every day, knowing that the Ascended could arrive at any time to slaughter without question or punishment? I would be just as wrathful.

A shudder worked its way through me as I stared at his profile, at the taut lines of his face, and the shadows under his eyes. I realized that maybe Casteel and I weren't all that different. "I understand."

His gaze flew to mine, his eyes wide. "What?"

"I understand why you're doing this. They have your brother, who was captured in the process of freeing you," I told him, my thoughts shifting to Ian. "I can understand that you'd go to extremes to get him back."

He turned to me. "Really?"

I nodded. "I would do the same. So, I can understand and still not like it. I can hate that I'm nothing more than a pawn to you and still understand why I am."

"You're not just a pawn to me, Poppy."

"Don't lie," I told him, my heart squeezing. "That's not doing either of us any favors."

He opened his mouth and then closed it, seeming to rethink what he'd been about to say.

"There's a reason I understand," I told him. "You would do anything to free your brother, and I will do anything to get back to mine. I'll agree to this if you promise to help me get to Ian."

"Poppy—"

"I know what he is, and you know that I have to see what he's become."

He turned fully to me. "And what if he has become just like the others?"

"Just because he's Ascended doesn't automatically mean he's evil—don't." I lifted a hand when he moved to speak again. "You said that they can control their bloodlust if they want. Many of the Ascended are evil, but just as many were good people before their Ascensions, and they had no idea what the truth was. My brother…" I drew in a shaky breath, squaring my shoulders. "I have to see for myself what he has become. So that is the deal. I will temporarily marry you and help you free your brother if you help me free mine."

Casteel's head tilted as he stared at me for several moments. I had no idea what he saw, but then he nodded. "I agree."

"Okay," I whispered.

"You're not going to fight me on this?"

I considered that. "Not in front of others. Why would I? If them believing we're getting married keeps me alive, then why wouldn't I go along with that?" I reasoned, frowning slightly. I would never have guessed that whiskey had such an amazing ability to clear one's thoughts. "I don't have a death wish. Neither do I have a desire to be caged and used as a bag of blood."

He flinched. It was small, but I saw it. "But in private, you'll fight me tooth and nail?" he surmised.

"Kieran knows what you've planned, doesn't he?"

He nodded.

I met his stare. "Then in front of him and in private, I will fight you tooth and nail. I will not pretend to be the docile fiancée without an audience."

"Understandable." He dragged his thumb over his glass. "But if you want to pretend to be just that in private—"

"Not going to happen."

Something glimmered in his golden eyes. "I think you will find that I can be impossibly charming."

I glared at him.

"Remember what you said about impossibilities?"

I did. "But this is truly impossible."

"I guess we will see."

"I guess we will," I told him, relaxing. This banter felt normal. At least, for us.

Casteel eyed me. "I feel like this is a trick, and you're two seconds from trying to plunge that knife into my heart again."

I coughed out a dry laugh. "What good would that do? You'd only be annoyed, and the knife is not nearly sharp enough to sever your head or pierce your incredibly thick skull."

He smirked, finishing off the whiskey left in his glass before moving away from the mantel. "But it would give you great satisfaction."

I considered that.

It would.

"I knew it," he murmured, placing the glass on the table.

A couple of moments passed as I felt Casteel's gaze on me. "Do Atlantians recognize the tradition of rings when they propose?" I asked. The Ascended didn't in Solis, but many of the mortals did. A ring was bestowed upon a couple's engagement, and then bands were exchanged upon marriage.

"We do."

"Then how believable is it that we are engaged if I don't have a ring?"

"Good point," he murmured.

"I want a ring," I announced. "I want an obscenely big one like I've seen some of the wives of wealthy merchants have. Their diamonds are so large they look like they should weigh down their hands."

He angled his body toward me. "I will find you a diamond so big it will enter the room before you do."

"Good." It took me a moment to realize that I was smiling. I wondered if I should be concerned by that as I thought everything over. I felt a little more at ease. What I had said to him about understanding why he was doing this was true. That didn't mean I had to like it or that reality didn't sting and hurt something fierce. But if Vikter had taught me anything, if I'd learned anything from Queen Ileana and my time as the Maiden, dealing with Duke Teerman and Lord Mazeen, it was that being pragmatic and rational was the only way to win a battle and survive a war. I would go along with this because this was how I stayed alive and got to Ian. I, like Casteel, would do anything for my brother. And that included going from one viper's nest to another.

Chapter 11

I was to be married.

That was the last thought I had before falling asleep and the first thought I had upon waking—both of which I'd done alone.

Casteel had left shortly after I agreed, Delano having summoned him. I ended up falling asleep, and the only reason I knew he'd returned in the middle of the night was because I'd woken at some point with the warmth of his body inches from mine. I'd lain there for far too long, listening to the steady sound of his breathing, fighting the urge to roll over and look at him. He was gone when I woke, and I was relieved—this time for different reasons than before.

I needed to wrap my head around what I had agreed to, and I tried to do so as I stood in front of the dimly lit vanity in the bathing chamber, tackling the knots in my hair as if they had the answers to all my questions.

The marriage was real…yet not. A business arrangement that would give both of us what we wanted. His brother. Land. My brother. Freedom. And maybe even an end to a war that hadn't even begun yet.

Well, hopefully, we would gain what we desired.

How could I not agree? If I said no, and Casteel truly let me go, stashing me away where no one could find me—if that were even possible—I would still need to see Ian. This way, I wasn't doing it alone. I may be Casteel's key to the King and Queen, but I had enough intelligence and common sense to recognize that he was also the safest and smartest path to my brother.

But that wasn't the only reason I had agreed.

Despite Casteel's lies and betrayals, I knew that I wouldn't have been able to walk away, leaving Casteel to save his brother and possibly even his people through different means. Even though I had been given little opportunity to discover who I was as a person, I knew enough about myself to realize that I wouldn't have found a moment of peace in whatever freedom I had. Not after everything I'd learned, and not when there was something I could do.

But marriage?

It had been so long since little-girl fantasies of weddings and the possibility of being tied to an Ascended—something that, at the time, I hadn't known would never happen—had filled me with fear and panic.

This marriage filled me with panic and fear too, but for very, very different reasons. We would have to behave as if we wanted one another in a way that went beyond the physical. We'd have to act as if we were in love. And that was dangerous. Even with my lack of experience in all things, I knew this. What I already felt for him in spite of everything felt like a slippery slope. It would be hard enough to pretend to be together so we could convince his people of our relationship and not be affected by it. There needed to be boundaries. Lines. I was still a pawn. Only now, I was an active one.

I couldn't forget that.

I wouldn't.

Another worry manifested. How were we going to convince anyone that we were in a loving relationship when I'd publicly refused the proposal and insinuated, rather clearly, that I thought he'd lost his mind?

How was I supposed to even act? All I had as examples were my parents, and from what I could remember, everything about their love—the long looks and the way they constantly touched one another—had been *natural*. Something that couldn't be faked or forced. And the rest of the relationships I'd seen regularly were those of the Ascended, and I'd never seen the Duke and Duchess touch each other. Even Ian never spoke of his wife in any of the letters he sent. Not once beyond announcing their marriage—something I hadn't been allowed to attend. Then, Queen Ileana's refusal to allow me to travel had been positioned as a safety concern. But now, I wondered if it was something more.

I should've questioned more then, but I had become complacent in the Ascended's absolute control of me. How did that happen? How did the people of Solis get to the point where so very few questioned handing over their children? Some even happily did so, feeling honored. Was it fear? Misinformation? Lack of access to education and resources? There were so many reasons why, and even more for those who had begun to suspect that things were not as they seemed, yet had made excuses.

Like I had.

Because seeing the truth was terrifying.

And what if Casteel's plan worked? I saw Ian and...dealt with how that turned out. Then what? Would the Ascended truly change? Would the people of Atlantia be satisfied? And how would we know if the Ascended were following the new rules, living a more restricted life? Even if they did, I doubted the divide between those who lived in places like Radiant Row and the slums by the Rise would suddenly evaporate. The wheel the Ascended created would continue to turn, wouldn't it? Or would losing the Queen and King scatter the rest of the Ascended, forcing them into a new way of life?

I didn't know the answers to any of that. All I did know was that the people of Solis couldn't continue to be preyed upon. And if I could help stop that, then I would.

That was a purpose far greater than the one I'd lived with as the Maiden. It was real. It would change lives. It made me feel as if I had been chosen for something that *mattered*.

But none of that told me how I was supposed to act in a *loving* relationship. The Ascended always came across as if they were somehow removed from physical needs, but I knew that wasn't always the case. Though Duke Teerman's and Lord Mazeen's perversions were not good examples of how to behave in a relationship.

My heart beat too fast in my chest as a knock sounded. A moment later, the door cracked open, and Kieran called out, "Want breakfast?"

"Yes." Dropping the brush, I hurried from the bathing

chamber.

Kieran held the door open for me. "Someone is very hungry."

I wasn't sure I could consume even a mouthful of food. I stepped out into the walkway to see that the snow had stopped, even though the wind still whipped through the trees, sending the fallen snow whirling across the yard.

"Will we be leaving soon?" I asked. "Since the snow has stopped?"

"I believe Alastir and some of the others will leave later today to check the roads to our east, to see if they're passable. I hope so since the storm didn't stretch very far to the west."

Meaning the roads from Masadonia, or even the capital, wouldn't be as impassable. "Do you think they realized we haven't shown at our next location yet?"

"I don't think so. We have time. Not much, but some," he said.

It was weird to feel relief, almost as if it were a betrayal of some sort, even though I knew it wasn't.

"So, Penellaphe. For once, I have a question for you," Kieran drawled as we entered the stairwell.

I glanced over at him. "Okay?"

"How's it feel to be on the verge of becoming a real Princess?"

"He told you already?" I didn't know why that should surprise me. Casteel had probably seen Kieran last night.

"Of course, he did. I probably knew his plans had changed before he did."

My eyes narrowed. "I'm willing to bet his plans changed when he realized I was part Atlantian."

He smiled, and the expression hid a wealth of mysteries. "His plans changed well before that. But like I said, he hadn't quite realized that."

"But you did? You know him *that* well?"

"I do."

"Well, good for you," I muttered.

He chuckled. "I can't wait to see how you two are going to pull this off."

My pulse skittered like a wild horse. "What does that mean?"

Kieran slid me a knowing look as we entered the bustling common area. "Not a minute has gone by since we left the Blood Forest that you aren't threatening Casteel's life."

"That's an exaggeration. There's definitely been… Several minutes have gone by." I cringed, but Kieran had a point.

"I guess we'll find out soon."

I was too nervous to wonder if anyone was shooting me hateful looks as we went into the otherwise empty banquet hall and took our seats at the table. Chairs had now replaced benches.

Food was brought out—sausage and eggs, along with those amazing biscuits. Somehow, I got past the twisting of my stomach to snatch one of those. I was far quieter this morning as I ate my food. The reason why appeared just as I finished what I could eat. Kieran looked over his shoulder, and I knew who had arrived.

Slowly, I peeked behind me. Casteel walked into the room with Alastir and several of the men at his side. Alastir spoke to him as Casteel looked straight to where Kieran and I sat. Our gazes seemed to lock for a moment, and then I quickly looked away, heart back to thundering in my chest.

"Casteel will announce you as his fiancée." Kieran lowered his cup. "It will be wise to behave appropriately."

My eyes narrowed on Kieran's profile. "Do you think I'm going to scream in Casteel's face and run off instead?"

A hint of a smile appeared. "I wouldn't be surprised."

Rolling my eyes, I peeked at the doors. The group had stopped just inside the room, speaking with Naill, who, like the rest of them, had a habit of seemingly appearing out of nowhere. "Do you think he'll believe us?"

"Yet another question?" Kieran leaned back, crossing his arms. "Seriously? Do you ever get tired of asking so many?"

"Apparently, you don't, since you just asked three of them."

He chuckled then. "I think it will be tough to convince Alastir."

I stared at him. "That's really motivational. Thank you."

"You're welcome."

One quick glance, and I saw that they were still by the doors. "How do you know he will announce that I agreed to the marriage? Did he tell you?"

"No."

"Then how do you know?"

"I just know things."

I pinned him with a bland look. "I know you two are close, but…" Something occurred to me. The bond. "I read that some Atlantians of a certain class and wolven have bonds."

"Did you?" he murmured.

"Yes. It is believed the wolven are duty-bound to protect the Atlantian they're bonded to."

"Are you going to eat that biscuit?" he asked.

Brows knitting, I shook my head. "You can have it."

Kieran picked up the roll and immediately began tearing it into tiny pieces, reminding me of how the small rodents the Healers kept in cages ripped apart their paper bedding.

I shoved that image out of my head. "I'm thinking the history texts had the part about the bond being with a certain Atlantian class wrong. It's a certain bloodline. Elemental."

"You'd be right." He popped a piece of the bread into his mouth. "I could live off this bread."

"The bread is…tasty." I kind of wished I hadn't let him have it. "The bond between you two is more than just you protecting him, isn't it?"

"We were bonded at birth, and the connection is a lot of things, Penellaphe."

I was about to demand details, like if he could somehow sense what Casteel was about to do or not, but the sound of approaching footsteps quelled the desire. My heart, which had only slowed down slightly, started pounding again. Casteel and the men were coming over, and I had no idea what I was supposed to do. Smile prettily and behave as if Casteel hung the very moon and stars each and every night? My shoulders tightened as I tried to picture myself doing that. And for some reason, the scars on my face became bigger and more visible in my mind.

"Are you hyperventilating?" Kieran asked.

"What?" I stared at my plate. "No."

"You're breathing very fast."

Was I? Oh gods, I was. Why was I behaving like—?

"You should calm yourself," he advised. "As I said, it is very unlikely that Alastir will believe Casteel. The others will follow his lead."

"Yet again," I muttered. "Not helpful."

I didn't get a chance to demand to know why Alastir would hold that kind of sway.

Before Kieran could respond, I heard Alastir say something to him, and honestly, it sounded like a different language. My ears only started to process sounds when I heard Casteel say my name.

Blood rushed to the tempo of a pounding drum as years of expected behavior and grooming kicked in on an unconscious level. I felt myself standing.

Casteel touched the small of my back, the contact light yet I felt it in nearly every part of my body. My gaze slowly lifted to his, and the intensity in those amber depths held me captive. I thought I saw something akin to concern settling into his features. Was I still breathing too fast?

"Penellaphe?" he repeated.

"I'm sorry." Feeling a little dizzy, I blinked. "Did you say something?"

"I asked if you were finished with breakfast." Casteel watched me closely.

"Yes." I nodded for extra emphasis.

"Good." He took hold of my hand as he tucked my hair back from my face, brushing the heavy strands over my shoulder. The act was an intimate gesture I wasn't used to, and the look that settled in my features told me that he *was* growing concerned.

I needed to pull myself together.

If I could stand and remain silent during Duke Teerman's lessons, I could behave as if I weren't about to fall to the floor now.

Fixing a smile to my face, I turned to Alastir as I pulled forth manners learned long ago. "Hello, Alastir. I hope you had a good evening?"

A slight curve to his lips formed as he inclined his head. "It was. Thank you for asking." He noted where Casteel held my hand and then arched a brow at Kieran. "It's very polite of her to ask, unlike either of you."

Kieran sounded as if he choked on air, and on my other side, I thought I heard a muffled snort. I squeezed Casteel's hand. Hard. "I'm learning that these two are not very well mannered," I said. "I apologize for their lack of consideration."

Alastir's gaze swiveled back to me as Emil grinned from where he stood, speaking with Naill. A deep laugh left Alastir, crinkling the skin around his eyes. My lips parted on a soft inhale. That laugh. All I could think of was Vikter, and my heart ached fiercely.

"These two are definitely not ones I'd consider well-behaved under any circumstances," Alastir replied.

Casteel looked down at me, and I thought I saw an apology in his stare, as if he weren't thrilled with how this might play out. He said nothing, even though Alastir waited, and others watched. He returned the squeeze, nowhere near as hard as I had done. Did he want me to...read him? I opened my senses, and what I tasted all of a sudden was a mix of sour and vanilla. Shame and sincerity. He wasn't proud of this. Either that, or I was deciphering his emotions wrong. That could be possible, but I didn't think so. I nodded, and his lashes lowered, shielding his eyes for the briefest moment.

And then I saw it.

The mask slipping into place, curving up the corner of his lip in a smug twist of a smile. His features sharpened, and when he opened his eyes again, they reminded me of chips of amber.

"I hear congratulations are in order," Alastir said, drawing my attention to him. The laughter had long since faded. "The Prince told me this morning that you accepted his proposal."

"I did."

"I must be honest, when he told me, I thought I might've drunk too much last night. I didn't believe him when he said he was marrying, especially the Maiden."

"She is not the Maiden," Casteel cut in swiftly. "Not

anymore." He let go of my hand and moved it to my back again.

I felt an inexplicable warming in my chest, one that left me greatly unsettled.

Alastir cocked an eyebrow. "I would imagine she's not," he said, and my eyes widened slightly. "But she *was* the Maiden." He shifted his attention to Casteel. "Who she was may be in the past, but that does not change that past."

The hand at my back flattened as Casteel replied, "The past is irrelevant."

"Do you really believe that?" Alastir mused.

"What I believe doesn't matter." Casteel's palm slid off my back, leaving behind a shiver. He took my hand once more. "What does matter is that everyone else believes that."

"Spoken like a true Prince. Your mother and father would be proud." Alastir grunted out a short, dry laugh as his gaze roamed over me once more, lingering on the side of my neck, where my hair had fallen over my shoulder. There was no doubt that he saw the faded marks. The line of his mouth tightened. "I'm glad you're here, Penellaphe, as we've only had a few moments to speak, and I have many questions."

"I can imagine," I murmured.

Casteel tugged gently on my hand. "Sit with me?"

Nodding, I started for the seat I'd just risen from, but Casteel moved to the chair at the head of the table. He sat, and it only struck me then where he planned for me to sit. Not in a chair but in his lap. I hesitated. There was no way I was sitting in his lap. Over my shoulder, I saw the others take their seats while Kieran moved to stand at Casteel's left, and Alastir took the chair to his right, where I'd been seated earlier.

Casteel looked up at me, the twist of his lips softening. What now filled his gaze was a challenge. My eyes narrowed, and he arched a brow. There was nowhere else to sit. The only other option would be to stand behind him like a servant, and I refused to do that. There *was* a space at the end—

"Would you like this seat, Penellaphe?" Alastir offered.

Knowing that seating at tables was often a demonstration of one's position, I knew I shouldn't accept the offer.

"My fiancée is upset with me," Casteel announced,

surprising me enough that I turned to him.

"I can't imagine Penellaphe ever being upset with you," Kieran commented, and I had the strongest urge to lean over and punch him.

"I know." Casteel's smile was wider now, more real. The dimple in his left cheek was starting to make an appearance, and the hint of fangs caused my stomach to dip at the same time my ire spiked. "But I admit, I deserve it."

I stilled, unsure what he was about.

"You're not even married, and you're already upsetting her?" Emil chuckled. "That's not a good start."

"No, it's not, which is why I must rectify this immediately. I'm sorry," he said, the smile fading as his eyes met mine. "Truly. It wasn't planned."

My skin pimpled. Was he apologizing for me not being prepared for this, in front of others?

Casteel shifted, curling an arm around my waist. So caught off guard by his words, I ended up sitting sideways in his lap. He dipped his chin, and his lips brushed the curve of my ear as he whispered, "I thought I would have time to speak to you first."

I nodded slightly.

His lips were a featherlight caress across my cheek, and then he said louder, "I didn't plan the proposal, and to be honest, it wasn't the very best, as many within Haven Keep witnessed, even those at the table. She actually told me no at first."

"That was not the only thing she said," Naill commented with a chuckle. "Told him he was out of his mind. Told him a lot of things."

Did that Atlantian have a death wish?

Casteel laughed. "It's true, but I won her over, didn't I?"

The answering masculine chuckles caused my skin to prickle with irritation. My tongue moved before I could stop myself. "That was after I threw a knife at your face."

Alastir made a coughing sound as Kieran's and my plates were removed and replaced with food. "Excuse me?"

"Yes." Casteel's eyes were like warm pools of gold. "That was after you threw the knife at me. I haven't been the best of suitors," he continued, lifting my left hand. "I promised her the largest diamond I could find as soon as we return home."

"Well," Alastir drew out the word as he picked up a fork. "That is something that can be easily fixed upon returning. Our Queen has just what you need in safekeeping."

His mother had a diamond ring? For Casteel? For when he married? My spine couldn't be more rigid. Why had I brought up the stupid jewelry? I didn't even care about it since I...well, I'd never been allowed to wear any beyond the golden chains of the veil.

"Casteel hasn't exactly been forthcoming with information on how you two met." Alastir bit into his sausage, not taking the time to slice and dice it as Kieran had. "I wanted to ask when we last spoke. How did you end up in the incorrigible hands of our Prince, Penellaphe? I imagined someone of your...status would've been hard to reach, especially by someone like him."

Casteel let out a low laugh. "You should have more faith in my abilities to achieve what I want."

I tensed, feeling like those words were meant more for me than Alastir.

"Be that as it may," Alastir said with a wry grin, "how did he find a way to you?"

Wondering how honest I was expected to be and precisely what kind of rumors he'd heard, I decided to be as truthful as possible. In the past, I'd learned that most lies were successful when the little information given was the truth. "He became my guard."

"Well, that's not how we met initially." Casteel's hand that rested on the curve of my hip moved, causing me to nearly jump out of my skin. "It was actually at a brothel."

Someone at the table sounded as if they choked on their food. I was betting it was Emil.

A fair brow rose as Alastir chewed slowly. "That was...unexpected."

"The Red Pearl isn't just a brothel," I corrected, turning a narrow-eyed glare on Casteel.

He grinned. "It's not?"

"Card games are played there."

"That wasn't the only games being played there, Princess."

His thumb moved along the inside of my hip, causing my stomach to whoosh. "Penellaphe had a habit of sneaking out and exploring the city at night."

I nibbled on the inside of my lip as I tore my gaze from Casteel. Had he known how often I did that? He had said that he'd been watching me for longer than I realized.

"What I know of the Maiden—and, yes, Casteel, I know she's no longer the Maiden, but that was what she was," he added before Casteel could correct him. "The Ascensions of the others were tied to yours, weren't they? And again, I am sorry that you were raised in such a web of lies told by the Ascended."

Several at the table cursed at the mention of the Ascended.

"Thank you. And yes, you're right." I frowned slightly. "Or they were. I don't know if their Ascensions will be carried out now."

"Hopefully, they won't," Delano remarked.

"I agree," I said quietly, thinking of Ian.

"Do you?" Alastir asked. "Truly?"

"I do," I admitted. "I didn't know who or what the Ascended really were. I, like most people within the Kingdom of Solis, only knew what I was shown."

"Then I expect many are blind to what is right in front of them," someone commented, a younger man with rich brown hair toward the end of the table.

"Many live in fear of being ripped apart by the Craven or displeasing the Ascended and angering the gods," I replied. Casteel's arm tightened around my waist, his hand squeezing my hip gently. Was that some sort of message? I had no idea, nor did I care. The people of Solis were victims just as much as the Atlantians were. "Many are also more worried about providing for their families and keeping them safe than they are about questioning what the Ascended tell them."

"Are they so distracted by their daily struggles that they don't question handing over their children to the Court or to gods they've never seen?" Alastir asked. "Or are they just that submissive?"

"I wouldn't confuse submission for distraction, and I wouldn't mistake obedience for stupidity when it's apparent that you know very little about the people of Solis," I stated coolly.

Alastir's gaze swung to mine.

"What they have been told about the Atlantians, about the gods and the Craven, is all they know. Generation after generation, they're taught to believe in the Rite and how much of an honor it is for their third sons and daughters to serve the gods. Raised to believe that only the Ascended and the gods stand between them and the Craven. I was raised the same way." I leaned forward, a little surprised to find that Casteel didn't stop me. "The gods belong to the people of Atlantia, do they not? Do your people believe in them even though they've never seen them?"

Silence fell around the table.

It was Kieran who answered. "The gods have slept for hundreds of years, and only the oldest among the Atlantians can remember seeing them. But we believe in them nonetheless."

I smiled tightly. "Just as the people of Solis believe in them."

"But not everyone within Solis follows King Jalara and Queen Ileana," Alastir pointed out. "There are many who have seen the truth, who support Atlantia."

"You're right. The Descenters." I exhaled slowly. "I know I've had my suspicions throughout my life. I'm sure many others have, as well, but for whatever reason, their eyes haven't been fully opened. I imagine a lot of that has to do with the stability of what one knows, even if it isn't comfortable. And I suppose a lot has to do with fear of acknowledging what is truly around us, what it means for us and those we care for."

Alastir leaned back, eyeing me. "It's admirable."

"What is?"

"Your utter lack of fear when speaking to me—talking to any of us—when you know what we are," he said. "What we are capable of."

I met his stare. "I'm not foolish enough to not feel fear when I know that any of you could kill me before I even have a chance to take my next breath. But fearing what you're capable of doesn't mean I fear you."

Casteel leaned in, his voice in my ear. "Still so incredibly brave," he murmured, and that inexplicable warming returned to my chest.

"I like her," Alastir said to Casteel after a heartbeat, and I thought he might actually mean that. Then, I did what Kieran had suggested. I used my abilities once more. My senses stretched out, connecting to Alastir. I didn't sense anger from him, but there was the tanginess I often associated with sadness. I wasn't sure what could've evoked that response, but I thought he was being honest.

"But back to how you and the Prince met at this…unique establishment. How was that possible?" Alastir's fingers tapped idly on the table, and I swore there was a collective sigh of relief that the topic had moved on. "With the Ascensions being tied to you, I was under the impression that you were well guarded and kept…" He trailed off as if he searched for the right word to use.

"Sheltered?" I suggested. "Caged? I was. For the most part," I added. "I wasn't permitted to travel freely, only allowed to leave my room with one of my guards or my companion, and that was only to attend classes with the Priestess or to walk the castle grounds during certain times."

Emil stopped, his cup halfway to his mouth, his brows knitting together. His eyes were a vibrant gold. "And the rest of the time, you were expected to remain in your room? Even for meals?"

I nodded.

The Atlantian looked stunned, and someone murmured under their breath.

"But you found a way to sneak out. I imagine that's extremely risky behavior. Someone could've taken you at any time during those explorations," Alastir pointed out.

What I felt from him was…more guarded than a few moments before, but I still didn't detect the acidic burn of anger or hatred. If anything, he was more reserved than the last time we'd spoken, as was I.

"Someone did take her. Obviously," Casteel spoke up then, his thumb now tracing a distractingly slow, steady circle.

"Ah, yes, you did take her." Alastir inclined his chin. "But do you really intend to keep her?"

Chapter 12

"I wouldn't be marrying her if I didn't plan on keeping her."

My hearing had to be faulty. Keep me? As if I were some sort of pet? Placing my hand over his as I fixed a smile on my face, I dug my nails into his flesh.

Casteel's thumb didn't miss a single sweep along my inner hip. "I can't help myself." His lips brushed my cheek, and it took everything in me not to elbow him in the throat. "Penellaphe intrigued me from the first moment I spoke to her."

Intrigued. That word again.

"I can see why." Alastir tilted his head. "She's utterly unique, and most likely not what one would expect from the Maiden."

"She is unique and brave, intelligent and beautiful," Casteel agreed, apparently no longer content to drive me out of my mind with just his thumb. His fingers were involved now, sliding out from his palm and then gliding back. "And completely unexpected. But she is not the Maiden, Alastir." His chin grazed my shoulder as he turned his head to the wolven. "And if you refer to her as the Maiden one more time, we are going to have a problem. Understand?"

This time, when my muscles tensed, it was in response to his words.

"Understood," Alastir murmured.

"Good." Casteel's chin drifted over the curve of my jaw as he sat back.

Alastir was quiet for a moment, and then he addressed the men. "Make sure the horses are ready for when we check the roads."

Everyone at the table rose—everyone but Delano and Naill. Those two remained even after Alastir flicked a pointed look in their direction.

"If I called those men back, they would heed my summons," Casteel began, his fingers still sliding along my waist and hip. "And those who remain will only leave this table once I command it."

Alastir faced Casteel. "I know this."

"Glad to hear that, because for a moment there, I thought you might have forgotten who commands whom here."

A shiver tiptoed down my spine, a reminder of whose lap I sat in. This was not Hawke. He was the Prince of a kingdom, and he would not be disobeyed.

"I haven't, Casteel. You know me better than that. Which is why I must speak openly."

"Then speak," Casteel replied quietly, and visions of him slamming his hand through Landell's chest danced before me.

"You wish for me to do so right now?" Alastir's gaze flicked to me briefly. "Even if what I have to say is something you might not want to be spoken at this time?"

A tingling sensation swept over me as Casteel's fingers stilled on my hip. For a moment, I thought he would send me away. "You'd be surprised by what Penellaphe already knows."

Alastir lifted his brows.

"He planned to ransom me in exchange for his brother," I announced, deciding it sounded a little better coming from me. Alastir's eyes widened slightly. "It's not a secret. Everyone at this table knows."

"And that has changed?" Alastir queried softly, but neither Casteel nor I had a chance to answer before he continued. "I've watched you grow from a small boy sitting at his mother's side to the man you are today, just as I watched Malik. And I wish every damn day that I would've gotten to watch him grow into the King he was destined to be. You two would do anything for each other, sacrifice anything." The *sacrifice anyone* went unspoken, but it still lingered in the space. "And I understand the sense of obligation you carry within you. I understand more than most do, as I'm sure you remember."

Tension crept into Casteel's body, and I knew that Alastir had struck a chord.

"I know it's not like you've suddenly given up on your brother, no matter how intrigued you may be." Alastir tipped toward us, his voice low. "Neither your mother nor your father wanted you to leave when you did. They understand why you felt you needed to, but you also know where they stand on this."

"I know where they stand," Casteel stated, and instinct told me that Alastir was referring to Prince Malik. "And where do *you* stand?"

"Where I always have, with the Kingdom of Atlantia," Alastir answered. "But I also would never expect you to give up on Malik. I wouldn't be able to if I were you, so I need to ask. Is this…engagement another ploy to gain your brother's freedom?"

The fact that Alastir zeroed right in on what Casteel was planning told me that he did know him as well as he claimed.

I realized then that it wouldn't be me who needed to convince Alastir of the engagement's authenticity. It would have to be Casteel. And if he couldn't? Then what?

"How does marrying Penellaphe have anything to do with my brother?" Casteel's voice was level.

"That's a good question." Alastir leaned back. "Perhaps you believe that taking what the Kingdom of Solis covets and putting her in line to be the eventual Queen of Atlantia will give you better bargaining power."

The fact that Alastir was yet again so on point with what Casteel planned should've stunned me. It didn't. What took me by surprise was the eventual *Queen of Atlantia* part.

I might've toppled out of the chair if it weren't for Casteel's arm around me. It struck me then that Casteel had left a very important part out when he discussed our arrangement.

He was to become King.

Oh, we had *so* much to talk about, it wasn't even funny.

"Maybe this would put all of us in a position of better bargaining power," Casteel remarked. I bit down on the inside of my lip. "But during the time spent at the capital and in Masadonia, I've come to accept that my brother is beyond my reach."

Lie. That was such a lie. But I said nothing because even I had the sense to remain quiet.

Alastir was silent for a long moment and then he exhaled heavily. "As much as I hate to say this, because I love both you and Malik as if you were my sons, I hope that is true. If only for your sake and the sake of the kingdom. It is far past time to let go."

I reached out with my senses again, this time not hesitating. Sincerity echoed through the invisible cord, tasting like warm vanilla.

"It is," Casteel said, and my ability stretched out toward him. The burst of agony was tangy, coating my insides.

My hand dropped to his out of instinct, and I only stopped myself at the last moment. He would know what I'd done. I slipped my hand away, clasping them in my lap.

"What about your obligations?" Alastir met Casteel's gaze with an unflinching one of his own. "What was expected of you before you left still awaits your return."

Casteel's fingers started moving again, along the curve of my hip. "Things change all the time."

What had been expected of Casteel upon his return? Questions bubbled to the tip of my tongue, but I held them back, figuring that the second I started asking them would be the moment they stopped talking. Right now, it was as if they had forgotten I sat between them.

"And things have changed since you left, Casteel. You've been gone for over two years," Alastir advised, picking up his cup. "There is unrest among our people, especially the wolven."

"I know that," Casteel answered as I glanced at Kieran. He stood with a hand on the hilt of his sword, but other than that, I wondered if it were possible for someone to be asleep while standing with their eyes open. He looked that bored. "And I will do everything I can to ease that unrest."

"By marrying someone who is only half-Atlantian? An outsider?" Alastir turned to me. "And I mean no offense by that,

Penellaphe. I sincerely do not."

"None taken," I advised. He was right. I would be an outsider to Casteel's people.

"She may only be half-Atlantian and raised in Solis, but my people will accept her because *I* accept her." Casteel stated this as if there were no other option. "You know, you were partly correct when you said that marrying her gives us bargaining power. It does. With her at my side, we have a better chance of gaining back our land."

Alastir sat back in his chair. "To avoid war?"

"Yes. Isn't that what you want? Isn't that better than sending our people off to die by the thousands?" Casteel demanded. "Do you want to see more wolven die?"

"Of course, not." Alastir shook his head. "I want to avoid war. I've already lost enough to the Ascended, as you know."

I felt a momentarily tensing in Casteel's body. "I do. Gods, I do know." He exhaled heavily, relaxing a bit, and I sensed that there was more, things not being said. "The part you were incorrect about is assuming that my only reason for marrying Penellaphe is for bargaining power, whether that be for my brother or the kingdom. If I didn't feel the way I do for her, I could've simply used her in the way I originally planned."

The truth stung, but the lies scraped over my skin like hot knives. I kept my face blank, showing no reaction.

"That is true." Alastir dragged his lower lip between his teeth. "I can only hope the unrest is manageable. I've been trying, but the young ones…they have a certain view on how things should be carried out. And your father has agreed with them more and more." Alastir's gaze fixed on the cup he held. "He hoped that your time in Solis would prove fruitful. He has learned that it has. However, he has plans now, Casteel. And he is still the King."

"Do those plans involve me?" There went the realization that I should remain quiet. Still, I couldn't hold myself back. For far too many years, I'd sat in silence while others around me discussed me, my life, and my future.

No more.

The look of surprise flickering across Alastir's expression

gave way to a faint smile. "I have a feeling that many things involve you now." His features sobered as his gaze shifted to the Prince. "I would like to speak to Penellaphe."

"About?" Casteel queried.

"About all of this. I want to talk to her alone," he requested.

Casteel leaned forward, pressing his chest to my back. "Why do you want that?"

"Do you really need to ask that question?" Alastir returned, his cheeks flushing with the first hints of genuine anger. "You will need my aid when it comes to convincing your father and the wolven that this is a worthy marriage—that this will benefit the kingdom, and that you truly chose her. You know that. Do you think I will go along with any of that if she is being forced into this?"

My respect for the elder wolven blew through the roof of the keep.

"No, I do not believe you will go along with it," Casteel answered. "If Penellaphe wishes to speak with you, I have no problem."

My heart rate kicked up, but when Alastir turned to me, I nodded. "I will speak with you."

"Perfect." Alastir gave me a tight smile as he rose. "Come. Let's walk."

Casteel's arm slipped from around me, and I stood. "Just so you know, Penellaphe doesn't need protection. She is more than capable of handling things herself. But that is my future you are walking away with. Guard her well. Your life depends on it."

"Is it true?" Alastir asked as we walked the narrow halls of the keep, my hand tucked into the crook of his arm. Dim light flickered from the oil sconces, casting shadows along the unfamiliar stone walls. "You can defend yourself? Is that with or without a weapon?"

"Both," I answered. "I have been trained with a dagger and a sword, as well as a bow. I have also been trained on how to fight, hand-to-hand."

Surprise and respect settled into his features as he looked down at me. "That is not common for the women of Solis, and especially not for one who was the Maiden."

"It's not," I agreed. "But I was so helpless when my parents died. I was a child, but my mother hadn't been able to fight back. If she could have, she might've survived. I just...I didn't want to be helpless like that again, and so many people, especially women, never have the opportunity to learn how to protect themselves. They have to rely on others—on the Ascended—and I...I'm beginning to realize that further strengthens the absolute control the Ascended have."

"But they allowed you to learn how to fight?"

Imagining the Duchess's or Duke's reaction to such news, I laughed softly. "No. My guardians would've had an absolute fit. But, honestly, I always thought..."

"Thought what?" he prodded when I trailed off.

I wasn't sure if I should share this, but something about Alastir put me at ease, and maybe that something was how much he reminded me of Vikter. "I always thought Queen Ileana would've approved if she'd learned that I could fight. I don't know why I believe that. It's just that...the Queen I knew—"

"Isn't the Queen others know," he supplied, and I nodded. "People have many different sides to them. Even the Ascended. How did you learn to fight?"

"One of my personal guards taught me in secret. His name was Vikter." A knot lodged in my throat and stayed there as I told Alastir about him and the risks he took. "He was like a father to me, and I...gods, I miss him so much."

Alastir had stopped walking as I spoke of Vikter, but he still held my arm. "He sounds like an amazing man."

"He was, and I—" I blinked back the hot rush of tears. "He should be alive today."

His gaze searched mine as he said, "And he died at the hands of Descenters who were following Prince Casteel's lead? How were you able to move past that?"

How? My stomach dipped. *I hadn't* moved past that. "I don't think I will ever get over that."

"And yet you've fallen in love with Casteel? He may not have held the sword—"

"But they killed in his name," I finished for him. "I know. Casteel knows that. He knows that he is responsible, and I know he loses sleep over it." My mouth dried as I said, "It hasn't been easy, but what I feel for him has nothing to do with Vikter." The lie rolled off my tongue smoothly enough. Maybe too easily. My heart lurched as wind beat at a nearby window. "Nothing about Casteel and I has been easy. I thought he was someone else entirely when we first met, but I started falling for him even then." And gods, that was the truth. "And so, here we are."

"Yes, here we are." Alastir gave a close-lipped smile as he shifted my arm so his hand held mine. "I've known Casteel since birth, as well as his brother. I knew his father before then, and his mother even longer than that. I remember when the Queen was married to a different King," he said quietly, and that alone told me that he was far older than I anticipated. "Casteel is like a son to me. In reality, he would've been a son of mine if fate had played out differently."

Would have been a son of mine? "What do you mean?"

The skin at his eyes creased as my gift suddenly pressed against my skin, responding to the sudden shift in his emotions. An agony so potent and raw that it reached out to me. I opened myself, unable to stop it, and immediately tensed at the turmoil rolling through him, thus passing to me. His grief cut so deeply, it made it hard to breathe. I started to use my gift differently, to lessen the pain.

"Did you know that Casteel has been in love before?"

His question threw me, causing me to drop the connection with him. Even then, the tangy bitterness of sorrow still filled the back of my throat. "Yes, I know that."

And that was all I knew. That he had been in love.

"Did he tell you that he was once engaged?"

Words left me. I shook my head.

A small, sad smile appeared. "I'm not surprised to hear that. He doesn't talk about her often. No matter how much I've tried in the past. And to be honest, I can't remember the last time he even said her name. I can't blame him for that, and neither should you. She is a wound that has healed, but still a wound nonetheless. He would be…" He looked down the hall, his shoulders tensing and then loosening. "He would be very upset with me to know that I spoke of Shea with you. And, truthfully, I am overstepping here. But you need to know why I was so surprised to learn of your engagement. I honestly didn't think Casteel would ever allow himself to feel like that again." His gaze met mine. "And you need to know why I hope his motivations for this marriage are true and rooted in his heart and not as a desperate bid to find his brother."

I didn't know which part of what he'd shared was the most shocking. That Casteel had been engaged—to a wolven—that he'd been in love with someone who was so obviously no longer alive, or that Alastir wanted the marriage between us to be real.

I cleared my throat. "Shea was your daughter?"

Alastir nodded. "She was. And it's strange, I barely know you, but you remind me of her. She too often spoke her mind, much to the ire of everyone around her. And she was capable of defending herself when needed." He laughed a little. "I would guess that is one of the things that has drawn Casteel to you. That allowed him to see beyond the veil, so to speak."

I didn't know what to think of any of that. "When did she…die? How?"

"It was quite some time ago, many years before you were born." His words were yet another reminder of how many years of experience Casteel had. "She is my daughter, but her death is not my story to share. That's Casteel's." His gaze met and held mine. "And I do hope it is one that he'll one day share with you."

I'd believed that the source of Casteel's grief had stemmed from his brother's capture, but I'd already discovered that some of it was from what had been done to him. And now I wondered just how much of it was tied to this man's daughter.

"I'm sorry to hear about your child," I said, meaning it. "And I won't say anything."

"I don't mind if you do. To be frank, I hope he does talk to you—talks to someone about her."

I was the last person who should be speaking to him about Shea. "Why are you telling me this, though? It doesn't sound like it's something I should bring up with him."

"It's not. At least, not now. I hope that he will open up and talk to someone one day, even if it's not me. The reason I'm telling you this is because Shea was no damsel. I can see that you aren't either. But I hope you are not so much like her that you don't ask for help or refuse it when you need it." He patted my hand. "I will forever be loyal to my kingdom, to the gods, and to the Da'Neers, but even if I never had a daughter, I could not stand by and watch a young woman be used against her will in such a way. War is cruel. There are casualties. But this would be unnecessarily cruel, and I will not stand for it."

My heart was pounding again. Could he sense that?

"Casteel has been determined to find his brother for decades, Penellaphe. Enough time to fill a mortal's lifespan. And while I hope he has finally moved on, that he will assume the role his kingdom desperately needs, most importantly, I wish that he is finally allowing himself to live. I want to believe that. Yet, I don't."

I tensed.

Alastir's gaze met mine. "So, that is why I'm offering you my aid. If you are being forced into this, I will help you escape. I will do everything in my power to ensure safe passage. Not to send you back to Solis. I will not hand you over to those who seek to abuse you in a different way. But I will make sure you are somewhere neither the Ascended nor Casteel can ever reach you. All you have to do is tell me, and this will be over for you."

The breath I took went nowhere as I processed his words—his offer. It was freedom. The same as Casteel offered, but without the strings of marriage and all the pretending and the risks involved. And I believed the sincerity of his offer. This man who'd just met me would risk the ire of his Prince, possibly even consequences that extended far beyond anger, to help a girl he barely knew. All because he was…

Because he was a *good* man.

And it was something I could see Vikter doing. It was something I knew Vikter had wished that he could've done once he realized how much being the Maiden was *killing* me, bit by bit, each and every day. Tears burned the backs of my eyes once more.

"Dear gods," Alastir uttered. "I think the threat of tears tells me everything I need to know. I'm sorry—"

"No. It's not that." I squeezed his hand. "It's just that your offer is unexpected. You're a good person and—and there are so few good people. It's something I think Vikter would've done, and it just made me think of him."

"And that's all?" He watched me closely, placing his other hand over mine.

"Yes," I said, holding his gaze. "I appreciate your offer. I appreciate what you are willing to do for me. But he's not using me. Not like that."

"You don't need my help, then?"

"I don't. I swear."

And I didn't. Not now.

If he'd come to me a day before, my answer probably would've been different. I would've said yes. I would've run. But he couldn't give me what Casteel could. Ian. And I couldn't walk away now, knowing that I could help change things for the people of Solis. The freedom Alastir offered wasn't the kind I needed.

Alastir sighed, and I could tell that he thought I was making a foolish choice. Maybe that meant he didn't believe Casteel. It could mean he felt bad for me because he believed me. I didn't know.

"If you ever change your mind," he said, his eyes sad, "you only need to tell me. Can you promise me that?"

I really felt like crying now. "I can promise that."

"Good." He smiled, and I...

I didn't even know what I was doing until I sprang forward and threw my arms around Alastir. I hugged him. The gesture stunned the man. For a moment, he didn't move, but then he put his arms around me.

"Sorry," I mumbled, pulling away. My face was hot.

He smiled then, one that crinkled the skin at the corners of his eyes. "You never need to apologize for a hug, Penellaphe. It's been far too long since I've had one, to be honest. Neither Casteel nor Kieran is the hugging type."

I laughed hoarsely. "I think if I tried to hug Kieran, he'd pass out."

"Most likely. Well, I think I know all that I need to," he said, yet he still sounded sad. I thought the emotion was either for his daughter, for Casteel, or even possibly for me. "I should probably get you back to the Prince."

I started to turn but stopped. I didn't know when we'd get a chance to speak privately again. "May I ask you something?" When Alastir nodded, I said, "You used to help move Atlantians or their descendants from Solis?"

"I did."

"I was thinking about my parents—about why they left the capital. It's possible that they knew what the Ascended planned or learned that they were descendants themselves. At least one of them. Were there others who did what you did?"

"There were others. Not many. And sadly, most never returned home." He stroked his chin with his thumb. "We assume they were captured, so there aren't many you could speak with."

I hadn't even dared to hope that there was anyone I could talk to. "I was just wondering if it was possible for my parents to have known that someone like you existed."

"Of course, it was. The King and Queen knew that we were actively searching for our people," he confirmed. "It's possible one of your parents learned of us from an Ascended." His head cocked. "So, you think that is what happened?"

"I don't know," I admitted, running a hand over where the knife was sheathed to my thigh. "I don't remember much about the night I was attacked, but I do remember that my father was quieter than usual during the trip. So was my mother. They seemed nervous instead of excited about starting a new life in a quieter place. And I...I think my father met with someone. I vaguely remember there being another person there."

"But your memories aren't clear enough." When I shook my head, he said, "That's fairly common after such a trauma."

It was. Or so I'd been told.

"After the war, many survivors claimed to have forgotten entire battles they fought. The emotions and the scars were still there, but the details were nothing but shadows," he explained. "The same with Casteel. He remembers very little of his time in captivity."

That wasn't true. He remembered it all, or at least enough to not have to search the shadows for details, but I didn't say that. I was surprised that he'd shared enough for me to know that he remembered and had not told Alastir.

"I have dreams. Sometimes they reveal a little more. Like opening a chest and letting more of the night out. But I don't know if those memories are real or not. The new ones, that is," I said. "Anyway, I don't know if it matters. I just want to know."

"Wanting to know is understandable. I understand." His features tightened for a moment, and then they smoothed out. "Most of those who knew to look for us used false last names. What were your parents' first names?"

I exhaled heavily. "Coralena and Leopold. Cora and Leo," I said, staring at the lamp, trying to remember what my father looked like. The memories of him had faded. "That's what they called each other."

"Coralena," Alastir said after a moment, clearing his throat. I looked at him, but he too was staring at the lamp. "That's a beautiful name. One unique enough that if they used their real first names, it would be remembered. When we arrive in Atlantia, I'll ask those who are still with us if they recall ever speaking with or about one with that name. It's a long shot, but you never know. The world, no matter how big, is often smaller than we realize."

Chapter 13

Alastir led me to a room I'd never been in before on the other side of the keep from the banquet hall. I knew Casteel was likely inside, simply given that the doors were guarded. The moment the doors swung open, the musty scent that hit me sparked joy in my heart.

Books.

Rows and rows of books.

I walked forward in a daze, barely aware of Alastir speaking, and completely unaware of anything else but the possibilities awaiting behind the thick and narrow, multicolored spines. I moved forward as if compelled—

An arm snagged me around the waist. I swallowed a squeak of surprise as I was pulled down. For the second time, I found myself in Casteel's lap.

So focused on the books, I hadn't even seen him sitting on the settee I'd walked past. I twisted toward him, ignoring the jump in my pulse as heavy, hooded, amber eyes met mine. "Was that necessary?"

"Always," he replied, his arms loose around me as several men filed out of the room, their gazes trained forward as if they didn't dare look in my direction.

The door clicked shut, leaving only Kieran behind, sitting in an armchair with his feet propped up on a cedar chest. I started to pull free of Casteel. I didn't make it very far.

His arms tightened. "How was your talk with Alastir?"

"It was okay," I said, immediately thinking of the woman Casteel had been engaged to. Shea. I wanted to ask about her. I wanted to know what'd happened. I wanted to know why he'd never mentioned her, even though I understood there had been no reason for him to bring her up with me. We'd once been friends. Or at least I'd believed so. Though that was also when I'd thought we could be more. But that was before I learned the truth. And even though we'd entered into this arrangement, I wasn't...well, I wasn't important to him in the way where he would share secrets.

But is that true? A voice whispered in the back of my mind. Casteel had shared with me what had been done to him while he'd been the Ascended's prisoner. He hadn't opened up with Alastir, the father of his once fiancée. What, if anything, did that mean? Either way, discussing the woman he'd once planned to marry for no other reason but that he loved her felt too...intimate. Like it was something true lovers would do.

And that was not us.

Alastir would have to pin his hopes on someone else.

"Just okay?" One dark brow rose.

An inexplicable heaviness settled in my chest as I nodded.

"He should be more detailed in his questioning," Kieran commented. "Should we be worried that Alastir is going to attempt to whisk you off?"

I shot him an arch look. "Why would you think that?"

"Because we both know what kind of man Alastir is," Casteel said, drawing my attention back to him. "He's probably worried that you're being forced into this marriage and likely offered you his aid in escape."

"You offered me a choice last night. If I didn't agree to the marriage, you wouldn't force me. We came to an agreement," I reminded him. "If I accepted Alastir's offer, would I be sitting here?"

"I suppose not." He watched me through half-lowered lashes. "Or, you could be waiting for when I least expect it. Though just so you know, I always expect you to do the unexpected."

My brows knitted. "You sound paranoid."

"As if I don't have a reason?"

"I'm offended that you think I'd go back on my word. I agreed, *Your Highness*." I smiled when I saw his jaw flex. "Alastir did offer his aid. I turned it down."

A moment passed. "Then I apologize for being paranoid, Princess."

I snorted. "Sure, you do."

"Now I'm offended that you doubt my sincerity."

I rolled my eyes. "I do have questions for you. Ones more important than what Alastir and I discussed."

"You have questions?" Mock surprise filled Kieran's tone. "I'm utterly shocked."

"I'm an open book," Casteel replied. "What would you like to know?"

An open book? Unlikely. "What plans does your father have?"

Casteel leaned into the cream-hued settee, looking impossibly at ease. "My father has many plans, Poppy." His gaze drifted over my face. In the back of my mind, I realized that he hadn't once called me Poppy while in front of Alastir. "But if they include you, those plans will swiftly become nothing but figments of the imagination."

"It sounded like I was what made your *activities* fruitful."

"Don't worry about my father," Casteel said, lifting his hand from my hip. He drew his thumb across my lower lip, causing an unwanted flutter in my chest. "He has bigger concerns right now than you."

My eyes narrowed as I caught his wrist. "Like the lack of land issue?" I pulled his hand away.

His eyes deepened to a warm amber. "I'm sure that is taking up much of his time, but he won't risk damaging his relationship with me to take any action against you."

I wanted to believe that. Getting back to Ian depended on

me staying alive and in one piece. Being a part of the King's plan probably wouldn't bode well for me remaining whole and hearty.

Especially given that the scheme probably included sending me back to the capital of Solis in pieces.

"I think you forgot to tell me something," I told him.

His brows rose. "I'm going to need more detail than that."

"Why? Because there's a lot of things you haven't told me?"

"A man must have his secrets. Isn't that part of the allure?"

Struggling for patience, I tried to count to ten. I made it to three. "Your secrets are the exact opposite of alluring. If there was an anti-allure potion, it would be exactly that."

"Damn," he murmured, eyes gleaming.

"Are you expected to become King upon your return?" I demanded. "Is that what's expected of you?"

The amusement faded from his eyes. "One of them. A King and Queen can only rule Atlantia for four hundred years. It's designed that way so change can occur. If a child of theirs doesn't assume the throne, then anyone can come forward and challenge for it. My parents' reign has extended beyond the timeframe. And because they don't believe Malik will return, they feel it is time for me to take on the role."

"Has anyone challenged the throne?"

"As far as I know, no."

But how would he know since he hadn't been home in years? "Did you not think it would be a good idea to tell me?"

"Not particularly."

"Oh, my gods," I started.

"Mainly because I knew it would freak you out," he added.

"Like right now," Kieran murmured.

"No one asked for your two cents," I snapped, and the wolven chuckled. I turned my glare back on Casteel. "Whether or not it would freak me out, I needed to know that—"

"It changes nothing," he cut in. "Just because my parents believe it is time for me to take the throne doesn't mean I have to or will. They cannot force me. My brother is the true heir to the Atlantian throne. Not me. And he will take his seat once I free him."

Pressing my lips together, I glanced at Kieran to gauge his

reaction to what Casteel had said, but he stared straight ahead, his expression unreadable. I doubted my senses would tell me anything more, but I knew that Casteel fully intended to save his brother. He didn't want to be King, even if it was past the time for a new one to be crowned. With that said, becoming Queen was not something I had to worry about. I started to stand.

Casteel's arm tightened. "Where are you going? I was so very comfortable with you in my lap."

"I'm sure you were, but there's no audience."

"What about me?" Kieran asked. "I'm still here."

"You don't count."

"Ouch," he murmured.

"But we're not in private, Princess. Wasn't that the deal you made? In public, you wouldn't fight me?"

My eyes narrowed. "There is no one else in this room. The doors are closed, and the deal we made didn't include sitting in your lap."

"I know." He sucked his plump lower lip between his teeth, exposing the edges of his fangs. "But I really enjoy it."

Muscles curled low in my stomach, and I really didn't care for how my body responded to his heated stare, and the glimpse of those fangs. It answered with a heady flush that I could only hope wasn't as visible as it felt. It also called forth a sharp, intense throbbing that settled in an area that made me want to squeeze my legs together. And I really hated the knowledge that he knew exactly how I responded to him. I let go of his wrist. "I don't care if you enjoy it."

"Lies," he murmured, tucking back my hair. "You enjoyed it, too."

"But do you know what I enjoyed more?" I leaned in, seeing the surprise flare in his eyes that quickly gave way to heat.

That lazy, half-hooded gaze returned. "I have a few ideas."

"I enjoyed throwing the knife at you and making you bleed," I said, jerking my head back from his touch. This time when I stood, he didn't stop me.

Casteel laughed, lowering his hand to the arm of the chair. "That was one of my ideas."

"You two are more convincing now than you were during

the whole time with Alastir," Kieran commented. "And if you can't convince Alastir that you're so in love with each other that he's forgotten his decades-long search for his brother, and you have forgiven his plans to ransom you, then there is no way you'll convince the King. And especially not your mother."

Unfortunately, Kieran had a point. "Alastir doesn't believe us. He didn't say that outright, but I could tell that he has serious doubts. He probably thinks I'm infatuated with you, and you're just using me."

A slow grin spread across Casteel's face, barely halting when he saw the look I gave him. His eyes still glimmered. "We'll just have to try harder then, won't we?"

I folded my arms. "How can anyone really believe us when I asked if you were out of your mind just a few nights ago?"

"A lot can happen in a few nights, Poppy. Especially with me."

"Your arrogance never ceases to amaze me," I muttered.

Casteel ignored that. "I think he will believe us. We have time to convince him, but now I'm sure I need to reassure him before he leaves to check the roads." Casteel rose.

"Reassure him of what?"

"He can be…sensitive. Therefore, I need to reassure him that I won't have him killed before we leave here," he replied, and I couldn't tell if he was being serious or not. "Would you like to stay in here for a while? There's a lot of books. None as interesting as Miss Willa's diary, though."

That damn diary.

"I would like to stay here," I said.

Casteel glanced at Kieran, who said, "I'll keep an eye on her."

"Do you all really think I'm in that much danger? Word of our engagement must have spread through the keep by now."

"I'm not taking any chances with you." Casteel moved forward, touching my cheek just below the scar. "Thank you."

"For what?" The touch of his fingertips was light, but a shiver still rolled through me.

"For choosing me."

I spent the rest of the day in the library, taking a late lunch of soup by the crackling fireplace as I thumbed through the dusty pages of short tales meant for children, and old records of those who'd once lived in New Haven. As I moved from row to row, I didn't think about what Alastir had told me or what awaited me once we left the keep. I lost myself to the freedom of being able to read any book I wanted. What I'd been allowed to read in Masadonia had been restricted to historical texts, and while Tawny often snuck far more interesting novels for me to enjoy, it was never enough.

Kieran was a quiet presence in the room, having picked up one of the books I'd discarded. I suspected that he was pleased with his task, only because I was too busy to ask him any questions.

It wasn't until after I'd finished the bowl of stewed vegetables and scoured all the shelves, except for the bottom row behind a large oak desk, that I found a text of particular interest. It was a thin novel, bound in gold-dyed leather, halfway hidden behind the numerous, thick records, the gold smothered in dirt. I pulled it out, coughing as a cloud of dust plumed.

"Please don't die," Kieran commented from where he sat. "Casteel would be most displeased."

Ignoring him, I wiped off the cover as I carried the book to the desk. I cracked it open, flipping through blank parchment faded to a dull yellow. I stopped when I saw the date. The gold-bound book was another set of records, but one far older than the rest. It was dated at least eight hundred years ago.

Turning the pages, I read through birth and death dates, occupations and house numbers, quickly noting that these records were very different. The span of years between the dates of birth and death caught my attention.

Hundreds of years.

These were records of the Atlantians who'd once lived in New Haven. The worn armchair creaked as I sat in it. Many of the names were illegible, the ink too faded, as were occupations.

Some were easier to decipher. Baker. Stable Master. Blacksmith. Healer. Scholar. It was strange to see these common skills listed beside dates that suggested they'd lived ten or more mortal lifespans. But I supposed that when Atlantia ruled over the kingdom, many of them lived very ordinary long lives. There were occupations and words unfamiliar to me, ones I saw repeated under the column that listed jobs, and words often in parentheses near the names that I could read.

"What is a wivern?" I asked, unsure if I'd pronounced it correctly.

"What?" Kieran looked up from the book that rested in his lap.

"I found records from when Atlantians lived here," I told him. "The word *wivern* appears frequently."

Kieran drew his legs off the chest and rose, placing his book where his feet were. He came to stand by my shoulder. "Where?"

"See?" I tapped a finger below the faded black ink. "There are words I don't recognize. Like here." I drew my finger down. "Ceeren."

"Hell." Kieran leaned forward, turning the pages back to the title page. "It's Atlantian records."

I arched a brow. "That's what I said."

"I'm surprised this remained here all these years." He flipped back to the page I'd been looking at.

"It was behind a couple of other records and covered in dust. It must've been forgotten."

"Definitely forgotten. The Ascended destroyed any and all records of the Atlantians who once lived here. No matter how inconsequential as a census."

"So, what does wivern mean?"

"A wivern was an Atlantian bloodline that was killed off during the war," he explained. "They too were of two worlds, mortal and animal."

"Like the wolven and changelings?"

He nodded. "Except the wivern could take the form of cats larger than those that roam the caves in the Wastelands. Here. Draken?" His arm brushed mine as he moved closer to point out a place farther down the page.

Air hissed out of Kieran's clenched teeth as he jerked back his arm. I turned, finding him standing several feet from me.

I lifted my brows, thinking that was a bit of an overreaction to his arm touching mine. "You okay?"

He stared at me, eyes wider than I'd ever seen before, but bright in an unnatural way. "You didn't feel that?"

"You touched my arm. That's all I felt." I watched him rub his arm. "What did you feel?"

"A shock," he said. "Like being struck by lightning."

"Have you been struck by lightning before?"

"No. It's a figure of speech." He glanced at the door before those too-bright eyes settled on me. "You really didn't feel that?"

I shook my head. "Maybe it was like that static charge you get when dragging your feet over the carpet." A faint smile tugged at my lips. "I used to do that all the time to Ian."

"Why doesn't that surprise me." Kieran lowered his hand. "The Prince is coming."

I opened my mouth, but the door opened a heartbeat later. Was Kieran's hearing that good?

Casteel strode in, his hair swept back from his face, and it was like all the air had been sucked out, and the library suddenly became three sizes smaller. It was simply him, his mere presence immediately taking over the space.

He glanced between Kieran and me. "You two look like you're having fun."

Based on the way Kieran still looked as if he'd seen a spirit, I doubted it.

"I found a book of records from when the Atlantians lived here." I picked up the book.

"Sounds real fun," Casteel drawled.

"Perfect timing." Kieran's expression smoothed out. "Your fiancée has questions."

The way he said the word *fiancée* made me want to throw the book at his head.

"Perhaps I have answers." Casteel leaned against the desk. "And, yes, before you ask, you're free to do as you please."

"Thank the gods," Kieran muttered, peeling himself away from the built-in bookshelves. He started toward the door. "Is all good with Alastir?"

Casteel nodded. "He and several of the men left to check the roads."

"Good." Kieran turned. "Have fun."

I watched him close the door. "He's acting weird."

"Is that so?"

"He got a static shock from his arm brushing mine, and he behaved as if I'd done it on purpose."

"You know how some electrical wiring can short out? Emit sparks or charges of energy?" When I nodded, he said, "Wolven can lose control over their forms if they come into contact with electricity, even at harmless levels. Sometimes, during a particularly bad lightning storm, they are often affected by it."

"Oh. Well, then." I paused. "He's still weird."

Casteel laughed, and the sound was deep and real and nice. "So, what did you have questions about?"

I looked up at him and wished I hadn't. The words he spoke before leaving to speak with Alastir came back to me. *Thank you for choosing me.* I didn't choose him, though. Not really.

Stomach fluttering nonetheless, I dragged my attention back to the book. "I found these words I didn't understand. Kieran was just explaining that the wivern could shift into large cats, and he was about to tell me what a draken is."

"Ah, this *is* an old book." He leaned over, scanning the pages. The scent of woodsmoke mixed with his scent. "A draken was a powerful bloodline, one able to sprout wings as wide as a horse, and talons as sharp as a blade. They could fly. Some could even breathe fire."

My chin snapped up, and I stared at him. "Like...like a dragon?"

Casteel nodded.

"I thought dragons were myths." I remembered reading stories about them in the books I'd borrowed from the city's library. Some even had drawings of the frightening beasts.

"Every myth is rooted in some fact," he answered.

"If there were draken who could fly and breathe fire, how in the world could the Ascended even gain the upper hand against Atlantia?" I asked.

"Because the draken were basically gone before the first vampry was even made." He picked up a strand of my hair and started to twist it around his finger. "If they had been there, nothing would remain of the Ascended but scorched earth."

I shivered. "What do you mean by *basically* gone."

"Well, my very curious Princess, legends state that many of the draken didn't die. That they slumber with the gods or protect their resting places."

"Are the legends true?"

He unraveled the strand of hair. "That, I cannot answer. I've never seen a draken, which is a shame. Would have loved to see one."

"So would I," I admitted, imagining that a draken would be a fierce but majestic sight.

Casteel was looking over the page as he spun my hair around his finger once more. "The ceeren were here? Huh. I wouldn't have guessed that."

"Why?" I snatched away my hair, pulling it free from his hand.

He pouted. "Because there is no sea or large body of water nearby. Ceeren were also of two worlds, part mortal and—"

"Water folk?" I whispered, heart lurching.

"I imagine some may have called them such. They would grow fins—not like a lamaea—" He grinned, and a hint of the dimple appeared. "Their fins were in the right places, but their bloodline also faded out before the war."

Was it a coincidence that Ian had written a story about two children befriending some water folk? I'd thought it nothing more than a figment of his imagination. But maybe he had discovered the ceeren.

"How did they die?"

"There's a lot of debate surrounding that one. Some of the older Atlantians say it's because they fell into a depression once Saion went to sleep, losing their will to live. Others believe that through generations of intermingling with other bloodlines, there simply were no pure ceeren left."

"I hope it was the latter," I said, even though that was a weird thing to hope for. "Them dying off because of a god going to sleep is far too sad."

"That it is." Casteel turned the page. "You should find this interesting." He dropped his finger to the middle of the page. "Senturion."

I refocused. "What is that?"

"A general term for multiple, old bloodlines who were warriors born and not trained." He placed his hand beside mine. "There were dozens at one time, each line marked by their own special talents that made them dangerous to face in combat. Many of the warrior lines died out hundreds of years before the Ascended."

"How?"

"All kingdoms are built from blood. Atlantia is no different," he explained. "The war that ended most of the warrior lines started with an uprising of elemental against the ruling line."

Remembering what Kieran had told me, I said, "The...the deities?"

"Someone has been talking with you."

"Kieran told me about some of them, but I don't understand. He made it sound like the deities held unquestionable authority—that they were the children of the gods and created the elementals."

"I'm sure Kieran would say that." He snorted. "But, yes, they created the elementals and most of the warrior lines, but there always comes a time when the creation seeks to rise above the creator. The elementals and several of the other lines orchestrated a massacre, managing to kill several deities, which I imagine wasn't entirely easy. A few of the warrior lines sided with the elementals, and some with the deities. The war didn't last as long as it did with the Ascended, but it was far more destructive. In the end, nearly all the deities had been slain, entire bloodlines were gone, and a deity still maintained the throne until he was finally cast aside and killed—this time for reasons that went beyond my ancestors deciding they were better fit to rule."

"And what was that?"

"I've already told you why, once before." He inclined his head when I glanced up at him. "He created the first vampry."

"King Malec? He was a deity?"

Casteel nodded.

Good gods, that meant that Casteel's mother had been married to a deity? "Had he been alive since the beginning? Or was he a descendent of the line?"

"He was the child of two ancient deities."

I gave a shake of my head, feeling as if my brain would implode. That didn't stop me from asking more questions. "What kind of talents did these warriors have?"

The dimple deepened as he said, "Some were able to use the earth in battle—summon the wind or rain. They were of the primordial line. Others could call upon the souls of those who were slain by the one they fought. The one listed near the top?" His pinky brushed mine, sending a shock of energy I hadn't felt when one had passed to Kieran. "Pryo? They could summon fire for their blades. Underneath that is one of the cimmerian line?"

His pinky slid over mine as I stared at the word written in ink too faded for my eyes. I nodded.

"They could call upon the night, blocking out the sun and leaving their foe blind to their movements."

"All of that...all of that sounds too fantastical," I admitted as his finger traced the line of mine, sending a wave of awareness through me.

"It would, but so are wolven to a lot of mortals." He had a point there. "And I imagine so are empaths."

"Empaths?"

"A warrior bloodline that died off shortly after the war, but these were even more unique, Poppy. The ones everyone dreaded to face in battle." His fingers slid over mine, and I looked up at him. "They were favored by the deities, as they were the only ones who could do what the empaths could—read the emotions of others and then turn that into a weapon, amplifying pain or fear. Sending an army running before a sword was even lifted."

My breath caught.

"This is the bloodline I believe you're descended from, Poppy. Or at least what I've been thinking." His hand returned to the desk. "Empath warriors. It's the only one that makes sense. A few could've been lost in Solis, unable to return to

Atlantia at the end of the war and therefore presumed dead. One of them at some point could've met a mortal, years and years later, or the child of two of them did, creating either the first generation that gave birth to you or—"

"Or one of my parents was...was an empath warrior." Stunned, I was unable to move. "Did they have a certain eye color? Because I don't have gold or hazel eyes."

"No. Yours are the color of an Atlantian spring—of dew-kissed leaves."

I blinked.

Casteel looked away, clearing his throat. "Anyway, the warrior bloodlines had no specific distinguishing traits."

Then my mother *or* father could've been one, or the child of them. "Is it possible that Queen Ileana or King Jalara were so close to them and had not known?"

"It is possible. But they would have known what the Ascended were if they were an empath warrior." Bracing his weight on his hand, Casteel dipped his head so we were almost at eye level. "So, I think they were first-generation. And like you, didn't understand why they couldn't sense emotions from the Ascended."

"But I can't use it as a weapon or anything like that."

"The abilities change once mortal blood is introduced." His gaze flickered over my face.

"How did they die?" I asked, and then immediately realized the answer. "They couldn't use their abilities against the Ascended, could they?"

"Either because they couldn't sense emotion or didn't know how to. They were still exceptional fighters. It would explain your almost natural talent with weapons." His voice softened. "Bolder and braver than any of the other lines."

My gaze fell to the faded ink. Empath warriors. Could it be that I was descended from a bloodline so powerful they could take out an army before a battle even began? One favored by the children of the gods? Could it be that I was a part of this bloodline? It sounded right. It felt like a final puzzle piece being found. It felt *right*. The corners of my lips tipped up, and I smiled.

"Beautiful," Casteel whispered.

Startled, my eyes flew to his. The moment our gazes connected, I couldn't look away. His head was so close to mine, his mouth even closer—close enough that if I tilted my head and leaned in an inch or two, our lips would touch. My heart started pounding. Did I want that? Did I not want that? I didn't move to put space between us. My eyes began to drift closed—

Casteel moved back, his head turning to the door. He slid off the desk just as a fist sounded. "Come in."

Naill entered, hand on his sword. "One of the watchers signaled that we have company, coming from the western roads."

"Who?" Casteel demanded.

"The Ascended."

Chapter 14

I was already standing when Casteel turned to me. "We must go," he clipped out.

I went to move around the desk but stopped. "Wait." Spinning around, I snatched the book and shoved it back where I'd found it, behind the other records.

Casteel noted my actions in silence, and when I came around the desk, he took my hand.

How could they have known that I was missing? It had to be too soon, especially given the storm. It had only clipped the western sides, but they would've expected it to slow us down.

"They've already entered the yard," Naill advised as we left the library, sending my stomach plummeting.

"Be smart," Casteel advised. And with one curt nod, Naill took off. "Come," he said to me.

Casteel led me in silence through the dimly lit, winding halls that felt like a maze designed to trap us. We reached an old wooden door that he pushed open with an arm, and entered the kitchens. The faces of those we passed were a blur as they stepped to the side, bowing at Casteel on sight.

"The Ascended are here," he said, and several gasps echoed. "Hide the youngest below and warn the others. Do not antagonize the Ascended."

An older man stepped forward, thumping his fist off his

chest. "From blood and ash."

Casteel placed his fist over his heart. "We will rise."

The people scattered before we reached the doors that led outside. We were near the stables, the air cold but still as I glanced up at the sky that had given way to night. We headed for the heavily wooded area, neither of us speaking until we were among the snow-heavy limbs. Only then did it strike me how much my life had changed.

I was running away from the Ascended.

Not toward them.

Casteel kept hold of my hand as he navigated the darkened woods.

"Where are we going?" I asked, my breath forming misty clouds.

"Just outside until I know for sure what is happening." He caught a bare, low-hanging branch, lifting it out of the way.

I kept close as we moved along the fringes of the forest. I realized we'd moved deeper into the woods as we circled the keep and then started to move closer. Perhaps a half-hour passed before the cold began to get to me. I shivered as I curled my free hand so that it was hidden under my sleeve.

"Sorry," he said gruffly. "I wish there'd been time to grab a cloak or at least your gloves."

"It's okay."

He glanced back at me, but I couldn't make out his expression. We continued on, drawing even closer to the keep.

Casteel stopped me. "Wait."

The tone of his voice sent a wave of warning through me. "What?"

He jerked his chin forward. "Something is happening."

"What?" I repeated and followed his gaze, struggling to see through the trees. "I don't have super-special Atlantian eyes."

"And I'm sure that fills you with wrathful envy."

It did.

"We need to be quiet."

I listened, which I was sure came as a shock to Casteel. We crept toward the edge of the woods, and as the trees thinned out, I could see that the yard was brightly lit, far more than I'd ever seen it.

And it wasn't empty. Not in the slightest.

Casteel stopped once more, this time tugging me to my knees beside him. Cold snow seeped through the cloth of my breeches. Unease blossomed as my gaze roamed over the men on horseback. There were dozens, with at least half of them stationed around a windowless carriage that was nearly black in the glow of the lit torches. But I didn't need special Atlantian eyes to know that the carriage wasn't black, nor did I need better lighting to recognize the symbol embossed on its side. The mantles draped over the armored shoulders weren't white, they were black.

And the carriage was crimson.

The emblem was a circle with an arrow piercing the center. The Royal Crest.

These men weren't Royal Guards—they were *the* guard. Members of the Royal Knights.

"They brought knights," I whispered the obvious, mainly because I needed to say it to believe what I was witnessing. I'd never seen a knight outside of the capital.

"Yes, they brought out the knights," the Prince replied, his tone flat but carrying a razor-sharp edge as he let go of my hand. "So, what are you going to do, Princess?"

I could feel the intensity of his stare as I watched the keep's doors swing open. Two knights appeared, their hands at the ready on the hilts of their broadswords as they led the inhabitants of the keep out into the cold. A mixture of disbelief and confusion thudded through me as the knights lined everyone up. I recognized Elijah and Magda immediately, as they were near one of the torches. For once, the man was quiet as he stood there, arms crossed over his broad chest. I didn't see Kieran, nor did I see Naill and Delano, but there were at least two dozen outside the keep, and there were…oh, gods, there were children among them, shivering without their cloaks as a fine flurry of snow continued to drift through the air. What if Alastir and his men returned in the midst of this? They would have to see them before they were seen.

"Will you go to them? Shout and alert your presence?"

Casteel demanded quietly.

"Why would I do that?" My head jerked in his direction. "I agreed to your proposal. I turned down Alastir's help."

"But that was before the Ascended were here. Right in front of you."

"Yes, that was before," I told him, my frustration forcing the truth out of me. "But that doesn't change what I've decided. I have more of a chance of reaching my brother through you than I do them."

Some emotion flickered across his features. "I still can't believe you were going to try to do that by yourself. You would've gotten nowhere near him alone, Poppy." His head tilted as his eyes narrowed. "Unless you weren't planning to do it by yourself. Good gods, were you going to allow the Ascended to find you? Was that what you planned on telling the first person you came across when you tried to escape? That you were the Maiden? Did you think they'd take you straight to the capital? To him? If so, then you're far more reckless than I ever gave you credit for."

Air left me in a ragged burst. "I figured it would be easier to escape them than you once I got where I needed to be."

He stared at me like I'd sprouted another head. "Once you got where you wanted to be, Poppy, you would be where *they* wanted you to be, alone and unprotected."

"As if that is any different with you." My lips thinned as I turned to the keep. One of the knights dismounted.

"You are protected with me, and you'll never be alone," he shot back.

There was a tug in my chest that I desperately ignored.

"And by the way, in case you were wondering, your plan would've turned out just as poorly as your little traipse through the woods did," he growled.

"Do you think this is the best time to rehash something that doesn't even matter?" I demanded.

"I think it matters."

"Well, then you're wrong."

"I am rarely ever wrong."

"Oh, my gods, I think I'd rather risk it with them than stand here with you for another second."

"Well, it's your lucky day. They're right there. Go to them. Tell them who you are."

"As if you'd let me do that," I spat, twisting toward him.

"As if you have any idea what I would or would not allow." His eyes were nearly luminous with his fury. "But you're right. I wouldn't allow *that*, because I refuse to carve your name into the wall down below."

I shuddered as my wide gaze connected with his. Casteel cursed, looking to the keep.

The knight who'd dismounted spoke, apparently not one of those who'd taken a vow of silence. "Is this everyone who resides in this keep?"

"Everyone and then some," answered Elijah. "We just finished dinner and were spending a little bit of time catching up."

"Interesting," the knight replied, stopping in front of him. "And yet the Lord who oversees New Haven is nowhere to be found inside that keep?"

They…they weren't here for me? But rather to check on Lord Halverston? My gaze darted to the carriage. But why would an Ascended come? With knights?

"As I already said, Lord Halverston is hunting with several of his men," Elijah replied, and I knew that was a lie. Lord Halverston, an Ascended, was dead, as were all the Ascended who once lived here. "He left a few nights ago and will be returning shortly. He has a hunting cabin—"

"We've checked the hunting cabin up by the moors," the knight cut him off. "He wasn't there. Didn't look like anyone had been there in quite some time."

"If he isn't there, then he must be on a hunt and decided to camp somewhere else." Elijah didn't miss a beat. "He was excited to get out there. It was all he could talk about for several nights. Said he missed the thrill of the hunt."

Elijah was a very convincing liar.

But not persuasive enough.

"Is that so?" Doubt dripped from the knight's tone.

"It is," Elijah bit out. "And to be really honest with you, I don't appreciate the insinuation that I'm not being truthful with you."

Well, he wasn't being even remotely truthful.

"And I also don't appreciate you and your knights with your fancy black armor and fancier black mantles showing up at this time of night," Elijah went on. "Dragging everyone out in the cold—including the children, as if they could somehow be of assistance to you."

"Careful, Elijah," Casteel murmured.

The carriage door opened without a sound, and a voice spilled out, one that was smooth and almost friendly. "Everyone inside New Haven can be of assistance if given the right motivation."

Magda placed a hand on Elijah's arm, most likely silencing whatever it was that was about to come out of the man's mouth.

"After all, as subjects of the Kingdom of Solis, very minimal motivation should be required if one is faithful to his or her King and Queen." The Ascended came into my line of sight. I knew that crescent-shaped face and long, raven-black hair.

"Lord Chaney," I whispered, pressing my hands against the bark of a tree. The Ascended wore no cloak or gloves, only a heavy tunic over dark breeches. "He's from Masadonia. Why would he be here looking for Halverston?"

That didn't make sense unless I…I was wrong to think they were here for the Lord of New Haven.

Casteel didn't answer, and the unease grew as I glanced at him. His chin was lowered, jaw set and hard as he stared forward. His hand curved around the hilt of his short sword.

"I do find Lord Halverston's absence concerning, which we will need to address appropriately," Chaney remarked, drawing my gaze back to him. "But I've come all this way on far more important business that must be handled first. I know we've never met, so I feel it's important to let you know that unlike the knights, I am not nearly as patient when it comes to humoring unhelpful subjects."

"I don't think your knights are all that patient either," Elijah replied.

Chaney chuckled, the sound as cold as the wind funneling

the snow along the ground. I didn't know much about Lord Chaney other than seeing him at the Council meetings. Sometimes, when I snuck about Castle Teerman, I overheard him with the Duke or Duchess. All the Ascended gave me the creeps, but Chaney appeared pleasant enough. He always nodded politely in my direction when we crossed paths, never stared too long, and he'd been kind to the staff as far as I knew.

"Well, then, please note that I'm even less patient." The Ascended stopped in front of one of the children, a boy I'd seen running from house to house when we first arrived in New Haven. He'd been outside the stables the night I learned the truth about Casteel. "I've been told that visitors arrived not too many days ago."

My spine went rigid. They had to be here for me, but how did they discover so quickly that we were here?

"You heard wrong, my Lord," Elijah answered. "There have been no visitors. Only those returning to the keep."

The Lord strolled past Elijah, his hands clasped behind his back. He stopped once more, this time in front of an elderly man who had his arm around another who looked as if he could barely stand. "I'm here on behalf of the Crown." He looked over his shoulder to Elijah. "So, I really hope you won't lie to me. To do so is akin to lying to the King and Queen, and that would be an act of treason. While they are more often than not our benevolent benefactors, they are still our rulers. Is that clear?"

"Crystal," Elijah replied stoically.

"Good." Chaney pivoted to face where Elijah stood, unclasping his hands. "I'm well aware that a group arrived recently. I may call them visitors. You might refer to them as 'those returning to the keep.' Semantics. So, I will let that slide. A young woman traveled with them. Where is she?"

I exhaled roughly, feeling nothing but a sense of rising dread.

It was Magda who spoke. "There was no woman that returned recently, my Lord."

My fingers dug into the bark as Chaney stared at her, too far away for me to read his expression. Even though I already knew what would happen, I opened my senses and stretched out, forming the intangible connection with the Lord.

I felt nothing. Vast. Endless. Empty. And it had been the same for the empath warriors, who were far stronger than I? Did the Ascended have no mortal emotions at all? Tiny bumps pimpled my skin as I shifted my senses toward Elijah. The moment I connected with him, I felt the hot, acidic burn of anger, and the iron taste of steely determination. He wasn't afraid. Not at all. I pulled my gift back.

Chaney snapped his fingers, and one of the knights stepped forward, opening the carriage door. I frowned, leaning forward as a slight form came into view, shoulders curved in, head bowed.

"Oh, my gods," I whispered, jerking back from the tree so fast that I lost my balance.

Casteel caught me before I toppled over. "Steady," he murmured.

"It's Mrs. Tulis," I told him, stunned.

"You need to go underground." He started to turn me.

I dug in my feet. "No."

"You don't need to see this," he argued.

But I had to.

I had to see this.

Casteel cursed, but he didn't force me to move.

Wearing nothing but a frayed, worn gown, the woman stopped a few feet from the carriage. She trembled so badly that I wondered how she remained standing. The wind tugged at the knot of her hair, lifting the strands that had already fallen. Her arms were curled around her chest—her *empty* arms.

"Where is her son?" I asked. Casteel shook his head when I looked at him.

"Tell me again, Mrs. Tulis," Chaney said, stopping once more. "Who arrived here just a few days ago?"

"It w-was the Maiden," she stammered, and my heart dropped. "The C-Chosen. She came with others from Masadonia." She took a tentative step toward Elijah. "I'm sorry. He—"

"That's enough, Mrs. Tulis." That was all Chaney needed to say, and she quieted at once, sinking into herself. "I'm sure all of you know who the Maiden is. She was being escorted to the capital. And as I'm sure you already know, New Haven is not part of the route one normally takes to get there. Stopping here wasn't part of the plan."

"There's no Maiden here. Not in any sense of the word," Elijah said, and a few of those standing in line chuckled.

"His mouth," murmured Casteel, "will be the death of him one day."

I feared that one day might come sooner than later when Chaney seemed to inhale deeply. "So, you say she's a liar?" he asked.

"All I'm saying is that there's no Maiden in this keep," Elijah answered, which technically wasn't a lie.

"All right." Chaney nodded and then moved fast like all Ascended could, almost as quickly as an Atlantian. One moment he was standing several feet from Mrs. Tulis. The next, he was behind her, his fingers sinking into her wind-swept hair. A vicious crack sounded as he jerked her head to the side.

Lurching forward, I clamped my hands over my mouth to silence the shout building in my throat. Elijah made a move toward the Lord, but he drew up short as several of the knights pulled their swords.

With wide, disbelieving eyes, I watched Lord Chaney lift his hands. Mrs. Tulis crumpled to the ground in a boneless heap at his feet. Even after seeing the underground chamber with all those names, I couldn't...I couldn't have prepared myself for what I saw. He'd snapped her neck. Just like that. He'd killed her as if she meant nothing, as if her life had no value. Slowly, I lowered my hands.

"Why?" Magda said, her fingers pressed to her rounded belly. "Why would you do that?"

Lord Chaney stepped over Mrs. Tulis's body as if she were nothing, absolutely forgettable. "Why would she go unpunished for lying?"

Oh, gods. A shudder racked me. She hadn't been lying. Magda knew that. All of them knew that.

"Unless it was you who is lying," he said. "And the only reason I can come up with for that is that several of you—or all of you—are Descenters. Like the one you accused of lying. After all, she once lived in Masadonia but disappeared along with her husband and son shortly before the Rite and after their very public request to refuse the Rite was denied. Her death was quick and just."

Her death was just? I couldn't believe what I was hearing. And how had he gotten ahold of her when she had been in New Haven? And where was Tobias?

"But back to the issue at hand. The Maiden is very important to the kingdom. Worth more than every single one of you," Chaney addressed the line of people. "Where is she?"

No one spoke.

Chaney looked at the only knight who spoke. Without saying a word, he lunged forward, thrusting his sword deep into the belly of a man standing in line.

Horror seized me as Casteel jumped up but stopped, growling under his breath. The air around him vibrated with rage, and my senses swelled as the man's agony rippled out across the yard. My throat tightened as I fought back the nearly overwhelming urge to connect with him. I couldn't allow that. It would be too much.

The man staggered, but he didn't scream. He didn't even shout from the pain. I imagined a giant pair of shears snipping away at all of the lines my gift was trying to connect to him...to Casteel...to all the others. Rage coated the air, falling heavier than the snow had, and I trembled with the effort to shut it down. To lock it all away before the need to ease the man's suffering and the fear and anger of the others overwhelmed me.

Before I made things worse.

Not a single member of the keep standing by twitched a muscle as the man lifted his head and spat in the knight's face.

The knight twisted the sword before tearing the blade free. Red spilled out of the man's stomach, thick and ropey as he went down on one knee.

"Fuck you," the man gritted out.

The second thrust of the sword was more of a swipe, cleaving the man's head from his shoulders. There were gasps. At least I thought there were, but the blood was pounding too heavily in my ears. It could've been me who reacted.

Casteel rose once more, his hands opening and closing at his sides. A muscle flexed along his jaw, and then he stretched his neck to the left and to the right before returning to kneel beside me.

Bile crept up my throat as the knight wiped the spit from his cheek with the back of his free hand.

"I will kill that one," Casteel vowed quietly, his voice colder than the air we breathed. "I will kill that one slowly and painfully."

One of the other knights stepped forward, grabbing a boy—the one who'd run from house to house when we first arrived in New Haven. He pressed the point of his sword under the child's chin.

My heart stopped.

"This is what they are truly like." Casteel curled his fingers around my chin, drawing my gaze to his. "That is what you once believed would be easier to manipulate, to escape."

I shuddered.

Casteel's gaze searched mine. "I know. I *understand*. Even after everything I've told you about the Ascended and what I've shown you, seeing it is still a shock." His voice softened, loosening some of the ice. "It's always different when you see it."

It was.

Chaney had turned back to the line. "If you've hidden the Maiden somewhere, you only need to tell me where. If others left with the Maiden, then you simply need to tell me where. Tell me where she is. It's that simple. Prove to me that you value your lives."

"And then what? You will leave this place? As if you'd let us live if we told you," Elijah snarled. "I may have moments of profound stupidity, but I'm not that dumb."

Chaney chuckled. "I believe that is debatable."

"Perhaps," Elijah replied, and I could practically hear the smirk in his tone. "But I'm not the one hiding behind a child."

The Ascended grew very still as the hairs on the back of my neck rose. "Are you suggesting that I'm a coward?"

"You said it." Elijah unfolded his arms. "Not me."

Casteel tugged my eyes back to his as he reached for his

boot with his other hand. "I wish you'd never had to see any of this."

He didn't give me a chance to respond. Rising so quickly, he was already near the edge of the trees in the blink of an eye.

It took me a moment to realize that the space where he'd knelt beside me wasn't entirely empty.

Lying on a cushion of dead leaves and snow was a blade the color of blood, and a handle made of smooth, ivory bone. A wolven dagger—*my* wolven dagger.

Slowly, I picked it up with a trembling hand, the weight familiar and welcomed. I looked to where Casteel moved like a shadow between the trees. How long had he had it with him, and why had he given it back to me now?

Because bloodstone could kill an Ascended.

He'd left me with a weapon that I could use in case the Ascended made it to me.

"You're looking for the Maiden?" Casteel called out, and the Lord spun around. Several of the knights flanked him.

Chaney tilted his head as Casteel walked into the clearing. "Who in the hell are you?"

"Who am I?" Casteel chuckled as if this were all a joke to him. "Who do you think I am?"

Rising slowly, I pressed against the base of a tree before moving around it. I stopped when I saw a flash of fawn-colored fur from the area of the stables. *Kieran.* He slunk along the side of the building, disappearing into its shadows.

"I don't know," Chaney replied. "But I'm hoping you're someone who can answer my question. I would hate to see such a young life cut short."

My fingers tightened around the bone handle of my weapon as I crept forward once more, my gaze swinging toward the knight. Could I get behind him before anyone saw me? Before Lord Chaney gave the go-ahead, and another life was ended? All it would take is one nod, and that child's life would be over.

The soft crunch of dried leaves whipped my head to the right. A large white wolven brushed against the tree I'd just been hiding behind, nearly blending in with the snow.

A sudden memory surfaced—of me lying in the cell after

the attack Jericho had led, bleeding out. A wolven with white fur had nudged my cheek and then howled. I'd thought it was Kieran, but it had been this wolf.

It had been Delano.

He looked at me, his pale blue eyes bright against the tufts of white fur. He made a soft chuffing sound as he drifted over to where I stood. His head reached beyond my hip, and I had the strangest urge to reach down and scratch his ear. I resisted, though. It didn't seem appropriate.

Casteel stopped in the middle of the yard, his arms at his sides. "I can answer your question. The Maiden is here."

That stopped me dead in my tracks.

"Is she?" Lord Chaney clapped his hands as he looked around the yard, to those lined up. "Now, how hard was that? I asked a question, and I received an answer."

"You should ask how he knows that the Maiden is here," Elijah said with a chuckle, and I saw Magda take a small step back.

Well aware of Delano at my heels, I moved forward as Lord Chaney stared at Casteel. I reached the last of the trees, stopping when Chaney demanded quietly, "You didn't say who you were. You going to answer that?"

"I am born of the first kingdom." Casteel's voice carried like the wind and snow, stroking over the knights, who all turned, one by one, to look in his direction. "Created from the blood and ash of all those who fell before me. I have risen to take back what is mine. I'm who you call the Dark One," he said, and chills danced across my skin. "Yes, I have the Maiden, and I'm not giving her back."

Lord Chaney *changed.*

Gone was the veneer of civility. His face contorted, cheekbones sharpening as his jaw dropped open. Those eyes burned like coal—like a *Craven's.* I stumbled back, bumping into Delano as I saw—

I saw the truth once more.

The Ascended bared his fangs as he hissed like a large serpent, dropping into a crouch.

"Mine are bigger than yours," Casteel responded in turn,

prowling forward.

Then the knights *changed*, at least half of them, exposing elongated canines as their lips peeled back. It felt like the ground moved under my feet, even though the entire world seemed to stop. There were Ascended among the Royal Army. That…that was unheard of. Only the Royals Ascended. That was what we'd been told—

And that was another lie, another fact exposed to everyone who stood here now. I immediately knew yet another truth. The Ascended didn't intend for anyone to leave the yard alive tonight.

Chapter 15

It was…it was chaos.

Half of the knights charged Casteel, and the others turned on the ones lined up—

Elijah snagged the arm of a knight who'd lifted a sword, smashing his closed fist down. The crack of bone drew a howl of pain as Elijah caught the sword and turned it on the guard. The sword was bloodstone, and it did what was intended, piercing the black armor and sinking deep into the knight's chest. Elijah pulled the blade free, and I expected to see the knight fall, just like a Craven, as Elijah spun, his sword clanging off another. There were shouts of pain and a godsawful hissing noise, but I couldn't pull my eyes away from the knight.

He didn't simply fall like a Craven would. Fissures appeared along his cheeks, spreading across his face and down his neck, forming a web of fractures that disappeared under the clothing and armor. His skin…*cracked*.

Strips of flesh peeled back and flaked off, shattering into dust that was caught on and swept away by the wind. Within seconds, nothing remained of the knight but the clothing and armor he'd once worn, left in a pile on the ground.

The Craven didn't die like that. Their bodies remained whole. That hadn't happened to the Duke, but he'd been killed with a cane fashioned from a tree from the Blood Forest. And that hadn't happened when I killed Lord Mazeen, but the blade was made of steel. Not bloodstone.

My gaze fell to my wolven dagger. That…that was what bloodstone did to an Ascended?

For a few very precious seconds, I was frozen where I stood, my gaze sweeping across the yard, over the clash of swords and bodies, over the blood splattering the snow.

The knights…they weren't just fighting the Descenters. They were *attacking* them. Many still had their swords in their scabbards. Their weapons were their fangs and their strength. They overpowered the mortals among the people of the keep almost immediately, faces twisted in snarls, fangs gleaming in the moonlight. They flew at them, jumping on some, driving them down to the ground like…like a Craven would. My knees felt strangely weak as I stood there.

Bloodlust.

Maybe they didn't screech like the Craven or appear decayed and half dead, but what I was seeing was clearly bloodlust.

Any lingering doubt I had about everything Casteel had claimed nearly vanished when I saw the chamber. But now, there was none. This was what the Ascended truly looked like, and I had never seen anything more terrifying.

Naill appeared. From where, I wasn't sure. He grabbed a knight by the nape of the neck, tearing him free from a man. He shoved a short sword through the knight's back, but it appeared to be too late for the man. He fell to the ground, his throat a mangled mess.

Delano suddenly rushed past me, jarring me from my stupor. With one powerful lunge, he took down a knight that had grabbed hold of a woman, his face buried in her neck—his teeth in her throat. The woman staggered a few feet, pressing her hand to the wound.

Blinking, I turned and saw Casteel shove a sword into a knight's chest and then spin, leaving the sword there. He grabbed the back of another knight's head, yanking it back. The Ascended's head dropped, and Casteel…

Air leaked out of my parted lips.

He tore through the knight's neck, ripping it open. Tossing the man aside, he spat out the blood as he grabbed the sword from the other's chest, pulling it free a second before the knight turned to ash.

I scanned the yard, no longer seeing Lord Chaney, but I did see a knight backing up—the one who held the child. He used the boy as a shield, keeping the sword under the young one's chin.

The wolven dagger practically vibrated in my hand, and I was *finally* moving. Instinct crowded out the horror, and it was like being on the Rise or recently when I'd faced the Craven. A sense of focus and calm settled over me as I darted into the yard, running for the carriage. Out of the corner of my eye, I saw Kieran leap upon a knight that had Elijah's back pinned against the stone wall of the keep. He grabbed the knight in his powerful wolven jaws, flinging him to the ground. Magda appeared, thrusting one of the bloodstone swords down.

I slowed as I moved along the back of the carriage, stopping at the edge. Peering around it, I saw the knight dragging the now-struggling boy toward the stables, a thick arm around his neck. In the moonlight, the child's wide, panicked eyes met mine a moment before the knight turned away.

"Keep fighting," the knight growled. "That really gets the blood pumping."

The child was no longer a shield.

He was food.

Fury pumped *my* blood as I slipped out from behind the carriage, crossing the distance between us as I flipped the heavy-handled dagger so I held it by its blade—just like Vikter had taught me.

The knight turned suddenly, dragging the boy around as if he were nothing more than a rag doll. He lifted the sword as his gaze, reddish black in the moonlight, flickered over me—over my face. The *scars*. His eyes widened in recognition. He knew who I was. His arm loosened, dropping a fraction as he lowered the sword.

I saw my chance.

I took it.

The dagger flew from my fingers, spinning through the air. The blade struck true, slicing through the knight's eye and embedding itself deep in his brain. His hand spasmed open, releasing the sword. It fell to the ground as tiny cracks in his flesh appeared, racing across his skin. They were thin but deep, and when he broke apart, it was almost as if he caved into himself.

"Damn," the little boy said, eyes wide. He turned, bending to pick up the dagger from the armor. He handed it to me. "You got him! You got him right in the eye! How did you do that? Will you show me?"

Relieved to see that the child wasn't remotely traumatized, my lips twitched. "Maybe—"

"A two for one special?" a voice sounded from behind us. "Perfect."

"Run and hide," I told the boy, shoving him away. Hoping he listened, I squared off with a knight. Blood and gore covered his mouth in thick clumps. I was beginning to think the vow of silence didn't apply when they weren't hiding what they were.

Either he hadn't been given a description of what I looked like, which didn't seem likely, or he was too lost to bloodlust. That sounded more probable. He bared his fangs, hissing as he bent. I saw now that their teeth were like those of the Craven. There weren't only two fangs, but four. Two on the top, and two on the bottom. Short and easily hidden, but no less deadly.

The knight charged me with all the grace of a barrat. Knowing that the armor would be hard for me to pierce, even with a bloodstone dagger, I braced myself. The moment his fingers grazed my arm, I stepped to the side as I swung the dagger down on the center of his chest with all my strength. My blow met resistance, but the knight's own body weight and momentum worked to my advantage. The blade pierced the armor and then the chest.

The knight's shout of pain and shock ended abruptly. Jerking the dagger free, I danced back as the fissures in his skin appeared. I didn't want to be anywhere near him when he broke apart. The thought of the ash, of the *pieces* of him, getting on me, in my hair or mouth—or oh, gods, in my eyes—made me want to vomit.

"Maiden?"

The hair along my neck rose at the sound of Lord Chaney's

voice. I turned around, my heart lodged in my throat. The fangs were hidden, his placid expression now set to one of awe. Blood seeped from a wound on his chest. It looked like someone had almost gotten him with a sword or dagger, but he'd been too fast. What had caused the lurch in my chest was what he held against him.

It was the boy.

The child either hadn't listened to me or wasn't fast enough. Lord Chaney had one hand curled under the child's throat. Thin rivulets of blood ran from where the Ascended's nails dug into the boy's skin.

"They told me you were scarred," the Lord said. His eyes were like the blackest fire as they flicked to the dagger. "I assumed they meant it was just a scratch or two, just a minor flaw. But it is you."

"It is me." I rapidly ran through the possible scenarios as the boy trembled. Almost all of them ended with the child's death, and I couldn't have that on my soul. Too many people had already died or were seriously wounded. Names would be carved in the chamber's walls, all because the Ascended had come for me. I only saw one way for the boy to survive. "You're here to save me." The words tasted of ash on my tongue. "Thank the gods."

Lord Chaney watched me closely. "Are you sure you're in need of saving? You killed two knights."

"One of them was trying to hurt the boy, and the other knight...he scared me," I forced out. "I thought they were going to hurt me. I didn't know there were Ascended among the Royal Knights."

A humorless half-smile appeared. "There's no need to be afraid now, Maiden," he said. "You're safe. Lay down the bloodstone."

The hairs were still at attention. The dagger was my only weapon against an Ascended. Without it, the paltry meat knife would be little to no help. Just like it would've if I had managed to escape the night prior. Casteel had been painfully right about how badly that would've gone, though now wasn't the time for self-recriminations. "You're hurting the boy."

The Lord's brows rose as the sound of fighting continued in the yard. "Am I?"

I nodded. "He's bleeding."

He didn't take his eyes off me. I knew I wouldn't be able to throw the dagger as I had before. The element of surprise was gone. "He's a Descenter, Maiden."

"He's just a child—"

"A child of those who sought to kidnap you. His safety should be the least of your worries. Why you stand before me unveiled, not only holding a bloodstone dagger but also with the knowledge of how to use it is far more concerning."

I almost laughed. Leave it to an Ascended to believe that my unveiled face and my ability to fight was more concerning than the fate of a child. "But he's just a little boy, and I believe he's a second son," I quickly lied. "He is destined to Ascend, and the gods will be very displeased if something were to happen to him, wouldn't they?"

"Ah, yes. I wouldn't want to displease the gods." His fingers eased, and the boy wheezed raggedly. The Lord placed his hands on the boy's tiny shoulders. "Lay down the dagger. You don't need it now. Then I shall let him go. I will take you far from here, back to your Queen. She is very worried about you, Maiden."

With the dagger, I had a chance. Lord Chaney was fast, and smarter than the knight. He wouldn't come at me like a wild boar. I'd have to be clever. But without my bloodstone weapon? I stood no chance. The Lord wouldn't kill me. The Ascended needed me. The child, however? He would kill him with little thought. My gaze dipped to the boy. He'd been at the stables, shouting, "From blood and ash" when the others called for me to be sent back to the Queen in pieces. But he was just a child.

Exhaling slowly, I opened my hand. The dagger slipped from my fingers. It hit the ground with a soft thunk that sounded like a door being closed. "I'm ready to go home." I steadied my voice. "To my Queen. Please?"

Lord Chaney smiled again, and dread knotted my stomach. He nodded, and that was the only warning I had before shocking pain exploded across the back of my head, and my world plummeted into darkness.

Jostled into consciousness, I woke to my head throbbing as if it were splitting in two and a dry, cottony feeling in the back of my mouth. The constant, rough rocking forced my eyes open. Everything was a blur of crimson.

I blinked until my vision cleared. A gas lamp cast a soft glow over the crimson. I was in a carriage, laid out on a cushioned bench draped in red. I drew in a deep breath and almost coughed on the heavy, too-sweet cologne.

"You wake."

My stomach dropped. Lord Chaney. I rose unsteadily, wincing as pain spiked intensely across the back of my skull. The Ascended came into view as I reached around and gingerly touched the skin. It was tender, and there was a small lump, but no blood, even though the area throbbed.

"You hit me," I said, my voice hoarse.

"I didn't hit you," Lord Chaney replied. He sat in an arrogant sprawl, arms resting along the back of the bench. "Sir Terrlynn was the one who struck you. It was distasteful but necessary."

"Why?" I quickly glanced around the carriage. There was nothing I could use as a weapon, and I doubted there was bloodstone or Blood Forest stakes hidden anywhere.

But I did have the…knife. Although, what was I going to do with a meat knife against an Ascended?

"We needed to make haste, and I feared you would somehow…unintentionally delay us." He shifted on the bench, lines of tension forming at the corners of his mouth.

My gaze dipped as I lowered my hand to the seat beside me. The wound across his chest was visible beneath the tear in his tunic. The reddish-pink skin was jagged, and the gash appeared deep. Ascended were known to heal rapidly from wounds, much like the Atlantians.

"How long have I been unconscious?" I asked. With no windows, I couldn't tell if it was day or night.

"You slept for about an hour."

My heart tripped over itself. An hour? Good gods, I couldn't believe he even escaped the keep—eluded Casteel. But the Prince had to have realized I'd been taken.

What if he thought I'd gone with the Ascended of my own accord, even after everything I'd seen and been told? Tightness seized my chest, but I couldn't worry about that now. I glanced at the door. Over the sound of the carriage wheels, I could hear the pounding of hooves. We weren't alone.

"If you're planning to escape, I would advise against such a foolish thing," Lord Chaney stated. "We are traveling at quite a speed, and I doubt you would survive such a fall. But if you did, know that we do not travel alone. Sir Terrlynn rides beside us, as do several knights and guards."

Drawing in a shallow breath, I ignored the sharp rise of nausea as I met the pitch-black eyes of the vampry. A chill swept over my skin. Even though I hadn't considered throwing myself out of the door of a speeding carriage, I was definitely planning on escaping. I had no idea how long I'd been in the library, but I figured we were several hours away from dawn, when the Lord and the knights would need to seek shelter from the sun. That would be my chance to escape.

And then what?

I had no idea, but I would have to figure that out when I got to that point. Until then, it would be best if I could convince the Lord that I was a willing participant in this.

"Why would you think I'd want to escape?" I asked as I leaned back, folding my hands in my lap as I crossed my ankles. I sat just like I would if I wore the veil. It was like slipping on a mask—a suffocating and toxic disguise. "I feared that no one would come for me. I'm surprised that you found me so quickly."

"We have eyes everywhere, Maiden," he replied, rubbing at the space above his wound. "Even in places where the Descenters are firmly entrenched."

"Is that how you found Mrs. Tulis? The woman who…who was with you?" In this very carriage, possibly where I was sitting. And now she was dead on the cold ground. Where was her son?

A tight smile appeared. "It was mere coincidence that we happened upon her. She was on foot, a few miles outside of New Haven, walking in the snow. She was nearly frozen when we found her. What an idiot." He let out a rough laugh, and I wanted to strike out at him, making his laugh the last breath he took. "She claimed that the Dark One had killed her husband."

Mrs. Tulis hadn't chosen any of Casteel's options. Heart sinking even further into grief, I suppressed a shudder. Had Casteel known that Mrs. Tulis had left? Could I blame her? She probably feared the same would happen to her.

"We were already en route to New Haven, only a handful of days behind you," he told me. "We discovered that several of those who were escorting you were not who they claimed. The Descenters had worked their way even into the highest ranks of our guards."

Did he mean Commander Jansen? It would make sense if they'd discovered that he had helped Casteel. If so, I knew Jansen was dead.

"So, Mrs. Tulis was an unexpected find, but she confirmed that a woman traveled with the Dark One, someone that others whispered was the Maiden," he told me, swallowing thickly. "She was right."

"But if you knew that, why did you kill her?" I asked, a part of me needing to understand such an action.

"She fled the city instead of obeying the order of the Rite."

I waited for him to say more, but there were no other words. I inhaled sharply, nearly gagging on the floral scent of his cologne. "And what of her child? Her son?"

Lord Chaney simply smiled. There was no explanation. Nothing. Dread knotted in my chest at the sight of the cold, inhuman curve of his lips. He couldn't have done something to the child. Right? My eyes closed briefly. My refusal didn't come from a place of naivety, but from the inability to fathom how one could smile if they had harmed an infant. But there were all those children, some so young, that were given over to the Temples during the Rite. No one ever saw them again for a reason, and it had nothing to do with their service to the gods.

"What of the boy?" I opened my eyes. "His parents may

have been Descenters, but he is only a child."

"He remains at the keep."

That was a small measure of relief, but I latched on to it. Anything to stop myself from vomiting as I fixed what I hoped was a serene expression on my face. A look of blind, devoted trust as he watched me, and I...watched him.

Lord Chaney could be considered a handsome man. I'd overheard a few of the Ladies in Wait, those second daughters given to the Court to Ascend, speak of him. But I didn't remember him being this pale. His skin was leached of all color, and I could see the faint blue veins underneath.

"Are you...well?" I asked. "The wound appears... quite fierce."

"It is a very...fierce wound." He continued massaging his chest. The lines bracketing his mouth deepened as his lips parted. "Penellaphe?"

I twitched at the sound of my name. "Yes, my Lord?"

He still hadn't blinked. Not once since I woke up, and wasn't that entirely unsettling? "You can stop pretending."

Ice hit my veins. "Pretending what?"

Chaney leaned toward me, and I tensed. His fingers stilled. "Tell me something, *Maiden*. Did you welcome the bite of an Atlantian? Perhaps even enjoy the forbidden blood kiss? Or did he force it upon you? Hold you down and take your blood against your will?"

That damn bite.

My fingernails dug into my palms. "It...it was not welcomed."

A hint of red churned in the black abyss of his eyes. Just like a Craven. Gods. "Is that so?" he asked.

I nodded.

"The Dark One bit you, and yet, you sit before me, not as a Craven. That must've come as a shock."

Gods, I'd forgotten that. How could I have forgotten that the Ascended had taught us that an Atlantian's bite was poisonous? "Yes, but I am the Chosen—"

"And you saw us tonight, out in the yard. You saw what we are," he interrupted. "Yet you do not seem surprised. You showed more shock and concern regarding that woman's death." He lifted a hand, placing it on the bench beside my knee. "You say you're relieved that I found you?"

"I am."

He laughed softly. "I don't believe you."

All of my senses went on alert as I spared a brief glance at his hand. The veins stood out starkly. He was not well. Not at all.

Chaney tsked softly under his breath. "The King and Queen are going to be so displeased."

I didn't dare take my eyes off him. "Displeased by what? You ordering a knight to strike me?"

"They may be unhappy to learn that, yes, but I do believe they'll be more disturbed to learn you've been compromised." The red burned brighter in his eyes. "And most likely in more ways than one."

The implication in his tone ignited my temper, and for a moment, I remembered that I wore no veil. "You should be more concerned about yourself." I met his stare. "You're not looking well, Lord Chaney. Perhaps the wound is more serious than you realize."

"That bastard Atlantian almost got my heart," he said, features turning hollow. "But I'll survive."

"I'm glad to hear that," I bit out.

"I'm sure you are." The carriage hit a rock, jostling me, but Chaney didn't seem to notice. "There was a reason I was charged with finding you. Do you know why that is?"

"Your patience and generosity?"

His chuckle was like nails dragging along my nerve endings. "I didn't know the Maiden was so feisty."

I arched a brow.

"I was chosen because I know what you truly are."

I forced my hands to unclench.

"I know what is really in your blood, and I dare say I know more than even you do."

"Is that so?"

His lips parted, and I wanted to recoil from the sight of his fangs—a reaction that was nothing like when I saw Casteel's. "You cannot even begin to comprehend why you were Chosen, but that's neither here nor there. You'll learn soon enough."

"And what is it that I will learn?"

His eyes, a kaleidoscope of red and black, fixed on me—on my neck. "That you will usher in a whole new era of Ascended."

Disgust rippled through me. "Do you think I don't already know that?"

"I don't think you can even possibly begin to understand what that means. But be that as it may, you were right. I am a bit more wounded than I let on. If it hadn't been bloodstone, it would be healing by now. I've said to the Queen and King, time and time again, that all the bloodstone needs to be destroyed. But without it, she worries that the Craven would then overwhelm the people."

"Can't have your food source being destroyed now, can you?" I said before I could stop myself.

"The Dark One has obviously been whispering in your ear." His tongue ran along his bottom lip. "He's obviously been doing more than that."

"It doesn't matter what he's been doing." I smiled just as coldly as he. "What does matter is that I know why I'm the Queen's favorite. I know what you all plan to do with me. I know you won't touch me. I'm needed alive so that I can either keep the Atlantian you have held in captivity fed or be used to make more Ascended."

His head tilted. "You're right about one thing. We do need you alive. That's about it."

Before I could even process what he said, that I was only right about one thing, he rose and moved toward me.

And I reacted.

Leaning back, I planted my booted foot in his chest and kicked him back to his bench.

His eyes widened as he laughed. "Dear Maiden, that was unnecessary. I just need a sip. The King and Queen never need to know. It will be our secret. One you would be wise to keep—"

I kicked out again, catching him in the chest once more.

He hissed in pain. "That wasn't very nice," he snarled as I shifted, reaching for the knife. "That actually hurt."

"That was the point." I unsheathed the blade, holding it

steady. "If you know as much as you think you do about me, then you'll realize I know how to use this. It may not kill you, but I can make you wish it would."

His burning black eyes widened as he held up his hands. "Now. Now." His tone was placating. Patronizing. "There's no need for threats of violence."

"There's not?" Keeping an eye on him, I scooted across the bench, toward the door.

He tracked my movements. "Did you forget about the speed in which we're traveling? The knights?"

"I'd rather take my chances of being trampled to death. At least I'll go to the grave knowing you'll probably be right behind me once the King and Queen learn that I'm dead because of you." I reached for the door—

Chaney struck.

I expected him to go for the knife. I reared back. The moment his hand reached around my ankle, I realized I had made a fatal miscalculation. He yanked hard, pulling me off the bench. My back cracked off the edge of the seat, sending a jolt to my already aching head as I went down hard in the cramped space.

He pulled me toward him, over the rough, dirty, wet floor, laughing the whole while. "There's no point in fighting—"

Gripping his knee, I sat up, swinging the knife with all my might into his chest—into the angry, seeping wound.

Chaney howled, lashing out. His fist caught my jaw, snapping my head back. Bright bursts of light crowded the sides of my vision as he fell back in his seat, clutching at his chest. I struggled to my feet. The carriage jerked, pitched me back and then forward. Grabbing his shoulder for balance, I climbed onto him. He twisted under me, moving onto his back and then rolled, throwing me to the side. I crashed into the back of the bench, hitting the cushions and then fell to the floor. Air punched out of my lungs in a painful rush. I started to sit up, but Chaney dropped on top of me.

"I don't know how the Teermans managed to be around you, knowing what you truly are. Not without stealing just a taste. You may only be half-Atlantian, but your blood is potent." His weight and the stench of his cologne was unbearable, suffocating as he gripped my left arm, yanking it to his mouth. "I just need a little bit. Then the damn throbbing in my chest will stop—"

"No!" I shouted, struggling wildly beneath him. All my years of training disappeared in a flood of panic. I kicked the bottom of the bench with the leg that wasn't pinned. I kicked him, the floor, the seat—

But it was no use.

The vampry's teeth shredded my skin, sinking into the flesh of my lower arm.

Chapter 16

My arm was on fire.

The flames blazed through my body, so intense and all-consuming, I feared it would stop my heart.

I was scared that it already had because I was burning alive, screaming as I pressed against the floor, trying to escape the pain, get away from what was happening, but it invaded every part of me. I could feel it—*him* drawing my blood into him, breaking off pieces of me with each swallow. It was nothing like when Casteel had bitten me. The pain did not ease. It didn't go away. It ratcheted up with each passing heartbeat.

He moaned, biting harder, digging his bottom teeth into my skin. Just like a Craven. Just like before. Like *that* night when I was too small and too young to fight back, too helpless.

The carriage screeched to a grinding halt, knocking Chaney loose. A moment of reprieve came where the burning ebbed enough for my brain to work again. My breath wheezed as my fingers spasmed around the handle of the knife. *The knife.* I still held it. I wasn't a child. I wasn't helpless any longer. *Move, Poppy. Move.*

Chaney latched on to my arm once more, and the pain was a hot coal against my skin, shoving me past the shock of pain before it could drag me under again.

I swung the knife down, driving it into his back, over and

over until he finally felt it, finally reacted with a bellow of rage as he tore his mouth free. He lurched backward and to the side, reaching for the knife. Clutching his shoulder, I held on, jabbing the knife into the wound, into his chest, his face—anywhere I could reach, and he went wild—as wild as me. A new wave of pain exploded along my arm, my cheek, and bright, dazzling lights once more danced across my vision. I screamed as something seemed to rip open inside me. My senses stretched out, attaching to the Ascended. Nothing. Nothing. Nothing but my pain, my rage. It pulsed and throbbed inside me, through me, down the cord, and through the entire carriage, becoming a tangible, third entity as I sliced the knife through his cheek. Chaney jerked back, yelping. Blood sprayed and spurted, running from his eyes and ears. I didn't stop. Not even when a crash sounded from the roof of the carriage. Not even when I thought I heard shouting from outside. I stabbed as many holes into the Lord as I could, until he sprang so many leaks, my hands were slick with his blood, my blood, and I kept thrusting the knife into him, over and over—

The carriage door ripped open, torn from its hinges. Cold air rushed in with the night, and the night was *enraged*. It washed over me, its intensity so stunning, it overwhelmed me, shutting down my senses.

And then Chaney was gone, along with the crushing weight and the heavy, too-sweet cologne, but I couldn't stop. Blinded by rage, pain, and an old, all-too-familiar panic, I kept stabbing at the air, at the night, at the shape that filled the gaping doorway, and then at what appeared above me. Until a hand caught my wrist—

"It's okay. Shh, it's okay, Poppy. Stop. Look at me," a voice demanded. "Look at me, Princess."

Princess.

The Ascended wouldn't call me that.

Breathing ragged, my wild gaze swiveled around the carriage, stopping when I found him. He hovered over me, cheeks spotted with blood. "*Hawke*," I whispered.

"Yeah. Yes." He sounded shredded and windblown. "It's me."

"I..I didn't want to go with him," I told him, needing him to know that *I* understood—that I really saw the Ascended for what they were, even before I woke up in the carriage. "He had a boy, and I—"

"I know. I found the wolven dagger by the stables. I knew you wouldn't have left that behind if you'd had a choice." Gently, he pried the knife from my hand, placing it on the bench. The normally striking lines of his face seemed fuzzy. "And here I thought I would make this grand entrance, rescuing you. I'm not sure you needed rescuing."

I wasn't so sure about that. My rolling gaze landed on the bloodied knife. Even as dazed as I was, as much as my thoughts were muddied, I knew I wouldn't have killed Chaney. I wasn't even sure how badly I'd wounded him. He would've recovered quickly, and he would've bitten me again. He would've kept biting me, feeding off me, and—

"Hey, stay with me." Casteel's soft voice intruded, ending the spiral of panic before I realized I was even falling down it. His fingers touched my chin, drawing my gaze from the knife. His eyes roamed over my face, lingering where my jaw throbbed viciously, and then his gaze dipped. Tension crept into his jaw. "He hurt you."

Lifting my head took more effort than I thought it would. It was strangely heavy as I looked down. The front of my tunic was ripped, streaked with red.

"You're bleeding," he said, his voice rough as he touched the skin below the corner of my lip. That too ached, but then his hands carefully peeled back the left sleeve of my tunic. He became as still as the statues inside Castle Teerman, as if he too were fashioned from the limestone they were made of.

His eyes were like shards of brilliant amber. "Did he bite you anyplace else?"

"No." I swallowed dryly, the rigidness seeping out of my muscles. "It hurt. It felt like a Craven's bite." A tremor rocked me. "It felt nothing like—"

His eyes met mine, and a long moment passed as he stared down at me like he…like he *cared*, as if he would do anything to take back the pain I felt. "He wanted it to hurt."

"Bastard," I whispered, letting my head fall back.

Casteel slipped his hand under my head before it could make contact with the hard floor. I wanted to tell him thank you, but my face hurt—my entire body ached, and my arm throbbed and throbbed.

"He could've killed you," he said, and for the first time since I'd met him, I thought he sounded weary. "You're only half-Atlantian."

Something about that was important—something Chaney had said. But my thoughts were like scattered wisps of smoke.

"Bloodlust would've consumed him, and he wouldn't have stopped. There nearly always has to be another vampry with them to get them to stop. And sometimes, that's not even enough. I didn't think…" His exhale was frayed, tattered. "I didn't think you'd be alive when I reached you."

Yet again, he sounded concerned, but that had to be the head injury I'd most definitely acquired. Or maybe it was the fading adrenaline.

Or perhaps the blood loss.

"Why?" he asked.

"He had…that boy. I had to do something," I forced my tongue to move. My eyelids were too heavy. Everything was too heavy, even as I felt Casteel gather me into his arms, lifting me from the carriage floor. "It was the only way he'd let the boy go."

"But he didn't," Casteel said as my eyes closed, and I slipped into oblivion. "He didn't let that boy go."

The journey back to the keep was a tumble of hazy images, broken pieces of dreams and pinwheeling stars. Casteel's face was so close to mine that I'd thought he would kiss me, but it seemed like a strange time for that. There were sounds. Voices I recognized, ones tinged with concern. Then a strange taste against my tongue that reminded me of spice, citrus, snow, and Casteel. Warmth like the summer sun invaded my veins, and when the heat started to seep into my muscles and spread across my skin, I thought I heard the trickle of water and smelled something sweet, like lilac. But Casteel was a heavy whisper against my skin, and then there was nothing.

When I opened my eyes again, confusion swept over me. I recognized the exposed rafters of the ceiling and the dark spice and pine scent that lingered on the blanket tucked around me, but I had no recollection of how I got back here. My gaze shifted to the gray light creeping through the small window. The last thing I remembered was Casteel carrying me out of the carriage. There were disjointed images, things that didn't make sense no matter how hard I tried.

"Poppy?"

Heart kicking suddenly against my ribs, I turned my head toward the sound of his voice.

Casteel was near the fireplace, rising from a chair. He was dressed as he had been when I saw him last, all in black. Only the swords were missing. He prowled slowly toward the bed, his face clear of the spots of blood. "How are you feeling?"

I had to tug down the cobwebs choking my thoughts to answer that question. "I...I feel okay." And I did. I felt like I'd spent an entire night in restful sleep.

He stopped by the edge of the bed, one eyebrow raised. "You don't sound like that's a good thing."

"I don't understand. I should—" My next breath caught in my throat as I pulled my arms out from under the blanket. The loose sleeves of the nightgown slipped down to reveal...skin that was more reddish pink than normal in two spots, but not an angry shade, not torn. Slowly, I lifted my fingers to my mouth and then to my jaw. The skin wasn't swollen there either. There was only a faint ache when I swallowed. I lowered my hands to the soft blanket as the spiced citrus and snow taste blossomed in the back of my mouth.

"Poppy?"

I swallowed again. "How did I get into this nightgown?"

There was a heartbeat of silence, and when I looked back at Casteel, both of his brows were raised. He seemed utterly caught off guard.

"Did you...did you do it?"

He blinked and then shook his head. "No. Magda did. We thought you'd be far more comfortable."

That meant Magda was alive.

"Is that all you have to ask?" he said.

My gaze fell back to the faint puncture wounds on my arm. "You gave me your blood."

"I did."

"Was I that badly injured?"

"You were bruised and bleeding, and that is bad enough," he stated, and I looked to him once more. "There was also a worrisome lump on the back of your head. Kieran didn't believe it was all that serious, but I...I will not take any chances." His jaw flexed. "And we cannot risk lingering here to allow time for you to heal. Others will be coming for you."

Others.

"They were following us," I said, clearing my throat. "Lord Chaney told me that they'd discovered that—"

"I know," he said, and a hint of a grin appeared. "I had a small conversation with the vampry, and I can be very persuasive when it comes to obtaining information."

Fragments of what Lord Chaney had said slowly pieced together. "He...he saw the bite mark on my throat, and he knew that I'd learned the truth." My brows knitted. "He said he couldn't understand how the Duke or Duchess had never fed from me—how they resisted knowing what I was. He said my blood is potent."

His jaw clenched. "To a vampry, Atlantian blood would taste like a fine wine. A full-blooded Atlantian would be like—"

"Aged whiskey?"

He cracked a small grin. "Very aged, and very smooth."

I shook my head. "Well, I guess the Teermans resisted because they knew the Queen and King would be mad. Plus, it would expose the truth about them." I toyed with the edge of the blanket. "Chaney was wounded."

"Elijah got a good swipe in before the coward ran off."

I wished I'd seen that, but something else Chaney had said slowly fought its way to the surface. "I told him...I told him that I knew why they needed me alive. He insinuated that I wasn't correct."

Casteel smirked. "Of course, he would. I doubt the Queen or King would want you to know the truth or to believe it. They want you willing, to not fight them—for them to be able to lie to you until they have you where they want. If he hadn't been wounded, he probably would've told you that everything was a lie. He would've worked to gain your trust."

"But the lure of my blood was too much?"

Casteel nodded.

My stomach twisted with nausea. "When I saw Lord Chaney, he always seemed…kind," I said. "And more mortal than the Duke or Mazeen."

"The Ascended are masters of hiding their true natures."

But so was Casteel.

My heart tripped over itself, still unable to think that all Ascended were like that. I thought of the Duchess, who'd told me to not waste one more moment thinking of Lord Mazeen when I questioned if I'd be punished or not. Maybe there was a reason I'd never seen her and the Duke touch one another. Just because she was a vampry, that didn't mean she was protected from his cruelty. And then I thought of Ian.

In the silence and in my desperation to not think about my brother, I thought of the knight—Sir Terrlynn. Inherently, I knew he was the one who'd spoken while in front of the keep, the one who had disemboweled the Descenter. "Did you kill the knight?"

"I did what he'd done. Sliced him open and let him bleed. He was a vampry, but it was not without pain." Casteel's eyes burned with golden fire. "And then I killed him."

"Good," I whispered.

A measure of surprise flickered across his face. "There was very little dignity in his death."

That was true. "But he's dead now?"

Casteel nodded.

"At least it was a…relatively quick death." I didn't feel even remotely bad that the knight had suffered. And maybe I should be concerned about that. I probably would be later. I took a deep breath. "How many were lost?"

How many names would be added to the walls?

"Four were killed, in addition to Mrs. Tulis. Six seriously wounded, but they will survive."

My heart ached. "What of the boy? He's okay, right?"

His gaze turned sheltered, and suddenly I remembered what Casteel had said. *He didn't let the boy go.* I rose onto my elbows. "The boy is okay, right? That's the only reason why I laid down my dagger. Chaney said he'd let the boy go."

"He did what all Ascended do. He lied." Tension bracketed his mouth as I jerked. "The only blessing was that it was a quick death. His neck was snapped. He wasn't fed upon."

For several moments, I couldn't think. I couldn't even speak as the image of the boy's wide, panic-stricken gaze filled my mind. Horror and grief seized me. "Why?" A knot clogged my throat. "Why would he do that? Why kill him and not even feed upon him? What was the point?"

"You're asking for an answer to something that not even I can fully comprehend," he replied quietly. "The vampry did it because he wanted to and because he could."

Closing my eyes, I pressed my lips together as my heart squeezed and twisted. Tears burned the backs of my eyes, and I wanted to—I wanted to *scream.* I wanted to rage at the pointlessness of it all.

I didn't know how long it took me to gain control, to not burst into tears or fall headfirst into the helplessness-induced rage. I'd done all that I could to save that boy, and it meant nothing. *Nothing.* He would still be just another name added to a long, endless list of them. And for what? And the Tulis's son? I knew in my heart of hearts that he too was dead. I exhaled raggedly as I lay back down, smoothing my hands over my face. My cheeks were damp.

Casteel remained quiet, silent and watchful. When I opened my eyes again, I asked, "What was his name?"

"Renfern Octis," he told me.

"And his parents?" I asked hoarsely.

"His parents died some time ago. His mother by a Craven, and his father to sickness. His uncle and aunt cared for him."

"Gods," I whispered, staring at the rafters. "I...I saw the

knight take him. I couldn't stand by and watch that happen."

"I'd hoped that you would, but I wouldn't have expected anything less from you."

My bleary gaze shifted to him. The words weren't spoken in annoyance. I thought I detected respect in them. "That's why you gave me my dagger."

Casteel said nothing.

"Do…do you have it?"

He nodded.

I started to ask for it back, but Casteel said, "No matter how much death I've seen, it never gets easier." His lashes lowered, shielding his gaze. "It's never less shocking. I'm glad for that, because I think if it ever does stop shocking me, I might stop valuing life. So, I welcome that shock and the grief. If not, I would be no better than an Ascended."

What I'd said to him the other day soured on my tongue. "I know you're not like them—like the Ascended. I shouldn't have said that to you."

Casteel stared at me for so long, I started to grow concerned. But then he said, "You're not going to ask if you'll turn into a Craven now? You're not angry that I gave you my blood?"

"I know I'm not going to turn into a Craven." I sat up easily and leaned against the headboard. "Did you use compulsion?"

"Not to make you drink. You were surprisingly amicable to that, which caused me to worry all the more," he told me, and I was suddenly grateful that I had no recollection of that. "Once you started to feel the…effects of my blood, I did use compulsion to help you sleep. I assumed you would appreciate that."

Considering how I'd reacted the last time, I *did* appreciate that. I drew a leg up under the blanket. "I'm not mad. I don't hurt, and I would've been in a lot of pain." I looked at my arm again, still shocked to see nothing more than faint marks. "How often can you give me your blood? I mean, would something happen if you continued to do it?"

"I hope that I don't have to continue doing so, but nothing would happen if I did." His lips pursed. "Or at least, I don't think so."

"What do you mean by 'at least' you think that?"

"Atlantians don't often share their blood with mortals, not even half-Atlantians." He sat on the edge of the bed. "In fact, it's forbidden."

"Is it because of your bloodline?"

"Our blood doesn't have much impact beyond its healing and aphrodisiac qualities to mortals. But you're not completely mortal. I imagine it may strengthen the part of you that is Atlantian, at least temporarily." He faced me again. "But there is a worry that sharing one's blood with those who have mortal blood could eventually lead to an Ascension."

"Oh." I could see why that would be a concern. "Would you get in trouble if it was discovered?"

"You don't need to worry about that."

"But I do," I blurted out.

An eyebrow raised. "Then you're worried about me, Princess?"

My skin flushed. "If something happens to you, then that would jeopardize what I want."

His head tilted as he studied me. A too-long stretch of silence passed. "No one who saw how injured you were either time will ever share that I gave my blood to you."

That was good to know. "But what would happen?"

He sighed. "Kieran was right. You do ask a lot of questions."

My eyes narrowed. "Curiosity is a sign of intelligence."

Casteel smiled at that. "That is what I hear." The dimple disappeared. "The King and Queen would be unhappy, but since I'm their son, they would probably yell at me, and that's about it."

I wasn't sure if he was telling the truth or not.

"I figured you'd be mad," he admitted.

"How can I be mad when you made sure that I'm not in pain?" I asked, and I truly wasn't. "It didn't hurt me. It doesn't hurt you, right? I'm just glad I don't have a throbbing headache and…" I looked at the faint marks. "I won't have yet another scar."

Two fingers pressed under my chin and lifted my gaze to his. "Your scars are beautiful," he said, and there was a swift, swelling motion in my chest that couldn't be deflated no matter what my brain yelled at it. "But I refuse to allow your body to be scarred again."

My heart started thumping once more. "You say that like you mean it."

"Because I do."

I wanted that to be true, and that was enough of a warning. I leaned away from his grasp. "When…when do we leave?"

"Naill is out scouting, making sure there is no unexpected traffic on the western roads. I can't leave until I am sure that there are no immediate threats to the keep," he explained, and that made sense. "I hope we will be able to leave by morning or the following day at the latest."

Nodding, I closed my eyes. When I started to see Lord Chaney's face, I shifted my thoughts beyond that to what I'd learned before the Ascended arrived. I'd likely discovered what bloodline I descended from—a line of warriors.

The need to get up, to move—to do something—hit me again, but this time, I had a purpose. "Are the injured ones in pain?"

Casteel's brows knitted. "They've been given what we have on hand to ease their pain. Magda left to retrieve more."

"I can help them." I scooted to the other side of the bed and pushed the blanket off.

He rose. "Poppy—"

"I can help," I repeated, coming to my feet. "You know I can. Why shouldn't I?" I raised my brows when he didn't answer. "There's no good reason for why I shouldn't."

"Other than that you were just injured?" he suggested.

"I'm fine, thanks to you." My hands opened and closed at my sides. "You know I hated not being able to use my abilities before, being forced to do nothing when I can help people. Don't do that to me."

"I'm not trying to do that to you."

"Then what are you trying to do?" I demanded. "These are your people. I want to help them. Let me do that."

"You don't understand." He thrust a hand through his hair. "The people here don't know you. They don't—"

"Trust me? Like me? I already knew that, Casteel. I don't need either of those things. That's not why I want to use my abilities."

Casteel fell quiet and stared at me for so long that I braced for an argument. "Then you should get changed," he said, turning away. "I'll get jealous if anyone else sees how pretty your legs are."

Chapter 17

I found myself in borrowed clothing once more as Casteel and I left the room. The heavy sweater was a deep, forest green, warm and soft, but this time, the pants were a size or two too big. Gathered around my waist with gold rope, the breeches were baggy through the entire leg. I was positive the tie was normally used to hold curtains back from a window. I felt a little foolish, like a small child playing dress-up in adult's clothing, but I wasn't going to complain. The clothes were warm and clean, smelling of lemongrass.

As we reached the bottom of the stairway, Casteel took my hand in his. A charge of awareness seemed to pass between our joined palms, traveling up my arm. I glanced up at Casteel in surprise.

He stared down at me, lips parted enough that I could see the hint of fangs. The amber hue of his eyes was luminous in the dim stairwell.

"Sparks," he murmured.

"What?"

Smiling slightly, he shook his head. "Come. There is something I want to give you when you're done with the injured."

Casteel pushed open the door before I could further question him about what he'd meant or what he planned to give me.

People huddled around the open doors of the front entrance of the keep, staring out. Wind had blown in a dusting of snow, but no one seemed too aware of the cold air creeping in.

"What are they looking at?" I asked.

"Something unexpected," Casteel replied, and my brows knitted in a frown.

Now beyond curious, I started toward the doors. Casteel didn't stop me. Becoming aware of the Prince's arrival, the people parted, bowing at the waist, their pale faces and distracted gazes returning to the outside.

Walking forward, I saw more standing outside, arms wrapped tightly around their waists. They faced the stable. As the bright morning rays stretched across the snow-covered ground, we rounded the corner of the keep.

I came to a complete stop, my hand going lax in Casteel's grip.

Ahead of us, where the space had been emptied, where Lord Chaney had found me the night before, was a tree.

My gaze lifted, following the wide, glistening bark and over the thick limbs stretching as tall as the keep, heavy with leaves gleaming crimson in the bright morning sun.

This was no freshly planted sapling. The tree was well rooted, as if it had stood there for decades, if not hundreds of years. Moisture seeped through the bark, beaded and rolled slowly to the tips of the leaves, falling in droplets of red, splashing against the snow.

A blood tree.

"How?" I whispered even though no one knew how the trees in the Blood Forest grew, why they bled. Why did one grow here overnight, where one hadn't stood before?

"They're saying it's an omen," Casteel answered quietly.

"Of what?"

"That the gods are watching." His grip tightened on my hand as I shivered. "That even though they still slumber, they are signaling that a great change is coming."

"Did you happen to forget about the blood tree?" I asked as we returned to the keep. "And that's why you didn't mention it?"

"To be honest, I had more pressing concerns."

I arched a brow. "Really? What is more pressing than an omen sent by the gods?"

"You waking up uninjured was more pressing than a vague, rather unhelpful message from the gods," he replied as we entered the banquet hall, and I almost tripped.

"You cannot be serious," I stated.

He frowned. "I'm completely serious."

There was no way he was being honest. The omen was far more important than anything that had to do with me. When was the last time the gods had sent any sort of message? There was nothing in the history books, and even if there had been, it was doubtful it would've been accurate.

But there was something more pressing than the blood tree, and it was what awaited us here.

The injured had been placed in a room adjacent to the banquet hall. Before the doors even opened, I could feel the pain radiating through the stone walls. My pulse tripped, even though my steps didn't slow.

Casteel stepped in before me, and was immediately greeted by Alastir.

"I see you've returned," Casteel said as I took in the room, thoughts of the blood tree fading. Six cots were set up, all of them occupied by men, except the last one. Red stained the bandage around her neck. I recognized her. One of the knights had grabbed her, and I was surprised to see that she had survived. But her skin was only a shade away from death, and she was impossibly still. An older woman sat beside her, hands pressed together as her lips moved in a silent prayer.

"And I see I should've returned earlier," Alastir commented.

"You returned soon enough, according to Elijah." Casteel clasped the older wolven's hand. "I heard you and your men took care of the rest of the knights."

Alastir nodded absently as he surveyed the room, lips set in a thin line. "Damn them. These people didn't deserve this."

"The Ascended will pay."

"Will they?" Alastir asked.

"It is a promise that won't be broken," Casteel answered.

Alastir let out a shuddering breath as he turned to me. "I'm glad to hear that you were safely returned, Penellaphe, and that they were unsuccessful in their attempts to retrieve you."

Unsure of what he'd been told, I nodded as I murmured my thanks. My skin buzzed with the need to move forward. Only one, the woman, seemed to have moved beyond pain. I twisted to Casteel.

Catching my eye, he nodded. I hurried forward, to the first man. He was an older gentleman with more gray than black in his hair. I didn't know what his injuries were, but his unfocused gray eyes tracked me. I opened myself, sucking in a sharp breath as anguish, both mental and physical, came from the beds and those perched beside them. It crowded out the air, choking and suffocating. My gaze briefly swept to the woman and then to the elder beside her. Some would not leave this room. Others knew this. Hands giving in to a slight tremor, I focused on the man before me.

"I'm sorry about what was done to you," I whispered, and the man said not a word as I placed my hand on his.

Normally, it took a few moments for me to call upon the kind of memories that led to the easing of pain. I'd think of the sandy beaches of the Stroud Sea, of holding my mother's hand. But this time, I felt warmth in the skin of my palm. I didn't have to pull upon anything, only thought of taking the pain. I knew the moment my gift reached him. His mouth went lax as his chest rose with a deeper, steadier breath. I held his hand until the clouds left his eyes. He stared, but did not speak, and neither did the man beside him, one too young to carry the haunted look in his eyes. I eased his pain from whatever wounds the blanket covered and from what ran deeper. *Grief.* Raw and potent.

"Who did you lose?" I asked once he'd stopped trembling, aware that no one was speaking. Not Alastir. Not Casteel, who shadowed me through the room.

"My…my grandfather," he said hoarsely. "How did you…how did you know?"

Shaking my head, I placed his arm by his side. "I'm sorry for your loss."

Eyes followed me as I made my way to the next man and knelt. In the back of my mind, I wondered if it was Casteel's blood that made it easier for me to use my gift or if it was because of the Culling. Either way, I was happy to find that it worked with little effort. Continuing to dwell upon happier times was not easy when death clouded the room.

The man before me was slipping in and out of consciousness, twitching and moaning softly as I placed my hand on his, channeling my energy into him. His sweat-dampened brows smoothed out within seconds.

"What did you do?" a young woman demanded as she fell to her knees beside the man, dropping an armful of clean towels. "What did she do?"

"It's okay." Casteel placed a hand on her shoulder. "She only eased his pain long enough for Magda to return."

"But how…?" She trailed off, her brown eyes widening as she placed a hand over her chest.

Meeting Casteel's gaze, I rose and went to another, one with eyes of winter. A wolven. I had no idea how old he was, but in mortal years, he appeared to be a decade or so older than me, his onyx-hued skin drawn into tense lines. A deep slash ran across his bared chest, where a sword had sliced open tissue and muscle.

"I'll heal," he said gruffly. "The others, not as easily."

"I know." I knelt. "That doesn't mean you need to be in pain."

"I suppose not." Curiosity seeped into his eyes as he lifted his hand.

I folded mine over it, and again, I sensed there was pain that ran deeper. Years and years' worth of sorrow. My palm warmed and tingled. "You also lost someone."

"A long time ago." His breath caught as his breathing slowed. "Now, I understand."

"Understand what?"

He wasn't looking at me. I followed his gaze to Casteel.

Behind him, Alastir stood as if he couldn't believe what he was seeing. Maybe we should've warned him.

"Jasper will be interested," the wolven said, a faint grin appearing as he leaned his head back against the flat pillow.

"I'm sure he will be," Casteel commented, eyes lightening. "Be well, Keev."

The wolven nodded, and I rose, curious as to who Jasper was as I moved to the man beside Keev, the one that had watched me the entire time. I started forward.

"No," the man gritted out, sweat coursing down his face. His eyes were a shade of golden hazel. "I don't want your touch."

I halted.

"No offense, my Prince." His too-shallow breaths filled the silence. "I don't want that."

Casteel nodded. "It's okay." He touched my lower back, urging me on.

I went, looking over my shoulder at the mortal with Atlantian blood. He watched me, his face already flushed with fever. I connected with him, and immediately severed the connection. The hot, acidic burst of hatred and the bitterness of distrust stunned me. Quickly looking away, I swallowed as my senses stretched out to every corner of the room, and I stumbled under the mixed rush of emotions and tastes. *Iced lemonade. Sour and tart fruit. Vanilla. Sugar.* Confusion and surprise. Fear and awe. Distrust. Amusement. My heart started kicking against my ribs.

Casteel's hand flattened against my back as he glanced down at me.

"I'm okay," I whispered as I cut off the connections, focusing only on the two women in front of me.

The older woman, her eyes a spun gold and brown, looked up at me, watched me as I shifted toward the all-too-still woman on the cot. I knew she was mortal, or at least partially. An Atlantian like Casteel would be healing, but she...

She couldn't have been all that much older than me, her skin free of lines and untouched by age. I lowered myself, even though I sensed...nothing from the woman.

"You don't have to do that," the older woman said.

Hand halting inches from the waxy, limp hand of the wounded woman, I looked across her.

"I know." She swallowed. "Your gifts would be wasted on my daughter."

"I..." I didn't know what to say.

She gazed down at the woman, touching her cheek and then her brow. "I heard of you before I came here. I lived in Masadonia for a time, a few years ago," she said, surprising me. "They whispered about you—the families of those you attended, that is."

I pulled back my hand, aware of how intently Casteel was listening.

"They said you gave dignity to those cursed." Her skin creased as she smiled at her daughter. "Ended their pain before you ended their suffering. I didn't believe them." A tear dropped onto the woman's chest. "I didn't believe anything raised by the Ascended could give something of such worth. I didn't believe." She lifted her gaze to mine.

My breath caught. Her eyes... Flecks of gold seemed to burn brighter as she stared at me, stared straight *into* me.

"You *are* a second daughter," she whispered, sending a chill through me. "Not a Maiden but Chosen nonetheless."

Unsettled by the emotions of those in the room and the shadow of death waiting to claim the young woman, I wished to go outside where a downpour could wash away the coating on my skin.

"Some of them were afraid of me," I blurted after Alastir had closed the door behind us. "That guy—the one who wouldn't let me touch him? He didn't trust me at all, and I could feel their fear."

Casteel's gaze narrowed on the door. "They don't understand what you can do."

"They've never seen anything like that." Alastir joined us by an empty table, his skin still pale. "I haven't seen anything like that in..."

"Not since there were empath warriors?" Casteel surmised. "I think that's the line Penellaphe is descended from. A few of them must've remained in Solis."

Alastir nodded as he eyed me. "When did your parents learn of your abilities? Or when did you first know of them?"

"I don't know the exact age, but it was before we left the capital. I don't know if the Ascended knew what I could do at that time."

"And you have a brother?" Alastir asked, and Casteel's head swiveled toward him. "Was he your full-blooded brother?"

"I believe so," I said, realizing that someone must've told him about Ian or that he'd learned of him when he first heard of me. "But if he's like me—half-Atlantian—then why would they have allowed him to become an Ascended?"

Alastir glanced back at Casteel. "You sure he is?"

"As sure as I can be without having seen the Ascension myself."

A thoughtful look crossed Alastir's face. "It's unlikely they would've turned him if he was of Atlantian descent, but...stranger things have happened." He looked over at me and then turned to Casteel. "Has she displayed any more of the empath traits?"

Casteel shook his head, and I assumed that Alastir referred to how the empath warriors could somehow use what they sensed against people.

"But why would they be afraid?" I asked. "They saw me help the first person."

"The people, even those who have lived in Solis, can be wary of things they haven't seen before and don't understand," Casteel explained, and it struck me then that maybe their reaction was why he hadn't wanted me to help in the first place.

"Some in Atlantia, our oldest who survived the war, would remember the empaths." Alastir touched the back of a chair, silent for a moment. "And that could be a problem. I'm sure you've seen that damn tree out there. The gods have sent a warning."

"Come now, Alastir, when did you become such a fatalist?"

Irritation flashed across Casteel's features. "The omen is not necessarily a warning. Change can be good just as much as it can be bad. And either way, it has nothing to do with her."

Damn straight, that omen had nothing to do with me. The mere idea that it did was ridiculous. I crossed my arms. "Why would the oldest of the Atlantians remembering the warriors be a problem?"

"You don't have anything to do with that omen. A great change coming doesn't necessarily mean something bad." Casteel's stance widened. "And the empath warriors' abilities were sometimes feared, mainly because very little could be hidden from them. And out of all the bloodlines, they were the closest to the deities."

Alastir arched a brow. "And because they could siphon the energy behind the emotions," he elaborated. "They could feed on others in that way. They were often called Soul Eaters."

"Soul Eaters?" I stiffened. "But I can't do that. I don't get anything from the people I help. I mean, I don't get energy or anything, and I can't amplify fear."

"I know that. We know that," Casteel reassured.

"But they don't know that." The wolven pulled his hand from the chair as he gave me a faint smile. It didn't reach his eyes. "Casteel is right. We just need to make sure they understand that you are not capable of what your ancestors could do. And once they get to know you, I believe they will no longer think of the small percentage of your ancestors that incited fear."

"Really?" Doubt filled me.

Alastir nodded. "Truly. This is not something you need to concern yourself with."

I really hoped that was the case since there was already enough to worry over.

He refocused on Casteel. "And don't be so sure that the omen has nothing to do with her—with both of you. You two are to be married. Will that not usher in great change?"

Casteel's brows rose as his expression turned thoughtful. "Well, you do have a point there," he said, and my eyes narrowed. "Are you heading out soon?" When Alastir nodded, he took my hand in his, surprising me with how easily he did. The act seemed almost second-nature to him, but each time he held my hand, it was like a revelation to me. "Safe travels. We will see you in Spessa's End."

"Safe travels to you both." Alastir placed a gentle hand on my shoulder. "Thank you for coming to the people's aid, even if some didn't understand or appreciate."

I nodded, uncomfortable with the gratitude.

We parted ways with Alastir, walking across the banquet hall. "Is he leaving for Spessa's End already?"

"While you were resting, I spoke with Emil. After what happened, we thought it was better if we traveled east in smaller groups to avoid drawing attention."

"Makes sense," I murmured. "You really think that the omen has to do with our marriage?"

"Could be," he said, but we were nowhere private enough for me to point out that the marriage wasn't real. Not in a way where it would usher in any great change.

Unless our plan worked. *That* would bring about great change.

My thoughts shifted to what else had happened in the room, hopefully dissipating the still-oily feeling on my skin. "The mother in there said the same thing as the woman in the Red Pearl. That I was a second daughter but not like I thought." Glancing over my shoulder, I saw Alastir at the door. The poor man still looked like a breeze might knock him over. "I didn't get it then, but now I think she meant I was second-generation."

"What woman in the Red Pearl?"

"The one who sent me up to the room that you were in. Obviously."

His brows snapped together as he looked down at me. "I have no idea what woman you're talking about."

"Really?" I replied, tone dry. "The one you had send me to your room. I think she was a Seer—a changeling."

"I didn't have any woman send you to that room, especially not a changeling," he said. "I knew who you were the moment I pulled that hood back, but I had no one send you to my room."

I stared up at him. "Are you serious?"

"Why would I lie about something like that? I already told

you that I knew who you were that night."

"Then how…?" I trailed off as Casteel hung a sharp left, pushing open a door and pulling me inside a room that smelled of soil and herbs. The door clicked shut behind us. I looked around, spying cans of vegetables, bushels of potatoes, and satchels of dried herbs. "Did you just pull me into a pantry?"

"I did." Casteel's chin dipped as he stepped into me. Dark hair toppled forward onto his forehead.

I stepped back, bumping into a shelf. Jars rattled. He was so tall, I had to crane my neck all the way back to meet his gaze. "Why?"

"I wanted a moment alone." He placed his hands on the cupboard above my head. "With you."

Senses hyperaware, I watched him lean in as a confusing tremor of anticipation coiled its way down my spine. "And you needed this moment alone in a pantry?"

He turned his head slightly, lining up his mouth with mine. "I just *needed.*"

Tiny shivers hit every part of me. I opened my mouth to tell him that whatever he needed didn't involve him and me in a pantry, but nothing came out. No protests. No warnings. I simply stared up at him, waiting and…wanting.

"I know how hard that had to be for you." His lashes swept down as his breath danced over my lips. "Going in there with your abilities, opening yourself up to their pain."

My fingers curled around the edge of a shelf. "It was nothing."

"That's a lie, Princess." His mouth was closer, just a breath from mine. "You did it even though you felt their fear and distrust. It was everything."

I felt my lips part. "And that's what you needed to tell me in the pantry?"

He shook his head, causing my breath to hitch when his lips glanced off the corner of mine. "I wasn't done."

"Sorry," I murmured. "Please, continue."

"Thank you for your permission," he replied, and I could hear the smile in his voice. "There are many times when I'm in utter awe of you."

I stilled. Every part of me.

"I shouldn't be surprised by what you're capable of," he went on. "What you're willing to do. But I am. I'm always in awe of you."

A tugging sensation in my chest stole a little of my breath. "Is that what you needed when you pulled me into the pantry?"

"I'm still not done, Princess."

My pulse thrummed. "No?"

"No." His forehead dropped to mine. "There is one more thing I need. Something that I've needed for days. Weeks. Months. Maybe forever." The bridge of his nose brushed mine. "But I know you won't allow it. Not like this."

The pounding in my chest moved lower. "What...what have you needed for so long?"

"*You.*"

I shuddered.

"So, maybe, just for a few minutes, when no one is looking—when there's no one but us—we can pretend."

Leaning into the cupboard, I felt dizzy, as if I weren't getting enough air into my lungs. "Pretend?"

"We pretend that there's no yesterday. No tomorrow. It's just us, right now, and I can be Hawke," he said in the heated space between us. I shook once more. He touched my cheek, sending a bolt of awareness through me. His fingers drifted over my chin, my lower lip. "You can just be Poppy, and we can simply share a kiss."

"A kiss?"

He nodded. "Just pretend." His lips now a whisper against my cheek. "Just a kiss."

I shouldn't.

There had to be a hundred reasons why. It blurred the lines of who we were. I'd told him it would never happen again. He was using me. I was using him. Kissing wasn't wise. Even with all that I didn't know, I knew enough to realize that it never stopped with a touch of the lips, even when it did. There was always *more*. Wanting. Needing.

And I wasn't sure how I even felt about him since my feelings toward him seemed to change every five minutes. But either way, I shouldn't allow anything like this. If I did, everything would be harder, even more confusing than it already was. Tawny could perfectly sum up what it was now in two words: a mess.

But a woman was about to die.

Her mother said I was still Chosen.

A man in there didn't want my touch.

Some in that room *feared* me.

Hated me.

I could still feel Lord Chaney's teeth in my flesh even though there were no wounds.

I could still see the burning coal of his eyes, and feel how I was nothing more than an object to him. Food. Sustenance. A thing.

And I didn't want to feel any of that.

I wanted to bask in Casteel's awe of me, and maybe…maybe I already knew, deep down, how I truly felt about him.

"Just pretend?" I trembled as the tips of his fingers skated down the side of my throat, around to the nape of my neck.

"Pretend." His lips hovered above mine once more, right there, teasing.

I closed my eyes, my voice barely more than a whisper. "Yes."

Chapter 18

Like before, the night of the Rite, when we'd been under the willow tree in the gardens and I'd asked him to kiss me, he hadn't wasted a moment.

Except he'd been Hawke then, and we hadn't been pretending.

His lips brushed over mine, once and then twice, so incredibly soft and gentle that it threatened to unravel all pretenses. I shuddered and felt his lips curve against mine. I knew he grinned. I knew that if I opened my eyes, I'd see that infuriatingly tempting dimple of his. The touch at the back of my neck and against my cheek, just below the scar, was featherlight as he seemed to map out the feel of my lips with his, slowly, leisurely reacquainting himself. Tiny shivers skittered through me.

But I wanted more. Already.

Impatience burned through me. Lifting my hands from the shelf, I gripped the front of his tunic and pulled him against me. "I thought you were going to kiss me."

"Isn't that what I'm doing?"

I shook my head. "That's not what you can do."

He chuckled against my lips. "You're right. It's not."

Then he truly kissed me.

He claimed my lips as if he were staking a claim to my very soul. The possibility that he was already well on his way to doing so should've served as a dire warning, but I was far too immersed, far too gone at the feel of him, lost in how demanding his lips were. He tugged on my lower lip with his fangs, urging my lips to part. Gasping, I yielded to him. The kiss deepened, and his tongue slid over mine. I let out a little breathless moan against his hot mouth. The taste of him, his smell…all of him invaded me, scalding me.

We kissed and kissed, and I…I still wanted *more*. Wanted to keep pretending as liquid fire poured through me, erasing the icy touch of Lord Chaney, washing away the suffocating feel of the room where death had surely come and gone by now, and all the unknown of what awaited.

He knew this, sensed this, and he gave me what I desperately needed.

His hand finally, finally moved from my cheek, trailing down, smoothing over my breast. There was a reverence to his touch, as if he worshiped me as he slid his hand under the hem of my sweater. Flesh against flesh. My body jerked as his fingers skimmed over the patchwork of scars and then moved farther up, over the lines of my ribs, the bottom swell of my breast. I moaned into his mouth as his thumb reached the turgid peak. Sharp spikes of pleasure twisted through me.

He made a deep, dark sound that rumbled through me as the hand at my neck dropped to the small of my back. He pulled me away from the cupboard, against the hard length of his body, and still, he devoured me with his lips, branded me with his touch. The hunger in him should've scared me, but all it did was inflame the same need within me.

We were only pretending…

But this felt so very real.

He felt all too real, his lips against mine, my chin—his touch at my breast, my back, and against my body. My head fell back as his mouth trailed a blazing path to the healed bite. I felt the hot wetness of his tongue, the wicked sharpness of his fangs as he scraped them along my flesh. I cried out, my entire body tensing, coiling in delight and forbidden anticipation.

"Poppy," he breathed, maybe pleaded. I wasn't sure. His tongue flicked over my skin.

Would he bite me?

Did I want that?

Would I stop him?

My body already knew the answer as I reached up, sinking my hand into the soft strands of his hair.

"You want that?" he whispered against my sensitive skin. "Don't you?"

I shuddered, unable to answer.

"You do."

An aching pulse stole my breath, and then, in a feat of impressive strength, he shifted his hands under my thighs and lifted me as he turned. My back hit the door as he hooked my legs around his waist. His body met mine, and he pressed in, the hardest parts of him against the softest parts of me.

I moaned as his mouth closed over my neck. He drew the skin between his sharp teeth, and my hips lifted from the door, pushing against his.

He drew harder on the skin, wringing another cry from deep within me, but he didn't break the flesh. He didn't draw blood. Instead, he teased and taunted until every nerve ending felt stretched to its breaking point, until I rocked against him, with him.

And when his mouth finally returned to mine, I knew we were both quickly losing control.

We were pretending.

Even as he kissed as if he drank from my lips. Even as he ground against me, and I dug my fingers into his shoulders and then the material covering his chest. We were pretending.

Slowly, the kisses slowed, his hips still pinning mine to the door. He was breathing as raggedly as I was when he lifted his mouth from mine. "I think…I think that is enough."

Was it?

Letting my head fall back against the door, I nodded as I swallowed. It had to be enough because this was insanity—it was leading to more insanity. It seemed like he was minutes away from stripping me bare and taking me against the door. It felt like

I was seconds away from begging him to. My grip on his shirt loosened as I opened my eyes.

Casteel stared down at me, his lips swollen, eyes a vivid, molten gold. Gods, he was shamelessly beautiful, and he looked as thoroughly undone as I felt.

He made a deep, rumbling sound. "Don't look at me like that."

"Like what?" I didn't recognize the throaty voice.

"Like you don't think that was enough." His hand smoothed over my hip, cupping my rear as he pulled my lower body away from the door and against his ridge of thick hardness. He caught my gasp with a quick, deep kiss I wanted to sink into.

But the kiss ended, and he gently eased my legs down. He stayed close for several moments, his forehead resting against mine as he smoothed the strands of my hair back with hands I swore trembled slightly. My knees felt oddly weak when he took a step back, putting space between us. Our gazes met, and the aching want in me pounded along with my heart.

"That was..." I bit my lip, having no idea what I was going to say.

"You don't have to say anything." He returned to where I stood, catching a strand of my hair and tucking it behind my ear. "It's probably best that we don't."

"Right," I whispered, wanting to press my cheek into his hand but somehow resisting.

He smiled slightly. "I do have something that you need. A gift. One I planned to give to you when we left the room. Before I became...sidetracked."

Sidetracked? Was that what this was for him? Was it more for me?

"It's not a ring," he said. "But it's something I think you'll appreciate nonetheless."

My brows furrowed in confusion. "What kind of gift?"

"The best kind," he said. "Retribution."

I had no idea how Casteel could be so cool and collected after that kiss, but as I glanced over at him, he looked like he'd just attended a reading of *The History of The War of Two Kings and the Kingdom of Solis*, which was as stimulating as watching grass grow.

It was almost like what had occurred in the pantry was a figment of my imagination, and if it weren't for the feeling of aching unfulfillment, I would seriously be doubting what had happened. But it wasn't. It was real. He'd kissed me, and he'd done so like his very life depended on it.

Was he truly that unaffected, and if so, what was the point in pretending?

Before I could use my senses, Casteel opened a heavy wooden door. The musty, damp scent was immediately recognizable.

"My gift is in the dungeon?" I asked, my steps slowing as we made our way down the cramped stairwell. My stomach churned at the scent.

"It may seem like a strange place for a gift, but you'll understand in a moment."

Ignoring the paranoid voice that whispered that this was some sort of trap, I moved along. After agreeing to the marriage, I doubted he planned to throw me into a cell. Still, it was unsettling to be here again, where I'd almost died.

A shadow peeled away from the wall as we reached the torch-lit hall. It was Kieran. The wolven's pale gaze flicked from Casteel to me. "How are you feeling?"

"Okay. You?" I asked for some reason, and then felt my cheeks flush. There was no way he could know what'd happened in the pantry, even with his extra-special wolven—

Unless he knew because of the bond.

I really needed to figure out more about that bond.

His lips curved into a grin. "Just dandy." He looked at his Prince. "And you?"

"The answer is the same as when you last asked," Casteel said, and my brows pinched.

I turned to him. "Were you injured?"

"Would you fret with worry if I was?"

The corners of my lips turned down. No? Yes? "Not

particularly."

"Ouch." He pressed a hand to his chest. "You wound me yet again."

"He's not wounded," Kieran answered. "At least, not physically. Emotionally, I believe you left him shredded."

I rolled my eyes. "Then why ask if he's okay if he's not hurt?"

Kieran started to reply, but Casteel beat him to it. "He's a worrywart. Constantly fearing that I've been injured or that I've overexerted myself. Wanting to know if I've gotten eight hours of rest and eaten three square meals a day."

"Yeah, that's exactly it," Kieran replied drolly.

Casteel flashed him a grin and then motioned to me. "Come. Your gift awaits."

Having no idea what the two of them were going on about, I trailed after the Prince, beginning to suspect what my gift was. *Retribution*. The rich iron scent of blood was heavy in the air. Fresh. The sickeningly sweet floral undertone lingering beneath the blood confirmed my suspicions before I even saw what awaited me in the cell Casteel had stopped in front of.

Chained to the wall, arms spread wide and legs bound, stood Lord Chaney. He'd definitely seen better days. One eye was gone. Deep gouges streaked his face, caused by the knife I'd wielded. Blood leaked from his parted mouth in a continuous trickle. His shirt had been split open, revealing that the gash I'd seen earlier was part of three deep slashes in his chest. Claws had also scored his skin just below his throat and across his narrow torso. The shackles around his wrists and ankles were spiky, digging into his skin and drawing blood. He had to be in immeasurable pain.

There wasn't an ounce of pity in me as I stared at the vampry.

"You didn't kill him," I said, and the Ascended opened one eye. It was more red than black.

"No." Casteel leaned a hip against the bars, angling his body toward mine. "I wanted to. I still do. Badly. But he didn't wound me, it wasn't my skin he tore into. Not my blood he stole."

My heart was hammering once again as I dragged my gaze

from the vampry to Casteel.

"Retribution is yours, if you want it," he said. "And if not, I will be your blade, the thing that ends his miserable existence. It's your choice." Reaching into his boot, he pulled a blade free and held it between us. It was my wolven dagger. "Either way, this belongs to you, whether it finds its way into the heart of an Ascended today or not."

Wordlessly, I curled my fingers around the bone handle, welcoming the cool weight once more. I looked into the cell again.

"He doesn't speak now?" I asked. The Ascended hadn't been able to keep quiet before.

"I tore out his tongue," Kieran announced, and both Casteel and I looked at him. "What?" The wolven shrugged. "He annoyed me."

"Well," Casteel murmured. "Okay, then."

The Ascended made a pitiful whimper, drawing my gaze back to him. All the empathy welling up in my chest nearly strangled me.

But it wasn't for the monster before me.

It was for Mrs. Tulis, whose neck he'd snapped without even so much as a thought. And for her son, Tobias, who I knew no longer had a future. It was for the man the knight had slaughtered on Chaney's command, and those who'd died. It was for the ones who lay in the room off the banquet hall, and for the woman who was most likely dead by now. The burn in my throat and in my eyes was for the boy, who the Ascended had killed just because he could.

Just because he wanted to.

"Open the cell," I ordered.

Kieran stepped forward and unlocked the cell door, and my feet carried me in.

Perhaps this was wrong. Definitely not something the Maiden would do, but I wasn't the Maiden anymore. Truthfully, I'd never been. But even so, a life for a life wasn't right. I knew that. Just as I knew that the hand that now held the dagger had held the hand of the wounded, easing pain instead of causing more.

Casteel or Kieran could end Chaney's life, as could any number of those within the keep who were also owed retribution. The blood didn't need to be on my hands.

But blood had been spilled because of me.

I stopped in front of Lord Chaney and looked up, staring into the one burning eye. There was so much coldness there. The emptiness was vast as he glared at me, straining against the shackles, drawing more blood as he attempted to reach me. A reverberating, whining groan emanated from the Ascended. If he could get free, he would come at me like a Craven, teeth snapping, tearing into my flesh. He would kill me in his hunger, consequences be damned. What I was to the Ascended wouldn't matter. He would feed and feed, and if he hadn't been the one to come to New Haven, he would continue to kill and kill. I stared into the eye, and all I saw were his victims' faces, knowing that many more would remain nameless.

The dagger practically hummed against my palm.

What I'd done to Lord Mazeen had been an act borne of grief and rage, but it still had been an act of revenge. There had been something in the core of who I was that had allowed me to strike the Ascended down. Whatever it was, it was something that Casteel recognized. It was why he had given me this *gift*. He knew I was capable, and maybe that should disturb me. It probably would later.

Or maybe it wouldn't.

I no longer knew what would haunt me, if what used to keep me up at night still would. I was changing, not just day by day, but hour by hour it seemed. And what had governed me before when I wore the veil, no longer ruled over me now.

I held Lord Chaney's gaze. I didn't look away. I didn't say a word as I accepted the Prince's gift, thrusting the bloodstone into the heart of the Ascended.

I watched until the red glow faded from his eye. I watched as his flesh cracked and peeled back, flaking off and scattering as the shackles clattered against the stone wall. I didn't turn until nothing remained but a fine dusting of ash, drifting slowly to the floor.

Sometime later, I sat at the desk in the library, skimming the Atlantian records. I barely saw the letters, even the ones I could read. My thoughts were in a million different places, and I couldn't focus. Sitting back in the chair, I sighed heavily.

"Is there something you wanted to discuss?" Kieran looked up from whatever book he had been thumbing through. Casteel had left him in charge of me while he met with the families of those who had lost a loved one. He hadn't asked if I wanted to take part, but I had enough common sense to realize that my presence would either be unwelcomed or a distraction. What he was doing right now wasn't about me.

"Or is there something you want to ask?" Kieran added. "I'm sure there is something you'd like to ask."

I frowned at the wolven. "There's nothing I want to ask."

"Then why are you sighing every five minutes?"

"I'm not sighing every five minutes. Actually, there *is* something I want to ask," I realized, and his expression turned bland. "This bond you have with Casteel. What does it actually entail? Like are you able to know his thoughts? If something were to happen to him, does it happen to you?"

"I shouldn't be surprised by how incredibly random that was, but I am."

"You're welcome," I quipped.

He closed the book. "I can't read Casteel's thoughts, nor can he read mine."

Thank the gods.

"I can sense his emotions, probably in a way similar to how you can read others. And he can sense mine," he continued. "If something were to happen to him, if he were weakened severely, the bond would allow him to pull energy from me."

I tipped forward. "And when he was held captive?"

Kieran didn't answer for a long moment. "When he left Atlantia, I had no idea what he was about. He didn't want me to go, expressly forbade it, actually."

"And you listened?"

"He forbade it as my Prince. Even I have to obey at times." He grinned. "I wish I hadn't—hell, if I'd known what he was going to do, I would've done everything I could to make him understand how idiotic it was. And if that hadn't worked..." Kieran drew a leg off the coffee table. "I knew he'd been injured when I suddenly fell sick, without any warning. I knew it was no simple injury when the sickness robbed me of all my strength. I knew he'd been captured when I could no longer walk, and no amount of food or water could ease the hunger or keep the weight on me."

"My gods," I whispered. "He was held for—"

"Five decades," Kieran said.

"And you were...you were ill that entire time?"

He nodded.

"Is his brother...is Prince Malik bonded?"

Kieran's features hardened and then smoothed out. "The wolven he was bonded to died while attempting to free him."

Sitting back, I dragged my hands down my face. "What would happen if he were to die? If you died?"

"If either of us were to die, the other would be weakened but would eventually recover."

"So, what does the bond really do? Passes energy between you if you need it?"

He nodded. "The bond is an oath that requires that I obey him and protect him, even at the cost of my own life. Nothing alive today supersedes those bonds."

"And will he do the same for you?"

"He would. It's not required, but all elementals who are bonded would."

Thinking that over, I carefully closed the record book. "How did the bonds get started?"

"The gods," he answered. "When their children—the deities—were first born in this land, they summoned the once wild kiyou wolves and gave them mortal forms so they could serve as their protectors and guides in a world that was unknown to them. They were the first wolven. Eventually, as the elementals began to outnumber the deities, the bonds shifted to them." He leaned forward, resting his arms on his knees. "Not all elementals are bonded. Delano isn't bonded to an elemental."

"What of Casteel's parents?"

"Their wolven died in the war."

"Gods," I whispered. "And Alastir? Is he not bonded?"

"He was until the war," he said, and that was all he needed to say for me to know that whoever he had been bonded to had not survived. "The bonding doesn't often occur now. It's not required of a wolven, and many have simply chosen not to. And if it were still required, there are simply not enough wolven for that to occur widely."

"Because of the war?"

Kieran nodded.

I let my head fall back against the chair. "Is that why the wolven are the most vocal about taking back the land?"

"It is."

"They don't want war." I stared at the ceiling. "They want retribution."

There was no reply. There didn't need to be. I already knew the answer.

"What about you?" I asked. "What do you want?"

"I want what Casteel wants."

"Because of the bond?" I arched a brow.

"Because war should only be a last resort," he answered. "And like Casteel, if it comes to that, I will have to pick up my sword, but I hope it does not."

"Same," I whispered, letting my thoughts drift. "You've seen the blood tree?"

"I have."

"Casteel said the others are saying it's an omen of great change. Alastir said it probably has to do with my marriage to Casteel." I thought of his first reaction. "Do you think it's a warning?"

His eyes met mine. "I think he's right. Your marriage will bring change to both kingdoms, one way or another."

One way or another. Whether we succeeded and prevented a war or failed. I shivered. Neither of us spoke after that. Not until I rose what felt like a small eternity later. "There's something I want to do."

Kieran eyed me and then stood. "Lead the way."

He followed me outside the library and through the hall. Those we passed on the way to the common area gave us a wide berth, and I could feel their stares—some brief, others longer. I didn't need to open my senses to know that some gazes were those of distrust. Word of what I'd done earlier must've made its rounds.

I kept my head high as those in groups whispered to one another. If Kieran heard them, he showed no reaction as we walked outside, under a sky shaded in violet and the deeper blue of the encroaching night. Not wanting to see the blood tree, I didn't look toward the stables. The wind had died, and the only sound was the snow crunching under my boots.

The walk through the woods and to the chamber of names underground was silent. Kieran said nothing as I picked up the chisel and hammer and began searching for an empty space, finding it after several minutes. Halfway down the wall, to the left of the entrance, new names had been carved, the etchings still carrying a layer of stone dust.

The last name was Renfern Octis.

Chest aching, I traced his name and then the dates below it. He'd only been eleven.

Eleven.

I placed the chisel against stone and hammered a name and then two more, the last after I thought I was finished. I knew no birthdates, but I added the last date.

Mrs. Tulis.

Her son, Tobias.

And then I carved Mr. Tulis's name into the wall. His death may not have come at the hands of the Ascended, but it was they who'd driven him to his death.

Chapter 19

How could——?

Momma!

Jerking upright with a scream lodged in my throat, I reached out blindly, my hand smacking on the nightstand until my fingers closed around the handle of the wolven dagger.

"Poppy," came Casteel's sleep-roughened voice from beside me, startling me. When had he come back? It had to have been after I'd fallen asleep. "Is it a nightmare?"

Swallowing hard, I nodded as I closed my eyes. Immediately, I saw my mother's horrified face and the pain in her gaze. There was so much blood—running down the front of her gown, pouring from the wounds in her chest. Not bites. Not—

Chest squeezing too tight, air wheezed from my lungs. My eyes flew open, but I could swear I heard the screams. Not shrieks. But screams, and the scent…the scent of burning wood.

The bed shifted as Casteel sat up. Gently, he pried my fingers from the dagger. "I'm just putting this down. It's still within reach in case you want to stab me."

I watched him lean over me, placing it on my other side. "I don't want to stab you," I croaked out.

"That would be a first," he teased, and I hiccupped a shaky laugh. "Try to remember you said that later when I'm sure I'll give you a reason to stab me."

I shook my head, lifting shaking hands to my face. "I'm sorry." I dragged my hair back. "I didn't mean to wake you. I know we have to leave early."

Delano had returned after the awkward dinner in the banquet hall, where people either stared or whispered until Casteel's cool gaze silenced them. The roads were clear enough that Casteel felt it was safe to leave New Haven.

"What did I tell you before?" Casteel asked. "Don't apologize. It's not your fault. Don't worry about it."

That was easier said than done.

"Do you think you can go back to sleep?"

"Yeah." I lay back down, curled on my side. The flames in the fireplace rippled softly, and the longer I stared at them, the more images from the nightmare started to piece themselves together. The mist…it had been as thick as smoke. It had almost smelled like burnt wood and something pungent. Wasn't that what Ian and I had thought it was at first? Was that why I'd left to find my father? I tried to picture his face, to see his eyes, but no matter how hard I tried, I couldn't. All I could see was red. So much red—on the walls and pooled on the floor, bodies shredded open. But no Craven. There had been no Craven feeding on those bodies. Why? Why was there so much blood—?

A surge of restless energy poured back through me, drumming up the residual fear and panic. I couldn't lay here. I couldn't close my eyes.

Sitting up, I started to move from the bed, but Casteel hooked his arm around my waist. "I can't lay here. I can't sleep. I just need—"

"To forget." In the fire's glow, he touched my cheek, bringing my gaze to his. "I know. I get it. I do."

Sucking in too-shallow breaths, I knew he of all people did understand. I folded my hands over my face. "I don't want to think about that night." Tears burned my throat, and I hated them—hated this glaring weakness. "I want to forget."

"But you need to feel to do that. You need to replace that

fear with something else. That's why you used to explore the city at night," he said, pulling my hands away from my face. "But there's no city for you to run off to. All you have is me."

All you have is me.

My heart twisted itself up into a knot.

"Let me help you replace the fear and helplessness. I can erase it. I promise," he whispered, guiding me back until I was lying down once more. "Let me be enough, at least for tonight."

"I…" I ran out of words as he shifted so he blocked out the fire's glow, leaving me in the darkness of the room.

"There's just us. No one else." His lips brushed my cheek, causing me to gasp. "Like earlier, in the pantry, we can pretend."

I closed my eyes.

"Right now, in the dark, I'm just Hawke." His arm eased from my waist as his hand drifted over my hip and down my thigh, to where the gown tangled around my legs. "You're just Poppy, and I can help you."

Maybe it was the nightmare. It could've been the darkness and the sudden, throbbing ache that sprang to life. Or perhaps it was because in the darkness we could be Hawke and Poppy, with no past and no future. And pretending…pretending made none of this real. Maybe all of those things were the reason I turned my head to his. Our lips brushed.

"Pretend," I whispered, and I…I kissed him.

Casteel let me explore his mouth, holding himself still, all except for his hand. He slowly drew his palm up my hip, my stomach, and moved it between my breasts, dragging the hem of the gown up until it gathered below my neck. Cool air followed, teasing my exposed skin.

I kissed him, trembling when I felt his palm on my breast. The tip hardened to an almost painful point. His thumb moved lazily over the peak and then to the other as he said, "I wish you could see what I'm about to do."

I wet my lips as he pulled away, his thumb dragging over the rosy, puckered skin. Then he did something with his thumb and forefinger, causing my entire body to jolt, and a rush of wet warmth to pool between my thighs.

"Gods," I gasped.

"Mmm." His mouth coasted along the skin of my neck again. "You like that?"

There was no point in answering that. He knew it, and he did it again. My hips moved on reflex, spurred on by the rapidly building ache between my thighs. He hadn't—we hadn't—touched like this since the woods after I'd stabbed him, but my body hadn't forgotten. I was blossoming with heat.

His mouth closed over my breast, and the combination of his tongue and the sharp rasp of his fangs caused me to kick my head back. A breathy moan left me as my eyes peeled open wide. He tugged at the skin with his mouth as his hand drifted down my stomach and lower, over the very center of me. It was the lightest, softest touch, teasing and taunting.

"You're very wet, Poppy," he murmured against the aching peak of my breast. "I like that. A lot."

Incapable of embarrassment or being shocked by the rawness of his words, I could only whimper as his finger moved in slow, lazy strokes.

"I also like how quickly you respond to my touch." He nipped at the skin of my other breast as he swirled his thumb around the sensitive flesh. "Want me to do something about it?"

I panted for breath. "Yes."

Casteel answered by pressing down on the bundle of nerves. Crying out, I arched against his hand, and I felt like I was drenched, drowning already. Just as his mouth closed over my breast once more, he slipped a finger inside me. A strangled sort of sound left me, and there was no room for thoughts of a night from long ago or worries for the morning that was quickly approaching. My heart thundered in my chest.

He dragged that finger in and out as he lifted his head, and even though I couldn't see, I knew he could. I knew he watched his hand between my spread thighs. I knew he was fixated on what he was doing, on the way I lifted my hips to meet his thrusts. He watched as he eased another finger into the tight wetness. My eyes drifted shut again, and I knew this was what he'd wanted to do earlier, in the pantry. I gave in to this, into the wet heat and the darkness and the wickedness of his touch. Casteel groaned as I ground my hips against his hand.

"That's it." His voice was rough. "Ride my fingers."

I did just that, rocking against his hands as the stirrings of release ratcheted up. Then tension, still painfully unfamiliar, spun and spun until it felt like too much. "Oh, gods, I can't..." I pressed my hips against the bed.

"You can." He kept going, thrusting his fingers inside me. "You will."

It was too much, too intense, and there was no escaping it. He hooked his fingers deep inside me, and lava flowed through my blood. And just when I thought I would surely erupt into flames...

"That's it." His voice was gruff and thick.

Biting down on my lip as the tension curled and twisted deeper, tighter, I buried my face against the crook of his arm. His lips brushed my cheek as he pressed his thumb to the tight bundle of nerves. My hips lifted from the bed as all the tension shattered. It was like lightning in my veins. The sweetest kind of agony, scattering my thoughts as the release rippled and eased as he withdrew his fingers. Sated and stunned, I went utterly boneless, exhausted and limp as Casteel gathered me close. The blanket settled over me—over us—as he pulled me against his chest. Under my cheek, his heart thudded steadily.

The heart I'd pierced not all that long ago.

Casteel held me tightly, closely, his hand continuously sliding up and down the length of my spine. I didn't know if he even realized what kind of comfort his closeness or his touch brought. Maybe he did, and that was why he remained in the room even knowing that I could wake him at any point in the night. There were other rooms, other far quieter and definitely less complicated beds, but he was here. He held me, soothing my ragged nerves after chasing away the lingering horror of a night I wanted nothing more than to forget. He helped me forget while offering pleasure and bliss to replace the fear and hopelessness, and he did this while taking nothing in return.

I fell back asleep, into the darkness where I was just Poppy, and he was simply Hawke.

We were leaving.

For Atlantia.

Those dark, private moments in the middle of the night seemed like an eternity ago instead of mere hours as I took a too-shallow breath. I studied those with us. Naill and Delano were with Elijah, and I had no idea if they were in on the plan Casteel had concocted, so I remained quiet. I'd spent the better part of the morning stressing over how I was supposed to act. The concern that had faded in the aftermath of the arrival of the Ascended and everything else had now returned with a vengeance.

"Would you like anything else before we leave?" Casteel asked, and then I felt a slight tug on my braid. "Poppy?"

Realizing that he was speaking to me, I shook my head. "No. I'm fine. Thank you."

Both Kieran and Casteel stared at me, and the silence stretched on so long that I had to look to see if they were still there. Looking over my shoulder, I found both of them staring down at me, their expressions near mirrors of perplexity.

"What?" I demanded.

"Nothing." Casteel blinked. "You're ready, then?"

I nodded.

Watching me as if I were a coiled snake about to strike, he extended his hand. I started to rise without accepting his palm but caught myself. A quick glance told me that the others waited near the door. Figuring that refusing such a simple gesture wouldn't be a good start at convincing others that we were together, I placed my hand in his.

The contact of his skin against mine sent another charged jolt through me. My eyes flew to his, but there was no knowledge to be gained from his heavily hooded gaze this time as he helped me stand.

"Is everything ready?" Kieran asked.

"It is," he replied. "Elijah thinks we'll make it to Spessa's End by the end of the week if we don't make a lot of stops."

"It's doable," Kieran agreed. "And advisable."

"The people here have only a few days before the Ascended send others looking for her," Casteel said as he reached between us, plucking up the edge of my braid. "They'll send scouts and probably more knights." Dropping my plait over my shoulder, he then reached for my satchel.

Kieran nodded. "Magda returned earlier this morning. She said she thinks most will be ready to travel in a day or so."

"Good." Casteel glanced down at me. Unsure what to do, I decided on silence as the best course of action. After all, it used to be second-nature, even though I'd struggled to remain quiet when I first donned the veil. Kieran thought I asked a lot of questions now, there would be a wolven-shaped hole in the wall in his desperation to get away from me if he'd known me when I was younger.

Sending me a curious look, Casteel started toward the others. Naill and Delano nodded in my direction, saying nothing. It was Elijah who spoke. "I haven't gotten a chance to thank you for what you did yesterday—helping those who accepted it."

Shifting uncomfortably, I cleared my throat. "I just hope I helped."

"You did. Pain is the biggest obstacle healing faces, and you stepping in when you did is a big reason why we won't be sitting around here for longer than we should." A big smile parted his beard. "I also haven't gotten the chance to congratulate either of you on the upcoming nuptials. To be honest, every day I half-expected to find the Prince sliced up in all the ways a man fears."

I blinked slowly.

Casteel chuckled deeply. "You're not the only one. I expected to be picking up pieces of myself." He glanced down at me, his lips slightly parted. "But I was once told that the best relationships are the ones where passions run high."

My brows started to pucker.

"I wonder who told you that," Kieran said.

"It was me." Elijah laughed as he clapped his hand on Kieran's shoulder, causing the wolven to stumble. Skin crinkled around golden-brown hazel eyes, and even though I wished the topic was about anything other than this, I was happy to see him smile and laugh after what'd happened here. But it made me wonder if it was because he'd become so accustomed to the death that the effects weren't long-lasting. "Told him that if a woman fights with that kind of passion and makes you work that hard to earn even a smile, then that's the kind of woman you want by your side in and out of the bedchamber."

My mouth opened, but I truly had nothing to say.

"I've always thought you had a wolven somewhere in your bloodline," Kieran commented.

Elijah scoffed. "Told you before, there's just piss and whiskey in my line."

"Maybe that's the real bloodline you descend from," Casteel murmured as he led me past them.

I raised my brows but said nothing as we entered the empty hall and then exited out into the yard. The snow had stopped, but my breath formed misty clouds. I was so going to regret leaving my cloak behind, even soaked with the stench of Craven blood.

As we made our way to the stables, unease formed upon the sight of leaves that glistened like rubies in the sunlight. No one was out there staring at it this morning, but I could swear the blood tree had grown even wider than it had been the day before. Crimson hued sap still seeped across the snow in a network of thin lines of red, reminding me of veins or roots.

Three horses were led out already, their ears perked as a stable hand held their reins, nervously glancing toward the blood tree. Casteel walked us past them, where Setti waited inside the stables. The massive black horse had been named after the God of War's warhorse. I used to think that the beautiful horse had big hooves to fill, but now, knowing the truth, I imagined Setti filled them just fine.

As we approached the horse, Casteel let go of my hand. My palm missed the warmth, which was something I'd never share. I walked up to Setti as Casteel walked around to secure my satchel to where his own bag hung. My gaze crawled across the barn, stopping on a pole with a deep groove. Knowing what had caused that mark, I resisted the desire to look away from where Phillips had been killed with a bolt fired by Casteel. But I made myself look, to remember. Phillips had somehow figured out the truth, or at the very least, that Casteel was not who he claimed. He'd tried to help me escape, but I hadn't listened. I had no idea if Phillips had known the truth about the Ascended. He could have, but that didn't matter. He was dead, regardless.

Exhaling slowly, I saw the very same bow attached to Setti's side. It was curved like the ones I'd used, but this one had a handle and an arrow already nocked in place. The weapon was unlike any I'd ever seen. It had to be Atlantian.

I extended my hand to the horse, allowing him to sniff me. "Remember me?"

Setti sniffed as Casteel finished with the straps. The horse nudged my fingers, and I grinned as I gently patted the bridge of his nose.

"I think he missed you." Casteel joined me. "And I think he's been spoiled by all the attention you've showered upon him."

I didn't think it was possible to spoil any animal too much. I scratched him behind his ear.

Casteel was closer, and out of the corner of my eye, I saw him stroke a hand down Setti's mane. Looking to the back of the barn, he lowered his hand. "I'll be right back."

Nibbling on my lower lip, I peeked over my shoulder. Casteel strode across the barn to where an older woman had appeared. She held something dark in her hands. Setti nudged my fingers again, demanding my attention.

"All right. All right." I resumed petting him. "Sorry."

Stroking the long, graceful neck, I saw that Delano and Naill were already mounted. Kieran walked toward his horse, but it didn't appear as if Elijah was coming with us.

A moment later, Casteel returned. "Here," he said. "You're going to need this until we reach Spessa's End."

This turned out to be a cloak, a black one lined with soft fur. I turned to take it, but Casteel moved behind me, draping it over my shoulders.

"I had one of the seamstresses make it since salvaging the old one was out of the question," he continued as he reached around me.

I didn't dare breathe too deeply as his fingers worked the

buttons under my throat. I tried not to focus on how close he was or how—I swallowed a gasp as the backs of his fingers brushed my breasts, reminding me of last night. I really didn't need to think about that.

His arms grazed my chest. How many buttons were there? I looked down and almost groaned. The line of shiny black discs ended just below the chest.

"Just so you know, I burned it along with the Craven," he went on, and my pulse thrummed as his chin grazed my cheek. "We lucked out that one of the seamstresses already had this mostly finished. There. Now, you'll be less likely to spend the entire trip begging for my body heat. Though, I'd be more than happy to appease such a request."

I was sure he would be. "Thank you," I murmured.

His hands slipped away from the buttons to my shoulders and then down my arms, leaving shivers in their wake. Shivers that spread down my front. Looking up, I saw Elijah heading our way, and I almost waved at him in relief.

"One moment," Casteel called out, and Elijah stopped. A moment later, he turned me in his arms so that I was facing him. "Are you all right?"

Lifting my gaze to his, I briefly wondered how he could have such incredibly thick lashes. "Yes."

His gaze searched mine. "You're being very quiet."

I was, but how did I explain that it was because I had no idea how I was supposed to behave? I was sure that he'd probably find that silly, my lack of knowledge so great that I had no idea how to even pretend.

"Is it what you did in the cell?" he asked.

"No," I answered quickly.

"Is it the people here?"

I shook my head.

His features tensed. "Then is it about last night?"

"No," I said without hesitation. Probably too quickly based on the sudden flare of light in his eyes. "I'm just a little tired."

He watched me intently. "I'm not sure it's that."

"It is," I told him. "It's not what happened last night or anything else. You know I didn't get a lot of sleep."

He eyed me in a way that said he wasn't quite sure he believed my response, but after a moment, he nodded. Stepping back, he motioned for Elijah to join us.

"I still think you'll make good time," Elijah said as he grasped Setti's reins.

"Let's hope so." Casteel's hands settled on my hips.

I froze.

"Put one foot in the stirrup," he reminded me gently. "And then grab the horn. I'll lift you."

Feeling about seven different kinds of inadequate, I reached up and gripped the horn. Most people learned to ride by the time they hit their teens.

"You're not familiar with horses, eh?" Elijah asked.

I shook my head, expecting to hear mockery in his tone, or at the very least, disbelief. I didn't hear any of that.

"Never would've guessed that, seeing you over here all comfy with this temperamental ass."

"Hey," Casteel said. "You saying things like that is why he's a temperamental ass towards you."

Elijah laughed as Setti's ears lowered. "Make sure he teaches you how to ride," he said as Casteel lifted me with ease. "You seem like a natural."

"That's on an exceedingly long to-do list of things I plan to teach her," Casteel replied as I settled in the saddle.

Did he really plan to do that? Excitement sparked. If I could ride and control a horse, I'd be able to travel easily once I was free. It would be a necessary skill, to be honest.

Wait.

What were the other things he planned?

The grin Elijah sent to Casteel didn't go unnoticed. "I bet you do."

Heat flooded my face, even though I only had an inkling of what the innuendo meant.

"You still think you'll have the first group out within two days?" Casteel asked as he swung up behind me with startling ease. I was sure if I tried that, I'd end up belly-flopping across the saddle and then sliding off it.

"I hope to get the first group out by tomorrow morning,"

Elijah told him.

"Good. I'll be waiting for them to arrive in Spessa's End before I continue on to Atlantia. At least then, I will feel a little better about crossing the Skotos," he said. "But I don't want you to wait too long. Just because the western roads are clear now, you know they won't stay that way for long."

"And you know I'm not leaving until the last one is well on the way home."

Thinking of all the people being forced to abandon their homes saddened me. It didn't matter that it had been planned long before my arrival. I'd sped up those plans.

"I know. That is why you've been entrusted with these people." Casteel took the reins Elijah handed him. "I expect to see you home, my friend."

"You will." Elijah looked at me. "Keep our Prince in line and do so vigilantly. I expect to hear many stories that involve you throwing down with him."

"You really don't need to encourage her." Casteel curled an arm around my waist, and a heartbeat later, I was nestled between his thighs, my back pressed to his front.

Although I hadn't forgotten about the lack of personal space while on horseback, my memories of it had dimmed. I wasn't sure I needed the cloak, but I knew from past experience that there was no point in sitting straight as a pole. All I would succeed in doing was causing my back to ache and my bones to feel jostled. And besides, I didn't think a happy…fiancée would pull away from their intended husband.

And, truthfully, I didn't want to. I had no idea how much of that desire had to do with avoiding how uncomfortable it would be, or if it was because of last night, his gift, the pantry, the secrets he shared, and all the moments in between.

Elijah bent his arm, pressing his fist to his heart. "From blood and ash."

"We will rise," Casteel finished, and my stomach dipped in response. Those words were the mark of the Dark One, his promise to his people and his supporters scattered throughout the kingdoms that they would rise once again.

Those words had once been a harbinger of chaos, the

bringer of pain and death. And now, the Dark One sat behind me.

I was to marry him.

Temporarily.

And I'd allowed him to kiss me. To touch.

Because we were pretending.

None of this was real.

"Until next time." Elijah bowed in my direction.

"I hope your travels are uneventful," I said, surprising myself, and maybe even Casteel, because his arm tightened in response. I meant it, because…well, I liked the way Elijah always laughed.

Even when it annoyed me.

And the people here didn't need to experience any more violence or heartbreak.

"As do I." Elijah grinned, stepping back. "Though I doubt she needs it, keep her safe, Prince."

"I always keep what is mine safe," Casteel murmured, and my eyes narrowed as he gave Setti a soft nudge.

Setti trotted forward. The other three were waiting, and we ended up in the middle of the group as we rode out into the yard and passed the eerie warning the gods had left behind. My heart matched the steady thud of Setti's hooves as I gripped the pommel.

"Where are your gloves?" Casteel asked.

I found my voice after a moment. "In the satchel."

"They won't do any good there." He switched the reins to the hand that was at my waist, and then he was handing them over. "Spessa's End is farther south. It will be warmer there."

I took the gloves, slowly pulling them on while my heart leapt. Up ahead, the roofs of homes came into view. Sparing a look behind me, I saw only the edges of the stone keep before it too disappeared.

The mixture of nervousness and anticipation swirling inside me was a strange companion as I turned back around. In a few minutes, once we left the Rise surrounding New Haven, there would be no more chances to escape if I wanted to. We would be traveling too far to the east. I had to be fully committed to this deal I'd struck with Casteel—to his plan. Because now, there was no turning back.

"By the way, I'm not yours," I told him. "I don't belong to anyone but myself. Nothing changes that."

"What if I just wanted a piece of you?" He shifted the reins to his other hand. "A tiny piece that belonged to me? I can think of a few I would love to have, Princess."

My cheeks warmed. "I bet you can."

His laugh was rough and deep. "Tell me what piece of you I can have. It can be any piece of your choosing. Whatever it is, I'll take it." His chin grazed my cheek. "It will be my most prized possession."

I didn't offer Casteel a piece of me as we rode forward, joining the others. There was no reason to because what he didn't know was that he already held too many of them.

Chapter 20

"You've been entirely too quiet today," Casteel pointed out again, several hours into the ride to Spessa's End.

"Have I?" I asked, knowing full well there was no point denying it. The back of my neck tightened. Conversation had hummed all around me. Jokes had been shared. Playful insults were often traded, and while Casteel was their Prince, his status didn't give him immunity. Few questions and comments had been directed at me, mostly about my training and how I was able to keep it hidden. Other than explaining how I trained with Vikter, I remained silent.

There was less opportunity for me to mess up that way.

"You have," he said.

Aware of how close Delano and Naill were, riding only a few paces behind us, I said, "I've been...caught up in the scenery."

"The scenery?" he repeated. "You've been engrossed in staring at...trees?"

My brow creased as I nodded. Tall pines crowded the road to Spessa's End, growing so close to one another, their branches stretched from tree to tree. Very little could be seen beyond them.

"I had no idea you were so invested in the common evergreen."

The corners of my lips turned down as I stiffened, pulling away from where I'd been leaning into Casteel. "I would think you'd be grateful that I'm quiet."

"Why in the world would you think I'd be grateful for that?"

I sent him an arched brow over my shoulder. "Really?" I drawled in a low voice.

His eyes narrowed, and as I returned to staring at the snow-tipped pines, he nudged Setti forward. The large horse responded at once, drawing ahead of the group. "What's really going on with you?" he asked, his voice low.

"I have no idea what you're talking about." I lifted my head at the flutter of wings. A bird, larger than I'd ever seen, took flight from the top of one of the pines, soaring gracefully into the sky. The wingspan was enormous, at least several feet. "Good gods, what kind of bird is that?"

"I do believe it's a silver hawk. They're known to snatch small animals and even children if they're hungry enough."

My eyes widened. "I'd heard stories about birds that could pick up children, but I thought they were just tales."

"I'm sure many things in these woods are the subject of such tales, but there is only one tale I'm interested in hearing." Using his arm around my waist to tug me back against him, his voice was just above my ear as he added, "And that is why you're suddenly as quiet as a ghost."

"Do you need to hold me this tightly to ask that question?" I snapped.

He chuckled. "There she is—my Princess."

"I've been here this whole time, and I'm not your Princess."

"Technically, you *are* my Princess, and no, you haven't been here the whole time," he replied. "The Poppy I know isn't quiet and meek. At least not the one without the veil."

I stared ahead mutinously as his observation struck too close to home for comfort.

"And this Poppy, the one who says nothing, only showed up this morning," he went on. "You say it's not because you chose to be the one who ended that bastard Ascended's life. I know you well enough to believe that."

"I don't know why you think you know me so well," I retorted, even though he did know more about me than anyone, including Vikter, Tawny, and my brother.

"I know that you did what you felt was right and that is the end of that. You're not one to wallow in your choices," he said, and he *was* right. Ugh. "You said it wasn't because of last night, and I'm inclined to believe that to be the truth."

"If I said I didn't care what you believe, would it make a difference and force you to be quiet?"

"No."

I sighed.

"I'm a wagering sort of man, so I'm willing to bet it has everything to do with our *understanding*."

Irritation flared hotly. Why did he have to be so observant? It was annoying.

"So, instead of telling me nothing is wrong, I'm hoping you'll be honest with me."

"I'm hoping that hawk returns, and instead of snatching up poor helpless animals and children, it grabs you."

Casteel laughed, the sound rumbling through me. I knew if I turned around, I would see the hint of fangs and those damn dimples. "I fear that your hopes will go unanswered."

"As per usual," I muttered.

He ignored that. "I'm not going to let this go, and you of all people should know that I'm persistent when I want something."

A shiver curled down my spine, and the hand that had ended up between the folds of my cloak at some point during the journey, slid from my hip to my stomach. Swallowing hard, I ordered myself to think of anything that didn't involve his hand and how low it sat on my belly.

"Talk to me, Poppy," he whispered near my ear as his fingers began to move. Every cell in my body seemed to focus on those digits. "Please?"

Please.

The soft request caught me off guard. It was so rare to hear that word pass his lips, even before his identity had been revealed. I gave a small shake of my head. "I…I don't know how to act."

He angled his head so he could look at me. "What do you mean?"

His fingers were still moving, tracing circles that swept above my navel and then below. My face felt hot, and I wasn't sure if it was due to embarrassment or the slow, lazy pace of his movements, which reminded me too much of those dark, early morning hours. "I don't know how I'm supposed to behave in a way that will convince others that we're…together."

His fingers halted for a heartbeat and then started moving once more. "You just need to be yourself, Poppy."

That sounded easier said than done. "Being myself would likely mean arguing with you constantly—"

"And threatening to stab me," he interjected. "I know."

"How is me threatening to stab you going to convince anyone that this engagement is real?"

"I'll admit, that would lead the average person to believe there were no fond feelings between us, but no one would believe that I would choose a submissive Maiden over my brother. They'd expect me to fall for someone as fiery as she is kind, brave…even to a fault. Someone who pushes back." His fingers now moved up and down in a straight line, but for once, his words were far more distracting. "They'd expect someone like you, to be honest. Not the veiled Maiden. That is not who you are."

Unsettled by what he'd said, my grip tightened on the pommel. "You're right. I'm not the veiled Maiden. Not anymore, but I…" My gaze lifted to the strip of gray sky. "It's what I'm used to, I guess. I'm not used to this."

"I imagine you're not used to any of this, and I don't mean the whole being kidnapped part."

A wry grin twisted my lips. "All of this is new. The lack of the veil and being allowed to speak whenever I want, to whomever I want. Or being able to use my abilities and not hide them. I can't even remember the last time I ate supper at a table with more than just one or two people. I'm not used to being in a room full of individuals, being the center of attention, yet somehow still invisible to them. I…" I trailed off before I admitted what had found its way to the surface. I wasn't sure if even I knew who I was without the veil and all its limitations, because even though there were still rules, new ones to follow, this was unlike anything before. "I guess what I was like as the Maiden—"

"What you were forced to be like as the Maiden," he corrected softly.

I nodded. "I guess it's what I'm comfortable with when I don't know what's expected of me. And silence—docility—was always expected."

"But was it easy?"

The sweep of his fingers, drifting even lower, snagged my attention, sending a flash of molten heat through me and causing me to wonder if I had the foresight to set boundaries with this whole agreement. Surely, what he was doing with his hand wouldn't convince anyone of our relationship since it was hidden beneath the cloak.

"Princess?" he murmured, his lips grazing my ear.

I exhaled shakily, hoping that what Kieran had said about Casteel and a wolven's ability to scent desire was grossly exaggerated. "I…I often wanted to scream—just scream for no good reason, in the middle of the Great Hall during the City Council meetings. I would've loved to have screamed right in Priestess Analia's face."

He barked out a short, rough laugh. "I would've expected a far more violent desire when it came to that bitch. And I still don't use that word often, yet I use it proudly when it comes to her."

I grinned, feeling a savage joy at seeing the Priestess's eyes widen when Hawke had put her in her place. "And I…I hated just standing there and listening to the Duke get upset because I didn't walk quietly enough—"

"He seriously lectured you about that?"

"Yes." I laughed, but there was nothing funny about any of this. "He'd lecture me about anything. Find any reason for a *lesson*. Not standing straight enough. Being too quiet. Not speaking quickly enough when spoken to—when I was allowed to respond, which was everchanging. I…" I shook my head. "I wanted to scream in his face—no, that's not true. I wanted to punch him. Often. With my fists." I paused. "With a dagger."

Casteel was silent for a moment. "How did you deal with him? That's something I can't wrap my head around. You're not weak. You're not a pushover. That's inherently the opposite of who you are. How did you never push back?"

I stiffened, feeling shame creep in. "I couldn't."

"I know that," he immediately reassured. "I didn't mean to suggest that you could have. You were trapped. Just like I was, and if anyone thinks you should have, then they have never been in a position where they had to do anything to survive."

I relaxed a little. "I just...you know, it took a couple of times for me to learn how to disassociate from it. I would be there, but I would think of something—anything—else. Sometimes, I thought about all the ways I would one day pay him back for every foul thing he did or said. Other times, I imagined training with Vikter. When it was too hard to focus, I just counted. I would count as high as I could."

He seemed to have stopped breathing. "I'm glad I killed him."

"Me, too." I cleared my throat. "Anyway, it wasn't always easy, but sometimes, it was...easier to just do what they wanted, to be what they expected. I know that sounds terrible."

"Maybe to those who've never survived a cane to the skin for no reason." His voice had hardened. "We all do what we need to survive. I did countless things I never thought I would do," he admitted freely without an ounce of shame. And I...

I envied that, but our situations were different. His was a matter of survival, life and death. Mine was not that. "But I think choosing the easier path is why I ignored my suspicions about the Ascended, or at least, it helped to dismiss them."

"I don't think you were alone in choosing that path. I'm sure many others in Solis have shared your suspicions, but it was easier to look past them, even if that meant suffering or sacrifice."

I nodded. "Because the alternative would be the upending of everything you believe to be true. And not only that, it comes with the realization of the part you played. At least for me, it does. I was toted out to the people, put on display to remind everyone that the gods could choose anyone—that they too could be Blessed one day. And I always knew I wasn't Chosen," I whispered the last part, my chest heavy. "But I went along with it. And the whole time, they were stealing children to feed on. Taking good people and turning them into monsters. The easier choice I made too often didn't make me a part of the problem."

Casteel said nothing, but his fingers still moved idly.

"It made me a part of the system that bound an entire kingdom in chains created of fear and false beliefs." I turned my cheek toward him. "You know that's true."

"Yes." His breath danced along the corner of my lips. "It is true."

I lowered my gaze to the hardened soil of the road.

"But you know what else is true? Right now, you are destroying an intricate section of the system that has chained an entire kingdom for hundreds of years," he added. "You should never forget that you were once an accessory, but you also shouldn't forget what you are now a part of."

I looked forward, at the narrow road ahead and the snow-heavy needles. "But does the present really make amends for the past?"

Casteel didn't answer immediately. "Who is the judge of that? The gods? They sleep. Society? How can they make decisions unbiasedly when they are prejudiced by their own sins?" he questioned, and I had no answer. "Let me ask you this. Do you blame Vikter?"

I frowned. "For what?"

"He was like a father to you, Poppy. He had to know how much you struggled with the whole Maiden thing. Even if he didn't realize how much you struggled, he had to have seen it."

The last conversation I'd had with Vikter, right before the attack at the Rite, had been about how I truly felt being the Maiden.

"And he knew what the Duke was doing to you, didn't he? But he didn't stop it," he added quietly.

I craned my head to the side. "What could he have done? If he spoke one word or intervened, he would've been fired and ostracized, and that is a fate close to a death sentence. Or, he would've been killed. And then I wouldn't have been trained. I never would've learned how to defend myself. Vikter did everything he could," I defended vehemently. "Just like my mother and father did the night they were killed."

"But one could argue that the right thing would've been to intervene. To stop the Duke from hurting you," he said. "And I know I'm not one to talk about doing the right thing, but he could've chosen the more difficult path. Either way, you don't hold it against him. And if you did, you've forgiven him, right?"

Heart aching, I faced forward. "There was nothing to forgive. But he...you heard what he said to me before he died."

"He apologized for failing you," Casteel confirmed.

Tears burned the backs of my eyes. His last words ever spoken were brutal. I hadn't regretted what I'd said to him before the attack, but now? Now, I wished I hadn't spoken so freely. I would do anything for Vikter to have died feeling as if he'd done right by me. And he had done just that to the best of his ability. He was the reason I could hold a sword and fire an arrow, fight with my hands and my mind.

"I think Vikter knew that you never held his inaction against him, but whether or not he believed he'd done all that he could was up to him," Casteel continued softly. "I think it comes down to whether you can make amends with yourself."

I saw the point he was making, but I didn't know if anything I did from this moment on would be enough to erase being a silent party to the Ascended.

"In the meantime, while you try to figure out if you can make amends with yourself, it helps to find someone to blame. And in your case—and Vikter's—blame can be shared."

"With the Ascended?" I surmised.

"Do you not agree?"

The Ascended created the system Vikter and I and everyone else became a part of, unintentionally reinforced, and ultimately became victims of in different ways. My mother hadn't been able to defend herself or me because of the limitations the Ascended placed upon women. Families handed over their children to the Court or to the Temples because the Ascended taught them it was the only way to appease the gods and then used the very monsters they created to reinforce those fears. Mr. Tulis made the choice to shove a knife deep inside me, but the kingdom the Ascended created was what drove him to that. Vikter could never speak against the Duke without repercussions that would've either had him removed from my life completely or ended his. And I...

I had my freedom stripped from me and was kept so sheltered that I could turn to no one with my suspicions. And the Queen, she who cared for me so tenderly, was the foundation of that system. There was no denying that. Nor was there any denying that the system would only strengthen and grow unless access to the Atlantians was cut off. Even without the ability to make more Ascended, they would still be strong if they remained in control. If Casteel's father did not go to war against them.

But war was never one-sided. Casualties always piled up on both sides, and the losses were always the greatest among the most innocent. Many of those who would be free if Atlantia went to war with Solis would die before they even realized how much they'd been chained.

"Yes. They are to blame," I said finally, raggedly. I had no idea how we strayed so far off topic. Brushing a stray piece of hair back from my face, I cleared my throat. "So, there is your answer to why I've been quiet. If I'd known that insulting and threatening you would convince others of our agreement, I would've pulled a knife on you this morning in the banquet hall."

"Well, I wouldn't go that far," he said, squeezing me. "But if I may make a suggestion? I would stop calling our engagement an agreement or understanding. That sounds entirely too business-like. As if we're discussing the trade of milk cows."

"But isn't that what this is?"

"I would say that what we have is a very intimate agreement. So, no."

"What we have is simply an impersonal agreement and nothing more."

"Impersonal? Is that so?" His hand drifted lower, over the flap of buttons on my pants.

My breath hitched. "Yes."

"Truly?"

"*Yes,*" I hissed.

"Interesting. It didn't seem impersonal last night," he murmured, and then caught the lobe of my ear between his teeth. I gasped, my eyes wide as the little nip set fire to my blood. Slowly freeing the sensitive flesh, he chuckled as his lips touched the space behind my ear, and then I felt the indecent thrill of his sharp teeth dragging over the skin of my throat.

For a moment, all thoughts scattered. My boiling blood roared in my ears, through my body, tightening my breasts and settling between my legs, where his fingers ventured dangerously close. They made those tiny circles that tugged at the seam of my pants, rubbing it against my very center. My back arched without thought, and a hidden, reckless part of me wished I could will those fingers lower—

"And now?" he repeated. "Sure doesn't feel impersonal."

I reacted without thought, slamming my elbow into his stomach. Casteel grunted out a curse.

"Please don't fight atop the horse," Delano called out from somewhere behind us. "None of us wish to watch Setti trample either of you."

"Speak for yourself," came Kieran's droll voice.

Casteel straightened behind me. "Don't worry. Neither of us will fall. It was just a love tap."

"That did not look like a love tap," Naill commented.

"That's because it was a very passionate one," Casteel replied.

"You're about to get a love tap to your face," I muttered under my breath.

Casteel curled his arm more firmly around my waist as he laughed. "There's the vicious little creature. I missed her."

"Whatever," I grumbled.

He leaned into me, lowering his voice once more. "Back to the original subject at hand, our *engagement* is far more believable when you're hitting me than when you're standing by quietly."

My brows snapped together. "That sounds like a very dysfunctional…engagement."

"You can't spell dysfunctional without fun, now can you?"

"That…I don't even know what to say to that."

"My point is that you just need to be yourself, Princess. Couples argue. They fight. Most don't go around stabbing or punching the other—"

"Most don't start off being lied to or kidnapped," I interrupted.

"True, which has led to the stabbing and punching, but people who are in love enough to marry—the ones that people know are together before they even realize it—never consist of just one person, one personality, or one will. They fight. They argue. They disagree. They make up. They talk. They agree. The one thing they never are is perfect."

"Are you telling me that the key is for us to fight and make up?" I asked, because there was no way anyone could look at us, see the way we behaved toward each other, and think we were madly in love. They probably thought we were insane.

"What I'm telling you is that there is no one way anyone behaves in a relationship. There isn't a textbook of things to do or how to behave with the exception of the stabbing. I take back my fun in dysfunctional statement."

"Thank the gods."

"I just want to make sure you understand that, so when you're free and if you decide to leave—"

"If? You mean when I leave?"

"Yes. My apologies," he demurred. "*When* you leave and go out into the world and find yourself a mate who has never lied—"

"Or kidnapped me?"

"Or kidnapped you, there should be no stabbing or punching. Only kisses and promises upheld until dying breaths and beyond," he said. "That is what you deserve from who you choose to love."

I didn't know what to make of that—of him speaking of me…me loving someone else—loving someone for real. Acid pooled in my stomach.

"The thing is, you won't mess up if you get mad. You won't do the wrong thing. Each couple is different. Some spend their time whispering sweet words in each other's ears. Some spend the time baiting one another. Both enjoying being the tiger in the cat and mouse chase. That is us," he said. "Or who we appear to others. This won't be hard. Not with the passion between us, and before you try to lie and say there is none, just know that it would provoke me into proving I'm right."

The last thing I needed was for him to prove that he was right. There was passion between us, whether it was right or wrong, and I supposed it would be far harder to do this if we couldn't physically bear one another's touch.

And what he said made too much sense. Not the nonsense about us both being the cat in the cat and mouse chase, which made no sense whatsoever. However, the part about there being no textbook to follow, no guidelines did make sense. So much so, it felt like something I should've known.

"You probably think I'm foolish for not knowing—"

"I don't think you're foolish. I never have—well, I take that back. I thought you were pretty foolish when you tried to escape," he said, and my eyes rolled. "You've never been in a relationship, and you really haven't been around many normal ones, so I understand why you wouldn't be sure how to act. And it's not like this is a normal situation."

Feeling a little better, I relaxed some. "And you've been in a relationship. I mean, you said you've been in love before."

"I have."

I watched the snow slip from branches as we passed, thinking of Alastir's daughter. Shea. That was such a beautiful name, and maybe since Casteel had shared things with me before, he would be willing to talk about her. "What…what happened?"

His fingers stilled and he was quiet for so long that I didn't think he'd answer, which made me all the more curious. But then he spoke. "She's gone."

Even though I already knew that, I felt a piercing ache in my heart, and I opened myself to him without giving it much thought. The moment I connected with him, I was hit by a wave of anguish so potent that it almost shielded the thread of anger underneath. I'd been right. Casteel's pain and sadness wasn't just for his brother. It was also for this faceless woman.

I thought about what Casteel had told me the night of the Rite, before the attack. He'd taken me to the willow in the gardens, and he'd told me about a place he used to go with his brother and his best friend. A cavern they had turned into their own private world. He'd said that he'd lost his brother and then his best friend a few years later. Could that best friend have been Shea, this woman he loved?

But his pain...

Before I even knew what I was doing, I'd let go of the saddle and started to remove my glove—

"Don't," he warned softly, and my hands froze. "I appreciate the gesture, but I don't need you to take away my pain, nor do I want that."

Still connected to him, I couldn't imagine how that was possible. The agony that waited beneath the smirks and the teasing glances—under all his masks—was nearly unbearable. It threatened to drag me to the frozen ground. Being trampled by Setti was almost preferable to what festered from the wounds that couldn't be seen. "Why wouldn't you want that?"

"Because the pain is a reminder and a warning. One I plan to never forget."

I severed the connection as nausea threatened to creep up my throat. "Did she...did she die because of the Ascended?"

"Everything that has rotted in my life has been tied to the Ascended," he said, his hand returning to my hip.

"I'm tied to the Ascended," I said before I could stop myself, before I could ignore the strange stinging.

Casteel didn't respond. He didn't say anything. Seconds ticked by and turned into minutes, and it felt as if there was a band tightening around my chest.

Staring straight ahead, I spent the next however many hours wondering how he could stand to even be near me—be close to someone tied to the Ascended as I was. They took his brother. They took the person he loved. They took his freedom. What else could they take from him?

His life?

A chill swept over my skin as I sat straight, my hands clutching the saddle. The idea of Casteel dying, of him no longer being there with those frustrating smirks and teasing glances, his quick-witted replies, and those damn, infuriating dimples? I couldn't even consider it. He was too vivid, too bright to think of him no longer being there.

But he would be gone one day. When this was all over and we parted ways, he would be gone from my life. That was what I wanted—what I planned.

Then why did I suddenly feel like crying?

We camped out near the road, several hours after the sun had set. It was cold, but not nearly as cold as it had been in the Blood Forest. Casteel hadn't spoken much beyond offering me food or asking if I needed a break, but as I lay there in the middle of the starless night, he returned to my side, stretching out behind me. I woke in his arms.

The next three days were just like that.

Casteel barely spoke. Whatever he felt, and I didn't open myself up to him to truly know, was a shadow colder than the nights. So many times, I wanted to ask—I wanted to tell him that I knew about Shea. That I was sorry he'd lost her. I wanted to ask questions about her—about them. I wanted him to do what Alastir had said he hadn't. I wanted him to talk, because I knew his silence fed his anguish. I said nothing, though, telling myself it wasn't my place. That the less I knew, the better.

But he came to my side in the night, and he was there when a nightmare found me, waking me before I could give sound to the screams building inside me. He held me in silence, his hand stroking my back until I fell back to sleep.

The nightmares…they were different. Patchy, as if I were popping in and out of them instead of following the events of the night as before. They didn't make any sense to me, either. Not the wounds on my mother, not the screams or the choking smoke. Not that creepy voice whispering about bleeding poppies. It was like the nightmares weren't real anymore.

That was what I was thinking about as we saddled the horses and traveled the road to Spessa's End on the fourth day. I had no idea how much time had passed when I saw something in the trees to my left. I couldn't make out what it was, and just when I thought I was seeing things, I saw it again, several trees down the road.

It hung from a limb stripped of pine needles and bare of snow. A rope shaped into some kind of symbol—a circle. I twisted in my seat, but I couldn't find where it had been in the mass of trees. The arm around my waist tightened, the first reaction from Casteel in days. I could feel the tension in his arm as I scanned the woods.

The shape tugged at the recesses of my memory. It looked like something I'd seen before. To the right, I saw it again—a brown rope hanging from another bare limb, fashioned almost like a noose, but with a stick or something crossing through the center.

I'd seen something similar in the Blood Forest. Except it had been created out of rocks and had reminded me of the Royal Crest. But now that I could see this one more clearly, I realized it was only *like* the Crest.

It wasn't a straight line like an arrow, situated at a slant, but one that was slanted in the opposite direction. And that…that wasn't a stick bound to the rope. It was too ashen in color, the ends knobby.

Oh, gods.

It was a *bone*.

Setti slowed, and Casteel's arm slid away from me.

Slowly, I lifted my gaze, and trepidation took hold. There were dozens of them hanging amongst the trees, all different, at dizzying heights.

"Casteel?" I said quietly. "Do you see what's in the trees?"

"Yes."

"I saw the same shapes in the Blood Forest."

"Cas," Kieran's voice was low, barely audible.

"I know," he answered, and I heard a quiet snap of a clasp. When his arm came back around me, he held the strange bow in my lap. As close as it was, I could see that the nocked arrow was thicker than normal, and although I'd seen the kind of damage the bolt could do, it was still somehow unfathomable.

I stared at the bow and the bloodstone arrow. "Is it

Craven?" I asked, having seen the rocks right before they arrived. I looked down, seeing no mist.

"I don't think Craven have started to decorate trees with craft projects, Princess," he said, and my heart gave a stupid little leap. It was the first time he'd called me that in days. He shifted the handle of the bow into my hand. "The lovely decorations are courtesy of the Dead Bones Clan."

"The what?" I turned my head toward his.

"They used to live all across Solis, especially where the Blood Forest is now, but they've since relocated to these woods and hills over the past several decades."

"I've never heard of them."

"There are a lot of things the Ascended don't share with the people of Solis. Like the fact that there are people who live and survive outside the protection of the Rise."

"How?" I demanded. Many of the villages outfitted with smaller Rises were often overrun by Craven.

"They survive by any means necessary. For this clan, one of those means is by slaughtering anyone they view as a threat. Supposedly, they eat who they kill and will often use the flesh for masks and the bones—well, you already saw what they like to do with the bones. You know what they say—waste not, want not."

My mouth dropped open. "I…"

"Yeah, Princess, there really aren't any words. We try to avoid them when we pass through here. Normally, we don't have any problems. But in case we do." He folded a hand over mine. "Feel this metal piece? It's the trigger. You aim this bow just like you would a normal one, but instead of pulling the string back, you press on this, and it fires the arrow."

I had so many questions, but I curled my fingers around the wooden handle, getting a feel for its weight. Instinct told me that the important thing was to focus on his instructions. "Okay."

"The arrow is nocked the same, except it's held in place. All you need to do is aim and pull the trigger. Bloodstone bolts will also kill mortals," he instructed. "You know what to do if we have any problems with these people. Stay alive."

I started to respond, but Kieran shouted. No more than a second later, Casteel jerked me back against him. The handle of the bow pressed into my stomach as something whizzed mere inches from my face. My head jerked to the right as a branch on the other side of the road snapped in two, taken down by—

"In the trees!" Naill shouted. "To the left!"

Casteel wheeled Setti, guiding the powerful horse around so that I was facing to the right. He shifted in the saddle, his body pressing mine down as flat as I could go—

There was another shot, and then Casteel was gone from Setti's back, driven to the ground.

Chapter 21

"Casteel!" I shouted, my heart slamming against my ribs. Twisting in the saddle, I gripped the bow as I looked down.

Rolling out of the path of Setti's hooves, Casteel rose to his knees. My stomach dropped at the sight of the *arrows* jutting out of his back. One was lodged in his left shoulder. Another was near the center of his back, just to the right. Blood already darkened his black cloak.

"Solis bastards!" someone shouted from the trees. "You're going to die today!"

Another arrow blew past my face, missing me by inches. Panic exploded in my chest as Setti pranced in a tight circle, startled. *He's okay,* I told myself as I gripped the saddle horn with my other hand. He was Atlantian. Two arrows couldn't take him down. *He's okay.* I'd stabbed him in the actual heart, and he'd been fine. *He's okay*—

Setti reared. My grip on the pommel slipped. I had no idea how to control a horse, and if I let go to grab the reins, I would fall. I was nowhere near as fast as Casteel. My wild gaze darted over the heavy tree line as Naill shouted a curse, taking an arrow to the leg. Setti slammed down on his front hooves, rattling me to my very bones. I lost my grip and slipped. The sky turned sideways—

An arm snagged me from behind. The scent of rich spice

and citrus in fresh snow enveloped me. Casteel yanked me down as Delano suddenly appeared on Setti's other side. Catching Setti's reins, he rose to a crouch on the saddle and leapt onto the horse's back, keeping his mount's reins in his other hand. Sliding into the seat, he dug his heels in, urging Setti and his horse into the woods to the right.

A blur of fawn-colored fur shot past us, into the woods. *Kieran*. Several heartbeats later, I heard a yelp and a high-pitched scream as Casteel all but carried me into the trees to the right.

"Fucking wolven!" a man hooted, his enthusiastic response quite at odds with what came out of his mouth next. "This just became our lucky day, boys! The gods are good!"

Casteel spun suddenly, shielding my body with his. He jerked and growled out a sharp curse, and I knew he'd taken another arrow.

"This is getting extremely annoying," he snarled, thrusting me behind a tree. He tossed the quiver of arrows I hadn't seen him grab toward me. "Don't get shot. That will be even more annoying."

"How about you try not getting shot *again*." An arrow now protruded from Casteel's lower back, and he was still standing there. In the back of my mind, I knew why. He was Atlantian. But all I could think as I saw the three arrows pierced through him was...what if he weren't?

He'd be dead, and I...

"But I make wearing arrows look good, don't I?" Casteel twisted sharply, his hand snapping out. He caught the next arrow intended for him.

I stared at him.

"I don't know why any of you think this is your lucky day," he yelled back as he turned around. He shattered the arrow in his fist. "It's really not. Not when my cloak has been ruined. And I really liked it. It was warm, and now it has godsdamn holes in it. How will that keep me warm?"

Something about him being more upset about his ruined cloak than he was about having *multiple* holes in his body had a strange, calming effect on me. My hands stopped trembling as I focused on the pines across the road. I knew how to fire a bow. I was very good at it. Vikter had claimed that I was one of the best archers he'd seen. I had the steady hands for it, the watchful eye, and the quick reflexes. That was why Casteel had handed the bow over to me. He knew I could use it.

And I had the steady hands now.

A sound began, a great wave of rattling that reminded me of those wooden toys with beads inside that infants often enjoyed. It seemed to come from all directions, like the rasping of dry bones. The hairs on my neck stood on end.

Rapidly scanning the other side of the road for any movement that wasn't fawn-colored, I lifted the bow as Naill joined Casteel. My finger curled around the trigger as I kept searching—

A muddied brown shape briefly appeared between the pines, and I didn't hesitate. Not for a second. I leveled the bow just as my target lifted his weapon, taking aim at Naill. I pressed on the trigger.

The bolt released with a whoosh, flying across the road. I already knew I'd hit my target when I reached for another heavier, thicker arrow.

Movement caught my eyes. I looked just in time to see Casteel launch into the air. He jumped higher than he stood, which was well over six feet. My lips parted as he landed on a limb, shaking free pine needles and snow dust. All I could see was his arm punch into the shadows of the limb. A second later, he yanked a mortal out, tossing him to the ground—

Delano shot out from the forest. In his wolven form, he was nothing more than a streak of white fur. He caught the mortal before he hit the ground, whipping his large head and shaking the man like a dog did its favorite toy. I heard a cracking sound, and then Delano dropped the broken mortal. Blood streaked Delano's fur as he lunged, catching another clansman around the throat that Casteel had thrown from the tree from...dear gods...from higher up.

Dragging my eyes from what I was unlikely to ever forget, I nocked another bolt, firing at another mortal that popped out from between two trees. Loading the bow, I twisted at the waist, leaned out—

"Damn bloodsuckers! Boys, be fast!" that first voice came again, somewhere from the trees. "We ain't dealing with just wolven! Aim for the head!"

Okay, the fact that this Dead Bones Clan knew about the wolven and the Atlantians was interesting. And I—

Fiery pain lanced across my skin as an arrow shot by me, grazing my arm. I sucked in a sharp breath as I darted back behind the elm, shaking my wrist as if that would somehow lessen the burn.

It didn't help all that much.

Screams of pain pierced through the distant snarls. Gritting my teeth, I looked over my shoulder, no longer seeing Casteel or Delano. Naill was gone too. I stayed still until I saw a shifting of shadows and a flash of movement to my left. I zeroed in on it.

I fired the bolt just as the sound of pounding feet whipped my attention to the right. A man ran at me—at least I thought the tall, broad shape was a man, but I couldn't be sure. His face was covered by something that looked like leather. Clumps of brown hair poked out from the mask. He carried no bow, but rather some sort of club, and he was fast for someone his size.

"Shit," I whispered, whirling toward the quiver. I grabbed a bolt and nocked it quickly.

The man swung the club before I could fire. I ducked but wasn't fast enough. His club caught the bow, knocking it from my grip with one shattering blow. He laughed. "What kind of bitch are you?" he asked as I jumped back. I recognized the man's voice. He'd been the one shouting, and now that he was only a foot or so from me, I could see why I thought his mask was made of leather.

And I could also see that Casteel hadn't been joking when he said that the Dead Bones Clan operated on the waste-not-want-not creed.

It was skin.

Human skin that had been stretched to fit over his head, stitched in jagged pieces around the openings that had been created for the eyes and mouth. My stomach churned, but I didn't cave to the rising nausea.

"Are you part dog, or do you like to suck on things?" he

asked, switching the club to his left hand. "If you got something you can suck on." He reached d[...] what I could only assume he was referencing. "Yo[...] a mess, but your mouth looks just fine."

Heart pounding, I darted out of reach of the club as he swung it again. I reached inside my cloak, unsheathing my dagger. I stilled, waiting as my fingers opened and closed around the handle. I had to be quick and smart. I'd only have one chance.

"I bet you're one of those wolven bitches. Hear they like their women all cut up." He made a calling sound, one used to summon a dog, and my grip tightened. "Tell me, girl. What kind of bitch are you?"

He lifted the club again, and I made my move. Shooting forward, I slipped under his arm and grabbed the dirty tunic. Thrusting the dagger up, I used every ounce of strength I had to drive it deep under his chin.

"I'm *this* kind of bitch," I growled. The muscles under the mask pieced together by human flesh went lax as I jerked the knife free.

Blood spurted in a hot spray. Whatever he was about to say ended on a gurgle. The club fell from his hand, and then he toppled like a tree, straight and forward, taking me down with him.

I hit the pine-needled, snow-crusted ground with a grunt as air punched out of my lungs. The man was limp, his grotesquely masked face smashed into my shoulder.

"Dammit," I muttered as his heavy weight sank into me. He smelled like rot and other things I didn't want to think about. I tipped my head back against the ground. "This is just great."

A flutter of wings drew my gaze to the sky. My eyes narrowed as that large hawk from before appeared overhead, gracefully circling before disappearing into the trees. A wing, caressed by the sun, gleamed silver. I really hoped my new cloak didn't end up drenched in blood.

Sighing, I gathered up my strength and shoved at the man, managing to get him at least partway off my chest. I drew in a deep breath—

The man was suddenly lifted up and tossed aside like he was nothing more than a bag of small rocks. I had no idea where he landed. All I could do was stare at Casteel.

He stood above me, his face splattered with dots of red. "You're bleeding."

"You have three arrows sticking out of you."

"You've been injured. Where?" He knelt beside me, ignoring my somewhat unnecessary observation.

"I'm fine." I sat up, my eyes glued to the arrow jutting from his stomach as I sheathed my dagger. "Does it hurt?"

"What?"

"The *arrows*." I paused as he grasped my left arm, pushing the cloak aside. "The arrows that are sticking out of your body."

"It's nothing more than an annoyance." He turned my arm, and I winced. "Sorry," he said gruffly as he exposed the tear in the sleeve of my tunic.

"They're inside your body," I repeated. "How can that only be an annoyance? Is it because you're from an elemental bloodline?"

"Yes." His features sharpened as he carefully peeled back the edge of my sweater. "The wounds will heal as soon as I pull the arrows out."

"Then why haven't you done that yet?"

"Because they will not fester, unlike your wound if dirt gets into it." His gaze flicked up, and his eyes snagged my focus. The pupils seemed larger. "Are you worried about me, Princess?"

I clamped my mouth shut.

"You are, aren't you? I heard you scream my name when I fell from the horse," he continued, and it was weird for him to tease after riding in silence for hours—and with three arrows sticking out of him. "Your concern warms the same heart you've so grievously wounded."

I shot him a glare. "You're no good to me dead."

One side of his lips quirked up as he stared at my arm. "Looks like a flesh wound. You'll live."

"I told you I was fine."

"Still needs to be covered." He rose, bringing me with him. Stepping back, he tore off a piece of his cloak. "Not the most hygienic of options, but it will work until we reach Spessa's End."

The crunch of needles drew my gaze. I saw Delano slinking between the pines, still in his wolven form. Streaks of red stained his fur. His pale-eyed gaze moved from Casteel to me, and then he took off in a powerful lunge, darting between the trees.

"Where is he going?"

"Probably to retrieve the horses," Casteel answered.

I glanced up at him. He stood beside me, holding my arm in one hand and the cloth in the other, but he made no move to cover the seeping wound. He was just standing there, the hollows of his cheeks shadowed.

The throbbing in my arm fell to the wayside as concern *did* take root. "Are you sure you're all right?" I asked. "Maybe you should pull those arrows out or something."

His throat worked on a swallow, and his lips parted. There was the barest hint of fangs.

"Casteel," Kieran called out from behind us.

The Prince blinked, lifting his head to look over my shoulder. His pupils seemed even bigger, crowding out the amber of his irises. Instinct sent a shiver of warning through me. "I'm fine."

"You sure about that?" Kieran asked.

I watched Casteel closely, wondering what was wrong with him. "Your eyes," I whispered. "The pupils are really large."

"They do that sometimes." He cleared his throat, finally moving as he repeated louder, "I'm fine." He wrapped the strip of cloak around my upper arm. "This may hurt."

It didn't feel all that great as he tightened the makeshift bandage, tying it so it stayed in place. Once done, he lowered my arm and draped the cloak over it. I watched him step back and look down at himself, still…well, still concerned for him. "Thank you."

His gaze flew to mine, and there seemed to be a bit of surprise in those odd eyes. He nodded and then looked at Kieran. "Are there any left?"

"Those alive ran back to whatever homes they'd fashioned for themselves," Kieran stated. "Naill is scouting up ahead to make sure we don't run into any more."

Wanting to know how these people knew what Kieran and Casteel were, I twisted at the waist—

Every single thought fled. My mouth dropped open. "You're naked!"

"I am," Kieran replied.

And he was.

Like completely naked, and I saw way too much tawny-hued skin. *Way* too much. I quickly spun around, my wide eyes clashing with Casteel's.

"You should see your face right now." Casteel gripped the arrow in his stomach. "It looks like you've been sunbathing."

"Because he's naked," I hissed. "Like, super naked."

"What do you think happens when he shifts forms?"

"The last time his pants actually stayed on!"

"And sometimes they don't." Casteel shrugged.

"Those pants were looser, I suppose," Kieran stated. "There's no need to be embarrassed. It's only skin."

What I saw was *not* only skin. He was…well, his body was a lot like Casteel's. Lean, hard muscle and…

I wasn't going to think about what I saw.

At a loss for what to say, I blurted out in a whisper, "He has to be cold!"

"Wolven body temperatures run higher than normal. I'm just a little chilled," Kieran commented. "As I'm sure you noticed."

Casteel smirked. "I doubt she knows what you're referencing."

I inhaled deeply through my nose and exhaled slowly. "I know exactly what he's referencing, thank you very much."

"How do you know that?" Casteel lifted his brows, and I noticed that his pupils seemed to have returned to their normal size. "If you know what that means, then someone has been very naughty."

"I know that because—" I sucked in air as he yanked the arrow free. "Oh, my gods."

"It looks worse than it is." He tossed the arrow aside and then reached for the one in his left shoulder.

I started to turn away but remembered that what was behind me was far more traumatizing. "I hope you have an extra set of clothes," I said to Kieran.

"I do. As soon as Delano arrives with the horses, I'll be all prim and proper again."

I flinched as Casteel pulled the second arrow out. "I don't think you've ever been prim and proper."

"That's true," Kieran said, and I thought he'd moved closer. "You took out the mouthy one?"

I nodded as Casteel cursed when the arrow he'd been pulling on most likely got stuck on something important. Like an organ.

"With your dagger?" Kieran sounded impressed.

"That and my sparkling personality."

The wolven snorted. "It was probably the latter that did him in."

My stomach twisted as Casteel ripped out the third and final arrow. I swallowed. *Hard.* "I think he broke the bow, though."

"But he didn't break you." Casteel straightened his tunic, the tension bracketing his mouth easing. "And that's all that matters."

Once Delano returned with the horses, and Naill reported back that the road ahead appeared clear, we continued on our way.

With a completely clothed Kieran, thank the gods.

We rode on in silence, everyone watchful and alert for signs of the Dead Bones Clan. The sky was darkening to a midnight blue as the road eventually widened, and the temperatures dropped even more. As soon as the crowd of elms thinned out, I figured it was safe to speak. I was practically bursting to do so. "I have so many questions about the Dead Bones Clan."

"Shocking," muttered Kieran, who rode to our left.

Casteel laughed softly, and that was the first sound he'd really made since climbing back onto the horse. I wondered—not worried—that he was still hurting from the arrows, but if I asked,

I would then be subjected to his overdramatic teasing.

"Can't promise we'll be able to answer those questions, but what would you like to know?" he asked, his arm loose around me.

"Why did the Dead Bones Clan attack like that?" I started there. "I get that they survive outside a Rise that way, but it's obvious we weren't Craven."

"The Dead Bones Clan isn't just anti-Craven. They are anti...everyone," Naill said from behind us. "Sometimes, they let people pass on the road. Sometimes they don't. We can only hope that Alastir and his group made it through, but they were armed. As will be those who are behind us."

Gods, I hadn't even thought of them. I hoped they made it. I liked Alastir, and I really hoped the people of New Haven didn't run into any more trouble.

"If they got Alastir and that group, they probably wouldn't have come after us. I'm betting they're hungry," Kieran said, and my lips curled.

"I heard one of them talk about how they wanted to make a cloak out of my fur," Delano said from where he rode to our right. His brows were furrowed. "My fur should be reserved for something far more luxurious than a cloak. I bit him extra hard for that."

My lips twitched as Casteel said, "From what I've learned about them, when the war broke out, they escaped to these woods. I don't think anyone knows anymore whether they've always had a penchant for flesh—eating and wearing it."

I didn't want to think about their penchant for flesh. "They knew what you all were," I pointed out.

"You've got to remember that they're remnants of a time when Atlantia ruled over the entire kingdom," Casteel said. "I imagine that each generation learned about us through stories told by their elders. With them outside the control of the Ascended, our histories weren't rewritten or lost."

"Okay, but they still tried to kill you."

"Kill *us*," Casteel corrected, and my stomach dipped. "This road has seen a lot of Atlantians and wolven throughout the centuries. I doubt their attack-first-and-ask-questions-later mentality fostered any fondness once they realized that we would not be felled by arrows or clubs." He shifted as if he sought to get more comfortable. "Plus, wolven fur does make for very nice cloaks."

Naill laughed as the wolven cursed.

"But they used to live in one of the towns near the Blood Forest. At some point over the past several hundred years, they ended up here," Casteel continued. "I've traveled this road before and never had dealings with them until now."

That explained why I saw the symbols there and then here. "How have they escaped the Ascended's notice?"

"Who's to say they have?" Naill countered.

"Well, they're still alive," I reasoned. "So, I would think they have."

Kieran drew ahead. "Due to the Dead Bones Clan often attacking on sight and with what has to be their dwindling numbers, I think they probably aren't worth the Ascended's time."

Looking behind us, I wondered exactly how many lived in the woods. Hundreds? Thousands? If there were thousands, the Ascended would definitely make it worth their time. Thousands could stage a revolt. Maybe not a successful one, but one that could cause many problems, especially since the clan was in possession of the kind of knowledge the Ascended wouldn't want known.

"And the Ascended don't often send people out here," Delano added. "That may change once they realize you're missing, but only the gods know the last time anyone sent by them came this far or went beyond."

Something about his voice caused me to look at him. In the fading light, I could see the hard, unyielding lines of his face. "Why is that?"

"You'll see," Casteel answered.

And that was all he said—all anyone said as night descended, and the moon rose, casting silvery light over the hills the forest had given way to.

With my mind occupied with everything that had happened and what I'd learned before the first arrow had shot across the road, I didn't think it was at all possible that I would find myself dozing. But that was exactly what happened as I felt myself easing into the space between Casteel's arms. At some point, I ended up leaning back against him, and when I realized that, I jerked upright.

"I'm sorry," I mumbled, muscles weary as I forced myself to sit straight. I saw that we were spaced out again, Delano and Naill several feet ahead with Kieran keeping pace beside us.

"For what?"

"You were shot." I smothered a yawn. "At least three times."

"I'm already healed. You're fine." When I didn't move, he used his arm around my waist to tug me back.

The gods help me, but I didn't resist.

"Relax," he whispered atop of my head. "We should reach Spessa's End soon."

I stared up at the twinkling stars, wondering how there could be so many. I didn't know why I asked what I did. "Does it bother you?"

"What, Princess?"

"Having to be so close to someone who represents the Ascended," I asked. "After they took so much from you."

A moment passed. "I would do anything for my brother."

Yes, I truly realized that he would.

"And you're part Atlantian," he tacked on. "That helps."

I couldn't tell if he was joking or not, but then Kieran spoke about the increasing clouds. The subject changed, I drifted and drifted...

We camped in the meadows we came upon, and in the morning, the first thing I realized was that we didn't need our cloaks once the sun rose. I knew that meant we had to be getting close. The day was a blur of open fields and unending blue skies, and when the sun fell, we didn't stop. We continued on.

Then the horses slowed. The first thing I saw was an endless pool of the deepest onyx. It was like the sky had kissed the ground.

"Stygian Bay," I whispered,

"The rumored gateway to the Temples of Eternity, Rhain's

land," Casteel answered.

"Are they true? The rumors?"

"Would you believe me if I said yes, Princess?" He tugged me back so I leaned into him once more. "You're warm," he offered in way of explanation.

"Thought Atlantians didn't get cold."

"Don't point out my inconsistencies."

Maybe it was because I was tired. Perhaps it was the stillness and the beauty of the Bay. I didn't know what it was, but I laughed. "It's not even that cold now."

He made a sound, a soft rumble that I felt more than heard. "You don't do that enough. You never have."

I felt a twist in my chest, one I forced myself to breathe through. "Is the Bay the actual gateway to the real Temples of Rhain?" I asked instead.

His breath was warm against my cheek as he said, "Stygian Bay is where Rhain sleeps, deep below. It borders Pompay, and its southern coast reaches Spessa's End."

A jolt of surprise widened my eyes. The god really slept there?

"Are we in Spessa's End?"

"No," Kieran answered. "We're about a day's ride from there. We've reached Pompay."

Pompay—the last Atlantian stronghold.

What I saw taking shape out of the darkness of night stole whatever I was about to say.

First, it was the Rise or what was left of the crumbling walls. Only sections by the entry stood, where no gate existed, stretching dizzying heights into the sky. The rest couldn't be more than five feet, and most of that was the piles of broken stone.

We rode into a town that no longer existed. Burnt-out homes lined the road, most missing entire walls or were destroyed down to their foundations. No people were about, no candlelight from any windows of the homes that at least had four walls and a roof. Only the sound of the horses' hooves clattering off the cobblestones could be heard as we traveled farther, past larger buildings with toppled pillars—structures I imagined once held meetings or offered entertainment. Trees were nothing more than skeletons, dead and decaying, and there was no sign of life anywhere. Whatever had happened here hadn't occurred during the war. The land would have reclaimed the buildings and streets by now if that were the case.

"What happened here?" I winced at the sound of my voice. It felt wrong to speak, to shatter the silence of what appeared to be a graveyard of a town.

"The Ascended feared that with its roots as a once prosperous Atlantian city, Pompay would become a haven for Descenters. But they had little reason to believe that," Casteel said, his voice hushed. "There were Descenters here, only because there had been no sitting Royal to rule the town after the war, but they were mostly mortals—farmers and the like. But no Ascended wanted to rule so far east, so they razed the town to the ground."

"What of the people who lived here?" I asked, afraid I already knew the answer.

Casteel didn't speak because the answer to my question appeared before me as we rounded a bend in the road. It went on for as far as the eye could see, stone mound upon stone mound, lit only by the silvery moonlight. There were hundreds of them, so many that I couldn't quite believe what I was seeing, even though I knew that what I saw was reality. Pompay was a slaughtered town, truly a graveyard.

"They came in the night some forty or so years ago," Delano said. "An army of Ascended. They swarmed this town like a plague, feeding upon every man, woman, and child. Those who were not killed turned into Craven and spilled out from Pompay in search of blood."

Gods.

"The ones who died were left behind to rot in the summer heat and to freeze in the winter," Kieran said. "Their bodies remained where they'd fallen. A lone person by a tree, dozens in the street." He cleared his throat. "Couples found in their beds. Entire families in their homes, mothers and fathers clutching their children to them."

"We buried them," Casteel told me. "It took some time, but

we buried all that remained. Six hundred and fifty-six of them."

Good gods.

I closed my eyes against the tide of sorrow and shock that flooded me, but I could not unsee the piles and piles of stones of so many senseless deaths.

Casteel's exhale was rough. "So now you know why the Ascended don't often travel this far."

I did know.

I saw.

"I...I don't know how I'm shocked," I admitted. "After everything I've seen, I don't understand how I can't believe this."

Casteel's arm tightened around me, but it was Naill who spoke, echoing what the Prince had said earlier. "I don't think this is something you can ever get used to. At least, I wouldn't want to. I want to be shocked. I need to be," the dark-skinned Atlantian told me. "If not, then the line that separates us from the vamprys would be much too thin."

Chapter 22

We rode on in silence, passing the endless mounds of stones and the ruins of homes and businesses. We stopped just outside the city on the coast of the Bay.

I found little sleep that night, seeing the stone graveyard every time I closed my eyes. Surprisingly, when I did rest, there were no nightmares. When we left at dawn the following morning, I knew the haunting ruins of the city would stay with me for the rest of my life. And as we traveled along Stygian Bay, I feared what awaited us in Spessa's End.

With the sun beginning its steady climb, glittering off the midnight Bay, the cloaks and gloves became unnecessary. However, with each burnt-out building or dilapidated farm we passed, I was chilled all over again.

When Casteel caught me staring at some toppled marble columns among the reddish reeds, he asked, "You didn't expect this, did you?"

I shook my head. "I didn't know it was like this. Actually, I didn't know much about Pompay or Spessa's End, but I never thought this was the case. I believed the towns still existed. So did Vikter. He talked about wanting to visit the Bay."

"So few travel this far out that there is little risk of the people of Solis ever discovering what was done to the towns or the people."

"And there's little risk of them discovering what has been rebuilt," Delano added.

Eventually, the day gave way to night, and cooler air was ushered back in. The empty fields were replaced by a heavily wooded area that bordered the fields we rode near. I was beginning to wonder if Spessa's End even existed or where we'd be staying when we reached the other side of the black Bay when I heard the soft, lilting call of a songbird.

Casteel shifted behind me, lifting his head. He mimicked the cry with one of his own. I started to turn to him in surprise when the call was returned. It wasn't songbirds. They were signals. The moment I realized that, I finally saw the signs of a city.

Moonlight bathed the sandstone walls of the Rise in silver. Nowhere near as tall as the ones surrounding the larger cities in Solis, the structure still stretched at least a dozen feet into the air, and I could make out numerous square-shaped parapets spaced several feet apart.

Ahead, heavy iron doors shuddered and then groaned, inching open. Torches jutted out from the deep and wide walls of the Rise, casting light around the perimeter. The courtyard was mostly left to the shadows, but farther along, light flickered like a staggered sea of low-hanging stars.

"Was this not destroyed? Or was it rebuilt?" I asked as we rode through the Rise.

"The Rise suffered some damage but remained mostly intact. We've been able to repair those sections. See the lights? That's Stygian Fortress. It belonged to the caretakers of the Bay and was reinforced during the War of Two Kings," Casteel explained. "The fortress was largely unscathed, even after the war. I suppose the Ascended were afraid to incur the wrath of Rhain by destroying the dwelling, so they left it standing."

"And the caretakers?" I was half afraid to ask.

"They are buried beyond, in stone graves with the rest of the original people of Spessa's End," he answered.

Sick—I truly felt sick. Two entire towns destroyed. And for

what? All because the Ascended feared the truth and didn't want to rule so far east? This was a kind of evil, senseless and inconceivable, and I knew that Spessa's End and Pompay probably weren't the only ones. New Haven would most likely face the same fate, and the only small blessing was that Elijah was moving the people out before they too ended up with only a pile of stones as a marker of the lives they led.

"But we've reclaimed Spessa's End, built back as much as we were able to," Casteel said. "And the Ascended have no idea."

"What do you mean?"

"You'll see." Casteel's thumb made a sweep along my hip. "I've found a temporary answer to our land issues."

Before I could question further, a form took shape on the road, halting any answers to my questions. Setti slowed as I tensed, my hand slipping to the dagger on my thigh out of instinct.

Casteel's hand folded over mine. "He's a friendly."

"Sorry," I murmured.

"Don't be," he said in a low voice. "I'd rather you be prepared than be too trusting."

A torch flamed to life, casting a reddish glow over the face of a young man. He wasn't alone. A wolven stood beside him, a smaller one with fur the color of the Bay. Without warning, the wolven bounded toward us, jumping and prancing about like a...an excited puppy that recognized visitors.

"Someone is happy to see you," Kieran remarked.

Casteel chuckled as he tightened Setti's reins. "Careful, Beckett. You don't want to get too close to the horse."

The young wolven danced back as his tail wagged frantically before he wiggled his way toward Delano.

"Your Highness," the young man who held the torch said with a voice pitched with awe. He dropped to one knee, bowing his head, and I was half afraid he'd lose his grip on the torch.

"There's no need for that," Casteel said, drawing us closer to the young man. He shifted behind me. "Is that you, Quentyn?"

The man's head bobbed. "Yes, Your Highness—I mean, my Prince. It is I."

"Gods, you've grown at least a foot or two since I last saw you." The smile was evident in Casteel's tone, and I almost turned to see it. "Did Alastir drag you out here?"

"I wanted to go with him," Quentyn answered. "So did Beckett."

"Maybe you can tell him to rise." Kieran rode past the young boy. "The longer he continues to kneel, the larger your ego will grow."

"Don't know if that's possible," Naill said under his breath.

I raised a brow.

Casteel laughed. "You can rise, Quentyn. And call me Casteel, like everyone else."

Quentyn rose so fast that I had no idea how he didn't light his head on fire in the process. Admiration filled the boyish face. It was too dark for me to make out his eyes as he glanced curiously in my direction. "We've been waiting for you, hopeful that you'd make it here tonight."

"Where's Alastir?" Casteel asked as the wolven trotted between Delano and us.

"He's retired for the evening."

Casteel snorted. "More like he passed out. He was talking about some whiskey he'd gotten his hands on when I last saw him."

"I...uh, do believe that the whiskey may have aided in his inability to stay awake," Quentyn answered sheepishly.

I grinned, unable to help myself.

"But we made sure fires were lit in the rooms since it does get chilly here at night," Quentyn continued, glancing up at me curiously.

"Allow me to introduce my fiancée." Casteel took note of his questioning looks. "This is Penellaphe."

Fiancée.

My grip on the saddle loosened, and I wondered if the dizziness was just my imagination. I didn't think I'd ever get used to hearing him say that.

"Alastir said you were bringing a lady with you—your fiancée." The torch bobbed along with him. "I mean, congratulations! To you both. You hear that, Beckett? This is our

Prince's fiancée."

Beckett, the wolven, bounced happily across the road, disappearing into the brush.

"Penellaphe, this is Quentyn Da'Lahr. The overly excited pup is Beckett Davenwill, a great-nephew of Alastir."

Act like yourself. That was what Casteel had advised earlier. What would I normally do? Sitting here and staring at the young man as if I had no brain between my ears was not how I'd behave. I would smile and say hello. I could do that.

Fixing what I hoped was a normal smile on my face, I gave Quentyn a small wave. "It's a pleasure to meet you."

"It's an honor to meet you!" Quentyn offered a jaunty wave with the torch in return.

The enthusiasm in his voice and greeting softened my smile, and it no longer felt like it was plastered there.

I felt rather proud of myself as we passed a copse of trees, and the fort came into view. Torches and lanterns warmed the sand-colored stone of the ancient fortress, which rose higher than the Rise. Massive columns supported walkways that connected the roof of the stronghold to the Rise.

Arriving at the stables, Casteel demounted with ease and then settled his hands on my hips, lifting me from the saddle. My pulse thrummed as my body slid against his, our heavy cloaks proving to be no real barrier. The hands at my hips tightened. I looked up, his gaze catching mine. For a moment, neither of us moved as we stared at each other. There was an intent in the shape of his lips, one my body seemed to inherently recognize and respond to. I suddenly felt entirely too tight and yet too loose at the same time. His head tilted, sending my blood pumping. Anticipation was swift and sweet, and I knew I should pull away. We didn't have to be *this* convincing, but I didn't move. I couldn't. I was snared like a rabbit.

"The rooms are right over here," Quentyn announced, breaking the spell. Casteel turned, grabbing our bags as Quentyn headed toward our left. I patted Setti goodnight and then followed Quentyn.

"None of the rooms on the upper levels are all that useable, but the ones on the ground level are pretty nice." He stopped suddenly. "Oh—one second. Be right back."

Blood still thrumming, I watched Quentyn dart through an open doorway, into a lit room. "He…um, he seems young."

"He just went through the Culling," Casteel explained, and I thought his voice sounded thicker, richer.

"I'm surprised to see him out here," Kieran said, having reappeared. "And that one"—he nodded behind us—"especially."

I looked to find Delano leading the horses toward the stables. The small wolven trotted beside him, ears perked as Delano spoke to him, tail wagging frantically.

"Both are far too young." Naill joined us. "I was under the impression that none of the young had moved out here."

"As was I." Casteel squinted. "The last I saw of Beckett, he could barely control holding one form or the other."

I blinked. "Is that common?"

Kieran nodded. "It takes at least two decades for us to gain control over our two halves. Any slight change of emotion can send us to four legs or two."

"That has to be…inconvenient."

He laughed dryly. "You have no idea."

"Have Atlantians relocated to Spessa's End?" I asked. "Is that what you meant by a temporary fix to the land issue?"

Casteel nodded. "It hasn't made a huge impact. Not yet. But it has freed up some of the homes and land. Those who've moved out here have been hand-selected for the most part. Old enough and trained in case the Ascended do happen to venture to these parts, but that hasn't happened since the Ascended laid siege to the town."

"How many people live here now?" I asked.

"A hundred, give or take a few."

Irritation pricked at me as my gaze swept over the smooth stone façade of the fortress. Why was Casteel just now telling me this instead of when he first spoke of the land and the population issue in Atlantia? Or at any point after that? Better yet, why was I irritated that he hadn't? Was this information even necessary for me to know? Probably not, but it still…frustrated me.

The young Atlantian reappeared, carrying a bundle. "Alastir

said that you may be in need of clothing, and we were able to gather some items. I don't know if any of this will be helpful, but it's clean, and I'm sure we'll be able to get you more in the morning."

I took the light bundle. "I'm sure it will be of use. Thank you."

Quentyn beamed before pivoting on his heel. Kieran lingered back as we followed the Atlantian through the covered walkway. He chattered, telling us about the wildlife he'd seen as we passed several dark rooms and then continued around the side of the fortress where it was evident that no rooms were near. He swore he saw a cave cat, even though Alastir told him that there were none still alive in this area.

The first thing I saw was a terrace. Wind caught the pinned curtains, causing the material to snap softly. As Quentyn unlocked the door, I was able to make out a chaise lounge at one end, and several low-to-the-floor chairs.

Quentyn handed the key over to Casteel and then opened the door. "Alastir made sure the room was aired out and a fire lit since the nights get kind of cold here."

A lamp turned on, casting light throughout the spacious, private living quarters outfitted with plush couches and a dining table.

"There are pitchers of fresh water by the fireplace." Quentyn opened another set of doors, and I caught the scent of lemon and vanilla.

If the living area had been a surprise, the bedchamber was an utter shock. The fireplace sat in the corner, and as Quentyn indicated, several pitchers sat on the floor before it. In the center of the room was a canopied four-poster bed with gauzy white curtains. Across from it were double lattice doors that appeared to lead out to another terrace. On the other side was an entryway to a bathing chamber. All I could do was stare.

"If either of you would like, I can get more water for the bath," Quentyn offered.

Casteel looked to me, and I shook my head. It was far too late for all that work. "That won't be necessary, but thank you."

"If you're sure." When I nodded, Quentyn added, "I cannot

wait to have a shower where the only thing I have to do is turn a knob."

"Shower?"

Casteel shot me a half-grin. "Instead of sitting in the bath, you stand. The clean water comes from the ceiling. It's much like standing in a rain shower—a warm one."

I stared at him.

A dimple appeared in his cheek as he turned to the other Atlantian. "She doesn't believe that we have running hot water in Atlantia."

Quentyn's eyes grew to the size of small saucers. "He speaks the truth. I always took it for granted. I will never do that again."

Marveling over the concept of a standing bath that felt like a warm rain shower, I didn't even realize that Quentyn had left until Casteel spoke.

"Are you hungry?" he asked, placing our bags at the foot of the bed.

I shook my head, having filled up on the baked bars and nuts Casteel had brought with us. "I can't believe these rooms." I touched one of the curtains on the bed. "They're beautiful."

"My father would stay in this one or the other room that faces the Bay when he traveled to Spessa's End. Both rooms have been updated as much as possible."

I turned back to him. "I expected rooms with the bare necessities."

"We eventually plan to fix up the rooms on the second floor. That will allow for more to stay here while the homes are either being repaired or rebuilt." His gaze roamed over me. "I want to check your arm."

"It doesn't even hurt," I told him, placing the small bundle of clothing on a settee that sat in the corner near the bed.

"Be that as it may, I would still like to see it."

Knowing that he wouldn't let it go, I unhooked my cloak and hung it on a hook near the fireplace and then pulled up the sleeve of my sweater tunic. I started to tug at the knot, wondering if he'd tied it in a manner that required scissors to remove.

"Let me." He approached me as silently as always. His

fingers were warm as they grazed my skin. He had the knot untied in a heartbeat. The bandage slipped away, revealing a thin slash that had stopped bleeding some time ago. His thumb slid over the skin near the wound. "This doesn't hurt?"

"I swear." I bit the inside of my cheek. It didn't hurt. His touch, nor the area. The smooth swipe of his thumb felt...pleasant and shivery.

His chest rose with a deep breath and then he dropped my arm, taking a step back. "I'm going to check in with Quentyn and the others. Go ahead and make yourself comfortable. I'm sure you must be tired. Just make sure you clean the wound."

"I will."

His gaze met mine, and all I could think about was those moments outside, after he'd helped me down from Setti. Would he have kissed me? Would I have allowed it? I imagined we would have to kiss in front of people.

"Get some rest, Poppy."

Casteel was gone before I could even formulate a response, and I knew I should be relieved by that. But I...

I wasn't sure what I was.

Turning to the settee, I walked over to the bundle of clothing. There was a thin lilac-hued sleeping robe and a thicker, forest green tunic that would definitely come in handy.

Unhooking the sheath, I parted the curtain and was greeted by soft furs and a mountain of pillows.

"Goodness," I murmured, placing the sheath on the bed.

Using only one of the warmed pitchers, I carried it into the adjoining chamber. Half afraid Casteel would return while I stood naked, I cleaned up as quickly as possible in the much cooler room, making sure to clean out the wound with fresh water and a mint-scented bar of soap. Once I was finished, I slipped on the soft robe, tying the sash around my waist. Digging my brush out of my bag, I undid my braid and worked through the tangles in my hair as I stared at the doorway to the living area.

Sometime later, while under the blanket, I wasn't thinking about the Dead Bones Clan, the marriage, or what had happened at the keep. I wasn't even thinking about what the sun would reveal about Spessa's End come morning, or how strange it was that Casteel had left the room so quickly. I lay there thinking of all those stone graves, burnt-out and rundown homes in Pompay and in the fields between the two cities. If Tawny were here, she would be convinced that spirits roamed the night.

I shivered as my eyes drifted shut, wondering how the Ascended had been allowed to grow to this kind of power where they could destroy entire cities with no recourse.

And the only answer was a bitter one.

So very few had questioned what the Ascended claimed, and I'd simply accepted what they said, never truly giving life to any of the suspicions I had. That went beyond submission and straight into willful ignorance.

Shame slithered through me, another tell-tale sign that in many small ways, I'd been a part of the problem. A spoke in the wheel of the very system that brutalized hundreds of thousands, including myself.

The fire must've been fed at some point during the night because a pleasant heat surrounded my body. I couldn't even remember being this toasty in my bedchamber back in Masadonia. That was my first thought as I slowly came awake.

I didn't want to wake up and leave the warmth of the bed nor the heady scent of dark, lush spice and pine. Snuggling down against the warm, hard bed, a contented sigh escaped me.

Wait.

The *hard* bed?

That…that didn't make any sense. The bed had been soft, the kind that you sank into. But now it was warm, hard, and smooth against my cheek and hand. Not only that, the bed was wrapped around my waist, my hip—

My eyes flew open. Tiny particles of dust floated in the morning sunlight seeping through the terrace doors across from the bed. The curtains had been tied back, and I knew I hadn't done that before I fell asleep.

And I wasn't lying on the bed, at least not completely. What was under my cheek wasn't a pillow. It was a chest that rose and fell steadily. Beneath my hand wasn't the worn texture of the blanket, but a stomach. The bed wasn't wrapped around me. It was a heavy arm over my waist and a callused palm against my hip—my *bare* hip.

Oh my gods, I was using Casteel as my own personal pillow.

And based on the fact that I was lying on him, it was me who had sought him out in my sleep. When had he even returned to the room? Did that matter at the moment? It didn't as I became aware of every place our bodies met.

This was nothing like curling up together while camping on the road. There was no excuse for being all tangled up in him.

I lay there frozen, my breath in my throat. My breasts were pressed against the side of his body. One of his thighs was tucked between mine, the soft buckskin of his breeches nestled against a very, very intimate part of me. The robe had parted below the sash in my sleep. There was nothing between his palm and my skin, and that hand spanned my hip, the tips of his fingers resting against the curve of my rear.

A sweet, hot feeling swept over me, and my eyes drifted shut. I knew I shouldn't feel this. It was reckless and stupid and felt oh so dangerous. Instead of basking in how his body felt against mine, I should be plotting a way to somehow extract myself from him without waking him up, but my brain went in a totally different direction. It was almost like I could...pretend again. That this was okay. That *Hawke* was holding me in his sleep, and that this was just one of many mornings we woke up like this. He'd kiss me and touch me, fitting our bodies together, and this would happen because we were lovers about to marry for no reason other than the fact that we wanted and desired and needed each other. My breath caught again, and my pulse quickened. Heated lightning danced over my skin and zipped through my veins. I could almost imagine the hand on my hip slipping more to my behind and then lower still. Those fingers of his were capable of eliciting sensations I hadn't even known were possible, not even after reading the scandalous diary of Miss Willa Colyns. My entire world concentrated on the memory of his fingers skimming over the sensitive skin of my inner thighs and then slipping inside me. A throbbing ache settled in my core, and a tiny part of me wished I had never experienced such pleasure at his hands. If I hadn't, I wouldn't want this now, but that was only a small part. The rest couldn't regret experiencing something so powerful and beautiful when I'd spent most of my life being forbidden to know what pleasure felt like.

But I shouldn't be thinking about this—about what it had been like for him and me, and how he made me feel even now. Because in the early morning hours, when it was just me, I could admit that what he elicited from me went beyond the physical.

It didn't seem to matter that I really shouldn't desire any of this, but my body didn't care about what was right and wrong. I still shivered with need as my toes curled.

Casteel shifted against me, and my heart seemed to stop in my chest. He was asleep, but could he still…sense my desire? His arm tightened, pulling me more firmly against him. His thigh pressed against the apex of mine. A shocking, aching pulse ricocheted through me in hot, tight waves. Suddenly, even my brain betrayed me. I was bombarded with images and sensations—the wicked memory of his mouth nuzzling my neck, the slide and scrape of sharp teeth, and the burst of pain that had so quickly turned into intense pleasure. There was a wildfire in my blood, pooling in my core. In the furthest reaches of my mind, I knew this was the slippery slope I feared would come with this…arrangement of ours. Sharing a bed. Pretending to be…in love. Touching and kissing. *Pretending…*

Pretending I already wasn't slipping down that slope.

His arm loosened, but I was still pressed against him, my heart pounding so fast I would be surprised if he didn't feel it. Was he still asleep? Each breath I took scorched my lungs as I carefully lifted my cheek.

His head was turned slightly away from me. A tumble of dark waves falling over his forehead. The line of his brow and the curve of his jaw were relaxed. Thick lashes shielded his eyes, and his lips were parted as his chest continued to rise and fall in deep, steady breaths.

Unable to look away, I was snared by how peaceful Casteel

appeared while asleep, how young and vulnerable. Seeing him like this, I never would've guessed that he was over two hundred years old or that he was capable of such feral, deadly action.

My gaze drifted over his features, settling on his full mouth. I should've known the first time I saw him that he wasn't mortal. No one looked like him. At least no one from the Kingdom of Solis, including even the most beautiful Ascended. Why had he wanted me? Why did he still want me? But the night he'd helped replace the panic and fear from the nightmare with something good, something *wanted*, he hadn't sought any pleasure for himself. Did that mean he didn't want that…from me any longer?

Those questions didn't come from the niggle of insecurity that I did everything to keep hidden, but simply from pure logic. I knew what half of me looked like. I knew how people saw the other half. Many wouldn't consider me undeniably attractive even though I had heard people claim that attraction didn't always stem from the physical. But I wasn't sure if that was true. It wasn't like I had a lot of experience with such things. Queen Ileana had once told me that beauty was more than straight, smooth lines as she showed me the Star, a diamond highly coveted throughout the Kingdom for its rarity and luminous, silver appearance.

"*The most beautiful things in all the kingdom often have jagged and uneven lines, scars which intensify the beauty in intricate ways our eyes nor our minds can detect or even begin to understand,*" the Queen had said as she turned the diamond in her hand, light catching on its irregular dips and peaks. "*Without them, they would just be common and ordinary, like all the other smoothly cut diamonds you can find anywhere you look. Beauty, my sweet child, is often broken and barbed, and always unexpected.*"

I wasn't sure if what she said held true for people. It didn't seem that way, because Casteel was all smooth, straight lines, and he was magnificent.

Why he wanted me or how he could when there were others with equally smooth, straight lines didn't matter. What did was the fact that I was staring at him while he slept, and that was borderline creepy.

Tugging my gaze away, I bit down on my lip as I decided that this would very much be like ripping a bandage from a wound. I would need to just move. Do it fast and well, and hope that he didn't wake until I fixed the stupid robe or before he realized I was sleeping on him. I started to pull away—

Without any warning, Casteel moved. There was no time to even respond. He was shockingly fast as he rolled me under him, a hand curled around my throat. I gasped in shock.

Casteel's eyes were so dilated that only a thin strip of amber shone as his lips peeled back, revealing sharp, slightly elongated fangs. A low, feral growl of warning rumbled out of him and vibrated through me.

"Casteel!" I forced out around the hold on my throat. "What is wrong with you?"

The grip on my neck tightened, forcing a harsh breath out of me. Instinct took over, breaking through the coating of surprise as I swung at him with my fist, fully planning to bring it down on his arm, breaking his hold on me. It never happened.

He caught my hand, thrusting it down to the bed. I strained against him, but his hand was like a band of steel. Lifting my left hand, I sank my fingers into his hair and pulled hard, jerking his head back. "Let go of me!"

The sound that came from him sent goosebumps rushing across my skin as he easily resisted, leveling his head once more.

There was no visible amber to his eyes now, and the way he looked at me was like…like he had no idea who I was. As if he didn't see me.

My heart stopped. Something…something wasn't right. "Casteel?"

The only answer was a snarl that reminded me of a very large, cornered wild animal as those nearly black eyes moved down the length of me. He didn't seem to recognize his name or me.

At once, I remembered what he'd told me. He had nightmares, and sometimes when he woke, he didn't know where he was. That had to be what was happening here.

I willed my heart to steady. "Casteel, it's me—"

The rumbling warning came once more. His nostrils flared

as he inhaled sharply. Modesty be damned. I didn't care that everything from the waist down was clearly visible because of a nightmare or something else, whatever was going on, it had a grip on him. I had a horrible suspicion that I was seconds away from turning into breakfast.

Remembering the dagger I'd placed under the pillow, I reached behind me, grasping the handle as Casteel shifted above me, his hand leaving my throat to curl around my hip—

Shock splashed through me as I felt the curve of his chin against my lower stomach. Oh, gods, what was he doing? I snatched up the blade, sitting up as far as I could with one hand still pinned to the bed by his. I pressed the dagger against his neck.

He seemed completely unaware as warm breath danced lower. Tension clamped down on my chest, and coiled even lower—unexpectedly and crazily. Because he was—

Oh, *gods*.

It didn't matter what I thought. Neither did the indecent throbbing echoing from within me or the way my entire body seemed to clench tightly as his breath neared the space between my thighs. Another growl came from the back of his throat, this one different, deeper and coarser.

"I don't know what is wrong with you, Casteel, but you need to let go of me." I put pressure on his throat with the blade. "Or we will find out what happens to an Atlantian when their throat is cut."

That seemed to catch his attention because he stilled and lifted his gaze. Those all-black eyes shook me. I willed my hand to stay steady. I knew if he decided to strike, there'd be very little I could do to stop him. I could make him bleed if given the chance, maybe even worse. "Get off me," I ordered. "Now."

He was incredibly still as he stared down at me, like a predator who had sighted its prey and was about to pounce. I tensed as my gift came alive, spilling out from me in the way it did when I was in a crowd of heightened emotions. There was no stopping it. The connection was made, and his feelings rushed through me in a wave of...*gnawing* darkness and insatiable hunger. The kind I had experienced myself on more than one occasion when Duke Teerman was disappointed with something I did or didn't do and I was denied food until I learned to do better. The longest had been three days, and that hunger had been the kind that twisted up the insides in painful need. That wasn't the only thing I felt. Under the feeling of utter emptiness was a lush, dark spice coating my mouth and stoking the banked flames inside me.

Casteel was hungry.

Starving.

Was it for blood? He'd said that Atlantians needed the blood of their own. Had he been…feeding? Surely, he had. There were Atlantians here. He'd bitten me a few days ago. He'd drunk from me, but not a lot. I had no idea how potent my blood was, but if it could make vamprys, I imagined it held some allure to him. I also had no idea how often an Atlantian needed to feed, but that sumptuous, heavy feeling coursing through the connection sparked a primal sort of knowledge that this wasn't just about satisfying a physical hunger.

But under the hunger, I didn't feel any other emotions. The razor-sharp sadness that always cut through him was absent. I didn't know if any part of Casteel or even Hawke was inside him now.

My heart pounded as I tugged on my left arm, the one still pinned to the bed beside my waist. His grip loosened, and he then let go, but he didn't move. I was overly aware of how close his breath, his mouth was to the most sensitive part of me and where I knew a major artery waited. His head turned just the slightest bit, and his chin grazed the crease of my thigh. Several inches lower, closer to the knee, were the gouges in my skin that looked like claw marks but had been made by the teeth of a Craven. I felt none of the horror and fear as I had then, nor the revulsion and certainty of death. All I felt was a delicious ache.

The hand that held the knife to his throat trembled as a forbidden pulse of arousal thundered through me. It was wrong, and I shouldn't feel the heat, the dampness gathering there. But it also felt right, and so natural, even while *none* of this seemed natural.

He made that sound again, the rolling rumble, and my entire

body shuddered. I could barely breathe, let alone think. My senses were firing all at once, and when he dipped his head, my arm went lax, bending to accommodate. My fingers spasmed open, and the knife fell to the bed beside me.

What are you doing? What is wrong with you? What are you—?

He gripped my hips with both hands, lifting me, and then his mouth was on me, obliterating the panicky questions. The air left my lungs as his tongue sliced over the very center of me. This wasn't like the last time, the only time. There was no teasing, slow exploration as he guided me into the wicked act. This time, he *devoured* me, capturing my flesh with his mouth, delving into the warmth and dampness with firm, determined strokes of his tongue. He fed from me as if I were the sweetest nectar, the source of the very life force he needed. I was consumed.

Crying out as my head kicked back, I was lost in the raw sensations. My body moved of its own accord—or tried to. He held me firmly in place, and there was no matching the sinful assault, no escaping it even if I wanted to. Fierce heat built inside me, twisting and tightening as everything in me seemed to concentrate on where he was. My back arched as I grasped the sheets fitted to the bed. His lips moved against me, his tongue inside me, and the sharp graze of his teeth scraped the bundle of nerves. The sensation echoed in the healed bite mark on my neck. It was too much. I screamed as I shattered, breaking apart into a thousand satin-garbed shards of pleasure as intense, stunning release rolled through me in undulating waves.

I was still trembling when I felt him lift his head. Blinking my eyes open in a daze, I lowered my chin and what little air had entered my lungs left me.

His eyes were pitch-black now, no amber to be seen, but they weren't empty and cold like the Ascended's. They were endless and heated, but equally disconcerting to look into. His glistening lips parted—

A terrace door swung open, and a gust of wind swept through the room and over the bed as Kieran stormed inside, his hand on the hilt of his sword.

He drew up short, brows inching up on his forehead. I had no idea what he could see or how much Casteel's body shielded since the curtains had been pulled back. "I heard you scream," Kieran said in way of explanation. "Obviously, I misread the situation."

There was no time to feel the burn of mortification. Casteel's head swung in Kieran's direction. A violent snarl of warning doused the languid heat in my body. That was a far different sound than what I'd heard from him, even when he first woke. This promised blood-soaked death.

"Shit," Kieran muttered, his pale blue gaze widening on the Atlantian. "Cas, my brother, I warned you this would happen."

I had no idea what Kieran had warned Casteel about, but I could see his muscles tensing, preparing, and my gift...oh gods, my gift was still open, still connected to him. What I felt from him then truly scared me. The acidic sting of anger mingled with a charred taste I was unfamiliar with, but whatever it was, it was bad enough that I feared for Kieran's life.

And I wasn't exactly sure when I started to care if the wolven lived or died, but his death would be...it would be yet another unnecessary one. I didn't want that.

"Casteel," I tried, hoping that would garner his attention, and not of the murderous variety.

He didn't seem to hear me, his chin dropping even lower as his fingers slid from my hips. Snarling, he bared his fangs.

"I hope you're listening, Poppy," Kieran said, voice low and unbelievably calm as he let go of the hilt of his sword. "When he lunges for me, I need you to run. Go to the area near the stables. It will have double doors. Find Naill or Delano. Get ready."

Get ready? He expected me to run? Besides the fact that I rarely ran for help, I doubted that I would even make it to the door.

"Casteel," I tried again, and when I felt the power coiling in him, I did the only thing I could think of. Using my gift, I reached out and placed my hand on his arm. I thought of every wonderful feeling I'd ever felt. Walking on the beach with my mother holding one hand and my father holding the other with Ian dancing in front of us, kicking up sand. I sent that through the connection, through the contact of my flesh to his, using the same technique I did to temporarily give a reprieve from pain. I didn't know why I said what I did next, other than I needed to. "It's okay, Hawke."

His entire body jerked as if an invisible hand had grabbed him by his shoulder and pulled. Chest rising and falling in rapid, short pants, his back bowed as his hands landed on either side of my hips. He didn't move. Not for several long moments, but slowly, through my abilities, I no longer had the charred taste in my mouth, and I felt something under the hunger—a cyclone of shame and sadness.

Slowly, he lifted his head and opened his eyes. I let out a ragged breath. They were amber, the only black his pupils. His gaze met mine, and a long moment stretched out between us. Swallowing thickly, I dropped my hand as he looked down.

"Honeydew," Casteel whispered. He grabbed the halves of my robe, tugging it over my hips and my thighs. His hands lingered there, a faint tremor coursing through them as he lifted his gaze to mine once more. "I'm sorry."

And then he rose from the bed and walked out of the terrace doors, past Kieran, without saying another word.

Chapter 23

Sunlight streamed in through the terrace doors, and for several moments, all I could do was sit there and stare at the open door. I couldn't believe what'd happened, from the moment I woke up, all tangled up with him, until he left the bedchamber. What had happened to him left me confused. And my actions, what I'd done and allowed, left me stunned and in a daze.

Casteel had lost his mind.

I'd lost *my* mind.

Kieran closed the door, cutting off the rush of sweet-scented air and snapping me from my thoughts. My gaze cut to where he stood in front of the fireplace. The flames had calmed, no longer stirred by the wind. "Did he hurt you?"

"What?" My voice was hoarse as I blinked.

"Did he hurt you, Penellaphe?" Kieran repeated, his voice softening.

"No. He…" I looked at my bare legs. He hadn't hurt me. He could've, and I wasn't even sure if he hadn't wanted to, but he'd done the furthest thing from hurting me. Reaching for the blanket, I tugged it to my waist.

A muscle flexed in Kieran's jaw. "He didn't force himself on you?"

"Gods, no." I shoved the hair back from my face and caught sight of the knife. It remained where I'd dropped it on the bed. Casteel hadn't forced anything, and the truth was, I could've stopped what'd happened at any point if I wanted to. I could've wounded him enough to attempt an escape. But I hadn't because I…I'd *wanted* what'd happened. I'd woken up wanting that. And I didn't know if Casteel had sensed my desire through whatever had its claws in him, but regardless, I had wanted that.

Him.

I searched for remorse or shame, anything that would show that I regretted what'd taken place, but there was nothing. Like before, there was just vast confusion and irritation with myself because I knew better—knew that things like this just aided in me falling more and more for him. Not too long ago, I had told him that nothing like that would ever happen again, and I'd proven that I couldn't trust myself to make good life choices—not once or twice but three times. The pantry. The nightmare. And now, this. How could I want him so badly that I didn't care about what he did or who he was? Or what he might do to me?

"What happened?" Kieran asked.

It took a couple of moments for me to gather my thoughts. "He woke up, and it was like he didn't recognize me. He was snarling, and his eyes were pitch-black." I left out quite a bit there as I looked at Kieran, but I was sure he already knew a great deal of what'd happened. "His eyes reminded me of an Ascended. Is he…will he be okay?"

Kieran's face was impressively blank, considering what had just happened. "He should be once he cools down."

"Cools down? I think he needs more than that." I glanced at the door. "He was about to attack you."

"In that moment, he saw me as a challenge." He paused. "A threat."

"To who? Him?"

"You."

My heart turned over heavily. "That doesn't make sense."

Kieran folded his arms over his broad chest. "Under the right or, I suppose *extreme* circumstances, those of his kind can become quite possessive."

"With what? Their meals?"

"Did he bite you?"

"Other than the first time?" I resisted the urge to touch the nearly faded mark on my throat. "No."

Something akin to disappointment flickered over his face, and without thinking, I opened my gift and reached out to him. There would be time later to feel guilt over prying when it didn't seem exactly necessary. What I felt wasn't what I imagined disappointment to feel like. This was thick and cloying, reminding me of too-heavy cream. *Concern.* He felt concern. I pulled my senses back.

"What was wrong with him?" I asked, even though I already suspected I knew.

He watched me for a moment. "He'll be fine. Although, I suggest you take this time to prepare yourself before he returns."

Frustration surged, and I narrowed my eyes. "Thanks for the suggestion, but you didn't answer my question. You said that you warned him. About what?"

Kieran said nothing.

Never able to remain seated when anger started pumping through my blood, I grabbed the dagger and shoved off the blanket, standing.

He raised an eyebrow at me. "You plan to use that?"

"Why does everyone think I'm going to stab them when I pick up anything that's not blunt?"

"Well," Kieran replied blandly, "you do have a habit of doing exactly that."

I started to argue but quickly realized that, unfortunately, he had a point. "Only when it's deserved." I placed the dagger on the small wooden table. "And it's not my fault that some of you deserve to be stabbed. Repeatedly."

He inclined his head as if he agreed with the point I'd made. "You shouldn't worry about him—"

"And you should answer my question." I faced him. "Something was obviously wrong with him. He wasn't in control, and I felt his hunger. He was starving."

"So you used your abilities?" A faint smile appeared. "Glad you took my advice."

I rolled my eyes. "I know that Atlantians need to feed off other Atlantians. He told me that they don't need the blood of mortals, but of their own kind. That they need to feed. But he never said why. I may not be a scholar on all things Atlantian, but I'm guessing the black eyes and him being ready to bite your head off are a couple of the reasons Atlantians need to feed?"

"The black eyes, yes. But the wanting to bite my head off probably had more to do with whatever morning activities you two were indulging in."

My face flamed hotly, and it took everything in me to ignore that. "He needs to feed—" I thought about earlier, after the Dead Bones Clan attack. "That's why he was staring at my arm in the woods! When you asked if he was okay. He was hungry then. That's why he was…all growly and wanted to bite your head off."

"Part of the reason. Yes." Kieran looked away, dragging his teeth over his lip. A long moment passed. "He needs to feed. I could tell he was getting to the edge, but he's not about to tip over it. He's not that close."

Unease blossomed. "How can he not be close? He didn't recognize you or me."

His gaze slid back to mine. "If he was closer to the edge, he would've ripped my head off, and you would be Ascending as we speak, forbidden or not. Or, you'd be dead. If he was too close to the edge, one drop of your blood would've sent him over. You most likely would've died, and when he realized what he'd done, he would've…I don't even want to think about what he would've done."

I sucked in a sharp breath, unsure which of those two options was worse. Well, Kieran getting his head torn off sounded way more painful and…messy than what could've happened to me.

If Casteel had been too close to the edge, if he'd fed and then ended up turning me, I would become…an Ascended. Unable to control my bloodlust. Unable to walk in the sun. Virtually immortal. But what kind of life was that?

Though what kind of life would I even have with Casteel? By the time I was old and gray, he would look as he did now. Young. Vital. He would—

Wait. Why was I even thinking about a future—our

future—when there really wasn't one? Maybe I truly had lost my mind.

I felt like I needed to sit down. "If this was him not close to the edge, then I don't think I want to see him on it."

"No, you do not." Kieran tipped his head back against the wall. "Did he wake up normally, or was he startled awake?"

Thinking of what I'd been doing and fantasizing about before he'd woken up, I was glad that Kieran wasn't looking at me. "I think I woke him up. I moved, and that's when he sort of launched himself at me."

"That makes sense," he murmured, eyes closing. "I don't like talking about him—about this kind of stuff. If he knew I was, he probably *would* rip my head off. I'd deserve it because there are things only he should be allowed to repeat. But I think you need to know this even though I'm not sure you deserve to be privy to the knowledge."

"Why wouldn't I be deserving?" I asked. It wasn't like I was the one running around and kidnapping people. Casteel was.

"Because this is something only close friends and loved ones should be privy to, and you are neither."

Well, he had a point there. But I already knew what Kieran didn't think would be right to share. "He told me before that he had nightmares, and that sometimes when he woke, he didn't know where he was."

In any other situation, I would've laughed upon seeing Kieran so surprised. But none of this was funny. "He told you?"

I nodded. "I had a nightmare—I have bad ones—and after one of them woke him, he told me about his."

Kieran's expression smoothed out. "Yes. He has nightmares. You know what was done to him when he was held by the Ascended. Sometimes, he finds himself back there, caged and used, his blood nor his body his."

This time, I sat down before even realizing it, though I wasn't surprised to find myself there. The heaviness of his words had put me there, and the reminder of the agony and horror of what Casteel had faced kept me there.

"When he has those nightmares he told you about, and if he's startled awake, sometimes his mind gets stuck in that madness," Kieran went on. And if anyone knew how nightmares could feel so very real, it was me. "And if he hasn't fed, he can slip a little into the animal they turned him into."

A monster.

Shuddering, I closed my eyes. What had he said when I'd called him a monster? *I wasn't born that way. I was* made *this way.* But he wasn't that. My heart ached as fiercely as it had when Casteel had told me about his captivity.

Letting out a shaky breath, I opened my eyes to find Kieran watching me. "He's not an animal," I said, and I wasn't sure why I'd said it, but I needed to. "I don't know what he is, but he's not that. He's not a monster."

"No, he's not." His head tilted to the side. "I think you would've liked him if you had met him before all of this."

Uncomfortable with how much I would've preferred that, I folded one arm over my waist.

A sad, wry smile formed on Kieran's face, almost as if he knew what I was thinking. "I imagine a lot would be different."

I nodded slowly, pulling myself out of the well of sorrow that was a cavern in my chest. "Why hasn't he fed? There were Atlantians at the keep, right? There are Atlantians here."

Kieran nodded. "There are many he could've fed from but he hasn't."

"Why? Why would he let it get to this point?"

He raised an eyebrow. "That's a damn good question, isn't it?"

My damn good question didn't have an answer, and it plagued me as I washed up and dressed in the baggy pants and the deep green tunic that had been in the bundle Quentyn had given me. Other unanswered questions bothered me, as well. Why wouldn't Casteel have fed? Were the nightmares also partly responsible for the cutting sadness that clung to him? If this was him not too close to the edge, then what was he like when he was at the edge? What would've happened if he hadn't...well, fed from me differently?

And why in the world had I allowed him, when he was obviously not in his right mind, to do what he'd done? And *why* had he done that? Did bloodlust elicit such actions? Or was it because he'd sensed my arousal? My cheeks burned, and I wasn't sure I wanted to know the answer to that question.

Either way, I had been wrong when I said that I didn't have a death wish. Because what if he had been teetering on that edge and he'd used that mouth for something else?

My stomach dipped as I ran a brush through my tangled hair. In the soft lamplight, the strands reminded me more of a ruby-hued wine than a blazing fire, like it often did in the sun. I angled my head to the side. The bite marks were no longer visible, but I left my hair down anyway and then stepped back into the bedchamber.

Kieran stood by the terrace doors, staring out them. I wasn't exactly surprised to see that he was still here. "Are you on babysitting duty? I agreed to the marriage," I said as I picked up the thigh sheath. The word *marriage* still sounded strange on my tongue. "I'm not going to run."

He turned to me. "I was waiting to see if you'd like to get some breakfast."

"Oh." I slid the wolven dagger into the holder and then straightened the hem of the tunic. The top was more form-fitting than I was used to, but it was clean. I glanced at the door. "Should we...should we wait for Casteel?"

He turned to me. "That won't be necessary. He'll find us when he's ready."

I nibbled on my lower lip. It didn't feel right to go off when he was...well, going through whatever he was. And it also felt weird to be so concerned about him.

"Are you hungry right now?" Kieran asked, dragging my attention back to him. "Or would you like to see the Bay?"

"The Bay," I chose, knowing my stomach was still too tied up in knots to eat anything yet.

"Good." Kieran turned and opened the door.

Warmer air than I expected greeted us as we walked outside and across the yard. Within a few moments, I shoved the sleeves of my sweater up. "I didn't expect it to be this nice here—weather-wise."

"Next to Carsodonia, we're at the most southern part of Solis. It'll get cooler at night, especially as the season turns, but the days will remain pleasant."

"Just like the capital." I tipped my head back, letting the sun wash over my face as I heard the sound of distant voices and laughter coming from what I assumed was beyond the fortress. "Were you at the capital with Casteel?"

"For a time, yes. I wasn't exactly a fan," he said, and I glanced over at him with a raised brow. He shrugged a shoulder. "Too many Ascended. Too many people crowded together."

"And there aren't too many people crowded in Atlantia?" I asked as we walked past a crumbling stone wall. The black waters of Stygian Bay glittered like pools of obsidian, still and vast. It went on as far as I could see, disappearing into the horizon.

"Not yet, but if we continue growing, our cities will be as crowded."

Reaching the top of a slight hill, I turned, unable to see anything beyond the fortress walls. "But you have Spessa's End."

Kieran nodded, and I still couldn't believe that there was anything here. I started down the hill, and the grass gave way to sand. There was no damp scent as we drew close to the broken piers that jutted up from the water like decayed fingers. The air smelled of lavender, except I saw none of the purple-tipped plants. I stared at the lifeless, midnight waters, wondering when or if the god that slumbered within the Bay would wake. If so, what would the God of Common Men and Endings think of the world he'd left behind, of what was being done to the mortals he cared for in death?

Looking down, a sudden urge swept through me. "It has been years since I felt sand under my feet."

"Now is a better time than any to feel it again, I suppose."

His dry response didn't deter me as I yanked off my boots and socks. A grin tugged at my lips as I wiggled my toes in the warm, coarse sand.

Kieran snorted. "Malik used to do the same as soon as he reached the sand. Tear off his shoes so he could feel it against his feet."

A heaviness settled over me as I walked toward the Bay, leaving my shoes and socks behind in a pile. "What was Malik like? I mean, what is he like?"

Kieran followed a few steps behind me, silent for a long moment. "He was kind and generous but also a wicked prankster. Casteel was always the far more serious one." He joined me. "He was the brother you would've thought was being groomed from birth to be King."

Casteel, the serious one? That surprised me more than the fact that a god slept in the Bay.

My thoughts must've been visible on my face because he said, "The way Casteel is with you—the teasing and trying to get a rise out of you—isn't how he is with most."

"So, it's an act?"

"No, Casteel is just more…alive when he's with you," he said, and I—

I thought my jaw might hit the sand.

"And Malik was the life and soul of the family," Kieran continued. I picked my mouth up off the ground. "And the past tense is correct. Even if he lives, he will not be who he used to be."

"But he'll have his family to help him remember—his parents, Casteel, you," I reasoned. "All of you can help him remember who he once was."

Kieran didn't respond.

I looked at him. "Do you…do you think he still lives?"

"He has to. Even if the vamprys have been capturing Atlantians all these years, full-blooded or half, they would not allow the Prince to die. With him, it takes less blood to complete the Ascension. He's too much of a prize to let wither and die."

Stomach churning, I briefly closed my eyes. While a large part of me hoped he still lived, a small part almost wished he didn't. Whatever existence he had under the Ascended's control was no life.

The question that was already answered surfaced again. How could the Ascended be allowed to continue?

They couldn't be.

If Casteel and I were successful, then would I seriously be content spending the rest of my life safely hidden away while the Ascended continued ruling the people of Solis with fear? Stealing their children and who knew how many other people? If the Queen and King lived or died, wouldn't the other Ascended simply find another Atlantian to continue making more Ascended, even if it were forbidden?

Casteel wanted to avoid war, but how could anyone be sure that the Royals would change? That they wouldn't seek to go back to the way things were?

Kieran shifted slightly, looking over his shoulder. I followed his gaze, squinting. Three or four people walked past the crumbling walls, their clothing a vibrant array of golds and blues.

"Who are they?"

"Not entirely sure who they are," Kieran answered, turning back around. "But most of the people here are older Descenters and Atlantians and wolven."

I watched them until I could no longer see them, my stomach twisting into tiny knots. How would they respond to me? Friendly and outgoing like Elijah and Alastir, or would they be like the rest?

"Casteel and I came here once when we were younger, before the town was razed," Kieran said, catching my attention. "It was one of the first times we'd left Atlantia. Malik was with us, and the people who lived here, those who were half-Atlantian or supporters knew who we were and behaved as if Rhain himself had risen from the Bay."

Not one but two Princes in their midst must have stirred up some excitement.

"A lot of people crowded the edges of the Bay." He squinted as if he were trying to see what had once been here. "A small girl slipped on the embankment and fell into the water. There was panic and helplessness as everyone stood at the edge."

I sat down, several feet from the water's edge. "No one jumped in after her?"

He shook his head. "No mortal enters these waters and returns. The people believed that Rhain's sentries would capture anyone who dared, grabbing their ankles and pulling them down below." One side of his lips quirked up in a wry grin as he lowered himself to the spot beside me. "But Cas jumped in. Didn't even think twice about it. Just dove right in, even though the girl had slipped under and hadn't resurfaced."

I turned back to the Bay. "Did he find her?"

"He did. Pulled her back to the water's edge where Malik and—" He drew in a deep breath, stretching out a leg. "One of our friends was able to force the water from her lungs. The girl breathed. She lived. And those who were unaware of what Malik and Cas were, truly believed they were gods."

I was happy to hear that the girl had lived, and I hoped that what happened to this town came long after her time. But my brain got stuck on something. Kieran had almost said a name for this *friend*, and I had a good idea who it was.

"Was it Shea who came here with you all?"

"What?" Kieran's head snapped in my direction. "How do you know her name?" His eyes narrowed, and before I could respond, he muttered, "Alastir."

I nodded. "Alastir told me about her. That Casteel was once engaged to his daughter."

His features sharpened. "Alastir shouldn't have said anything."

"Why? That was his daughter," I argued. "He lost her, too, and before you get mad at him, he even told me he probably shouldn't have brought her up. I haven't said anything to Casteel." Well, that was kind of true.

"But, of course, you have questions."

"I do," I admitted.

Kieran slowly shook his head as he stared out over the Bay. "You're not asking for my advice, but I'm going to give it to you, nonetheless. This time, I truly hope you listen." His icy blue eyes met mine. "Don't bring up Shea with Cas. That is a road you don't want to travel with him. Ever."

My brows lifted. "But she's a part of him and—"

"And why does that matter to you?" he challenged. "This marriage will only be temporary, correct? Why do you need to know about those who shaped who he is today? That kind of knowledge is for those who plan on a future."

I snapped my mouth shut as frustration boiled inside me. Kieran was right, but…

Sighing, I looked over my shoulder, able to see the upper walls of the fortress. Had Casteel cooled down? "Are you sure he'll be okay?"

Kieran's head inclined as he studied me. "Do you want an honest answer or one that will make this easier for you?"

"You said earlier that he'd be okay," I pointed out as dread blossomed to life.

"He will be." He paused. "For now."

"What is that supposed to mean?"

"It means that he'll be okay for a little longer, but he needs to feed. He's gone too long."

Dread pumped through me, alive and well. "When was the last time he fed?"

"I'm not sure, but it had to be when we were in Masadonia." He dragged a hand over his head and then dropped it, glancing back to the water. "Normally, he'd be able to go for weeks without feeding, but he's given you blood twice, and then he was wounded. That moved him closer to the edge."

"He didn't need to give me his blood last time."

His gaze swiveled back to mine. "I know. I told him not to, but he did it anyway. He didn't want to see you in pain."

I sucked in a short breath. "And now he's in pain because of that. Because of me?"

"It's not because of you, Penellaphe. It was his choice. Just as it has been his choice not to feed."

"I still don't get that." Frustrated, I picked up a fistful of sand. "Why would he do this to himself? I felt his hunger, Kieran. It was intense, and the longer he goes, it will only get worse—"

"And you will be more at risk."

I stilled, even though my heart thundered. "I thought he was the only person I was safe with. Isn't that what you said?"

"You are, but when an Atlantian doesn't feed, no one is safe. Not even those they care about or even love."

Air left me in a singular rush. Love? "He doesn't care for me."

Kieran stared back at me. "If it helps you to believe that, then by all means, continue. But that doesn't make it true."

I glared at him. "And just because you spout vague statements doesn't make whatever you're saying true either."

"He gave you his blood when you didn't need it, just so you wouldn't be in pain when you woke—"

"And so I didn't delay in leaving New Haven!"

"Funny how we weren't planning to leave the moment you woke anyway," he replied. "Which you're conveniently forgetting."

I clamped my mouth shut.

"Even if that were the case, which it isn't, if he didn't care, he wouldn't have been concerned over you being uncomfortable during our travels, would he? And if he didn't care, he would've used a hundred different compulsions at this point, no matter how temporary, to keep you better controlled, something that would make all our lives easier."

My eyes narrowed.

"He wouldn't be marrying you, risking the ire of not just his entire kingdom but also his parents, who you will soon discover are *not* two people you want to anger just so you have a chance to make it through this alive, free from the Ascended and from him. If that is what you choose," he went on. "But more importantly, he would've stuck to the plan he spent years cultivating, and we would've already been halfway to Carsodonia to exchange you for his brother. Yet, here we are. And the only reason why any of that changed is because once he got to know you, he started to care for you."

I wanted Kieran to take back those words because they did things to my heart, and even worse, dangerous things to my mind.

"You're annoying," I muttered.

"The truth often is. But you want to know an even more annoying truth?"

"Not really."

"Too bad, because you need to hear this. He cares for you just like *you* care for him despite the lies and the betrayal," Kieran stated. "That's why, even when you were the Maiden, you shared your secrets with him and allowed him things you would've never permitted anyone else. That's why you didn't use that dagger strapped to your thigh this morning, even though you knew how to use it against an Atlantian. That's why you want to know more about Shea. It's why, even now, you are concerned about him." His eyes flashed an intense blue. "And just so you know, the only reason I didn't end your life the second I learned that you stabbed him in the heart is because he cares for you. Is that less vague enough for you, Penellaphe?"

My lips parted on a shaky inhale. I didn't want to hear what he said. I didn't want to recognize the truth of his words. Acknowledging them was...it felt irrevocable.

Because caring for Casteel meant more than just wanting him. It meant either forgiving or forgetting his lies and betrayals, and I didn't know if that was right or wrong. Because him caring for me meant more than just an agreement or pretending, and the implications of all of that was...well, it was terrifying for a multitude of reasons. Kieran could be wrong. Casteel could care for me, but not deeply. While I would...oh, gods, I already knew what it meant for me to care for him—what I desperately wished wasn't the case.

That I'd started falling in love with him when we first met and hadn't stopped.

But beyond that, I was the Maiden—a person his people, his family, would most likely loathe. I was only half-Atlantian. I would age and die, and he would be who he was today for so many years, it would feel like an eternity to me.

I stared at the sand, feeling more out of my element now than I had since this whole thing started. "The night before I learned who he really was, I had already decided that I could no longer be the Maiden. It wasn't just because of him. Maybe how I felt about him was the start of me realizing that I could never live in the skin of the Maiden, but I wanted to stay with him," I admitted, my voice hoarse and barely above a whisper. "Even though I thought he was a Royal Guard and would have to basically go into hiding with me, I wanted to be with him—to stay with him somehow. Because he made me feel.... He made me feel like I was *alive*." I swallowed hard. "I did care for him. I cared for him a lot."

"He was Casteel then just like he's Hawke now," Kieran stated quietly, drawing my gaze to him. "And you know that. You just aren't ready to accept it."

I briefly squeezed my eyes shut. Still, caring for him could cause a chain of reactions I wouldn't be able to prevent. Caring for him felt like I was betraying not just Vikter and Rylan and all of those who'd died because of him, but also myself. That I forgave his lies and his misdeeds. Still caring meant...

"Still caring for him would only lead to heartache," I whispered, knowing the truth right then and there. I did care. I never stopped caring. And acknowledging that felt as if I'd slipped under the black water.

"It doesn't have to," Kieran said. "But even so, sometimes, the heartbreak that comes with loving someone is worth it, even if loving that person means eventually saying goodbye to them."

The roughness in his tone spoke more than his words shared. "You sound like you have experience with that."

"I do." A long moment of silence passed between us. "Do you know what happens when an Atlantian cares for someone?"

I shook my head, wanting to know more about this person that he'd loved but had to say goodbye to.

Kieran didn't give me a chance. "They find the idea of feeding from someone else repellent. It's too intimate for them to even consider. And if the partner is mortal? It usually takes the mortal proving to the other that it's okay for them to feed, and in some cases, the Atlantian is lost to the darkness of hunger. That's why he hasn't fed."

My heart thudded against my ribs as I told myself that couldn't be the case with Casteel. It just couldn't.

Kieran was quiet only for a few minutes. "Cas told me once that he felt as if he already knew you after speaking with you just a few times."

I wiggled my toes in the sand once more. "I asked him about that."

"This is my surprised face," Kieran murmured, and when I looked at him, his expression was the same as always. Bored with a hint of amusement.

My lips twitched despite the insanity of our conversation as I turned back to the sparkling, sun-drenched midnight water. "He told me he believed it was the Atlantian blood in him, recognizing mine."

"And you felt the same?"

I nodded. "Is that a possibility?"

"Possibly," he said after a moment. "But I don't think that's the case. I think it's something deeper than that. Something intangible, far rarer and stronger than bloodlines and even the gods. Something powerful enough that it has ushered in great change in the past."

Tensing, I had a feeling I didn't want to know what he thought. That whatever it was would be even more earth-shattering than what he'd already shared. It'd be words given life that I wouldn't be able to control.

"I think you're heartmates."

Chapter 24

Heartmates.

Kieran didn't elaborate on what that meant, and I didn't ask for more information. I'd never heard of such a thing, and I didn't want to.

Processing the idea of Casteel caring about me was complicated enough without adding yet another intangible element to it.

But what Kieran had said—all of it— lingered throughout breakfast, robbing the food of all taste as my gaze kept roaming back toward the white banners hanging on the walls of the dining hall, spaced six feet apart. In the center of each of them was an emblem embossed in gold, shaped like the sun and its rays. And at the center of the sun was a sword lying diagonally atop an arrow.

I knew I was staring at the Atlantian Crest.

We ate at a narrow table in a dining room that'd once served the people of Spessa's End but now was empty except for Quentyn, who had brought the eggs, crispy bacon, and biscuits out to us when we arrived. He chatted with Kieran, his energy from the night before seeming just as high. I tried to focus on the conversation, aware of how different this was from the last time Kieran and I had shared food. Quentyn didn't ignore me or treat me with barely contained dislike. If he knew I had once been the

Maiden, he didn't care. And that was, well…it would've been something to revel in if I didn't keep looking around to see if Casteel appeared, or if my mind wasn't so wrapped up in what Kieran had said.

I couldn't focus on the fact that Casteel may care for me. I couldn't even dwell on the revelation that I'd moved past the stage of caring for him quite some time ago. There was no amount of time or space for me to even come to terms with any of that and what it meant.

What I turned over and over in my mind was the reality that Casteel needed to feed, and if what Kieran had said was true, I needed to convince him to do so from someone else or…*I* needed to feed him.

But there really wasn't an option between the two. Naill and Delano knew I was half-Atlantian, and if the others, whoever else was here, didn't know, they would learn soon enough. Casteel feeding from someone else wouldn't exactly convince anyone of our intent to marry, would it?

It would have to be me.

My stomach dipped as the bite of bacon scratched its way down my throat. Would I be okay with that? I thought of what it had been like when he'd bitten me before, and I picked up the glass of water, nearly downing the entirety of it. It wouldn't exactly be a hardship. It would be…

Gods, it would be intense.

Nothing like when Lord Chaney had bitten me. Nothing like a Craven's bite.

"The one thing I'm not looking forward to is traveling back through the mountains," Quentyn said, drawing me out of my thoughts. I'd discovered when I first saw him in the bright lamplight that he was fair-haired, not blond-white like Delano, but more…golden. He was young, slim as a reed and already taller than me. There was a delicacy to his features, one that drew the eye and held it, and I imagined the beauty in the lines of his face would only increase as he got older. His eyes were a vibrant shade of amber, just like Casteel's, but curved upward at the outer corners in a way that made his eyes seem like he was always smiling.

"Yeah, I'm not looking forward to that part of the trip either," Kieran agreed.

"Are you talking about the Skotos Mountains?" I asked, glancing toward the doors for what probably had to be the hundredth time since Kieran and I had sat down.

Quentyn nodded as he looked over at me. When he first saw me, his gaze had snagged on the left side of my face, but that was all. He hadn't continued to stare. He hadn't quickly looked away in embarrassment, either. He saw them and seemed to move on from them, and I appreciated that. "The mist, man. The *mist*. During the day, it thins out a bit, but at night? You can barely see a few feet in front of you."

I remembered what Kieran had said about the long mountain range. "And that's…Atlantian magic?"

"Yes. It's designed to ward off travelers, making them think there are Craven in the mountains, but there are none," Kieran said, eyeing my plate. "You going to eat the rest of that bacon?"

"No." I nudged my plate toward him. "How does Atlantian magic work?"

"That's a complicated question with an even more convoluted answer." Kieran picked up a slice of bacon from my plate. "And I know you're gearing up for a hundred more questions."

I totally was.

"But the easiest answer is that the magic is tied to the gods," he said.

Well, that only caused me to have more questions and made me think of the Blood Forest tree, the omen, that had appeared out of thin air in New Haven.

"And besides, the mist isn't just a mist," Kieran added between mouthfuls of bacon. "Is it, Quentyn?"

"No." The young man's eyes widened. "It's more like an…alarm system."

"It responds to travelers, even Atlantians, and the way it responds is different for everyone. Larger groups seem to trigger it." Quentyn's fingers tapped nonstop on the table. "That's why we split up into groups no larger than three."

All of that sounded…concerning. "And traveling through

the mountains is the only way?"

"It is, but don't worry too much." Quentyn smiled. "We didn't have too much of a problem when we came through it before."

Too much of a problem?

"Which reminds me, I can make some extra bacon for when we leave." He popped up from the chair. "If you like?"

Kieran paused with the second slice halfway to his mouth. "When it comes to bacon, the answer is always yes."

The young Atlantian laughed as he glanced over his shoulder. The door opened, and my heart launched itself into my throat as my gaze crawled over the faces of the men and women who entered. My shoulders lowered as I recognized none of the faces. There was a half-dozen.

"You guys hungry?" Quentyn called out and was greeted with several enthusiastic replies. Turning around, he shrugged as he said, "I like to cook."

And then, with a nod at both of us, he raced off to the kitchen area.

I watched the group of newcomers split into two, seating themselves at the round tables near the door. All of them nodded in acknowledgment, but none approached. A woman with dark hair glanced over her shoulder. She had golden eyes. An Atlantian. As did the man who stared from where he sat across from her.

Ignoring the nervous fluttering in my stomach, I offered a smile.

The woman turned back around, and the man faced another beside him.

Sighing, I turned to Kieran. "When do you think we will leave?"

"If Elijah was able to get the first group out a day after we left, they'll probably be at least two days. Since the group would be larger, they won't be traveling as fast as we did." He wiped the sheen of grease from his fingers on a napkin. "But we're less than a half-day's ride from the mountains, so we should reach them by tomorrow afternoon, which will allow us to cross halfway before nightfall. And then we'll be in Atlantia."

My heart skipped a beat. I hadn't realized that we were now so close to what was basically an unofficial boundary line. "Just like that?"

He smiled slightly as one of the younger men with light brown hair bent his head to the woman, whispering. "Just like that."

Leaning back in my chair, I peeked over at the people. Their postures seemed awfully stiff. I bit down on the inside of my lip and opened my senses, letting them stretch out. The moment their bitter and sour-tasting emotions came back to me, I immediately wished I hadn't let my gift free. Distrust and dislike were often hard to separate, but in some cases, they were joined. Like now.

They had to know who I was. It was the only reason they'd feel this way.

"You've been quieter than expected," Kieran commented.

I shut down my senses, offering a shrug. "I've been thinking." Which wasn't exactly a lie. I'd done a whole lot of thinking during breakfast.

"Great."

I shot him an arch look. "It's really your fault, by the way."

"Probably should've kept my mouth shut."

"I sort of wished you had."

"But I didn't."

"No," I sighed, picking at the napkin on the table. "Where is he?"

"Who?"

My head tipped to the side. "Like you don't know."

"I know a lot of hes."

"Hes isn't a word," I muttered. "Where is Casteel? Is he…?"

"Is he what?" he quietly asked when I didn't continue.

"What if he's not okay?" I glared at him. "If he was closer to the edge than you realized, what if he's out there, feeding off…random people."

"I haven't known you for long." He gave a shake of his head, and I thought maybe he was searching for patience. "But sometimes, the things your mind conjures worry me."

"I think it's a valid concern," I grumbled.

"I imagine he's cooled down, gotten himself ready, and is speaking with people." Kieran looked at me from the side of his eye. "Glad to see that you're acknowledging that you care for him and are questioning his wellbeing."

I started to tell him that I wasn't, but that would have been an obvious lie. Kieran knew it. I knew it. And I hated everyone, but especially Kieran.

Something occurred to me in that moment, and I got up close and personal with abject horror. I had no idea what I was going to say to him about this morning. Not about the whole feeding thing. I knew what I needed to do to make sure he didn't go all Ascended-eyed on me again. But the other *thing*? Could I just pretend like it didn't happen?

That seemed like a successful plan.

Shoulders slumping, I changed the subject. "Can I ask you something?"

"I have a feeling if I said no, it wouldn't stop you."

He was right. It wouldn't. I kept my voice incredibly low. "Casteel said that if I refused the marriage, he'd let me go. That he would take me somewhere safe. Was he telling the truth?"

Kieran looked at me, brows raised. "So, you're basically asking me to betray him?"

"I'm not asking—okay. I am."

"He wasn't lying," Kieran said after a moment. "If you had refused, he would've let you go. But I doubt you would've been free of him."

The corners of my lips turned down. "If I'm not free of him, how would he have let me go?"

Kieran lifted a shoulder in a shrug. "Those two things aren't mutually exclusive."

My frown increased, but then I shook my head as I looked to the door. Knowing he wasn't lying meant something. It meant a lot because Casteel would do *anything* to get his brother back.

Except he wouldn't force me to marry him to achieve what he wanted. He wouldn't use me as ransom, and for the first time since all of this began, I truly realized his plans to use me had changed long before I was even aware—probably even before *he* was aware they had. It wasn't just his claim or what Kieran said. It was all of that and Casteel's own actions. I just didn't want to accept it—to see or understand. Because while Casteel wasn't a monster, he *was* capable of doing monstrous things to get what he wanted. But I *was* exempt. He wasn't the good guy—the savior or the saint. He'd killed to free his brother. He'd used countless others—mortals and Atlantians alike—to free his sibling. And he still would. To him, the means justified the end.

But Casteel had drawn a line that he wouldn't cross.

And that line was me.

Truly acknowledging that was terrifying. Already, my heart was pounding, and that swelling sensation had returned, filling my chest. And that scared me. Ignoring and denying what I felt for him was easier when I could convince myself that I was nothing more than a pawn—another means to justify the end.

Now, there was no ignoring or denying anything.

I didn't know if that meant what Kieran had claimed—that Casteel and I were heartmates, but it did mean something. What that changed for me—for us—I also didn't know.

I took a breath. It went nowhere, and it felt like the floor was moving—the whole world was shifting under me, even though I was sitting. "I'm going to do it."

"I'm half-afraid to ask what it is you're going to do."

Folding my arms across my chest, I rolled my eyes. "I'm going to offer myself up…for dinner basically. To Casteel," I tacked on.

"As dinner?"

"Basically." I peeked at Kieran, and I could tell he was trying not to laugh.

"Only a part of me is surprised, but I'm relieved." And it did seem like his shoulders looked less hunched. "He needs you."

I'd just returned to the rooms Casteel and I had been given, hoping he'd returned, when Alastir knocked on the main door.

Letting him inside, I told myself not to stress over Casteel's continued absence. He had to be okay...*ish*, and it was still pretty early in the morning.

Alastir was dressed in an outfit far more suited for the temperate weather, wearing only a white button-down shirt and breeches. I was half-tempted to cut the sleeves off the sweater, even though it remained cool in the rooms.

"I won't take up too much of your time," he said, sitting on the edge of the settee as he brushed back a lock of hair from his face. "I just wanted to check in on you after hearing that you had a far more eventful trip here than I."

I sat across from him in one of the thickly cushioned armchairs. "Most of it was rather uneventful up until I learned of the Dead Bones Clan with firsthand experience."

"I couldn't believe when Casteel told me they had attacked your group," he responded, and the measure of relief that came with that was ridiculous. He had to have spoken with Alastir this morning. "To be honest, I figured they were mostly gone by now."

"Well, they are definitely a few members short now." The image of Casteel tossing the men from the trees filled my mind. "I still can't believe the Ascended have either allowed them to live out there or don't know about them." I glanced around, shaking my head. "Part of me can't even believe they don't know about this. I was shocked when I saw it."

"Solis is a powerful kingdom, but they are also an arrogant one. I don't believe they even considered once that Atlantia might quietly take back some of their lands."

"Casteel had once said something similar—about their arrogance."

He nodded. "Did Casteel not tell you about Spessa's End? How he hopes to eventually move hundreds here?"

I nibbled on my lip, unsure if I should lie or not, but I decided that doing so would be silly. It was clear I had no idea. "He hadn't yet."

A slight frown pulled at his lips. "I honestly expected he would. Reclaiming Spessa's End is incredibly important to him and the kingdom. And, it was entirely his idea. Something he convinced his father and mother of."

Irritation reared its head again, but so did something heavier. Embarrassed because this seemed like something a fiancée should know about, I shifted uncomfortably in my chair. "I'm sure he planned to tell me, but with everything going on…"

Alastir nodded, but I could see the skepticism in his gaze. "I'm sure he would've, and that it was a simple oversight. Not an issue of trust or inattentiveness."

I stiffened, having not even thought of an issue of trust, but…but that would make sense, wouldn't it? What was being done here in Spessa's End would be highly coveted information to the Ascended. If they found out, it could mean yet another raid on the town, the destruction of what they were building here—whatever that was. I wasn't exactly sure since I'd only caught glimpses of it. Was that why Casteel hadn't shared any information until I was far enough away from the Ascended that I was no longer a risk to Spessa's End if I were captured or if I…reneged on our deal? Did he think I would ever say something that would put innocent people in harm's way?

Innocent people I had assumed were guilty not all that long ago.

Unsettled by my thoughts, I asked Alastir about his trip. From there, he spoke of the upcoming journey. I relaxed as he talked. It was his voice and his raspy laugh, so familiar and so like Vikter's. There was a calming quality to it, and I was so grateful for his visit that when it became clear that he would soon be leaving, I wanted to find an excuse for him to stay.

"There was another reason I wanted to speak with you," he said as he leaned in. "When I spoke with Casteel this morning, he appeared…well, as if he were strung too tight. Then I learned that he'd been wounded when your group was set upon by the Dead Bones Clan."

Keeping my face blank, I nodded. "He was wounded."

"I don't know how much you know about Atlantians and their needs or customs like the Joining, or what happens when they choose to be with someone, but he may need to feed. And with you not being accustomed to the Atlantian ways, I wanted to make sure you knew," he said, his gentle smile creasing the skin at the corners of his eyes.

There was a sudden knot in my throat, and I almost launched myself at the poor man, but I somehow managed not to repeat that awkward moment. "I know he needs to feed. He will." I felt my cheeks heat. "But what is the Joining?"

Alastir's eyes widened. "He didn't tell you?"

My shoulders started to slump. "Should he have?"

"I would think so." His eyes narrowed slightly. "It may be expected, especially since you're not a full-blooded Atlantian, but it—well, it wouldn't exactly be the easiest of conversations with someone who didn't grow up in Atlantia." He started to stand. "And it's one I was eternally grateful I never needed to explain to my daughter."

"Wait." I lifted a hand. "What is it?"

"You should ask Casteel."

"You should tell me since you brought it up," I pointed out. "What is this thing? The Joining?"

Alastir was still for a moment, and then he closed his eyes. "This is going to be an incredibly awkward conversation."

I started to grin. "Now, I'm really interested."

"And you will likely change your tune fairly quickly." He rubbed his chin. "Gods, he probably never told you because of your background."

"My background?" My brows rose. "As the Maiden?"

He nodded. "In your own words, you said you were quite sheltered, but even if you weren't, what you're about to hear would have come as a shock."

"Okay?" Curiosity burned through me.

"The Joining is a very old tradition—one that isn't often done. And thank the gods for that." His upper lip curled in distaste. "It's quite crass."

Now was probably not a good time to admit that I was even more curious.

"When a bonded elemental takes on a partner, the bond can be extended to that person. It requires an exchange of blood between the three—or the four if the partner is also bonded. And the exchange of blood...well, it is quite..." He cleared his throat as his cheeks flushed. "It can become very *intimate*. In a way that would most likely make you very uncomfortable."

There were many times in my life that I was shocked by something. The last several weeks had been one surprise after another, but this...

Even as sheltered as I was, I had a pretty good idea of what Alastir was trying to say thanks to Miss Willa Colyns' diary. "Do you mean sex?"

His face was as red as mine felt. "Unfortunately."

I stared at him, mouth open, but I had absolutely no words.

"But," he said quickly, "like I said, it is a very old tradition, and while some of my younger brothers and sisters are far more open to the archaic traditions, it's not one often practiced these days for...well, for obvious reasons."

"I..." I felt hot and cold at the same time. "But you said that it may be expected since I'm not a full-blooded Atlantian. Why?"

"Why?" He blinked at me, and then his expression smoothed out. "Penellaphe, my dear, have you and Casteel not discussed the future? At all?"

The look in his expression caused acid to pool in my stomach. It was one of parental patience, the kind when a child was in over his or her head and needed an adult to rescue them.

"You will age, and while Casteel will also, he will do so in a way that, in eighty years, he will look the same and—"

"And I will be old and gray if I even survive that long," I cut in, and then lied through my teeth. "We've talked about that."

His gaze searched mine. "The Joining would not only ensure that the wolven would be duty-bound to protect your life, but the bond would tie your life to the elemental and the wolven. You would live as long as the wolven did, however long that may be."

Yet again, I was utterly speechless. So many things raced through my mind, but what came to the forefront was the fact that I knew why Casteel had never mentioned this. Tension crept into my muscles, and the heaviness in my chest felt suffocating. There was no need for this...this thing to take place. No matter what Kieran thought, Casteel didn't plan for us to remain married.

Chapter 25

The realization had a far more chilling effect than it should, and it was all Kieran's stupid heartmates conversation's fault.

And come to think of it, why in the hell hadn't Kieran brought this up?

Then I thought of having this conversation with Kieran, and I wanted to take a wire brush to my brain. As handsome as I believed Kieran to be, I just...I couldn't even begin to imagine doing something like that with him.

With him *and* Casteel.

I looked around for a glass of water, but there was none.

"You don't need to worry about this. I don't think he'd expect something like that. Casteel is not about the old traditions," Alastir said.

"But would the wolven expect that?" I asked, and then the worst thing ever spewed from my mouth. "Would Shea have done it?"

Alastir's eyes widened.

I immediately wished I hadn't said anything. "I'm sorry. I imagine as a wolven, she wouldn't have been expected to. And I shouldn't have brought her up—"

"No. No, it's okay." Alastir stretched forward, placing his hand on mine. "Don't apologize. I'm actually glad you're willing to speak of her." He smiled again, squeezing my hand before leaning back. "Although she was a wolven, it is a tradition that some would've expected to be honored, and Kieran's oath would have also extended to her. She was..." He pressed his lips together, and a long moment passed. "Shea never backed down from anything, no matter if others found it distasteful or crude. She would've done anything for Casteel."

And would Casteel have gone through with it?

Gods, I didn't even want to think about that.

I swallowed as I sank into the chair. My head started racing again.

"I've taken up enough of your time." Alastir once again began to rise.

"Wait," I nearly yelled as something occurred to me. "If the Joining can extend a mortal's life, then why didn't King Malec do that with Isbeth—his mistress? Instead of making her a vampry? Or wasn't he bonded?"

Alastir stared at me as if I'd suggested whole-heartedly embracing the Ascended's way of life. "King Malec had a bonded wolven. Actually, he had more than one since he often outlived them. But it wouldn't have worked on a mortal. The partner has to carry Atlantian blood in them, and even if that woman had Atlantian blood in her, it would've been a grave insult to the Queen. One that went beyond carrying on affairs. Any wolven of worth would've refused. That much, I know." His gaze met mine and held. "How old do you think I am?"

His question threw me. "I...I don't know. Far older than you look, I imagine."

"I've seen eight hundred years."

Good gods.

"And the reason I know his bonded wolven would've refused if asked?" Alastir stated. "It's because I was his last, and it was I who alerted the Queen to what Malec had done, shattering an unbreakable oath."

Sometime after Alastir left, the tub was filled with warm water, courtesy of Casteel, according to the two mortals—a younger man and woman with curious eyes. They didn't ask questions or linger longer than necessary and let me know that if I put my clothing and the nightgown in the wicker basket they'd placed outside the door, my clothes would be laundered. While I'd hoped to see Casteel, I appreciated the gesture, and I was also relieved that he hadn't returned.

I needed time to process...*everything.*

So, I made use of the bath, washing my hair, and then I slipped on the robe, tightening it around my waist. The sun was now high, but there was a chill in the room that wasn't present outside. I sat in front of the fire, slowly working the tangles free from my hair as my mind wandered from one utterly shocking topic to another.

Alastir had been Malec's bonded wolven? And the Joining? My gods, would the people of Atlantia actually expect that of me—from the three of us? The heat of embarrassment almost drove me away from the fire. It wasn't that I was disgusted or repulsed. What people decided to do and with whom or how many was their business. And the way Miss Willa had written about sharing herself with more than one partner was never discussed in a way that made me uncomfortable.

Well, that wasn't exactly true.

Mostly, I didn't understand how all of it worked. Not the physical aspect. She'd gone into quite a lot of detail regarding that. But more so, it all sounded so very complicated. I just couldn't even wrap my head around something like that when everything with Casteel was already so damn convoluted.

And why was I even concerning myself with this? Obviously, this was not something Casteel planned. But had he planned to do it with Shea?

"Stop it," I hissed, forcing my thoughts elsewhere. Unsurprisingly, they came right back to *him.*

What was a serious Casteel even like? Was that another mask he wore? I'd seen glimpses of that version of him whenever he asserted his authority, but he was so quick to tease and make light with me.

He's just more alive when he's with you.

Placing the brush on the floor, I closed my eyes and thought of Shea. Had he been that way with her? I doubted he'd donned any masks with her. Most likely, he had been an entirely different person then.

What'd happened to her? All I knew was that the Ascended were involved in her fate. How did she die? How long were she and Casteel together? Did she love him, too?

Of course, she did.

Even with little to no experience, I knew better than to travel down that road. I'd seen how Casteel reacted before, and while I might not have ever been in a relationship or loved, I knew people either wouldn't or couldn't talk about certain things. Things that could only be shared with those you loved, those you truly trusted.

I think you're heartmates.

There was a snag in my chest as I bit down on my lower lip. After learning about the Joining, I knew Kieran was totally off-base on the whole heartmates thing, but I still wanted to travel that road with Casteel. I wanted to know about who he used to be before he lost Shea, lost his brother. And I wanted to know all of that because I...I *cared* about him. Because I'd never stopped falling.

Gods.

I was in so much trouble.

And there was a high likelihood that Alastir had realized what I had when we spoke. That Casteel hadn't trusted me with the knowledge of Spessa's End. Worse yet, there was no way he believed our engagement was real.

Sitting with my head tipped back and eyes closed was how Casteel found me when he walked into the room. Impossibly, all thoughts I'd been wrapped up in vanished, replaced by what I made up my mind to do.

"What are you doing?" he asked, and I heard the door close behind him.

"Brushing my hair." Straightening, I opened my eyes, but I didn't turn around.

"Wouldn't you need the brush in your hand to do that?" He

sounded closer.

"Yes." A hundred silver hawks fluttered in my chest.

A moment later, he was sitting beside me, one knee bent and the other curled, resting against mine. Slowly, I looked over at him. The moment our gazes connected, the air whooshed out of my lungs. I didn't know if it had to do with what Kieran had told me or everything else.

"I'm sorry," he said. "I'm sorry about this morning—about losing control like that. It will never happen again."

My skin pimpled. His apology was unexpected, but I wasn't sure if I wanted it. What happened seemed mostly out of his control, and his apology…it made me respect him. I nodded.

"I planned on talking to you earlier than this. I came back after…well, I came back, and you were gone."

"I was with Kieran," I told him. "We went down to the Bay and then had breakfast."

A faint smile appeared. "I heard."

My brows lifted. "You did?"

He nodded. "The people here told me."

I didn't point out how the people here hadn't spoken to me during our brief encounter but felt the need to report to him that they had seen me.

"I came back to see if you had returned as soon as I could."

"It's okay." I swallowed. "Thank you for the bath."

"I should be the one thanking you."

"For what?"

"For knowing how to reach me this morning," he said, and heat raced across my face.

I toyed with the end of the sash as I glanced at him. Words rose and died on the tip of my tongue. He stared at the flames, the lines of his face nowhere near relaxed. Something occurred to me then, in my desperation to not think about this morning. "Whenever you introduce me to people, why are you so insistent that no one refers to me as the Maiden?"

"That's an incredibly random question."

It was. "I'm beginning to realize I'm an incredibly random person."

The half-smile returned. "I like it. Forces me to stay on my toes when I'm around you. But to answer your question, the less people think of you as the Maiden, the more they will think of you as the half-Atlantian who's captured my heart." There was an odd hollowness to his words, and when he looked at me, I noticed faint blue shadows under his eyes. "And the less likely they will be to want to harm you."

I nodded as I opened my senses to him. The connection was shockingly fast, and within a heartbeat, his hunger hit me— his hunger and his sadness, the latter more bitter than normal, and heavy—so damn heavy. He hadn't felt that way earlier. Was it because of what'd happened this morning or something else?

"It's also not who you are anymore," he added, and I pulled back my gift, realizing that closing it down had been easier since Casteel had given me his blood the second time. "It's not who you ever were."

"No, it's not."

"Did you ever accept it?" He planted a hand on the floor beside me and leaned over an inch or two. "Was there ever a point where you wanted to be what they made you?"

I had never been asked that before, and it took me some time to figure out how to answer. "There were times when I wanted to make the Queen happy—to make the Teermans pleased with me. So, I tried to be good—to be what was expected of me, but it was like...wearing a mask. I tried but the mask cracked quickly enough."

"Forcing a warrior to don a veil of submission was never going to last."

Feeling my cheeks warm, I looked away. "I don't know about the warrior part—"

"I do," he insisted. "From the moment you stayed instead of walking out of that room at the Red Pearl, I knew you had a warrior's strength and bravery. It's why you went to Rylan's funeral. It's what drove you out to the Rise when the Craven attacked and fought back—fought me. It's why you didn't bow under Alastir's remarks when you first met him but rather challenged his beliefs. Hell, it's what drove you to learn how to fight in the first place." A dimple appeared in his right cheek. "It's your bloodline—it's you."

The warmth in my chest had little to do with the fire. "I'm still a little annoyed that I'm not of the changeling line and I can't shift forms."

Casteel laughed, and the sound was as real and sunny as my chest felt. And when his gaze snagged on mine, I finally found the courage of the warrior he claimed I was.

And started with perhaps the most embarrassing thing ever. "I spoke with Alastir earlier."

"He mentioned that he was going to visit with you."

"He did, and he…he told me about the Joining."

Casteel's head swung toward mine so fast, I was surprised he didn't crack his neck. "He did *what?*"

"Do I really need to repeat that?"

"What did he tell you?"

"He told me what it is." I focused on my brush. "That it's a blood exchange that often turns into something, um, more intimate."

"Good gods, he did not."

"He did."

"I…" Casteel suddenly broke out into deep, thunderous laughter. The kind that was so loud and hard, it sounded like it hurt.

My wide gaze shot to him.

"I'm sorry," he gasped. "It's just that I would've paid good money to see him try to explain that to you."

I narrowed my eyes. "Would you have?"

"Hell, yes, I would've. Oh, gods." Dragging a hand through his hair, he looked over at me. "Let me guess? He said it was crude and disgusting?"

"Yeah. Pretty much."

"Gods, what an old alarmist." He laughed again, shoulders shaking. "I wish I could've seen your face."

"Well, since I learned about it from him, I wished I could've punched you in your face."

"I bet you did."

"I don't know what is so funny. He said people might expect it from us—especially because I'm not full-blooded Atlantian!"

"First off," he said, struggling for breath, "I don't think anyone is going to expect that."

From you seemed to hang unsaid between us.

"And while it is an intimate ritual, one that isn't often done anymore, it is not always sexual. For some, I'm sure it becomes that *naturally*. And hey, to each their own. They're consenting adults, and you do you, you know? I'm not going to judge."

"I'm not judging either."

He cocked an eyebrow. "You're not?"

"I'm not," I insisted.

"So, you're interested then?" he murmured.

"That is not where I was going with that."

"Uh-huh."

I ignored the way he said that. "Is it true that a mortal with Atlantian blood would be given a longer lifespan?"

Casteel nodded.

"Has that been done before?"

"I haven't known any bonded elementals who have taken a mortal with Atlantian blood," he answered. "As far as I know, there hasn't been. And it's a lot to ask of a wolven. That kind of blood bond goes both ways. If the wolven dies, so does the other, and if the mortal with Atlantian blood dies, the wolven would also."

"Oh." I blinked slowly. "Alastir didn't mention that."

"Wait." He swung his head toward mine. "Do you even know what could happen during that ritual that would make it so very crude—"

"I know what could happen," I snapped.

"Is it because of that diary?"

"Shut up."

"Did you bookmark the chapters detailing how Willa spent afternoons entertaining not one but two suitors, one in front and the other—?"

"You seem to know a lot about that book."

"I love that fucking book," he said, and my jaw ached from how hard I was clenching it. "So, you're interested then, Princess. What a wild side you have."

"That is not what I said!" My cheeks flushed.

"I know." He chuckled. "I'm sorry. I'm being an ass."

"At least you recognize it."

"I just...I was not expecting this. But you do have a very...*adventurous* personality."

"I hate you," I growled.

"Not *that* adventurous, huh?" Casteel laughed again. "Look, I know you're not looking for this marriage to go beyond the necessary," he said, and that strange, stupid ache in my chest pulsed. "So, it's not even something you need to worry about. But the Joining is meant to strengthen the bond that's already there, and ensure that the partner is also a part of that bond. It's not done lightly, and again, it is not always a sexual thing. I know it's been done where everyone kept their body parts to themselves."

My brows lifted. "Then why did Alastir make it sound like it was a..."

"A dirty thing?" He grinned. "Because he's old and overdramatic and thinks he's being helpful."

"Why——?" I cut myself off before I could ask why *he'd* never brought it up. I already knew why. Just like I knew why he hadn't told me about Spessa's End.

"What?"

I shook my head, changing the subject. "Alastir said he was Malec's bonded wolven."

"That he was. Did he tell you he told my mother that Malec had Ascended Isbeth?" When I nodded, Casteel let his head fall back. "Alastir broke his oath, severing his bond. That has...well, that has rarely happened. Alastir can sometimes say too much, but he's a good man."

I nodded slowly, watching him as he closed his eyes. "Your mother didn't leave him then?"

"No."

"Did she stay with him because she loved him?"

"You know, I really don't know. She doesn't talk about him, but you have to wonder given she named her first son a name so similar," he said. I wondered how their father felt about that. "When my mother confronted Malec, she did so privately, but what he'd done still got out. And others followed suit. In a way, it all happened so quickly."

"And here we are," I murmured.

"Here we are," he confirmed.

Drawing in a deep breath, I said what needed to be said. "I know you need to feed. I know you're close to the edge, and you haven't fed from anyone else."

"Someone has been talking," he replied flatly. "And I doubt it was Alastir."

"Someone needed to. What happens if you don't feed, other than the black eyes? If you do tip over the edge?" I asked. "You never really explained beyond it being a very bad thing."

He looked away, dragging his lip between his teeth. "It's like being…dead inside, worse than an Ascended. We fall into bloodlust, but it's a violent madness, like that of a Craven. But we don't decay or rot." He shook his head. "Once we tip over the edge, we grow stronger with each feeding, but it's like a disease of the mind because we become nothing more than rabid animals. Very few come back from that."

I remembered what he said the Ascended did to him— withheld blood until he was ravenous. "Did the Ascended withhold blood from you often?"

"There'd be years when they kept me well fed." The twist of his lips was a mockery of a smile. "Then they'd give me enough so I didn't die, and sometimes, that wasn't enough."

Years.

Sorrow gripped my heart—for him, for his brother, and any other who was going through that. But mostly for Casteel because he knew exactly what his brother was facing. "But you came back."

"There were times when I didn't think I would, Poppy." He stared into the flames, his voice barely audible. "When I forgot how much time had passed. When I forgot who I was and what mattered to me. It was like parts of my brain had turned dark." He dragged a hand through his hair and then dropped it to his knee. "But I came back. Not the same. Never the same. But I found parts of who I used to be."

I swallowed against the knot in my throat. "I'm—"

"Don't say you're sorry." He cut me a sharp look that

would've stung my feelings before, but I understood it—understood him. Sympathy wasn't always wanted. "You did nothing you should apologize for."

"You're right. I was going to say I'm glad you found yourself."

A harsh laugh burst from him. "Truly, Poppy? Are you really?"

"Yeah, I guess I am." I lifted a shoulder in a shrug. "You may have come back as an asshole, but that's better than being lost in your own mind. I wouldn't wish that on anyone."

The laugh that left him was softer, and it tugged at my lips. "True." He dragged a hand down his face. "Anyway, I know what it's like to be close to the edge. I've been past it. I'm fine."

"But you're not, Casteel."

His eyes widened slightly as he looked at me.

"What?"

"It's just that you hardly say my name."

"Should I call you Your Highness?"

"Gods," he choked out. "No."

I did grin a little at that, and he saw it and stared as if I'd just pulled off an amazing feat. I had no idea why a grin from me would do that.

I refocused on the task at hand. "I felt it. I felt your hunger this morning," I told him. "I know you're starving, and I know how that feels, at least to some extent. The Duke would forbid me food sometimes when he was angry. You need to feed."

"First off, knowing that the Duke did that, I want to kill him all over again. But secondly, blood wasn't the only thing I was starved for this morning." His eyes were heated honey. "And I think you know that."

My pulse skittered, and my voice sounded raspier than normal when I said, "If you won't do that—if you can't—then you need to take my blood."

Casteel jerked back as if I'd smacked him. He rose to his feet in the next instant. "Poppy—"

"You can't continue on this way." I stood, not nearly as gracefully as he had. "What if you get injured again?"

"I'll be fine." He took a step back from me. "I told you. I

won't lose control again."

"I don't think you have a choice in that, do you? It's just a part of who you are. You need Atlantian blood. You haven't fed from anyone else, so maybe you'll do it from me. It's not like you haven't bitten me before."

The angles of his face stood out in stark relief. "I haven't forgotten that."

"Then this shouldn't be a big deal. You need blood. I have the blood. Let's get it over with."

He laughed, but it was without humor. "Get it over with? As if this will just be another business arrangement?"

I lifted my chin. "If that's what it needs to be, then it will."

"So, you're okay with being that? Being the source of my strength, considering everything that I've done to you? Adding this to a long list of things you don't want to do but feel you need to?"

"Well, when you put it that way…" I threw up my hands in frustration. "Maybe I'd rather be the source of your sanity so I don't have to worry about you tearing into my neck between now and whenever this is over."

His chest rose with a deep, shuddering breath as his shoulders bunched with tension.

"Can you really say that it won't happen again? Look me straight in the face and tell me you truly believe that you'll be able to stop next time," I demanded. When his nostrils flared and he said nothing, I knew the truth. And I knew I had to admit another truth, one that I wouldn't be able to take back. "I felt your hunger, Casteel, and I don't *need* to do this. I stopped doing things I didn't want to do the moment I took off the damn veil. I want to help you. Because as stupid as this may make me, and only the gods know why, I care about you! So, yeah, I don't want to have my throat ripped open, and I also don't want to know that you're suffering for no reason."

Trembling and stomach twisting, I felt like I'd just stripped myself bare. "There's probably something wrong with me—actually, there's definitely something wrong with me. Obviously. But if you—" I forced the words out before they choked me. "If you care about me at all, you won't want to put me at risk. You'll take what I'm offering with a thank you and stop acting like an idiot!"

Casteel stared at me, his brows raised, and then, after what felt like an eternity, his shoulders lowered. "I'm so incredibly unworthy of you," he whispered, and I shivered, remembering the only other time he'd said that to me. It was the night I'd shared my body, my heart, and my soul with him. He lifted his head and seemed to take another breath. "Okay."

I exhaled slowly. "Okay."

"On one condition," he said. "I won't do this alone. Not after...not after not feeding for so long. I won't risk that. I...I could take too much. Do you agree?"

At first, the idea of someone else being present made me uncomfortable, but then I remembered how his bite had felt before. Maybe having someone present would curtail that.

So, I nodded. "I agree."

Chapter 26

My bare feet curled against the wood floor as Kieran looked between Casteel and me, and I really wished I hadn't learned of the Joining and how it could sometimes become...*intimate*.

Kieran being here while Casteel fed felt extremely intimate.

Casteel hadn't been gone more than a few minutes, and I stood in the same spot as when he'd left, as if I'd been glued to the floor. It wasn't that I had doubts. I just couldn't believe I'd offered to do this—that not only did I want to do this but that I had also admitted that I cared for him. It felt like my life had once again changed irrevocably in a span of minutes.

"I don't need to take a lot," Casteel said to Kieran, who looked like he was about to go to war. Actually, they'd been battling with each other for the last ten minutes or so. Casteel was hesitating, and Kieran was about to throw him at me.

The wolven stood there, arms crossed, and eyes glittering. "You need to take more than a sip or two. You need to feed like you normally would."

A muscle throbbed in Casteel's jaw as he looked over to where I stood. I felt like I needed to say something, to offer reassurance because Casteel actually looked like he was a second from bolting. "Take what you need," I told him, willing my voice steady.

Casteel stared at me, and for a moment, I saw a glint of incredulity in his gaze, and then his lashes lowered.

My heart thumped painfully against my chest as Casteel opened his eyes.

He took one step and then stopped. His chest rose and fell sharply. "This is your last chance to change your mind. Are you sure about this?"

Swallowing hard, I nodded. "Yes."

His eyes closed once more, and when they reopened this time, only the thinnest strip of amber was visible. He dipped his chin, and the sharpness of hunger etched deeply into his features. "You know what to do." His voice was rougher, barely recognizable as he spoke to where Kieran loomed. "If I don't stop."

But would Kieran intervene? My heart skipped a beat. A tendril of fear curled itself around the forbidden, wicked swell of anticipation within me.

Kieran moved behind me, and then I felt his fingers along the right side of my neck. I jumped a little, telling myself not to think about the Joining. To not even go there. Because if I did, I would be the one bolting from the room. "I'm just going to monitor your pulse," he said quietly. "Just to be sure."

My gaze fixed on Casteel. He reminded me of a caged animal whose cell was about to be unlocked. "Do you normally have to do that when…when he feeds?"

"No." His fingers were cool against my neck. "But he's too close to the edge right now."

Too close to the edge…

Then it was too late for doubts.

Casteel was suddenly before me, the scent of lush spice and pine almost overwhelming. His fingers threaded through my hair, but he didn't yank, even though I could feel his body vibrating with need.

I didn't know if I consciously chose to connect with him at the moment or if my gift took control. His hunger immediately reached me, settling in my chest and stomach in a gnawing ache that seemed bottomless. And underneath that, the heaviness of concern.

His cheek grazed mine as he eased my head back and to the side. "There will only be a heartbeat of pain." His breath was warm on my throat, his voice ragged. "I swear."

Then he struck.

Fiery pain stole my breath, and my body jerked, interrupting the connection I'd forged with him. Instinct drove me to take a step back, but I bumped into Kieran. His hand landed on my shoulder, holding me there, and then Casteel's arm swept around my waist. The pain flared brighter, stunning me, and then...

The heartbeat came and went.

Casteel's mouth tugged at my skin, and I felt that staggering pull in every part of my body. The pain flashed out as quickly as it had overtaken me. All that was left, all that existed in the world was the feel of his mouth at my throat, the deep, long draws of my blood leaving me and filling him. My eyes had been open, fixed on the dull white plaster of the ceiling, but now they drifted shut as my lips parted. He drank from me, the fingers in my hair curling. His mouth lifted—

"That's not enough," Kieran said. "That's nowhere near enough, Cas."

Casteel's forehead pressed to my shoulder as the hand against my back fisted the material of my robe.

The connection thrummed intensely, and I could still feel his hunger. It had eased a bit, but it was still acute. Kieran was right. He hadn't taken enough.

Tentatively, I lifted my hands and touched his arms. Not his bare skin. I didn't know if easing his pain would cause him to stop or not. "I'm okay." My voice sounded breathless as if I had run circles around the fortress. "You need more. Take it."

"She speaks the truth." Kieran placed his hand above mine, squeezing Casteel's arm. "Feed."

Casteel shuddered, and then he lifted his head slightly. His lips grazed my jaw, and then the line of my neck, sending a shiver down my spine as I bit down on the inside of my cheek. His lips pressed to the skin above the bite, a whisper of a kiss that startled me, and then his mouth closed over the tingling skin once more.

Every part of my body seemed to focus on where his mouth

was fastened to my throat. Thoughts scattered as an ache blossomed to life low in my stomach and between my thighs. I tried to remember that Kieran was there, monitoring my pulse, and what we were doing was almost like...like a life-saving procedure, but I couldn't hold onto any of those thoughts. With each pull against my skin, each tug that seemed to reach all the way to my toes, that throb pulsed, and the ache grew and grew, heating my blood and my skin.

I needed to think about anything but what it felt to have Casteel at my neck, his lips moving, the muscles of his arms bunching under my palms. But it was no use, and—oh, gods—the connection to him, it was still open. There was hunger, yes, but there was also more. A spicy, smoky flavor filled the back of my throat. The taste, the feeling, was heady and overwhelmed my senses. My body jerked with a pounding flood of desire that weakened my legs. I didn't know how I was still standing or if Casteel or Kieran held me up. Each breath I took seemed too shallow as the ache moved to my breasts. Tension coiled tightly inside me, to the point of near anguish—a razor-sharp type of pleasure that left its own version of scars.

A sound came from Casteel, a throaty rumble. And then he moved suddenly, tugging deeply at my throat as he pressed into me—pressed me back against Kieran with unexpected strength. The wolven hit the wall behind us with a grunt as Casteel trapped us both. His mouth moved against my neck as his hips jerked against my belly—

Oh, gods.

I could feel him against me. I could feel him inside me—his desire and mine, churning and twisted together. A dull roaring sound filled my ears, and I was suddenly drowning in a torrent of sensations that came at me in endless waves. Trepidation and concern over what was happening while we weren't alone, with Kieran there, lodged behind us, fully aware of what was occurring. Shame over the rush of slick dampness Casteel answered with a grind of his hips as his hands dropped to my waist. Desire that somehow merged with something deeper, something irrevocable, and disbelief as I curled my arm around his neck, as I held him, wanting to drown in this fire. Until I realized I already was.

I didn't know at what point things had spun so out of control. When the way he held me, the way he pressed against me was no longer about quenching his thirst and more about assuaging a different hunger. I didn't know exactly when I lost the fight against my body. I didn't know when I'd stopped thinking about the fact that it wasn't just Casteel's body that touched mine, it wasn't his chest that my head fell back against.

Was it the bite? Was it the need and the want that had been stroked to life the night at the Red Pearl that had never gone away, becoming the fire in my blood that simmered any time I was close to Casteel? Was it something reckless and wicked inside me, in the core of who I was, that allowed me to let go and to forget…*everything*? Or was it all of those things combined? I didn't know—I didn't know anything when Casteel's hands trembled as they slid down my thigh, over the robe. He lifted me onto the tips of my toes, and then higher, drawing one leg around his waist. The lower half of the robe parted and the upper part slipped off my left shoulder. When his hardness pressed against the softest part of me, all I knew was that I had become the flames in my blood, something utterly unfamiliar to me, something daring and shameless. I was the fire, and Casteel was the air that fed it.

Casteel's hips sank into mine, and my body answered without conscious thought, churning against him as he fed and fed. The tension coiled tighter. In the back of my mind, I didn't know if it was the bite or the feel of him between my thighs that was quickly driving me precariously close to the edge.

"That's enough," Kieran said. His voice should've been a shock, but it was only a source of frustration. "That's enough, Casteel."

Body throbbing, I opened my eyes in a daze as Casteel's chest rose swiftly against mine. A moment passed, and then whatever air I had left abandoned me as I felt the wet, sinful lap of his tongue below the bite and then against it. The tension pulsed again, and then his mouth lifted from my neck. That was as far as he moved for several moments, and then he stepped back, taking me with him as my heart and blood kept pounding and I continued to *ache*. One of his arms folded over my waist, his other hand returning to my hair, guiding my head down. I buried my face in his neck, taking in his scent and just *breathing*. Both of my legs were curled around his waist, and I wasn't even sure when that had happened, but he held me there, no space between our bodies as he looked over my shoulder at Kieran.

"Thank you," he said roughly.

"You're okay?" Kieran asked, and I felt Casteel nod. "Penellaphe?"

My tongue felt heavy, but I managed to work out a muffled, "Yes."

"Good." The air stirred around us as Kieran brushed past. The door creaked open, and cool wind teased the bare parts of my skin, but it did nothing to stifle the heat.

"Thank you," Casteel said again to Kieran, and then the door closed. His head turned to mine. "Thank *you*," he whispered.

I said nothing as I held him, caught in a storm of…desire. Casteel moved, bending and lowering me to the bed. The back of my head rested on the pillow as his hands slid out from underneath me. I felt the bed dip with his weight as he sat beside me, and I opened my eyes.

Casteel was close, his hands on either side of my head as he hovered over me. I could see that the robe had slipped even farther, revealing the upper swell of my breast. The tips of my breasts tented the thin material of the soft robe. And lower, one entire leg was visible, all the way to the crease of my thigh and hip. I should fix the robe, cover myself. I should be embarrassed, but I didn't move my hands. It wasn't that I couldn't. I simply didn't as I shifted my gaze to his.

Those eyes blazed like heated honey, beautiful and consuming. Neither of us spoke as his chest rose and fell, his breaths as rapid as mine. His muscles were rigid as he held himself in check. I knew that was what he was doing, because I was still connected to him, open to him for longer than I had ever been open to anyone, and I no longer felt the gnawing hunger. What I felt was rich and smoky, and nearly as intense. My breath hitched, and I burned even more.

His lips parted, and the tips of his fangs appeared. The bite tingled so sharply that a shivery wave crashed through me, causing my thighs to squeeze, and my hips to twitch.

Casteel's eyes closed as he drew in a ragged breath. "Poppy…" There was a wealth of need in that one word, in my name. I trembled. Then his eyes opened again, and they were nearly luminous. "You've already given so much of yourself, done so much for me," he said, and I thought he spoke of more than just my blood. His mouth lowered, and the anticipation swelled. He stopped mere inches from my mouth as his hand curved around my hip. "Let me do this for you. Let me take away the ache."

My heart clamored even as my entire body went tight. I needed to say no. There were a hundred different reasons for that. But that wasn't what came out of my mouth in a husky voice that was not mine. "But what about your ache?"

A fine tremor coursed through him. "This isn't about me." His hand drifted over my stomach, to where my skin was bared at the left hip. "Let me thank you the only way I can right now. Let me show you my gratitude."

I could barely breathe or think. I pulled my senses back, thinking that would help clear my mind, but my desire still beat at me, in tune with my unsteady heart. And I realized that I was still the fire. I still wanted, right or wrong, just like I had this morning, which felt like an eternity ago.

I was vaguely aware of my head moving in a nod, and then Casteel's chin dipped, and his lips grazed mine. He turned me onto my side, away from him, as he stretched out behind me. Confused, I looked over my shoulder at him as he shifted onto his elbow and met my gaze.

"You're so brave," he murmured, tugging me into the cradle of his hips. The robe had slipped, and there was nothing but his breeches between the curve of my rear and the hard length of him now. I bit down on my lip as he skimmed his hand down my thigh, lifting my leg up, just enough for one of his to slide between mine.

He drew his hand up my side, over my arm, and then moved back down. "And strong."

The robe slipped more, seeming to follow his hand. I looked to see that the material had parted even more, exposing one breast. Warmth suffused my cheeks when I saw the evidence of my desire in the turgid peak. His hand closed over my breast, drawing a gasp from me as his thumb swirled over the nub. My back arched into the touch, into him.

"So generous," he rasped, sliding his hand down lower, below my navel and over my bare hip then lower still. His fingers met the wetness gathering there, and then he cupped me. His touch was like a brand as he idly drew one finger over the very center of me in light, playful strokes that caused my entire body to twitch. He continued with those featherlight touches until I thought I would stretch beyond my skin, that I surely would ignite, and then he sank a finger inside me. My head kicked back against his chest as a breathy sound escaped me. "So fucking beautiful," he gritted out, withdrawing his finger until he was almost free of my body and then inching it back in.

He angled his hand so his thumb danced over the sensitive bundle of nerves as he continued to stroke with that long, talented finger of his, pumping it slowly in and out, taking more and more of my breath with each thrust of his digit. He worked his other arm around me, folding it across my chest. He palmed the too-tight breast as he worked in a second finger, stretching me, feeding the fire even more.

I cried out, pressing against his hand, against him. His breath came in rough bursts as I turned my head to see him watching his hands, watching me lift and grind against it. I slipped into the balmy sensation, falling maddeningly into it. Reality fell away. I hadn't been the captive. He hadn't been the captor. We weren't partners in an agreement, each using the other. It was just us, his skilled fingers and hands, the warmth of his arms, the glorious tightening within me, and when he trembled, cursing as I rode his hand, rode the hard length that pressed against me from behind. It was all those things, and the sudden thrill of power and control.

He started to angle his body so there was space between us, but I'd given in to the fire. I reached back, curled my fingers around his hip, and dug in my nails in a silent demand.

Casteel obeyed.

He submitted with another curse and a brief, hot pass of his lips across the curve of mine as his fingers plunged harder, deeper. I rocked against him, and there was no rhythm as we both moved and strained. The curl low in my stomach spun and spun—

"Poppy, I—" He broke off as I placed my other hand over his, holding him to me as *I* worked him.

And it happened—the tightening and curling, all of it unraveled, stroking out through every limb. I moaned as release powered through me, as I shuddered around his fingers, and *he* shuddered against me, still moving those damn digits of his and eliciting every whipping wave of sensation he could until my hands fell away from him, and I went limp. Until his breathing steadied against my cheek. Then, slowly, he eased out of me.

His hand didn't move far though, instead gliding up and stopping just below my navel. He tugged the halves of my robe closed with his other hand, holding it in place just below my breasts. There was something about the act that seemed…gentle.

Slowly, I became aware of a dampness against my lower back and the upper swells of my behind. I tipped my head back and to the side.

His head rested on the pillow behind mine, his features relaxed in a way that I'd only seen when he slept. Those eyes of his were heavy and hooded as his gaze met mine.

And then the strangest thing occurred. Pink crept into his cheeks as he shifted his hips away from me. "Sorry," he said thickly, a boyish grin appearing on his lips. "That wasn't supposed to happen."

I looked down. There was a spot along the front of his pants that was a darker black. Damp. My cheeks colored as my gaze flew to his.

"That hasn't happened since…" The grin turned sheepish, and between that and the faint blush staining his cheeks, it was like seeing someone totally different. "Well, that's never happened before."

"Really?" I asked, surprised by the throatiness of my voice.

"Really." His gaze searched mine. "I didn't want—I mean,

of course, I wanted that. I wanted more. I always want more when it comes to you." The hue of his eyes brightened once more, and my toes curled. "But I wanted it to be about you."

Gods, there was also something so tender about the way he said that. "It was about me. You tried to put space between us." I turned my head away, my gaze falling to his hands. "I'm the one who didn't allow that."

"And I liked that." A pause. "A lot. Obviously."

My lips twitched.

"Who knew you could be so demanding," he continued, and I rolled my eyes. "I also liked that. Obviously."

I grinned.

His exhale was soft, tickling the back of my neck. "What you did for me? Offering to feed me? I know that had to be scary."

It wasn't. Not really.

"And I just want you to know that I…" He cleared his throat. "There really aren't words, other than thank you."

I stared at his fingers and the tendons of his hands, searching for some hint of regret or shame. I was sure the embarrassment would come later when I saw Kieran, but I didn't regret offering my blood to Casteel. And like before, I didn't wish that what happened afterward hadn't. It didn't feel shameful or wrong. It had felt natural, as if some inherent knowledge said that it was common for that level of intimacy to come from feeding. To give way to *more*. That if I'd grown up in Atlantia, that if he and I were different people, what we'd shared afterward would be common. Once again, it felt like…like the ground we held had changed and shifted under us.

"You don't need to thank me." I closed my eyes. "It was my choice."

Casteel eased his arm out from under me, and the bed shifted as his weight left it. A languid warmth settled over me as I watched him make his way to where his bag lay at the foot of the bed. He

pulled something out and then disappeared into the bathing chamber, closing the door behind him. I heard the faint sounds of fresh water from pitchers being emptied into the basin. Water splashed, and I wondered how he was able to withstand the coldness of it.

I wiggled my toes against the blanket bunched at the foot of the bed, thinking I should rise or at least pull the blanket up, but I was too comfortable to make the effort. My eyes drifted shut, reopening when I heard the door open. Casteel strode out, wearing only those loose cotton pants that hung indecently low on his hips. I shouldn't look, and I definitely shouldn't stare, but I soaked in the sight of the lean, coiled muscles of his abdomen and the defined lines of his chest and shoulders. His form was evidence of years spent wielding a sword and using his body as a weapon, but to look like him...

It should be forbidden.

Casteel caught my gaze, and his full lips curved. The dimple in his right cheek appeared.

And then the left one.

"I like that," Casteel said.

"What?"

"You looking at me."

I watched him toss the rolled-up pair of breeches into his bag. "I'm not looking at you."

"My mistake, then," he murmured, the dimple in his right cheek remained. He straightened, and the muscles along his spine did interesting, fascinating things.

I waited for him to tease me about what we'd done, for him to point out that yet again, and twice in one day, I'd proven myself wrong when it came to him.

The teasing never came.

He disappeared from my line of sight, and I somehow managed to not turn and watch him. A handful of moments passed, and then the bed dipped under his weight once more. Surprise whispered through me. I should've known the moment I saw him in those pants that he wasn't leaving the room, but I guessed I hadn't expected him to stay. It was so early in the day, barely noon.

Reaching down, Casteel grabbed the blanket and tugged it up over me—over us—and then he snuggled in behind me like he had before.

Silence stretched, filling the room, and then he said, "Can I...can I just hold you?" he asked, and I'd never heard him sound so uncertain. "There are things I should be doing, and I know we're not in public, and I know that what we shared doesn't change anything, but...can I...can we just pretend?"

My heart thumped heavily again, and I didn't know if it was the effect of the feeding or what we'd done afterward. Or if it was the softness of his request, the vulnerability in it, and the feeling that things had shifted even more between us. It could've been all of those things that led me to say, "You can."

Casteel's exhale was ragged, but he didn't move. When I looked over my shoulder, his eyes were closed, his lips parted. I wondered if he was all right. "Casteel?"

Thick lashes swept up, revealing extraordinarily bright amber eyes. "I...I didn't think you'd let me."

Lying my head back down, I wet my lips. "Should I have not?"

"Yes? No? I don't know." Casteel moved then, slipping one arm under me and the other around me. He tugged me close, sealing my back to his chest. "No takebacks now, though."

I allowed myself a small smile as I sank into his embrace, his warmth. And I permitted myself one other thing.

I let myself enjoy it.

Chapter 27

Pulling one of Casteel's clean tunics over my head, I looked down at myself and sighed. Between the too loose breeches and the oversized shirt, which nearly reached my knees, I looked a bit ridiculous. But the plain black shirt was far better than the too-heavy sweater.

We hadn't dozed that long, maybe a little over an hour before I woke to find him propped up on his elbow, watching me. When I asked what he was doing, he simply responded with, *"Enjoying the scenery."*

I'd blushed a thousand shades of red, and he'd smiled before lowering his head and brushing his lips over my forehead. Then he'd said that he had an idea, and that was how I ended up in the baggy breeches and one of his shirts.

Glancing at the oval mirror before leaving the bathing chamber, I caught sight of the side of my neck. The patch of skin around the two red puncture wounds was faintly pink. I touched the skin, finding the area tender but not painful. When I left the bed, I'd noted that the shadows under Casteel's eyes were gone, as was the sharpness to his features. It was amazing how quickly my blood had affected him.

It was also amazing how his bite had affected *me*.

The moment his mouth had closed over my skin and the initial pain of his bite vanished, it was like tumbling into a world where the only thing that mattered was him and the feel of him drawing a piece of me deep inside him. What Kieran had shared with me before about heartmates hadn't mattered. The realization that Casteel had possibly kept the truth of Spessa's End from me because he either feared I would share what I knew if captured or he hadn't trusted me with the information until I was far enough outside the Ascended's reach was no longer a concern. Neither was the shock of learning about the Joining. There had been no shame over being trapped between Kieran and Casteel as Kieran had been all but pinned to the wall by Casteel's need. I'd become a flame, and none of that had mattered.

But now?

Now, there was embarrassment when I thought of Kieran—the wolven who must have known about the tradition. Something Casteel had never told me about because it hadn't been relevant for him to do so. The marriage was temporary. An act that I wasn't sure was as innocent as Casteel made it out to be—at least not most of the time. But I didn't feel shame for what Kieran had witnessed. I didn't know if I was supposed to, but it didn't feel like something to be ashamed of. My reaction to Casteel was natural, and even if what came afterward when Casteel expressed his gratitude was foolishly reckless when it came to my heart, it had also felt *right*.

Flushing at Casteel's apparent lack of control, I scooped my hair out from the tunic's collar, leaving it down. He'd said that had never happened before, and I couldn't fathom why he'd lie about that. The fact that it'd happened with me was inconceivable, but there was an odd sense of power there, too, one as old as time itself. The kind of power that I imagined Miss Willa and the women at the Red Pearl, the ones who worked there and were patrons of the establishment, had mastered.

Hearing Casteel's footsteps in the bedchamber, I tore my gaze from the mirror and slid open the pocket door.

Casteel had managed to change his clothing. Somewhat. He'd donned his breeches and boots, but the white tunic still dangled from his fingertips. Something about the hard lines of his chest and stomach were utterly fascinating, but my earlier boldness had left me.

"So, about my idea," he said, lifting the shirt over his head.

"I'm half afraid to ask." I moved to the terrace doors. He'd opened one after we woke. Warm sunlight spilled across the tile floor.

His laugh was muffled as the shirt slipped over his head. "I'm wounded."

With his back to me, I grinned. "I'm sure you are."

"Completely." Facing me, he left the shirt untucked. "Since it's early in the day, I thought we could take a little field trip."

Excitement bubbled to life as I shoved up one long sleeve. "To where?"

"I thought you might like to see the real Spessa's End."

I opened my mouth to ask if he truly trusted me with what I saw, but I managed to stop myself.

His gaze flickered over me. "What?"

"I would like that," I said instead.

Casteel's head cocked as he studied me for a moment, almost as if he didn't believe my answer. "I'm glad to hear that." He came forward, stopping in front of me. "But there is a caveat."

"What is that?" I asked as he lifted my arm.

He folded over the edges of the sleeves, forming a cuff. "We continue to *pretend*."

My heart skipped a beat. "That you're just Hawke?"

"And you're just Poppy." He rolled up the sleeve, halting just below my elbow. "Want the sleeves higher?"

Knowing that he was asking because of the pale scars on my inner elbows, I nodded.

There was a glimmer of approval in his eyes as he tucked the sleeve so it was above my elbow. "We don't spend the rest of the afternoon thinking about the past."

"Or worrying about the future?" I said.

He nodded as he motioned for me to lift my other arm. "We will just be Hawke and Poppy. That's all."

I watched him roll up the other sleeve. "No one else will treat you as Hawke. They won't see me as Poppy."

His gaze lifted to mine. "No one else matters. Just you and me."

Another skip of another beat. There was no denying that it would be incredibly ill-advised of me to pretend anymore. It blurred everything, and pretending...well, it didn't feel like that to me. But there was also no denying that I wanted exactly what he offered.

And since when did something being foolish ever stop me?

Besides, I wanted to see Spessa's End.

Telling myself that was the main reason, I nodded. "I agree to your conditions."

The dimple appeared in his right cheek. "So, it's a deal?"

"Yes."

"Then we must seal the deal," he told me. "And do you know how Atlantians seal a deal? They do so with a kiss."

"Really?" I asked doubtfully. "That sounds incredibly problematic."

"Perhaps."

"And it also sounds like a lie."

Casteel nodded. "It is."

There was no silencing the laugh. It burst from me. And Casteel—he moved so unbelievably fast. His head dipped, and his mouth was on mine before the laugh even faded. The shock of his lips against mine sent a jolt through me. The kiss was...it was as intoxicating as his bite, as everything about him was. And when his fingers sifted through my hair, guiding my head back, there were no protests to be found. The kiss deepened, and the touch of his fangs, his tongue on mine, sent a hot, tight shudder through me.

"Sorry," he whispered against my lips. "I know I should've asked first, but your laugh... It undoes me, Poppy." He slid his hands over my cheeks, his fingers not hesitating when they reached the scars. "You're more than welcome to punch me for it."

I didn't want to punch him. I wanted him to kiss me again. A soft breath left me. "I guess the deal is sealed now, isn't it?"

He gave an audible swallow. "That it is." Drawing back, he took my hand. "Come. If we spend another moment here, I don't think we'll make it from this room."

My eyes widened. There was no mistaking the seriousness of his words, and another shiver danced across my skin.

Casteel led me out through the terrace and into the

courtyard, his hand still firmly around mine. I looked off toward the sun-drenched Rise and squinted. "Are there people on the Rise?"

"There are, and they were also there last night. You just couldn't see them."

"Mortal eyesight sucks," I muttered, and he smirked. "But I thought the Ascended weren't a threat this far east."

"They haven't been, but I'd rather be safe than sorry."

Our boots trod softly over the patchy grass and sand. "Alastir said that rebuilding Spessa's End was your idea."

"For the most part," he said, and that was *all* he said as we neared the stables. I felt the sting of disappointment, but then I reminded myself that today wasn't about the future. "You up for riding? It's not that far of a distance to walk, but I'm feeling lazy."

"I'm fine with either."

"Perfect. Because I have another idea," he said. A moment later, an older man strode out of the open door of the tack room. "How are you doing, Coulton?"

The man came forward, dragging a handkerchief over his bald head. The closer he got, I realized he was a wolven. His eyes were the blue of a winter morning. "Good." He bowed his head in greeting. "And you?"

"Never been better."

A grin appeared as Coulton's gaze slid to me. The smile halted as he suddenly took a step back. He stared at me, and I tensed, my hands tightening on reflex—squeezing Casteel's. I immediately forced my grip to relax. Either it was the scars, or the wolven realized who I was—who I *used* to be. The Maiden. I reminded myself that I couldn't necessarily blame him for his reaction.

"Is everything okay, Coulton?" Casteel asked, tone flat.

The wolven blinked and then his smile reappeared. "Yeah. Yes. Sorry. It's just I had the weirdest sensation." He looked at his Prince, the olive tone skin deepening to a ruddy color. "Like a staticky, charged feeling." He shoved the handkerchief into the front pocket of his sleeveless shirt. "Is this her? Your fiancée?"

Wanting to believe that the wolven spoke the truth, I knew

better than to believe something simply because I wanted it to be true. I opened my senses and reached out to him. The invisible connection formed, and I expected the bitter taste, the choking heaviness of distrust and dislike. That's not what I felt. The cool splash against the back of my throat was surprise, followed by the tart sensation of confusion. It felt like he was speaking the truth.

"This is Penellaphe," Casteel said. "My fiancée."

Hearing the coolness in Casteel's tone, I stepped forward and extended my hand as I smiled. "It's nice to meet you, Coulton."

A smile appeared, one that stretched across the wolven's entire face. "It's an honor to meet you." The wolven took my hand, and his eyes widened. Through the connection, I felt his surprise once more. "There it is again. That feeling of static." He laughed, still holding my hand as he shook his head. "Perhaps it is you, Penellaphe."

Having felt nothing, I said, "I'm not sure about that."

"I don't know. You feel as if you're…full of energy. Heard you descended from Atlantia." He squeezed my hand and then let go as he looked at Casteel. "I imagine it's from a powerful line."

Casteel tilted his head as my brow puckered. "I believe she is."

"Are you here for Setti?" Coulton asked. "If so, he's out in the pasture."

"No. He needs his rest. I just need two horses."

"Two horses?" I questioned.

"That's my other idea." Casteel's features relaxed into a grin. "To teach you how to ride by yourself."

"What?" I whispered.

"Ah. I've got the perfect horses for that." Coulton pivoted, walking toward the stalls along the right side of the stables. "There are two older mares in here. Great temperament. Not likely to take off."

"You think this is a good idea?" I asked.

"Now seems like a better time than most," he told me. "And you're going to do just fine after being on Setti."

I wasn't so sure about that as Coulton led out a stocky, white and brown horse along with a fawn-colored one. Neither were as large as Setti but they were still big enough to trample me to death.

"Which one do you think is the best fit?" Casteel asked.

"Molly here is a good girl." Coulton patted the side of the spotted one. "She'll be gentle."

Once they were saddled, Casteel nudged me toward Molly. "You'll do just fine," he told me, voice low as Coulton held onto both horses' leads. "I'll keep her reins until you're ready."

Nervous and a little scared, I pushed past that. I'd always wanted to learn how to ride, and it was a necessary skill that I lacked. Now was as good a time as ever.

I stroked Molly's muzzle as I walked over to her side, swallowing. Casteel followed, and I knew he was going to help me up. "If I fall, try to catch me."

"I can do that."

"Please don't kill me," I murmured as I reached up, gripping the saddle. "Being killed by a horse named Molly would be embarrassing."

Both of them chuckled, but as I placed my foot in the stirrup, Casteel said to the wolven, "You have the reins?"

"Molly isn't going anywhere."

I hauled myself up, remembering at the very last second to swing my leg over. A moment later, I was seated, and I'd done it by myself. I looked down at Casteel.

He smiled, and I felt a catch in my chest. Both of his dimples appeared. "Now, I'll have no excuse to touch you inappropriately in an appropriate setting."

"I'm sure you'll find another way," Coulton remarked.

"That is true." Casteel bit his lower lip. "I am very inventive."

I rolled my eyes, even though I was practically bursting at the seams with pride. This may not seem like a big deal to many, but it was to me.

Casteel kept his eyes on me as he mounted the other horse, who turned out to be named Teddy. I almost laughed when Casteel frowned at the name.

"Ready?" he asked once he held both reins.

Holding on to the horn of the saddle, I nodded. "I hope Setti doesn't get jealous."

"He will if he sees you."

Saying goodbye to Coulton, Casteel led us out of the stables. The first couple of steps sent my heart pounding because it felt like I would fall at any second. But Casteel talked me through it, reminding me that it was no different than when he was behind me.

Casteel went through the basics of controlling a horse as he led us around the side of the fortress and along the crumbling wall.

"To get a horse to stop, you close your fingers around the reins, squeeze, and pull back slightly. The horse will feel the tug and know to stop," he said, showing the technique. "You can also use your legs," he explained, showing what he meant. When I nodded, he continued. "To get a horse to walk, you squeeze with your legs again, but you do it here." He pointed at the side of the horse. "Or you push with your seat—leaning forward. Anytime you want the horse to listen to the command, you lift the reins. That's a signal to them that a command is coming. Want to try it?"

I nodded. Keeping hold of the saddle, I waited for Casteel to lift the reins, putting light tension on Molly's halter, and then I pressed my knee against the area Casteel had pointed to. Molly lumbered forward.

Smiling, I turned to Casteel. "I did it."

He stared at me. "And now I want to kiss you, but I can't because you're on your own horse." The corners of his lips turned down. "This was a bad idea."

I laughed.

"A really bad idea."

As we traveled around the side of the fortress, he went through some more basic commands while having me stop and start Molly. I grew more confident with each try, and so focused on the horse, I didn't even notice that we'd cleared the fortress until I looked up and saw a thicket of trees ahead. We entered them slowly, and Casteel navigated both horses down the earthen path.

"Coulton had a strange reaction to you," he said as the bushy leaves filtered the sun.

"He did, but I think he was being honest. His reaction wasn't something negative. I know because I used my gift."

"I realized that when you stepped forward. Very smart of you to do that."

"I...being able to read emotions to gauge someone's intentions isn't infallible," I said, starting to grow used to being in the saddle alone. "But most people can't hide their emotions from themselves."

"It gives you an upper hand. It's what gave the empaths the upper hand."

"You're not worried that I read your emotions?" I peeked over at him.

"I'd rather you use everything you have in your arsenal than be worried about what you're picking up from me."

"I think most people would prefer that I not do it."

"I'm not most people."

No, he was not.

"You asked earlier if Spessa's End was my idea. It was a combination of mine and Kieran's," he said after a few moments, surprising me with his willingness now to talk about this place. "We came here often when we were younger, along with my brother."

I already knew that those trips also included Shea, but I kept that to myself.

"It's just a day's ride through the mountains, and half of that from there to Saion's Cove, a city in Atlantia," he went on. "We came here a lot—Malik and me. More than our parents ever realized. We'd inspected every inch of this land, finding all its secrets while our parents believed we were in the Cove. They would have had our heads if they'd known how many times we crossed over into Solis."

"Wasn't that dangerous, though?"

"That was what made it so alluring." A brief grin appeared. "But even when Spessa's End was once populated, the Ascended didn't travel the road east all that often. Not many knew who we were, and while here, we could just be brothers."

Instead of Princes of a fallen kingdom.

"Anyway, Kieran and I both realized the potential of this place with the fortress and the Rise being largely intact." Casteel shifted in his saddle, holding the reins lightly in his grasp. "With this land being so close to Atlantia, it's important."

I didn't think that was the only reason why it was important to him.

"It took a bit to convince my father and mother. They didn't think it would give us enough to bear the risk, but they eventually relented. Although my father has become increasingly supportive of taking back all the land, my mother has been the voice of caution. She doesn't want another war, but she knows that we cannot continue as we are. We need this land. We need more, but for now, I hope it will give us enough that if the risk one day presents itself, it will be worth it."

I considered that, and something occurred to me. "Then Spessa's End is a part of Atlantia."

"All of Solis was once Atlantia, but I've reclaimed this land. This is Atlantian soil."

My heart stammered as I looked over at him. "Does that mean we could...we could be married here?"

"Yes." He held my gaze for a moment and then looked ahead. "But that's not what this afternoon is about, Poppy."

"I know," I said, but my heart still pounded with the knowledge that this was Atlantian soil. That marriage may come sooner rather than later.

A shout from ahead startled me, and my jump caused Molly to lurch forward. Casteel steadied the reins.

"You okay?" he asked.

I nodded. "What was that?"

"Training, I imagine."

"Training?"

He inclined his head toward me. "Even though the risk is low, we watch from the Rise, and we train those who can defend the city if need be."

Interest more than piqued, I faced forward. We rode to the edges of a field that had been cleared of grass. A large stone pavilion sat on the other side of the open space, butted up to the dense stand of trees. White and golden curtains rippled in the breeze, rolling and lifting gently, revealing a handful of people seated inside.

But it was what I saw standing in the center of the glen that left me speechless.

Women stood on the flattened land, at least a dozen of them, dressed like no woman would dare in Solis. Wearing black pants and sleeveless tunics, the sun glinted off the golden rings encircling their upper arms.

"Who are they?" I asked.

"Them?" Casteel inclined his head toward the group. "Remember the women I told you about the night I found you on the battlements of the Rise?"

I did. "Women who could cut a man down without blinking an eye."

"You failed to mention the other part." He looked at me, a teasing smoke-filled smile tugging at the corners of his lips. "About being less magnificent—"

"I didn't forget," I cut him off. "I chose not to mention it."

He chuckled, but before he could explain further, a mass of movement snagged my attention. Men dressed the same as the women poured out from the shadows of the surrounding trees, racing across the field. The women were vastly outnumbered. There had to be three to four times more men.

The women turned, all but one, who stood apart from the others, closest to the approaching men. A tall blonde, her hair pulled back in a thick braid. She was watching us, seemingly unaware of the behemoth of a man, larger than even Elijah, racing toward her, a golden sword raised—

She turned at the last second, my lips parting as she caught the man by the throat. Letting out a long, wavering cry that was taken up by the other women, she drove the man down, slamming him into the ground. Dirt exploded on impact, hanging in the air as she gripped his arm, twisting until he dropped his sword. It seemed to fall into her waiting hand, and within a heartbeat, she had it pointed at his throat.

I looked out over the clearing, and only the women stood,

each of them weaponless at the start, having disarmed the men. Now, they held swords or spears, pointed at the men's throats or far more interesting areas.

"They are the kingdom's elite, each one skilled and deadlier than the one before," Casteel said, and I could feel his gaze on me. "They are the Guardians of the Atlantian armies."

Unable to take my eyes off the women, I watched them extend their hands to the men. They helped them to their feet.

"They are the last of their bloodline, born into a long succession of warriors who will defend Atlantia to their last breath."

"And they're all women?"

"They are."

The Guardians and the men took notice of our presence. The tall blonde stepped forward, placing her closed fist over her heart. The other women followed suit while the men bowed from their waists. Casteel acknowledged their gestures by placing his fist over his heart.

I was absolutely awestruck as Casteel nudged our horses around the edge of the field, grateful that he had control of Molly. My eyes were still glued to the women as they handed the weapons back to the men. I just…it was almost like I couldn't believe what my eyes were telling me. To grow up in a society where the sharpest object a woman was permitted to handle was a knitting needle, I was stunned. And I was fascinated as one of the women showed a man a better way to grip the sword.

"They're training them, aren't they?" I asked.

"Yes," Casteel answered. "The Guardians always train our warriors, here and beyond the Skotos."

"So, there are more?" I watched a wolven with black and white fur prowl out from the pavilion, approaching the blonde. The wolven nearly reached her chest.

"There are about two hundred of them left," he said as the Guardian smiled at that wolven. "But one of them is equal to twenty trained warriors."

I finally dragged my awed gaze from them. "Do they have…unique abilities courtesy of their bloodline?"

"Only the females born within that bloodline. They are like

elementals in terms of strength and mortality, and they do need blood."

"Are any other warrior bloodlines still alive?" I asked as we entered the other side of the woods.

Casteel shook his head. "They are the only ones left." He paused. "Besides you."

Besides me.

It was strange to hear that, knowing I was descended from a line of warriors. "I may not be the only one," I said, and Casteel focused ahead. "I know it's unlikely that Ian is my full-blooded brother, but that doesn't mean there aren't others out there that no one knows about, including the Ascended."

"That's true, but I think it would be highly doubtful that any of them have gone undetected by this point." His gaze followed a sparrow as it flew across the path. "Makes me think of the first Maiden—if she did exist—and how many more were potentially discovered that we will never know about. And it also makes me think about the time I was held by the Ascended. They always used mortals with Atlantian blood to feed me."

I resisted the urge to reach out to him with my senses, already knowing what I would find.

"Some were young, just past maturity. Some were older, their hair gray and bodies already breaking down with age," he said after a few moments. "I tried to keep count of how many had been brought into my cage, but I...I wasn't able to. Even so, between Malik and me, I don't know how there could be any more out there."

Ian had been the last to Ascend, and it had only been him. Before that, it had been several years since the last Ascension. Dread surged through me. Ascensions had been carried out annually for several years, but then they'd all but stopped when I was a child. The implications of that brought forth the concern I'd had before. What if Malik was no longer alive?

Kieran and Casteel both believed that Malik lived, but there was no evidence of that. And I wanted to know if Casteel had truly considered that. I bit down on my lip.

"You look like you want to say something," he observed.

I did, but how could I ask what I wanted? I didn't think I

should, so I said what I also believed I needed to say. "You did what you needed to do to survive. I hope you truly believe that."

Casteel didn't answer, and when I looked over at him and saw the vast emptiness in his expression, my heart ached. Because I knew.

I knew he didn't.

And all I wanted in that moment was to bring warmth back to him. "I still want to stab you."

His head shot in my direction.

"Just not as frequently," I amended.

One side of his lips curled up, and then he laughed. The sound was rough and a little hoarse, but it was real. "I would be disappointed if you didn't."

I looked forward, smiling. "That is such a weird statement."

"What can I say? I have a thing for women with violent tendencies."

"That doesn't sound any better," I said, even though I wondered if Shea had been that way. Prone to stabbing him when she was angry? I wasn't so sure about that, considering what he'd said I deserved when this was all over. A relationship with no stabbing or punching. Or kidnapping.

I shoved those thoughts aside before they could weigh me down. We were pretending, and that meant there was no future, even if we couldn't escape the past.

Luckily, a distraction arose a few moments later. Riding out of the wooded area, I finally saw what Casteel had built.

My grip loosened on the saddle as I took in a piece of Atlantia hidden away in Solis.

Stygian Bay glistened like the darkest hour of night to our right. Ahead of us was a town the size of New Haven. Yet again, I was struck speechless as we rode along the dirt road. I only half-noticed those who acknowledged our arrival, who either bowed or called out.

One-story homes made of sandstone and clay dotted the gently rolling landscape. There had to be around a hundred of them, and each one was spaced out to accommodate private, curtained terraces, and small gardens. As we drew closer to the homes, I could see that the gardens were full of ripe tomatoes and tall stalks of corn, cabbage, and other vegetables planted in neat rows. The only homes in Solis that had any land beyond a patch barely large enough to grow a tree were the ones in places like Radiant Row.

"My gods," I whispered as I looked around.

"I'm hoping that's an exclamation of approval," Casteel stated as we neared the crest of a small hill.

"It is. These homes... And the gardens? I've never seen anything like it."

"Food supply is far easier to manage when each household harvests as much as they can," he said, drawing Molly closer to him when the mare appeared to take note of a vivid, yellow butterfly. "All the gardens were planted by farmers who have experience with crops. Those who agreed to settle in Spessa's End were required to apprentice with farmers to learn how to keep them healthy and spot disease. With the temperatures rarely dropping below freezing at night, we're able to grow some of the crops longer than places farther north."

In Solis, food had to be paid for or grown, but very few had the land to grow anything, which meant that many spent the bulk of their income to acquire food. If there was no money, there simply was nothing to eat.

As soon as we reached the top of the hill, the scent of grilled meat replaced the sweetly scented breeze. It was then that I realized I hadn't truly seen anything yet. The town center lay in the valley between the homes. There were other buildings— larger than the houses, numerous columned pavilions adorned with bright canopies or curtains, housing various markets. There were businesses—butchers, seamstresses, blacksmiths, and bakers, and in the very center and raised higher than any of the other buildings was the ruins of what had once been a great coliseum. Or so it appeared. Only half of the structure remained.

"Concerts and games were once played there," Casteel said, having followed my gaze. "I remember sitting in those seats, watching plays."

Thinking of all the souls that had once filled the massive coliseum twisted my heart. "Will it be repaired?"

"I don't know yet," he admitted as we traveled down the

sloping hill. "I never wanted to tear it down. It's become a monument in a way, a reminder of what once stood here. Perhaps one day we will repair it."

There were more people in the town center, drifting between the pavilions and stalls. Pretending that he was just Hawke and I was Poppy ended as the people either rushed forward to greet Casteel or lingered back until others passed on.

There were wolven and Atlantians among the Descenters, and out of the blur of faces, I realized that all of them seemed genuinely happy to see Casteel. Most called him by name and not by his title, which was something not tolerated in Solis. All Royals were addressed as Lord or Lady, and to not do so was seen as greatly disrespectful, and worse yet, potentially a sign of being a Descenter.

I watched Casteel as he grinned or laughed at something someone said, asked about a family member or friend, seemingly as fascinated with them as I had been with the Guardians. I smiled when he introduced me to those who approached. *My fiancée. My fiancée. My fiancée.* I listened as he spoke to many, addressing them by name, and he was attentive and welcoming as we traveled along. If this wasn't another mask—if this was who he was with his people—he was a Prince that anyone would be honored to rule beside.

Something nameless and unknown inside of me *softened* and then opened up even as my senses thrummed under my skin, stretching and throbbing in response to the cyclone of conflicting emotions spilling out of the crowd and into the air around me.

I noticed that, more often than not, the people's reaction to me was far more subdued. Smiles went from warm and genuine to cold and tight. Welcoming glances became ones of curiosity or turned blank. Some gazes lingered on the scars for the briefest of moments while others openly stared. There were quickly averted gazes, and mumbled greetings.

Even as I struggled to keep my senses in check—even though I knew that many of the people of Atlantia didn't welcome me—I started *pretending* again.

But this time he was Casteel, and I was Poppy, and he truly was my Prince.

Chapter 28

"There's someone I'd like you to meet," Casteel said as we rode past the town center, beyond the crowds of people.

The tightness in my chest eased with the crowd's dispersal, but balls of nervous energy formed in my stomach. Would this person be friendly? Would they stare?

"You okay?" he asked as he guided the horses to a stop outside of one of the homes where vines with tiny pink flowers climbed the terrace's latticework.

I nodded as my gaze shifted up the road, drawn by the clang of a hammer. Homes were being built. Men were on the roofs, their skin damp with sweat, and women ran tools over the exterior walls, smoothing out the clay.

A young wolven loped out from the inside of the house, dancing around the women's legs, tail wagging. Remembering what was said the night before about not many young being here, I figured it was Beckett. A grin tugged at my lips as he nudged a spade with his nose, rolling it toward one of the women.

Casteel dismounted as the door to the house opened wider. Kieran strode out, his brows rising upon seeing me astride my own horse.

Before I could even feel embarrassment over what had happened this morning, he opened his mouth. "Dear gods, you have her on her own horse? Soon, she'll be running one of us over instead of stabbing us."

My eyes narrowed. "This is who you wanted me to meet?" I asked. "Not sure if you realize this or not, but I'm well aware of who he is."

Casteel laughed as he came to my side. "It's not him I want you to meet." He held Molly steady. "You want to dismount on your own?"

I nodded, rising and drawing one leg up and over the saddle. I lowered myself to the ground, nowhere near as gracefully, but I did it.

Kieran applauded. "Good job."

"Shut up."

The wolven laughed as one of the workers called out Casteel's name.

Casteel looked over, squinting. He touched my lower back. "I'll be right back."

I nodded as I turned to Molly, scratching her behind the ear as I watched Casteel jog toward the house.

"By the way," Kieran approached me, "I hope you're not embarrassed about this morning."

"I'm not embarrassed," I whispered.

"You're not?" He sounded doubtful. "You won't look at me."

"I was just looking at you a few moments ago."

"Only because you wanted to do violent and terrible things to me."

I smiled because that was true.

"You look like you want to do that now."

Brows raised, I looked at him. "Happy? I'm looking at you now."

A half-grin appeared. "Yes, but your face is as red as a tomato."

"Whatever," I muttered.

"And you still look like you want to murder me."

I sighed.

He adjusted Molly's halter as he said, "You know what you felt during the feeding and what surely came afterward is only natural."

"Thanks, but I don't need you to tell me this."

"Then maybe you would like some advice?"

"Not really."

"I'm going to give it to you anyway."

"Of course, you are."

"If you wish for future feedings—and I'm sure you realize there will be future ones—to be less intimate, you could offer him your wrist."

I spun toward Kieran. "Well, that information is so very helpful now."

Kieran laughed, not even bothering to move out of the way when I punched his arm.

"Ouch," he murmured. "That was actually hard."

"Do I even want to know why you just hit Kieran?" Casteel asked as he rejoined us.

Kieran's eyes lit as he opened his mouth—

"No," I jumped in, shooting Kieran a look that promised death if he spoke as Casteel came to stand beside me. "You do not."

Grinning, Kieran backed up. "When has she ever needed a reason to be violent?"

"Good point." Casteel glanced down at me, one side of his lips quirking. The damn dimple winked into existence. "I guess I should be grateful that she didn't stab you."

"There's always later," I muttered.

A throaty, feminine laugh snapped my head around. "You're right, Kieran. I like her."

Standing barefoot in the terrace's doorway was a stunning woman dressed in black leggings and a bright yellow, sleeveless tunic that fit the curve of her hips and chest. Golden cuffs encircled her wrists and upper arms. Her jet-black hair, braided in narrow, tight rows, nearly reached her waist. The pale, wintry blue eyes were a striking contrast to skin as beautiful as the rich black of the night-blooming roses. There was some vague familiarity about the slant of her cheeks and the shape of her brow, but I knew I'd never met the female wolven before.

"Because she insinuated that I could be stabbed later?" Kieran muttered. "Shocker."

Oh, gods, I really needed to stop talking about stabbing people.

The woman laughed. "Of course." She stepped out of the doorway, her gaze flicking to Casteel. "Why are you standing there so quiet?"

"I am not interrupting you." Casteel held up his hands. "The last time I did, you knocked me on my ass."

I blinked.

"That is not why I knocked you on your ass," she replied. "I don't exactly remember why I did it, but I'm sure it was because you did something to deserve it."

The corners of my lips turned up.

"Since both of them have no manners, I'll introduce myself. I'm Vonetta, but everyone calls me Netta. I'm Kieran's sister."

Shock rippled through me. "You have a sister," I blurted out.

Vonetta shot her brother a look. "Wow, Kieran."

"Hey, Casteel never said I had one either."

"Don't drag me into this," Casteel remarked.

"My feelings are hurt, and I am the baby of the family. My feelings should never be hurt," she tossed over her shoulder. "I expect an extra batch of the candied fruit."

"As soon as I have an hour to make some, I will."

"You have had plenty of hours to do so already." Facing me, she extended a hand. Her nails were painted a yellow as brilliant as her tunic.

"I'm Penellaphe," I said, taking her hand. The moment our skin touched, her eyes widened. "Did you just feel something weird?"

"Yeah. Like a static charge," she answered as Casteel moved in closer. She let go of my hand. "That's strange."

"Coulton felt the same thing," Casteel said.

"And I felt something like that back in New Haven," Kieran reminded me.

"That's right." I clasped my hands together. "I'd forgotten."

"Well, I'm kind of offended now," he muttered.

"Do you feel anything like that?" I asked Casteel, recalling a similar feeling a few times we'd touched.

"I have," he said, head tilted as he examined me closely, like I was a strange new species. "I thought it was my imagination."

"I've felt it when I've touched you." I turned back to the siblings. "But I didn't feel anything now or when Coulton or Kieran felt something earlier."

"Apparently, we're not as special as Casteel," Vonetta commented.

"You should've already known that," he replied.

She shot him a look. "You saying something like that was probably why I knocked you on your ass the last time."

I laughed. "I like her."

"Of course, you do." Casteel sighed as he placed his hand on my back. But when I looked up at him, he had that look to him again. Like he'd lost his breath. Swallowing, he looked over at Kieran's sister. "Are you going to invite us in?"

"Are you going to be less annoying?"

"Probably not, but since I'm your *Prince*...."

"Whatever. Fine." Then she smiled. "Come in. I just finished making sandwiches."

The living area was a round, cozy area full of color. Thick sky-blue floor cushions circled a low-to-the-ground white table. Bright orange and deep purple throw pillows covered a black settee. The breeze let in by the open windows and terrace doors lazily turned the blades of a ceiling fan. A stack of books on an end table by the settee snagged my attention as Casteel tugged me down onto one of the cushions on the floor while Vonetta and Kieran disappeared through a rounded archway.

"Is lemonade fine?" Vonetta's voice carried out from the other room. "Kieran made it, so it's more sweet than sour."

Casteel glanced at me, and when I nodded, he called out, "That's perfect."

A few moments later, Kieran returned carrying four glasses, which he placed on the table before dropping onto the cushion on the other side of Casteel.

"Thank you," I said, picking up the cool glass. Ice cubes clinked together, and I realized there must be a cold room underground somewhere since there appeared to be no electricity running in Spessa's End yet.

"Don't be polite," Kieran remarked. "It weirds me out."

I cracked a grin at that as I took a sip. The sweet and sour mix was perfect. "This is actually really good."

"Kieran is a master at making drinks," Casteel shifted back on one arm, leaning slightly into my shoulder. "Especially the kind involving alcohol."

"A man must have his talents."

"Even if said talents are generally useless," Vonetta commented as she entered, carrying a silver tray loaded with sandwiches cut into narrow strips and a large bowl of strawberries dusted with sugar.

"I'll remember that the next time you ask me to make you a drink," Kieran replied.

Vonetta snorted as she sat beside me. "I hope you like cucumber sandwiches. Other than cold cuts, it's the only sandwich I can manage."

"They're one of my favorites. Thank you," I said, picking one up. "And it's the only sandwich I've ever made, actually."

"Really?" Casteel asked, handing me one of the napkins from the tray.

I nodded. "I wasn't allowed to cook or to learn how, but I did sneak into the kitchens sometimes and watch," I admitted, and then felt silly the moment the words had left my mouth. I had no idea how much Vonetta even knew about my past. Heat crept up my throat as I sat back a little, distancing myself from Casteel. I quickly shoved half the sandwich into my mouth.

"Kieran told me a little bit of what it was like for you," Vonetta said, her tone soft. "But honestly, the not being allowed to learn how to cook part sounds amazing."

I glanced up at her in confusion as Casteel reclaimed the short distance that separated us. His arm pressed to mine as he reached for a sandwich and then remained there.

"I don't mean the not having a choice part. That sounds terrible. That *is* terrible." She took a drink of lemonade. "But if I didn't have to learn, then I'd have an excuse for why I'm horrible at cooking. Our poor mother spent many moons attempting to teach me how to bake bread. I'd rather sharpen a sword than knead yeast. Of course, Mom excels equally at both."

"As do I." Kieran grinned, and his sister rolled her eyes.

"Sounds like you and Poppy have that in common," Casteel said, wiping his fingers on the napkin. It said something about his relationship with Kieran's sister that he'd called me that in front of her. "She also has a fondness for sharp, deadly objects."

"I do," I confirmed.

Vonetta grinned. "Yet another reason to like you," she said. "So, what do you think of Spessa's End so far?"

Finishing off the last of the sandwich, I then told her how I hadn't been aware of what had happened to Pompay and Spessa's End. "I'm amazed by what has been done here—the homes are so much nicer than what most people have in Solis. And the gardens? There is nothing like that there. After seeing Pompay, I expected nothing but ruins."

"Solis sounds like a really cruddy place," she stated.

Casteel snorted. "Understatement of the year, Netta."

"There are nice parts, but so very few people have access to them." I picked up a plump strawberry. "And there are good people there. Scared individuals who don't know any other way to live than what they were born into."

She nodded as she brushed several braids back over her shoulder. "Hopefully, that changes soon."

I agreed, and the conversation moved on from there. Casteel asked about Kieran and Vonetta's parents. I learned that her mother was named Kirha and that Vonetta planned to travel home to see them soon. Their mother had a birthday coming up. They talked about how many new homes they felt would be completed in the next couple of months, and Vonetta mentioned a few people that she knew were interested in settling here. She asked about the potential for electricity, which led to a conversation about power grids and lines that sounded like a different language to me. I learned that Vonetta's role in Spessa's End was like one of a Rise Guard, and the way Vonetta and Casteel traded insults made it clear that the three of them had grown up together. The friendship between them was so real, that it made me fiercely yearn for the same thing—made me think of Tawny. She would love Kieran's sister.

Vonetta then asked about how I'd learned to fight, and

minutes ticked away, the sandwiches disappeared, and throughout the afternoon, there was never more than a few minutes where some part of Casteel's body wasn't in contact with mine. Whether it was his arm resting against mine or his knee, or him messing with my hair, tucking it behind my ear, or fixing the sleeves on my borrowed tunic. The constant contact, the small touches here and there, made it all too easy to forget that we were *pretending*.

And it was hard not to notice, at least for me, how different Vonetta was toward me compared to the others. It could be because she was Kieran's sister and Casteel's friend, but the wolven in general had entirely different reactions toward me. They weren't distrustful, and while I did briefly open my senses to Vonetta when I caught her staring at me strangely, all I felt from her was curiosity.

"So, the whole static charge thing," Vonetta brought back up after Kieran had cleared the table. "I want to see if it happens again."

My brows lifted, but I was also curious. I extended my hand, and a moment later, Vonetta placed her palm flat to mine. She frowned slightly. "Do you feel anything?"

"No." She sounded disappointed.

"I only felt it once," Kieran remarked, letting an arm dangle over a bent knee. "Actually, come to think of it. What does she smell like to you?"

I drew my hand back, twisting toward Kieran. "That's right. You said I smelled like a dead person."

"I didn't say you smelled like a dead person," he countered. "I said you smelled *of* death."

"How is that different?" I demanded.

"That's a good question." Casteel turned his head, brows lifting. "You're really smelling her, aren't you, Netta?"

I looked to find Vonetta's head close to mine. "Please don't say I smell *of* death."

"You don't." She drew back. "But there is a unique scent to you." Her dark brows knitted together. "You smell...*old*."

"Um." I shifted uncomfortably. "I'm not sure if that's any better."

Casteel dipped his head, and I felt the bridge of his nose along the side of my neck. "You don't smell like that to me," he murmured, and a shiver curled its way down my spine. "You smell like honeydew."

Oh, my *gods*....

"I'm not saying she smells like mothballs and stale peppermint candy," Vonetta said, and Kieran laughed. "It's just... I don't know how to explain what I mean."

"I think I understand." Casteel sat back.

"You do?" I questioned.

He nodded. "Your blood tastes old to me—old in a way that it's rich. Powerful for someone who is not full-blooded Atlantian. It's probably the bloodline."

Vonetta tilted her head. "And what kind of—?"

A sudden, loud crash from outside interrupted us. Shouts of alarm rang out, and all three of them were on their feet in a matter of seconds.

"Sounds like that came from up the street where the houses are being worked on," Vonetta said as I rose to my feet. Casteel was already out the terrace doors, Kieran following quickly behind him.

I trailed them out into the late-afternoon sun. We didn't have to go far. Alastir rushed down the dirt-packed road, carrying the limp form of a small wolven.

Beckett.

I already knew he was in pain. I could feel it pinging against my skin, hot and sharp. I swallowed hard.

"What happened?" Casteel demanded.

"Beckett was being—well, he was being Beckett." Alastir's face was pale as he gently laid his nephew down in a patch of grass. The wolven's growl ended in a whimper. "A piece of the roof collapsed, and he couldn't move out of the way quick enough."

"Shit," Casteel grunted, kneeling beside Beckett.

Emil appeared behind Alastir. "Where is the Healer?"

"Talia is in the training fields," a mortal woman said. "Someone was injured during practice."

"Go and summon her. Tell her to come as soon as she

can," Casteel ordered one of the wolven. The man took off, shifting into his wolven form in a blur of speed. "It's okay, Beckett. We're getting help."

Beckett's chest rose and fell rapidly, and his mouth hung open. The whites of his eyes were stark against his dark fur. My senses stretched and pushed at my skin, and I tensed, trying to prepare myself as I opened up. Burning, acute pain rolled through the connection, stealing my breath. It was throbbing and endless, painting the soft grass in shades of red and soaking the sky in embers. This was definitely no minor hurt.

"I think his back legs are broken," Alastir said, his hands trembling as he placed them on the ground. "He needs to shift. He needs to do it now."

"Oh, no," Vonetta whispered.

"If he doesn't, the bones will start healing before we can straighten them."

"I know," Casteel said as I severed the connection before his physical pain overwhelmed me. "Beckett, you have to shift. I know it hurts, but you have to shift."

The young wolven whimpered as he shuddered.

"He's in too much pain." I stepped around Vonetta.

"He's too young," Kieran said in a low voice, to no one in particular. "He won't be able to do it."

My gift hummed, demanding to be used as it guided me toward the wolven. My fingers tingled with the urge. Vonetta caught my arm. "Don't get too close, Penellaphe." Concern clouded her pale eyes. "An injured wolven is a very dangerous one, no matter how young."

"It's okay. I can help him." I stepped to the side, slipping free of her grip as I searched out Casteel's gaze. "I can help him."

Casteel was still for a half a second and then nodded. "Come to his back. Beside me and away from those teeth."

Aware of Kieran shadowing my steps and us gaining an audience, I lowered to my knees. Beckett's rear legs were twisted at awful, unnatural angles. Beckett growled, lifting his head and kicking out with his front leg, both weak attempts to warn us off, but I knew he could strike a lot more quickly.

"Can you do it?" Alastir whispered. "What you did in New

Haven?"

I nodded.

"If you can help him and he's able to shift," Casteel spoke low and fast, "that'll make it so much easier for Talia."

"Okay," I said as Casteel angled his body so he would have to go through him first if the wolven reared. "I'm not going to hurt you, Beckett. I promise."

Lips peeled back, revealing canines sharp enough to pierce skin and strong enough to crunch bones. I tried not to think of that as I placed my hand on his back. Opening myself up again so I could monitor his pain, I swallowed back the bile crowding my throat. His pain…it made me want to throw up. I started to drum up warm, happy memories—

Something… something different happened the moment my fingers sank into Beckett's soft fur.

The tingling sensation in my palms ramped up as if static danced over my skin, and my hands heated. The wolven twitched, whimpering quietly as a muted glow appeared between my fingers, peeking through the strands of fur before washing over my hands.

My lips parted. "Uh…"

"That's not normal," Casteel observed, a dark eyebrow raised. "Right?"

Out of the corner of my eyes, I registered Emil's mouth drop open. I saw the same reaction from most of those around us. Alastir rocked backward, paling even further as he stared at me. Whispers and gasps echoed around me.

"Well," I heard Vonetta say. "I think you forgot to tell me something, Kieran."

I don't know what Kieran said in response. I heard Casteel whisper my name, but I shook my head as Beckett's head lowered to the grass. I could feel his pain lessening. "It's working, but I've never seen it do this before."

"You mean you've never seen your hands glow?" he asked. "Like twin stars?"

"They're not glowing that brightly," I denied.

"Yeah, they kind of are," Kieran murmured, and Emil nodded when I looked up.

"Okay. Whatever," I muttered. My hands were glowing brightly now. "I'll freak out over that later."

Beckett's breathing steadied, and the whites of his eyes became less visible.

"Sweet gods of mercy," someone murmured.

"Princess?"

"Hmm?" I focused on Beckett. Emotional pain was harder to cut through and whatever release I brought was incredibly short-lived, but physical pain took longer to ease. I believed it had to do with all the important nerves and veins, and physical pain almost always carried an emotional anguish with it, especially if it was as intense as it was for Beckett. Easing his pain was two-fold, but the throbbing was dulling, becoming little more than an ache. He only needed a few more moments.

"Poppy," Casteel called, and this time, I looked over at him. Sunlight glinted off the curve of his cheek as his gaze swept over me, around me. "You're glowing. Not just your hands. *You*."

Chapter 29

Good gods, I *was*.

A silvery glow radiated out from under the sleeves of my tunic.

"You look like moonlight," Casteel whispered, and it wasn't the sunlight reflecting over his cheek. It was me.

The fur thinned under my fingers, replaced by clammy skin as Beckett shifted into his mortal form. I lifted my hands, rocking back on my rear as Vonetta swept forward, draping a blanket she must've grabbed over the boy's waist. His legs…they were a mottled, angry shade of red and violet, but they were straight and no longer twisted.

Aided by Alastir, Beckett sat up, his pale, sweat-slick face quickly gaining color. Someone was talking. Maybe Casteel asking if he were in pain? Beckett didn't answer as he stared at me, eyes as wide as saucers.

"Am I still glowing?" My hands weren't, but maybe my face was? Because it felt like everyone was staring at me.

Casteel shook his head and then looked down at Beckett. "I think…I think you healed his legs."

"No." I glanced down at my hands—at my normal, flesh-toned palms. "I can't do that."

"But you did," Casteel insisted.

Beckett still stared at me. So did Alastir. And Emil. And

everyone else.

"I can't," I repeated.

"Can you move your legs?" Kieran asked, and when Beckett continued to do nothing but stare, the wolven leaned over me and snapped his fingers. "Beckett. Focus. Can you move your legs?"

The young wolven blinked as if he were waking up from a spell. He drew his left leg up, wincing, but then extended it with little trouble. Then he repeated it with the right. "I... I can move them. There's pain but nothing like before. Thank you." Astounded eyes met mine. "I don't know how to repay you. Thank you." Before I could tell him there was no need for repayment, he twisted at the waist toward the Prince. "I'm sorry. I didn't mean for this to happen. It's not anyone's fault. I wasn't paying attention—"

"It's all right." Casteel placed his hand on the boy's slim shoulder. "You don't need to apologize. You're okay, and that's all that matters."

"I know." His eyes glistened as he fought back emotion. "I should've—"

"You have nothing to apologize for," Casteel repeated.

Beckett exhaled roughly as he fisted the blanket lying over him. He bent his left leg once more, sucking his lip between his teeth. Maybe his legs hadn't been as injured as we thought they were.

Casteel rocked back as his gaze flicked from me to Alastir. "You think you can get him to the training fields? You can take one of our horses. I want Talia to look at him."

Alastir blinked, dragging his gaze from me. "Of course."

Sliding an arm under Beckett's shoulders, Emil helped him stand. He took a tentative step while holding the cloak to his midsection, smiling in relief when his legs held his weight.

"Thank you," Alastir said to me.

I could only nod. "I don't think he was as badly hurt as we thought."

"Yes," Alastir said, but he didn't sound like he believed me.

Rising then, Casteel turned to the others. "Beckett will be fine. The Healer will take a look at him."

The people, a mixture of wolven, Atlantian, and mortal nodded, but there was a thickness to the air, and it settled over my skin like a coarse blanket. I didn't dare look up as Casteel ushered the group away. *It* was palpable. The crowd's emotions. Raw and unfettered. I closed my eyes, trembling with the effort it took to keep my senses locked down, but it was no use. I split open, and the whirl of spinning emotions poured into me. Shock. Confusion. Awe. More shock. Something extremely bitter. *Fear.* Why would anyone fear me?

"Poppy." Casteel touched my shoulder, jolting me. "Are you all right?"

I opened my eyes, letting out a ragged breath of relief when I noticed that it was just him—him and Kieran and Vonetta. I didn't dare look too far. If I did, I would never be able to close myself down.

"You really left some pretty big details out when you told me about her," Vonetta said, and I almost laughed at how annoyed she sounded.

"I...I don't know how that happened—how I healed him or started glowing." I craned my neck to look back at Vonetta. "I can relieve people's pain with my touch, but only temporarily."

"And you can read emotions," she said, obviously knowing enough about my bloodline. "You're an empath."

I nodded and looked to where Casteel knelt beside me. He was looking over his shoulder to where the others had gone back to the house. "But I've never done that before," I said, and Casteel faced me. "I honestly don't think he was as badly hurt as we feared."

"His legs were completely broken," Vonetta said. "They were smashed and twisted."

"I..." I shook my head. "That's impossible."

"It's really not. The empaths could heal."

"Did they glow?"

"Not that I know of," Vonetta said. "But they were all gone before I was born."

"It could be the Culling." Casteel's brows knitted as he placed a hand on the grass. "And you're on land that has been reclaimed as Atlantia. You're on Atlantian soil. That could impact your abilities." His eyes met mine. "And it could be my blood. What I've given you stays in you."

I leaned forward, keeping my voice low. "Your blood is making me glow?"

His lips twitched. "I don't think my blood is the sole reason why you glowed like moonlight."

"It's not funny," I snapped.

"I'm not laughing."

"You're trying not to laugh," I accused. "Don't even deny it."

Casteel laughed then, holding up his hands. "It's just you look...adorably confused, and now you look adorably violent."

I shook my head at him. "There is something so wrong with you."

He arched a brow and then looked to where Kieran and Vonetta stood. "Can one of you check on Beckett? See how he's doing?"

"Of course," Kieran answered as I pushed to my feet.

"I'll go with you," his sister said, giving me a little wave. "I'm going to have so many questions for you later."

I had many for myself.

I watched them start down the road and then turned to Casteel. Beyond him, I saw that the others had returned to repairing the section of the roof that had fallen. "They were scared of me. Not all of them but some. I could feel it."

Casteel's lashes were lowered, shielding his eyes as he looked down at me.

"Remember Alastir being concerned about what some of the older Atlantians would think if they realized what bloodline I descended from?"

"I do." He took my hand, leading me to where his horse remained.

"Do they think I'm—what did he say some called the empaths?"

"Soul Eaters."

I shuddered at the name, pulling my hand free from his. "Is that what they think I am? That I'm feeding off pain?" Or their fear could've stemmed from the fact that I'd literally *glowed.* I would also be concerned if I saw that. "Did you ever think that when you learned that I could ease the pain of others? That I was this—this Soul Eater thing?"

"Not once." He turned to me again. "Soul Eaters are practically on par with a *lamaea* at this point. I didn't even think you were half-Atlantian then, remember?"

I searched his face, but there was nothing hidden in his expression or his unflinching gaze. "I don't know how any of that happened," I admitted as I turned to Teddy, stroking the horse's side. "Normally, I have to think about something happy to channel that feeling into others. But this time, all it took was for me to place my hands on Beckett. My skin tingled more than normal, and my hands heated, but that was all that was different."

"When was the last time you used your gift in that way?" He caught a piece of my hair, tucking it back.

"It was…when I healed the people in New Haven. That was the last time."

"And now you're technically on Atlantian soil." He stood beside me, resting his arms on the saddle. He'd rolled up the sleeves of his shirt, and the dusting of dark hair along his tan forearms seemed scandalous. "I don't know if it's that or the Culling, but there could be more changes."

I really hoped those changes didn't involve glowing any other colors. "Maybe his legs weren't even broken—"

"His legs were most definitely broken. You saw them."

I stepped back from the horse, folding my arms over my waist as I stared at the light blue curtains rippling out from the terrace across the street. "Your people already dislike me because I was the Maiden. And now they're going to think I'm a Soul Eater. I really don't think marrying me is going to change that."

"The people just haven't seen anything like that before. They need time to grow used to it, and they will accept you," he said. "I do think you should hold off on using your abilities, though—"

"I'm not going to hide." I met his stare with an equally hard one. "I'm not going to ignore those in pain—people I can help. I won't do that."

"I'm not asking you to hide your abilities." He drew his arms from the saddle. "All I'm asking is that you hold off until we understand more. Use your abilities when there isn't a crowd to witness it. That way, we control the narrative."

My stomach tumbled. "Is there a narrative we need to control?"

"There is always a narrative." He dragged his hair back from his face with his fingers. The unruly waves immediately toppled over his forehead. "What you did for Beckett was nothing short of amazing," he bit out, shifting the topic. "I hope you know that."

My brows inched up my forehead. "You don't sound like you're amazed. You sound angry."

"That's because the damn Soul Eater thing is overshadowing the fact that you healed broken bones with your *touch*." He stepped in closer to me, a predatory intent to his stare. "I don't think you understand what you did for that boy."

"I know what I did." I unfolded my arms. "I…I healed him."

"You didn't do only that." He took another step, his eyes now like chips of amber.

Heart thumping, I backed up against the warm clay and stone of Vonetta's house. "I didn't?"

Placing his hands on either side of my head, he leaned in. "If a wolven suffers a broken bone, they must immediately shift to prevent permanent damage to the bone, the nerves, and the soft tissue. They have minutes to shift, and he was already at that point or damn near close to it."

"Okay?" I whispered, wondering why he still sounded frustrated.

"He would've lost his legs, Poppy. You prevented that."

"Then why do you sound angry with me?" I demanded.

"I'm not," he growled.

"You sure about that?"

"One hundred percent sure."

"Are you…hungry again?" I asked, even though his eyes remained normal, and I knew he didn't need blood yet.

"Not for blood." He dipped his head then, and all the air

fled my lungs. His mouth was a mere inch from mine.

Was he going to kiss me?

People could see us. People could already be watching. But the intensity in his stare told me that wasn't the point. Whatever he felt wasn't for show.

"I don't think you know your own feelings." I flattened my palms against the warm stone and clay.

"If you open your senses to me right now, you'll know exactly what I'm feeling. Do it."

"I don't want to."

"Why?" His warm breath danced across my parted lips.

"Because I don't want to." A flutter started in my chest.

"Or is it because you don't want to know that it's taking everything in me not to ruin yet another pair of your pants by ripping them off and fucking you so hard that days from now, you'll still be able to feel the extent of my gratitude."

My eyes never felt bigger. The sharp, swift curl low in my stomach never felt more reckless, more demanding, more *alive*.

I swallowed—swallowed hard. "That seems like an odd way to thank me."

He dropped his forehead to mine. "It's the only way I know how."

"A simple thank you would suffice."

"No. It would not."

I couldn't think of what to say, even though there was a lot I should. We stood there for several moments, and at any time, if either of us turned our heads just the slightest, our lips would have met. And I…

I thought I would be lost.

Or maybe found.

Casteel shuddered as a sound I was sure a wolven could make rumbled through him. Every muscle in me tensed deliciously, but he stepped back as he took my hand. Without saying another word, he led me to the horse and hoisted me onto the saddle.

Once he settled behind me, he folded his arm around my waist. "As much as I wish we could spend the rest of the day pretending," he said as his lips brushed along my jaw. "There's something we must discuss."

Drawing in a deep, steadying breath, I nodded. "About our future?"

"Can I point out that I like how you say, 'our future?'"

"I would prefer that you not, but since you already have, I assume that's a yes?"

"It is." Casteel guided the older mare down the road. "We must talk about our marriage."

"What about it?"

"I think you already know, Princess."

I squinted at the setting sun. From the moment I'd learned that Spessa's End had been reclaimed, I had a feeling this conversation was coming.

"What I'm about to say will probably concern you. I don't want it to."

I tensed. "When you start conversations like that, it will inevitably cause me concern."

"Understandable, but know that what guides my decisions is an abundance of caution and anticipation of potential issues," he said.

"Just so you know, this is the most unromantic conversation having to do with marriage that I've ever heard."

"I cannot disagree with that," he replied, and goosebumps pimpled my skin in response to the seriousness of his tone. "I'd originally planned for us to marry once we reached Saion's Cove and then travel to Evaemon, the heart of Atlantia."

"Is that where your parents live?"

"Yes."

"You planned for us to marry before I met your parents?"

"It would make things far less complicated if we did," he reasoned.

I may have been sheltered my entire life, but I was no fool. "You want to marry before they have a chance to stop us."

"They can't stop us," he reminded me, shifting Teddy's reins into my hands. "I don't need their permission."

Curling my fingers around the reins, I said, "But you'd want their approval?"

"Of course, I would. Who wouldn't want their parents'

approval?"

But that wasn't necessary for us since the marriage was temporary.

"As I've said before, I think they will be suspicious of my intentions, especially my mother. She knows I haven't given up my brother." He showed me how to guide Teddy so we weren't going straight through the town center, but on the outskirts. "Both she and my father will seek to find numerous reasons why we should delay the marriage."

If we couldn't convince Alastir, I truly had no idea how we would sway his parents. "Once we're married, then there's nothing to be delayed."

"Exactly." His hand settled back on my hip. "This is another part that I don't want you to overthink even though I know you probably will."

"And I will probably have a good reason to do so."

"That's debatable, but nonetheless, I feel it would be in our best interests to wed here, in Spessa's End."

Although I suspected as much, my heart still skipped several beats. "In your best interests?"

"In *our* best interests," he repeated. "Sooner or later, people would've learned of your abilities to relieve pain. If not by the arrival of those from New Haven, someone other than Beckett would've been injured. I just wasn't expecting today. And while I don't believe many will look upon you with fear for long or think of you as a Soul Eater, it would be wise for us to marry before anyone thinks to do something incredibly idiotic."

Something incredibly idiotic translated into someone attempting to kill me.

"And we have everything here that we need to marry," Casteel said as we climbed the sloping hill. "Or we will shortly."

"What are those things that we need?"

"Well, rings, of course."

I rolled my eyes. "I wasn't being serious about the ring."

"I know, but I still plan to gift you the largest diamond you've ever seen," he said, and I could hear the smile in his voice. "But a simple Atlantian band will have to suffice for now."

There were several more skips in my heart.

"The ceremony can be small. But we will need an officiant," he continued. "Any head of a bloodline can officiate a marriage."

"Alastir?"

"No. He does not speak for the wolven, even though he is among the oldest," Casteel explained. "The wolven who does is named Jasper. And, luckily, he'll be arriving in Spessa's End by tomorrow. We can be married by the evening."

My chest felt tight. In a little over twenty-four hours, we could be married. A rush of confusing emotions as conflicting as the ones the people had felt when I healed Beckett hit me.

I had to focus on the plan and not everything else. My mouth was dry as I asked, "And then we continue to Atlantia?"

"Yes."

I frowned slightly. "But what is the point? If we marry before we even cross the Skotos Mountains, couldn't we then send word to Carsodonia?"

"Besides the fact that my mother might legitimately murder me for not taking my new bride home to meet her, our marriage will need to be recognized by the King and Queen. You will need to be crowned."

"Crowned?" My head jerked to the side.

He arched a brow. "You will become a Princess, Poppy. You will need to be crowned. Then you'll have the same authority as I do. Your position in Atlantia then cannot be questioned by the King or Queen of Solis."

"That…that seems like semantics."

"More like politics. And since King Jalara was alive during Atlantia's rule, he will know that a Prince or Princess not recognized by the Crown holds no power or authority in Atlantia."

I shook my head as I faced forward. Politics was nonsense to me. We'd crested the hill and reached the woods. With the setting sun, there was only the faintest traces of sunlight filtering through the trees. "And you believe that your parents will accept our marriage?"

"They will."

"You do realize that Alastir doesn't quite believe our engagement is genuine," I pointed out. "If your parents don't believe us, why do you think they will crown me?"

"Because we will convince them," Casteel said, and he said it like there was little possibility of anything else occurring.

But I wasn't so sure.

"What are you thinking?" Casteel asked after several silent moments.

"I'm thinking many things," I admitted. "But I know you're lying."

Casteel stiffened behind me. "I'm not—"

"I don't mean that you're lying to mislead me," I quickly added. "But you're lying to protect me. You're more concerned about the Soul Eater thing than you're willing to admit. And you're more worried about your parents' reactions than you're willing to say. That is why you want to marry now."

Casteel still remained tense. "Are you reading my emotions?"

I smiled faintly. "I don't need to read your thoughts to know any of that."

He was quiet and then said, "Poppy—"

"Not that you've asked, and I'm *assuming* you were getting around to it, but yes," I cut him off. "I will marry you in Spessa's End."

Chapter 30

"I don't think this is wise," Alastir said as he sat in the chair across from Casteel and me the following day.

Casteel stretched out his legs, crossing them at the ankles. He looked utterly at ease but I knew better. I hadn't opened my senses. Part of me was half afraid that if I did, I would start glowing silver even though I hadn't when I tested it out on Casteel upon returning to our rooms the night before.

But I *knew*.

It was as if I had opened myself up to him. There were no tastes in the back of my throat, but I knew he was annoyed with Alastir and struggling to remain patient. I knew he was also bored with the conversation five seconds after it began. These were not speculations. I *knew* this to be true, because when I did open myself up to him, I felt those exact emotions.

Just like I had when I woke this morning to Casteel watching me from where he lay beside me and knew he was hungry. Not for blood. Hungry like he had been when we stood outside Vonetta's house. What I'd felt from him had brought forth a heady reaction from my body, and when he left the bed without touching me, I felt his confusion.

Then, when Vonetta showed up with clothing that I had yet

to go through and a basket of powdery doughnuts, I'd looked at her and had known that she felt no ill feelings toward me. There was curiosity and a low-level buzz of wariness, but she didn't distrust or dislike me. When I opened my senses to her, what I felt confirmed that.

And now, I could feel Alastir's dismay simply by looking at him. It was thick like curdled milk.

What I felt was not my imagination, that much I knew. This was my abilities changing yet again, possibly even growing stronger.

"I do not think you should marry without the King's and Queen's permission," Alastir said.

"You know I don't need their permission."

"But that doesn't mean you shouldn't request it. Even if they reject this marriage, you can still proceed, but at least you would be doing so with their knowledge," Alastir argued. "Marrying here or in Saion's Cove without their consent or knowledge will cause a spectacle, Casteel."

"It would only cause a spectacle if people realize they were unaware." Casteel crossed his arms. "Which is something no one should realize since it's not improbable for me to have sent word home to them."

Alastir leaned forward. "Casteel, I really think—"

"You're not going to change his mind," I interjected, nearly as weary with the conversation as Casteel was.

"And what about yours?" Alastir demanded. "Would you wish to meet your future mother-in-law before or after you've married her son? Or does what you want even matter?"

The pulse of fury from Casteel was a warning, but it was my irritation with that question that led me to say, "If I hadn't agreed with Casteel, we wouldn't even be having this conversation with you."

"Penellaphe, trust me when I say that this is not something either of you needs to rush into," he said, gentling his voice, but I felt a thread of…anger that was not mine or Casteel's. "You have time. All the time in the world."

But we didn't. "In a perfect world, I would've loved to have been courted in a way that didn't involve kidnappings or fleeing the Ascended."

"Or being stabbed," Casteel murmured under his breath.

I turned to him.

He winked.

He actually winked at me.

Taking a deep breath, I focused on Alastir. "But that is not the real world. The reality is that I'd rather marry before learning all the ways his parents will most likely object," I told him, and that was the gods' honest truth. Temporary or not, who in their right mind would want to subject themselves to that?

Alastir's features softened. "You don't know that they will."

"Yes. I do," I stated, aware of Casteel's gaze and the absence of the all-too-brief amusement. I sat forward. "The only people here who have been even remotely friendly to me are the wolven and some of the men who traveled with you. None of the people of Spessa's End have, and I *know* exactly how they feel about me."

Any denials died on Alastir's tongue.

"There is no reason for me to believe that his parents won't share the same worries or concerns as the people do," I continued. "I'd rather marry without actually being able to replay all of their concerns in my head during the ceremony."

Alastir sat back, rubbing his fingers over his brow. "I can understand that. I really can, but our King and Queen—"

"Will be shocked and probably greatly annoyed that I have married someone they have never laid eyes on, not to mention someone who is only half-Atlantian and was once the Maiden," Casteel interrupted. "But as soon as they get to know her, none of that will matter. They will come to love her as fiercely as I do."

My heart stuttered and squeezed as I looked at Casteel, and I knew—I *knew* he hadn't planned to say that last part, or at least he hadn't meant to say it like that. His surprise was sharp and cool, and the moment his gaze met mine, I looked away.

I swallowed the ragged breath I wanted to exhale. "How is Beckett?" I asked. Vonetta had said that the young wolven was walking with barely a limp, but it was time to change the subject.

"It is like he wasn't injured at all," Alastir replied. "What you did for him—"

"I was only trying to ease his pain," I said again. "I don't even know if I'll be able to do something like that again."

Alastir nodded, but he didn't seem too convinced of, well, anything. And then, he left. Alone, I turned to Casteel.

"That was fun, wasn't it?" he asked.

I didn't know what it was about how he'd said that, but I laughed. "Almost more than I could handle."

He smiled, his body finally relaxing to match his posture. "I could tell."

My gaze flickered over him, and I...I knew the anger and frustration had faded. The sadness was there, lingering beneath it all, but there was a strange sense of contentedness, too.

"Are you reading my emotions?"

"No." I paused. "Sort of?"

"What does that mean?"

"I'm not sure what it means." I glanced down at my hands. "Ever since I woke this morning, I can read emotions without opening myself—without having to concentrate. I focus, and if I want to know...I know."

"And if you don't want to know?"

I frowned. "Then I don't. I don't know if crowds will be different."

"Because they sometimes overwhelm you."

He remembered. I nodded.

"That's..." He trailed off, and I looked over at him. "What am I feeling now?"

"I...you're feeling curiosity. Not concern."

His head tilted. "Why would I feel concern?"

"Aren't you worried that I will develop more empath traits?"

"If you're thinking that I'm worried about you becoming a Soul Eater and feeding off my emotions, you'd be wasting your energy."

I frowned at him. "I would hope you wouldn't think that."

"What I do think is it's all amazing," he said. "You're amazing."

I rolled my eyes.

"Especially when you shut Alastir up. That is a talent that

even I haven't mastered." He sat forward, stopping so that we were nearly at eye level. "My parents will likely be displeased, but they will welcome you. I'm not saying that to make you feel better. I mean it. Their anger or disappointment will not be directed at you."

I actually believed that.

And I almost believed what he said to Alastir about his parents loving me as fiercely as he did. Heartmates.

Casteel curled his fingers around my chin, drawing my gaze back to his. "What?" His gaze searched mine. "What are you thinking? I know you are thinking about something. You always get this look on your face when you're thinking about something you don't want to share."

"What kind of look do I get?"

"Your nose wrinkles."

"What? It does not."

"It does."

I couldn't tell if he was being serious or not. "I wasn't thinking anything."

"Lies." His thumb swept over my bottom lip. "Tell me."

His gaze caught and held mine, and my heart started pounding. I fell into his warm amber depths, and I could feel my mask cracking. "I was thinking…I was thinking that you can be very convincing when you speak to others about how you feel about me."

"Is that so?"

"Yes," I whispered.

He dragged his lower lip through his teeth as his lashes lowered. "But not convincing enough."

I knew he spoke of Alastir, but I thought if he were any more convincing, *I* would start to believe him.

His lashes lifted. "There's something I want to show you."

Astride Setti once more, Casteel controlled the reins as he led us through the woods, riding in the kind of companionable silence

I'd felt with few people before. He hadn't gone straight, toward the town. He veered left, where the canopy of trees was quite a bit thicker and the woods were dense for as far as I could see.

"Look," Casteel said, nodding toward our right.

Turning my head, there was no stopping the smile that lifted the corners of my lips and spread across my face. Before us was a stunning field of flowers with showy red petals and black whorls, swaying slightly in a breeze.

"*Poppies.*" A light laugh escaped me at the unexpected sight. "I'd never seen so many in one place." My gaze swept over them. "It's beautiful."

"Yeah," he agreed after a moment, clearing his throat as he shifted behind me. "It is." The horse started to move along the edge of the woods and the poppies. "They're grown here in the meadows for medicinal use."

I arched a brow. "You don't worry about people using them for other reasons?"

"Do the fields look empty to you?" When I nodded, he tapped my hip lightly with his fingers. "There are sentries in there, camouflaged so they're hidden. The fields are monitored at all times so no one with the knowledge of how to cultivate the poppies can use them for ill-gotten gain."

"Goodness," I murmured, half expecting someone to pop up from the rows. "That's smart. I've heard it's becoming a problem in some of the cities."

"While I was in Carsodonia, it ran rampant, and I saw it taking hold in Masadonia, too. But can you really blame those who live under such conditions, desiring an escape, no matter how temporary? Many of them who lose hours and days in opium dens are those who gave their children to the Court or to the Temples," he said. "It may not be right, but I can understand why."

"I can, too. I mean, they're seeking peace, even if it doesn't last." Sadness crowded out the beauty of the field.

"This is only part of what I wanted to show you." He urged Setti forward, pulling me from my thoughts. "Something I think you will appreciate."

"I appreciated the poppies," I admitted with a faint flush.

"I'm glad to hear that." His chin grazed the side of my head as his arm tightened briefly around my waist, pulling me more fully against his chest.

The movement left me a little breathless. It always did, and it was something he did often. I wondered if he was aware of it as he took us deeper into the forest. Was it a purposeful gesture or one he wasn't even aware of? The act reminded me of what I remembered seeing my father do. He always seemed to be pulling my mother close to him, as if he couldn't bear for there to be any space between them. I didn't think that was the reason for Casteel. Maybe it was just a method of communication for him.

Yet again, I found myself wishing that Tawny were here. I could ask her. She would know.

Sighing, I allowed myself to soak in the dappled sunlight of the forest, the chirps of nearby birds, and the scent of rich soil and...something sweet?

I sat up straighter as I caught sight of wolven-eye blue and soft purple lilac blossoms. The display was magnificent, climbing a rocky hill and spilling over in thick, spirals of color. It wasn't until we grew closer that I realized there was an opening in the hill, a gap of blackness behind a curtain of blue and purple.

My heart began to pound as Casteel stopped the horse once more and we dismounted, leaving Setti to graze. I thought I had an idea of what Casteel was going to show me as he took my hand, leading me to the nearly hidden entry that one most likely wouldn't find if they weren't looking for it.

"It's a little dark in a part of this," he warned me, sweeping aside the heavy fall of flowers. "But it won't last long."

A little dark was an understatement as we entered the hill. I could see nothing in the cool air. My grip on his hand tightened. "Can you really see anything?"

"I can."

"I don't believe you."

A low laugh came from in front of me. "You're wrinkling your nose right now."

I totally was. "All right, then."

"Do you remember the caverns I mentioned before?" he asked. "The ones that I came to with my brother?"

The ones that he'd also come to with the girl he'd once loved. Yes, I remembered, and it was exactly what I suspected when I saw the entryway. Disbelief still seized me in the darkness. Was he really bringing me to a place he'd once shared with his brother—with Shea when he sought to escape confusing conversations that his parents were having? I almost couldn't believe he would bring me here.

"Yes," I answered, finding my voice. Up ahead, I could see faint light breaking through the darkness. "I thought they were in Atlantia."

"They are. And here. But what you can't see is that many tunnels branch off from this one. Some of them run for miles, all the way to the Skotos Mountains and then beyond them, to the bluffs by the sea," he explained. "Malik and I spent endless hours and days trying to map them out, but we never found the tunnels that passed through the mountains."

I could easily picture little boys spending an entire childhood racing through the tunnels. My brother would've been the same.

"This is a part of them," he said as sunlight began to seep through the fissures in the ceiling of the cave. "The best part in my opinion."

Damp, sweetly scented air reached us as Casteel turned to our left, where streams of sunlight washed over deep gray stone walls. He let go of my hand and hopped down a foot or so. "There's a slight drop here." Turning back to me, he placed his hands on my hips and lifted me down.

He didn't let go when my feet were steady on the rock floor. He remained there, our chests inches apart. I looked up, and his eyes immediately locked onto mine. A shivery sense of awareness passed between us, one nearly impossible to ignore as we stood there. There were shadows in his eyes and around his mouth, and that sent my heart racing all over again.

And it didn't slow as he backed up, his hands slipping away from my hips. A ragged exhale left me as he turned and walked forward. I felt like a bowstring pulled too taut as I got my legs moving.

The lilacs had crept their way into the cavern, rising over the walls and streaming over the ceiling. Wisps of steam danced in the slivers of sunlight as Casteel stopped in front of what appeared to be some sort of rock pool.

"Hot springs," he said, kneeling down and running his fingers through the water. It bubbled in response, fizzing. "It's not the only one in the cave system, but it's the largest."

I stopped beside him, staring at the springs. It was large, about the size of the Great Hall in Teerman Castle, the edges irregular. Outcroppings of rocks jutted from the frothy water in several places. "How deep is it?"

"It'd probably reach your shoulders through most of it." He rose fluidly. "It does get a little deeper farther out, near the entrance to another cavern. You'll see that area is dark, so I would stay away from that if you can't swim."

"I used to be able to," I told him, bending down. Warm water fizzed around my fingers. "But I don't know if I remember."

"I can help you remember when we have more time," he offered, and I tipped my head back to look at him. "We will be expected at dinner tonight, but we still have a little more time to...just be."

We.

As if we were a unit, a lock and a key.

The night before, I had eaten in my room while Casteel left to do, well, something princely. I wasn't even sure if he'd eaten when he returned after the sun had set, and he joined me on the terrace. We didn't speak much then either, and it had been...comforting.

I turned back to the pool. "How much time do we have?"

"About an hour."

An hour seemed like a lifetime.

"You shouldn't waste a minute of it," he said, almost as if he'd read my thoughts. "I'm going to check on the horse. I'll be back in a couple of minutes."

Looking over my shoulder, I watched as he disappeared into the tunnel, leaving me in privacy to undress.

He was always so...unexpected, his actions and words a constant contradiction. Considerate and then demanding.

Teasing endlessly and then cold as looming death. Violent beyond all thought and then unbelievably gentle. I knew I could spend a dozen years by his side and never fully see all his facets—all the masks he wore.

Dragging in the sweetly scented air, I tore my gaze from him and quickly undressed, leaving my clothes and boots in a messy pile. The grass was cool under my feet, and the breeze warm against my skin as I walked forward. Water teased my toes, warm and frothy. I carefully eased down the earthen steps, delighted as the water quickly reach my hips, lapping around my skin as I moved farther out. Heady, pleasant warmth seeped through my skin, into muscles sore from hours of riding. The lush scent of the water soothed my nerves as it fizzed around my breasts, reaching just above them. Stopping in the middle of the pool, I tipped my head back and let out a soft sigh.

In an instant, I knew why Casteel favored this place. With just enough sunlight filtering through the cracks above to see by, the soothing, lulling sound of birds chattering, and the heady fragrance of lilacs climbing the walls, it was a mystical, private hideaway seemingly fashioned from the imagination—a place you could spend a lifetime.

Or at least I felt like I could stay here forever, enjoying all the little bubbles tickling my bare skin as the white-tipped foamy water rinsed away more than the dust from the road. It swept aside the fear of the magic in the mountains and washed away the lingering questions I had about myself, about what had happened when I touched Beckett, about my future, and about *him.*

I turned, stirring the gently churning water.

Casteel stood at the edge. He'd moved there quietly, so I had no idea how long he'd stood there, or what he saw. There was a hardness to the line of his jaw as he stared at me, and when he spoke, there was a roughness in his voice that hadn't been there before. I saw hunger I'd mistaken for anger when we stood outside Vonetta's house. "Do you find the springs to your liking?"

"I do." I dragged my arms through the water, watching it fizz and bubble in response. "I've never seen anything like this." Lifting my gaze back to him, I reached for the edge of my soaked braid. I began unknotting the plait as he tugged off one boot. "There are springs in Masadonia that Tawny and I snuck off to a time or two, but the water was cold, and we couldn't stay in long. She would…" I sighed as a twinge of melancholy threatened my peace. "She would love this place."

"You're sad. I can hear it in your voice. I'm sorry that you miss her," he expressed, removing his other boot. The socks followed. "I know how hard it is to be apart from those you care about."

"You do." And he did, far more than I did. Hair unbound, I let it lay over my shoulder. "But she is safe for now."

"For now," he agreed, reaching behind his head. He gripped the collar of his tunic and pulled it over his head and then down his arms, revealing the broad width of his shoulders first and then the delineated lines of his chest and the trim hardness of his stomach.

A different kind of nervousness than before rose within me and then abated as he tossed the cloth aside. He was undressing, and I should look away. I should feel embarrassed by his soon-to-be blatant nudity. But I didn't avert my gaze as his hands dropped to the line of buttons on his breeches. Heat crept into my cheeks as he slid them down his hips. The way his body was angled gave only a tantalizing glimpse of sleek muscles. His pants landed with his tunic, and then he looked to where I waited.

Our gazes met and held, and I didn't know what got into me, if it was the warm, bubbling water, the serene beauty of the lake and the dreamlike surrealism of being in Atlantia, or maybe it was the hunger he'd spoken of earlier. Whatever it was, I lowered my eyes and let myself look. My gaze drifted over his chest again, then down the coiled muscles of his stomach and over pale nicks and grooves. I got a little hung up on the indentations on either side of his hips and then my breath quickened.

He wanted me, shamelessly so. I didn't understand how or why. He *cared* for me, but I was only partly beautiful. I was no seductress, and ill-experienced to boot, and he had only been drawn to me in the beginning because he needed me to free his brother. But he desired me. Even I knew that.

I forced my gaze lower, to the Royal Crest branded onto his skin, just below his hip. His hand drifted over the brand, halting as if he sought to hide it for a moment, and then rose over the numerous slices across his stomach. My gaze followed.

Anger rushed me. That kind of premeditated cruelty was disturbing. "I..." I started to apologize for what had been done to him, but I caught myself. My eyes met his once more. "I wish they could feel the same pain they inflicted upon you."

A slight flicker of surprise lit his features. "Even your Queen, who cared for you so tenderly?"

My heart turned over heavily. "I don't think I will ever be able to reconcile the Queen you knew and the one who cared for me. But, yes. Even her."

His head cocked. "You mean that."

I nodded, because I did.

A half-grin appeared. "So incredibly violent."

This time, I didn't even bother to correct him. "Perhaps a little."

His deep, rich laugh echoed throughout the cavern, daring me to forget what had come to pass and what lay in wait, challenging me to take what I wanted.

I sank under the water, eyes closed. Bubbling, swishing liquid danced over my face and through my hair. What did I want? *Him.* I wanted his hands on me, washing away all the reasons why I shouldn't. I wanted to feel his skin against mine, crowding out the world around us. I wanted the touch of his lips, chasing away any logical protests before they could form. I wanted his mouth on mine, kissing away the lies his lips once spoke. I wanted his hands on me, soothing away the sting of guilt and the feeling that I was betraying myself. I wanted to feel him inside me so I couldn't feel anything but him. I wanted to be so completely devoured by him that there was no room for the fear that he would become a scar upon my sure-to-be-broken heart. Because...because what if Kieran was wrong? What if after Casteel accomplished what he wanted, when he fulfilled his end of the bargain, all that remained was lies and betrayals?

I wanted to believe we were heartmates in spite of everything that made that seem impossible.

I stayed underwater, desperately searching for strength and common sense. I stayed until my lungs burned. When I broke the surface, there was still nothing but want and need for him. Hands trembling, I scooped the hair back from my face as I blinked away the dampness clinging to my lashes and lost my breath, lost a little bit more of myself.

Casteel had entered the pool.

He stood several feet away, having already gone under the water himself. His midnight hair was slicked back from his face, and water sluiced down his chest. So much taller than me, the frothing water only reached just above his navel. He looked very much like I imagined a god would, the fractured rays of sunlight glistening off his damp skin.

His intense gaze snagged mine, and that sense of awareness from before returned, passing between us. It was like a strike of lightning, thickening the already balmy air.

"I've been thinking," he said, gliding through the water toward me.

"You have?" My pulse pounded everywhere.

He nodded. "I have."

I had to crane my neck back as he stopped only a handful of inches in front of me. "Do I want to know what you've been thinking about?"

"You'll probably say no." He drifted forward, his movements graceful and purposeful, and I moved backward. "But that will be a lie."

"How would you know?"

"I know a lie when I see one," he replied, crowding me back against the smooth rock wall. "More importantly, I know when you lie."

There was a catch in my breath as he placed his hands on the rock like he'd done earlier. Could he sense my desire? Even in all this water and under the potent scent of lilac? I pressed against the warm rock, thinking that it was impossible for my heart to beat any faster. "What are you thinking about?"

"My idea." His breath coasted over my cheek. "You might be interested in it."

"Doubtful," I murmured.

"You haven't even heard what it is yet, Princess." Those lips grazed the curve of my jaw, and the edges of his damp hair touched my cheek, causing me to gasp. "Yeah, I definitely know you'll be interested."

Edginess swamped me as my head tipped back against the rock without conscious thought. "Why don't you tell me what it is, and I will let you know if I'm interested?"

His chuckle was rough as one of his hands left the rock. My stomach hollowed as his fingers met the bare skin of my waist. "Only if you promise not to lie."

"If you can tell when I'm lying—" A shaky breath left me as he shifted closer, his chest brushing mine with each breath he took. The contact sent a wave of shivers through me, tightening the tips of my breasts to almost painful points.

"What were you saying, Princess?" he asked, and I felt him smile against my cheek.

What was I saying? It took a moment for me to remember. "If you know I'm lying, why would it matter if I told the truth?"

"Because you know that the truth is important." The hand left my waist, trailing down my hip, stirring the water. Bubbles danced over my legs, between them. A wicked feeling curled low in my core. "The truth is permission."

My unfocused gaze crept over the cones of blue and purple blossoms. "Is it?"

"It is." He paused. "Did you know that the bite, until it's fully healed, becomes an erogenous zone? A point of pleasure? It can give you the same feelings as the bite. Almost. Did you know?"

I thought I did. "No."

"Want me to show you?" he offered. "I know you're a curious sort."

"Yes," I whispered, dizzy with anticipation.

"Remember, Princess. This is just to assuage your curiosity. Nothing more."

"I know." My fingers curled against the rock.

"Good." Then his mouth closed over the bite. He sucked on the skin, drawing it between his teeth. My back arched, dragging the hard peaks of my breasts against his chest. I shuddered, becoming liquid.

Good gods…

"Did I ever tell you what you taste like?" His tongue lapped over the sensitive mark.

"Honeydew?" I whispered, eyes drifting shut as I turned my head toward his, seeking what I knew I shouldn't want.

"You dirty girl. I'm not talking about that." He nipped at my jaw, drawing another gasp from me. "I'm talking about your blood, but now you've dragged my mind into unseemly places."

"Your mind always resides in unseemly places."

He laughed deeply. "I can't deny that." His nose brushed mine as his mouth drew closer to my lips. "Your blood tastes old to me, powerful but light. Like moonlight. Now I know why."

"How does anything taste like moonlight?"

"Magic, I imagine. Now stop distracting me when I'm trying to tell you about my idea."

"I'm not—" I bit down on my lip as his hand slipped down my thigh. "I'm not being distracting."

"Oh, yes. You're always so damn distracting," he chided gently.

"Sounds like that's your problem."

"It is both our problems."

"What are you asking permission for?" I sounded breathless, as if I were standing on an edge. "What is this idea?"

"If you want," he said, his chest rising and falling against mine, sending darts of forbidden pleasure through me. "We can pretend again." His hand slid along my thigh, higher and higher—

The tips of his fingers reached evidence of what I knew he'd already sensed. My hips jerked at the illicit thrill as a breathy moan parted my lips.

He dragged his mouth over mine. It wasn't a kiss, just a passing glance of his mouth against mine. "You can pretend." Cool air seeped in as he lifted his head. "You can pretend that this isn't because you don't have a need of me."

My heart felt like a trapped butterfly as I opened my eyes. His were blazing, a heated honey. "I don't."

The curve of his lips was cruelly sensual. "You can pretend

that this—" He eased a finger inside me, just the tip, but I rose up on my toes. His eyes turned luminous as his gaze drifted over my face and then lower to where my breasts had risen up above the churning water. He lifted his gaze to mine as he pressed his finger in further, and I could feel my inner muscles clenching around him. "That this has nothing to do with you wanting me."

"I don't," I told him, even as I lifted my hips off the rock, pressing against his hand, against him.

Casteel hissed as my stomach brushed the hot, hard length of him. He pushed me back to the rock, trapping his hand between us as his chest flattened against mine. The skin-to-skin contact, the way he slowly pumped his finger, shorted out my senses. "You can pretend that it's just the sensitive bite on your neck causing you to squirm against my hand."

I was squirming as best I could.

"You can pretend that's the reason you wish it was my cock you were grabbing onto so tightly." His head dipped to mine once more. "We can both pretend, and we both can…"

"Can what?" I breathed. "Just be Hawke and Poppy?"

For a moment, the hardness etched onto his features slipped and then cracked, revealing the near-desperate need underneath. A need for *me*. For us.

What if Kieran was right?

I could barely breathe, let alone think, but I knew what he meant. Gods, did I ever. And in this moment, we wanted the same. Perhaps we needed the same—to just feel and let everything else fall to the wayside. To just be here, in these seconds and minutes and no place else. Could we do that? Maybe he could. Perhaps this was all about slaking a physical need for him, even as inexplicable as that was. Why couldn't I? I wanted what he could give me. Pleasure. Momentary escape. Experience. A sense of freedom. Because that's what release felt like. How was that a betrayal to anyone, including myself? Wasn't denying it more treacherous? Or was I lying to myself even now? And if so, did that even matter?

His touched stilled as he searched my face for an answer. And in that moment, I realized that this was my life. What existed between Casteel and I was neither right nor wrong. It was messy and complicated, and maybe I'd regret this later as I gave him more and more pieces of me, but I wanted him.

And I was so done denying myself *anything*.

I was done lying to him and to myself.

"Only on one condition," I said.

"You have a condition now?"

I nodded, my heart thundering. "I don't want to pretend," I whispered. "I'm Poppy and you're Casteel, and this is real."

Chapter 31

"Can you agree to that?" I asked.

His eyes drifted shut for a heartbeat, all the striking lines of his face were tense. "Always," he whispered. "Yes."

I reacted and pulled away from the rock. Closing the distance between our mouths, I kissed him. I knew the moment my lips touched Casteel's, the very second his lips parted, that this was *real*.

I lifted my hands from the rock, looping them around his neck as I took what I wanted, tasting him on the tip of my tongue, reveling in the decadent thrill of his sharp teeth. I didn't know what I was doing, only that instinct guided me. I moved my lips against his, nipping and exploring and learning.

And Casteel didn't seem at all bothered by the artless inexperience. If anything, it seemed to inflame him. He gave me what I wanted. Kissing me with a wild sort of abandon that bordered on crazed.

When he ended the kiss, he was breathing just as heavily as I was. "We're not pretending, Poppy? No more? You want me. Knowing *everything*, you want me."

"What do you think?" I moved against his hand in demand.

His other hand dropped to my hip, stilling my movements. "I need to hear you say it, Princess."

Of course, he did.

"Yes," I nearly cursed. "I want you."

"Good." He slipped his hand from between my legs. "Because this is real."

Before I could feel the loss of his wicked hand, he gripped my thighs and lifted me. I gasped, hands slipping over his shoulders as more than half of my body left the water.

"Hook your legs around my waist," he commanded softly. "Do it."

I did as he requested without complaint. It was rare. I hoped he recognized that.

He moved his hands back to my hips as he looked down to where my breasts were pillowed against his chest. "I would love to take my time because there are so many different ways I'd love to be *real* with you. Lay you out on the rocks and lick every inch of your body. Make you come that way. And then I'd want you on your knees and your mouth around my cock."

I shuddered at the depraved images his words brought forth. That act had been in Miss Willa's diary, and it had seemed abhorrent when I'd read it. But now? It sounded...*intriguing*. "I—I don't know how to do that."

"I don't think you could do it wrong," he told me, eyes flaring intently. "But I'd show you. I'd show you how to use your mouth and tongue. If we had time, we would play." His hands tightened at my waist. "But we don't have time, Princess."

"No." My heart pounded. "We don't."

His gaze held mine. "I'm glad we're on the same page." The muscles under my hands bunched as he said, "Princess?"

"Your Highness?"

Those eyes of his turned to molten amber. "I'm going to need you to hold onto me and not let go, because I'm about to fuck you like I promised."

I gasped at his lewd—deliciously so—words. "Yes. Please."

Casteel didn't respond with words. He did so with action, guiding me down until I felt him nudging my entrance. I bit down on my lip.

"Lower your legs," he demanded. "Just a little—there. That's perfect." His lips returned to mine. "You're perfect."

"I—" My words ended in a cry that he captured with a kiss. He filled me, stretching me until I wasn't sure if this position would work. Or if *I* would work. We'd only done this twice. I'd only done this twice. But I held on, my fingers digging into his skin as he kept sinking into me, deeper and deeper until there was no space between us, and Casteel shook.

He dragged one hand down my back, folding his arm around me. And then he...he held me there, against his chest, buried deep inside. "You okay?" he rasped, lips brushing mine. "Poppy?"

I nodded, easing my grip on his shoulders.

"You sure?"

"Yes," I whispered, my eyes closed. It didn't hurt. It didn't feel exactly comfortable, but I knew there was more. I shifted, wiggling my hips.

He groaned my name. "Poppy..."

I ignored the way my heart clenched in response to his voice. I didn't want that. I wanted the hardness between my legs and inside me, needed what it made me feel. I didn't want my heart getting involved.

I squirmed, gasping as pleasure sparked.

"Gods, Poppy. I'm trying—" A sound rumbled from him, vibrating through me. "I'm trying to make sure you're ready."

"I'm ready," I told him. *I've been ready.*

He cursed, but then he moved, thrusting his hips up as the hand on mine pulled down. My eyes went wide at the raw sensation of him moving inside me, slow and deep. I sighed, muscles I didn't realize were even tense relaxing.

"That's it." His words were barely a whisper. "Gods, you feel..." The hand guiding me spasmed and then loosened as I lifted myself on his length. "You feel like all I could ever want."

I'd never wanted to believe something more in my life, and that realization threatened everything.

"We're being real," I reminded him, seeking out his mouth. "Don't lie to me now."

He went rigid against me for a handful of seconds, and then

he bit out a harsh laugh. "You're right." His hand fisted in my hair, pulling my head back. "We don't need to lie now."

His mouth covered mine, and one of his fangs scraped my lip, dragging a husky moan from me. A staggered heartbeat later, we were back at that rock, one of his arms around me and the other hand in my hair, the only things between the hard surface and my skin as he rolled into me, pinning my hips.

And then he did what he promised.

Casteel *fucked*.

His hips slammed into mine, and the way I was held there, all I could do was whatever he demanded. I held on as the frothy water foamed and bubbled violently around us. Each thrust of his hips felt as greedy as the strokes of my tongue against his. Every plunge of his hips felt more like an act of possession than the one before. My head fell back but never reached the rock because of his hand, and the world was a kaleidoscope of broken sunlight, slate-colored walls, and vibrant petals. I tightened—everything in me tightened as his head dropped to my shoulder, his body grinding into mine. I curled myself around him, pressing my face into his neck, tasting the sweet water and the salt of his skin. My pulse thundered through me, his just as strong against my cheek. Our bodies moved in a frenzy, and it felt like he was everywhere at once, stealing my breath. There was no hesitation. No slowing down or coming up for air. We were both swept away in the madness, lost in the tension coiling tighter and tighter. I thought it would shatter me, shatter us both, but he gave me what I wanted so badly.

The feel of his skin against mine crowded out the world until there was only us. The touch of his lips against my neck, my cheek, had already chased away any protests. His mouth found mine once more as his hands held me so tightly to him, so carefully, preventing the sting of guilt from even forming. He moved so deeply inside me that I couldn't feel anything but him, and when release found me, it also found him, devouring us both, leaving no room to fear what awaited and making what seemed impossible, possible.

I felt weightless in Casteel's arms, cheek resting on his shoulder and feet floating several inches above the pool's floor. I'd attempted to move away earlier, after the last of the pleasure abated and reality started to seep in with the fading sunlight. I didn't make it far, though. Casteel didn't let me. He kept his arms around me.

"Not yet," he'd said as he guided my cheek to his shoulder.

It felt like permission. I didn't fight him. I blamed a lot of things for this, even though I had no desire to fight him then. The warmth of the pool and his skin for starters. The way he moved his hand up and down my spine was entirely too soothing. The languidness in my body was also at fault, and so was the truth that it felt lovely to be held, especially like this, with no barriers between us.

After being forbidden human touch for so long, his nakedness was like being offered a platter of the most decadent chocolates and sweets. I traced tiny circles on his other shoulder, wishing I had the courage to explore the hardness, the indents and scars. Instead, I satisfied my curiosity with the way his skin felt under my fingers and how his body felt like steel wrapped in satin.

And I...gods, I soaked in every moment, my eyes glued to the side of his neck, the damp curl of his hair. In the secret chambers of my heart, I cherished these moments.

I didn't know how long we stayed like that, nothing but the sound of the water and the calls of the birds outside around us. Casteel seemed to know exactly when someone neared the cave.

"It's Kieran. He's the only one who would know to find me here." He gently disentangled himself from me, and I thought I felt his lips brush over the crown of my head. "I'll be right back."

I sank to my shoulders as he glided through the water and then rose. I got an eyeful, one that shouldn't have heated my face as much as it did given what we'd done. He stopped to grab his pants, but didn't pull them on.

Casteel walked out of the cavern as naked as the day he was

born, and if he didn't stop to put on those pants, Kieran was about to get one hell of an eyeful.

"Okay, then," I whispered and then laughed, the sound echoing in the chamber.

My head fell back as I stared at the slivers of sunlight, searching for remorse or shame. Like before, I only found uncertainty. Not for what we'd shared, but for what it meant. We hadn't been pretending.

What we'd shared had been real. No games. No pretenses. No half-truths.

I dragged my teeth over my lower lip. It felt swollen from his kisses. I lifted my fingers to my mouth, shivering as I thought of how he'd claimed it just as thoroughly as he'd done with the rest of my body.

I turned at the sound of Casteel's footsteps. Thank all the gods, he was halfway clothed. The flap of buttons was undone, though, and I had no idea how the pants stayed on his hips. He carried a white bundle in his hands, which he laid carefully on the floor of the cave.

"Kieran figured we were headed here. He brought some fresh clothes for both of us and a towel."

I couldn't even fathom how Kieran had been that intuitive, and I probably didn't want to know.

He extended a hand, offering a thick, white towel. "It goes without saying that I prefer the naked, wet version of you. But it's time to dry off and be presentable."

I shook my head as I moved forward, slowing when the bubbling water started to drop below my chest. Why was I hesitating? It wasn't like he hadn't seen my breasts, the scars, and everything else. He was waiting, watching me, and hadn't I done the same earlier? Watched him undress unabashedly? Shoring up courage, I continued on, and the strangest thing happened. Each step became easier, even as the water dropped to my ribcage and then to my navel. Even as Casteel's gaze followed the water level. His lips parted slightly, and I was confident that Nyktos himself could arrive, and Casteel wouldn't look away from me. I realized there was power in that, in being a source of distraction for him. The edges of his fangs dragged over his lower lip as the water fizzed around my inner thighs and then lower. Pretending or not, he enjoyed what he saw as I climbed the earthen steps.

"I'll help." He spread the towel wide. "I know you don't need it, but I want to."

I said nothing as I stood in front of him, bare as he'd been. He stepped in behind me, rubbing the towel over my wet hair.

"This should be dried first," he explained, and I was fully aware that he was staring down at me as he squeezed the excess water from my hair. I knew he saw the tips of my breasts pucker and could see the flush I felt tinting my skin.

"Wouldn't want you to catch a cold," he said, voice rough. "That's what I hear about wet hair."

"Uh-huh." My jaw worked as a smile tugged at my lips.

"I'm just being thorough." He slid the towel down my arms, all the way to the tips of my fingers and then across my back. "You'll thank me later."

"For being thorough?"

"Among other things." He dragged the cloth over my stomach and then up, catching the water between my breasts. His hands lingered there before he turned me to him.

He knelt before me, sending my stomach tumbling as he drew the towel up my left leg, then my right, and finally between them. I sucked in a sharp breath, swaying slightly.

"Just being thorough," he reminded me, his eyes hooded. "I wouldn't want you unnecessarily wet, Princess."

I had a feeling he meant something else.

The towel smoothed over my backside. "I think you're all dry now." His gaze slowly made its way to mine. "Mostly."

Yes.

Mostly.

Grinning, he leaned his head down and kissed the faded, jagged scar on my inner thigh. The act startled me out of the pleasant haze. I watched him rise, a thousand different thoughts racing through my head as he wrapped the towel around me.

I grabbed hold of the edges. "Casteel—"

"I know." He placed a finger over my lips. "What we've done here stays here."

I blinked, stung at once by words I wasn't sure I even

understood. I wasn't going to say that. I honestly didn't know what I was going to say.

He turned, picking up the white shirt, which was such a contrast against his tan skin. A lock of dark hair toppled over his forehead, softening his features as he bent his head, buttoning his pants. There was a curl low in my stomach. How could he make such an ordinary act as dressing appear so sensual?

I honestly didn't need to stand there and watch him dress. Dropping the towel, I quickly put on my clothes.

"Here." Casteel fixed my sleeves again.

I didn't know exactly what it was about that moment that made me think of the consequences of what we'd just done. The fact that it hadn't even crossed my mind until now showed that I needed to make better life choices.

"You said that you took prevention for pregnancy," I said, recalling that he'd taken an herb that rendered both males and females temporarily infertile. "Are you still covered?"

"Yes. I'm careful, Poppy," he said without hesitation, gathering up our clothing and my boots. "I wouldn't risk a child."

Between us.

He hadn't said that, but it hung in the air nonetheless. And there was another odd, irrational bite. One which made no sense because of the idea of having a child with anyone was more terrifying than finding an actual creature with fins for legs and tails for arms under my bed.

There was something obviously wrong with me because it still hurt.

Because what was real to him wasn't the same for me.

Word of what I'd done to Beckett had spread. I knew this because everyone stared as I lifted a spoonful of thick herbal soup.

Well, not everyone.

Two Atlantians had commandeered Casteel's attention. So

had Kieran. I had no idea where Delano and Naill had disappeared to, and it could literally be anywhere since we were in one of the larger buildings in the town center. But the rest were either sneaking peeks in my direction or outright staring.

The mortals and Atlantians who sat at the table before us. The wolven interspersed throughout the rest of the tables. They all stared. Not that I could blame them. I *had* glowed silver, and I had healed someone with my touch. I'd be staring at someone who I'd heard or seen do that, too. But it was what was behind those stares that unnerved me. The air fairly vibrated with emotion, and like before, I hadn't needed to concentrate, to open myself to feel the near hostility of most around me.

Swallowing the rich, flavorful soup, I lifted my gaze to the banners that hung on either side of the door. They rippled softly in the breeze coming through the open windows, which caught the blades of several fans, keeping the packed room cool.

A soft touch to my arm drew my attention to my right, where Alastir sat. "Would you like to take your dinner in your private quarters?" he asked quietly. "If so, I can escort you back to the fort."

I lowered my spoon as I glanced to where Casteel sat at the head of the table. He was listening to an Atlantian as he rooted around on a plate of cheeses, inspecting each one as if he were looking for the perfect one or flaws. I refocused on Alastir. "Do I look that uncomfortable?"

A tight, worried smile appeared. "You've barely touched your food."

It was hard to eat while people stared. My gaze flickered over the crowded room. Part of me wanted to excuse myself and return to my bedchamber, but this was only one of many dinners or events where I would be the object of interest. Plus, hiding in my quarters may be the easier option, but it would also be more cowardly. And besides, no one was projecting their emotions. There wasn't a screamer among them, so I could ignore them. Mostly.

"I'm fine," I decided.

His smile didn't reach his eyes. "I know it must be hard to be around so many who aren't welcoming of you and know how they feel. I would not think ill of you if you don't want to expose yourself to that. And just know that anyone who has spent even a few minutes in your presence does not feel that way. The rest will come to know you, I'm sure. But until then, I apologize for their behavior."

He squeezed my arm gently. "Did you know that this was once a very busy trading post?"

I swallowed the knot his words formed in my chest.

"When Atlantia ruled over the entire kingdom, this was the first and last major city before you crossed the Skotos Mountains. There used to be…thousands that once passed through here," he said, sighing as his gaze coasted over the bare walls. "It was such a shame to see what became of this place, but Casteel and these people are slowly restoring it and bringing new life."

Quentyn strode out from an area where the food had been prepared, carrying a large pitcher. Another trailed behind him, shorter and younger with a slight limp. It took me a moment to recognize the boy with the black hair and tan skin. I'd only seen him in his wolven form and very briefly as a mortal, but his skin had been pale and clammy then.

Beckett.

I watched him refill the glasses at the end of the table and make his way toward us. As he refilled his great-uncle's glass, he finally looked at me.

"We already met," he whispered. "Kind of."

"Beckett," I said. "How are you feeling?"

"Almost perfect." He poured water into my glass as he glanced back at Alastir before dipping his chin. "Thank you. I can't say that enough."

"You already have."

A wide, toothy grin broke out across his face but quickly faded, and I felt a sharp spike of…of *fear* before he moved on to the other side of the table.

Was he now afraid of me?

I sat back as the knot in my chest expanded. I couldn't understand why. I'd healed him—how I'd done that, I had no idea—but Beckett had to know that I wasn't someone to fear.

"Penellaphe? Are you all right?"

A ragged breath left me as I looked at Alastir. "Yeah. Yes." I smiled as I turned my attention back to him. "They seem very helpful. Beckett and Quentyn."

"Respecting your elders is drilled into the young from a very early age. You will often find the youngest helping to serve food and drink at many dinner tables throughout Atlantia," Casteel explained, having overheard me.

Alastir snorted. "Except for you. You always had your nose in a book at the dinner table."

Surprise distracted me from Beckett's response. "What were you reading?"

"Usually history books or my studies," he answered, one side of his lips tipping up. "I was an utterly boring child most of the time."

My eyes connected with Kieran's briefly, reminding me of what he'd shared about Casteel being the serious one.

"Well, your brother made up for that," Alastir said, shaking his head. "You didn't want Malik serving you anything at dinner."

My gaze flew back to Casteel, and I watched his smile grow. I didn't know what I expected, but it was so rare that anyone spoke of his brother.

"Malik would often...experiment with the drinks and food," Casteel said when he caught my gaze. "And you did not want to be on the receiving end of those experiments."

"I'm half afraid to ask," I said.

"But you will," Kieran murmured.

I ignored the wolven.

So did Casteel. "He would add lemon and pepper to juice, salt to dishes meant to be sweet, and generally ruin whatever it was that you were excited to eat."

"That's terrible," I said, laughing.

He leaned over, lashes lowering as he said. "And yet, you laugh."

"Yes."

Casteel lifted his gaze, and the heat in it sent a shiver dancing over my skin. "Probably because it sounds like something you'd do."

"Possibly."

He chuckled as he straightened, turning back to the other table as he returned to picking through the cheese.

"How many—?" I stopped as Casteel's hand brushed mine. He placed a hunk of cheese on my plate, one that had been thinly sliced. I glanced over at him. He was now listening to another mortal from the table behind ours. "Thank you."

He nodded.

I picked up the cheese, smiling slightly before eating a piece of it. A sudden burst of laughter drew my attention. Kieran had risen, moved to sit with a few men at the end of the table. The laugh had come from where Beckett and Quentyn sat with Emil and some other men who'd traveled with Alastir. Wondering what had made Emil laugh so loudly, I tugged my attention away.

My gaze collided with that of two mortals. They were older. Males. One of them spoke in the other's ear. The second man with neatly trimmed blond hair curled his lip. His disgust soured the cheese.

I took a drink, washing away the taste. That wasn't the first unfriendly stare or mannerism I'd received, all done when Casteel was distracted—like now, since he'd risen to speak with a woman who was all bones and wrinkled skin. My grip tightened on the glass. Each time I caught one of their looks or stares, I wanted to ask if they needed assistance with something. I wanted to hold their stares until they grew as uncomfortable as I felt, but I said nothing. I did nothing. Just like when the Priestess scolded me, or the Duke lectured me.

"Don't pay them any mind," Alastir murmured quietly.

I placed my glass on the table.

"They just don't know you," he repeated. His smile was as false as the one I often wore as the Maiden. "Their distrust or even dislike of you is something you must get used to as their Princess and soon-to-be Queen."

Queen.

My entire body seized. That wasn't going to happen, I reminded myself. Even if the impossible happened and Casteel and I—well, I couldn't even finish that thought. Casteel didn't want to become King.

"If you don't wish to step back and remove yourself from this situation, then you can't let it show that their feelings are getting to you. You can't let Casteel know, lest we have another Landell situation on our hands," he continued. "I don't know for sure what he feels for you, but one thing is evident. He will act upon any perceived insult to your honor. There is power there, Penellaphe. You are the neck that turns the head of the kingdom."

I stared at him.

"I'm sorry. You probably don't understand any of that. You weren't prepared for this. That's not your fault," he said, and yet, it sort of felt like it was. "None of this is. His engagement to you is utterly unexpected."

"I'm sure their dislike of me has more to do with who I was and not that I'm marrying their Prince." I thought about that. "Or it's an equal combination of the two."

"That, and they have all heard that he originally planned to use you for ransom. They don't understand how love has blossomed from that. Neither do I, even after his claims of love."

"Stranger things have happened," I muttered as Casteel moved toward the entryway just as the door opened. A tall man walked in, black ink swirling over the swarthy skin of both arms, all the way up to his shoulders. His hair was shaggy, a silvery hue that had nothing to do with his age. There were only faint lines at the corners of his eyes when he smiled upon seeing Casteel.

"I'm sure they have," Alastir said, lowering his voice as Casteel clasped hands with the silvery-haired man. Was that Jasper? He was too far away for me to see his eyes. "But I've known him his entire life. More importantly, I've seen him in love, Penellaphe."

By an act of sheer will, I kept my face blank as I looked at Alastir. I couldn't...I couldn't believe he'd said that. But all I felt from him was concern.

"They were expecting someone else as their Princess," he went on. "It's not just you."

"Someone who was not the Maiden?" I surmised.

"Well, of course. But as you know, he was expected to marry upon his return—" He snapped his mouth shut as his brows lowered. "He didn't tell you?"

A strange thumping started in my body. "Didn't tell me what?" Alastir started to look away, but I grabbed his arm. "Didn't tell me what?" I demanded.

"Good gods, that idiotic boy." He pinched the bridge of his nose, and I felt the flare of annoyance in him. "One of these days, I will learn to keep my mouth shut."

I sure hoped not, since it was clear there was a lot I'd never hear if it weren't for him.

"Why do I have a feeling I'm the idiotic boy you speak of?" Casteel asked as he returned to his seat. The smile on his face faded as he took in Alastir's and my expressions. "What have you two been whispering about?"

"I don't think now is the time—" Alastir started.

"I think now is the perfect time," I cut in, well aware that those around us were starting to pay attention.

"As do I." Casteel eyed Alastir. "Speak."

That one command demanded a response. Alastir shook his head, jaw tight as he said, "You didn't tell her that you were already promised to another."

Chapter 32

The sudden roaring in my ears made me think I hadn't heard Alastir correctly. Or maybe it was because my heart pounded so hard that I'd misheard.

But I hadn't, had I? Because, suddenly, I remembered everything Alastir had said the morning I met him. He'd spoken of obligations upon Casteel's return. Marriage was definitely an obligation.

A sharp slice of pain tore through my chest. It felt like a *crack*, and it sounded like thunder in my ears. How no one else heard it was beyond me.

Slowly, as if I were caught in the stage between waking and sleep, I turned to Casteel. He was speaking, but I couldn't hear him, and I couldn't believe what I'd heard.

What I'd just learned.

Promised to another when I met him in the Red Pearl and he'd been my first kiss, when I knew him as Hawke and had grown to trust him, desire him, and care for him. *Promised to another* when he'd taken me under the willow and told me that he didn't care what I was, but rather who I was. When he showed me the kind of pleasure we could find with each other, first in the Blood Forest and then again in New Haven. *Promised to another* when I learned the truth of who he was and when we took from each other in the woods outside of the keep, when I fed him, and he *thanked* me afterward.

Promised to another when he proposed marriage as the only way for us to get what we wanted. *Promised to another* when he said that we could pretend. *Promised to another* as Kieran claimed we were heartmates, and I decided to give him my blood.

Promised to another when I told him in the cavern that it had to be *real.*

Somehow, even though I knew that the arrangement between us had not been borne of love, and I wasn't sure Kieran knew what he was talking about when it came to the heartmates thing, this betrayal still stabbed more deeply than all Casteel's other betrayals.

And if that wasn't a wake-up call that I'd already slipped too far, I didn't know what would be.

Pain I didn't want to lay claim to ripped through me so fiercely that I thought I would be split in two, but snapping on its heels was an anger so intense that my entire body vibrated with it.

Only seconds passed between when Alastir spoke and the bitter, acidic burn of rage pouring like a rainstorm through me.

"Promised to another?" I demanded, my voice surprisingly steady but so damn raw. I didn't care that we were in a room full of people who disliked me.

"It's not what you think, Penellaphe."

My brows flew up. "It's not? Because I imagine that promised to another means the same thing in Atlantia as it does in Solis."

"What it means doesn't matter." His eyes were an icy golden color as he stared down at me with an expression I couldn't believe I was seeing. *He* looked shocked. *He* looked angry with me. And I could not believe what I was hearing or seeing or living.

And he felt angry. Even with my own volatile emotions I could still feel the cool splash of surprise from him and the burn of anger underneath it.

"How could you—?" he started, jaw flexing. His chest rose with a heavy breath. "The promise was an oath I never took. Did I, Alastir?" He tore his gaze from me. "Can you claim otherwise?"

"It was all but agreed to," Alastir responded. His anger burned through my senses, scorching my skin. "You know what your father has planned for decades, Casteel."

Decades.

A part of me recognized that Casteel denied what Alastir had stated and that Alastir had basically confirmed such. So, there was a slight lessening of my fury, a halt to the continuing cracking in my chest, but the pain and the anger were still there. This had been discussed for *decades*? For longer than I'd actually breathed life? Did it not occur to Casteel to tell me any of this? To warn me? I pulled my senses back, closing them down.

Vaguely, I became aware of the silver-haired man and Kieran approaching. They were close enough to hear everything—close enough for me to see that the newcomer was a wolven, and that the curve of his jaw and the lines of his cheek seemed familiar.

"You mean that for decades my father assumed that I would eventually agree, but not once did I ever give him or anyone an indication of such," Casteel fired back. "You know that. How in the world did this even come up?"

"How in the world did you not think to tell her?" Alastir demanded.

There was a soft inhale from the tables of Descenters, and the silver-haired man murmured, "I have the best timing."

My gaze shot to his and locked. The pale blue eyes flared brightly, nearly luminous as his lips parted. They moved, but there was no sound. His surprise was like freezing rain, sudden and all-consuming. He jerked, taking a step back. Was it my scars? Or did he feel that weird static charge even though we didn't touch?

"Do you think I don't know why you brought this up?" Casteel queried in a voice too soft, snapping my attention back to him. "It is weak of you."

Alastir tensed beside me. "Did you just call me weak?"

A smirk twisted Casteel's lips. "What you just did was weak of you. If you think that equates to weakness of mind or body, that is on you. Not me."

The wolven had recovered from his reaction to me. He placed his hands on the table, and when he spoke, his voice was low. "You should both calm down."

"I'm perfectly calm, Jasper," Casteel replied.

This *was* Jasper. The wolven who was supposed to marry us. Great.

"Since you're bound and determined to have this conversation right now when you should've had it in private ages ago, then let's have it out for all to witness since everyone here has been thinking it from the moment they learned of your engagement," Alastir snarled. "You may not have agreed, but an entire kingdom, including Gianna, believed you would marry upon your return."

Who in the hell was Gianna? Was that her name? The one the King and Queen expected Casteel to marry when he returned?

"This has nothing to do with Gianna," Casteel replied curtly.

"I can actually agree with that," Alastir returned. "It has everything to do with the kingdom—your land and your people and your obligation to them. Marrying Gianna would've strengthened the relationship between the wolven and the Atlantians."

Jasper's head snapped in Alastir's direction. "You are overstepping, Alastir. You do not speak for the entirety of our people."

The older wolven burned with rage beside me, but there was a connection there, one that harkened back to Landell, to one of the things he'd said in response to Casteel stating his intention to make me the Princess. He'd said that it was supposed to be an honor meant to bring all of their people together.

"I know what my obligations are." Casteel's words fell like chips of ice. "And I know exactly what my father expects of me. Those two things are not mutually exclusive, nor would marrying a wolven suddenly erase the deaths of over half of their people. Anyone who believes that is a fool."

"I didn't say I agreed with it." Alastir picked up his drink.

"Perhaps this conversation should occur at another time," Emil stressed, having moved to Alastir's side. He looked to Jasper as if to say, "*do something.*"

Jasper sat in the chair Kieran had occupied, and quite frankly, he stared at Alastir as if he hoped the man would continue.

"You mean when we don't have one of *them* sitting right there?" a man spoke, an Atlantian who I thought had been at the house Beckett was injured at. "Who was raised in the pit of vipers and is most likely just as poisonous as the nest she grew up in? When we are *this* close to finally seeking retribution against them?"

Casteel opened his mouth, but something unlocked inside me, raising its head. And whatever it was breathed fire. Years of grooming to remain silent and demure, to allow people to do and say whatever they wanted to me caught fire and burned to embers and ash. I was simply faster in my response. "I'm not one of *them*," I said, and the focus of the entire room shifted in my direction. All except Casteel. He still watched the Atlantian, and I had a wicked suspicion that we were seconds away from repeating what had happened to Landell. "I was their Maiden, and even though I suspected the Ascended were hiding things, I fully admit to not opening my eyes to who they truly were until I met Casteel. But I was never one of them." I met the Atlantian's stare, tasting his anger and distrust, feeling it swell inside me, fueling my burning fury as if he were a lit match. "And the next time you want to call me a poisonous viper, at least have the courage to do so while looking me straight in the eye."

Silence.

Ian would've said it was so silent you could hear a cricket sneeze.

And then Jasper let out a low whistle.

The Atlantian snapped out of his stupor. "You were their Maiden. The Chosen. The Queen's favorite. Isn't that what they say?"

"Dante," Emil warned, shooting the fair-haired Atlantian a sharp look. "No one asked for your opinion on this."

"But I'm glad he gave it since I'm well aware that he is not the only one thinking this," I said, flicking my gaze over the room. "Yes, I was the Queen's favorite, and I was raised in a cage so pretty that it took a very long time for me to see it for what it was. The Ascended planned to use my blood to make more vamprys. That was why I was their Maiden. Would you feel loyalty to your captors? Because I do not."

Casteel looked at me then, his gaze still icy, but something else moved in those depths. There was no time to figure out what it was. And at the moment, I frankly didn't care.

"If that is the truth, then I salute you." Dante raised a glass. "We all salute you, and I mean that seriously. It's truly few and far between these days that anyone from Solis has had their eyes opened. No offense to those who have who are present."

There were several murmurs before Dante continued. "To learn that you're of Atlantian descent does explain why you're important to them, but you—"

"Are of better use to you dead?" I interrupted as Quentyn and Beckett came out of the kitchen, carrying freshly baked bread. They stopped, their eyes widening.

Dante lowered his glass, staring at me.

"I know many of you would prefer to send me back to Queen Ileana in pieces, as does the King, I'm sure." I lifted my chin even as a fine tremor shook my hands. "Part of me can't blame any of you for wanting that, especially after learning the truth about them."

A muscle clenched in the Atlantian's jaw, but it was Alastir who spoke. "I told you, Casteel. I said that you would encounter pushback if you proceeded with this."

So did Landell.

"And what did I tell you when you said that before?" Casteel asked.

"That this is what you want. That she is what you want," Alastir said, and my heart twisted in my chest. "And you know I want to believe that. Everyone in this room does."

I doubted that.

"And the King and Queen will want to believe that," Alastir said. "Especially Eloana. But you've spent decades trying to free your brother instead of accepting what the rest of us have come to terms with. You refused your duties to your people because you weren't ready to let him go, something that I could understand even if it pained me. The last time you left, you had to know that there was no longer any hope that he'd return to us, but you still went, gone for years—gone for so long that your mother began to fear that you too had suffered the same fate as Malik," he said, and my heart squeezed for a wholly different reason while Casteel showed no reaction. "But you're returning home with the most guarded jewel of the Ascended. There are few who truly believe this doesn't have anything to do with your brother."

"If I hadn't accepted my brother's fate, I wouldn't be leaving Solis," Casteel said, and only Kieran and I knew how much it cost him to speak those words. "It's no secret that I planned to use Penellaphe as ransom. I spent those years far from home working to get close to her." This he directed not just to Alastir but to the entire room. "I succeeded, and when the time was right, I made my move. I took her."

Casteel spoke the truth that was still hard to hear. "I took her, and I kept her, but not to use her. Somewhere along the way, I no longer saw her as a bargaining chip or a tool for revenge. I saw her for who she was. Who she is—this beautiful, strong, intelligent, endlessly curious and kind woman who was as much a victim of the Ascended as any Atlantians. I fell in love with her, probably long before I even realized I had." He laughed, the sound rough. And gods, it sounded so real that my throat knotted. "My plans changed. What I believed about Malik changed. And this was before I learned what she was. That she is part Atlantian. She is the reason I came home."

My gaze collided with Kieran's, and he nodded as if to confirm what Casteel said.

But how could it be?

When he'd been expected to marry someone else for decades and never once told me? Then again, he had yet to really say a word about Shea.

Pressing my lips together, I looked away. If only all of what he'd said was true. The future would be different. Everything would be different. I wished he hadn't spoken those words at all.

The old woman Casteel had talked to earlier spoke up. "And you knew that he originally planned to use you?"

"I didn't at first, not until after he'd already gained my trust and that of the Ascended in charge of me. When I found out…" I trailed off, thinking my reaction was best not known.

"She stabbed me in the heart with a bloodstone dagger," Casteel finished instead.

The old woman blinked while Jasper gave a sudden bark of laughter. "I'm sorry," he said. "But damn…are you for real?"

"It's true," Kieran confirmed. "She thought it would kill him."

Emil started to grin but one look from Casteel stopped that in its tracks.

Shifting in the suddenly uncomfortable chair, I wondered how in the world that piece of knowledge helped anything. "I was a little angry."

Casteel arched a brow as he glanced at me. "A little?"

I narrowed my eyes. "Okay. I was very angry."

"I didn't know that," Alastir said from behind the rim of his cup.

"Obviously, Casteel takes after his father when it comes to women with sharp objects," Jasper commented with a snort. "I feel like I'm missing some vital information that Delano conveniently left out when he met me halfway."

I frowned, but at least I knew where Delano had been.

"You stabbed Casteel?" Jasper repeated. "In the heart? With bloodstone. And you thought it would kill him?"

"In my defense, I felt bad afterward."

"She did cry," Casteel remarked.

I was going to stab him again.

"But I trusted him, and he betrayed that," I continued. "I was the Maiden, nearly groomed my entire life to remain pure and focused only on my Ascension. I was Chosen to be given to the gods, even though I never chose the life. And I don't know what you know of me, but I had no control over where I went, who I spoke to or could speak with. I was veiled, unable to even look someone in the eye if they were allowed to speak with me. I didn't get to choose what I ate, when I left my chambers, or who was allowed to even touch me. But he was the first thing I'd ever truly chosen for myself."

My voice cracked slightly as the knot expanded. I took a shallow breath, feeling Casteel's gaze on me, but I refused to look at him. I couldn't, because I didn't want to know what he was feeling.

"I chose him when I knew him as Hawke," I forced myself to continue, to say what I needed to say so that everyone in the room could hear me even if it felt like I was scraping at a wound in my chest with rusty nails. "I didn't know what that would mean at that time, other than I wanted to have something that I actually wanted for myself. I'd already begun to question things—the Ascended and if I could be or do what they required of me. I'd already begun to realize that I couldn't live like I was any longer. That the Maiden wasn't me, and I was better and stronger and meant for something other than that. But he...he was the catalyst in a way. And I chose him. I chose him because he made me feel like I was something other than the Maiden, and he saw *me* when no one else ever really did. He made me feel alive. He valued me for who I am and didn't try to control me. And then it all seemed like a lie once I realized the truth of who he was and why he was a part of my life."

Neither Alastir nor Jasper spoke. I could still feel Casteel's stare.

I swallowed, but the knot was still there. "So, yes, I was very angry, but what I felt for him before remained, and after learning the entire truth about the Ascended and what had happened to him and to his brother, I could understand why he set out to use me. That doesn't mean that it was okay, but I could understand why. I refused his proposal at first, just so you know. Accepting him and...and allowing myself to feel what I did for him was a betrayal to those who were lost in all of this, and it felt like a betrayal to myself. But I still chose him despite it all."

I closed my eyes. Up until this moment, I'd spoken the truth, some of it new to me, and I did so for the first time in front of Casteel. What came next was easier because it was the lie. "We've moved past how we met. At least, I have. He loves me, and I wouldn't be here in a room full of people who have spent the entire dinner staring at me in distaste or distrust,"—I opened my eyes, slowly looking across the table, to the two mortal men—"if what we felt for one another wasn't real. I surely would not be on my way to an entire kingdom who will likely whisper each time they see me, distrust everything there is about me, and look upon me as if I deserve not even minimal respect."

The two men looked away, their cheeks flushing.

"I..." Dante sat down. "I don't know what to say."

"You,"—Casteel cleared his throat—"you don't have to say anything. You, all of you, just need to accept that this is real."

Real.

Alastir leaned back, his gaze heavy and somber.

It was Jasper who spoke, with a faint lift of his lips. "If you've chosen her, then how can we not do the same?"

Hatred.

That was what I tasted in the back of my throat, what I inhaled with every breath as I sat at the table. It came from different directions at different times, pinging around the room even though most of the tension had left once it didn't appear as if Casteel would tear out the hearts of Alastir or Dante. Most returned to their dinners and conversation. Except for Casteel, who watched me, and the silver-haired wolven who also studied me as if I were some sort of puzzle.

But several others in the room didn't stare and remained silent. People who hadn't projected their emotions before but did so now.

Their anger coated every drink I took or piece of food I swallowed with a bitter taste. It took no leap of logic to realize that they weren't happy with what Casteel or Jasper had said. Nor anything I'd said had changed what they believed of me. It wasn't all of them, thank the gods, but it was enough for me to know that I was still not welcome here.

Restlessness hummed through me, an almost nervous sort

of energy as I tried and failed to shut off the emotions of others. I didn't know why I couldn't when reading the emotions only when I wanted to had become so much easier throughout the day. Was it because I was tired? Maybe it was what happened with Beckett or possibly even what I'd done in the cavern with Casteel.

Or perhaps it was learning that Casteel had kept yet another thing from me?

It was probably all of those things that played a role in my sudden failure to shut down my abilities.

I looked at my plate of mostly untouched food, and I...I simply did not want to sit here any longer.

And I was tired of doing things I didn't want to do.

"Excuse me," I said to no one in particular, rising from my seat.

Jasper watched me but said nothing as I stepped around the chair. I walked past the tables, aware of conversations halting as I passed. I kept my chin high, wishing I'd had the forethought to go through the clothing Vonetta had brought over. Nothing took the dignity out of one's exit like wearing clothing several sizes too large.

But I doubted being dressed in pretty tunics or even the richest of gowns would've changed a damn thing.

I pushed open one of the doors and stepped outside, dragging in deep breaths clean of others' emotions. Stars had already started to glimmer in the deepening sky, and I stared upward. I was finally able to close myself off.

Turning, I spotted Delano and Naill sitting on the crumbling wall that led to the Bay. I didn't try to read them, and it worked. Their emotions weren't forced onto me.

"You look like you could use a drink." Delano offered the bottle of brown liquid he held. "It's whiskey."

I walked over, taking the bottle by the neck. "Thank you," I said, lifting it. The woody aroma was powerful.

"Tastes like horse piss," Naill said. "Fair warning."

I nodded, tipping the bottle to my mouth and taking a long swallow. The liquor burned my throat and eyes. Coughing, I pressed the back of my hand to my mouth as I handed the bottle to Delano. "I don't know what horse piss tastes like, but I'm sure that's a good comparison."

Naill chuckled.

"We were getting ready to head in there." Delano stretched out his legs, crossing them at the ankles. "But we figured we'd wait until the air cleared a bit."

"Good choice," I muttered.

"Looks like the room is airing out now." Naill's gaze flicked over my shoulder.

The muscles in the back of my neck tightened. "Please tell me that's not him."

"Well, I suppose it depends on who *him* is," Delano drawled.

I turned to see Casteel coming down the steps and across the short distance that separated us, his gaze locked onto mine.

"I have a feeling the air is going to get a bit thick out here." Naill hopped off the wall. "I think it's time we head inside."

"Wise call," Casteel remarked, his gaze, nearly feral, never leaving mine.

Delano pushed off the wall. "Please, no stabbing. All of that makes me anxious."

I crossed my arms. "No promises."

Casteel smirked but said nothing as Naill and Delano made their way back into the fort. He stared at me.

I stared at him. "Do you need something?"

"That's a loaded question."

"I was hoping it was a rhetorical one with the answer being: *obviously, no,*" I said.

"Sorry to disappoint you," he replied. "Why did you leave?"

"I wanted a few moments to myself, but apparently, that isn't going to happen."

A muscle flexed in his jaw. "I'm sorry, Poppy."

My brows lifted as I focused on him. There was still a potent thread of anger in him, and I didn't delve deeper into the layers of emotions. "About what exactly?"

"About more than one thing, apparently," he replied, and my eyes narrowed. "But I'd like to start with how my people have behaved toward you. I hate that they've made you feel so unwelcome, and I hate that you know how they feel. I can promise you that will change."

"You...you really believe that you can change that? You can't," I told him before he answered. "They will either accept me or not. Either way, I expected this, and there's no way you didn't. You just hoped I wouldn't read them."

"I *wished* you wouldn't have known," he corrected. "How could I not wish that? And I do believe how they feel about you will change."

Pressing my lips together, I looked away. I didn't think it was impossible for them to change. Feelings were not stagnant. Neither were opinions or beliefs, and if we stopped believing people were capable of change, then the world might as well be left to burn.

"We need to talk and not about the people in that room," he said.

I turned from him to where the reflection of the moon rippled across the Bay. "That's the last thing I want to do right now."

"Do you have better ideas?" He stepped closer, the heat and scent of him reaching me. "I know I do."

My gaze shot to him. "If you're suggesting what I think you are, I am going to stab you in the heart again."

Casteel's eyes flashed a warm honey. "Don't tempt me with empty promises."

"You are so twisted."

"Alastir was right. I do take after my father when it comes to women with sharp objects," he said.

"I don't care."

He ignored that. "My mother has stabbed my father a time or a dozen over the years. He claims he deserved it each time, and truthfully, he never seemed all that torn up about being stabbed. Probably had something to do with the fact that they'd be holed up in their private chambers for days after a spat."

"Glad to know the disturbed apple doesn't fall too far from the crazy tree."

He chuckled.

The door opened behind us, and Kieran prowled out.

"Don't yell at me," he said as the door swung closed behind him. "But my father wants to speak to you."

"Your father?" I frowned, and then it occurred to me. "Jasper?"

Kieran nodded, and now I knew why I thought some of Jasper's features were familiar.

A muscle flexed in Casteel's jaw once more. "He's going to—"

"Go speak with Jasper," I cut in. "Because as I already said, I don't really want to talk to you right now."

"Keep telling yourself that, and maybe it'll be true." Casteel turned to Kieran as I came *this* close to punching him. "I really hope your father has a good reason for wanting to speak with me right this moment."

"Knowing him, he probably just wants to laugh at you," Kieran replied. "So have fun with that."

Casteel flipped Kieran off as he stalked back toward the doors.

"Very princely," Kieran called after him and then turned to me. "Come, Penellaphe. I'll take you back to your room. Then I must ensure that Casteel actually doesn't end up slaughtering someone, because my father is sure to drive him crazy."

"I don't—" Exhaling heavily, I was too irritated to even argue. "Whatever."

Kieran extended an arm and waited. Swallowing a mouthful of curses, I walked past him.

"That was a spectacular dinner," he said as we rounded the fortress.

"Wasn't it?"

He snorted.

Neither of us spoke as he walked me back to my room. It was only when he went to close the door that I asked, "Your father is the what? Leader of the wolven?"

"He speaks for them, yes. Brings any concerns or ideas to the King and Queen."

Remembering that Vonetta planned to travel home to visit their mother, I asked, "Is your father normally in Spessa's End?"

"He comes quite regularly to check on the wolven that are

here. Sometimes, our mother travels with him, but she's due soon."

For a moment, what he'd said didn't make sense. And then it did. "Your mother is pregnant?"

A faint grin appeared. "You look so surprised."

"I'm sorry. It's just that…you're around Casteel's age, right?"

"We're the same age. Vonetta—who won't be the baby of the family much longer—was born sixty years after me," he answered. "My father is nearly six hundred years old—my mother four hundred. Next to Alastir, he is one of the oldest wolven still alive."

"That's a…hell of an age gap between children," I murmured.

"Not when you think about how long it takes to rear a wolven. Beckett may resemble a mortal who is no older than thirteen, but in reality, he is older than you by many years. So is Quentyn."

That made sense. Casteel had said that aging slowed once an Atlantian entered the Culling. Quentyn may look my age or slightly younger, but he was most likely years older than me. "How did your father come to this position?"

"Not many wolven survived the war, so there simply wasn't a lot to choose from," he explained, and that…that was sad to consider. "Are you sure that is what you want to ask me about?"

It was.

And it wasn't.

Another question burned through me, but I wasn't going to ask that.

Kieran hesitated and then nodded. "Then goodnight, Penellaphe."

"Goodnight," I murmured, standing there until the door closed. Then I was alone. Alone with only my feelings, my own thoughts.

Promised to another.

Weariness enveloped me as I slowly walked into the bedroom. I went to the clothing Vonetta had brought over, relieved to see not a single item of white. I picked up a dark blue tunic with fine gold threading along the hem and edging. It was sleeveless and long, with slits up the sides. There was another that was gold, nearly the color of an elemental's eyes. I smoothed my hand over the soft, cottony material. There was another shirt of emerald green, one with frilly sleeves and a fancy neckline. I set the tops aside, finding two pairs of black leggings that were as thick as breeches, and both appeared as if they'd fit me. A hooded cloak made of cotton was folded on top of several new undergarments. Vonetta had mentioned the cloak, and now that I saw it, I knew she was right when she'd said it was far more suitable than the heavier winter cloaks.

But it was what lay underneath that confused me.

It was a splash of blue nearly as pale as a wolven's eyes. I picked up the slippery, silky material, my eyes widening at the tiny straps and minimal length.

The thing was indecent.

But the nightgown I'd been given in New Haven was far too heavy for nights that didn't drop below freezing, and this...this *nightgown* didn't actually require a sash to stay closed, so there was that.

Dropping it onto the bed, I turned around and I had no idea how long I stood there before I sprang forward, racing back into the living area. I went to the door, placing my hands on it. Tentatively, I reached down and turned the handle.

The door opened.

I quickly closed it and slowly backed up, waiting for Kieran to return, to realize that he'd left the door unlocked. When he didn't—when no one came—my hands trembled. And when I realized that no one had locked the door behind me earlier today or even the first night Casteel and I arrived, my arms began to shake.

I wasn't caged anymore. A willing captive. I just hadn't noticed that none of the doors had been locked from the outside.

Gods.

Realizing that did something to me. It unlocked the rawest emotion inside me, and it hit me hard. Sinking to the floor, I clasped my hands over my face as tears poured from me. The doors were *unlocked*. There were no guards, no one to govern me.

If I wanted, I could simply walk out and go…well, wherever I wanted. I didn't have to sneak out or pick a lock. The tears…they were borne of relief, and they were tinged with earlier hurts and older ones that had scarred many years ago. They were weighted with the knowledge of future pain, and they fell from the realization that tonight, when I sat at that table, I had finally shed the veil of the Maiden by defending myself. It wasn't that I hadn't done it before. I'd stood up for myself with Casteel and Kieran, and even Alastir, but tonight was different. Because there was no returning to the silence, to that submission. It didn't matter if I was the neck that turned the head of a kingdom or an outsider in a room full of people who had every right to distrust me. Staying silent was only temporarily easier than shattering the silence, and that realization was painful. It shone a light on all the times I could've spoken up—could've risked whatever consequences. All of those things fed my tears.

I cried. I cried until my head ached. I cried until there was nothing left in me, and I was just a hollow vessel, and then…then I pulled myself together.

Because I was no longer a captive.

I was no longer the Maiden.

And what I felt for Casteel—what I was only beginning to accept—was something I had to deal with.

What I said tonight at dinner? It was true. All of it. Even that last part was true, wasn't it? That even if I hadn't entirely forgiven him for his lies or the deaths he'd caused, I'd accepted them because they were a part of his past—our past—and they didn't change how I felt, right or wrong. That was what I'd denied for so long.

I loved him.

I was in love with him, even though that love had been built on a foundation of lies. I loved him even though there was so much I didn't know about him. I loved him even though I knew I was a willing pawn to him.

And this didn't happen overnight. It shouldn't come as a shock, because I was already in love with him the moment my heart broke when I learned the truth of who he was. I fell in love with him when he was Hawke, and I kept falling once I learned that he was Casteel. And I knew it wasn't because he was my first *everything*. I knew it wasn't my naivety or lack of experience.

It was because he made me feel *seen,* and he made me feel *alive* even when I genuinely wanted to cause physical harm to him. I kept falling when he never once told me not to pick up a sword or bow and instead handed one to me. I fell and fell when I realized that Casteel wore many masks for many reasons. What I felt only grew when I realized that he would, in fact, kill whoever insulted me, no matter how wrong that was. And that love...it entrenched itself deeply when I realized the kind of strength and will he had within him to survive what he had and to *still* find the pieces of who he used to be.

And the catch in my breath, the shiver and the ache whenever he looked at me, when his eyes were like twin golden flames, whenever he touched me, it went beyond lust. I didn't need experience to recognize the difference. He didn't have pieces of me. He had my whole heart, and he had from the moment he allowed me to protect myself, from the moment he stood beside me instead of in front of me.

And that realization was terrifying. Scared me more than a horde of Craven or murderous Ascended ever could. Because I had to deal with what Casteel felt and what he didn't.

The reason Casteel hadn't told me about this Gianna was the same reason he hadn't told me about the Joining or about Spessa's End. Kieran could be right, and he could be wrong. Casteel may care for me—care for me enough to not want to see undue harm befall me, and Casteel did want me physically, but that didn't mean we were heartmates. That didn't mean he loved me. And no amount of pretending would change that or how I felt.

I had to deal.

And I would.

Because my agreement with Casteel remained. I wouldn't back out because of how I felt or that my feelings were hurt. My brother was more important than that.

I lifted my head, bleary eyes focused on the ancient stone walls. The people of Solis were more important than how I felt, so were all those who called Atlantia home. Casteel's brother was more important, as were all those names on the walls of the underground chambers.

Casteel and I could change things. We could stop the Ascended, and that was what mattered.

Climbing to my feet, I shakily made my way to the small bathing chamber, grateful that Casteel hadn't returned while I'd been having a complete breakdown and moment of realization. I splashed away the tears staining my face and then undressed, pulling on the nightgown that could barely be called clothing. The cool material skimmed my breasts and hips, ending just below my rear. Tomorrow, I would question whether or not women actually slept in this…this scrap of silk, but tonight, I was too tired to even be concerned with it. After locking the doors, I took my dagger to the bed, placing in under the pillow. Pulling the blanket up over me, I tried not to think about how everything smelled of Casteel. I closed my aching eyes, and as weary as I was from *everything*, I immediately drifted into the oblivion of nothing.

It was the bed shifting under unexpected weight that woke me sometime later. Rolling onto my side, I slipped the dagger from under the pillow.

A hand caught my wrist in the shadows of the room, and a voice whispered, "Are you going to stab me in the heart? Again?"

Chapter 33

The scent of rich spice and pine reached me the second after the words.

Casteel.

My racing heart didn't slow. "Why don't you let go of my wrist and find out?"

"That sounds like a yes if I ever heard one," he replied as my eyes adjusted. The glow of the lamp outside the canopy cast most of him in shadow, but he was close enough that I could see the arch of a brow and the amused tilt to his lips.

Promised to someone else.

Anger was a heatwave that swept away any lingering sleep. "Let me go."

"I don't know if I should." His thumb moved in an idle circle along the inside of my wrist as he said, "Someone is likely to be very irritated if you stab me, and I end up bleeding all over the bed."

"You could always clean up after yourself."

"There's something innately wrong with the idea of being stabbed and then having to clean up my own blood."

I pushed against his hold, but my hand remained pinned to the bed. "There's something innately wrong with you being in here! How did you even get in? I locked the doors."

"Did you?"

"I did…" I sighed. "Key. You have a key."

"Perhaps." His head tilted. "Have you been crying?"

"What? No," I lied.

"Then why are your eyes swollen?"

"Probably because I'm tired. I was sleeping, but you woke me up."

"I wanted to come back sooner—it seems I always want to come back sooner," he said, seeming to have accepted my answer. "Especially when you're wearing something so interesting."

The blanket had slipped to my waist in sleep, exposing the low neckline of the nightgown. Heat crept down my neck and across the swells of my breasts. "It was the only thing in here for me to wear other than the robe."

"I like it." He shifted, seeming to get comfortable as he reached out with his other hand, fingering the strap. "Such ridiculous, tiny straps. I like them."

I knocked his hand away. "You can let go. I'm not going to stab you."

"I find that oddly disappointing."

"And I find that extremely disturbing."

He laughed deeply, letting go of my wrist. I started to move, but he was so much faster, shifting so he was above me. The warmth of his body pressed against my chest as one of his long legs ended up between mine, shorting out my senses. A flash of heat rolled through me as every part of my body became overly aware of how close he was.

"What are you doing?" I demanded.

"Making sure you're comfortable."

"And how will you accomplish that by lying on top of me?"

"I won't." A shadowy grin appeared. "I'm doing that because I like lying on top of you."

"Well, I don't," I bit out, pulse thundering.

His chest brushed against mine, sending a velvet shiver through me. "That's a lie."

"It's not." I lifted the dagger to his neck. "Truly."

"Do you remember what happened the last time you held a dagger to my throat?" His fingertips touched my cheek and slid lower, over my jaw. "I do."

A lick of pleasure followed his fingers. "That was a temporary loss of sanity."

"That's my favorite kind." He dragged his fingers down my throat and over the line of my collarbone. "I really do like these straps."

"I really don't care."

His fingers slipped under it as his hand curved on my shoulder. "You lie so sweetly."

I ignored that. "Casteel—"

"But not as sweetly as you say my name."

I let out a little growl. "You are…"

"Marvelous? Charming? Undeniable?"

"Increasingly annoying."

"But you still haven't used that dagger at my neck."

"I'm trying to think of the people who will have to clean up the mess."

"How thoughtful of you." He toyed with the strap. "Have I told you that you're beautiful?"

"What?" The shift in conversation threw me.

"I might have, but I couldn't remember if I did," he went on, tugging gently on the strap. "Then I thought that it wasn't something you could say too often. You're beautiful, Poppy."

My stupid, stupid heart skipped. "Is that why you decided to wake me up in the middle of the night?"

"You're beautiful." His head tilted, and I gasped at the feel of his lips on the longer scar of my cheek. He kissed that one and then the shorter one, above my eye. "Both halves, and you should never question why anyone would find you utterly, irrevocably, and distractingly beautiful."

The skipping was back, but I ignored it. "That is a lot of adjectives."

"I can come up with more."

"That won't be necessary," I advised. "So, now that you've told me this, you can get off me."

He smiled against my cheek. "But you're comfortable, Princess, and you make me feel…well, you just make me feel."

What did I make him feel? Lust? Amusement? Entertained?

The urge to read him was hard to ignore. "That's not a reason."

"That's the only reason."

Irritation pricked at my skin even as his breath danced over my lips and his fingers skimmed the outer swell of my breast. "Well, good for you, but I don't need you to be here."

"See, that's the problem." His voice dropped to a whisper as his hand slid over the silk of the gown. The material was so thin, it served no barrier against the brand of his palm. "You don't need me."

"That doesn't sound like a problem to me."

"But…" Casteel's lips glanced off mine, causing my breath to hitch as his hand slipped under the blanket and over my hip. His fingers reached bare skin, and a rush of damp heat pooled. "But you want me."

Muscles coiled tight in my stomach and then lower as I pressed the sharp edge of the blade to his throat, nicking his skin. "Not now," I told him.

Undaunted by the knife, he lowered his mouth. And when he spoke, his lips played over mine. "I can sense your arousal, Princess."

There was no denying that. I could lie all I wanted, but it didn't change that it took effort not to lift my hips against his, to not think of how he'd felt earlier, thick and hard inside me. But the wound in my chest from what I'd realized was still there, and the memory of how shockingly painful it was to think he'd already been engaged had been a warning I needed to heed before I lost sight of what was important.

"Just because my body wants you, doesn't mean any other part of me does."

"Then maybe we should pretend more?" he offered, his fingers drifting closer to where I ached. If he reached that area, I knew I would be lost.

It wasn't that he had that kind of power. It was that my desire for him did.

"Or maybe we stop pretending," he said. "I liked that better, to be honest."

So did I, but what was real to us was different.

Heart thumping, I tilted my head back. My lips touched his

as I said, "Since you'll be home soon, I'm sure there are other beds you could visit that don't require you to *pretend*. I'm sure they're probably numerous. But you could always start with Gianna's."

Casteel went still, his hand halting its movements on my inner thigh, and then he lifted his head. "That cannot be a serious statement."

"Did I sound like I was teasing?"

He rolled off me, and I caught myself before I did something irrational like stop him. I sat up, clutching the dagger as he left the bed so quickly, it was almost like he hadn't even been there.

A bitter sensation hit my veins, and I closed my eyes. I'd gotten what I wanted—he was no longer in the bed. So why didn't I feel relief?

"I can't believe you really said that."

My eyes flew open in disbelief. "You can't?"

He was a shadow through the curtains. "Hell no, I can't."

I scrambled across the blanket, shoving the panel aside as I nearly toppled out of the bed. A thin line of blood trickled down his neck, even though the wound I'd inflicted had already healed.

Standing, I slammed the dagger onto the nightstand because there was a good chance I would use it. Especially when I turned to him and caught the slow perusal that moved from the tips of my toes all the way up the bare skin of my legs to the fluttery hem and the low neckline of the gown. Heated amber eyes met mine.

I gritted my teeth. "You were promised to another, Casteel."

"Were you not listening when I made it very clear that it was a promise I never made?"

"I was listening very closely."

"Apparently, not close enough." Casteel's eyes narrowed as he stared down at me. "You know, I'm glad you brought this up. I'd momentarily forgotten that this was something we needed to discuss. You really believed that I was already engaged to someone else, didn't you?"

"Are you for real?" I choked, hands closing into fists.

"Really?"

"Last time I checked, I was real." He crossed his arms.

"Then why in the hell would you be surprised that I would think something like that? That you wouldn't tell me? You and your wonderful history of lies and half-truths?"

The heat was gone from his gaze, replaced by a splash of surprise, and then his eyes narrowed again. "Here's the whole truth, Poppy. Yes, I was expected to marry. I was expected by many, I'm sure. It was something my father had discussed for decades, but he never asked if it was what I wanted. Something you should be familiar with."

I flinched. I was all too familiar with that. "I thought Atlantians rarely married if they weren't in love."

"They don't. But as I'm sure you remember, my parents reign should've already come to an end. It should've happened decades ago. My father believed that perhaps if I married, I would stop searching for Malik and do what he thought was right. He knew that I cared for Gianna, that we were close, and thought she would be a good fit."

Gianna. That name. It sounded rare and exquisite. If this was something discussed for actual decades, then there had to be a history between them, and the sudden hot burst in the back of my throat tasted like an emotion I had no right to claim. "Make a good Princess, you mean?"

"I imagine that she would, but to answer your question, I never really said anything about it because I didn't want to hurt her or for her to feel as if I were rejecting her," he said. "She doesn't need that when it wasn't like she pursued me on her own."

But she *had* pursued him? I managed not to ask that question. "But you never said anything to me about her—about this expectation."

"Honest to gods, Poppy, I'd forgotten about it until Alastir mentioned the obligations. Far more important things have occupied my mind. And I figured that my father would've surely let go of the idea," he said. "At no point did I ever think that Alastir would bring it up like that. But he's—" He shook his head. "You can decide not to believe me, but that's the truth.

And even if I had remembered, why would I mention a promise I *never* made to a woman, to another who I was trying to convince to marry me?"

"Maybe so I would've been prepared to hear that?" I nearly shouted. "So I didn't sit there and think that you were engaged to someone else when you and I—" I cut myself off.

"While you and I did what, Poppy? Kissed. Gave each other pleasure? Had sex? Fucked? Made love?"

I sucked in a shrill breath. "Made love?" I whispered.

"I know that's not what we were doing," he said, his eyes flashing a frigid gold. "You wouldn't think for one second that I was engaged to someone else if that was what we were doing."

"I don't understand how that has anything to do with this," I admitted. "And I also don't understand why you're upset."

"Because *I* cannot understand how you actually believed I could be engaged to someone else and do the things I've done with you."

"You speak like I know everything about you!" I threw up my arms in frustration. "Just so you know, being able to sense emotions doesn't tell me everything about a person. Yet you act like I know you. But I hardly do when you pick and choose what you will tell me and when. You only tell me what you want me to know, and I have to piece together what you have shared about yourself to form any opinions. And then I have to decide whether or not you're lying!"

Casteel stepped forward. "Except for when I needed to feed, I have been nothing but honest with you since you learned who I really was."

"Even if that is the case, I still don't know you well enough to know what you would or would not do."

"Have you even really tried?" he asked.

"I have!"

His brows flew up. "Really? Is that what you're doing every time it looks like you want to ask something but force yourself to be quiet?"

"I do that because you either tell me nothing, or you tune me out when I ask about things!" I started to turn away and then whipped back around. "Tell me about the conversations you and your brother escaped? The ones that drove you to the caverns. Tell me why you refuse to take the throne even when you know your brother won't be fit to do it when you free him," I demanded. "Tell me why you thought it was okay in the first fucking place to kidnap me and use me as ransom before you even knew me!" Frustration crowded my throat. "Tell me why it never occurred to you to mention the Joining. Tell me about Gianna, Casteel. Does she care for you? Does she want this engagement? Do you care for her?"

He exhaled roughly, shaking his head, but I wasn't done.

"Tell me why you never told me the truth about Spessa's End until I was here? Was it because you didn't trust me with that information? Tell me about *her*. The one you loved and lost because of the Ascended. Tell me what happened to her. Will you even say her name?" My chest rose and fell with rapid breaths, and my anger overwhelmed my senses, blocking out his emotions completely. "Tell me how you can stand to be near me when I represent the people who took so much from you. Tell me why you really came to my room tonight. Tell me something that matters! That is real."

Casteel's chest rose with a heavy breath. "You want something real?"

"*Yes.*"

"I came to your room tonight to learn if what you said at dinner was true. That I was the first person to ever see you. That I was the first thing you ever chose for yourself. That you chose me when you knew me as Hawke, and even after you learned the truth, you still chose me," he growled, his eyes luminous. "I came here tonight to learn if you really felt like you were betraying Vikter and Rylan, all the others and yourself. I came here to see if that'd changed. Was all of that *real,* or were you just *pretending*?"

I took a step back, entirely too exposed, and it had nothing to do with the ridiculous nightgown. I hadn't expected him to go there. I wasn't sure why, but I hadn't.

He shook his head as he barked out a short, humorless laugh. "Yeah. Silence. As usual. That's why there was never a reason to tell you any of those things you've demanded from me."

I stared up at him, hands and arms trembling. "I don't know what you want from me."

"Everything," he bit out between clenched teeth. "I want *everything.*"

A shiver broke out over my skin. "I...I don't understand what that means," I whispered. And inexplicably, the back of my throat burned. Apparently, I hadn't cried out all the tears I had to give because they were now threatening to break free again. "I don't understand any of this. Not you. Not me. How I'm supposed to feel. How I'm supposed to forget everything. I don't—" Pressing my lips together, I smoothed fingers over my face, over the scars he'd kissed. I dropped my hands. "I don't understand."

The sharp lines of his face softened, and it was like watching a mask slip away before my eyes. He stepped forward and then stopped. "Do you think I understand any of this, Poppy? None of this was supposed to happen. I had plans. Capture you and use you. Free my brother and, maybe, if the gods were good, prevent a war—or at least lessen the bloodshed."

Casteel turned sideways, shoving a hand through his hair. "That was the plan. And fuck if it didn't go off the rails the moment you walked into the godsdamn Red Pearl." His eyes closed. "And each time—every damn time—I spoke to you, each time I saw your smile or heard you laugh, and the more I got to know you, the less those plans made sense. And trust me, Poppy, those plans made way more fucking sense than this—than all of his."

The breath I took got stuck as I grew incredibly still.

"I'm a Prince. A kingdom of people is counting on me to solve their problems—even the ones they're unaware of, but I...I couldn't do it. I couldn't give you to them, not even for my brother." He turned to me, his eyes nearly luminous. "All because when I'm with you, I don't think about the kingdom full of people counting on me. I don't find myself in the middle of the day, when it's too quiet, back in those fucking cages. I don't sit and think of everything I know they're doing to my brother. Beating him. Starving him. Raping him. Turning him into a monster worse than even they can imagine. When I'm with you, I don't think about that."

I curled my hands against my chest—against my thundering heart as his features blurred. And finally, I felt him. His pain. His confusion. His *wonder.*

"I forget." He quieted as he shook his head in confusion. "I forget about him—about my people, and I don't even understand how that's possible. But I did. I do. And you want to know something about *her?* About Shea?"

I gasped at the sound of her name on his lips.

"Never once did I forget any of my obligations with her. Never once did I stop thinking about Malik," he said, stunning me. "And you—you have it all wrong. There is a reason I don't speak her name. It has nothing to do with the Ascended, and while it sure as hell has to do with how I feel about her, it's not what you think."

Casteel stepped toward me once more, his eyes entirely too wide as he said, "And, truthfully, I have no idea how *you* can even bear my touch after my lies, after what I did and caused. All I do know is that I didn't plan any of this in the beginning, Poppy. I didn't plan on being drawn to you. I didn't plan to want you. I didn't plan on risking everything to keep you. I didn't—"

A fist pounded on the door, startling me so badly I almost jumped.

"If you value your life right now,"—Casteel raised his voice—"you will walk away and pretend you were never here."

"I wish I could. Trust me," came Emil's voice. "But this is important."

"Doubtful," Casteel muttered, and I almost laughed at the world-weary look that settled into his features.

But then Emil said, "The sky is on fire."

Chapter 34

Very few things were more important than what Casteel was saying, what he was admitting to me—and what was left unsaid.

The sky being on fire was one of them.

Casteel watched with near unnerving intensity as I pulled on a pair of leggings and then added the cloak over the ridiculous nightgown. Shoving my feet into my boots, I hurried to where he waited between the two rooms. We went to the main door, but Casteel stopped before opening it.

He turned to me, his gaze immediately finding mine. "This conversation isn't over."

"I know," I told him, and I did. "I have a lot of questions."

The laugh was quick, but nothing like the one before. It was real, and some of the sharpness faded from his features. "Of course, you do."

Emil was waiting for us beyond the terrace, and as I stepped out into the courtyard, my mouth dropped open.

A hazy, burnt-orange-red glow illuminated the sky beyond the Rise.

"What in the hell?" Casteel demanded.

"The sky really is on fire," I whispered. "Is it another omen? From the gods?"

"I sure hope not," Emil responded. "Because if so, that can't be good. Delano already left to see if he can find out what it is."

Casteel nodded. "I don't think it's that." He started walking around the corner of the fortress, but then stopped. Turning to me, he extended his hand.

I placed mine in his without hesitation. His grip was warm and strong, and that jolt of energy was there, traveling up my arm.

I have no idea how you can even bear my touch.

I wanted to tell him right then that I could bear his touch because I loved him.

But it didn't seem like a good idea with the sky being on fire.

Casteel prowled forward. "How long ago did you guys realize this was happening?"

"Ten minutes, if that. Are you going up onto the Rise?" Emil asked as we crossed the courtyard, heading for one of the entry points to the Rise.

"I figure it would give us a better view." He led me inside a stairwell lit by oil lanterns. "Did anyone go with Delano?"

Emil followed behind as we climbed the spiraling stone stairs. "I think Dante went out with him. Probably thought it would be safer."

"Possibly," Casteel murmured.

Reaching the top of the Rise, my steps faltered for a moment. What appeared to be the entire western sky was aglow.

"Good gods," Emil muttered, coming to a stop.

Casteel and I walked across the roof of the Rise, the cool air chilling my skin. Several people stood in and near the parapets, their bodies outlined in red.

One of them turned. Kieran. His father was beside him, facing the glowing sky. A Guardian stood on the ledge, the moonlight glinting off the golden swords strapped to her sides. She looked over her shoulder, placing her fist over her heart.

Casteel greeted her with the same gesture as a gust of wind lifted the wispy strands of her hair that wasn't held back. Mine also blew as I slipped my hand free of his and entered an empty peak. The wind...an acrid scent carried on it, reminding me of...

I placed my hand on the stone. "I don't think it's the sky

that's on fire."

The Guardian looked over at me, saying nothing as Casteel entered the parapet. "Neither do I."

"While I'm relieved it's not the sky burning," Jasper said. "Something is."

Something big was, but what could it be? There was nothing but fields and ruined cities that way.

"How far away do you think the fire is?" the Guardian asked.

"Hard to tell." Casteel placed his hands beside mine. "I would say about a day's or more ride, maybe even farther depending on the size."

"A day's ride?" I frowned. "That would be…what? Pompay? What could burn there to create this?"

"If it's farther out, it would have to be a massive fire to be seen from here," Casteel said, shaking his head. "Delano is fast. In his wolven form, he'll reach Pompay in no time. We'll know soon enough what the cause is."

"Until then, Your Highness?" the Guardian asked.

"Until then, we make sure there is no panic. Those who were at the dinner will have most likely seen this and are taking tales of the burning sky home. Go and make sure there is no panic, Nova."

The Guardian nodded and then stepped off the ledge. She strode across the roof, disappearing into one of the stairwells.

"And what do we do?" Kieran asked as he stared at the unnatural sky.

"We wait," Casteel said. "That's all we can do for now."

Dawn crept across Spessa's End in splashes of violet and pink, but to the west, it looked like the sun had fallen to the land. With each passing hour, the scents of smoke and burning wood grew.

Pulling the halves of the cloak around me, I stared down at the dirt road ahead, searching for signs of Delano or Dante, but I saw nothing. I couldn't even see the Guardians I knew were out beyond the wall, hidden in the tall grass. Endless hours had passed since we'd climbed the Rise, and though I didn't need to remain, I wanted to be here the moment we found out what burned—and, hopefully, what'd caused it.

Leaning against the parapet wall, I glanced over my shoulder. Casteel stood several feet away, speaking to Kieran and Alastir. I sensed...concern from all three of them, and I wondered if they had the same fear that *I* wasn't willing to voice.

I turned back to the western sky, unsettled by the reddish-orange glow. Whatever burned was no normal fire.

"The sky brings back old memories."

I jolted at the sound of Jasper's voice. He'd entered the parapet without me realizing. The silver-haired wolven was tall—taller than his son and Casteel. He propped a hip against the wall and stared at the burning sky.

"Entire towns were burned," he continued. "Some by accident. Others on purpose. There'd be weeks where, no matter what direction you looked, the sky appeared to burn. It was something I'd hoped never to see again." His gaze slid to mine. "I don't think we've been officially introduced."

"No, we haven't." I found nothing but concern and curiosity whirling through him. "Penellaphe Balfour."

"Jasper Contou," he told me, and I realized I'd never known Kieran's last name. "Balfour? That is an old Solis name."

"Alastir said the same."

"He would know." Jasper glanced to where the others stood. "So, I was under the impression I'm to officiate a wedding?"

I bit down on my lip, wondering if Casteel still planned to marry me while here. We'd only planned to be in Spessa's End until the first group from New Haven arrived, which should be today. But with the fire?

"A highly anticipated and yet also extremely unexpected wedding, I might add." He smiled then, and I felt a trickle of amusement from him.

Perhaps the day before, I would've responded with something appropriately vague, spoke in a way that was becoming of the Maiden, but that part of me was gone. "I don't know if Casteel still plans to marry me while we're here," I answered, meeting his pale gaze. "You speak for the wolven?"

He nodded.

"So, I imagine you probably expected him to marry someone else."

His amusement rose a notch. "Considering that Casteel has never once indicated that he was interested in settling down with anyone, I didn't expect anything from him."

There was a catch in my heart. It wasn't that I didn't believe Casteel when he said that he hadn't agreed to marry Gianna, but it was…well, it was a relief to know that the wolven who spoke for his people hadn't expected the marriage. "But did you expect him to marry a wolven? From what I've learned, there has been discontent among the wolven, and I'm guessing there was hope that a marriage between Casteel and a wolven would ease those troubles."

There was a slight hardening of Jasper's jaw, and I felt a hot spike of anger. "I am of the same mind as Casteel. A marriage between our two peoples would've done very little to assuage concerns or to end the need for retribution against the Ascended. Valyn is also intelligent enough to know that," he said, referring to the King by his first name. "But when you hear enough whispers, you begin to believe whatever those whispers tell you."

I frowned as I looked at Casteel—at those who stood with him. Was Jasper suggesting that the union between Casteel and a wolven had been an idea fed to the King? Alastir was an advisor to the Crown, but while he had doubts regarding our relationship's authenticity, he didn't appear against it. But what had Casteel said to Alastir last night at dinner? That he knew why he'd brought up the expectation. Perhaps it had been Alastir's idea in hopes that it would help ease the unrest. I couldn't exactly fault him for that.

"I imagine I will still be officiating a wedding," Jasper mused.

I lifted my brows as I refocused on him. "You don't doubt our intentions?"

"Not after meeting you."

"I'm not sure if that was a compliment or not," I admitted,

even though nothing I sensed from him indicated that he was being facetious.

His grin grew even wider. "You seem to have no problem speaking your mind for someone raised to be the Maiden."

"Not always," I confessed, shivering as a gust of smoke-tinged wind whipped across the roof. "You seem to have no issue speaking with me even though I was the Maiden."

"And are apparently capable of healing broken bones with just the touch of your hands."

I looked at him in surprise.

"I heard what you did for Beckett. I told Alastir that little idiot shouldn't be out here." There was a fondness to his tone. "Young wolven can be very accident-prone due to their general curiosity about literally everything, which leads to a near-catastrophic level of inattentiveness."

I grinned. "But he'll be okay."

"Because of you."

Looking back at the sky, I exhaled softly. "I've never done that before."

"I heard that, too. From my daughter and son. They also said you appeared...*old.*"

Good gods, I'd forgotten about that amidst everything that'd happened after that conversation. "Do I smell like death to you, too?"

He laughed. "You do not smell *of* death, but you do have a...different scent. One I can't exactly place, but that feels familiar." Jasper was quiet for a moment, and I suddenly remembered the wolven in New Haven—the one who had spoken Jasper's name and said that Jasper would be interested in meeting me. "When Delano said you most likely descend from an empath bloodline and Kieran confirmed such, I didn't believe them. And now I really don't."

My gaze shot to his. "Why not?"

The wolven inclined his head. "Because very few empaths could actually heal with their touch, and I've never heard of an empath who glowed like the moonlight. That doesn't mean none ever did, but the ones I knew sure as hell didn't."

Unease stirred. "Are you suggesting that I'm not descended

from that bloodline?"

"I don't know." Honesty rang in the silver-haired wolven's words as he studied me. "You are a mystery in many ways, Penellaphe."

Casteel's approach silenced any response I might have had. "I truly hope you're not filling her head with tales about me."

"Are they tales I should know?" I asked.

"Depends." Casteel eyed Kieran's father. "If they involve anything that happened between when I was a babe through my Culling, the answer would be no."

My brows rose. "Well, now I'm definitely interested."

Pushing away from the wall, Jasper chuckled. "I haven't spun any tales." He paused. "Yet."

Casteel's eyes narrowed as he stood beside me. "How about you keep spinning tales to a minimum?"

"But I'm very interested in spun tales," I remarked.

Jasper grinned again, and this time, with the light of the sun, there was no mistaking the resemblance between him and Kieran. "We have time. I'll make sure of it." He winked in my direction before clasping a hand on Casteel's shoulder and leaving the parapet.

"It's amusing to me that Alastir knows to keep his mouth shut when it comes to embarrassing stories concerning my most formative years, and yet speaks freely about things that should be given a second thought," Casteel said, watching Jasper join his son and Alastir. Beckett had arrived, and when he smiled up at Jasper, I couldn't help but think of the bolt of fear I'd felt from him. "And yet, meanwhile, Jasper is the exact opposite."

"I'm really interested in your formative years."

"I'm sure you are." Casteel angled his body toward mine, and it was the first time since Emil had knocked on the door that we were somewhat alone.

There was so much to say as we stared at one another. So many questions and words left unsaid, but neither of us spoke as he gathered the edges of my cloak, pulling the thin material tighter around me. His hands remained there, balled in the material below mine as his gaze roamed over my face.

"You don't need to stay up here, Poppy," he said after a

moment.

"I know, but I want to be here when Delano comes back." I looked down at his hands. "Besides, I doubt I'd be able to sleep."

"You could try."

"So could you."

"Even if I wasn't the Prince, I would be up here," he replied.

I lifted my gaze to his. "Even if I wasn't about to become a Princess, I would be up here."

Casteel became so still, I wondered if he breathed. I sensed an acute rush of emotions flow through him, so swift and sudden, I couldn't make out what they were. That could've been my shock, though, because I'd never felt anything like that from him before.

Then he moved, lifting a hand. He hesitated as if to see if I would pull away. When I didn't, he cupped my left cheek. His fingers splayed across the scars. "I don't think I've ever heard you refer to yourself as the Princess."

Had I not?

His gaze searched mine, and a long, tense moment passed. "There is so much we still need to talk about."

"I know," I whispered. "But it has to wait. I know that, too."

"But until then?" He stepped into me, causing my breath to snag. "I am honored that you are standing beside me now."

I didn't know what to say, and I realized that sometimes nothing needed to be said.

"Are you hungry?" he asked. "Thirsty?"

I shook my head as he lifted his gaze to the western sky.

"But you're cold."

"Just a little."

"A little is too much." He lowered his hand to my shoulder and turned me so I faced the west. I allowed it.

And when he folded his arms around me, pulling my back against his front, I only tensed for a few seconds. I allowed that too and relaxed into his warm embrace, letting my head rest against his chest. Casteel seemed to let out a breath, and for several minutes, we just stood there. Together.

It was in those moments that I thought about what the wolven had said. "Jasper sort of indicated that he doesn't think I'm descended from the empath bloodline."

"He did?"

"He said he's never heard of or knew any that glowed silver."

"Neither have I," he said. "But no other bloodline makes sense. The only other thing I can think of also doesn't make sense."

"And what would that be?"

"That neither of your parents were purely mortal. But if that were the case, and you're a mixture of two lines, it seems hard to believe that both your mother and father would've gone unnoticed by the Ascended."

"And that would mean that Ian would also be part Atlantian."

"Possibly."

My heart tripped over itself. Casteel was right. It didn't make sense. Because why would Ian have Ascended then?

If he actually had.

"It is possible that you come from an empath line that was rare and older," Casteel said. "Just because we haven't heard of or seen it, doesn't mean it didn't exist."

He was right.

Something occurred to me then as I watched the western sky. "Was Jasper chosen as the speaker for his people because Alastir was already your parents' advisor?"

"Alastir could've been both, but Jasper…well, he has a sense for things. Not like you. He's just more in tune with people and even animals."

I thought about that. "Kieran's the same way, isn't he?"

His chin grazed the top of my head. "Jasper once said there was a Seer somewhere in his bloodline—a changeling—and he'd gotten a watered-down version. When I was younger, I used to think he was just telling stories, but he seemed to know things. Like when it was about to storm, or what side to hedge his bets on. Sometimes, he knew what I was going to do before I even did it."

Just like Kieran.

"And Vonetta isn't like that?"

"She takes after her mother more—well, except for the cooking, but definitely the ass-kicking," he said.

I smiled. "I asked Jasper if he expected you to marry."

There was no tensing or stiffening as he said, "And what did he say?"

"That he didn't," I told him, closing my eyes. "That's what I don't understand."

"Poppy—"

"I mean, I don't understand how the speaker for the wolven doesn't expect you to marry a wolven, but some of your people do. Other wolven did." Namely Landell. "And, apparently, your father. And I guess even Alastir at one point."

"Well, Alastir did expect it. I know that for sure. I'm almost confident it was his idea," he said, confirming my suspicions. "After all, Gianna is his great-niece—Beckett's older cousin."

"*What?*" I opened my eyes just as I heard the distant call of a songbird. A signal that was answered with a closer call and then by one of the Guardians, who stood at the other end of the Rise.

"They're back," Casteel said.

I turned in his arms, our gazes meeting for the briefest of moments, and then we both moved. We weren't the only ones hurrying to the courtyard. Alastir and Jasper were right behind us, along with Kieran.

Emil and Vonetta lifted the barricade, and the heavy iron doors parted as Casteel strode to the center. I squinted, seeing nothing—

Then ahead, on the dirt road, a white blur racing towards us—white fur matted with reddish-brown.

"Shit," Casteel grunted, running out the doors. Someone else cursed, shouting for him to stay back, but he was already halfway to Delano.

Who was hurt.

Who was also alone.

I took off, the cloak billowing out behind me.

"Dammit." That was definitely Kieran.

I didn't slow down, reaching Casteel and Delano just as the

wolven collapsed, sending clouds of dirt into the air. My heart stopped as I read the fiery agony in him. The physical pain snapped my senses open in the way they had before I woke the day before. The cord stretched out, connecting with him, and the pain caused my steps to falter.

Kieran caught my arm, righting me. I started to thank him, but he was already past me as Casteel dropped to his knees.

I reached them just as Jasper did. "Why am I not surprised that both the Prince and our soon-to-be Princess are outside the walls of safety?" he said.

"Welcome to my world," Kieran muttered.

"He's in pain," I said, moving to where Casteel knelt. Once I did, I could see the wound in Delano's side, under his front leg—his right arm. The blood there was fresher, leaking from a puncture wound.

"He's unconscious," Casteel bit out, looking up the empty road and then back at me. "Can you—?"

I was already on my knees on the other side of Delano, my hands tingling with heat. "I don't know what will happen," I said, glancing over at Casteel. "I don't know if I will ease his pain or anything more beyond that."

Eyes like chips of amber met mine. "Do whatever you can."

Aware of the Guardians surrounding us as Alastir knelt behind Casteel, I sank my hands into the soft wolven fur. Like with Beckett, before I could start to pull from the all-too-shallow well of good, happy memories, the heat intensified. A faint glow surrounded my hands as I felt Delano's pain rise suddenly, sharply, and then ease.

"Gods," Jasper whispered hoarsely.

"I'm glowing again, aren't I?" I asked.

"Yes," Casteel answered. "Like moonlight. Beautiful."

Delano shuddered as I felt the last of his pain trickle away. His ears twitched and then perked. A moment later, he lifted his head, stretching to look back at me as I lifted my hands.

"Hi," I said, and I swore the wolven smiled.

"Delano?" Casteel leaned forward. "Can you shift?"

The wolven turned back to Casteel and shuddered again. As the fur thinned, Kieran whipped off his shirt, draping it over

Delano's midsection just as his legs lengthened, claws retracted, and pale skin replaced fur. A moment later, Delano was in his mortal form.

I rocked back. Watching a wolven change forms would never cease to amaze me.

Delano lifted his right arm as he sat up, wiping the blood off to reveal no wound. Just a pinker, ragged patch of skin. He lowered his arm, eyes meeting mine.

"Delano," Casteel said. "What in the hell happened?"

Tearing his gaze from me, he turned to Casteel, his chest rising and falling with steady breaths. "They're coming. The Ascended."

Chapter 35

"They're burning everything," Delano said between mouthfuls of roasted meat and gulps of water as we sat in a room inside the fortress, off from the dining hall. "All of what was left of Pompay. All of the woods from Pompay to—to Gods, possibly all the way to New Haven. The Dead Bones Clan?" His bare shoulders tensed as he reached for the water. "I don't see how they could've gotten out of there. They have to all be gone."

My empty stomach churned with nausea. I was no fan of their people-eating and skin-wearing habits, but that didn't mean I wished they'd all be murdered. Especially after learning that they'd survived the war and the Ascended by hiding out in those woods.

"As soon as we saw Pompay, we knew it wasn't normal. There weren't that many there. Maybe two dozen guards. But to create that kind of fire? To the point that the air is nearly black with smoke? We knew there had to be more." His knuckles bleached white from how tightly he held his glass.

We.

But only he'd returned, and I knew what that meant.

I looked to where Casteel stood on the other side of the table.

His expression was utterly devoid of emotion, but I could feel the vast, icy rage inside him. "Did you see more?"

"We skirted past them, traveling farther west. That's where

we saw them—saw the rest. We got close—as close as we could. To see how many there were." He downed half the glass of water. "They have camps, Cas. Horses. Wagons pulling supplies."

Alastir, who'd been standing since we entered the room, sat in a chair, his face pale as Delano lifted his fingers, one by one, from the glass. "There have to be hundreds of them, close to eight hundred or so, I'd guess. A godsdamn army."

I sat back. From the moment I'd realized that the sky wasn't actually burning, I had already suspected that the Ascended were behind the fire. My hours on the Rise were spent preparing myself for what I already knew. The knowledge that the Ascended were coming wasn't what shook me. It was the sheer *numbers* of them.

"Hell," Jasper muttered.

"One of them saw us as we left their camp. Arrows. That's what got me. Got Dante."

"Was he killed?" Casteel asked.

Delano nodded as he stared at the plate. "Got him in the head."

Alastir swore, rising once more. "Dante didn't know when to shut up." He turned, clasping the back of his chair. "But he was a good man. Honorable."

"I know." A muscle flexed in Casteel's jaw.

"I couldn't stop to heal," Delano said. "The moment the arrow hit me, and I saw that Dante was dead, I ran. I would've gotten here sooner but I was weakening."

"It's okay. You got here." Casteel unfolded his arms and placed a hand on the wolven's shoulder. "That is what matters."

Delano nodded, but I knew he didn't believe that. I could feel it. The anger—directed at the Ascended and at himself.

"You ran how many miles?" I asked. "With a wound that most likely punctured a lung. You did more than most could ever think to do."

Delano's eyes met mine. "And you healed me with the touch of your fingers."

"And that was nowhere near as difficult or as impressive as what you did."

The centers of Delano's cheeks pinkened as Casteel added,

"She speaks the truth. And you're the first person to ever impress her. I'm jealous."

I rolled my eyes.

Casteel squeezed Delano's shoulder once more and then asked, "Did you see any sign of Elijah? Or anyone from New Haven?"

With a shake of Delano's head, a heavy, somber pall settled over the room.

"There are other ways they could've traveled—routes that would take significantly longer. But that doesn't mean Elijah and the people didn't get out of New Haven," Kieran said, speaking for the first time. "They could've headed north and then come down through the foothills of the Skotos to avoid the Ascended."

"I know." Casteel crossed his arms. "Did you see any Ascended? Any knights?"

"No, but there were windowless carriages and wagons with high walls, completely sheltered. It's possible some are with them."

"That's one bit of good news then," Casteel said.

"How is that good news?" Alastir turned to him. "There are hundreds on their way here. An army."

"It's good because hundreds of mortals means Spessa's End has a chance," Casteel answered.

"A slim chance." Alastir returned to his seat. "You may be optimistic. I respect that, but even with the Guardians we have here, that will not be enough to hold back an army of hundreds."

A chill settled in my bones as I looked around the table, around the room and the stone walls that had already witnessed one city fall. "We can't let Spessa's End fall."

Several pairs of eyes turned to me, but it was Casteel's gaze that I met. "And we won't," he said. "Nova?"

The tall Guardian with the braided blond hair stepped forward. It was the one who'd watched us the day I saw them training. "Yes, my Prince?"

"Remind me of how many people we have that are capable of defending the town?"

"Less than a hundred who are trained or capable of

physically fighting," she answered, and Emil let out a low curse. "Our older population is trained with the bow, though. We would have about twenty archers."

Twenty archers was better than nothing, but it wasn't enough. Everyone knew that.

"We have an additional twenty-three from my and Alastir's groups." A muscle flexed along Casteel's jaw. "When do you think they'll reach Spessa's End?"

"They're in two groups," Delano said. "The smaller one is closer, about a day's ride out. I imagine they could be here by nightfall." The tension in the room intensified. "The larger group will take longer to arrive. Probably two days, but those guesses are based on whether the first group waits for the larger group."

"And how many are in the first group?" Jasper asked.

"Two hundred? Maybe three."

That was the smaller group? Dear gods… "There is no way they don't know what has been happening here if they've sent nearly a thousand or more soldiers," I said. "They're coming, ready for a fight."

"Someone must have talked," Emil said as he pushed off the wall. "They had to have forced the information from someone. Possibly a Descenter who traveled here or was aware."

"Or someone at New Haven," Alastir said, and my chest seized with dread.

"They're probably not entirely aware of what has been rebuilt here, but they know with it being this close to the Skotos, they're not coming unprepared. The size of the army could be more show than force in hopes of scaring us into giving them what they want." Jasper, seated a few empty seats down the table from me, twisted in my direction. "Which I assume is you."

I already knew that. Whether they knew what Spessa's End had become or not, they were coming for their Maiden. Their blood supply. The future of their Ascensions in one shape or form, and they'd brought an army to gain what they wanted, fully prepared to do so through force.

And people would…they would die. Possibly even some of those in this very room. All of them were the closest things to immortal there were, but none of them were gods. And even with everyone willing and able to fight, we were vastly outnumbered. People would die because they were harboring me, just like the people in New Haven.

Like Renfern.

My stomach and chest twisted with the iciness of apprehension. I couldn't live with that again.

"They cannot have what they want," Casteel snarled as his gaze shot to mine. "*Ever.*"

I stilled as he held my gaze. There was a vow in his words, one that spoke volumes—one that said he knew where my thoughts had gone.

"They're here for me," I said, holding his stare and willing him to hear what I couldn't say in front of others. "We cannot risk—"

"Yes, we can," he cut me off, eyes burning an intense yellow. "And, yes, I will. They cannot have you." Bending forward, he placed his hands on the table. "Whatever you're thinking, you have it wrong. They're not going to turn and walk away if they have you. You know that, Poppy. You saw that firsthand with Lord Chaney. They will get what they want and *still* lay waste to everything before them just because they can. That is what they do. And once they have you, they will use you to wreak more havoc and destruction. By giving yourself to them, you won't be saving lives. You'll be destroying more of them."

Casteel was right, and I hated that. It made me feel like there was nothing I could do to stop this—to fight back.

But that was wrong.

There *was* something I could do. I could fight.

Casteel dragged his gaze from mine. "We need reinforcements, and we need them quickly. Alastir, I need you to cross the Skotos. Alert those at the Pillars and Saion's Cove to what is happening. Send as many of our soldiers that can make it to Spessa's End within two days," Casteel ordered, to which the wolven already began rising from his chair to obey. Casteel wasn't done yet. He turned to Kieran. "I want you to travel with him just in case something happens."

"What?" Kieran exclaimed, obviously as shocked as I was to hear Casteel's demand. "There is a damn army of Solis heading this way, and you're sending me to Atlantia?"

"I am. You're fast. You're strong. And you will not weaken or falter if something happens to Alastir." Casteel met the wolven's astonished stare. "You will not fail us."

My heart started thumping hard because I knew. I knew in my bones why Casteel was sending Kieran away.

"My Prince," Nova spoke up. "I know you feel that it is your duty to remain here, but it is you who should travel beyond the Skotos. You should leave immediately and head for safety."

"I have to agree with her," Alastir chimed in. "The Ascended may think you're the Dark One, but they may know who you really are—the living heir to the Kingdom of Atlantia. You are the last person who should be here."

I tensed at Alastir's words, but Casteel showed no reaction to him being referred to as the living heir to the kingdom. "I value both of your thoughts and opinions, but you all know I will not leave Spessa's End to defend itself. Not when I helped to convince those here to come and make their homes in this place."

"Everyone who came here knew the risks involved," Alastir argued. "Your life cannot be put at risk for Spessa's End."

Casteel inclined his head. "If I'm not willing to risk my life for Spessa's End, how dare I ask the people here to do so? That is not what a Prince does—at least not a good one."

A wealth of respect for Casteel rose so swiftly in me, it took my breath. I didn't understand how he couldn't see it practically radiating from me. He wasn't willing to ask those to risk what he would not, and no one could argue that. Not even Alastir.

He exhaled heavily and then nodded.

"I should be here with you." Kieran stepped closer to Casteel. "My duty is to defend your life with mine. That is what I'm bonded to do, the oath I took. How can I do that running away from the battle?" His voice lowered. "Don't do this, Cas."

My heart twisted as I stared at them. Casteel was sending his bonded wolven away. One look at Kieran told me that he knew it, too. Casteel was removing any chance that Kieran would risk his life to save his.

Just as he'd done when he left to kill the Queen and King of

Solis.

And that meant that Casteel truly understood the likelihood that Spessa's End wouldn't hold until or if reinforcements arrived.

"You took an oath to protect me, and you will," Casteel said. "You're not running away from the battle. You will be keeping safe what is most important to me, and that is Poppy."

I jolted. "Wait. What?"

"You will leave with them. It will be hard," he said, still holding Kieran's gaze. "There will be no breaks, and you will need to listen to everything Kieran tells you, especially when it's night in the mountains, but—"

"I'm not leaving," I cut him off.

"You can't be here," Casteel replied. "Not when they come. This is not up for discussion."

I shot to my feet. "Let me make one thing clear. I don't know if you realize this or not, Casteel, but I'm not duty-bound to obey a single thing you say."

Casteel stiffened.

"And maybe you should actually look at me when you try to order me to do things," I tacked on.

He turned to me, his head cocked. "I'm looking at you now."

"But are you listening?"

"Oh, man," Delano murmured under his breath as the rest of the room went dead silent. "Someone is getting stabbed again."

Someone, I think it was Jasper, snorted.

"Oh, I'm listening," Casteel replied. "Maybe you should try that. Along with this thing called common sense."

"Definitely getting stabbed," Kieran confirmed.

I stepped around the table, aware that Delano appeared to be sinking into his chair. "Are you serious?"

"Are you armed?" Casteel asked with a smirk. "You are, aren't you?"

"I'm so confused by what is happening here," Nova whispered with a slight frown.

"Apparently, she already stabbed him once," Jasper

informed the Guardian. "In the heart."

Nova looked at me.

"And she cut me earlier tonight. Threw a knife right at my face another time," Casteel ticked off his fingers. "Then this one time, in the woods, she—"

"No one wants to hear about how many times I've made you bleed," I snapped.

"I do," Jasper remarked.

Emil raised his hand. "So do I."

"Look, not only is it not wise for the one thing they want to be here within their grasp, I don't want to worry about you handing yourself over," Casteel stated. "You know...like before."

"That is not a mistake I will make again," I stated.

"But you were just thinking about it, weren't you?" He stepped to the side so Delano was no longer seated between us.

"I was," I admitted. "For a couple of minutes. But you were right."

His brows lifted. "Blessed be the gods, someone mark the date and time. She just admitted I was right."

"Oh, shut up," I bit back.

"Fine with me. Conversation is over. You'll leave with Alastir and Kieran immediately." He started to turn.

"I am not leaving." I lifted my chin when he spun back to me. "You'll have to make me. You'll have to drag me all the way to Atlantia yourself."

His chin dipped as anger pounded through him, reaching me. "Or I could just compel you."

My skin went cold. "You wouldn't dare."

His jaw flexed, and then he spat out a curse. The ice left me. He wouldn't do that. "This is different, Poppy. Different than the Rise or the Craven or the Dead Bones Clan."

"You should leave," the Guardian spoke. "I saw what you can do—out there with Delano. But that will be of no use when it's time to fight. You will be nothing but a distraction to our Prince. You will be a liability."

Slowly, I turned to the woman. "Excuse me?"

Nova stared back at me. "I mean no offense. I'm only stating facts."

"Your facts are grossly incorrect," I told her. "Just to point out the most obvious of your inaccuracies, what I did for Delano would actually come in handy when and if people are injured. *That*,"—I sent a dark look in Casteel's direction—"is common sense."

Her eyes narrowed.

"As far as me being a liability? I'm just as good with a sword as I am with a bow, and I'm damn good with a bow. Probably better than most here. I am an asset," I said. "And as far as being a distraction to Casteel, that's his weakness. Not mine."

Nova's chin lifted, and I felt...I felt a measure of respect from the Guardian. It was buried under layers of wariness, but it was there.

"She's not lying," Casteel said, watching me. "Penellaphe can fight, and her skill with a sword and aim with the arrow are leagues above that of a trained soldier. She is never a liability."

My gaze shifted to him. "So then it's settled?"

His lips thinned as he shook his head.

"You need my help," I told him, drawing in a shallow breath. "And I *need* to be here. They are coming for me, and I have to be able to do something. I need to fight back, not stand by and do nothing."

Casteel's eyes met mine and stayed, and I thought maybe he understood then. Why I couldn't walk away. Why doing so would make me feel helpless. But even then, I braced for more of a fight. Because this *was* different. This was battle, and I could feel the mess of emotions in him. The conflict.

But then he nodded. "Okay. You stay," he said, and I breathed out a sigh of relief. "We'll discuss what exactly that means later."

My eyes narrowed.

"What of me?" Kieran demanded then. "If Penellaphe is staying—"

"There still needs to be two of you," Casteel interrupted, and I sensed the bone-deep weariness in him. "Delano can't make the trip, and you're faster than Naill and most Atlantians here."

Kieran stiffened while his father watched on in silence.

"And this is an order?"

Meeting Kieran's eyes, Casteel nodded. "Yes. It is."

The wolven's jaw worked so hard, I was surprised we didn't hear it crack. He shook his head. Disbelief and anger radiated from him, but I felt something else, something deeper that was warm and stronger than the anger. "I know why you're doing this," Kieran whispered.

Casteel said nothing for a long moment and then said, "It's not the only reason."

Words went unsaid between them, but were understood nonetheless. Whatever it was caused Kieran to nod, to accept Casteel's order. Then Kieran moved forward, clasping Casteel around the back of the neck. "If you get yourself killed," Kieran said, "I'm going to be pissed."

One side of Casteel's lips kicked up. "I won't fall, my brother." Casteel pulled him in for a tight, one-armed hug. "That, I can promise you."

Exhaling raggedly, Kieran returned the embrace. Maybe I was just tired. I didn't know, but I wanted to cry as I watched them, even though I wouldn't let myself consider the possibility that they would not see each other again. That their bond could be severed. Kieran stepped back, looking at his father.

Jasper was already on his feet, moving to his son. "I've always been proud of you." He curved a hand around the back of Kieran's head. "I've always had confidence in you. I know we will see each other again."

Kieran nodded, and as he pulled away from his father, I took a tentative step forward. "Kieran?"

He looked at me.

"Please...please try to be careful," I said.

He lifted his brows. "Are you worried about me?"

Crossing my arms, I nodded.

"Don't be nice to me," he replied, and I sensed amusement from him. "It weirds me out."

"Sorry."

He smiled then as he walked to where I stood. "You don't sound remotely sorry."

I grinned at him.

"Do me a favor," Kieran said, looking down at me. "Protect your Prince, *Poppy*."

I didn't see Casteel for the rest of the day.

After saying goodbye to Alastir, I returned to the room while he left to go and speak with the people of Spessa's End. I'd started to ask to go with him, but upon remembering the townspeople's reactions the night before, I realized I would only be a distraction. The kind that could prove deadly to the people of Spessa's End if they were busy staring at me instead of listening to Casteel.

I'd expected him to return, not so much to finish our conversation since there were far more important things going on, but because he needed to sleep.

But the morning gave way to the afternoon, and Casteel still didn't show. I didn't stay in the room. I prepared.

Luckily, Vonetta had been near when I stepped out into the courtyard, and she was willing to indulge me in a training session. Handling a sword or a bow wasn't a technique you forgot, but it was one that could become rusty with neglect.

Plus, she was a wolven, faster and stronger than a mortal, and fighting her would be a lot like fighting a knight. I needed the practice.

We drew a bit of a crowd, but Casteel was still with the people. According to Vonetta, he was helping to determine who could fight.

When I saw Casteel again, it was when Delano brought me to the small room off the dining room where dinner was spent discussing strategies. The fact that Casteel had thought to include me in the meeting didn't go unnoticed by me or by anyone else in the room.

By the time night arrived, and I'd returned to the bedchamber, Casteel still hadn't. I spent several hours nervously pacing and thinking about things—about everything that had happened before Casteel entered my life, and everything that had happened since. I thought about my gift—how it was changing, how I glowed like moonlight. And I thought about all that Casteel had said and what had been left unsaid.

I thought about how I was so damn tired of pretending.

At some point, after walking myself ragged, I finally fell asleep, dressed just in case the Ascended showed. I wasn't even sure what woke me, but when I opened my eyes, the grayish light of dawn crept into the room, and Casteel was in the bed beside me, propped up against a mountain of pillows. His long legs stretched out in front of him, crossed at the ankles, feet bare. His hands were loose in his lap. He was awake, looking at me.

"Are you watching me sleep?"

"Not now. I was a few minutes ago," he admitted, one side of his lips curving up. "Now, I'm talking to you."

"That's creepy," I murmured. "The watching me while I sleep part."

"Possibly."

"You have no shame." I rolled onto my back.

He smiled faintly at that, but it didn't reach his eyes—eyes that were tired.

"Have you slept at all?"

"Not yet."

The mess that was my hair toppled over my shoulders as I sat up. "I know you're this insanely powerful elemental, but you need to rest."

That half-grin appeared, the dimple in his right cheek peeking. "Are you worried about me, Princess?"

I started to tell him no. To deny that I was because that was what I'd always done. It was the easiest—and the safest—but I was tired.

Of lying.

Of pretending.

That was something else I'd thought about as I stood on the Rise overnight after preparing myself for the inevitable. I thought about *my* future. Who I used to be, who I was becoming, and who I wanted to be. And it was strange how revelations felt like they happened all of a sudden, but in reality, it took many small, almost indiscernible moments over the course of weeks, months, and years. Bottom line, I knew I didn't want to be someone who hid anymore, whether behind a veil, to others, or to myself.

Just like I'd said at dinner, I hadn't changed because of Casteel. I'd been in the process long before he came into my life, but he *was* a catalyst. Just like all those times I'd snuck out to explore, the books I'd been forbidden yet read, and when I smiled at the Duke, knowing I'd be punished later. Vikter's death was also a turning point.

"I am," I told him. "I am worried about you."

Casteel stared at me, and I didn't need to read him to know that my answer had shocked him.

"They're going to come. The Ascended could be here by tonight. You need to sleep. To be rested." I paused. "And maybe stop staring at me."

"I…" He blinked, and then his body relaxed once more. "I will rest. We both will. But I need…we need to finish our conversation. It can't wait." His gaze returned to mine. "Not any longer."

My heart kicked around in my chest as I leaned back against the pillows. "Where…where do we start?"

He laughed softly. "Gods, I think I know where to start. You asked if I have any shame? I do have some." He looked over at me. "Almost all the shame I've ever felt has to do with you. I hated lying to you, Poppy. I hated that I was capable of planning to take you—to use you—without ever knowing you. That I even have that capability inside me. I can feel shame for that, but if given the chance to do it again, I would do it exactly the same."

Casteel's gaze flickered over my face. "I wasn't lying earlier when I said I didn't plan for any of this to happen. It's not that I wasn't willing to use everything I had to gain your trust. If it took pretty words and kisses and my body, I would've used them all. I would have done anything to free Malik."

But he wouldn't.

He *didn't*.

"That's what the night in the Red Pearl was about. When you asked me why I would kiss you? Why I stayed in the room with you? It was because I knew I could use that to my advantage. I feel shame for that, but I wouldn't have done anything differently." He let his head fall back against the pillows, his gaze never leaving mine. "But I didn't...I didn't plan on actually enjoying your company. I didn't plan on coming to look forward to talking to you. And I didn't plan on the guilt that came with my actions. I didn't plan on...well, I didn't plan on caring about you."

My breath snagged in my chest as a tremble coursed through me.

"I planned on taking you the night of the Rite. When I led you out to the garden. To the willow. Kieran and the others were waiting for us. I was going to take you then, while everyone else was busy, and before you even had an idea of what was happening."

"But you didn't."

"If I had, you never would've witnessed Vikter's death. You wouldn't have seen any of that. Honest to gods, Poppy, I had no idea they were going to attack—"

"I know. I believe you." And I did. His shoulders loosened. "Why didn't you take me?"

"I don't know." His brows knitted. "No. That's a lie. I didn't take you then because I knew the moment I did, you would stop looking at me like...like I was just Hawke. You would stop opening up to me. Talking to me. Seeing me. You'd hate me. I wasn't ready for that."

I wasn't ready for him to admit that.

He swallowed as his gaze lifted to the bed's canopy. "When I touched you in the Blood Forest, I knew I shouldn't have, but I...I wanted to be your first. I needed to be your first everything. Kiss. Touch. Pleasure."

Oh, gods...

His jaw worked as he slowly shook his head. "Kieran...fuck, I thought he might actually punch me when he realized what I'd done. But he knew and..." Casteel cleared his throat. "The night in New Haven, when I came to your room, I didn't plan that. I wanted it. Gods, did I ever. It was all I could think about it seemed, and damn if that wasn't a fucking difference, but I didn't plan to do that with you when you had no idea who I was."

Pressure clamped down on my chest. "That's why you didn't want me to call you Hawke that night. I thought it was because that wasn't technically your name."

"It's because you didn't know who that name was attached to." He dragged his teeth across his lip. "I should've walked out of that room. If I were a better man, I would've. I feel shame for that, but gods, I don't regret it. How terrible is that?"

"I..." My throat sealed, and it took a bit for me to unclog it. "I hated that you weren't honest with me then, but I don't regret it. I never did."

His gaze swung to mine. "Don't say stuff like that."

"Why?"

"Because it makes me want to strip you naked and sink so deep in you that neither of us will know where we start and end." His eyes flared an intense gold. "And then we'd never finish this conversation."

"Oh," I whispered, his words sending a heated wave through me. "Okay, then."

The smile returned, but it was quick to disappear. "What I said that night still holds true. I'm not worthy of you. I knew that then. I know that still. But that hasn't stopped me from wanting you. That hasn't stopped me from concocting a plan where I can have you, if only until this is over. It didn't stop me from wanting everything from you. From pretending that I could have everything, Poppy."

I wasn't sure if I was even breathing.

"And I know you're probably still angry with me about wanting to leave, wanting you to go with Kieran, but I..." He closed his eyes. "After what was done to me and everything that happened afterward, I didn't think I was capable of truly wanting or needing someone like I do you. I didn't believe it was possible. And there have been so many times, *too* many times, that I've wanted this to be real."

"What part did you want to be real?"

"All of it. That I had accepted my brother's fate. That I was bringing home my wife, and that...there was this future I no longer believed I would have. That was all I could think about earlier. The idea of you being here when they came. I felt the fear already. When that bastard Ascended took you at New Haven? I thought I'd lost you." He swallowed again. "And I know too much has happened for any of that to be real. I know I've hurt you. I know when you said you carried the guilt for my actions, you weren't lying. And I'm...gods, Poppy, I'm sorry. You don't deserve that. You don't deserve everything that I've laid at your feet, and you sure as hell don't deserve the fact that I'm still trying to hold onto you. That when it comes time for you to leave, I'm still going to want you. Even when you inevitably do leave, I'll still want you."

He would've let you go, but I doubt you would've been free of him.

Isn't that what Kieran had said?

"I don't know what any of that means. I've long since stopped trying to figure it out." His lashes lowered, shielding his gaze. "Can you tell me? Can you read me and tell me?"

In that moment, I couldn't concentrate enough to read a book, but I knew what I needed from him. "Tell me about her."

Casteel's gaze met mine, and he looked...fractured as he looked away, returning to stare at his hands. He was silent for so long that I didn't think he would speak. That he wouldn't say anything, but then he answered.

"We...we grew up together—Shea and me. Our families were close, obviously, and we were friends at first. Somehow, at some point, it became something more. I don't even know how or when, but I loved her. At least, I think that's what I felt. She was brave and smart. Wild. I thought I would spend my entire life with her, and then I got myself captured, and she came for me."

My heart sank and plummeted even further when he moved suddenly, rising from the bed.

"I don't even know how many times she and Malik came for me. It had to be dozens, and you see, they never gave up on me. They believed I was alive. All those years, they kept searching for me." He thrust a hand through his hair. "And then they found me. I barely recognized them when they appeared in front of my cell. I thought I was hallucinating—imagining that my brother and Shea were there, all but carrying me out of the dungeon into the tunnels. I was in bad shape. Hadn't fed in a while. Weak. Disoriented. I don't even know exactly when the two Ascended appeared, but they were suddenly there as if they'd be waiting for us. They had been."

I scooted to the edge of the bed as he walked over to the terrace doors. "What do you mean?"

"I mean they knew I was going to be freed that day. They knew that my brother—the true heir—was coming. An Atlantian older and stronger than me, and he was going to be within their reach."

Understanding started to creep in, and I didn't want it to be true. Oh, gods, I didn't.

"There was a fight, and all I remember was Shea pulling me away—tugging me away from Malik, taking me through this maze of tunnels." He exhaled roughly. "All she kept saying was that she was sorry. That she had no choice."

I lifted my hands to my mouth, almost wishing he wouldn't continue.

"One of the Ascended came after us, cornered us, and he...he told me everything. Taunted me with it. Shea had been caught when she and Malik had split up while looking for me. The Ascended were going to kill her, and she told them who she was with. She gave up my brother in exchange for her life."

"Oh, gods," I whispered, heart cracking as his pain reached out to me, mingling with my own.

"They thought she was going to leave me behind. That's why they agreed. A two for one special." He laughed, but it was harsh. "They weren't prepared for Malik to put up such a fight. That was how Shea got me out. I didn't believe the Ascended. I tried to protect her, and then she tried to barter again. My life for hers. And I...once it seeped through the haze, through the hunger, that she was the reason they had my brother instead of me, and that she would hand me over to them again, I lost it. I killed the Ascended. I killed her. With my bare hands. I don't even know if it was panic that drove her actions. It had to be. She wasn't a bad person, but it couldn't have been love."

"No, it couldn't have been," I said. "I know I don't have experience, but if you love someone, you could never do that to them. I'm sorry to even say that. I didn't know her, but I just know you could never do that to someone you love."

"No. You couldn't. I know that." His head bowed. "I think she did love me at some point. Why else would she continue searching for me? Or maybe she felt that was what was expected of her. I don't know. But I would've chosen death if that meant saving the one I loved." He dragged a hand over his face as he kept his back to me. "I tried to find Malik after...after that, but couldn't find my way through the tunnels. I fucking stumbled out onto the beach at some point, and by the luck of the gods, a man found me."

He lowered his hand. "So, that's why I don't talk about her. That's why I don't speak her name, because as much as I once loved her, I hate her now. And I hate what I did."

I shuddered, unable to find words—because there were none.

"Alastir doesn't know." He turned to me then. "Only Kieran and my brother know the truth. Alastir can never know that his daughter betrayed Malik—our kingdom. It's not that I'm trying to protect myself. I can deal with him learning that she died by my hands, but it would kill him to learn the truth of what she did."

"I won't ever say anything," I promised. "I don't know how you've kept that to yourself. It has to..." I trailed off, letting out a ragged breath. "It has to eat you up inside."

"I rather it do that than let the truth destroy a man who has been nothing but loyal to our kingdom and people." He leaned against the wall, eyes closing again. "And Shea? I don't know if it's right or wrong that people believe she died a hero. I don't care if it's wrong."

I stared at him, seeing what I never thought existed under any of the masks he wore. His body had been tortured as well as his soul. "I wish I knew what to say. I wish you never had to do that after everything else you'd been through. I hate that you feel guilt, and I know you do. She betrayed you. She betrayed herself. And I'm sorry."

Casteel opened his mouth.

"I know you don't want my sympathies, but you have them, nonetheless. That doesn't mean I pity you. It's just that..." I stopped searching his emotions then. "I understand why you never wanted to speak of her."

And I understood now why Kieran advised me to never go down that road.

Casteel nodded as he turned back to the terrace doors.

There was something I didn't understand. "Gianna is Alastir's great-niece and the marriage to her was his idea?" When he nodded, I said, "And he was okay with you marrying his niece when you were once with his daughter?"

"He was."

I wrinkled my nose. "Maybe it's just me, but that would weird me out. Granted, I don't live for hundreds of years or—"

"It was one of the reasons I could never agree to that union," he said. "And it's not Gianna's fault. She's a good person. You'd like her."

I wasn't sure about that.

"But she...she looks like Shea. Not exactly, but the resemblance is there, and it was weird, even to me. But even if she looked nothing like her, I never thought of her in that way."

Unsure of how to feel about the knowledge that this Gianna actually looked like Shea—a woman Casteel had once loved and was betrayed by, I thought it over. After a few moments, I realized that none of that with Gianna and Alastir actually mattered. It was just...background noise. What mattered was us.

"I know why you sent Kieran to Atlantia," I told him. "You wanted to make sure he didn't risk his life to save yours."

He was quiet for a moment. "It's not the only reason. Alastir will call for our forces and then he will go straight to my father and mother—tell them that I plan to marry, and he'll express his doubts. That's the last thing anyone needs."

That was what Casteel had meant when he spoke to Kieran—what had caused the wolven to relent.

Knowing how much it had cost him to talk about Shea and now knowing what he carried with him, it made what I said next easier than expected. "I was telling the truth last night at dinner."

Chapter 36

Slowly, Casteel turned to me.

"It was the truth when I said you were the first thing I'd ever truly chosen for myself. It's also true that I chose you when you were just Hawke, and it's not just because you were the first person to ever really see me. That had something to do with it, of course, but if I wanted to experience pretty words or pleasure, I could've donned the mask once more and went back to the Red Pearl. I…I wanted you." My cheeks heated, but I continued. "It was true that I had already begun to suspect the Ascended, and whether I could be the Maiden. And I chose you because you made me feel like I was *someone*, that I was a person and not merely an object. You saw me and accepted me, but what you don't know is that the night I asked you to stay with me, I had already left behind the veil. I'd made my choice. I wanted to find a way to be with you even though I had no idea if you wanted that. And if you didn't, it would've…it would've hurt, but I was no longer the Maiden. I fell for you when you were Hawke, and I kept falling for you when you became Casteel."

His eyes widened.

"And I couldn't understand how I kept falling for you. I was so angry with you—with myself for not seeing the truth. And it felt like a betrayal to Vikter and Rylan, the others. And myself."

His chest rose with a heavy breath. "And you still feel that way? Like it's a betrayal to keep falling for me?" He took a step and then another toward me before stopping. "If so, I understand, Poppy. Some things can't—"

"Some things can't be forgotten or forgiven," I said, rubbing my damp hands over my knees. "But I think I realized, or have come to accept, that even then, some things can't be changed or stopped. That they still matter but don't. That those emotions are powerful, but not as strong as others. That what I felt for you had nothing to do with what you did or didn't do. It had nothing to do with Vikter or anyone else. And acknowledging that felt like permission to...to feel. And that scared me."

I placed my hand against my chest. "It still terrifies me because I have never felt this way about anyone, and I know...I know it has nothing to do with you being my first or there being, well, limited options in my life. It's you. It's me. It's us. What I feel? Like how I want to take your pain away and yet throttle you at the same moment? How your stupid dimples are infuriating, but I look for them every time you smile because I know that's a real smile. I don't know why I look forward to arguing with you, but I do. You're clever, and you are kinder than even you realize—even though I know you have earned the title of the Dark One. You are a puzzle I want to figure out, but at the same time, don't. And when I realized you have so many masks—so many layers, I kept wanting to peel them back, even though I fear it will only hurt more in the end."

I shook my head as I curled my fingers around the collar of my tunic. "I don't understand any of this. Like how do I want to stab you and kiss you at the same time? And I know you said that I deserve to be with someone who didn't kidnap me, or someone I don't want to stab—"

"Forget I said that," he said, closer to me when I looked up. "I have no idea what I was talking about. Maybe I didn't even say that."

My lips twitched. "You totally said that."

"You're right. I did. Forget it." His eyes searched mine. "Tell me why this terrifies you. Please?"

My breath snagged. "Because you...you could break my heart again. And what we're doing? It's bigger than us, and even your brother. You have to know that. We could actually change things. Not just for your people, but also for the people of Solis."

"I know that," he whispered, his chest rising and falling rapidly, his eyes luminous.

"And things are already complicated and messy, and acknowledging what I want—what I feel—just makes it all the more complicated and scary. Because this time…" Tears burned the back of my throat. "This time, I don't know how I will get over that. I know that probably makes me sound weak and immature or whatever, but it's just something I know."

"It's not weak." Casteel came forward, but he didn't stand there. He didn't sit beside me. He lowered himself to his knees in front of me. "Your heart, Poppy? It is a gift I do not deserve." He placed his hands on my knees as he lifted his gaze to mine. "But it is one I will protect until my dying breath. I don't know what that means." He stopped, curling his fingers into the leggings, into my skin. "Okay. Fuck. I do know what that means. It's why I'm in awe of everything you say or do—everything you are. It's why you're the first thing I think about when I wake and the last thought I have when I fall asleep, replacing everything else. It's why when I'm with you, I can be quiet. I can just *be*. You know what that means."

He took one of my hands and pressed it to his chest—his heart. "Tell me what that means. Please."

Please.

Twice in one conversation he'd said that, a word that didn't pass his lips often. And how could I refuse?

I didn't just focus on him to get what I was now learning was a cursory reading of his emotions. I opened myself, forming the invisible tether to him and what he felt. It came back to me in a rush, and it was shocking.

Not the heavy and thick-like-cream feel of concern. He worried—about what was going to happen to his brother, his kingdom, to me. It wasn't the cool splash of surprise that made me think he didn't quite believe this conversation. The tangy, almost bitter taste of sadness was minimal, and the only time his agony hadn't been raw and nearly overpowering was when I'd taken his pain from him. That surprised me, yes, but what shocked me more was the sweetness on the tip of my tongue.

"Do you feel that?" he asked. "What does it feel like?"

"Like…it reminds me of chocolate and berries." I blinked back tears. "Berries—strawberries? I've felt that from Vikter—

from Ian and my parents. But I've never felt it like this—like it's more decadent somehow."

And I thought I knew what it was. It was the emotion behind the long looks and the seeking touches. The feeling behind the way his arm always tightened around me when we rode together and why he was always messing with my hair. It was the emotion that drove him to draw that line he wouldn't cross with me. It was why he wouldn't use compulsion, and it was what allowed him to want to protect me but demanded that he allow me to protect myself. It was how when he was with me, he didn't think of his kingdom, his brother, or the time he'd been a captive.

And it was one of many things forbidden to me as the Maiden.

It was *love*.

"Don't cry." He lifted my hand to his mouth and kissed the center of my palm.

"I'm not crying. I'm not sad," I told him, and he grinned. The stupid dimple in his right cheek appeared. "I hate that stupid dimple."

"You know what I think?" He kissed the tip of my finger.

"I don't care."

The dimple in his left cheek appeared. "I think you feel the exact opposite when it comes to my stupid dimples."

He was right, and I shuddered.

Casteel let go of my hands and stretched up, cupping my cheeks. He leaned in, pressing his forehead to mine, and I swore I felt his hands tremble. "*Always*," he whispered in the breath we shared. "Your heart *was* always safe with me. It always will be. There is *nothing* I will protect more fiercely or with more devotion, Poppy. Trust in that—in what you feel from me. In me."

Trust.

As Casteel, he'd never asked me to trust him. He knew how fragile that was. One crack could bring it all down.

But I knew what I felt.

I nodded. "I don't want to pretend anymore."

"Neither do I."

"I...I don't know what that means for us," I whispered. "Your people and your parents...they don't trust me. You're basically the closest thing to immortal there is, and I'm...my lifespan is a blink. What do we do now?"

"We don't worry about my people or my parents or our lifespans. Not right now. Not even later. We take this day by day. This is new to you, and in a way, it's new to me. Let's make a deal."

"You and your deals."

His lips curved into a smile against mine. "Let's make a deal that we don't borrow tomorrow's problems today."

Tomorrow always came soon enough, but I nodded. Because in the same breath, tomorrow wasn't today's problem. "I can agree to that."

"Good." He drew back, and I thought there was a sheen to his eyes. "If we're going to do this, for real, then I feel like I need to make amends. And I know the list of things I should apologize for is long, but I think I should start with this." He moved then, rising so he was on one knee before me.

My heart hadn't stopped racing and swelling from the moment we started to really talk. But now, it beat so fast, I didn't know how I didn't pass out. He took my hand, and I wondered if he could feel it trembling.

He could.

Casteel folded both hands around mine, steadying my hand. "Penellaphe Balfour?" He stared up at me, and there was no teasing glint to his eyes, no smirk to his lips. No mask. Just him. Casteel Hawkethrone Da'Neer. "Will you do me the honor of allowing me to one day become worthy of you? Will you marry me? Today?"

"Yes. I will give you the honor of becoming my husband, because you're already worthy of me."

Casteel's eyes closed as he shuddered.

"I will marry you." I dipped down, kissing his forehead. "Today."

It was like nothing and everything changed after I accepted Casteel's proposal.

I stood in the bathing chamber, skin mostly dry as I tied the sash on the robe. A pink flush stained my cheeks, and there was a near feverish brightness to my eyes.

It was strange, the nervous flutter in my chest and stomach. Marrying Casteel wasn't something new, but it was real now, and that changed everything.

What was also strange was the unexpected feeling of lightness, as if a tremendous, suffocating weight had been lifted from me. I hadn't expected that. I'd thought more guilt would settle on me after admitting what I felt to Casteel. Instead, the guilt and the feeling that I was betraying others and myself had left me.

As I dragged the brush through my drying hair, I realized the guilt had actually left me in the cavern. I just hadn't realized it.

And even though a lot of unknown still faced us—the encroaching Ascended and what felt like the first act in a war that hadn't been decreed yet. How Casteel's parents would respond to the news of his marriage, and if his people would ever accept me. His brother and mine, and the whole biological differences between us that would one day become an issue, gods willing, when I aged and he barely showed signs of the passing decades—I was going to do exactly what Casteel had said.

We wouldn't borrow from tomorrow's problems. Or even the problems we could very well face in a handful of hours. Because I was about to marry the man I'd fallen in love with.

The man I *knew* felt the same, even if he hadn't spoken the words.

I was happy.

I was scared.

I was hopeful.

I was excited.

And all of those emotions were real.

A knock on the main door drew me from the bathroom. I opened it to find Vonetta waiting, a splash of red draped over one arm and holding a small pouch in the other.

"I hear there's going to be a wedding today," Vonetta announced as she swept into the room. "One that Kieran is going to be so irritated he's not here for."

"I sort of, kind of, wish he was too. Not that I'll ever admit that to him," I said, and she laughed. Closing the door, I followed her into the bedroom. "It doesn't seem right that he's not here when Casteel marries."

"It does feel weird, but I'm relieved. Not that he's missing the wedding." She looked over her shoulder at me as she laid what turned out to be a gown across the chaise. "But because he won't be here *later*."

"I know."

"Casteel is...he has a good heart. What he did by sending Kieran away? They're bonded, and I...I don't know if anyone else would've done that."

"He does have a good heart," I agreed, feeling my cheeks flush. Vocally complimenting Casteel wasn't something I did often.

A smile appeared as she turned back to the gown, straightening the skirt. "Anyway, Kieran is probably glad he's not here for the actual ceremony part."

My heart skipped a beat. I knew very little about an Atlantian wedding ceremony. The ones in Solis sometimes lasted days. The bride would cut her hair, and there was bathing in water anointed by the Priestesses and Priests. There were no vows, but many feasts. A particular part always came to mind when I thought of the Atlantians. "Can I ask you something?"

"Ask away." Vonetta faced me.

"I learned about the Joining a few days ago." I fiddled with the sash on my robe. "Casteel said it's not something that's done often, but is it something the wolven would expect? Or the Atlantians?"

"It really depends on the parties involved. Sometimes, the blood exchange is done, and other times it's not. But the choice to do so gives the impression of there being a stronger...well, for lack of a better word, *bond*." She shrugged, and I couldn't help but notice that she didn't appear weirded out, nor did she speak about it as if it were something sexual or shameful. "It doesn't always happen at the wedding. I've known it to occur before and after."

I nodded.

"But I don't think anyone expects you to do that," she added quickly.

My brows pinched. "Why?"

She studied me for a moment and then said, "You're not full-blooded Atlantian. There's never been a Joining with one who has mortal blood."

"Because it extends the life of the mortal?" I asked.

"I imagine that has something to do with it. And it's not often a bonded Atlantian of an elemental line marries one with mortal blood. It's not forbidden like the act of Ascending is," she said, referencing the making of a vampry. "It simply hasn't been done."

I didn't know what to think of that. If the Joining extended my lifespan, that could resolve at least one of tomorrow's problems, but I wasn't sure how I felt about tying my life to another's or even the idea of living that long.

"Anyway, Casteel stopped by when he was looking for my father and asked if I had anything that would be deserving of a Princess to wear to her wedding. I told him no. That all I owned was deserving of a Queen," she replied, and I grinned at that. "Brides in Atlantia typically wear a veil of red or yellow to ward off evil spirits and bad blessings, but he mentioned that the veil would be a no-go."

Gods…

That was incredibly thoughtful.

"So I thought the red gown would be perfect. And it should fit, with the exception of being a bit on the long side, so just don't run around in it."

"I'll try not to."

She picked it up, handing it to me. "Underneath is a red slip. Just basic. You should get changed. I have a feeling they'll be here soon."

The flutter in my chest increased until it felt like a nest of a dozen birds had taken flight while Vonetta went into the living room. I quickly dressed, donning the silky slip that barely reached my thighs and then stepped into the loosely draped gown of silk and chiffon. Gathered at the waist and form-fitting through the bust, it reminded me of the gown I'd worn the night of the Rite. The skirt of the dress was sheer to the thigh, forming two gauzy panels, and delicate golden thread was woven throughout the entire dress, stitched to form delicate vines. The neckline was looser than the rest of the bodice and the straps were fitted so they lay just off the shoulders. There was no hiding the scars in this kind of dress, but I...I was done hiding them anyway.

"The gown is beautiful," I called out. A moment later, Vonetta returned.

She smiled when she saw me. "Definitely no running, though."

I looked down to where the dress formed a crimson puddle against the tile. "Definitely not."

"Come. Sit. Let me see if I can do something with your hair," she said, tossing the pouch. "Just hold onto this."

Catching the pouch, I found it surprisingly weighty. I sat on the chaise, wondering what was in it while Vonetta retrieved the brush and an army of pins from the bathing chamber.

"I thought I had a lot of hair," she said, gathering the sides of my hair. "But damn, you almost have me beat."

Running my fingers over the velvety pouch, I thought of Tawny. "A friend of mine would sometimes help me braid it. Not braids like yours, but a couple that she would then twist into a knot so my hair wouldn't be visible under the veil."

"Your friend? Is she back in Solis?" she asked after a couple of moments.

"Yes. Her name is Tawny. You would like her, and she would love you. She's a second daughter—meaning she is destined to Ascend," I explained as she twisted and plaited the sides of my mostly dry hair. "She has no idea what the Ascended are truly like, and I have no idea if she'll Ascend now with me being gone."

"Kieran and Casteel once told me that a lot of the people of Solis are innocent—that they are unaware of what the Ascended really are. I used to find that hard to believe," she admitted as she gathered the braided sides and began to twist them into a knot at the back of my head. "But the more Descenters I met, the more I learned that the Ascended are masters at hiding the truth."

"They are." I swallowed as I stared at where the curtains were secured to the posts and swayed slightly in the breeze from the open doors. My mind disobeyed me. I thought of tonight, and the possibility that the first group of Ascended may reach Spessa's End. "I hate what's about to happen," I blurted out.

Her fingers stilled. "The wedding?"

"No. Gods. I'm actually looking forward to that," I said, letting out a little laugh.

"You sound like that surprises you."

"It does," I admitted softly. "I was thinking about the Ascended. What they may do when they reach here. I...I hate that I'm the reason everything you all built here is now at risk."

"We were always at risk," Vonetta said. "Sooner or later, we would've been discovered, and there would be a fight. We all knew that when we agreed to come here."

But like with New Haven, I was the catalyst that made things happen sooner, before they were ready.

"I imagine most brides don't think of sieges on the night of their weddings."

"But you're not most brides, are you?"

Gods, she had no idea how true that was.

"You're about to marry the handsome, albeit annoying as hell, Prince of Atlantia, Penellaphe." Her warm hands brushed my shoulders as she gathered up the rest of my hair, letting it lay against my back. "And from what I've learned about you from my brother and Casteel, the Ascended have already stolen a lot of joy from you. Don't let them steal this."

I drew in a deep breath and nodded. "I won't."

"Good. Can you open the pouch?" she asked. "And hand me what's in it."

Looking down, I unraveled the string and reached inside. My lips parted as I pulled out several strands of diamonds.

"Pretty, isn't it? It's not the nicest of necklaces, but I like its simplicity."

"This is simple?" I stared at the bright diamonds strung

across three layers of chains. There had to be at least half a dozen diamonds per chain.

"Compared to the standard in Atlantia? Yes."

I thought of the diamond Casteel had promised, and my eyes widened.

"Diamonds are also a tradition here." Vonetta took the necklace from me, and I lifted the hair that she had left down. "They are the joyous tears of the gods given form," she explained, securing the clasp. "Wearing them means the gods are with you even as they slumber. Did they have such a tradition in Solis?"

I shook my head as I fixed the strands. "Diamonds only represent wealth in Solis. Those who had the means would hold celebrations that lasted days. I've never been to one, but from what I know, the Ascended took center stage during the weddings. Not the gods. I can't even imagine a wedding that takes days to complete. Are they like that in Atlantia?"

"They could typically last a few hours, which is why Kieran would be glad to be missing that part." She walked around the chaise. "But with my father officiating the wedding, I doubt it will last more than a few minutes."

"Oh, thank the gods," I exclaimed as I stood. "I'm sorry. Days or hours is just…it's too long."

Vonetta laughed as I roamed into the bathing chamber. "You may luck out with the ceremony, but I imagine that once you reach Evaemon, the King and Queen will demand a celebration in your honor and to introduce you to your subjects. That will last days."

My subjects. Days-long celebrations.

I couldn't think of that as I looked at my reflection. The three rows of diamonds glittered in the soft lamplight. The dress and my hair—all of it was beautiful, and it was more than I expected or hoped for…or even what I knew I needed.

I spun toward her. "Thank you for this—for all of this. It means a lot, Vonetta."

"It's not a big deal, but you're welcome."

It was a big deal to look and feel like a bride when it was real. "Will you be at the wedding?" I asked and then laughed. "I don't even know where the wedding will be held."

"I can be if you'd like. And if you call me Netta. That's what my friends call me, and since I'm attending your wedding, I imagine we're friends."

I smiled as I nodded. "As long as you call me Poppy. That's what *my* friends call *me*."

"That I can do. By the way, the wedding will be here. Outside, actually. They are always outside, no matter the weather, and you won't wear shoes."

"Because both need to be standing on Atlantian soil?" I surmised.

"Correct." She brushed several braids over her shoulder. "And it's time. They're here."

"Wolven senses must be amazing," I said as my heart started to pound once more.

She grinned. "They are, but I saw my father walk past the window."

"Oh." I laughed. "Well, then."

"You ready?"

Nodding. I started to follow her out but then stopped. "One second."

Hurrying to the bed, I picked up the wolven dagger and secured it around my thigh.

"Planning to stab him during the ceremony?" Vonetta asked.

"Why does everyone act like I'm seconds away from stabbing Casteel?" I demanded.

"Apparently, you have a habit of it."

"I only stabbed him…a few times." I turned, fixing the skirt of the gown. "The dagger was given to me by someone I care about. He was like a father to me, and in a way, he'll be with me when I do something he never thought I'd be able to do."

Something I knew Vikter would've been happy to see, even though I was marrying the Prince of Atlantia. In my heart of hearts, I knew that all that would have mattered to Vikter was that I wanted this and that I was cherished.

And I knew both were true. They had been true for longer than I realized.

Chapter 37

The sun was high above our heads, the breeze pleasant, and the sandy dirt and grass warm under my bare feet as I walked willingly toward him.

Hawke.

The Dark One.

Prince Casteel Da'Neer.

Other people waited outside in the courtyard. Jasper was there. Naill and Delano stood behind Casteel, to his left. Guardians were on the Rise, keeping watch, and Vonetta was behind me. But all I saw was Casteel.

He cut a striking figure in all black, possessing the wild and primal beauty that always reminded me of the cave cat I'd once seen. He stood barefoot in the soil reclaimed by Atlantia. And I didn't think he saw anyone else as I walked forward. He stared at me with eyes luminous even in the sunlight, and an almost startled look etched upon his features as if he were utterly caught off guard. I'd seen that look before, especially when I smiled or laughed. He too seemed unaware of anyone else, even as Vonetta walked ahead and spoke to him. He stared, even as he reached into his pocket and handed her something. And when I let my senses reach him, I felt what I always did from him, except the tartness of conflict was gone, and the chocolate and berries taste was far stronger.

I couldn't take my eyes off him, not until Vonetta returned to my side and pressed something warm and metallic against my palm.

"The ring. For Casteel," she whispered. "He had the blacksmith make them."

I looked down at the gleaming, golden band. There was some sort of inscription on the inside, but I couldn't make out what it was.

Curling my fingers around the band, I didn't remember how I got there, but suddenly, I was standing in front of Casteel. He stared at me like I imagined one would if they saw a god standing before them.

"You look…" Casteel cleared his throat as the shadows of clouds drifted over the courtyard. "You look beautiful, Poppy. Absolutely…" His gaze roamed over me, from the braids in my hair, to the diamonds at my neck and then down the fitted bodice to the sheer layers of the skirt that rippled in the wind. A slow grin spread across his lips. The dimple in his right cheek appeared, and then the left. He dipped his head, his lips brushing against the shell of my ear as he spoke. "Am I seeing things, or is that your dagger strapped to your thigh?"

I grinned. "You're not seeing things."

"You're an absolutely stunning, murderous little creature," he murmured.

"There'll be time for all the sweet whispers later," Jasper said, and when Casteel pulled back, there was a fire in his eyes. "You do look quite lovely, Penellaphe."

"Thank you," I said.

"What about me?" Casteel asked, and behind him, Naill sighed.

"You look passable."

"That was rude," he replied.

"Would you like to go sit in the shade and nurse your wounded feelings? Like you did when you were young and inevitably injured yourself doing something incredibly stupid?"

Casteel's brows lowered as he looked over at Jasper. "This marriage ceremony is starting off in a really weird way."

"True." The wolven chuckled. "Let's get this started,

because I'm sure you're more eager to finish the ceremony than you are to start it."

Casteel shot the wolven a dark look, and I wondered exactly what that meant.

"I need both of you to face me," Jasper instructed, and then he waited until we did just that. He smiled at me, and my emotions were too scattered to read his, but there was fondness in his gaze. "I don't know how much you know about Atlantian marriages or how they differ from what is done in Solis, but I'll walk you through it, okay?"

"Okay," I whispered.

"Good. It's pretty simple. There are no vows. None that are spoken, anyway," he continued as the clouds overhead cast us in shadows. He briefly glanced up at the sky, raising a brow. "Each of you holds your rings in your left hands and joins your right together."

Casteel held his right hand palm up as I looked over at him. There was no smile on his face then. Just a certain intent to the set of his lips and in his gaze. Pulse pounding, I placed my right hand in his. The jolt traveled up my arm, and based on the slight widening of his eyes, I knew he felt it, too.

"Lower to your knees. Casteel first," Jasper said, and he did just that. "Now you, Penellaphe."

Casteel's hand tightened on mine as I moved to my knees, our gazes remaining locked.

"Place your rings in the soil between you so that they overlap," Jasper said, and Casteel placed a golden band, one smaller than the one I held, on the sandy soil. I placed the larger one on top so the openings overlapped.

Casteel knew the next steps. He didn't look away from me as he picked up the dirt and sprinkled it over the rings. He nodded, and I did the same, feeling the grainy dirt sift between my fingers as I repeated his actions.

Thick clouds gathered above us as Casteel whispered, "This next part may hurt, but only for a few moments."

Trusting him, I nodded.

"Lift your left hands, palms up." Jasper knelt before us, and with a brief glance, I saw that he held a dagger—one I'd never seen before. Like the swords the Guardians carried, the blade was gold. "I will make a cut in each of your palms. It will hurt for a moment, and you will do with your blood what you did with the soil. The wound will heal at once, but you both will carry the mark until the union is ended by death or decree."

I wasn't sure how a wound of mine would heal immediately. "And that is all?"

"Usually, these proceedings are a bit more drawn-out, but this will be it. At least for the parts I'm involved in." A teasing glint filled Jasper's pale eyes. "Casteel will have to fill you in on the rest."

"I will." Casteel gave me a quick grin. "Gladly."

A shiver broke out over my skin as I lifted my left hand, palm up. Casteel did the same as he leaned over, crossing the distance between us. His lips brushed mine as he said, "Just a moment of pain."

"I know," I whispered. "I trust you."

I heard the breath Casteel took, and I knew what that meant for me to say that, for him to hear it.

"Unworthy," he whispered, and then he kissed me at the exact moment I felt the sharp sting of Jasper's dagger against my palm. The kiss was as brief as the pain, but so much sweeter.

Casteel withdrew, pressing our hands together, palm to palm. He threaded his fingers through mine as he guided our joined hands to the rings. Air hitched in my throat as I watched my blood—*our* blood—slide down our palms, to our wrists. A drop and then two fell, splashing the rings.

Jasper was quiet as Casteel eased his hand from mine. He picked up the smaller ring, his right hand still clasping mine. "I'll put the ring on you, and then you'll put the other ring on me."

I nodded.

"Turn your palm up to the sky," he said quietly. When I turned my hand over, my eyes widened.

The cut had closed, but across the center of my palm was a thin swirl of vibrant gold that shimmered even with the sunlight obscured by clouds. "How…?"

Casteel grinned at me. "Magic."

It had to be that.

My hand was surprisingly steady as he slipped the dirt-and blood-streaked ring over my pointer finger. It was a little loose, but I didn't believe it would slip off.

"Your turn."

I picked up his and held my breath as I fitted it over his finger.

And then I watched in stunned silence as the dirt and blood seeped into the rings. The bands flared an intense gold and then faded, their surfaces now pristine.

"It is done," Jasper said, rising. "You are husband and wife."

The day turned to night.

My lips parted as I looked up. The gathering clouds had turned the sky the black of midnight, from the east to the west, to the south and north. Not a single trace of sunlight could be seen, even though it couldn't be more than an hour or two past noon.

"My gods," Vonetta whispered.

Casteel rose swiftly, bringing me with him. He pulled me to his side as he stared up at the black sky.

"Is this an omen?" I asked.

"It is," Jasper confirmed, his voice rough. "I haven't seen anything like this since...Gods, since your mother and father married. And even then, Casteel, it wasn't like *this*."

Casteel lowered his gaze to the wolven.

"This is an omen. A powerful one." Jasper shook his head in wonder. "A good one from the King of Gods." The unnatural clouds started to scatter, and sunlight broke through as Jasper smiled. "Nyktos, even asleep, approves of this union."

The gold band glimmered in the sunlight cascading through the windows of our bedchamber. Slowly, I turned my hand over. The swirl of shimmering gold followed the line closest to my fingers. I dragged my thumb over the curling line. The heavy dusting of gold didn't disappear, and I...I couldn't believe I was married.

That I'd gone from being Penellaphe Balfour, to the Maiden, and now, Penellaphe Da'Neer.

"I hope you're not already having second thoughts. But if so, it's not going to rub off."

My head jerked up as Casteel strode out from the bathing chamber. "I'm not trying to rub it off." I watched him walk around the bed, my heart already tripping in my chest. "And I'm not having second thoughts. I just don't understand how this is possible—the gold on my hand. How the blood and dirt just...sank into the rings and disappeared."

"When I said it was magic, I was only half teasing." He sat beside me, taking my hand. The contact sent a jolt of awareness through me. "It's the gods. Their magic." He ran his finger along the mark. "And this is like a tattoo but goes deeper than ink. All married Atlantians have this imprint until their marriage ends."

"Through death or decree?"

Dark waves tumbled over his forehead as he nodded. "The mark will then disappear."

That would be a terrible way to discover that someone died. I shivered.

Casteel's gaze lifted to mine. "Did you not believe in the gods at all?"

I started to say yes, that I did, but it was more complicated than that. "I believed what I'd been taught about the gods by the Ascended. The only magic was the Blessing. Other than that, they were like...silent sentinels who watched over us, and that it was our duty to serve them through the Rite." I laughed— laughed at myself. "Now when I say that out loud, I recognize how ridiculous it sounds. How blind I'd been."

"It only sounds that way to someone taught differently from birth."

"We thought their magic was the Ascension. That the Ascended were proof of that power," I said as Casteel trailed his fingers to the ring around my pointer finger. I realized something. "It surprised me when you placed the ring on my pointer finger. In Solis, the ring is worn on the fourth finger, but the line the imprint is on is closest to the pointer finger."

"Clever girl," he murmured, brushing back the strands of

hair that had fallen over my shoulder. "The line in your palm is believed to be the one connected to your heart. That is why the imprint is made there."

"It's sort of beautiful," I admitted.

"It is," he said, and I could feel his gaze on me. My breath caught. "I don't know about you, but I'm feeling all kinds of special," he added as he skimmed his fingers over the back of my neck and then the delicate chains of the necklace. "It has been several hundred years since Nyktos has made his approval of a union known."

My pulse skipped. "Not since your parents."

"So I've heard. My father would boast about it. Tell any who listened that the day turned to night when the ceremony was completed. I don't think Malik or I believed him, but he wasn't lying."

"And Nyktos hasn't done that for anyone since then?"

"Apparently, not. That is good news, Poppy."

"Unlike the Blood Forest tree that appeared in New Haven?"

"We don't know if that was good or bad," he replied. "We just know it was really weird."

I laughed, unable to help myself, and it felt good to do that. To not fight a laugh or a smile, and to be happy.

That look crossed Casteel's features again. The one he wore when I approached him before the ceremony. The one he wore every time he heard me laugh or smile. "Why?" Curiosity filled me. "Why do you look like that when I laugh? Or smile?"

"Because it's a beautiful sound and smile and you don't do it nearly enough." A slight flush crept across his cheeks as he looked at my hand. "And every time I hear it, it feels like I've heard it before—and I mean, like before I even met you. Like deja vu but different."

That made me think of what Kieran had shared. "What does heartmates mean?" I blurted out.

Casteel's gaze returned to mine. "How have you heard of heartmates but not the marriage imprint?"

"Well…" I drew out the word. "You see, you have this bonded wolven that often says very vague, mostly unhelpful things."

He laughed at that. "He does, doesn't he? He spoke to you about heartmates? When?"

"A few days ago." What felt like an eternity ago. "He said he thought we were heartmates, and I thought he was crazy. He didn't tell me what it meant other than something about it being more powerful than bloodlines and gods."

"That was vague." A smile played across his lips. It was a tired expression, but real. I saw a hint of both dimples. "Heartmates is…it's almost more of a legend than Nyktos giving his approval for a union. Not fable, but so rare that it has become myth." He toyed with a diamond teardrop as his lashes lowered. "It started at the beginning of recorded time, when one of the ancient deities fell so deeply in love with a mortal that he pleaded for the gods to bestow the gift of long life on the one he chose. They refused, even though he was one of their favorite children. And they refused each and every year, as the one he loved grew older, and he remained the same. Then, when his lover was old and gray, the body no longer able to support life, his lover left to join Rhain, where not even he could travel. Heartbroken, the deity did not eat or drink, and it didn't matter that the gods pleaded with him. Even Nyktos himself came to this land and begged him to live. He told him that he couldn't, not when a piece of his soul had left him when his lover died. It was a piece he would never get back, and without it, he had no will. Eventually, he became dust."

"That's…that's really sad."

"Some say all great love stories are."

"Some people are stupid."

He laughed again. "But I'm not finished. The gods realized their mistake. That they had underestimated the capacity for love—of two souls and two hearts that were somehow meant to be joined. They were heartmates. The gods knew they could not bring their child or his lover back, but when it happened again, with another of their children, an ancient daughter who'd had many lovers come and go throughout the years, they relented. When she came to them to ask that her mortal lover be given the gift of life, they agreed, but on two conditions. Both were presented with nearly impossible trials designed to prove their love. If they succeeded, the deity had to agree to be the source of her lover's life. Her lover would need to drink from her to remain by her side. Of course, she agreed, and they completed their trials. They would do anything for the other half of their souls and hearts."

My eyes widened as understanding swept through me. "Her lover was the first Atlantian."

He nodded. "Yes, the elemental line. It happened again and again throughout the centuries. An ancient deity would find their heartmate in a wolven, and they'd complete their trials to prove their love. Some believed that was how the changelings and other bloodlines began. Or, an Atlantian would find their heartmate in a mortal, therefore creating another line once the gods gifted them with life. That kind of love was rare—is still rare. When acknowledged by both, it's the type that means they would do anything for each other, even die. And heartmates have always been linked to those who have created something new or ushered in great change. It is said that King Malec and Isbeth were heartmates."

"But if they were heartmates, then why didn't the gods offer the trials and then grant her the same gift of life they did for the other heartmates?"

"If they had, then the first vampry wouldn't have been created, and the world...the world would be a vastly different place." Casteel followed the direction of my thoughts. "But creating life is complex and full of unknowns, even for the gods. They never foresaw Malec being inventive enough to drain Isbeth of her blood and replace it with his in his desperation to save her. But the problem was, they'd already gone to sleep by then and were too deep in their slumber to hear Malec's pleas."

"Gods," I whispered. "That is sort of tragic. I mean, his actions started...all of this. And yes, he was already married, but it's still tragic."

"It is."

"And the gods are still asleep, unable to offer the trials and grant those gifts now."

"But not too deep asleep to not be aware of what is

happening," he said. "Do you no longer think what Kieran said is so crazy?"

My heart flip-flopped. "I...I don't know. What about you?"

A smile full of secrets appeared. "I don't know either."

My eyes started to narrow, but then something occurred to me. "Wait. There's something I don't understand. Malec was a descendent of the ancient deities, right?"

"Right."

"Then how did he turn Isbeth into a vampry? The other deities—when their heartmates were given their blood, they weren't turned into vamprys."

"That's because the others were not drained of blood. They were given the gift of life by the gods," he explained. "The transformation is not the same."

"Sort of like one is sanctioned by the gods and the other isn't?"

"Sort of." He shifted closer, dropping his hand to rest on the bed beside my hip. His head lowered slightly, and I allowed myself to read him.

He was feeling a lot of things, one of them I rarely felt from him. It reminded me of what it felt like to sneak into the city Atheneum and find an interesting book, or when I watched the night-blooming roses open. Times when I was content. He was content. He was also wary, and I thought that was for what could come tonight. And he was...he was so very tired.

"You still haven't slept. You need to sleep." I started to reach for him, but stopped, unsure of myself. We were married now. More importantly, it was real—this was real, what we felt for each other. "The Ascended could be here tonight."

"I know." He lifted his head. "I will rest, but there is something else I want to do."

My chest got suddenly tight as my mind went in a completely inappropriate direction.

"We are married. It's official, except for the crowning, but there is another tradition."

My throat dried. "The Joining?"

He blinked once and then twice. "I'm trying very hard not to laugh."

"What? That is a tradition, right? I asked Vonetta about it—"

"Oh, my gods." He dragged his hand down his face.

"And she said—"

"It's not about that," he cut in. "It's about us. Just you and me, and the tradition of sharing ourselves with one another."

"Oh," I whispered, and now my mind was happily playing around in a very inappropriate place. "Like...sex?"

He stared at me. "I really enjoy the way your mind works, but that's not exactly what I was talking about."

"Well." My face heated. "This is awkward."

Casteel laughed as he cupped my cheek. "Don't feel awkward. I meant it when I said I love the way your mind works. But it's a tradition for a couple to share blood after a wedding. It's not required. Like I said, it's merely tradition, one meant to strengthen the bonds of marriage. Not doing it doesn't change anything—"

"But doing it changes what?"

"It...it's an act of trust." His hand slid from my face. "It's a pledge to share everything. It's mostly symbolic."

My heart was pounding again, and the bodice of the dress suddenly felt too tight. It was clear that this was something he wanted, even if it was only symbolic. Possibly even something he'd once envisioned himself doing with Shea before...well, *before*. I felt a surge of anger and pity for a woman who'd been dead for more years than I'd been alive, but it still took a lot for me to push those feelings aside.

"And I know the idea of drinking blood isn't exactly appetizing to you. So, I understand if you don't—"

"I do."

He leaned back, his eyes turning bright. "Is it because you want to or because I'm asking."

"How often have I done things you've wanted, but I haven't?"

He laughed. "Good point." The humor faded from his eyes, replaced by a devouring sort of intensity. "If you're sure. One hundred percent sure?"

"I am."

"Thank fuck." He started to reach for me but drew up short. "We need to take off that dress. Netta will have my ass if I return it to her wrinkled." His gaze lifted to mine. "And I have a feeling it's going to get very wrinkled."

So did I.

Pulse thrumming, I stood and reached for one strap. Casteel followed, taking hold of the other. "Are there buttons?"

I shook my head.

"Thank the gods again," he murmured as he dragged the strap free of my arm. "Because I would likely just give up and tear the thing."

"You usually have better patience than that." The dress gathered at my hips.

"Sometimes." Eyeing the slip, he helped me step out of the gown. "But not when it comes to you."

"I don't think that's true," I said as he started to toss the gown. I stopped him. "I'll take that."

His lips pursed as I laid the gown on the chaise. He waited for me at the corner of the bed. "I really have a thing for you and little ridiculous straps." He reached out, placing his hands on my ribs. He pulled the material taut against me. "And your breasts, but they are not ridiculous or little. Regardless, I have a thing for them, too."

"Thank you?" I said as he walked around me, sliding his hand across my stomach. He laughed, and the sound was part relief and part need. I didn't need my abilities to know that. I started to reach for the clasp on the necklace.

"Leave it." He glanced down. "And the dagger."

My brows raised. "Seriously?"

"When will you realize I speak the truth?" The tilt of his lips was wicked. "It turns me on when you're armed with something sharp."

"There's something so entirely wrong with you."

He came around to my front. "But you like what's wrong with me."

"There is something wrong with me, too." I looked up at him. "Because I do."

"I know." He touched my cheek. "I've always known you

like that I enjoy when you make me bleed."

Casteel kissed me and it felt like the first time our lips had ever touched. In a way, it was a first kiss, and Casteel and I had more than one first. With each truth, each change, it was like starting all over again but with all the experience and memories. And kissing Casteel was like daring to kiss the sun. I placed my hands against his chest, feeling the warmth of his skin through his shirt and this—all of this—was another first, because I kissed without once worrying if I should, without wondering if I would regret it. I kissed with abandon, and there was a freedom in that I had never known before.

He pulled me against him, one arm around my waist as his mouth trailed over the curve of my jaw and then down my throat. I tensed with wicked anticipation.

"There are other places, you know? Where I can drink from you."

"Like where?"

"Places that are far more sensitive than the neck." He dragged his hand down my shoulder, cupping my breast through the slip. His thumb found the aching peak. "Like here for example. Would you like that? Don't answer yet. There are other places even more sensitive. More interesting." He moved again, over the curve of my hip and lower still. He gathered up the silk. "Lift your arms."

I stretched my arms above my head, shivering as his clothing brushed my newly bared skin.

The slip landed on the floor, and then his hand was at my hip again. My thigh. I closed my eyes as I felt his lips at my neck.

His fingers trailed along my thigh, the ring around his finger cool against my skin. "There's a vein there, right along your leg, with all these little veins branching off. I'm thinking you'd really like that."

I shuddered. "Will you do that now?"

"I would, except I'm feeling incredibly archaic right now, and I want the world to see my fresh mark on your throat," he said. "And if the whole world saw that mark between your pretty thighs, I'd have to then kill the whole world."

"That's excessive."

"I feel excessive, Princess. There's another place, one that won't supply that much blood, but I think it will be your favorite." His hand cupped me then, between the legs, and his thumb pressed against the bundle of nerves, driving me to the tips of my toes. "Right there. I could taste you and feed from you at the same time."

A sharp curl of pleasure twisted through me. "Sounds indecent."

"Extremely indecent," he agreed. "You don't have to choose. Later, because there will be a later," he promised, and my chest squeezed, "we'll try every single one of those places, and you can tell me which is your favorite. What do you think about that?"

"I think…" A breathy moan escaped as his finger slid inside me. "I'm going to enjoy being very indecent."

"I can tell." He chuckled against my skin as he moved me backward, his finger moving slowly, shallowly. He guided me onto my back and then withdrew from me. "Both of us will."

As he moved from the bed, he slowed to kiss the scars along my stomach and then those on my legs. Then he stepped back, standing above me. I was completely on display, wearing nothing but the necklace and the dagger. Shyness crept into me, but I didn't move to hide anything from him. I let him look his fill.

"Beautiful. I want you to know that. You're beautiful. Every inch of you."

Like before, I couldn't help but feel that way when he looked at me like that.

His hands dropped to the flap of buttons on his pants. "Watch me."

I watched him undress as I'd done in the cavern. If he thought every inch of me was beautiful, then he hadn't looked in a mirror. All that sun-kissed skin and lean muscle. His scars weren't flaws. Not even the brand. They were a map of his strength, of what he'd overcome and a reminder that he'd found pieces of himself.

It struck me then how he could find my skin so flawless. He saw what I saw when I looked at him.

And he had since he first saw me without the veil.

Emotion clogged my throat, and I was half-afraid I'd start crying, but then he moved to me. The hard length of his body came over mine. My senses were nearly overwhelmed by the coarse hair of his legs against my skin, the weight and warmth of his body as he settled between my thighs, the feel of his chest brushing mine, and the hardness pressing at the softest part of me.

He curled his hand in my hair, tipping my head back. "You have no idea how long I've waited to do this. To be inside you as I take a part of you inside me. To feel you come around my cock while I taste your blood on my tongue. It feels like forever."

A shudder wracked my body as I drew my legs up over his. He gasped as the motion brought him closer. I wrapped my legs around his hips and lifted mine. We both made a sound then as he entered me just enough to send a wave of shivers up my spine. Casteel's head dropped to my throat as his fingers tightened in my hair.

"Then why wait any longer?" I asked.

He didn't.

His fangs pierced my skin at the same moment he thrust forward. I cried out, caught between acute pain and keen pleasure. I couldn't breathe or move, even as his mouth closed over the punctures, and he drew deeply, his hips rolling against mine.

And then there was no more pain. Just pounding, relentless pleasure that erupted from deep inside me, and he got what he'd wanted at the start. Release powered through me as I gripped his shoulders, breathed his name as he drank from me and moved inside me, and then—

His hand was at my thigh. He lifted his mouth from my neck, his lips glossy and red. He held the dagger, and in a daze, I watched him drag the blade over his chest. Just an inch or two. Blood welled.

"Drink," he gasped, lifting my head to his pectoral.

"Drink from me, Poppy."

It had to be his bite and the feeling of him inside me, of my body tightening around him. There was no hesitation. I kissed the cut, and my mouth tingled as blood touched my lips, my tongue. Warm and thick, it coated my mouth. I swallowed the decadent, lush taste of him.

"Gods." Casteel shuddered as he held me there, folding his other arm under my shoulder.

There was a burst of vivid colors—blues and purples. Lilacs. Was that the sweet taste of his blood? Was it more? There was a sound in my ears suddenly, a trickle of water—

Casteel started to move again. His blood…it was pure sin and addictive as I imagined the flower my nickname was derived from was. I could drown in it, in the sensations he elicited from me. When he pulled my head back, I started to protest, but then his mouth was on mine, and we were both lost.

There was no sense of rhythm or pace. We were frenzied. The effects of his blood and bite and my blood became madness. Tension built again, coiling deeply, stroking tighter with every deep, plunging thrust of our hips. The pressure spun until it whipped out, rocking me to my core again, and he was right there with me, toppling over the edge and falling and falling.

And he didn't stop.

He kept moving over me, in me, his mouth gliding over mine. He took me, and I seized him. We were a tangle of legs and arms, of flesh and fire, and the build was slower. Everything was slower as we took our time, acting as if we had all the time in the world, even though we didn't. And when we were finally spent, we didn't let go of each other. Not even as he finally drifted to sleep, his arms still tight around me. Not even when I joined him, my cheek resting upon the place I'd once thrust a dagger into.

And that was how we woke hours later, after the sun had set, to the long trill of a songbird. A call that was answered.

A signal.

I sat up, staring into the darkness beyond the terrace doors.

Casteel's chest pressed to my back a moment before he kissed my shoulder. "They're here."

Chapter 38

Moonlight glinted off the golden swords strapped to Casteel's side as we walked across the Rise. Delano, who had met us at the door, had given them to him.

The short-sleeved, lightweight cloak I wore over the dark blue tunic and leggings had been Casteel's idea. If any Ascended were among those nearing Spessa's End, they may be able to see me with their heightened vision. That was the only condition Casteel had given when I rose from the bed.

"The hood goes up as soon as they arrive, and it stays up for as long as it can," he'd said. "Don't make yourself a target."

"I have good news, potentially bad news, and hopefully good news," Emil said as he met us just outside a battlement. "Our scouts have reported that it's the smaller group that's set to arrive."

"How many?" Casteel asked.

"About two hundred."

"I think I can guess what the potentially bad news is," Casteel said. "Since it wouldn't have taken this long to arrive, they waited on the larger army and for night to fall."

Meaning, there were most likely vampry among them, and there was at least several hundred more not far behind.

"That and they've brought what appears to be catapults with them," Emil said. "These walls may be damaged by whatever they plan to throw at us, but I doubt they will have anything that can take them down if they remained standing throughout the War of Two Kings."

"These walls will not fall," Casteel vowed.

"What is the hopefully good news?" I asked.

"Since they waited for their larger armies to join them, it's hopefully given us time for reinforcements to arrive," Naill answered as he crossed the Rise.

"*Hopefully* being the operative word," Emil added. "There are a lot of what-ifs here. Alastir and Kieran would've had to travel nonstop. A sizable group of our soldiers would've had to be near Saion's Cove and ready to travel."

Fear trickled through me, but I didn't give it room to breathe—to grow. Having fear wasn't a weakness. Only the foolish and the false claimed to feel no fear, but that emotion could spread like a plague if given too much thought. I couldn't think of what could happen—if we weren't able to hold off the Ascended. If Kieran and Alastir hadn't been able to send reinforcements in time.

"And that's not taking into consideration the mist in the Skotos and how it would've responded to such a presence." Emil paused. "*Your Highness.*"

I jolted at the title. "Excuse me?"

Casteel glanced at me, a slight grin appearing in the moonlight. "In case you've forgotten, I'm a Prince."

My eyes narrowed. "I haven't forgotten."

"And we're married," he continued. "Which makes you a Princess."

"I know that, but the Princess thing isn't official. I haven't been...crowned or whatever."

"It's customary to refer to you as Your Highness or my Princess, even before the crowning," Naill explained.

"Can we not?" I asked.

"It would be considered a great dishonor." Naill paused. "*Your Highness.*"

I looked at him, and the Atlantian smiled innocently at me.

Casteel snorted.

"By the way, congratulations on the marriage," Emil said, drawing my gaze to him. My senses told me he was sincere. "I have a feeling you will make a very interesting Queen."

Queen?

Oh gods, how in the world did I forget that in the whole this-marriage-is-now-for-real thing? There was no way Malik would be in any shape to lead the kingdom once and if he was freed. Casteel would take the throne. Eventually. And I would be...

Okay.

I was not going to think about that.

"Then we will be calling you—Your Majesty," Emil said, winking at me. "Isn't that right, Cas?"

"Right," he replied flatly, placing his hand on my hip. "Both of you should be getting into position."

Emil and Naill made a great show of bowing before they left. "What was that about?" I asked. "You sending them off like that?"

"It's official," Casteel said, watching Emil as he stopped to speak to one of the Guardians. "I'm going to have to kill him."

My head whipped in his direction. "What? Why?"

"I don't like the way he looks at you."

Confused, I glanced back to where Emil was walking toward the stairwell. "How does he look at me?"

His hand was a scalding brand on my hip, even through the layers of clothing. "He looks at you like I do."

My brows lifted. "That's not true. You look at me like..."

Those heated amber eyes met mine. "How do I look at you, Princess?"

"You look at me like..." I cleared my throat. "Like you want to eat me."

Casteel's eyes narrowed into thin slits as his gaze return to Emil. "Exactly," he snarled.

I stared at him and then laughed. His gaze flew to mine, his eyes bright and wide like they always were when I laughed. "You're actually jealous."

"Of course, I am. At least I can acknowledge that."

And he was jealous. I could feel it, an ashy coating in the back of my throat. "You are…"

"Devilishly handsome? Wickedly clever?" He turned back to the western sky, where it still carried the haze of fire. "Stunningly charismatic?"

"That wasn't what I was going for," I told him. "More like ridiculous."

"Endearingly ridiculous," he corrected.

I rolled my eyes. "You know, not once have I even considered seeking the affections of another. Not since I met you."

"I know." He bent his head, brushing his lips over my brow. "My jealousy is not rooted in anything you've done."

"Or in logic."

"That we will have to disagree on. I know how he looks at you."

"I think you're seeing things."

"I know what I see." He pulled back, his eyes meeting mine. "Every time I look at you, I see a gift I'm not worthy of."

My breath caught as my heart swelled. It wasn't new—him saying things like that. What *was* new was me believing them. "You are worthy," I told him. "Most of the time."

He cracked a grin. "I think that's the nicest thing you've ever said to me."

I wondered if that was true as we stepped into a parapet. Bows and stocked quivers were placed against the wall. I looked down at the dark road and fields ahead, seeing nothing.

"Are they down there?" I asked, recalling what I'd learned when they discussed strategies. "The wolven?"

"They are in the fields, well hidden, even from vampry eyes." He placed his hands on the stone ledge, and the ring on his finger snagged my gaze. "The Guardians are in place, waiting for my lead. Those who can wield a sword are in the courtyard, and the others, the ones skilled with a bow, will be up here."

Pulling my gaze from his ring, I looked over my shoulder. They were already arriving. Mortals who were too old to lift more than a bow. The Guardians escorted them to different parapets. The trickle of fear returned as I turned back to Casteel. "How many do we have? The final count?"

His jaw hardened. "One hundred and twenty-six."

I pressed my lips together and closed my eyes as I forced myself to take a deep, even breath.

"I wish you'd gone with Alastir and Kieran," he said quietly. "You would be far away from here. Safe."

I opened my eyes.

Casteel stared into the darkness. "But I'm glad you're here. Spessa's End needs you. I need you." He looked at me then. "But I still wish you weren't here."

I could accept that. "I wish you weren't here," I whispered. "I wish they weren't coming." I let a little of the fear through. "We still plan to free your brother and see mine, right? We still plan to prevent a war?"

He nodded.

"But after tonight?" I swallowed as I looked out to the western sky. "It may be too late. War has come to us."

"It's never too late. Not even after blood has been drawn and lives have been lost," he said. "Things can *always* be stopped."

I hoped so. I really did.

He turned to me, touching my cheek. "We may be absurdly outnumbered, but everyone who picks up a bow or sword to fight for Spessa's End, for Atlantia, does so because they want to. Not for money. Not because joining the army was their only option. Not out of fear. We fight to live. We fight to protect what we've built here. We fight to protect one another. None of them—the Ascended, the knights, Solis soldiers—will fight with heart, and that makes the difference."

I blew out a steadier breath. "It does."

He was quiet for a moment, and then I felt his lips against my cheek, against the scars. "I will ask one other thing of you, Poppy. Stay up here. No matter what. Stay up here and use the bow. And if something were to happen to me, run. Go to the cavern. Kieran will know to find you there—"

"That's asking two things of me." Pressure clamped down on my chest.

"You are what they want," he said. "With you, they will be

able to do more harm to both Atlantia and Solis than if anything happens to me."

"If anything happens to you—" I cut myself off, unable to go there when everything between us now was still so new, when it would breathe life into the fear I already felt. "These people need you more than they need me."

"Poppy—"

"Do not ask me to do that." I looked at him. "Do not ask me to run and hide while someone I care about is hurt or worse. I will not do that again."

He closed his eyes. "This is not the same."

I started to demand how it wasn't when I heard the low call of warning from the fields. Both of us turned as fire sparked and a torch flamed to life in the distance, one after another until light spilled across the empty road.

Casteel signaled back as he reached for the hood of my cloak, pulling it up. As he fastened the row of buttons at my throat, the archers rushed forward, dropping behind the battlement walls.

Heart rate kicking up and breaths becoming too quick, I picked up a bow and an arrow out of the quiver—it was the kind I was familiar with—and stepped back so I wouldn't be seen beyond the stone walls. Casteel remained where he stood, the only person visible to the approaching regiment. Instead of what marched forward, I stared at him, focused on the straight line of his spine and the proud lift of his chin. And as the silence gave way to the sound of dozens of boots and hooves falling upon the packed earth and the creak of wooden wheels turning, my senses stretched out to him. There was the bitter taste of fear, because he was no fool, but it was such a small amount because he was no coward.

"This kind of reminds me," he noted, "of the night on the Rise in Masadonia. Except you're not wearing slippers and a rather indecent nightgown. I don't know if I should be relieved or disappointed."

My heart slowed, and my breaths were no longer shallow. My spine straightened, and my chin lifted. "You should be grateful. You won't be distracted tonight."

He laughed softly. "Still a little disappointed."

I smiled as my grip tightened on the bow.

There were no more words then as we watched the soldiers of Solis draw closer, shoving torches into the road and embankments. Their front lines were mortal soldiers, carrying heavy broadswords and wearing plates of leather. Horses pulled three catapults, and beyond them were the archers and mounted soldiers in metal armor, wearing black mantles. Knights. They were maybe two dozen or so of them. Not many, but enough to be a problem.

The knights parted as a windowless, crimson carriage rolled forward between two of the wooden catapults. There was something in them. I squinted. Sacks? It wasn't gunpowder or other projectiles. Instead of relief, unease blossomed.

Soldiers parted, making way for the carriage that bore the Royal Crest. Several of the knights rode forward, surrounding the conveyance as the wheels stopped, protecting whoever was inside.

It had to be a Royal.

The door opened, and someone stepped out—someone so heavily cloaked that when they moved around the door, I could not tell if it was a man or a woman who walked forward, flanked by knights. Whoever it was, took their sweet old time, stopping once they stood in front of the soldiers. Gloved hands rose, shoving back the hood.

"You have got to be kidding me," I muttered under my breath.

Duchess Teerman stood before the Rise, her face as pale and pretty as I remembered, but she wore no finery in her brown hair tonight. It was pulled back from her face in a simple twist as she stared up at the Rise.

And it was then when I truly feared what I would discover when I saw Ian with my own eyes. Duchess Teerman had been kind—well, she had never been particularly cruel to me. She'd been as cold and unreachable as most Ascended were, but when I killed Lord Mazeen, she had told me not to waste a moment more thinking of him. I believed that perhaps she too had been a victim of the Duke's perversities. Maybe she had been, but the fact that she was here could only mean one thing.

She was the enemy.

Would that make Ian one, too?

Her berry-red lips curved into a tight, humorless smile. "Hawke Flynn," she said, her voice too familiar as I quietly nocked an arrow. "Or is there another name you prefer?"

"It doesn't matter what name you call me," he answered, sounding about as bored as Kieran did during, well, everything.

"It would be rude if I called you by a false name," she replied, clasping her hands together. The soldiers and knights remained silent and still behind her. "I don't want to be rude."

"I go by several names. The Dark One. Bastard. Cas. Prince Casteel Da'Neer," he said, and there was no mistaking the slight widening of her eyes. She hadn't known that—who he truly was. "Call me whatever you like as long as you know it will be my voice that will be the last sound you hear."

"Prince Casteel," she spoke the words as if she'd been presented with an entire chocolate cake...or with an elemental Atlantian. She laughed. "Oh, I've heard all about you from *our* Queen and King. They always wondered where you disappeared to. What happened to you. Now I can tell them that their favorite pet is well and alive."

Pet? The grip of the bow dug into my palm.

"You know, I might just let you live, Duchess. Just so you can return to your King and Queen to let them know their favorite *pet* cannot wait to see them again."

Teerman smiled even broader. "I'll be sure to do so. That is if you allow me to live." There was a coyness to her tone that skated across my nerves. Was she flirting with him? "But before you get to the killing, I'm here to prevent death."

"Is that so?" Casteel asked.

She nodded. "You have to know that there are more than those who stand behind me." A hand extended with all the elegance of a ballroom dancer. "One of your dogs made it back to you, did he not? The other, well, our horses have been well fed."

Nausea seized me. She couldn't be serious. I wanted to vomit.

"You know that we outnumber whatever you have behind those walls. There can't be many living in ruins," she said, giving away the knowledge that she knew very little of Spessa's End. That eased some of the horror churning within me. "Even if it were hundreds of Descenters with a few—albeit one less—overgrown mutts, you will not walk away from this. So, I am here to prevent that."

"And I am here to tell you that if you refer to a wolven as a dog one more time, I will strike you down before those knights have a chance to blink," Casteel warned.

"My apologies." Teerman bowed her head. "I meant no offense."

Really? I rolled my eyes so hard that it was no wonder they didn't get stuck back there.

"I do hope we can come to an agreement. Believe it or not, spilled blood makes me squeamish," she said. "It's so…wasteful. So, most of my armies have remained back in a show of good faith. In hopes that you will listen."

"It doesn't appear as if I have the choice *not* to listen. So, please. Speak."

The Duchess heard the insolence in his tone. It showed in the tensing of her jaw. "You have what belongs to us. We want it back. Give us the Maiden."

Belonged to them? It? I drew on every ounce of willpower I had not to lift the bow and send a bloodstone arrow straight through her mouth.

"Give the Maiden back to us, and we will leave this pit of bones untouched for you to cross back to whatever remains of your once-great kingdom."

If her words represented the entirety of the Ascended, they truly had no idea what they were up against. What kind of hailstorm could descend upon them if something did happen to Atlantia's Prince.

"And if I did, you would just walk away? Allow me and mine to live?"

"For now? Yes. You're far too valuable to kill if we can capture you, but right now, the Maiden is the priority." Her pitch-black eyes reflected no light. "And there will be more chances to capture you later. You'll be back. For your brother, correct? Isn't that why you took our Maiden? To ransom her for him?"

Casteel stiffened, and the fact that he remained silent was evidence of his willpower.

"I hate to be the bearer of bad news, but there will be no ransom. You either give her to us or…"

When Casteel said nothing, she inclined her head, searching the battlements. "Penellaphe? Is she up there? I've heard you have grown quite…familiar with her."

Casteel said nothing as I stared down at her, not allowing myself to think too hard on how she could've learned that.

"If you are up there, Penellaphe, please say something. Show yourself," she called. "I know you must think terrible things of us now, about our Queen and King. But I can explain everything. We can keep you safe as we always have." Her gaze flickered past where Casteel stood. "I know you miss your brother. He's learned of your capture, and he's sick with worry. I can bring you to him."

I *almost* stepped forward, *almost* opened my mouth. She knew how to get to me, but she also must've thought I was an incredible imbecile if she thought that would work.

"Do you know what happened to the last Ascended who came looking for the Maiden?" Casteel asked.

"I do," Duchess Teerman replied. "That will not happen here."

"Are you sure?" he retorted. "Because what you seek never belonged to you in the first place."

"That's where you're wrong," Teerman countered. "She belongs to the Queen."

My self-control snapped, and I moved before I could stop myself, reaching the battlement as I said, "I belong to no one, and especially not her."

Casteel slowly turned his head toward me. "This is not staying unseen," he said in a low voice. "In case you're unsure."

"Sorry," I muttered.

Duchess Teerman's tight, toothless smile returned. "There you are. You were up there this entire time. Why didn't you say something earlier?" She held up her hand. "No need to answer that. I'm sure it's because of what you've been told—one very biased side of the story."

"I've heard enough to know the truth," I told her. "Have those who stand behind you? Do the soldiers know the truth of what you are? Of what the King and the Queen are?"

"You have no idea what Queen Ileana is, and neither does the false Prince standing beside you," she replied. "And you're wrong, Penellaphe. You belong to the Queen. Just like the first Maiden did."

"The first Maiden? The one I supposedly killed but never met?" Casteel demanded. "The one that probably doesn't even exist?"

"I may have insinuated that you were directly responsible for her fate," the Duchess replied. "But the first Maiden was very real, and she too belonged to the Queen. Just like you do, Penellaphe. As did your mother."

"My mother?" The string of the bow was taut between my fingers as I kept the arrow pointed down. "My mother was her friend. Or at least that was what I was told."

"Your mother was so much more than that," she called back. "I'll tell you everything about her—about you."

"She knows nothing," Casteel said. "The Ascended are masters of manipulation."

"I know." And I did. "There is nothing you can say that I will believe. I know about the Rite. I know what happens to the third sons and daughters. I know how the Ascension works. I know why you need me."

"But do you know that your mother was Queen Ileana's daughter? That you are the Queen's granddaughter? That is why you are the Maiden. The Chosen."

My lips parted on a sharp inhale.

"You're not even a good liar," Casteel snarled. "What you're suggesting is impossible. Ascended cannot have children."

The Duchess tilted her head. "Who said that Queen Ileana is an Ascended?"

"Every Ascended in Solis has claimed as much. Your history books have stated it," I exclaimed. "The Queen herself has called herself an Ascended. Are you seriously trying to say she is not what she is? When she does not age? When she does not walk in the sun?"

"They were lies designed to protect the truth—to protect your mother and you," she replied.

"Protect me?" I laughed, and the sound was harsh to my ears. "Is that what you call keeping me locked in my rooms? Forcing me to wear the veil and forbidding me to speak, eat, or walk without permission? Is that what the Duke was doing when he took a cane to my back simply because I breathed too loudly or didn't respond in a way he found appropriate? When he put his hands on me? Allowed others to do the same?" I demanded as Casteel stiffened even more. Anger flooded me, and I almost lifted the bow then, almost released the arrow. "Is that how you and the Queen *protected* me? Don't tell me you didn't know. You did, and you allowed it."

Duchess Teerman's porcelain features hardened. "I did what I could when I could. If he hadn't met his fate at the hands of the one beside you, he surely would have once the Queen knew."

"You mean, my grandmother? Who sent Lord Chaney after me? Who bit me?" I demanded. "Who most likely would've killed me?"

"I didn't know that," she argued. "But I can explain—"

"Shut up," I said, done with her, done with their lies. "Just shut up. There is nothing you can say or do that will make me believe you. So get whatever it is you think you're going to do here over with, *Jacinda*."

Her features sharpened at the use of her first name, something she sporadically required from me.

"Feisty," Casteel murmured. "I like it."

"I'm this close to shooting her in the face with an arrow," I warned him.

"I like that, too," he replied.

The Duchess stepped forward. "I can see that nothing I say at this time will help make this go smoothly. Perhaps the gifts I brought will change both of your minds."

Casteel straightened as she tilted her head back, toward the soldiers. Several moved to the catapults. Soldiers gripped the sacks, emptying whatever was in them and then knelt as releases were thrown. I tensed as metal groaned.

The catapults swung forward, one after the other, releasing the *gifts* as Casteel grabbed me, shielding my body with his.

But what was sent at us flew high above us. They flung through the air, over the battlements. We turned as they hit the stone walls behind us. The sound of them, the fleshy smack, the smear they left behind on the walls that could be seen even in the moonlight and along the floor as they tumbled forward, turned my stomach as the bow loosened in my grip. The nocked arrow trembled.

One had long, black hair.

Another a shroud of silver.

A glimpse of skin that was once a beautiful onyx.

An expression frozen in fear for an eternity.

Heads. They were *heads*.

So many of them.

Magda.

The mother of the woman who'd died.

Keev, the wolven.

The Atlantian man who'd refused my touch.

A head rolled to a stop by Casteel's feet. The moment I saw the blood-stained beard, my throat sealed.

Elijah.

Chapter 39

I staggered back a step, my horrified gaze lifted to Casteel and then to where Duchess Teerman *had* stood. She was no longer there. I turned back to Casteel.

His chest expanded, but no breath left him as he stared down at the *gift*.

"Casteel," I whispered.

Slowly, he turned from the grotesque sight and eyes nearly as black as an Ascended's met mine.

And I knew there would be no more talking.

Locking down my senses and shutting off my emotions, my horror and fury, I exhaled roughly.

"Kill as many of them as you can." Releasing the golden swords from his sides, he spun back to the edge and leapt.

He *leapt* from the top of the Rise, a dozen feet or more above the field.

Rushing to the edge, his name was a scream not given sound. He landed in a crouch, swords at his sides as he rose before an army of *hundreds*.

"Nice of you to join us," a knight called out. "The Dark One all alone? The odds are not in your favor."

"I am never alone," Casteel growled.

Piercing screams rang from every side of me, pitching and falling in a battle cry that would send a bolt of dread through the most seasoned warrior.

The *Guardians*.

They moved as silently as wraiths, appearing on the battlements. They swept their swords above their heads, bringing them together in a thunderous clap. Sparks erupted from the swords, igniting. I sucked in a breath as golden flames spiraled over the blades, encasing the stone blades in fire. Flames erupted across the Rise. Then they too went over the side, one by one, falling like golden stars. By the time they landed, Casteel was nothing more than a blur among leather and armor, cutting a path into the line before they even knew he was there as he headed straight for the carriage. He was going to kill the Duchess.

And for once I cared nothing for dignity in death.

Drawing in a deep, steadying breath, I lifted the bow and nocked the arrow once more as the first wolven burst from the shadows, taking a guard down from his horse. To my left and right, the oldest among those here lifted their bows. I searched for flashes of black—of mantles that signified a knight instead of a guard and took aim as the others spilled out from the trees that crowded the right walls of the Rise.

Catching sight of a knight on horseback, charging a man who'd shoved a sword deep into the chest of a soldier, I took aim. The knight's hand whipped out, and a barbed chain uncurled. The metal and spikes spun with dizzying speed as I focused on the one weak area not armored.

I released the string. The arrow flew across the distance, striking the knight in the eye. The impact knocked the knight from the horse, his body disintegrating as it fell to the ground.

Quentyn skidded into the space beside me, placing a shield against the stone walls. He stretched up, peering over the wall, jaw hard as he leveled his bow.

"Where's Beckett?" I asked, not having seen him.

"He's with the ones who can't fight."

I nodded. "The ones with black mantles are knights. Vamprys. Aim for their heads."

"Got it." His eyes squinted.

Notching another arrow, I scanned for Casteel, spotting him in the middle of the Royal Army ranks, sweeping his sword through the neck of one and the stomach of another. My gaze skipped over flaming swords, cutting down those with fire. A knight raced toward a Guardian. I released an arrow, and it caught him in the mouth.

"Archers!" a knight shouted. "On the battlements."

Aiming at a guard who rushed toward a wolven, I only saw the arrow pierce the leather, spinning the mortal to the ground a second before a volley of arrows ripped through the air.

"Incoming!" someone yelled.

"Down!" Quentyn shouted as he lifted a shield that had to weigh nearly as much as he did. We knelt as the arrows zinged down, clanging off stone and the metal of the shield. Shouts of pain tugged at my senses, telling me that some had found their marks.

Quentyn lowered the shield, and I popped back up as I placed an arrow over the bow.

"Do you see him?" Quentyn asked, releasing an arrow. "The Prince?"

I shook my head as I surveyed the chaos below. There was too much going on—there were too many. I could barely even see the Guardians' flaming swords in the clash of regular swords and bodies. "He'll be okay," I told Quentyn—told myself—as I pulled back the string, forgetting about the knights. I focused on the soldiers, going through a quiver of ammunition before several of them broke through the wolven and Guardians. A dozen or more reached the door. The shouts from below caused my gift to swell inside me. I knew they were going to make it inside.

Another wave of arrows went up, and I cursed as we ducked under the shield again. Several clattered off, hitting the floor beside us. Screams tore through the air. My gaze swung in the direction of the stairs. There weren't enough out there to hold them back. They'd keep coming, just like Craven would. They'd swarm us before the larger army even arrived.

And I was up here, hiding behind a shield.

My gaze met Quentyn's. "You're really good with a bow?"

He nodded. "I think so."

"Good. Cover me."

"What?" His golden eyes widened.

"When you see me down there, cover me." I dropped the bow.

"You can't go out there! Casteel—I mean, the Prince will—"

"Expect little else from me," I told him. "Cover me."

Without waiting, I darted toward the stairs, unsheathing my dagger as I raced past the gruesome gifts. I sped down the winding staircase, my steps slowing as I heard the clang of stone against stone.

They'd made it inside the Rise.

I inched down the rest of the steps, keeping close to the wall.

A body stumbled across the mouth of the stairs, falling to the ground. A Royal Guard appeared. All I saw was a young face splattered with blood. A face too young. Blue eyes. Did he know what he fought for? He had to. He had been out there when the Duchess spoke. It didn't matter either way.

Sword dripping with blood, he halted for a fraction of a second. That was all I needed. I sprang forward, shoving the dagger under his chin. His breath gurgled as he pinwheeled backward, the sword clanging off the ground.

Stepping out of the stairwell, I switched the dagger to my left hand and picked up the fallen sword. Testing its weight, I scanned the torch-lit yard, the bodies standing and the ones falling. And then I did what Vikter had taught me through our hours of training.

I closed it down.

Shut it all down.

The horror. What my eyes wanted my brain and heart to recognize. The fear, especially the fear—of being injured, of stumbling, of missing my mark, of dying—of losing those I cared about. Vikter had once told me that when you fought, you had to do so as if each breath may be your last.

I stalked forward, the cloak billowing out from behind me,

catching in the blood-rich wind. And all I saw when a soldier turned to me were the faces of their *gifts*.

The soldier raised his sword, his face a mask of violence. There were different kinds of bloodlust. What vampry and Ascended felt, and what mortals experienced when violence spilled into the air. I dipped under his arm, spinning back as I thrust the sword into his back. Yanking the blade free, I turned, shoving the dagger deep into the chest of another soldier. The bloodstone pierced leather and bone.

Whirling, I sliced through the neck of a soldier who went to drive their sword down on one who'd fallen. Wet warmth hit my cheeks as I turned, shoving my elbow into the throat of another. Bones crunched and air wheezed behind me as the pain of those around me scraped even harder at my senses.

Reaching up, I tore free the buttons at my neck. The hood slipped down, and I shrugged off the cloak. It fell to the ground behind me as I broke into a run, racing out of the Rise and into the battle we were sure to lose.

It was…madness.

Swords crashing against swords. Screams of pain and shouts of fury. Glimpses of fur and thick claws and flaming swords as the Guardians cut through mortal and vampry alike.

A man moaned as he clutched his bloodied stomach. He was a Descenter, and I started to stop, to either ease his pain or heal him—

An arrow whizzed past my head, striking a guard rushing toward me. Quentyn was *very* good with a bow.

I stepped back from the fallen man, knowing that now was not the time for that particular set of skills. As much as it hurt, as wrong as it felt, I turned away.

And then…I fell into the madness as I thrust my sword into the stomach of a soldier who couldn't have been much older than I was. I let my thirst for vengeance seize me as my blade sliced through the neck of another. I didn't hesitate or pull back when I saw recognition flare in the eyes the moment they saw the scars on my face. It took only moments out on the field to know that they'd been given orders not to harm me. It was clear they didn't expect me to be down here, to be fighting, and it was an advantage for me, one I used. Because orders from an Ascended hadn't sent me out here. I chose to be here. I kicked out, catching a knight at the knees before he could lift the spiked ball he wielded. He fell to his back, and I drove the sword down.

Bright, twin flames passed mere feet from my face as a Guardian kicked off the back of a falling soldier. The dark-haired Guardian spun in mid-air, catching two in the chest. The fiery blades sliced through leather and bone. Landing in a crouch, she rose with the fluid grace of a goddess, her eyes briefly meeting mine. She nodded before disappearing into the crush of soldiers.

A sudden yelp from a wolven spun me around. A fawn-colored one that reminded me of Kieran but smaller, limped backward away from a knight, blood coursing down the hind leg. Vonetta? I wasn't sure as I shifted the sword to my left hand and withdrew the wolven dagger. The knight lifted the sword as the wolven bared her teeth, crouching on the wounded leg. Flipping the dagger so I held it by the blade, I cocked back my arm and threw it. The bloodstone struck the knight in the forehead, taking him down before he even knew what'd hit him as I shoved the sword into the gut of another soldier who reached for me. The wolven whipped toward me and suddenly launched into the air. My breath caught as she crashed into a soldier behind me. They went down, her jaws locked on his neck. She shook her head, flinging the soldier like he was nothing more than a rag doll. Bone cracked as I turned, scanning the mass of bodies standing and on the ground. There were wolven among the fallen. Faces I recognized. I retrieved my dagger from the dusty ground as a wolven the color of snow darted past me. *Delano.* I turned, catching sight of Casteel behind the catapults.

Blood streaked his face as he spun out his blades, catching two soldiers in the chest. Yanking the swords free, he stretched his neck, and my heart stuttered. There was a wound on his neck and shoulder, ragged and seeping blood. Surrounded, he roared, fangs bared as he caught a soldier by the throat, ripping into flesh as Delano took a knight down from his horse, his claws tearing through the metal armor like it was nothing more than loose soil. Another wolven shot across the field—an impossibly large, silver one. Jasper? He grabbed the knight's arm as he swung the sword toward Delano and...good gods, he tore it straight off, sword and all.

I would have to vomit about that later.

Another knight leapt from his horse, landing like a mountain behind Casteel. He tossed a soldier aside to get to Casteel, flinging the mortal into the side of a catapult. The crunch of bones told me that the soldier wouldn't be getting back up.

I picked up my pace, jumping over a body and closing the distance just as the knight went for Casteel. Grabbing a fistful of the knight's hair, I yanked his head back as I thrust the wolven dagger into the weak space at the base of his skull, angling it upward. The knight shuddered as I let go, his body breaking apart.

Casteel spun then, fangs bared and mouth streaked with crimson. The sword he swung at me halted a mere inch from my neck. His breath came out in short, ragged bursts.

"You're welcome," I panted. "For saving your life."

Breathing raggedly, he jerked the sword back. A wide, bloody smile broke out across his face. "Would this be an inappropriate time to let you know I'm incredibly turned on by you right now?"

"Yes." My gaze shifted to the guard staggering to his feet behind him. "Highly inappropriate."

"Well, too bad." Casteel pivoted, and the guard's head went in a different direction of his body. "I find you highly arousing."

My lips curved up as I turned, seeing the carriage. "Is she in the carriage? The Duchess?"

"I believe so." He looked over his shoulder at me. "You want to kill her?"

I nodded.

"You're going to have to beat me to it."

Jamming the dagger into a soldier's throat, I said, "Doable."

Casteel's laugh was wild as he caught the arm of a knight, spinning him as he drew one of his swords around, cutting through the soldier's neck. I started forward when fire sparked to life in the waiting darkness of the western road. I drew up short, breathing heavily as the spark repeated itself, over and over and over. The sparks flew into the air—

Arrows.

Casteel crashed into me, grabbing me around the waist as he shoved us under the catapult. His body flattened over mine, pressing me into the hard, blood-and-dirt-packed earth.

The arrows fell, striking Solis soldiers and those who fought on Atlantia's side alike. I jerked back against Casteel at the sound of arrows piercing flesh, at the sudden intense flares of light all around us as the fire swept over bodies, igniting the catapult beside us. The world descended into chaos and death.

Chapter 40

Chills of dread were like icy fingers on the back of my neck and down the line of my spine as Casteel lifted his head, and his chest rose against my back with each heavy breath. Swallowing hard, I followed his gaze. The larger division had arrived, and we…we were engulfed.

An army of Solis soldiers ran forward, overcoming the carriage as they drew unmarred swords. They swarmed the road and fields outside the Rise, and then the Rise itself.

The chill of dread seeped into my skin and bones as I closed my eyes. There hadn't been enough time for Kieran and Alastir.

Casteel shifted so he was beside me. His fingers touched my cheek, and I opened my eyes. Even with the blood covering him, he was still the most beautiful man I'd ever seen, and I suddenly wished we'd accepted our pasts and opened up to one another sooner than we had. There would've been time then to really get to know each other. Maybe just a few days or weeks, but I could've discovered if I'd read his favorite book and he could've learned that strawberries were just as much a weakness for me as cheese was. He could've told me about the conversations that drove him and Malik to the caverns, and I could've shared the dreams I'd had when I was a child, before I was veiled as the Maiden. We could've explored each other, and he could've proven just how sensitive all those other areas he'd mentioned were.

Because now, there was a good chance we were out of time before we even had it.

He smiled at me, but there were no dimples. The expression didn't reach his eyes, and I felt tears stinging mine. "It'll be okay."

"I know," I said, even though I knew it wouldn't be.

"I'm getting you out of here."

A knot formed in my throat. "I can stop this. They won't harm me. I can go—"

"They cannot have you, Poppy. I know what they will do to you." His bloody fingers splayed across my cheek. "I cannot breathe when I think about that. I'm getting you out of here."

A knot formed in my throat. "What about the others? Naill? Delano? Von—"

"They will take care of themselves," he swore. "I need to get you out of here. That is all that matters right now."

But it wasn't.

Spessa's End mattered. The people mattered. "What about the people? The ones who can't fight."

"They'll be warned. We had plans in place in case this happened. They'll be warned, and they'll have time to get out. They're in a better position to do so than us. We'll have to fight our way out." His eyes held mine. "You understand that?"

I nodded as the knot expanded. "I'm sorry—about Spessa's End." My voice cracked. "About Elijah. About all of them—"

"You are what matters now." Casteel kissed me, and it was hard and fierce. A clash of teeth and fangs that tasted of blood and desperation. "You do. We do. Us surviving this. That is what matters."

Dragging in a deep breath, I cleared my mind of the panic and sorrow, and nodded.

"You ready, Poppy?"

"Yes."

He smiled again, but this time, his dimples appeared. "Let's kick some ass."

"Let's," I whispered.

Casteel rolled out from under the catapult and shot to his

feet, thrusting his sword into the first soldier. I followed, climbing to my feet. I'd been wrong earlier. I hadn't truly known madness until then—until they came from all sides, reaching for me when they realized who I was, stabbing and lurching at Casteel.

Sweat and blood slicked my skin, my grip on my sword and dagger perilous. I smelled and tasted and saw death. Each handful of feet we gained, we were surrounded again. The ground became oily with offal. My boots sliding as I screamed, driving the dagger into a chest. My muscles shrieked with protest as I swung the sword, slicing into necks and stomachs and *arms*—at anyone that got too close.

A blow caught my cheek, causing me to stumble into Casteel. Catching myself, I kicked out, dropping the man to his knees. I didn't think twice as I drove the sword through his skull, and I couldn't keep my senses locked down anymore. They opened, seizing my breath as my senses stretched out, forming connections with those around us, and…oh, gods, there was so much fear. The bitterness mixed with the taste of the blood, choking me as I swung, my arm knocking into Casteel's as I stabbed at a man—

A man who was *afraid*.

They were afraid to die, afraid not to fight, and just…*afraid.* I shuddered as I turned, seeing faces young and old, white and brown and black. Their emotions poured into me. I couldn't shut it off. Couldn't take the time to concentrate as I moved in front of a blow meant for Casteel. A blow that was pulled back only at the last second, and then I killed him. I killed the man who projected terror into the air.

And something…something was happening inside me. It was waking up, stretching and expanding, filling my veins and causing my skin to hum as I leapt forward, slamming the wolven dagger deep into a chest, swallowing the soldier's fear and drowning in his agony—in their fear and agony.

A hand grabbed my braid, yanking me back. My feet went out from under me, and Casteel spun. More hot blood sprayed the air, our faces. Our gazes connected as he helped me stand, and then we spun back around, hearts pounding as we tripped over bodies, as soldiers pressed in, as orders were shouted—*take her, kill him, seize them both.* As something exploded from deep within me, inhaling all the fear and agony and primal emotions, and all of it rose inside me. The swirling, churning mass of emotions clawed at my insides, my throat, and I needed to shut it down. I had to shut it all off—

I dropped the sword as I brought the dagger to my own throat. "Stop!" I shouted. "Stop, or I will slit my throat."

Casteel whirled toward me. "Poppy—"

"I'll do it," I warned as one of the soldiers stepped up to Casteel. "I'll cut my throat wide-open if any of you take another step forward. I doubt any of you will live if that happens. He'll take you down."

"I'm about to take *you* down," Casteel growled.

I ignored him. "And if he doesn't, what do you think the Duchess will do? The Queen? They'll do what you did to your men. You'll die. Every last one of you. That, I can promise."

Faces paled and glances were exchanged. Several stepped back—

The sky was ripped apart by deep wails, by snapping growls and piercing howls that came from the woods and everywhere at once it seemed. It was a crescendo, a call that kept rising and rising, and was answered by yips and barks that seemed to come from the trees, from the bush surrounding the left side of the Rise, and from the western road.

The soldiers before us started to turn—

Wolven raced out from the forest, streaking over the ground and launching into the air. They were a sea of fur and claws, taking down soldiers, tearing through armor and flesh. I saw Jasper and Delano among them, Vonetta too, but there were…there had to be dozens and dozens of them, and their timing…

Their timing had been impeccable.

A large brown wolven lifted its head, ears perked. Another and another did the same, luminous pale eyes locking onto mine.

Slowly, I lowered the knife from my throat.

All of a sudden, it sounded like the Rise was coming down around us. Like a thousand boulders tumbling and falling to the ground from the sky, but the Rise still stood, and nothing, not even the stars had fallen. I swung toward Casteel.

He smirked, eyes lit from within as he took a step back, exhaling deeply.

What reminded me of thunder grew louder, and as I turned, I realized that what I'd heard was the pounding of hooves.

Pale horses poured out from between the trees and filled the western road, mud and blood streaking their legs as they kicked up dirt and grass. Moonlight glinted off golden armor and raised swords. Those blades—those horses—mowed through the lines and rows of soldiers as white banners streamed and rippled behind the pale mounts, banners bearing the golden sword and arrow lying across the sun. The crest of Atlantia.

Atlantia had come, and there were *hundreds* of them.

Tired muscles in my arms loosened as they charged past us, stirring the blood-soaked air and lifting the tendrils of hair that had escaped my braid. They set fire to the remaining catapults, to the wagons as they swarmed the Solis army, and I knew none would be left alive.

As the wolven followed the army, a warm, damp nose bumped my left hand, and I looked down into the pale blue eyes of a large, fawn-colored wolven.

Kieran nudged my hand again, and I opened it, revealing the golden mark and the ring on my finger.

"Yeah," I said hoarsely. "You missed it."

His ears perked as he looked over to where Casteel stood.

"You missed a lot," the Prince said.

Kieran trotted over to him as I turned and saw the crimson carriage untouched.

Was she still in there? Or had she run?

I was walking before I knew, running toward the carriage, barely aware of Casteel shouting my name. I tore open the carriage door, and the Duchess hissed from the dimly lit interior. She lurched forward, catching herself on the door when she saw me.

Her eyes widened with surprise. "Penellaphe—"

I punched her in the face.

The Duchess stumbled backward, falling between the seats

as she cupped her nose. Blood poured out between her fingers. "That hurt," she seethed, glaring up at me as I climbed into the carriage.

"Things are going to hurt way worse than that," I promised.

She lowered her hands. "When did you become so violent, Maiden?"

"I was always violent." I caught her arm as she reached for something. My fingers curled around her cool skin. "And I was never the Maiden."

"But you were. You always were."

"Where is my brother?" I demanded.

"Come with me, and I'll show you."

I shook my head. "Where is Casteel's brother?"

"With yours," she said, and I didn't believe her.

"Is he alive?"

"Which one?"

"Prince Malik."

"How else would we have been able to Ascend Tawny if he wasn't?"

I let go of her wrist as my stomach sunk. "You lie."

"Why lie about that?"

"Because the Ascended do nothing but lie!"

"You know that Tawny couldn't wait to Ascend." She rose to her knees. "She was ecstatic when I told her the Queen had petitioned the gods for an exception, that she would Ascend. I sent her to the capital. The Queen did it for you. I told her how close you and Tawny are."

"Shut up."

"She wants you to be comfortable when you return home, her blooded granddaughter—" Her eyes widened as she caught sight of my hand. "What is that?" The Duchess scrambled forward, clasping my left wrist. "The imprint." She stared at the golden swirl across my palm. "You're married."

I pulled my hand free as she rocked backward, laughing.

"You're married? To the Prince of Atlantia?" Pitch-black eyes lifted to mine as a wide smile broke out across her face, revealing the fangs of both her upper and lower jaw. "If I'd known, none of this would've been necessary. You. Born of flesh and fire. The Queen will be so thrilled to learn you've done what she could never accomplish. Seized Atlantia right out from under them, under *her*. Our Queen will be so proud of—"

"Shut up," I snarled, thrusting the bloodstone blade deep into her chest.

Duchess Teerman's eyes widened only a fraction in surprise. I met her stare, holding the dagger there until the cracks formed in her skin, until the light went out of her eyes and her body caved in around the blade of the wolven bone and bloodstone dagger.

And just like an Ascended, I felt nothing but a sudden iciness as I watched Duchess Teerman turn to ash.

I turned.

Casteel stood outside the door, the lines and angles of his features sharp in the moonlight. "You beat me to her."

"I did."

A long moment passed. "Did she say anything to you?"

"No." I swallowed thickly. "She said nothing."

"Are you okay?"

I nodded. "Are you?"

He said nothing as the sounds of battle grew fainter, and I tentatively opened my senses. His emotions ran the gambit, a swirling storm that was hard for even me to make sense of.

"No one comes near this carriage," he said, speaking to whoever was beyond the opening. He hoisted himself up into the conveyance. The ceiling was just high enough for him to stand. "I'm very conflicted right now."

"You are?"

He nodded as the door swung closed behind him. "I'm furious with you for threatening your own life. For even thinking that was a suitable option."

"What else could I do?" I demanded, lowering the dagger. "They were—"

"I'm not done yet, Princess."

My brows flew up. "Do I look like I care if you're done?"

A shadow of a smile appeared in the dim glow. "I'm *livid* that you would do something like that."

"Well, I'm *annoyed* that you don't seem to realize that, at that moment, we were out of options," I snapped.

"Still not done," he said.

"Guess what? I don't care."

His eyes deepened to a heated honey. "I'm furious, and yet, at the same time, I'm in awe. Because I know you would've done it. You would've killed yourself to save the lives of those who still stood. You would've done it to save me."

Backing up as he came forward, I stepped on the cloak and whatever else the Duchess had been wearing. "You don't sound like you're in awe."

"That's because I don't want to be awed by something so incredibly reckless." His chin dipped, and his voice deepened. "And that's because I *need* you."

A sudden hot flush chased away the coldness stirring inside me.

"I need to feel your lips on mine." He planted his hands on the carriage wall, caging me in. "I need to feel your breath in my lungs. I need to feel your life inside me. I just *need* you. It's an ache. This need. Can I have you? All of you?"

I didn't know who moved first. If it was him or me or both of us. It didn't matter. We came together, the kiss just as wild as the one under the catapult, and it said everything that words couldn't communicate at the moment. We kissed as if we hadn't expected to have the luxury to do it again. And for far too many minutes, I knew we both believed that.

We'd been on the cusp of either being separated or killed, and that kiss...and what came next in that shadowy carriage was proof of how rattled we both were by the knowledge that we could've lost each other just as we'd truly found one another.

And it was more than that which allowed me not to care where we were, what I'd done in here and what was happening outside these thin walls, when he slipped the dagger from my hand, sheathing it on my thigh. Or when he turned and lifted me, placing me on my knees on the cushioned bench as he tugged the leggings and undergarments to my knees. What allowed me not to care was what the Duchess had said before I killed her, the utter coldness and emptiness I'd felt as I watched her die, and the haunting intuition that there had been some truth to her words.

Casteel placed my hands on the wall as he scraped the sharp edge of a fang along the side of my throat, sending a bolt of wanton heat and dampness through me.

"This is so inappropriate," I panted.

"I don't give a fuck." He nipped at my skin again, and my entire body arched. "Brace yourself."

I did, but nothing could've prepared me for what happened. He struck as fast as a viper, sinking his fangs deep into my throat at the same moment he thrust into me. The twisting shock of pain and pleasure stole my breath and fixed my wide eyes on the ceiling—on the circle with an arrow piercing the center embossed in black and crimson. Infinity. Power.

The Ascended Royal Crest.

And then...then I became that fire again, the flame.

There was nothing but an excess of pleasure and ecstasy, intensified by the deep, rumbling sounds he made, the hand that slipped between my thighs, and those wickedly skilled fingers.

A new madness engulfed us, one not too different from what I'd felt when I stepped out into the courtyard. And maybe all the death we saw and inflicted also drove us to this moment, to the hungry way his mouth moved at my neck and the nearly greedy way my hips pushed back against his. The feel of each other was a reminder that we were alive. That we'd survived. That there would be time for all those things I'd thought of as we were pinned to the ground under the catapult. That even as uncertain as our future was, there *was* one. And when the storm inside of us crested and took us both over the edge, I knew it was also the intensity of what we felt for one another, what we had both been fighting, that drove us.

That drove Casteel to abandon his people to save me.

That drove me to hold a dagger to my own throat, ready to slice deep to save him.

The intensity of the emotion, how all-consuming it suddenly felt, didn't make sense. My head fell back against his chest, and he kissed the corner of my mouth, the longer scar, and then the shorter one, I didn't care.

"You already have me," I whispered.

Chapter 41

The field I'd seen the Guardians training in was littered with cots occupied by the injured and the dead. Most were mortal. Twenty Descenters or those of Atlantian descent that had settled in Spessa's End had perished. At least fifty of Atlantian descent who'd arrived with the army had died, and double that occupied the cots. A dozen or so wolven were injured beyond their capabilities to heal themselves. The elemental Atlantians that had made up the vast majority of the army had healed themselves. None of the Guardians had fallen, and only a few were among the injured.

The Atlantian army had been successful, though, even with the casualties. They'd seized control by the time Casteel and I stepped out of the carriage to find Kieran and several Atlantian warriors standing guard.

I couldn't even muster an ounce of embarrassment at the knowledge that some realized what had happened inside the carriage.

Only one soldier in the entirety of the Solis army had been left alive. Casteel and a few others had left hours ago, escorting a young boy barely beyond the cusp of manhood to the scorched land of Pompay, charged with the task of relaying a warning.

And a message.

Atlantia had reclaimed Spessa's End, and any who came for

the town would meet the same fate as those before them. The message was also an opportunity. Casteel had initiated a part of his original plan. The Battle of Spessa's End didn't have to be the first of many to come. The Prince and *Princess* of Atlantia were willing to meet with the King and Queen of Solis to discuss the kingdoms' futures.

I didn't envy the boy who was tasked with delivering the message.

And I didn't envy any of the family and friends of those who had lost loved ones. Each time I saw someone I knew standing, I'd been overcome with relief.

"Thank you," a raspy voice drew my attention. An older wolven had taken a nasty blow to the arm, nearly severing it. He was the last one to be checked. I'd healed him. Like I'd healed all of those who'd allowed me to try.

Some had refused my touch, like those in New Haven had. My chest squeezed painfully as Elijah's image took form in my mind.

I cleared my throat. "You're welcome." Back and arms aching, I started to rise. "I don't know if your arm is completely healed, so you should have a Healer look at it as soon as possible."

The wolven caught my left arm before I could move. His eyes widened slightly at the contact, and I wondered if he'd felt the strange, electric-like current that others had when he touched me. He slowly turned my hand over. "It's true, then?" he asked, looking at the golden swirl across my palm. "You've married our Prince?"

I nodded as my heart skipped. This middle-aged wolven, with his head of ropey black-and-silver dreads had been the first to ask.

"Others are saying you fought beside him the entire battle."

"I started on the Rise, but I did go down."

"And yet, you're here. You've been here this whole time, healing others," he said, his pale eyes sharp. "With your touch."

"How could I not when I can help?" And I had helped. Talia the Healer I'd caught a brief glimpse of, had her hands full with those who refused my aid. So, after the battle, I had taken the time to wash the blood from my face and hands, even though it was still caked to my clothing and dried under my fingernails.

He nodded as he let go of my wrist and laid his head back on the cot. "Kieran said you were of the empath bloodline."

I nodded again.

"I've never seen an empath glow silver before," he said. "And I remember them. I was a young boy then, and there was only a handful still alive, but I'd remember something like that."

Wondering how old this wolven was, I said, "Jasper said the same."

"Not surprised to hear that. He knows things," the wolven said. "Except when to keep his mouth closed.

I smiled wearily. "That's what I hear."

"You must be descended from an old empath line."

"What else could I be?" I asked, not really expecting an answer.

"Yes," he murmured. "What else?"

I looked over my shoulder, spotting Quentyn and Beckett moving among the injured and recovering. "Water and food are being brought. Is there anything else you need?"

"No." The wolven eyed me as I stood. "But you should be careful, Princess."

I stilled.

"I've watched the others watching you. Our Prince may have chosen you. You may have fought beside him and for them. You may have healed many of us," he said with a voice full of gravel. "But they didn't choose you, and many aren't old enough to even remember the empath bloodlines. Those who are, remember what they could do—what they were called."

"Soul Eaters? I can't do that," I said, even as my heart started pumping. "I can't drain a person of emotion."

"But they don't know that." His gaze shifted to the cots. "Is there someone here? To watch over you?" He started to sit up. "You shouldn't be out here alone with the Prince—"

"I'm fine." Gently, I pressed him onto his back. "I'm armed and can take care of myself."

"I don't doubt that, but—" His features tightened, almost as if he were in pain, but I knew he wasn't. "I shouldn't say this. It's damn near treasonous, but you healed me. I owe you."

"You don't owe me."

"It would've taken days, maybe even longer for me to heal that wound, and that is if I kept my arm. I'm a wolven, Princess. That does not mean I can grow back limbs."

I glanced at the pale pink mark that nearly encircled the entirety of his biceps. The gods had to have favored him to keep that limb attached after that kind of injury.

"It's pretty well known among the armies that once the King knew of the Prince's plans to capture you, he began to make his own plans. I doubt he knows how much the Prince's plans have changed, but his have not."

A heaviness sat on my shoulders. "He plans to use me to send a message. I doubt I would be a message that was alive and breathing," I said. "I know."

"Then you should also know that Casteel is our Prince," the wolven said in a low voice. "But Valyn, his father, is our King."

"I know," I repeated, fixing a smile on my face.

"Do you?"

The heaviness intensified as I nodded again. "You should rest. At least until Talia can confirm you're healed."

The older wolven relented, unhappily, but with one last goodbye, I roamed the edges of the makeshift infirmary, scanning the field and the banners embossed with the Atlantian Crest.

I could feel eyes on me.

I'd felt them the entire time I moved through the field.

But with all the pain that had been echoing around me, I hadn't allowed myself to sense anything beyond the agony.

But they didn't choose you.

I flinched as the wolven's words played over and over in my head as I turned away from the field.

What the wolven had said about the King and the veiled warning hinting at where the Atlantian people's loyalty lay didn't come as much of a shock.

In the back of my mind, I'd already figured as much, hadn't I? And that was before they heard Duchess Teerman's ridiculous claims that I was Queen Ileana's granddaughter. The Queen was an Ascended. I was not of her blood nor born of flesh and fire—whatever that meant.

But I wasn't like other empaths, and even so, that bloodline sounded more feared than respected. I knew I wouldn't have many supporters in Atlantia. I barely had them here.

Casteel was the Prince of Atlantia, well-loved and respected. That much was obvious. But not a single person spoke ill of his father or mother, and I knew they were just as loved as he was. Casteel was the Prince, but his father was the King, and if he wanted me dead to send a message, his people would follow his lead. I didn't know if a ring or marriage imprint would change that when me fighting and killing to protect the people of Atlantia hadn't.

And Casteel…he had to know that. He always had to know that.

Sitting in the tub of warm soapy water, I had my arms locked around my legs, my knees pressed to my chest and my eyes closed. I recalled the warm sand under my feet, and the weight of my mother's and father's hands in mine. I remembered how easy Ian's smile was as he ran ahead, and the sound of my mother's laugh and the way my father stared at her like…

Like it was the most beautiful sound he'd ever heard.

The corners of my lips curved up. Thinking of those moments had eased the coldness that returned when I walked back to the fortress. What the Duchess had said and thoughts of Tawny haunted me, just like I knew they would. Along with worries about the King's plans and the loyalty of the Atlantian people.

I opened my eyes at the soft click of the bathing chamber door. The scent of rich, earthy spice, and crisp pine enveloped the soap's lemony scent as Casteel knelt beside me. The strands of his hair were damp, and the clothing he wore was clean and free of blood. When and where he'd cleaned up, I had no idea. I hadn't seen him since he left with the young Solis soldier.

"Hey," he said quietly, his gaze roaming over my face, lingering on a bruise I'd gained in the battle.

"Hi," I whispered.

One side of his lips curled up, and I felt my cheeks warm. I cleared my throat. "Is everything okay? With the soldier?"

He nodded. "He's on his way to Whitebridge." Reaching over, he gathered up several strands of my wet hair and draped it over my shoulder. He bared the bite mark on my throat, and I swore his grin deepened. "I hear I owe you a thank you."

I held my legs tighter. "For what?"

"You spent the entire day healing those you could and easing the pain of those you couldn't." Those twin amber jewels met mine. "Thank you."

I swallowed. "I only did what I could—what anyone with my abilities would do." At least, that's what I hoped. "Some of them wouldn't let me."

His fingers trailed over the damp skin of my back. "Some of them are idiots."

"They are your people."

"*Our* people," he corrected softly.

My breath caught, and a bit of panic and unease sparked at the realization that they were my people whether they liked it or not. "I'm…I'm sorry about Elijah and all of them. I liked him, and Magda was nice. But they…they were your friends."

His lashes lowered as he exhaled raggedly. "I've known Elijah since he was a boy, and I know how crazy that sounds since I look younger than him. He knew the risks, and I know he fought back. I know all of them did, but he didn't deserve that. None of them did."

"No, they didn't," I agreed softly.

"I should've made them all leave. Risked drawing the attention. I should've—"

"You did what you could. Some of those people couldn't travel because of their injuries, and none of them were ready to leave immediately," I argued. "What happened there isn't your fault."

Casteel said nothing.

"You know that, right? That was the Ascended. They are

responsible. Not you."

He nodded slowly. "I know that."

"Do you?"

Swallowing, he nodded, and I wasn't sure if that was the case. "I was told something odd earlier, when I returned to Spessa's End."

"I'm half afraid to ask."

There was a brief grin. "You remember when the wolven showed up during the battle?"

"How could I forget that?"

"Glad you haven't because that was when you had a knife to your throat—"

"I was trying to save you and the people," I reminded him. "We've already covered this."

"We did, but Kieran told me that he heard you calling him. He said the other wolven felt it, too. That they all veered in our direction. Jasper confirmed it," he said. "He said the same thing."

"I didn't. I mean, how?" I swallowed. "I was obviously feeling a lot in that moment. I felt like, I don't know, like I was about to lose control. But how is that even possible?

"I don't know, Poppy. I've never seen anything like that. I don't know how they could've picked up anything from you." He tugged on a strand of my wet hair and draped it over my bare shoulder. "Neither do they. I asked them when they came by just now. Both said they felt you calling for them—calling for help."

Goosebumps broke out over my skin. "Delano. Oh, my gods...."

"What?"

"When we were in New Haven and I was kept in the room, he burst inside at one point, swearing he heard me calling for him. But I hadn't."

Casteel's brows slashed over his eyes. "Did something happen at that time? Because if so and I wasn't told about it—"

"Nothing happened. I was mad—mad at you, because I was locked in the room," I explained. "He then said it must've been the wind, and it *was* windy then, so I forgot about it."

Casteel lifted another strand of hair. "That's bizarre."

I stared at him. "That's all you have to say to them *feeling* my call? That's bizarre?"

"Well, the definition of bizarre is something strange and unusual—"

"I know what bizarre means," I interrupted. "Is that another empath trait manifesting?"

His gaze met mine. "I've never heard of an empath being able to do that."

My stomach dipped. "Just like glowing silver and being able to heal—"

"You could be of two bloodlines," he cut in. "We talked about that before. It could be possible."

More possible than Queen Ileana being my grandmother. I had no idea what to think of the whole hearing my call thing, but what if that was an empath ability? People could project their pain and fear. What if that was what I was doing, and the wolven, for some reason, picked up on it? That seemed like it made logical sense.

"What do we do now?" I asked.

"Right now? At this very moment?" His smile was smoke as his gaze traveled over the bare skin he could see, which wasn't any of the interesting parts. "I have so many ideas."

"That's not what I was talking about," I said, even though I was glad to see the somberness leave his eyes.

"I know, but I'm distracted. It's not my fault. You're naked."

"You can't see anything."

"What I can see is enough." He lowered himself to his knees as he rested his arms on the edge of the tub. "So, I'm thoroughly distracted."

"You being distracted sounds like your problem and not mine," I told him.

He chuckled as he bent his head, kissing the patch of my knee that wasn't covered by my arms. "We'll leave for Atlantia tomorrow. The Atlantian armies that arrived will remain behind just in case the Ascended want to make a very bad life choice. Spessa's End will be protected."

There was a whooshing sensation in my chest. "So soon?"

"We would've already been there if things had gone as

planned." He leaned back. "We are married, but you haven't been crowned yet. That needs to happen."

I worried my lower lip. "I get that the crowning makes things official, but what will that really change? Your…" I briefly closed my eyes. "Our people still don't trust me or like me. Whatever. And your father still has his plans, right? For me?"

His brows lowered. "My father's plans have changed."

"What if they haven't?"

He studied me for a moment. "Did someone say something to you?"

Not wanting to potentially get the older wolven in trouble, I gave a slight shake of my head. "It's just…I know many don't accept me, even after the marriage and last night. You're the Prince and all. But he's the King—"

"And you're starting to sound like Alastir," he interrupted. "I'd almost think he got you all worked up again, but he stayed in Atlantia."

"It's not Alastir," I said. "But he did say that, and he has a point. I know you wanted to marry me partly because it offered me a level of protection—"

"Originally, Poppy. And that was only because I'd convinced myself that was the reason," he stated. "It wasn't the only reason. Neither was freeing my brother or preventing a war. I wanted you, and I wanted to find a way to try to keep you."

There was a different kind of snag in my chest now in response to his words. "You have me," I whispered the words I'd said to him in the carriage.

"I know." His gaze held mine. "And no one, not even my father or my mother, will change that."

I believed him.

I really did.

"No one will harm you," he vowed. "I will not allow it."

"Neither will I."

He smiled then, both dimples appearing. "I know. Come." Rising, he reached for the towel. "If you stay in there any longer, you will start to grow fins."

"Like a ceeren?"

A grin appeared. "Like a ceeren."

I didn't move though. "I lied to you."

Casteel arched a brow. "About?"

"You asked me if the Duchess had said anything to me before I killed her, and I said no. That was a lie."

A heartbeat passed. "What did she say?"

"I...I asked her about my brother and yours. She said they were together, but that's all she would say about them." I watched him return to kneeling beside me. "She told me that Tawny was going to Ascend without waiting—that it could've already happened. She said that the Queen knew how much I cared for Tawny and wanted her to be there, so when I returned home, I would feel comfortable."

"Gods." Casteel leaned over, cupping the back of my head. "You don't know if any of that is true. Any of it, Poppy. Your brother. Mine. Tawny. She—"

"She said that the Queen will be thrilled when she learns we've married. That if she knew that had happened, none of what took place last night would've been necessary," I told him, and he stilled. "She told me that I accomplished the one thing the Queen never could. That I took Atlantia."

"That doesn't make any sense, Poppy."

"I know," I said. "Neither does what she said about the Queen being my grandmother. It makes no sense at all. It's so far out there that, so unbelievable that I...I can't help but wonder if some of it is true."

Chapter 42

We rode east, toward Atlantia, under a sky that was a canvas of blues.

The men who'd traveled with Alastir were with us, even though the wolven hadn't made the trip back to Spessa's End. They were missing a few, more than just the wolven Dante, but our group had tripled, if not more, in size. We'd gained Jasper and several other wolven, who were returning to Atlantia. Vonetta had remained back in Spessa's End, but she had promised that she would see me soon as she planned to return for her mother's birthday and the upcoming birth of her little brother or sister.

The barren flatlands on either side of the heavily wooded area gave way to fields of tall reeds with tiny, white flowers. Beckett ran beside us in his wolven form, seeming to pull from an endless reserve of energy I found enviable. He would race ahead, disappearing among the wispy plants, only to pop up a few seconds later beside us once more. He never strayed too far from our side—or rather from Casteel's side. I figured Beckett's closeness had to do with his Prince's presence, and I was glad I picked up no fear from him—from any of those who traveled with us.

But the group was quiet, even Casteel, and there were so many reasons for the silence. There wasn't a single person here who hadn't lost someone in the battle or at New Haven.

I couldn't think of Elijah, of Magda and her unborn child, of any of them. I couldn't think of who would now add the names to the walls underground.

But I knew Casteel did. I knew that was why he'd fallen silent several times the night before, and I figured it had very little to do with what we'd talked about. He missed Elijah. Mourned him and all the others, and I knew he believed he'd failed them.

My thoughts were heavy, and it wore me down. The lack of sleep didn't help. Nightmares of the night of the Craven attack found me once more, and even though Casteel had been there when I woke, gasping for air with a scream burning through my throat, the horrors of the night found me again as soon as I fell back asleep.

I wasn't looking forward to tonight.

The sun was high above us when I realized the horizon I'd been staring at wasn't where the clouds met the land. I sat straighter, gripping the saddle as patches of dark green started to appear in the gray ahead. This mist. It was the mist obscuring the mountains, so thick that for however many miles we'd traveled, I'd believed it to be the sky.

"You see it now?" Casteel asked. "The Skotos?"

Heart stammering, I nodded. "The mist is so thick. If it's like this during the day, how much worse is it at night?"

"It'll thin out a bit once we get into the foothills." Casteel's arm remained secure around me as I stretched forward. "But at night—well, the mist is all around you."

I shivered as more of the mountains began to peek through the mist. A rocky cropping here, a cluster of trees there. "How did the armies get through the mist then?" I looked at Kieran. "How did you get here so quickly."

"The gods allowed it," he replied, and my brows rose. "The mist did not come for us. It thinned out at night, enough for us to continue forward."

I sat back against Casteel, hoping the gods would allow us the same.

Casteel burst the bubble of hope the next second. "The mist

is never as bad leaving Atlantia as it is entering."

"Great," I murmured.

"We're lucky that the Skotos Mountains are nowhere near as large as the range beyond," Naill said from where he rode on Jasper's other side.

"There are larger ones?" The Skotos Mountains were the largest in Solis, that I knew of anyway.

The Atlantian nodded. "It takes less than a day to cross where we're passing through. However, some peaks would take days." He shifted on his saddle. "But there are mountains in Atlantia that stretch so high into the sky, you see nothing else. Peaks so high that it would take weeks just to reach the top. And once there, even an Atlantian would find it difficult to breathe."

Tendrils of mist began to creep between the bushy reeds, forming little clouds above them.

Beckett dashed ahead, and within a heartbeat, was swallowed up by the mist. I sucked in a sharp breath, straining forward as I reached for my dagger—

"He's okay." Casteel's hand closed over mine. He squeezed gently. "See? There he is."

My heart didn't slow as the dark, furry head appeared above the mist, tongue lolling as he panted with excitement. "Are you sure there're no Craven here?"

Riding slightly ahead, Emil said, "There hasn't been a Craven this far east since the war."

I still remained alert as we neared a blanket of mist where only shadows of shapes existed behind it. Muscles tensed as every instinct in me wanted to grab the reins and pull Setti to a stop. We couldn't possibly pass through this. Who knew what waited on the other side? And what if they were wrong about the Craven? Goosebumps broke out across my skin as Jasper and Emil disappeared through the wall of mist. A shout built in my throat, lodging there when Delano vanished into the thick, grayish-white haze. I started to press back against Casteel—

He slowed Setti. "The first time I saw the wall of mist from the other side, I refused to pass through. It wasn't because of the Craven. I hadn't learned yet that they travel in the mist. It was that I feared we'd reached the very end of the kingdom, and that there was nothing beyond it," Casteel told me, his arm a band of steel around me. "I know that sounds silly, but I was young, less than a year from the Culling, and Kieran also feared passing through it."

I looked to our right, where Kieran kept pace with us. After everything I'd learned, I still found it hard to picture either of them afraid of anything.

"It was Malik who went through first," Casteel continued, dragging his hand around my waist in a slow, comforting circle. I looked down, my gaze snagging on the golden band he wore. "For a moment, I thought that was the last I saw of my brother, but then he came back. Told us there was nothing but weeds and sky on the other side."

"That wasn't what he told us at first," Kieran chimed in. "Malik claimed there were giants with three heads on the other side."

"He said what?"

Casteel laughed. "Yeah, he did. We believed him until he started laughing. Bastard doubled over with it." There was a fondness in his tone, and it was so rare to hear him speak of his brother without sadness and anger. "It will only take a few seconds to pass through. I promise."

As Naill entered the mist, I nodded jerkily. "If there are three-headed giants on the other side, I'm going to be very angry with both of you."

"If there are three-headed giants awaiting us, your anger will be the least of my concerns," Casteel replied, tone light with amusement. "Ready?"

Not really, but I said, "Yes."

Fighting the urge to close my eyes, I jerked as thin vapors stretched out from the rapidly approaching mass, a cool caress against my cheeks. Setti made a soft whinny as the tendrils curled around his legs, and then the mist enveloped us. I could see nothing. Nothing but the thick, choking, milky-white air. Panic bubbled up in me—

Casteel shifted behind me, pressing his lips to the space behind my ear as he whispered, "Think of all the things I could do to you." The hand at my hip glided over my thigh, and then up it, moving with predatory grace toward my very center. "That no one would ever be able to see. Not even you."

My breath snagged for a wholly different reason as his fingers danced over me. I tensed as muscles low in my stomach clenched in response and my head snapped to the side. I opened my mouth, but whatever I was about to say was forgotten when Casteel caught my lower lip between his teeth.

He slowly let go of my lip, but his mouth was still there, warm and solid against mine. "I have *so* many ideas."

My heart stuttered as a wave of shivers exploded over me. I could imagine what some of his ideas involved, and for a brief moment, I wasn't thinking about *anything*. A breathy sound left me, lost to the mist—

"You can open your eyes now," he murmured against my lips.

I hadn't even realized I'd closed them until he spoke, but now I knew why he'd done and said what he did. He'd sought to distract me, and it had worked, bringing a quick end to the rising panic.

"Thank you," I whispered, and his hand, which had made its way back to my hip, squeezed. I opened my eyes as he straightened behind me to see...

To see that the mist had thinned out to wispy coils around moss-shrouded rocks and the legs of the waiting horses. I blinked as I saw Beckett sitting before us, his tail swaying along the ground, stirring the mist as he craned his head back, looking up. I followed his gaze, lips parting on a sharp inhale as I saw what he looked upon.

Gold.

Glittering, luminous gold leaves soaked in the rays of sunlight that penetrated the mist.

"Beautiful, aren't they?" Delano asked, looking up.

"Yes." Awed, my gaze crept over the golden trees. "I've never seen anything like them." Even when the leaves changed colors in Masadonia with the weather, the yellows were muted and muddied. These leaves were pure, spun gold. "What kind of trees are they?"

"Trees of Aios," Casteel answered, referring to the Goddess

of Love, Fertility, and Beauty. I couldn't think of a better namesake. "They grew in the foothills and throughout the Skotos range after she went to sleep here, deep underground."

I glanced back at Casteel. "She sleeps here?"

His eyes, which were only a shade darker than the leaves, met mine. "She does."

"Some believe she is under the highest peak," Jasper said, drawing my wide-eyed gaze to his. "Where the trees of Aios flourish so intensely, you can see them from the Chambers of Nyktos."

"Chambers…of Nyktos?" I repeated.

"It's a Temple just beyond the Pillars," Emil explained. "Very beautiful. You must visit them."

"Does he sleep there?" I asked.

He smiled as he shook his head. "No one knows where Nyktos rests."

"Oh," I whispered.

"We should go ahead and split into smaller groups," Casteel cut in. "Kieran will ride with us. Beckett, you need to take human form and go with Delano and Naill."

I watched the wolven bound through the mist, causing Naill's horse to prance nervously. The Atlantian rolled his eyes as he looked at Casteel.

"He's good practice for whenever you decide to settle down and have children," Casteel said, and I could hear the smile in his words.

Naill looked like he might fall from his horse.

Having guided his horse to face us, Jasper smirked. "I fear after one night keeping an eye on Beckett, he will swear off children."

"Gods," Naill muttered as Beckett suddenly launched himself at a…gold leaf that had tumbled into his line of sight.

Quentyn shook his head as he watched his friend. "You should see him with the butterflies."

"I really don't want to." Naill sighed.

"We'll meet at the Gold Rock." Casteel addressed the group. "Remember, no one goes anywhere unaccompanied. Stay together in groups no larger than three." He turned to where

Beckett was finally sitting. "Do not explore. Do not answer any calls."

My stomach tumbled. Was Casteel referencing what the wolven believed they had heard from me?

"I expect to see everyone at Gold Rock, all in one piece with their minds intact," Casteel continued, and a shiver curled its way down my spine. "Be safe."

There were several nods as the group began to break apart, Beckett leaving with Naill and Delano, who said, "I'll make sure he shifts."

Quentyn stayed with Jasper and Emil, but before they headed to our right, Jasper rode to our side, clasping Casteel's hand. "Be safe, Cas. You've been gone far too long and are too close to home to not arrive."

"You have nothing to fear." Casteel's voice softened.

Jasper nodded, and then his attention shifted to me. "Stay close to them, Penellaphe. The magic in these mountains has a way of getting under your skin. Trust them but be wary of trusting what your eyes and ears tell you."

And with those parting words, he rode off, the now pale and quiet Quentyn in tow.

I looked over my shoulder at Casteel. "What in the hell is this mountain going to do?"

"Nothing," he replied, urging Setti forward. "As long as we don't allow it to."

Quiet.

Casteel and Kieran didn't speak. The thick moss along the path cushioned the horses' steps. There were no sounds of birds or any animal life, nor the echo of any wind rustling the golden canopy of leaves above us. With every passing hour, the temperature seemed to drop another couple of degrees as we climbed the mountain. The heavy cloak I'd all but forgotten while in Spessa's End was donned. Soon, a tingling numbness invaded my cheeks. It wasn't long after that when Casteel tugged the hood of the cloak up over my head and pulled the halves of his around me, too. We continued on in eerie silence and the unnatural beauty of the mountain. Gold leaves above glimmered, and along the ground, flecks of gold spotted the moss and glistened from the bark, reminding me of the Blood Forest.

All too soon, the beams of sunlight filtering through the leaves faded, and the streaks of mist thickened, blanketing the moss as we continued climbing. The fog grew, swirling around our legs and then our waists. The last of the sun reached us, and we forged on. Several hours into the evening, we stopped when the mist stretched above us.

Casteel guided Setti to a halt as he glanced around. I had no idea what he was looking for as I could see nothing but streams of white mist. "This appears to be as good a place as any," he said, his breath forming misty clouds as he turned to Kieran. "What do you think?"

The wolven was a faint shape behind the mist. "We've definitely reached the peak, so this should be fine."

Should be? "How can you tell we've reached the peak?"

"If we hadn't, we wouldn't be able to see more than a few inches in front of us," Kieran answered as he dismounted, stirring the mist.

I frowned. They could see more than a few inches?

Casteel shifted the reins to my hands. "Hold onto these. I'm going to get down and walk you two over to the tree."

Taking the reins, I wondered exactly what tree he was talking about. He swung off Setti's back, and for a moment, the gloom spun around him, seeming to swallow him. My heart kicked against my ribs. His face cleared the mist as he walked to Setti's front, curling his fingers around the horse's halter. He walked us through the chilled, churning air and then stopped, taking the reins from me as he spoke to Setti, crooning softly to the horse. I picked up something about carrots and orchard grass before he came back to my side.

Casteel lifted his hands to my hips, and I gripped his forearms as I leaned back, pulling a leg over the saddle. He helped me down, taking my hand as he unloaded one of the larger bags and the rolled blankets.

"Will it be like this?" I asked as he guided me forward, hating that I had to go blindly. "All night?"

"It will, but you'll get used to it."

"I don't think that's possible."

"How about here?" Kieran's voice came from somewhere. "The ground is pretty level."

"Perfect." Casteel seemed to know exactly where Kieran was because after a few moments, he appeared from within the mist.

Casteel let go of my hand, and I almost reached for it as I looked back, unable to see anything. "Do you think Setti will be okay?"

"He'll be fine," Casteel told me as he knelt. A flame sparked to life as he lit an oil lamp, chasing away a bit of the mist. "I'm going to give him some feed and then a blanket. He'll probably be asleep before us."

I had no idea how I would sleep tonight. The surroundings made the Blood Forest feel like a luxurious respite.

Another lantern came alive, held by Kieran. "I'm going to grab some branches."

Casteel glanced up. "Don't go too far."

"Yes, sir," Kieran answered with far too much enthusiasm.

I watched the yellow glow of his lantern until it disappeared. "Why aren't there any animals in these mountains?"

"They sense the magic and stay away." Casteel unrolled a thick canvas, one designed to keep the cold and damp from the ground from soaking through. As he spread out one of the blankets, the mist scattered a bit.

"Here." He took my gloved hand when I didn't move, drawing me down so I was seated in front of him. "I'm going to take care of Setti. I'll be right back, okay?"

I nodded. When he rose, I noticed he left the only source of light behind. "You don't need the lantern?"

"No." He started to turn and then stopped. "Don't let your curiosity get the best of you. Stay here. Please."

"You do not need to worry about me wandering off." I wasn't going to move more than a foot, and I didn't after he went back to feed Setti and make sure he was comfortable.

But I did lift a hand, waving it through the tendrils of fog gathering around me. The mist dispersed, only to seep back to dance and swirl around the finger I wore my ring on. It almost seemed alive, as if it were interacting with my movements and not simply impacted by them. My eyes squinted as a wisp of mist coiled down the left arm of my cloak. I jerked my arm back, and the mist recoiled and stayed there, a foot or so in front of me, waiting...

Biting my lip, I stretched forward, extending my fingers. The mist pulsed and then slowly expanded, forming a stream that grew what looked like ghostly fingers. The hand flattened against my left palm.

I gasped and drew back. The mist responded in kind, mimicking my movements.

"What are you doing over there?" Casteel's voice broke through the silence, seeming to startle the mist more than me. It scattered.

And then it struck me. "This isn't normal mist, is it? The mist is the *magic*."

"Yes," came his response. "And you're definitely doing something, aren't you?"

I shook my head in wonder. "No..." I dragged the word out as the magic twisted toward the sound of Casteel's voice. I rose onto my knees and stretched out, skimming just the tips of my fingers through the vapors. It *shimmied*. My brows rose. "Kieran said the magic here is tied to the gods. How is that possible if they sleep?"

"The short, very condensed version of a very convoluted reason is that even though the gods sleep, there is a level of consciousness still present. You already know that."

I did.

"They created the mist to protect the Pillars of Atlantia," he explained, and the mist turned back to him, as if it were listening. "But it's basically an extension of them, or at the very least, an extension of their will."

Something about being surrounded by a part of the gods' consciousness was incredibly bizarre. "What do the Pillars of Atlantia look like?"

"You'll see them tomorrow."

"But—"

"Some say patience is a virtue," his voice echoed back to me.

"Some deserve a punch in the face," I muttered, but I fell silent. As much as it perturbed me to admit, Casteel was right. I eventually grew used to the mist or, more appropriately, the magic. I wondered though…if it were an extension of the gods' will, then why did Atlantians trigger it? Then again, it had allowed the armies to pass through.

However, they were leaving instead of entering.

Casteel returned, as did Kieran. A small fire was lit, beating back the thickest of the magic. I took care of my personal needs, not far from Casteel's presence, which was not something I cared to ever repeat, and no amount of intimacy or openness would change that. Then we ate by the fire. It wasn't until afterward, when Kieran stretched out on the canvas that Casteel had laid down earlier, that I took a closer look at the sleeping arrangements.

There were three blankets, side by side and overlapping. My eyes widened as I stared at the two spaces beside Kieran.

"Are we sleeping here?" I demanded. "The three of us?"

"I was wondering when she was going to notice that," Kieran commented.

My gaze narrowed as the mist slipped over Kieran's chest. "Is it really necessary that the three of us sleep…so close?"

"Is it necessary for you to make it sound like we'd be doing something other than sleeping?" Casteel queried, and when my gaze shot to him, he grinned. "I mean, all we're doing is sleeping side by side." He reclined back on one hand as the dimple appeared in his cheek. "Unless you have a different idea. If so, I'm very curious to learn more about it, *wife.*

I stared at him as the mist seemed to still around us.

"What? I'm just a very curious soul."

"Did you forget that I'm armed?" I asked softly.

"Are you thinking about using it against me?" In the glow of the fire, both dimples appeared. "If so, this sleeping arrangement may get very uncomfortable for Kieran."

I immediately thought of the Joining, and the humor dancing across Casteel's face was evidence that he knew where my mind had gone.

"Or...interesting," came the wolven's response.

"I'm going to seriously hurt you both," I growled as the mist drifted away.

"And I'm so very...*intrigued* now," Casteel replied and then laughed as he patted the space beside him. "It's going to get even colder during the night, more so than when we were in the Blood Forest. In about an hour or so, you'll be grateful for the body heat."

That was highly unlikely.

"Which, by the way, is the only thing either of us is offering tonight," Casteel tacked on, the teasing gone from his gaze.

Kieran snorted and there was a taste of sugar on my tongue—amusement. "Yeah, I don't feel like having my head ripped off tonight."

"I doubt that will happen," I muttered.

Casteel moved then, catching my hand. He pulled me down beside him, and I didn't really fight him. The sleeping arrangements were awkward, but Casteel was my...he was my husband.

And it wasn't like Kieran hadn't already been in far more awkward situations with us.

Like when he'd seen me naked in the tub when we barely knew each other.

Or when he'd heard me screaming and walked in on Casteel and I, only to discover they were not shouts of fear or pain.

Or when Casteel had needed to feed.

I told myself to stop thinking about all of that as Casteel drew the blanket over us and then settled beside me. There was space between the three of us. Not much. Maybe an inch or so, and I so hoped I stayed still during the night.

And I really hoped that what Casteel had said about Kieran wasn't true—that he kicked in the middle of the night.

I wanted to turn toward Casteel. I liked...using him as a pillow. Okay. I just liked being close to him, but he was lying on his back, actually behaving himself, and so I stayed where I was, watching the mist as it moved in slow waves above us. After a couple of minutes, I tilted my head, and it seemed to do the same, tipping to the same side.

I glanced at Casteel. I thought his eyes were closed. When I looked at Kieran, it appeared to be the same with him. Could they really be asleep already? I drew a hand out from the blanket and lifted it a few inches. The mist dropped and stretched like before, forming wispy fingers.

"What are you doing?" Casteel asked.

The mist fell apart.

"You scared it," I grumbled.

"Scared what?" he asked.

"The mist—or magic. Whatever."

Casteel shifted onto his side. "You can't scare it," he said. "It's just magic. It's not like it's alive."

"Seems alive to me," I replied.

"That doesn't make sense," Kieran said tiredly.

"It interacts with you," I told them.

"It's your imagination." The wolven rolled, and I felt his knee brush my leg.

"It's not my imagination."

"The magic can play tricks on you," Casteel said, taking my hand and drawing it back under the blanket. "Make you think you're seeing things you aren't."

I frowned.

"You should sleep," he said. "The morning will come too soon."

Not soon enough for me.

In the quiet, my thoughts wandered. I thought of Renfern and how I wished I'd done something more, something different to change what'd happened to him and Elijah and all the others. I wondered if Phillips and Luddie, the guard and Huntsmen who'd traveled from Masadonia with us, had known the truth about the Ascended or if they had been a casualty of a quiet war. Just like Rylan and...and Vikter. My heart ached as I watched the mist slowly move above me. I missed Tawny, and I prayed that she hadn't gone through the Ascension. Then my mind veered to how the wolven had surrounded us. Could that have been me?

Had I projected something, and they simply answered?

I looked over at Kieran again. His eyes were closed. Did he really think it was me, calling to them?

I hated moments like this, when sleep evaded me and all that existed was things better not dwelled upon. I forced my thoughts away, and something occurred to me. "Are there any gods asleep under the Blood Forest?"

"What?" Casteel murmured, his voice thick with sleep.

I realized I'd woken him, though I didn't feel even remotely bad about that. I repeated my question.

"That is possibly the most random thing that's ever come out of your mouth," Kieran grumbled. "And I've heard you say some pretty random stuff."

"There are no gods under the Blood Forest—as far as I know," Casteel answered, his eyes closed. "What made you think of that?"

"The trees here remind me of the Blood Forest. Though gold instead of red."

"Hmm," Casteel murmured. "Makes sense."

"Maybe to you," Kieran grumbled.

"Do you know where Penellaphe sleeps?" I asked about the goddess I'd been named after.

Kieran sighed. "Not here, I can tell you that."

A small smile played across Casteel's lips. "I believed she slumbers under the Great Atheneum in Carsodonia."

"Really?" When Casteel nodded, I decided I didn't like the idea of the goddess of Wisdom, Loyalty, and Duty sleeping there, at the heart of the Ascended. "What about Theon?"

"The god of Accord and War and his twin Lailah rest beneath the Pillars of Atlantia," Casteel answered.

I opened my mouth—

"Please, don't," Kieran interrupted.

"Don't what?"

"Ask where every single god or goddess sleeps, because that will lead to more questions. I just know it will," he said, and I rolled my eyes. "You should be asleep like them, *Your Highness.*"

"Don't call me that," I snapped.

"Then go to sleep," Kieran ordered.

"I can't just fall asleep," I muttered. "I'm not like you two."

"I can always read to you," Casteel offered. "I still have a certain diary with me. There is a chapter I'm sure you'll be interested in. Miss Willa has the same sleeping arrangement—"

"No. Nope." I screwed my eyes closed. "Not necessary."

"Are you sure?" Casteel seemed to have wiggled closer. His entire leg pressed against mine.

"Yes."

He laughed softly, but I didn't dare say a word. I wouldn't put it past him to retrieve that damn diary and somehow be able to read those words with his extra-special Atlantian eyes. So, I lay there. I didn't know how much time passed before I fell asleep, but I knew I must've, because I suddenly became aware of how incredibly warm I felt. Every part of me had somehow escaped the cold of the mountain. Every part of me...

Slowly, I realized exactly why I was so toasty. I'd turned to Casteel in my sleep. He was on his back, and I'd all but climbed halfway on top of him. My head lay in the crook of his shoulder and chest. One of my legs was tossed over his, and the entire front of my body was fused to his side. One of his hands was curled around my shoulder.

But that wasn't the only explanation for why I was so warm. Heat pressed against my back. A heavy arm lay over my waist and a leg was tucked between mine.

If I had turned to Casteel in my sleep, Kieran had also turned, as if Casteel were a magnet that drew both of us.

My heart thudded as I lay there, unsure what to do. Should I wake them? Shrug Kieran off? I had a feeling that would wake them, and the last thing I wanted was for Kieran to discover the...the three of us cuddled together.

Both of them were incredibly warm, and there wasn't anything sinful about this. Well, the way I was half sprawled across Casteel didn't feel exactly innocent, but Kieran had most likely done what anyone would. He'd sought warmth in his sleep, and I couldn't exactly fault him for that.

What also didn't feel entirely innocent was where my hand rested. It was shamefully low on Casteel's stomach. I knew this because I could feel the imprint of the buttons against my palm.

If I moved my fingers more than an inch lower, I doubted he would remain asleep. The knowledge of that filled my head with all kinds of things I really shouldn't be thinking about at the moment, like what we'd done in the carriage...in the bedchamber, the cavern.

I mentally throat punched myself as I moved my hand away from that really fascinating part of Casteel, trying not to focus on the tautness of his lower stomach or the way his skin seemed to burn through his clothing—

Casteel's arm curled, tightening around my shoulder, drawing me closer. My breath snagged as his movement triggered Kieran. He shifted behind me, and my pulse felt like a trapped bird. A sleek, muscled thigh slid between mine, pressing in. I had no idea if it was Casteel's or Kieran's.

A hundred different thoughts and emotions exploded through me, so many, so fast, I couldn't make sense of them.

But neither of them woke, so I lay there, and my mind wandered again, not to places that would make this sleeping arrangement even more awkward or to sad ones.

I pretended.

Not like before with Casteel. I pretended that my brother was still a mortal, as was Tawny. That Casteel's brother was free, and that the Ascended weren't a reality. I pretended that tomorrow I would be arriving in a kingdom that welcomed me, to a King and Queen who would greet me with open arms. I pretended that Casteel and I were at the start of a life together, one that would be long and happy instead of one that felt like it could end at any minute. I pretended that we both aged, and that I was always reckless enough, brave enough to just let myself feel, to experience, to live without the past shadowing every choice I made, or the future looming over every decision.

That we always existed in the now and...*lived*.

Eventually, the warmth that both of them radiated, the steady, deep rise and fall of their chests, lulled me back to sleep. Sometime later, I drifted on the fringes of sleep once more, brought there by a whisper. A calling. A name.

"*Poppy...*"

Chapter 43

My entire being seized in recognition of that voice—one I couldn't pull from the depths of my imagination no matter how hard I tried.

But it was him—that was my father's voice calling my name.

My eyes opened to misty darkness and...and golden lamplight, and I realized I wasn't awake.

I was there once more, thrust back into the night that ended in blood-soaked screams.

"Poppy-flower, I know you're down there. Come out," he called. *"I need you to come to me, Poppy-flower."*

Chest twisting, I followed the sound of his voice, my lips moving but the voice coming out of me sounding so much younger. *"Papa? I was looking for you."*

"You found me, like you always do." The shadows pulsed and thickened in front of me, taking shape. He was tall—the tallest person I knew. *"You shouldn't be down here, my baby girl."*

I stared up at him, wishing I could see his face clearly. *"I wanted to go with you, Papa. I'm not scared."* But I was. I was trembling, and my tummy hurt.

"You're such a brave one, but you shouldn't be down here." He knelt, and eyes that matched mine took up my whole world. *"Where is your brother?"*

"With that woman who had cookies, but I want to be with you and—"

"You can't go with me." Cold hands landed on my shoulders,

and his face seemed to piece together. Square jaw covered with several days' worth of hair. Momma called it a beard and often complained about it, but I saw her rubbing her fingers over it when she thought Ian and I weren't looking. Straight nose. Dark brows. Eyes like pine. *"You need to stay here and keep your mother and brother safe."*

"This is her?" another voice asked from the darkness. A stranger's voice that wasn't completely unfamiliar.

"This is my daughter," Papa answered as he looked over his shoulder before smiling at me, but the smile was all wrong. Too tight. *"She doesn't know."*

"Understood," the voice came again, still familiar.

I didn't understand what he meant. All I knew was that he was going to leave, and I didn't want that.

"What a pretty little flower." The cold hands touched my cheeks. *"What a pretty poppy."* Papa leaned in, pressing his lips to the crown of my head. *"I love you more than all the stars in the sky."*

My breath choked. *"I love you more than all the fish in the seas."*

"That's my girl." Shouts from outside drew him away from me. *"Cora?"* he called for Momma. Only he ever called her that.

She drifted from the shadows, her features pained as she took my hand in her cold one. *"You should've known she would find a way down here."* She looked behind them, to where I couldn't see. *"You trust him?"*

"I do. He's going to lead us to safety."

Papa turned to me. *"Stay with your momma, baby."* Cold, cold hands touched my face again. *"Stay with her and find your brother. I'll be back for you soon."*

Mist poured in, taking Papa with it as it thinned out. I could hear his voice. He was speaking, but I couldn't make out what he said. I started to follow because I knew he wouldn't come back—

"Don't look, Poppy. Don't look over there," came Momma's hushed voice as she pulled on my hand. *"We must hide. Hurry."*

Confused, I tried to see her as she led me through the wispy void. *"I want Papa—"*

"Shh. We must be quiet. We must be quiet so Papa can come find us."

I stumbled after her, tripping when she stopped.

"Get in, Poppy. I need you to get in and be very quiet, okay? I need you to be as silent as a mouse no matter what. Do you understand?"

I shook my head. *"I wanna stay with you."*

"I'll be right here." Her damp, icy hands touched mine. *"I need you to be a big girl and listen to me. You have to hide—"*

A sound came, a shout that caused Momma to…to disappear for a moment. *"You've got to let go, baby. You need to hide, Poppy—"* Momma froze.

Time stilled as we stared at one another. Her skin thinned, revealing the delicate bones beneath. I shrank back—

"I'm sorry," a voice whispered.

Momma was yanked away from me. I stumbled after her, but it was too late. There was nothing but mist, and all that remained was her voice, her words. *"Howcouldyou?"*

"Momma?" I whispered, stepping forward, unable to make out what she said.

What a pretty little flower.
What a pretty poppy.
Pick it and watch it bleed.
Not so pretty any longer….

A hand gripped my arm, the skin paler than mine, spotted with red as leaves rattled like dry bones, and a low rumble filled the air. Shadows surrounded him as he tugged on my arm, the edges of his darkness washing over me—the edges of his black cloak covering me as I stumbled. He too was tall, but his face was a voice shrouded by cloth.

I needed to see his face.

I needed—

I was thrust back toward the screeching and the howls. And the fog—the mist that was around me and in me. It started to break apart, and the rumble grew below me in the ground. And a voice, a voice that sounded like spun gold and windchimes whispered *"stop, stop, stop"* over and over.

But I couldn't stop. I needed to see his face. The man in dark moved away, like a memory slipping through my fingers. I followed because it was important. This memory. Because someone else had been there with Momma. Someone who didn't want to be seen. I staggered forward—

"Poppy!" The voice was a jolt, a strike of lightning, and my eyes opened.

The mist had thickened in front of me, a whirling, churning mass. Specks of gold blinked in and out from within.

"No farther," the voice whispered, a voice so pure it was almost unbearable to hear. "What you seek is not to be found here."

"Stop." The mist solidified, took form, and became more golden. It was tall. *She* was tall. Tumbling waves of hair the color of fire twined together. A face blurred, but eyes the color of molten silver burned through the mist. Through me. "Go home. Take what is yours, and you will find what you seek there. The truth. Go *home*."

"Who are you?" I whispered. "Who——?"

An arm snagged me around the waist without any warning, drawing me back against a warm, hard chest. There was the scent of dark spices and pine as my feet were swept out from under me, and we went down, landing hard on the ground.

"Poppy. Gods. Poppy." Casteel turned me in his lap, one hand palming my cheek. He was breathing hard, his chest rising and falling rapidly as tendrils of mist drifted over his too-pale face. "Dear gods, Poppy, what in the hell were you doing?"

"I…" I looked around, seeing nothing but thick fog and Kieran standing above us, staring behind me and breathing just as heavily as Casteel. Confusion swept through me.

"What the hell were you doing?" Casteel demanded again, giving me a shake. His breathing was harsh, forming quick clouds in the cold. "You could've—you would've been broken, Poppy. Broken and shattered in a way I would never be able to fix."

I didn't understand what he was talking about, but he looked…he looked like I'd never seen him before. *Terrified*. Eyes wide and luminous, even in the mist, the planes and angles of his face stark.

He clasped my cheeks with his gloved hands. "I told you not to wander off."

"I…I didn't," I told him. "I was sleeping—I was dreaming. I heard…I heard my father calling my name——"

"Fucking mist," Kieran growled, waving a hand angrily

through the thick white.

"No. *No.* It was a dream, but it was real. I mean, it was pieces of the night the Craven attacked. Someone…someone else was there at the end." I started to pull away, but Casteel stopped me. "He was dressed, cloaked, and he was there that night." I twisted in Casteel's grip. "I was trying to see his face. If I could only see his face, I'd know who he was. I just…"

My lips parted as I stared into nothing. It wasn't a void simply absent of light. It was an *end.* A vast nothingness waited beyond the edge of a…cliff.

"Oh my gods," I whispered, shuddering as I realized how close I'd come to stepping off into…into *nothing.*

"It was the mist," Casteel said, his tone too gentle as he guided my stricken gaze back to his.

"She stopped me," I whispered.

"What?"

"Didn't you see her? She stopped me. Oh, my gods."

Casteel smoothed his thumb across my cheek, along the scar there. "No one else was here. It was just you and the mist."

"No. There was someone else." I looked over my shoulder, toward the emptiness. "I heard her voice. She kept telling me to stop, and then she appeared in front of me." I turned back to Casteel. "She was right *there.* Where there is…there is nothing. She told me to go no farther. That the truth wasn't here. She told me to go home and to…" I started shivering, and I couldn't stop. "To take what was mine. And that I would learn the truth."

"It's okay," Casteel assured me, but the look he exchanged with Kieran said the exact opposite. "Let's head back to camp."

"You didn't see her?"

"No, Princess." He kissed my forehead. "I only saw you about to—" He cut himself off. "It was only you."

As Casteel helped me stand, I knew the dream had been peeling back the layers of time, revealing pieces long-buried under trauma. And I knew I hadn't been alone. Someone…or some*thing* had stopped me from walking off the side of the mountain.

We started to—

The rumble I heard earlier returned, this time louder. Kieran cursed as Casteel whipped toward me. Before I could say a word, he lifted me in his arms and ran—ran as far as we could make it before he seemed to lose his balance. My heart seized as the mist scattered. Thrown to the side, Casteel's arm tightened around me as we fell into Kieran. He grabbed me—grabbed us—as we pressed into a tree that vibrated and rattled like a child's toy. Golden leaves shaken free drifted down to us, down to the earth that shook and groaned.

"What is happening?" I gasped, a hand clutching both Casteel's and Kieran's cloaks.

Casteel turned to me, but I couldn't hear what he was saying over the rumbling. At any moment, it felt like the entire mountain would rip open and swallow us whole. My wide eyes met his as my heart thundered.

And then it stopped.

The leaves stopped falling as the trees calmed, and the ground stilled.

"Is it over?" I whispered after several moments of silence.

"I think so." Casteel swallowed as his gaze lifted to where Kieran was slowly climbing to his feet behind me. Then his eyes met mine again. "Who did you say you saw? Who stopped you?"

"I don't know who it was, but it was a woman," I told him. "Why?"

"Because that was a god," Kieran said hoarsely. "Returning to their place of rest."

Within the first hour of our journey out of the Skotos Mountains, the magic of the mist lifted. The trees of Aios formed a glittering, golden ceiling as we descended the mountain, and I was able to remove my gloves. By the second hour, I considered shrugging off my cloak. The steadily rising temperatures should've lifted my spirits, but my mind was still on that mist-drenched cliff.

I had no idea if the cloaked man from my dream or his words were real or a hallucination. The latter seemed the likeliest explanation the longer I was awake. I'd never sleepwalked before, and I had no recollection of rising. That lent credence to the magic of the mountains preying upon me, but something or someone had stopped me. And Kieran had suggested that it had been Aios herself.

I glanced up at the golden trees. Could it truly have been the goddess? That seemed too fantastical to believe.

"Would you like something to eat?" Kieran asked, drawing me from my thoughts.

Casteel had asked the same question no more than thirty minutes ago, but my stomach was full of too many knots to eat more than a few slices of bacon Casteel had offered me that morning.

"If you would like something to drink, just let me know," Casteel said, and I nodded.

Throughout the morning, both had attempted to engage me in conversation or drown me in food and drink. I just…my mind was in too many places, in the past and in the future.

"I've been thinking about when we get to Atlantia," Casteel announced not too long after. "We need to resume those horseback riding lessons. You're going to need more than one if you plan to run into the capital of Solis on your own horse."

Excitement trickled through me. "I would like that."

"I'm sure Setti would enjoy it." Casteel guided the horse around a narrow bend. "He will probably expect daily visits from you. Though, I probably won't be happy," he went on. "I like you right here."

"I really hope you two don't turn into one of those couples who are constantly whispering sweet nothings at one another," muttered Kieran.

My brows lifted.

"Since we've been married, she's already told me to shut up—how many times? I'm pretty sure she's threatened to stab or punch me since then, too."

I did not recall either of those things.

"Well," Kieran said. "That's good news."

"But you're still going to hear me whisper things." Casteel's lips brushed the healing bite mark. "Just extremely dirty things."

"Shut up," I said.

Casteel laughed as his arm tightened around me, but I saw Kieran's gaze flick over me to Casteel, and I felt the Prince nod behind me. Kieran rode ahead, going far enough that I could barely make out the shape of him and his horse. I tensed, knowing there was no other reason for Kieran's actions than to give us space.

We rode in silence for a couple of minutes, and then Casteel said, "Last night wasn't your fault. It was the mist. Somehow, it was triggered, and it went after you. I shouldn't have yelled at you afterward. I'm sorry."

The sincerity in his tone startled me enough that I turned my head toward his. "I didn't think you yelled at me. You were just..."

"What?"

"You were just scared."

"I wasn't scared. I was fucking terrified," he admitted. "When we realized you were gone, we knew it wouldn't be easy to track you in the mist. I don't know how we found you so quickly, but thank the gods we did. Hell." He coughed out a dry laugh. "Maybe the gods actually have something to do with us finding you."

"Do you really think that was who I saw? Aios?"

"Honestly?" His breath touched my cheek. "We all felt the earth shake, and Nyktos did show us his approval. They seem to like you, Princess."

I worried my lower lip. "I know you don't think my dream was real—"

"I didn't say that. I think the mist got in your head, but that doesn't mean that what you saw or heard wasn't a real memory. It could've been real, and it could've been the mist. Both of those things. Either way, what happened last night wasn't your fault."

"But neither you nor Kieran almost walked off a cliff," I pointed out.

"That doesn't mean we weren't affected."

"You were?"

He was quiet and then said, "I had strange dreams last night."

"Like what?"

This time, he was silent for even longer. "I dreamt that you were...you were in the cage I was held in."

"Oh." My stomach dipped.

"And I...I couldn't free you." He shifted behind me as if he weren't comfortable, and I suddenly wished we were face-to-face.

My heart twisted in my chest. "That's not going to happen."

"I know, but the mist still preyed on my fear." His hand squeezed my hip. "And convinced me otherwise. That was how I woke to find you gone, gasping for air in disbelief."

Why the mist would lead him to dream of such a thing unsettled me greatly.

"Kieran woke like he was being chased by his own ghosts, roughly at the same time. I think the mist got to both of us in our sleep and that was why we had no idea you'd awakened and left."

Was that why neither of them seemed to have known we'd all been curled up together earlier in the night?

"What the mist did wasn't personal, and your susceptibility wasn't your fault. I should've been more aware. I should've expected something like that could happen."

"It sounds like you had your hands full."

"That's no excuse. I should've controlled the situation better."

I looked at him again over my shoulder, catching a glimpse of his hard jaw. "Compulsions aside, you can't control everything."

"Says who?"

"Says me."

A smirk appeared. "Well, you have me there. I can't control you. If I could, I suspect life would be easier, but I don't even want to try, to be honest. You keep things...intriguing."

Him and that damn word. Lips curving, I turned back around.

"Princess?"

"What?"

"I saw that. That little grin." He leaned in, dipping his chin against the side of my neck. "Why are there times you still hide your smiles from me?" His chest rose with a heavy breath as he sat back. "You have a beautiful smile. That and your laugh. And you...you never laughed enough as it was, but when you did..."

I closed my eyes.

"When you did, it was like the moment the damn mist finally cleared. Like when the first rays of sun break through the clouds after a heavy storm," he said without an ounce of embarrassment. "Your laugh is as beautiful as your smile, and when I told you it was like hearing something familiar? It wasn't a lie."

Letting out a shaky breath, I opened my eyes. The gold leaves glistened even more brightly now. "I...I didn't know that I was still doing that, and it makes me wonder if I did that before you. Smiling and laughter wasn't becoming of a Maiden, according to the Duke."

"I want to kill him again."

"As do I," I murmured.

We traveled on for a bit, Kieran was still far enough ahead that I couldn't see much of him. I thought about what I'd seen last night, what I did actually remember. "Do you remember the night I said that creepy rhyme in my sleep?"

"Not something I'm likely to forget," he replied dryly.

"My father used to say it to me."

Casteel stiffened behind me. "Come again?"

"Not the last bit—the part about picking the flower and watching it bleed," I told him. "I still don't know who said that. It could've been the Duke or some twisted part of myself. I don't know, but the first part—the pretty poppy part. I forgot that. He would say that to me. How could I forget that?"

His arm curled tighter. "I don't know, but bad memories always seem to have a way of being remembered over the good."

Wasn't that the truth?

"Did you dream of your father?"

"I did. I remembered finding him that night. At least, I think I did." My brow creased. "No, I'm sure that was real. I was looking for him. That's how my mother found me. He used to call her Cora." That was another thing I'd forgotten.

"Was that not her name?"

"Her name was Coralena."

"That's a beautiful name," he said, and it was. "What was your father's?"

"You don't know that?"

"No. I only knew that your name was Penellaphe at first, and it took a damn long time to discover you had a brother. And that was how I learned your last name," he told me. "To be honest, I didn't look into your parents. I didn't think there was a reason to."

"If you did, I doubt it would've given you any indication that I was...half-Atlantian." It still sounded strange to say that. "His name was Leopold, but my mother called him Leo or...or Lion."

"Lion," he repeated. "I like that. It fits that a Lion would have such a fierce daughter."

I smiled then, and I only knew that Casteel had seen it because he pressed his lips to the corner of my mouth. It felt like a thank you.

His arm squeezed me. "But back to the gods seeming to like you. Nyktos gave us his blessing basically. If that was Aios last night, and gods, it just might've been her, she woke to ensure your safety," he said, and there was a bit of awe in his voice. "I'm going to repeat that, Princess. A god woke from hundreds and hundreds of years of sleep to protect you. That is not something that has ever happened before as far as I know."

My pulse skittered. "Then why would it happen now? Why would they step in for me?" As soon as that question left me, Duchess Teerman's words came back to me. *You are Chosen.* Lies. Duchess Teerman had only spoken lies. "I mean, I'm not special."

"I'm going to have to disagree with the idea that you're not special. You are to me, and you are to the Kingdoms of Atlantia and Solis," Casteel said. "Together, we can change the now and the future. That's not the only reason you're special, but that could be why you've caught the sleeping eyes of the gods." He took my left hand in his. Our marked palms met, and there was that strange jolt of energy. "The gods favor you. Either way, this is good news, Poppy."

I threaded my fingers through his. "If the gods accept me,

how can your parents not? How can your—" I caught myself. "How can our people not?"

"Exactly." He kissed my cheek.

And for the first time since all of this started, hope sparked. Real hope that gaining the acceptance of his parents, of the people, would be possible. That they would stand beside us now when we returned to Solis to free his brother and to gain territory. That they would stand beside us afterward, when we returned. And if one day I became more than a Princess.

A lightness filled me, a warmth that made it impossible for that coldness to return.

We rode on then, eventually catching up to Kieran, and it wasn't too long before the sun-dappled gold-leaf trees gave way to lush green. I knew then that we'd passed the mountain and we were truly at the edge of the actual Kingdom of Atlantia.

Gold Rock was exactly as I expected. A large, round boulder that shimmered gold in the sunlight.

Jasper and two other groups were already there. Quentyn began waving the moment he saw us.

"Glad to see you made it," Emil said, bowing from where he stood by his horse. "And you."

The last part was directed toward me, and I recalled Casteel's jealousy. I stopped my grin then.

"What about me?" Kieran asked, dismounting.

"Should I lie and tell you I am thrilled?" the Atlantian replied, a hint of a grin on his face.

"It would make me feel like my life's complete, Emil."

"Naill and Delano haven't arrived yet?" Casteel asked as he dropped down. He reached for me as he said, "I figured they'd beat all of us."

"They haven't arrived yet," Jasper answered, looking tired as he leaned against the rock. "I thought you would've beat us here."

"Yeah?"

Jasper nodded as he covered a yawn with the back of his hand. "I cannot wait to become reacquainted with my bed," he said with a sigh as I started to unhook the buttons of my cloak. "Anyway, I hope the night was less eventful for you all."

"Nothing of interest happened with us," Casteel said, meeting my gaze as he brushed my hands aside. He began working the tiny buttons, and a wealth of gratitude rose. Not for him unbuttoning my cloak but for not mentioning what happened. "What about you all?"

"Weird dreams," Jasper muttered as he watched us— watched me.

"As if that's all," Emil commented as he rolled up the sleeves of his tunic. "I'm assuming you guys felt that last night— the shaking of the entire mountain."

Casteel nodded but didn't elaborate. I felt Jasper's attention focused on us—all the wolven that were present, actually—as Casteel folded my cloak and placed it in one of the saddlebags. The rest of our group arrived. None of them looked like they'd slept well, and it was strange to see Beckett in his mortal form and so subdued as we eventually continued on.

The patchy grass gave way to rolling hills that were a lush, vibrant green, and it wasn't too long before I wished I had changed into the sleeveless tunic.

Lifting a hand, I wiped a fine sheen of sweat from my forehead. "Is it warm like this always? I'm not complaining if it is."

"It's warm here, near the sea," Casteel answered, and I looked around, wondering what body of water he spoke of. "But farther inland, when you near the Mountains of Nyktos, you'll see more seasonal changes and colder temperatures."

I started to ask where this sea was when I saw them.

Graceful, gleaming white stone columns that stretched so far into the sky that if there had been clouds, they would've reached beyond them. A tumbling motion in my chest took my breath.

"The Pillars of Atlantia?" I whispered.

"Yes." Casteel's voice was soft in my ear.

A sense of wonder washed through me, one that ran deeper

than curiosity as we drew closer. I could see shadowy grooves in them, markings in a language I'd never seen before. The Pillars were more than just markers or even the resting place of Theon and Lailah. They were connected to a wall of the same stone, what appeared to be limestone and marble. It was as high as any Rise and continued on farther than I could see. We crested the hill, and I saw between the two pillars, seeing what awaited. Tiny bumps rose all over my skin as a hum seemed to vibrate in my blood in a long-forgotten hymn.

Casteel's chin grazed the side of my neck, followed by his lips. "Welcome home, Princess."

Chapter 44

Home.

Was this what the voice had meant last night? Was this truly home?

I wanted it to be more than I ever realized.

We passed through the Pillars, my heart thundering as I soaked in the sights before me with disbelieving eyes.

The first thing I noticed were the people along the walls, just inside the Pillars. How could I not see them? There were at least a hundred, dressed in black, sleeveless tunics and pants. Swords with gold handles were fitted to their sides. Crossbows like the one damaged in the fight with the Dead Bones Clan were strapped to their backs. The moment they saw Casteel, recognized him, they bowed, one after another in a wave, but it was those who stood on the ledges above that drew my attention.

Women.

There were more Guardians. They dropped to one knee in succession, placing their fists over their hearts.

I knew my eyes were wide. I knew I was staring, but all of them were staring, too—the men below and the women above— at us. I suddenly wished that I still wore my cloak, even with how warm the air was here. Or that my hair was free. Maybe then I wouldn't feel so exposed, my scars clearly displayed to these strangers' eyes.

Strangers I...I wanted to be accepted by.

I looked forward, and then I wasn't thinking of the scars or being accepted.

Leafy green trees lined the wide road, one smoother than any I knew of in Solis. It was made of some kind of dark stone that seemed fused together. The trees spread out into dense thickets of a lush forest, and ahead...

A city sprawled ahead, dipping and flowing with the valleys and hills—a city twice the size of Carsodonia. White and sand-colored structures gleamed under the sun, arcing gracefully with the landscape, some square and others circular. Some rose high, stretching into sleek towers, while others were buildings as wide as they were tall, and some remained closer to the ground. They reminded me of the Temples in Solis, but they weren't fashioned to mirror the night but to reflect the sun—to worship it. The roof of every building that I could see was green. Trees rose from them, vines swept down their sides, and bursts of color came from all sides.

Unlike the capital of Solis, where the city was stone and dirt, flashes of green surrounded buildings. Just as it had been in Spessa's End, no building appeared stacked on top of one another, crowded to the point where they could barely fit. At least not from what I could gather from this distance.

Beyond the city, where specks of white grazed in open pastures, past the heavily wooded area that followed, was a mountain that did disappear into the clouds. And in the face of that mountain were eleven statues that had to be as tall as the Atheneum in Masadonia. Each one held a lit torch from their outstretched arm, the flames burning as brightly as the setting sun.

These were the gods—all of them—watching over the city or standing guard.

I couldn't even begin to figure out how those statues were built to that size, raised onto the mountain. Or even how those torches were lit—how they remained lit.

"Saion's Cove is beautiful, isn't it?" Casteel didn't need to ask. It was the most beautiful city I'd ever seen, and I could imagine what the capital looked like. "You can't see the sea from here, but it's beyond the trees, to our right."

Thoughts of warm sand and salty air tugged at my heart as I followed his gaze. I saw the tops of columns through the trees. "What is in there?"

"The Chambers of Nyktos," he answered. "You can see the Seas of Saion from there, and the Isles of Bele," he added. "And, yes, the Goddess of the Hunt slumbers there.

"I have so many questions."

"There is not a single person surprised to hear that," Kieran remarked.

Delano laughed as he turned his head to the sky, basking in the sun.

A bell tolled, startling me. Leaves rattled as a flock of birds took flight from the nearby trees, their feathers a vivid green and blue. The bell tolled five more times.

I tensed. "Is something happening?" I looked around, and no one appeared concerned. I only ever heard a bell ring when there was an attack or something afoot.

Jasper smiled at me. "It is only telling the time. It's six in the evening," he explained. "It'll ring every hour until midnight and then resume at eight."

"Oh." That was clever. Ahead, I noticed someone on horseback riding toward us.

Casteel slowed the horse as Jasper said, "Here comes the welcoming party of one."

"Who is it?" I asked.

"Alastir," he told me. "He must've been waiting for us."

The advisor to the King and Queen arrived within a few minutes, a smile softening the deep scar in his forehead.

"You cannot believe how relieved I am to see you. All of you," Alastir said, and the strangest thing happened.

A shivery feeling of icy fingers danced across the back of my neck. Gods, he sounded so much like Vikter, but—

"You must tell me what became of Spessa's End." Alastir drew his horse up to our side, clasping Casteel's hand. "But I must warn you." His voice dropped low. "Your father and mother are here, and your arrival was spotted. They know you've come home."

My stomach fell beyond my feet. I hadn't planned on meeting his parents this quickly. They were supposed to be in the capital.

Casteel was of like mind. "What are they doing here?"

"They came as soon as they learned of the trouble in Spessa's End. Your damn father was about to cross the mountain. I assured him that our forces would make it…" He trailed off as he caught sight of the ring on Casteel's left hand. He turned Casteel's palm upward. His skin blanched. "You did it." He twisted in his saddle, looking toward my left hand. His gaze met mine. "You actually did it."

"We did," Casteel said. "Just like we told you."

"You missed it," Jasper chimed in as I picked up on the disbelief and concern radiating from Alastir. Which wasn't surprising. He'd wanted us to wait until Casteel spoke with his parents. "Day turned to night at the end of the ceremony. Nyktos gave his approval."

Alastir blinked as if he hadn't expected that. "Well, that is…that is good news. Perhaps that will be of aid when the King and Queen are made aware, but I need to speak with you Casteel, in private."

"Whatever you need to say to me, you can say in front of my *wife*," Casteel replied, and my already unstable stomach flipped.

Wife.

Why was that such a shock to hear? It was a pleasant surprise, though.

"This is a conversation regarding the kingdom and I mean no offense, but she is not a part of the Crown yet," Alastir replied. "Nor privy to such information."

Casteel stiffened behind me, and I knew he was about to push back, and the last thing I wanted was him to be standing here arguing with Alastir about what I was privy to when his parents arrived.

"It's okay. No offense taken," I said, tapping his arm. "I would like to stretch my legs a bit anyway."

Casteel wasn't at all happy about that, but Beckett offered, "I can show her the Chambers of Nyktos. It's not very far from here," he said. "That is, if you'd like."

"I would like that," I readily agreed, latching on to the offer as if it were a lifeline. "That's what I would like to do."

"Then that's what you will do," Casteel replied.

My heart was pumping so fast as Casteel dismounted and helped me get down that I wouldn't have been surprised if I fainted. How embarrassing would that be? The first time to faint...at the feet of my father and mother-in-law, the former the King who still planned to use me as a message.

But that would change. It had to. Not just because the gods favored me, but because what Casteel and I shared was *real*.

"One second." Casteel motioned at Beckett as Quentyn went to the young wolven's side. He drew me slightly away from the others, under the shade of one of the nearby trees. "I'm sorry about this," he said. "I had no idea they'd be here. I wanted to give you some time before I introduced you. That was what I planned."

"I know, and honestly, I'm glad that Alastir was here to warn us and that he wants to talk to you. It will give me some time to...I don't know." I felt my cheeks flush. "Prepare myself."

"You don't need to be nervous."

"Really?" I replied dryly.

"I'm trying to be helpful." A half-grin appeared and then vanished. "We've faced scarier things than parents caught off guard, and we will face far more frightening things. Just remember that this,"—he picked up my left hand and turned it over—"is real," he said, echoing my earlier thoughts. "We're real. No matter what."

I stared down at the dazzling gold swirl on my palm. "No matter what."

Curling a finger under my chin, he lifted my head, and his lips found mine. He kissed me, and it was no short peck on the lips. People watched us, but Casteel took his sweet time, and by the time he lifted his head, I felt faint for a whole different reason.

"No matter what," he repeated.

Nodding, I pulled away from him and turned to where Beckett waited, shifting his weight from one foot to the other.

"Poppy?"

I turned back to Casteel, and the moment I saw him, I felt the breath I took catch in my throat. The way he stared at me, the intensity in his fiery golden eyes, rooted me to the spot. What I felt from him...it tasted like the smoothest chocolate and the sweetest berries.

Casteel's chest rose with an uneven breath. "I'll come for you."

I love you.

That was what I thought Casteel was going to say. That was what I felt from him, but those words didn't pass his lips.

They hadn't passed mine either.

Whatever disappointment I might've felt was quickly lost to wonder as Beckett led me through the woods. The wolven hadn't been an excited chatterbox, and I could tell he was still wary of me. I picked up the faint trace of fear from him, and I imagined he was challenging himself to get past that by offering to take me to the Chambers.

The trees were full of the calls and chirps of birds, but as Beckett had said, the Chambers weren't that far. We left the wooded area fairly quickly.

The structure rose against the deep blue of the sky, the limestone and marble a glistening white in the sun.

We walked through a short field of tiny blue and yellow flowers. The closer I got, the more I realized how large the temple still was. It was nearly the length of Castle Teerman.

"Good gods," I said, glancing at Beckett. "This thing is huge."

He nodded as he quickly glanced at me. "It's one of the largest of the Temples here."

"Why is it called the Chambers?" I asked as we climbed the steep steps, welcoming the distraction. Vines scaled the wide steps, all the way to the top where they wrapped around the columns.

"It's because there are tombs underneath."

I stopped near the top and looked at him. "Seriously?"

A nervous giggle left him. "Yeah. The entrance to them is on the side. It's where some of the ancient ones have been buried—the deities, I mean."

"Sorry. Graveyards and tombs kind of weird me out," I admitted as I started walking again.

"Same." A quick smile appeared. "Especially these. You feel...I don't know, like those who are entombed are watching you."

A warm, salty breeze reached us as we came to the top. I didn't know where to look first. Pebbles and much larger rocks were scattered across the Atlantian Crest that had been engraved into the stone floors.

Statues of the gods stood between the columns, each one with one arm outstretched. Nyktos was the tallest of them all, and he stood in the very center of the Temple, the toes of his feet brushing the Atlantian Crest. All were sculpted so it appeared the sun rose behind them, and they held torches in their stone hands, empty of flames, of life.

Tearing my gaze from them, I walked to one side. The beauty of what I saw was stunning. I'd never seen water so clear. Bright blue, green, and even red coral was clearly visible underneath. Farther out, where the water deepened, it was a shade as blue as the sky above. I knew there were other things to see, like the trees of Aios that were visible from the Chambers, but I couldn't tear my gaze from the sea. The next breath I took was steady and calming as if I hadn't taken a breath as deep as this one in, well, forever. I blinked, realizing there were tears in my eyes. Normally, I wouldn't get choked up by seeing a body of water, but it...it felt like home.

"Thank you for healing my legs," Beckett said, startling me. As terrible as it was, I'd forgotten that he was there. "I know I said that before, but I, uh, I just wanted to say it again. You have no idea what you did for me."

It took me a moment before I trusted myself to speak. The poor kid was already uncomfortable around me. He didn't need me to start sobbing all over him. "You didn't need to thank me before, and you don't need to do it now." I touched the warm stone of a column. "I'm glad I could help."

Off in the distance, I could make out the Isles of Bele. They appeared large, as if they could house two or three towns the size of Spessa's End. There was something at the highest peak of the center island. A Temple? I started to ask Beckett what it was when I realized that he hadn't responded to me.

Pulling my gaze from the sparkling waters, I turned, and every muscle in my body immediately locked up. Beckett was gone.

But I wasn't alone.

Several people stood by the statue of Nyktos. Mostly men, but a few women. There were at least a dozen, a mix of Atlantian and mortal. Not a single wolven among them. But they were all dressed the same, wearing loose white pants and tighter, sleeveless shirts. Their arms were adorned with golden bands similar to those I'd seen on the Guardians in Spessa's End. Their attire, the way they stared at me, reminded me of the Priests and Priestesses in Solis.

Except the Priests and Priestesses didn't carry weapons. All of them wore a golden, narrow, long dagger strapped across their chests.

Goosebumps pimpled my skin. I recognized none of them, but I knew what they were feeling. Anger surged from them, thickening the air, and it mixed with my stinging disbelief as what was happening began to sink in. Instinct flared to life.

"You shouldn't be here," an Atlantian said, taking a step forward. "You should've never crossed the Skotos Mountains. Your mere presence is a taint, *Maiden*."

These people knew exactly who I was.

I quickly glanced at the exit—the only exit. They blocked it, and their anger—their hatred—it kept stretching out toward me, coating my skin like a too-coarse blanket, filling the back of my throat with hot acid. I severed the connection, picturing each cord being snipped away until there was nothing inside me but my pounding heart. Once I locked them out, I scanned the Temple again, this time looking for any sign of the young wolven. There was none, and everything inside me knew what had been done, even if I didn't understand why. He'd been so happy when I first met him. I'd healed him. No other wolven had been unkind toward me.

But he...he had led me here. He'd offered to bring me here, and then he'd left me.

Left me to those who I'd never seen or met before but who hated me nonetheless.

But they did not choose you.

My skin flushed hot and then cold. It had been a trap. One of opportunity or something planned, I had no idea. And I didn't know how this had been orchestrated—if these people had been waiting or for how long. But it didn't change what this was. The betrayal, the disappointment, and the bone-deep hurt sank its razor-sharp claws into me. I stared at the nameless faces, feeling as if my chest had cracked open.

It had been so silly of me to want these people to accept me. And so incredibly naive for me to take that flicker of hope and hold onto it. I wanted to scream. I wanted to...gods, I wanted to cry. And I wanted to rage.

But I couldn't.

I needed to stay calm. This was a trap, but they knew who I was, and that meant they also had to know that I was Casteel's wife. They couldn't seriously think to harm me. I needed to deescalate the situation somehow. The mortals wouldn't be a problem. The Atlantians standing before them could become one, however.

Still, I lowered my right hand to where my sweater hid the wolven dagger. "I'm sorry. I didn't know this area was forbidden, and I don't know what you've heard about me, but I am not an Ascended, and I never chose to be the Maiden. I fought against them at—"

"You're something worse," a woman interrupted, and I realized she held something in her closed fist. "We know what you really are. We know how you managed to gain the Prince's trust, *empath*. Soul Eater."

A prickly wave of dread skated over my skin. None of these people had been in Spessa's End or at New Haven. Had Alastir told someone? I doubted that Kieran would have during his brief return. At the moment, none of that mattered. What did was that what Alastir had said was right. So was Casteel, even though he hadn't wanted to say it. And I already suspected as much. Because of who I was and who I wasn't, they wouldn't accept me, and they feared me.

And that fear fed their hatred. That was the most dangerous of all. "I am not that either," I said, watching the woman's hand—their hands. A man held something, too. "I cannot feed off emotional energy or heighten fear. I didn't even know what I was until—"

"Close your mouth, whore," the Atlantian spat.

I blinked, shocked into silence by the slur.

"You speak out of both sides of your mouth," he continued. "Your lies may have worked on the others, but they will not work on us."

"You will not find what you seek here," a woman said, and I immediately thought of the voice I'd heard last night. "You will not destroy Atlantia from within. You may have warped the Prince's mind, but you will not succeed with us."

"I haven't done anything to him." My fingers curled under the hem of my sweater.

"Other than attempt to kill him?" another challenged as the clouds formed above us.

Well, that was hard to defend, and also something none of them should've known.

"Or led an army of Ascended to the walls of Spessa's End?" another claimed, and that was also hard to defend. "People died, didn't they?"

People had.

"The Ascended disguised you as a Maiden. Sending you right into the heart of Atlantia," the Atlantian man said, the one who had spoken first. "We will not let you destroy Atlantia. We will not allow you to destroy us all, whore of the Ascended."

"You have no idea what you're talking about." I fought my anger and was losing. I was too damn...*hurt*, and I refused to stand here and listen to them accuse me of working with the Ascended. I had *killed* countless people to defend Spessa's End. I had been prepared to end my own life to protect that town. "I speak nothing but the truth when I say I am sorry for all that you may have suffered at the hands of the Ascended. I can even understand your distrust and dislike of me, but if one of you calls me a whore one more time, you will regret it."

"Because of the Prince?" The Atlantian sneered. "Do you think we're not willing to die to protect our kingdom from even him? The Prince is already lost to us, just as Malik was."

"Your Prince is not lost to you." My fingers brushed the sheath of the dagger as the sun hid behind a dark cloud. "And it's not my *husband* you have to worry about. It's me."

Focused on the Atlantian, I'd forgotten about the woman— about what she held. I didn't even see her lift her arm. It was such a stupid misstep on my part. Vikter would be so disappointed.

Pain exploded, stunning me. I gasped, clutching my throbbing shoulder as I looked down.

A rock.

She'd thrown a *rock*.

I almost laughed, only because she could've thrown something worse. Like the dagger strapped to her chest. Anything more dangerous than a *rock*.

"That hurt," I bit out as the clouds darkened, becoming fat and heavy. The scent of rain filled the air, and in the distance, the warning of thunder rumbled. "But seriously? A rock?"

"You think we fear you?" the Atlantian male said, withdrawing his dagger. "You're not a threat when you can't touch us. We know how Soul Eaters feed. We know how you sense emotion. You must come into contact with flesh."

That was not how that worked. "There appears to be a lot of things you have no understanding of." I unsheathed the dagger. To hell with making the situation worse. "I am not your enemy, but you're quickly becoming mine."

"But you're not anything but a scarred whore for the Ascended," the woman replied calmly as thunder clapped, closer now.

Before I could even question how I could be both the Maiden and a whore, a new pain erupted along the side of my head, so sudden and shocking that I dropped the dagger as I staggered back. I quickly realized that the stoning was only meant to incapacitate me so they could get closer. Another rock hit me in the stomach, then my leg, my arms—

A streak of lightning lit the sky over the sea. Thunder boomed, echoing through the columns of the Temple as sudden agony lanced my brow when a rock connected with my forehead and the scarred skin there, so sharp and startling that it sent me to my knees. My hold on my senses loosened and then shattered. It was like a crevice cracked wide open in me as wet warmth trickled down my temple.

Ascended trash. Soul Eater. Whore. Words fell in time with their rocks, but it was what I felt from them that landed heavier blows.

"Enough," I whispered.

Their anger and hatred beat at me as I looked down, seeing my blood falling against the stone. I couldn't breathe. Their raw emotions were an endless rolling tide, and underneath it was a hum, a whirring from the very core of me. My skin vibrated. Just like it had when the soldiers surrounded Casteel and I before the wolven had arrived.

Something red splashed on the ground, tainting the pearly stone. More blood. Another drop joined it, seeping into the cracks. The marble trembled under my feet as roots appeared in the stone, thin as fragile veins, they crept out from the crack. I blinked a sting from my eyes, and the roots disappeared. Another splash of crimson fell and another, this one farther from where I stood.

It was blood.

But it wasn't mine.

It fell from above.

The skies bled.

Chapter 45

Dizzy, I lifted my head to see blood falling like rain from the crimson-hued cloud that stretched over the Temple and the cove.

It spattered the pristine white of the Temple floor, dampening my clothing and turning the white clothing of those who stood before me pink. It seemed to stun them as they cast their gazes to the sky.

"Tears of an angry god," someone whispered.

My gaze shifted to the blur of unfamiliar faces.

"It is an omen," the Atlantian who had unsheathed his dagger announced. "They're showing us that they know what must be done and what we will face."

"Enough," I said again.

"For Atlantia," a woman said. She was closer. A mortal with Atlantian blood and crimson streaking her face. An Atlantian stood beside her, his lips peeled back to expose his fangs and the hatred in his snarl reminded me of a Craven. Of an Ascended.

"From blood and ash." The Atlantian raised the dagger. "We will rise again, my brothers and sisters."

The hum in my blood grew, the buzz in my skin intensified, stronger than what I'd felt before, and that ancient sense of knowledge rose deep from my pain. The cords I could see so clearly rippled out from me, connecting me to each and every one of them. It gathered all their burning hatred and scorching loathing, their acidic bitterness and thirst for vengeance after years, decades, centuries of pain inflicted upon them. And I took it.

I took it all inside me, letting it pour into every vein, every cell until it choked me, until I tasted the blood, until I drowned in it. Until I tasted *death,* and it was sweet.

"Enough!" I screamed as the connection to them—to all of them—crackled with energy. The cords that had always been invisible, lit up in silver, becoming visible to not only my eyes but theirs.

"Your eyes," the Atlantian with the dagger gasped, staggering back.

Moonlight glow spilled out of me, seeping over the stone and rippling into the charged air as I stood. Thunder rolled endlessly, shaking the Temple and the nearby trees.

"Dear gods," the Atlantian whispered, his dagger slipping from his fingers to fall soundlessly to the tile. "Forgive us."

Too late.

The cords connecting me to all of them contracted as I threw out my arms. All the hate, the loathing, the bitterness and vengeance intensified, tripled, and then erupted from me, traveling through each of those cords, finding their way back home.

Lightning streaked overhead like a thousand screams as the group's rancid emotions choked them.

Hair blew back from faces. Clothing pulled taut against bodies. Feet slid over stone, and they went down, one after another after another as if they were nothing more than fragile saplings caught in a windstorm.

I watched as their vileness continued feeding back to them.

I watched as they clutched at their heads, writhing and spasming, screaming and *shrieking* until the bones in their throats caved in under their contempt.

And then…nothing.

Silence in and outside of me. I was empty again—no hatred, no anger, no pain. Empty and cold.

I sucked in air, staggering as the silver cords connected to them sparked and fizzled out. The rain eased and then stopped, forming pinkish puddles across the floor.

Those on the stone didn't move, they didn't thrash and squirm. Red. There was so much red around them that ran in rivulets to the puddles, deepening the pinkish hue. They lay still, their bodies twisted and contorted as if they had been thrown about by the gods themselves. Eyes wide and mouths hanging open, hands clenched tightly around rocks or their crushed throats.

I felt *nothing* from them.

The bells tolled again, this time rapidly with no pauses between the gongs, and the Temple shuddered. Stone cracked behind me. The scent of blood and rich soil spilled into the air. A shadow fell over me, stretched across the floor like hundreds of bare bone fingers.

Slowly, I turned around, and my gaze crawled up thick, glistening bark and across the bare limbs of a massive tree. Tiny golden buds formed all over and blossomed, thousands unfurling to reveal blood-red leaves.

A Blood Forest tree stood, rooted where my blood had first fallen.

Movement snagged my gaze. My head jerked to the left, and whatever breath I managed to get into my lungs fled.

They were sleek shadows prowling up the wide steps, hesitating there, surveying the bodies on the stone floor.

Heads turned to one another. Pairs of keen, frosted eyes lifted to where I stood before the blood tree, breathing heavily. I tensed.

Behind them, larger ones pressed forward. Two. Three. Four. So many more. There were *dozens*. Maybe even a hundred. Perhaps more. Each one greater than the one before them, their fur glossy in the sunlight as the clouds overhead scattered, their eyes an incandescent blue I'd never seen before. Their ears perked and nostrils twitched as they scented the air—the blood.

As they scented *me*.

I recognized the shock of Delano's white fur and then my heart twisted as I saw Kieran, his unnaturally bright eyes fixed on me, on the silvery light that still glowed around me.

Claws clicked on stone as they came forward, stepping over

the fallen, heads down low, slowly moving around me, circling me, making room…

Good gods.

The color of steel, the wolven was double the size of any I'd seen, nearly as tall as me. Maybe even taller, and it stalked forward, paws the size of two of my hands.

It was Jasper. During the battle at Spessa's End, I hadn't realized how large he was.

The silver wolven stopped in front of me, meeting my wide-eyed stare with those unnerving, glowing eyes, and I knew if I ran or reached for the fallen dagger to protect myself, I wouldn't make it an inch.

A shivery sense of awareness drew my gaze from Jasper, from the wolven, and beyond the statue of Nyktos.

Casteel came up the steps, his dark hair wet and windblown as if he'd run faster than the wind could travel. Faint traces of red streaked his face as he stalked forward, features stark and chin dipped low.

It struck me then, sort of dumbly, that Casteel looked like some kind of god standing there. In black, with his swords strapped to his sides, and the near brutal hardness that had settled into the striking planes and angles of his features, he reminded me of the god Theon.

Jasper turned to the Prince. The other wolven stopped circling me. Casteel's chest rose and fell heavily as he stepped around a body, stopping only when Jasper let out a low rumble of warning.

He drew up short, taking in me, the wolven, the bodies, and the lit torches. His eyes widened a fraction as something akin to understanding flickered across his face.

"My gods," he uttered. Golden eyes met and held mine as Casteel crossed his arms, withdrawing his swords.

Air lodged in my throat as pressure clamped down on my chest, squeezing my heart.

Casteel hadn't arrived alone.

Others were climbing the steps. Naill. Emil. Alastir. Familiar faces. Nameless ones. My senses flickered to life in me, sensing…sensing fear and awe and so many different emotions that I was afraid it would all overwhelm me again, and I would…

I didn't even know what I'd done.

Growls rumbled from the other wolven as two more crested the top of the stairs, followed by several dressed as the ones sprawled across the ground, their golden swords drawn. I should be concerned by them, but it was the two who had entered before them that captured my attention.

A tall, blond man, broad of shoulder and dressed in a white tunic stained from the blood rain, whose cut jaw, straight nose, and high cheekbones were painfully familiar. He drew up short, his hand going to the sword at his side.

"Impossible," breathed the woman who stood beside him, her hair a glossy onyx tucked back in a loose knot at the nape of her neck. The shape of her eyes and her mouth was also familiar, and she was beautiful, absolutely as breathtaking as the disbelief that poured from her.

Even if it weren't for the similarities, the crowns of twisted, bleached bone would've told me who they were.

Queen Eloana's hand pressed to the bodice of her simple, sleeveless lavender gown—a gown stained by the rain that had fallen. "Hawke…"

The silvery glow around me pulled back and faded, seeping into my skin as my entire body shuddered.

"What have you done?" she asked, her eyes as vibrant as her son's as she stepped forward. "What have you brought back?"

"It's not too late," Alastir spoke, startling me. "It's not, Eloana—"

"Yes." Her gaze swept back to me, to where the wolven surrounded me and then to her son.

My gaze swiveled back to Casteel. He stood right there, no more than a dozen feet or so from me, but it seemed like an impossible distance, an impassible gulf.

He stood right there.

Hawke.

Casteel.

The Prince of Atlantia.

The Dark One.

My husband.

My *heartmate*.

Casteel lowered to one knee, crossing the swords over his chest as he bowed his head between the vee of the deadly sharp blades. A stuttered heartbeat passed, and he lifted his chin just enough that he saw me.

The wolven sank onto their haunches, heads bowed, but their lips peeling back in snarls as those behind the King and Queen quietly advanced.

"Yes, it is," his mother spoke again, reaching up and curling her fingers around the twisted bones.

Queen Eloana removed her crown, and with wide eyes, I watched her place it on the Temple floor, at the feet of the statue of Nyktos.

With a whoosh of air, flames roared from the stone torch of Nyktos, flickering and dancing in the wind. The other torches followed suit, fire sparking to life, and the bones of the crown shimmered, the bleached whiteness of them cracking, slipping away and turning to ash, revealing the gilded bones underneath.

"Lower your swords," she commanded, her chin lifting even as she lowered to one knee, even as a potent, helpless sort of rage drenched the space around her, one that carried the stench of a long-buried fear come to fruition. "And bow before the…before the *last* descendent of the most ancient ones, she who carries the blood of the King of the Gods within her. Bow before your new Queen."

Get your free copy of the Red Pearl bonus scene at https://BookHip.com/LXDBMK

To see a full color version of the world map, visit https://TheBlueBoxPress.com/books/AKoFaFmap/

The Crown of Gilded Bones
A Blood and Ash Novel, Book 3
Coming April 20, 2021

Bow Before Your Queen Or Bleed Before Her...

She's been the victim and the survivor...

Poppy never dreamed she would find the love she's found with Prince Casteel. She wants to revel in her happiness but first they must free his brother and find hers. It's a dangerous mission and one with far-reaching consequences neither dreamed of. Because Poppy is the Chosen, the Blessed. The true ruler of Atlantia. She carries the blood of the King of Gods within her. By right the crown and the kingdom are hers.

The enemy and the warrior...

Poppy has only ever wanted to control her own life, not the lives of others, but now she must choose to either forsake her birthright or seize the gilded crown and become the Queen of Flesh and Fire. But as the kingdoms' dark sins and blood-drenched secrets finally unravel, a long-forgotten power rises to pose a genuine threat. And they will stop at nothing to ensure that the crown never sits upon Poppy's head.

A lover and heartmate...

But the greatest threat to them and to Atlantia is what awaits in the far west, where the Queen of Blood and Ash has her own plans, ones she has waited hundreds of years to carry out. Poppy and Casteel must consider the impossible—travel to the Lands of the Gods and wake the King himself. And as shocking secrets and the harshest betrayals come to light, and enemies emerge to threaten everything Poppy and Casteel have fought for, they will discover just how far they are willing to go for their people—and each other.

And now she will become Queen...

Discover More Jennifer L. Armentrout

If you're Team Hawke, you will love Caden.

If your Royal is Casteel, you'll fall for the Prince.

Discover the Summer King Trilogy...

The Prince: A Wicked Novella

She's everything he wants....

Cold. Heartless. Deadly. Whispers of his name alone bring fear to fae and mortals alike. *The Prince*. There is nothing in the mortal world more dangerous than him. Haunted by a past he couldn't control, all Caden desires is revenge against those who'd wronged him, trapping him in never-ending nightmare. And there is one person he knows can help him.

She's everything he can't have...

Raised within the Order, Brighton Jussier knows just how dangerous the Prince is, reformed or not. She'd seen firsthand what atrocities he could be capable of. The last thing she wants to do is help him, but he leaves her little choice. Forced to work alongside him, she begins to see the man under the bitter ice. Yearning for him feels like the definition of insanity, but there's no denying the heat in his touch and the wicked promise is his stare.

She's everything he'll take....

But there's someone out there who wants to return the Prince to his former self. A walking, breathing nightmare that is hell bent on destroying the world and everyone close to him. The last thing either of them needs is a distraction, but with the attraction growing between them each now, the one thing he wants more than anything may be the one thing that will be his undoing.

She's everything he'd die for....

* * * *

The King: A Wicked Novella

From #1 *New York Times* and *USA Today* bestselling author Jennifer L. Armentrout comes the next installment in her Wicked series.

As Caden and Brighton's attraction grows despite the odds stacked against a happily ever after, they must work together to stop an Ancient fae from releasing the Queen, who wants nothing more than to see Caden become the evil Prince once feared by fae and mortals alike.

* * * *

The Queen: A Wicked Novella

The King must have his Queen....

Bestowed the forbidden Summer's Kiss by the King of the Summer fae, Brighton Jussier is no longer *just* human. What she is, what she will become, no one knows for sure, but that isn't her biggest concern at the moment. Now Caden, the King, refuses to let her go, even at the cost of his Court. When the doorway to the Otherworld is breached, both Brighton and Caden must do the unthinkable—not just to survive themselves, but also to save mankind from the evil that threatens the world.

* * * *

From Blood and Ash

A Maiden…

Chosen from birth to usher in a new era, Poppy's life has never been her own. The life of the Maiden is solitary. Never to be touched. Never to be looked upon. Never to be spoken to. Never to experience pleasure. Waiting for the day of her Ascension, she would rather be with the guards, fighting back the evil that took her family, than preparing to be found worthy by the gods. But the choice has never been hers.

A Duty…

The entire kingdom's future rests on Poppy's shoulders, something she's not even quite sure she wants for herself. Because a Maiden has a heart. And a soul. And longing. And when Hawke, a golden-eyed guard honor bound to ensure her Ascension, enters her life, destiny and duty become tangled with desire and need. He incites her anger, makes her question everything she believes in, and tempts her with the forbidden.

A Kingdom…

Forsaken by the gods and feared by mortals, a fallen kingdom is rising once more, determined to take back what they believe is theirs through violence and vengeance. And as the shadow of those cursed draws closer, the line between what is forbidden and what is right becomes blurred. Poppy is not only on the verge of losing her heart and being found unworthy by the gods, but also her life when every blood-soaked thread that holds her world together begins to unravel.

* * * *

Dream of You: A Wait For You Novella

Abby Erickson isn't looking for a one-night stand, a relationship, or anything that involves any one-on-one time, but when she witnesses a shocking crime, she's thrust into the hands of the sexiest man she's ever seen - Colton Anders. His job is to protect her, but with every look, every touch, and every simmering kiss, she's in danger of not only losing her life but her heart also.

Discover 1001 Dark Nights Collection Seven

Go to www.1001DarkNights.com for more information.

THE BISHOP by Skye Warren
A Tanglewood Novella

TAKEN WITH YOU by Carrie Ann Ryan
A Fractured Connections Novella

DRAGON LOST by Donna Grant
A Dark Kings Novella

SEXY LOVE by Carly Phillips
A Sexy Series Novella

PROVOKE by Rachel Van Dyken
A Seaside Pictures Novella

RAFE by Sawyer Bennett
An Arizona Vengeance Novella

THE NAUGHTY PRINCESS by Claire Contreras
A Sexy Royals Novella

THE GRAVEYARD SHIFT by Darynda Jones
A Charley Davidson Novella

CHARMED by Lexi Blake
A Masters and Mercenaries Novella

SACRIFICE OF DARKNESS by Alexandra Ivy
A Guardians of Eternity Novella

THE QUEEN by Jen Armentrout
A Wicked Novella

BEGIN AGAIN by Jennifer Probst
A Stay Novella

VIXEN by Rebecca Zanetti
A Dark Protectors/Rebels Novella

SLASH by Laurelin Paige
A Slay Series Novella

THE DEAD HEAT OF SUMMER by Heather Graham
A Krewe of Hunters Novella

WILD FIRE by Kristen Ashley
A Chaos Novella

MORE THAN PROTECT YOU by Shayla Black
A More Than Words Novella

LOVE SONG by Kylie Scott
A Stage Dive Novella

CHERISH ME by J. Kenner
A Stark Ever After Novella

SHINE WITH ME by Kristen Proby
A With Me in Seattle Novella

And new from Blue Box Press:

TEASE ME by J. Kenner
A Stark International Novel

FROM BLOOD AND ASH by Jennifer L. Armentrout
A Blood and Ash Novel

QUEEN MOVE by Kennedy Ryan

THE HOUSE OF LONG AGO by Steve Berry and MJ Rose
A Cassiopeia Vitt Adventure

THE BUTTERFLY ROOM by Lucinda Riley

A KINGDOM OF FLESH AND FIRE by Jennifer L.
Armentrout
A Blood and Ash Novel

About Jennifer L. Armentrout

1 New York Times and International Bestselling author Jennifer lives in Shepherdstown, West Virginia. All the rumors you've heard about her state aren't true. When she's not hard at work writing. she spends her time reading, watching really bad zombie movies, pretending to write, and hanging out with her husband, their retired K-9 police dog Diesel, a crazy Border Jack puppy named Apollo, six judgmental alpacas, four fluffy sheep, and two goats.

Her dreams of becoming an author started in algebra class, where she spent most of her time writing short stories…which explains her dismal grades in math. Jennifer writes young adult paranormal, science fiction, fantasy, and contemporary romance. She is published with Tor Teen, Entangled Teen and Brazen, Disney/Hyperion and Harlequin Teen. Her book *Wicked* has been optioned by Passionflix and slated to begin filming in late 2018. Her young adult romantic suspense novel *DON'T LOOK BACK* was a 2014 nominated Best in Young Adult Fiction by YALSA and her novel *THE PROBLEM WITH FOREVER* is a 2017 RITA Award winning novel.

She also writes Adult and New Adult contemporary and paranormal romance under the name J. Lynn. She is published by Entangled Brazen and HarperCollins.

On Behalf of Blue Box Press,

Liz Berry, M.J. Rose, and Jillian Stein would like to thank~

Steve Berry
Doug Scofield
Benjamin Stein
Kim Guidroz
Social Butterfly PR
Ashley Wells
Chelle Olson
Hang Le
Stephanie Brown
Chris Graham
Jessica Johns
Dylan Stockton
Celia Taylor Mobley
Richard Blake
and Simon Lipskar